SANDEAGOZU

SANDEAGOZU

A NOVEL BY

JANANN V. JENNER

1817

HARPER & ROW, PUBLISHERS, NEW YORK

CAMBRIDGE, PHILADELPHIA, SAN FRANCISCO, WASHINGTON,
LONDON, MEXICO CITY, SÃO PAULO, SINGAPORE, SYDNEY

FIRST EDITION

Designer: Barbara DuPree Knowles

Illustrations by Robert Crawford

Copy editor: Bitite Vinklers

LIBRARY OF CONGRESS CATALOGING-IN-PUBLICATION DATA

Jenner, Janann V.
    Sandeagozu.

    1. Animals—Fiction.   I. Title.
PS3560.E516S3   1986   813'.54   86-45119
ISBN 0-06-015633-3

---

86 87 88 89 90 HC 10 9 8 7 6 5 4 3 2 1

BOOK

PROLOGUE

Falam, Burma
May, 1915

IN A LOW-CEILINGED burrow buttressed by the knotted roots of a silk-cotton tree the ancient python coiled about her eggs and scryed the minds of her unhatched children. In the slow reptilian way, slithering languidly like eels caught in a warm current, her thoughts moved within their small minds. Reaching deftly beneath the web of their first embryonic notions she sought the best of her hatchlings.

The pythoness was very old. In her lifetime she had guarded many such clutches and knew that these forty-two eggs would probably be her last. "I feel tired," the snake sighed. "I'm old and I'm tired and I want this to be over." It had been a particularly cold winter and for months she had coiled about her eggs, faithfully twitching to warm her babies in the way that only Burmese pythons can. She had imagined the cold winds swirling down from the high mountains, funneling into the river valleys and washing over the plateau. The chill winds shriveled and froze everything in their path, and as the temperature in the underground chamber had dropped the pythoness had heard her children whimper within their eggshells. She had known instinctively what to do and, although it had cost her dearly, she had warmed them, sacrificing her own flesh so that they would live. She had twitched and twitched her massive coils, and soon the babies luxuriated in egg pools of tropical warmth, even though the wind whistled above ground.

The mother remembered those nervous days and was glad that they were over. "Now," she thought, "for the Blessing." Python custom dictated that each brooding female could bestow a single blessing in her lifetime. This blessing would enable the chosen hatchling to develop the unique mental powers possessed by many members of the Elder Race, but most often reserved for those that the pythons called the Leather Skins: crocodiles and their kin. Bestowing her blessing was a heavy responsibility and the pythoness had already scryed the embryonic minds of most of her children. "There must be one unusual one in this clutch," she thought. "I can't waste the gift on an ordinary child. I must find the right one. They'll begin to hatch very soon and then it'll be too late."

Scrying was tiring work and the serpent was exhausted from her long fast. She shifted her position, gently coiling the yards of her body more closely around the heap of eggs. She thought of the veiled hatchling spirally packed within each soft shell and took care not to jostle or compress any egg as she resumed the mental search. The serpent knew that she was different from most other pythons. She was bigger and when she talked with the others in the hibernating chamber she could tell that she was smarter than most. "What would have happened to me if I'd been given the Blessing by my mother?" she had often wondered. "Would I have been very different?" The pythoness held this thought for a moment and then shrugged it away. There was no use wasting precious energy on an unanswerable question and, besides, it broke a Cardinal Rule of the Elder Race. With an inward sigh she reminded herself, "I must find the one to Bless. Then this will be over and I'll be free."

She was sifting the thoughts of a particularly appealing and ferocious youngster when she felt an unmistakable movement in one of the eggs. The pressure was as slight as the breath of air fanned by a damselfly's metallic wing and as stealthy as the midnight unfurling of a moonflower. Yet, like a bronzed trout leaping in a pool, the scrape of egg tooth against eggshell created a wake of sensations in the mill of the old snake's mind.

"Hatching has begun," she thought and forgot the blessing that she could bestow upon only one child. As if emerging from a clinging dream she felt the pangs of hunger reminding her that she hadn't eaten in nearly four months. Restlessly she flexed her back muscles, amazed at how light and small she felt. Her skin was loose and as she moved against the packed earth it ripped in places. "I hadn't realized it had been so long," she thought. "I wish I could get out of here, but I mustn't leave yet. Maybe there's something here to eat."

The pythoness knew that it was unlikely that anything edible had crawled into her burrow, yet she sampled the pocket of subterranean air with a hopeful flick of her rapid tongue. She could fnast only her own scent and the nasty odor of the pangolin who had once dug and then abandoned this hiding place. His smell clung to the walls of the blocked tunnel that led up to the burrow's concealed entrance. The old pythoness used her unique mental powers to conjure the image of the thick, crescent-shaped scales that covered his body. She saw the haphazard mess of matted hairs that stuck out between them. "Not very pretty," she thought, comparing his gross, horny scales with her own finely imbricate covering. "And I'm not even at my best."

She knew that her skin needed shedding. It had grown drab and scratched during her long confinement. The old pythoness had always prided herself on the enameled beauty of her scales and she thought of the gorgeous tan, black and white tapestry, of the rainbow sheen that waited below this ragged surface. She regarded her mental picture of the pangolin again, thinking, "I look haggard, but I'm glad I don't look like that: he hasn't even got a proper head." Both ends of the pangolin's body tapered to a blunt point and his eyes and ears were nearly invisible. The pythoness couldn't tell which end was meant to go first. "No matter," she thought disdainfully. "He's led around by the nose, no matter where it's located—just like all of his hot-blooded relatives." She thought of his narrow skull and suddenly felt sorry for the stupid earth digger. "Poor thing. Well, I guess everyone can't be a python. He's so ugly and, if that weren't bad enough, he doesn't even have the brains of a slug. If his scent didn't keep the ants away, I'm not sure I could have stood it for so long." She smelled the blocked entrance to the burrow once again and thought, "He stinks so—ugh. No wonder they live alone."

She fnasted the ceiling of the burrow and could sense the busy whisperings of the ants who clustered a few feet from her head. "They think he's still here," she thought smugly. She could sense their hunger as multiple pairs of antennae waved, surveying her. "They know about my eggs. That's for sure," she thought. As the pythoness had done so many times in the last months, she sent the ants another mental warning, reminding the minute predators of the thick claws and sticky tongue of the pangolin who lurked in this burrow. She saw their antennae mechanically flinch and they scuttled deeper into their lookout post. The ancient serpent smiled at her own cleverness, thinking, "They'll leave my babies alone now. The fear of that stinking pangolin will keep them away."

Ants are the implacable enemies of newly hatched snakes. She remembered the distraught young pythoness who had once wailed in the hibernating chamber, mourning the babies who had been eaten by ants. To the unspoken question of the elders the inexperienced mother had gasped, "I only left them overnight. I was so hungry—I couldn't wait any longer. No one ever told me about the ants."

The older serpents had listened to her lament. They had passed no judgment and offered no comfort. "This is how we learn," had been their reply and the bereft mother had wept alone. Eventually she had been trampled beneath the sharp hooves of a forest hog and the old pythoness had heard that the hog had rooted at her carcass for weeks. "Careless," the ancient snake thought. "That should never have happened. Perhaps it's just as well that her babies died early. Most of them must have taken after her."

The old pythoness' thoughts returned to the hatchlings that she guarded and she wondered, "How much longer?" She held her breath and concentrated on the eggs within her coils, hoping for a movement that would answer the question. She had begun to think that she had imagined the first hatching scrape, when it came again. This time the pressure was stronger and then it was echoed by a similar movement within a second egg. "They are beginning to stir," she thought. "It won't be long now. Soon the circle will be complete. Soon I'll eat again."

The side of her huge head was pressed against the ceiling of the burrow and through the bones that roofed her skull she heard a familiar pattern of vibrations. She had noticed these sounds intermittently during her long confinement and she knew that a family of chevrotains lived just above, sleeping in the daytime in one of the root-tangled cavities at the base of the enormous tree. She heard a delicate stamp and imagined a small, four-toed foot and thought, "Soon."

The pythoness had guarded many clutches of eggs and knew that it would be safe to leave when the hatchlings' first, tentative scrapings had built to a crescendo of slashing. She was cautious by nature and would wait until the first little python's snout protruded from a gash in the wall of his egg prison. Then she would abandon these children. As was the custom of the Elder Race, she would leave her little ones without saying goodbye, following the example of generations of brooding pythons. The old serpent thought again of the family of mouse deer who rested above ground, only a few feet away, and thought, "Soon. I'll get all of you very, very soon."

Her grim mouth watered as she imagined how she would ambush the female chevrotain and her twins. She felt another wave of egg movements against the dry scales of her flanks and by reflex scryed the mind of the baby who had awakened to find that his white-walled egg world had grown much too small. She saw him angrily scratch the egg tooth on the tip of his snout against the parchment that enclosed him. She smiled at his tiny, impotent fury. "This is not the one to Bless," she thought. "They all hatch out angry and ready to kill."

Waves of hunger made her think again of her long-awaited meal and of the liquid eye of the chevrotain who rested just above. "I'll hypnotize her," she planned. "Then the babies will be easy to grab." She imagined how she would speak to the female chevrotain, immobilizing her with a golden stare. She felt the warm body within her coils and felt the quick heart stop, crushed in mid-beat. The thin legs flopped limply and dry, stiff hairs tickled against her palate as she worked her jaws down over the trio of stripes that slashed the olive-brown throat. Mentally she loosened both jaws to engulf the soft, white-furred belly.

"Soon," she said to the two young chevrotains who dreamed of gamboling in a sunny meadow as they cuddled against their mother. "Your time will also come soon. But first, I must find the one to Bless."

The movements within the eggs were more insistent now and the young pythons would free themselves within minutes. "There isn't much time," the old female thought. "I must find the best one."

Once again she scryed the minds of the children who had awakened.

She moved among them with a touch as delicate as the tongue of a hummingbird probing for hidden sweets. "If only I could Bless them all," she thought, but knew that this was beyond even her mental powers. "I can choose only one. It must be the strongest, the smartest, the best."

Near the center of the pile of warm, moist eggs she found a hatchling who drove her egg tooth against the wall of her prison with calm, directed movements. Unlike her brothers and sisters this hatchling was unhurried and confident. She knew that she would be able to free herself. The old pythoness scryed this tiny mind and with a shock she saw the image of an emaciated, dry-eyed hag-fish of a python who huddled about a mass of dirty, white eggs. She realized that it was a picture of herself within the young one's mind. "This has never happened before," she thought. She looked again at herself, worn thin—hardly the regal beast that she thought herself to be. "This one *is* different," she thought. "Unusual . . . strange." She did not like the image that the little one held within her mind, but knew that it was mercilessly accurate. Quickly she noted that the child was twice as large as her nest mates. "She'll grow fast," the mother thought. "She's been given great gifts already. This is a lucky child. One like no other.

"This is the one," the old pythoness decided. As quickly as she planned to strike at the mother chevrotain, she swept the combined energy of fifty years of survival in the jungle into a single, gleaming mass and tempered that mass into a shining dart. Gently the old pythoness insinuated the dart into the cobwebby mass of yolky thoughts in the unformed portion of the little female's mind. Once more she scryed the unflattering image of herself and couldn't help altering it. She erased the dry, baggy skin and colored in her own pattern of ebony and white crescents in a field of tan scales that gleamed with an iridescent sheen. She added a regal curve to the scrawny neck and then made the image rear and hiss open-mouthed within the child's mind. She saw the hatchling gasp and cough. In a panic the baby ripped a hole in the eggshell and lay panting and dazed, gulping her first breaths of air. "That'll teach her to respect her elders," the mother python thought. Then she regarded her chosen child more kindly. "The gift will be there if she needs it." In a voice that could not be ignored she spoke to the child, saying, "I have given you a great gift. Survive and live to use it."

She did not remain within the baby snake's mind long enough to watch the result of her Blessing. Rather, she released her hold on the hatchling and fnasted the entire mass of her eggs. She knew that only a few from this clutch of forty-two would survive for even a month; even fewer would live a year and perhaps only one or two would survive long enough to mate or guard their own babies. She watched as more and more of the eggs were gashed open and many blunt snouts poked through the oozing holes.

She lost track of the child who had been Blessed. Satisfied that her job was complete, the old pythoness stealthily nosed a passage up through the debris that blocked the burrow's entrance.

A while later the snake's huge head appeared at the rear of the hiding place of the family of chevrotains. Her golden eye glittered and she spoke coldly within the mother's mind. "You can't move," she said in a matter-of-fact voice. "Now hold still. This will hardly hurt at all."

A moment later the old pythoness gripped the dazed mouse deer in one coil. In the next breath she turned to the babies, who lay flattened against the dust, ears drooping, frozen with fear. Faster than the clap of a pigeon's wing she suffocated them with a looped coil.

Below ground the ants watched as the mass of tiny pythons crawled free of their eggshells. One ant spoke to the sister who stood next to her, fascinated by the scent and movement of the small snakes who slithered to and fro, investigating the dark, wider world of their burrow.

"What pangolin?" the ant said irritably. "I don't know what you're talking about. I don't see any pangolin."

She began to move toward a hatchling who had not yet detached himself from his pliable eggshell. "Come on," she said to the crowd of sisters who still lingered in the opening near the ceiling of the python's burrow. "Don't be stupid. There's no danger down here. That pangolin left a long time ago."

The ant watched as her timid sisters followed her scent trail, singly and in groups. "Imagine," she thought, "the superstitious fools were just going to let all this go to waste. Just because of some silly notion about the ghost of a pangolin. Incredible. If they hadn't called me, who knows what would have happened to them when the Sisterhood found out. No getting around it: they're dumb. Just plain dumb. All ants are not created equal."

To her sisters she said, "Here's our chance." At once they attacked and stung the damp, inquisitive nose of the hatchling who was still attached to his eggshell. His scales were wet and soft and he offered no resistance. In moments the unlucky little python was a writhing mass covered by excited ants. They wasted no time in removing mouthfuls of his delicate flesh and carrying them back to their nest. They reduced twelve of the newly hatched serpents to earth-covered skeletons before the sun went down and in the ant city hunger was satiated for the day.

"We'll be back tomorrow," the ants cried as they trooped home, crops and abdomens distended with rich python meat. "And all the tomorrows after that."

The original leader was the last to quit the brooding chamber. "What did I tell you?" she was repeating once more to her duller sister. "There was no pangolin there. No pangolin at all."

Falam, Burma
January, 1916

"THIS IS FUN," thought the four-foot-long baby python as she undulated through the interlaced branches of the high bougainvillaea hedge behind the ruined pagoda. With a coil of her prehensile tail wrapped around one thin branch, she leaped upward. Her lithe curves scrambled for a hold on the swaying branch and she flowed to a more secure perch. "Now where is he?" she thought, paying no attention to the leaves that fluttered to the ground or to the thorns that scratched her wide belly scutes. With the fascinated intensity of a kitten stalking a half-crippled housefly, the serpent concentrated completely on her quarry: a tantalizing, olive-green lizard who always seemed to be just out of reach. Again and again he outwitted her, leading her higher and higher in the bougainvillaea, dodging at the last second to the opposite side of the branch they both occupied. "How does he do that?" the little snake wondered. Instinctively she lunged for him again and missed.

The lizard had won many races with young serpents in his time and he was unworried. This python was only a hatchling and he was sure he'd be able to outfox her. The male lizard was the owner of the length of the western side of the bougainvillaea hedge. He spent his days running along these thin branches, catching insects, parading before his harem of admiring females and keeping the young males properly respectful. "She'll never catch me," he thought. "I know this hedge as well as I know the scales between my toes." Keeping one eye on the snake, who was creeping closer, about to launch another attack, he surveyed the tangle of familiar branches. With a shock the lizard saw that an interloper was sunning on a nearby branch. "The nerve! What's he think he's doing?" the first lizard thought. "We'll have to see about this."

Purposefully he scuttled upward and lifted his body high on his frail legs. The flush of anger changed his skin from olive green to mauve. Keeping a watchful eye on the little python he turned his profile to her and to his opponent. He took a deep breath and angrily puffed out his throat pouch. He was gratified to see his young competitor blanch, turn the drab colors of an immature female and sheepishly lower his head. The dominant lizard suddenly ran at the interloper and sent him leaping down and out of sight. "And stay out," the first male thundered, lashing his tail back and forth. "This is private property."

Out of the corner of one quick eye he saw the sidelong glance of a particularly winsome female, who was delicately snapping chartreuse aphids from the underside of a bougainvillaea blossom. "Mine," the dominant male thought and, feeling omnipotent, he inflated his throat pouch three more times for good measure. He surveyed the length of his hedge and saw, far below, the dark earth where his females had buried his eggs. "My babies will hatch when the rains come," he thought. He saw the crowd of birds flitting in the flame-of-the-forest tree and for the first time noticed that its leafless branches were full of bright blossoms and fruit. "What a racket they make," the lizard thought. "It means that the dry season is coming. We will sleep soon."

The little female began to pump her head and shoulders up and down, signaling to the male. In response he flushed mauve again and, strutting sinuously toward her, puffed out his throat pouch again and again.

The little python had been at first surprised and then frightened by the bright spot of hot orange and yellow that unexpectedly bloomed beneath the bony chin of the lizard she had been chasing. The sudden appearance of color had made her draw back her head into a striking coil and she froze there, flicking her tongue nervously and wondering, "What's that? What's wrong with him?"

In the time it took her to fnast this new shape the lizard deflated his gular flag, changed the color of his skin and scuttled up and out of sight. He had completely disappeared.

The snake didn't understand that the lizard was gone. Only a moment ago he had been running from her; then he had suddenly changed shape and color and vanished. "Right before my eyes," she thought. "He must be there. He's small and tricky, but I can find him. I know I can." Her unblinking, amber stare surveyed the screen of leaves above, watching for movement. A breeze rustled the leaves, making her see lizard shapes all around. The little snake didn't know it, but her quarry had climbed even higher and now was completely out of sight, mating with his compliant female.

"Sooner or later he's got to breathe," the huntress thought, "and then I'll see him. I saw the frog that way, just this morning." The labial pits on her upper lip quopped faintly, telling her that some animal whose body temperature was slightly warmer than the leaves was hiding there. "But where?" she wondered. "I don't see anything." Once again she fnasted the leaves, seeking her invisible quarry. Her labial pits quopped even more faintly. "I don't believe it," she said to herself, "but he's gone. Completely gone." The snake sighed and slowly lowered her head to rest upon her finely scaled back. "I'll wait," she thought. "Maybe he'll show himself again."

Seen from above, the sinuous curve of thin python upon bougainvillaea branch mimicked the shape of a stout, climbing vine mottled with tan, black and white lichen. From this protected perch beneath the magenta and fuchsia blossoms the little serpent could see the glitter of the lacy, golden umbrella that shaded the apex of the pagoda where she prowled at night, feasting on mice and young rats. She could see the muddy curve of the river behind the pagoda and the corrugated tracks left by the crocodiles who basked and gossiped on the riverbank. She had often seen the crocodiles floating in the moonlit water, their rows of blocky scales washed with silver. Although she didn't understand all of their talk, she knew that they were revered as the smartest of the Elder Race. She was frightened of the Leather Skins, though; of the way their teeth glowed in the moonlight. She kept out of their way. "Besides," she thought, "U Vayu warned me about them. They may be very smart, but they can't always be trusted."

U Vayu was a crotchety, venerable python who lurked below the main altar of the pagoda. A servant of the temple, and protected by the monks who chanted there, U Vayu had obliquely hinted that if the young pythoness were lucky enough to receive a name during the hibernation which would begin soon, he just might become her teacher. "That's if you have the wit to survive," his cold voice had hissed within her mind. "Not everyone does, you know. And stay away from those crocodiles." He had given her a long, cold-eyed look and the little snake had felt an icicle of pain between her eyes. It was gone before she could shake her head. U Vayu had abruptly slithered away and he'd never spoken to her since. It was as if he'd forgotten that she existed.

Above the bougainvillaea hedge, almost too far away from her eyes to see clearly, were the bare branches of a huge tree. Although it had no leaves, hundreds of birds flitted back and forth in its branches, feasting on fruit. The birds had been busy there all day and some were settling down to roost. The little pythoness heard a harsh, rattling call reverberate through the branch upon which she curled. A shadow passed overhead and the bougainvillaea shook as the scaled claws of a heavy bird raked the screen of leaves just above her head. She clung to her branch tightly as it shuddered and dry leaves fluttered all around. She saw something with two long tails fall on the bare ground and in the next moment the bird landed beside it. With a coarse, loud cry the hornbill snagged the mating lizards in his cruelly curved nutcracker of a bill. He threw them into the air, expertly caught them, smashed them flat and swallowed.

The bird wiped his bill on the dry earth and shook his feathers, glancing upward at the bougainvillaea branches with an appraising eye. He blinked and his pupils seemed to widen with excitement. She saw his heavy beak open again but this time there was no rough cry.

The little python knew that the hornbill had seen her. Without thinking she spoke into the mind of the hard-faced bird, saying, "You don't see me, yellow-eyes. There is no snake here. You're scared of me." She wasn't sure where the voice had come from, but, to her amazement, the hornbill gave an astonished squawk and scrutinized the bougainvillaea branches to the left and right of her perch. He shook his head, making his mandibles clatter, and flew off, skimming heavily over the ground.

The little python remained in her hiding place until the sun went down, afraid that the hornbill might return and throw her into the air and smash her just like the lizards. She didn't understand why the bird hadn't attacked. Indeed, she had forgotten the voice that had spoken to the bird from somewhere deep within her mind. As she cautiously slithered out of the branches at dusk, labial pits quopping for danger, she thought, "If I can I'll ask U Vayu about it. He'll know what it means. U Vayu knows everything. He's the wisest serpent there is. Everyone says so."

In the months that had followed her hatching the little python had practiced and perfected the techniques that were necessary for her survival. Instinctively she had hidden beneath leaves until she'd shed her skin for the second time. She'd killed her first bird, a fledgling sparrow who'd fallen from his nest. She had been frightened by the sudden opening and shutting of his rubbery yellow bill, but had summoned her courage and strangled him anyway. Guided by instinct she had learned to efficiently stalk and kill prey through the first months of her life, and then, as the ponds and tanks dried up and the dry, cool winds hardened the grasses to stiff, brown stubble, she had sought a deep shelter in which to spend the dry, cold winter.

She coiled in the subterranean chamber with other pythons and, following their instructions, was musing on the colors and patterns of her tail. This is the traditional way for snakes of her kind of learn their names and, although most fail to do so, the method does work for a chosen few each year. All snakes and especially small ones have many predators. Most become hawk, owl or crow bait before they reach maturity, and because of this only a handful of pythons receive names each year. These lucky few are schooled by the older snakes in the hibernation chamber. They learn how to dodge the feathered talons that strike deep, how to fascinate rabbits into mute submission, how to grapple with cannibalistic cobras. If a snake has not received a name after one moon of the hibernation period, the older serpents take this as a sign that it will have a short life. The nameless one withdraws and prepares for the approach of death.

In this way generations of pythons have perpetuated the accumulated wisdom of their kind: only the strongest young snakes, those most likely to survive, are given the serpent lore that will help them thrive in a hungry, unfriendly world. The nameless baby snakes grow increasingly quiet with each day of hibernation. They are silent, except for commonplace courtesies to the eldest snake in the chamber. The old ones say that it is best that these hatchlings die, because they are invariably malformed or weak and, although the little pythoness trusted the wisdom of the archaic serpent ways, she felt sorry for the sad knot of intertwined nameless ones.

Even though she was a mere four and a half feet and still had the scar from her yolk sac on her pudgy belly, the little pythoness never doubted that she would find her true name. As she meditated on the dove-tailed, opalescent scales of the underside of her tail, her unique name entered her thoughts more quietly than a pebble sinking into the shadows of a pond. SHERAHI. She recognized it at once. Sherahi: no snake before her and no snake after her would bear this name. "Sher" meant tiger; "ahi" meant strangling snake. And that was what she was: a kind of snake fierce enough to strangle a water buffalo, a leopard or even a tiger. And she would vanquish these in the honorable way of her kind: by strangling, pitting her strength against that of her prey. She wouldn't stab home a poison and then retreat to cower until the prey died. "I am a killer," she thought in the cold way of her kin, "but at least I'm no needle-toothed coward. I will risk my life for every meal."

Coiled in the rocky shadows of the chamber, the old serpent, U Vayu, scryed her mind. Although he hid his jealous thoughts from the other pythons beneath a veneer of avuncular concern for the current batch of hatchlings, U Vayu secretly watched to see if the one who had received her mother's Blessing would also receive a name. U Vayu saw the hatchling recognize her true name and eavesdropped on her thoughts. In his hooded fashion he smiled at her bravado and hissed to himself, "Tiger killer, 'Sherahi'—a brave name. And brave words for an infant. 'Sherahi—tiger killer.' We'll see if she lasts even a year."

Falam, Burma
January, 1921

"DON'T BOTHER ME with your foolish questions, Sherahi," U Vayu snapped. "Can't you see that it's nearly time? They'll come for me soon. I must prepare. Go away and come back tomorrow or the next day or better still, the day after that."

"But, U Vayu," Sherahi said, nosing along the length of her old tutor's broad neck and pressing her small muzzle into his scales. She felt him slither off the broken wall, flowing down to the shadows at the base of the plaza's inner wall. Inwardly she smiled at his fussiness. Sherahi knew that U Vayu hated to be touched and she loved to provoke him.

Holding her head erect on a slender neck she followed, lashing her fifteen-foot length like a whipsnake as she tried to catch him. "Well, if you won't tell me about the rituals, U Vayu, will you give me permission to watch?"

"I have no control over you, Sherahi. A snake goes where he pleases. It is not mine to permit or deny. Do as you wish. Only, leave me be. I must compose myself." U Vayu slithered obliquely away from the ruined wall at the rear of the pagoda. Mentally, Sherahi followed the old python and watched him crawl from shadow to shadow until he slipped into the darkened arch that led into the temple. She saw him crouch motionless inside until his slitlike pupils expanded to their nighttime roundness. In the way of their kind his tongue flickered continually, sampling the surroundings, and Sherahi thought, "Caution. Always caution. That's the price he's paid for his long life. Caution and fear. U Vayu has probably never done anything just for the fun of it. He probably doesn't even know what it feels like to race the wind across an open meadow." She saw the old serpent crawl beneath the altar of the glinting statue of the Buddha and form a compact coil. He settled his wide head on the topmost curve of his neck and then suddenly glared at her. "Go away, Sherahi," he ordered in a voice that she had to obey and she felt him abruptly shut his mind to her intrusive probe. It was like the slamming of a heavy, metal-studded door. She heard his sibilant hiss and he repeated, "Go away, Sherahi. The rituals are serious. Not play for babies."

"The rituals. The rituals," Sherahi mimicked. "You'd think he lived only for them. If they're so important, then why do they happen only once every seven years? And why don't they take place in the temple itself, instead of behind it, out by the trash heap where that misshapen image leers out of the old wall? It doesn't make any sense."

Once again she heard U Vayu's warning hiss within her mind and sulked, "All right. I'm going." She sighed and slithered away from the dim temple where U Vayu coiled, moving swiftly across the open plaza of terra-cotta tiles that had been polished smooth by the bare feet of generations of worshipers and paused in the shadows at the base of the opposite wall. Sherahi felt the slick tiles and thought, "U Vayu told me that once this pagoda was a busy place. I wonder if he had any fun then?" Sherahi's thoughts were interrupted by the faint quopping of her labial pits and she fnasted the trail of a mother rat. She could see the scaly tail and twitching whiskers of the female who only a few moments ago had run hump-backed through these shadows. "I could catch her," thought Sherahi. "But I'm not really hungry. Besides, U Vayu said that it was important not to eat before the rituals. I don't want to have a meal in my stomach, just in case something happens. I don't like all these strangers who are gathering outside the wall. U Vayu said that most of them are harmless, but I'm not sure." She remembered the crocodile teeth that glowed white in the moonlight and her teacher's voice hissing, "You can never tell about humans. Except for the rituals we keep our distance from them."

The festivities would not begin until after dark and Sherahi climbed back into her favorite basking place on the tumbled-down wall to watch the sun slip below the horizon. Night fell as abruptly as it always does in the tropics, mantling the day with quick darkness. The pythoness was restless and edgy with excitement. "Tonight," she thought. "Something wonderful's going to happen tonight. I can feel it."

She undulated across the top of the wall toward the stout neem tree that grew next to the flame-of-the-forest tree. She would have liked to climb into its taller crown, but the branches only bore orange blossoms. "The dry season is coming," Sherahi thought. She wanted to watch the rituals from a protected lookout, so when she reached the neem tree she began to nose up into the lower branches, angling toward the trunk.

The only light was a faint, greenish glow on the horizon that marked the place where the sun had slipped from sight. The first few stars were weak points of light and in the distance a procession of torches bobbed along the road that led to the pagoda. "More strangers are coming," she thought. As she climbed, the snake pushed her wide belly scutes against minute irregularities in the bark and braced herself with lateral loops of her body. She used her labial pits and her tongue to wurp the length of each branch, seeking other beasts that might be lurking in the neem tree. "You never know who might be here," she said to herself, thinking of the pair of king cobras who patrolled the forest beyond the temple precincts. "Cobras don't like to climb trees, but who knows—they might be out on a dark night like this. Snake eaters. Ugh. The thought makes me sick. . . ." Sherahi imagined the shadow of a cobra's hood in every curve of branch and leaf. For a moment she considered retreating to the safety of her pagoda, but then she reassured herself. "Cobras don't climb trees," she reasoned. "This place is safe. I'm sure of it."

When she was halfway up the trunk she inched out onto a stout branch drooping over the wall that formed the rear boundary of the pagoda precincts. It gave her a better view of the encampment of strangers who had arrived the day before. U Vayu said that the monks had forbidden them to enter the temple grounds, but that they were always allowed to set up their tents and kitchens behind it, around the image-in-the-wall that they had come so far to worship. "It is very old," U Vayu had whispered. "Very sacred. Very mysterious."

"Very ugly, too," Sherahi had added and had laughed to see U Vayu inflate his neck indignantly.

"You look like a fat worm, U Vayu," Sherahi had giggled. Her tutor had not shared her hilarity.

Sherahi settled in a comfortable fork of the branches of the neem tree and fnasted the strange humans who sat on their haunches on the ground below, eating and smoking and scratching themselves in the light of scattered campfires.

"They're certainly raggedy," she thought. "And they are dressed in different colors. They're not like the monks at all."

Several men spread a cloth to the left of the image-in-the-wall. They sat cross-legged upon it and began the dreadful din that U Vayu had once told her humans called "music." It grated in Sherahi's deep ears and she picked her head up off the branch to avoid having to listen to the clashing cymbals, dinging gongs and wailing trumpets.

More of the ragged humans squatted on their heels before the image-in-the-wall. The men merely stared and seemed to mutter, while the women covered their faces and bowed. With their arms held behind their backs they swayed back and forth. "They're weaving like cobras," thought Sherahi. "I wonder what it means?" By the light of the central fire Sherahi saw that someone had splashed the image with red paint. "Not very neatly done," she thought, reminded of the fine, black lines and careful details that the monks painstakingly applied to the small images of Buddha that occupied dim niches around the inner walls of the pagoda. The image-in-the-wall was not of Buddha, but instead was a grotesque hybrid: a creature that was half human and half multiheaded serpent. A bouquet of hooded cobras reared aggressively above its human face. The heads of the serpents were incised in detail. Sherahi could see their teeth, head scutes and glaring stares, but the face of the human was oddly blank. The neck and armless torso wore swags of carefully detailed jewelry and the hips blended into a thick, sinuous tail whose S-shaped coils melded with the parent stone. Sherahi had examined this image many times and she had always been appalled at the slick surface of this otherwise perfect serpent's tail. It didn't have a single scale. "Not a proper snake," she always thought. "More like an eel. I'm glad it's one of them—instead of one of the Elder Race." She saw that the red paint had dripped down its smooth tail and had puddled onto the bare ground below. "Makes it even uglier," she thought and shuddered.

From her hiding place beneath the leaves of the neem tree Sherahi could see the central campfire, the musicians and the worshipers who milled around the image-in-the-wall. There was a veiled woman who sat alone, a heap of red skirts and gold-spattered veils. The others seemed to avoid her. "That's strange," thought Sherahi. There was a movement in the crowd below and she gave the veiled woman no further thought.

A small boy pointed and jumped up and down, clapping his hands, gnawing on his fingers. He pulled on his mother's skirts and soon all of the worshipers seemed to have been infected by his excitement. Sherahi saw them strain to see the torchlit procession that had appeared around the corner of the temple wall. Sherahi fnasted the oily smoke of torches and saw the cheekbones of the worshipers shine in the sudden glare. Their eyes went white.

It always made Sherahi's skin crawl to see human eyes turn white like that and she quickly looked away, thinking, "Why are their eyes so strange? Two colors. Ugh."

The procession passed below the neem tree and Sherahi buried her head in her coils to avoid the smoke. When she peered out again she saw that the faces of many of the worshipers were marked with the twisted grimace that U Vayu had told her was the "reflection of the emotion of fear." Eyes were wide and mouths worked and something told Sherahi that these people were speaking to their god. One woman, with tangled, gray-streaked hair, tore back her veil and clutched the slender arm of the veiled woman who knelt apart from the others. Sherahi could tell that she was pouring out a rapid stream of the inchoate sounds that humans used to communicate with one another. The veiled woman pulled her arm free. The circlet of golden bangles across her forehead glimmered as she shook her head from side to side. The first woman covered her face with gnarled, veiny hands and collapsed onto her knees. "What's wrong with her?" thought Sherahi. She looked more carefully at the veiled woman who waited beside the fire. Of all the strangers she was the only one who was not straining to gape at the torchlit procession as it circled three times around the image-in-the-wall. As if in a trance the woman gazed steadily up at the sacred carving. Sherahi caught the shine of a dark, wet eye behind the sheer crimson veil.

The procession stopped within the circle of light. The bearers were panting and nearly bent double beneath the weight of a bundle that hung from a stout pole they carried on their shoulders. "There's something very heavy in there," Sherahi thought. At a signal they gently set the blanket-covered mound onto the ground. Two of them lifted the pole and pulled it free while a third held the mouth of the bundle straight up. He kept the ends of the cloth firmly bunched, as if making doubly sure that it remained securely closed. Sherahi saw that a thick, purple cord was wrapped around the neck of the bundle. Its free ends had been daubed with the same red that dripped from the image-in-the-wall's chin.

The crowd pressed forward as a man dressed in a dirty white jacket and turban stepped into the circle of light. Cautiously he held the ends of the purple cord in one hand and stepped back a safe distance from the bundle. He held the other hand in the air, lifted his face to the image-in-the-wall and began to pray. His eyes were tightly closed and Sherahi could see that his teeth were red. She watched his lips move over his discolored broken teeth and wondered why so many humans had gaps in their rows of teeth, as he did. "Why don't new teeth grow in?" she wondered.

A spiraling movement within the bundle caught Sherahi's attention and she was about to scry it, when she saw an even larger movement in the scene below.

The veiled young woman had stepped forward and now took the purple cord from the white-jacketed man. As if in one breath the other humans scrambled back and crouched in a circle around her. Their faces formed a ruddy frieze. The woman held the purple cord between her closed palms. Meditatively she touched them to her forehead, to her mouth, to her chest. She nodded to the musicians and their wailing, clashing sounds stopped. Sherahi could hear the difference: it was as if the blood-sucking whine of a persistent mosquito had ceased. In a sibilant whoosh the snake released the breath that she hadn't realized she'd been holding.

The musicians put down their instruments and wiped their mouths on the backs of their hands. One of them took a folded leaf from a pocket and placed it between lip and gum. Another lit a fat cheroot and stood to stretch his cramped legs. "They're not interested in the ritual," Sherahi said to herself. "How can this be?" There was no answer to her question, though, and after a moment the drummer began to play. While the other musicians wandered off to join the crowd, he established and repeated a simple, syncopated rhythm. Sherahi saw it liven his fingers, and then the palms and heels of his hands. The rhythm moved up his forearms to his shoulders and soon it possessed his whole body.

The beat was so hypnotic that Sherahi found herself swaying within the neem tree. She felt the branch move below her and knew that she was shaking the leaves, but Sherahi didn't care. "No one'll see me up here," she thought. "They're all watching the ritual." She thought again of careful U Vayu, who never did anything impulsive, and continued to dance, just to spite him. "I'll never be timid like U Vayu and afraid of everything," Sherahi thought. "Never."

With one hand the woman lifted a crescent-shaped silver knife, which hung in a sheath at her belt. She cut the knotted purple cord; both hands clutched the mouth of the bag and stretched it up. From her rounded upper arms Sherahi guessed that she was a young woman, maybe even a girl. The border of her skirt was decorated with a wide band of woven chrysanthemums and there was a frayed rip in the hem. The woman bent over the bunched ends of cloth and the green and purple bangles on her wrists trembled. Sherahi could see that the palms of her hands were tattooed with a design that was strangely familiar. "I've seen that before," Sherahi thought. "But where?"

She thought no more about the arabesques that swirled on the woman's fingers, though, because something else was happening. Sherahi stopped swaying on the branch of the neem tree and held her breath as the tip of a serpent's nose protruded from between the woman's hands. Sherahi could see the labial pits that marked it as a python, a member of the Elder Race. "That's U Vayu," Sherahi thought as a cautious black tongue lashed to and fro.

"Get away," she wanted to warn the young woman. Sherahi had once seen U Vayu strangle a leopard. He didn't like humans and she knew that he could easily kill this small woman if he chose to. But the sight of U Vayu's huge head emerging from between the woman's hands stopped Sherahi's warning. His amber eyes glowed in the firelight and Sherahi saw the onlookers' eyes grow wide in their contorted faces.

The drum continued its rhythm and the woman called to the snake. U Vayu kept his eyes on hers and rose to meet her. She dropped the cloth that had restrained the serpent and slowly pulled the red gauze from her face. Sherahi was surprised to see that she was just an ordinary young woman. She wore intricate gold and glass jewelry; her hair hung down her back in a lank, oily braid; her cheeks were pitted with constellations of small scars. She was ordinary-looking, but her eyes seemed to mesmerize U Vayu.

The drumbeat changed slightly and now the woman and the serpent faced one another and began to dance in unison. U Vayu held his head high on the pillar of his neck. Sometimes he stood higher than the woman and his shadowed eyes regarded her archly. Sherahi found herself silently begging, "Please don't hurt her, U Vayu." The woman's arms were clasped behind her back and Sherahi saw that now the purple cord was twisted about her wrists. Her body undulated like a swimming snake and her tongue flickered. In the firelight it seemed to be forked. U Vayu matched her, move for move, and for a moment Sherahi forgot who was what and which was which. Then the woman's feet began to move, stamping a counterpoint to the drumbeat. The jingling of silver anklets and the slapping of heels seemed so familiar and full of joy that Sherahi could barely restrain herself from slithering down to join the pair. "I want to dance, too," she thought as she watched the fabric of the woman's skirt slowly encircle the huge, erect python. She saw the fabric shot with gold repeatedly cover and reveal the python's scales. U Vayu seemed to be swimming in a field of frayed flowers. Woman and serpent glowed in the firelight and slowly Sherahi began to understand. She watched them merge and draw apart and thought, "This is what U Vayu meant." Haltingly she said to herself, "I . . . I think I understand." It was as if a perfect-petaled lotus had blossomed within a part of her mind that she hadn't known was there. She imagined the image-in-the-wall and thought with amazement. "It isn't ugly, it's . . ."

Just then, something touched her neck and she found herself being pulled roughly from her perch within the branches of the neem tree. She fell heavily onto the plaza within the temple wall and felt many pairs of hot human hands grab her. Before she could rear and hiss to defend herself she was surrounded by darkness, and rough cloth was all around. Her jaws and neck were bruised and in her panic to escape she forgot all about U Vayu, the ritual and the blood-red image-in-the-wall.

As they tied the purple cord around the mouth of the rice sack the four boys grinned and pounded one another on the back in excitement.

"Twenty feet," one said gleefully. "At least twenty feet!"

"And sweet-tempered. He didn't even try to bite," another added.

"We'll be rich once we get to the market in Mandalay."

There was a muffled shout from within the darkened pagoda and the first boy looked over his shoulder and said, "Hurry. Someone's coming."

Hoisting the heavy sack behind them, the gang scaled the broken rear wall of the plaza and joined the boisterous revels that had already begun in the shadows on the edges of the sacred circle.

CHAPTER ONE

THE HAND CAUGHT Sherahi by surprise.

She was catnapping, musing on the journey to come, pleased that the rituals were starting again, planning nuances of movement that would mingle old forms with new. She would make Ruthie so proud of all of them. The length of her body was coiled within her new trunk while her head was cushioned on a nearby chair. She'd always liked traveling and was trying to remember how long it had been since the last trip when, without warning, the hand grabbed her head and shoved her completely inside the trunk. From the way the fingers touched her she knew that this person thought her slimy, loathsome, lethal. Before she could rear up and defend herself the lid slammed shut and she found herself a prisoner within the black and airless box.

Sherahi counted as one, two, three—was it four? six? nine?—blows were struck around the top of the trunk. "Locks," she thought. "Are they locking me here to suffocate?" Then the box began to move and she was roughly jostled against its sides.

Sherahi lashed back and forth in a fury, looking for a way out. Her teeth yearned to snag and slash the hand that had treated her with such disdain, such disrespect. Her thoughts were filled with images of a human hand turning white, then blue, then gray-purple as she strangled it in one coil and dropped it like the piece of offal that it was. She remembered the nightmare she had once had. Again she saw herself slithering along a dim corridor and an unidentified sadness overwhelmed her. "Is this it?" she wondered. "Is this the bad thing I dreamed about?"

The box stopped moving with a jolt. She could feel the crunch of gravel beneath heavy footsteps. It was loud at first and then diminished and disappeared. A short while later she sensed that it was getting dangerously hot inside the box as its sides grew warm and then uncomfortably hot. Sherahi adjusted her coils so that they touched as little of the hot wood as possible and was thankful for the insulating materials on the floor of the box. "What are they going to do now?" she wondered. "Leave me in the sun to roast to death?"

More time passed and the snake was relieved that the temperature held steady. It was hot inside the trunk, but this was not the heat that kills. Where had they taken her? Where was Ruthie? She put her nose against one of the air holes near the lid of the trunk and investigated her surroundings with a quick tongue. She seemed to be in a dark place surrounded by boxes. In this position her jawbones were in contact with the wood and she could hear the faraway scream of a whistle and the nearer rumble of a train.

The big python realized that this was to be the way in which she'd travel to the ritual: in the front of the train with the other baggage while Ruthie and the little ones rode in the coach. "Can this be possible?" she thought, lashing back and forth in a rage. "Has Ruthie lost her reason? Doesn't she know how foolhardy it is to try the patience of Sherahi the pythoness? Didn't she learn the last time?

"Do I have to destroy this trunk, too?" Sherahi wondered. She knew that would make Ruthie unhappy, but traveling in the baggage car was out of the question. After all, she wasn't baggage. She wasn't someone's prize cow going to the slaughterhouse; she wasn't a mindless chicken in a wooden cage dripping feathers and excrement over her clucking relatives stacked in cages below; she wasn't someone's property to be shipped hither and thither with no thought to her comfort. She was Sherahi, the most awesome and powerful pythoness in existence. And she was furious.

"Try to shut me in, will you?" she thought. She remembered Ruthie's disgustingly smooth skin with its fine coating of down. There wasn't a decent scale anywhere on her body except for the tips of her fingers and her obscene toes. "Try to lock me in, will you, little flat-face? Well, we'll see about that."

Sherahi planted one huge coil against each wall of the box, and, remembering that her relatives the sunbeam pythons (who were prodigious diggers in spite of being only four feet long) boasted that they could move boulders when they wanted to, she drew deep breaths and inflated her body. She was five times as long and had twenty times the strength of any puny, mud-dredging sunbeam python. She should be out of here in no time. She'd done it before. All she had to do was loosen one side of the box.

Again and again Sherahi drew deep breaths and pressed outward against the walls. With all the might of her twenty feet of bone buttressed by gristle, with all her layers of chevroned muscles bound to those bones, she shoved, pushed and willed the box to give way. She prayed to Shiva to help her smash this prison. She remembered Ganesha's flapping ears and prayed that he might lend her his elephantine strength and help her to open a way. The wood began to groan, to bend; she even thought she heard a crack but the locks were too strong. They held firm and Sherahi knew that she was trapped.

Like a hesitant bather dipping one toe into the ocean she asked herself again, "Is this it? Is this the bad thing that's going to happen?" And again there was no reply, only a tightening of the knot of dread within her chest.

For all her brawn Sherahi had no head for arithmetic. The traveling case actually had seven brass locks—and to make sure that the snake couldn't escape again, the box had been reinforced with a latticework of metal crossbands held with rivets. Ruthie Notar, known to her public as Naruda, Exotique Dancer and Snake Charmeuse, had no intention of paying for another python meal of a half dozen guinea fowl or for another Pomeranian puppy. After the last unfortunate incident she'd hired a locksmith to strengthen the big snake's traveling case. The man had been overly enthusiastic with his application of metal reinforcements (to say nothing of being charmed by Ruthie's green eyes) and now Sherahi's traveling case looked fit to hoard all the gold doubloons and pieces-of-eight, baroque pearls and square-cut emeralds of Bluebeard's treasure; or perhaps it could even restrain the Great Houdini himself.

From her vantage point, however, the pythoness couldn't appreciate all the fancy metalwork and she was far from enchanted with her newly renovated luggage. "Toadshit," she thought. "I'm stuck in this box and this time it's stronger than ever." She settled her body into the most comfortable coil she could manage in these cramped quarters and resolved to try to escape again as soon as she'd regained her strength. In the way of her kind, she began to wait and to think.

Sherahi thought of the old days, when she and Ruthie had first begun to travel together: the good days just after Ruthie had restored her sight. At that time Ruthie had treated her like something special. She'd kept her in a knotted cotton sack on the seat beside her and, when a journey was long, she would open the bag and let the serpent out. Sherahi remembered stretching across Ruthie's shoulders like a mottled mantilla, watching pinpoints of light swoop away in the darkness outside the window as the train swayed and clattered through the night. Once Ruthie had fallen asleep and the pythoness had coiled protectively about her, conscious of her responsibility for Ruthie's safety and thankful for the burden.

But that was a long time ago, when she had been only a youngster. It was before Bernie had entered their lives and long before the baby boas had arrived. It was so long ago, in fact, that the pythoness wondered if she would feel comfortable if she had Ruthie all to herself again. "I know too many of her secrets," the pythoness thought.

Sherahi found the air holes in the sides of the trunk again and flicked out her patent-leather tongue, fnasting the air. Nothing interesting-smelling was out there in the gloom—no other serpents, not even a potential meal. Nothing seemed alive, except for a cluster of cockroaches in one corner of the ceiling and they wouldn't wake up until dusk.

In an absent-minded way, more from habit than interest—in much the same way that a man eyes the passing scene as he sips espresso in a sidewalk café—Sherahi scanned the thoughts of the sleeping roaches.

The mind of one young, wingless roach was filled with a nightmare of gnashing teeth set in bloody gums. The teeth snapped closer and behind them on a heaving tongue were mutilated roach bodies that twitched as if still alive. Shattered antennae, broken wings and abdomens that trailed intestines like yellow spaghetti disappeared down a dark throat. The young roach whimpered as it slept. Sherahi shuddered and withdrew her scan.

"Will they be my only companions on this miserable journey?" she wondered. With her tongue and the Jacobson's organs in the roof of her mouth she began to fnast the shape-smells inside the baggage car, searching for other intelligence. One nearby suitcase smelled strongly of tomcat. Sherahi grew hopeful: a cat would be a good conversationalist, someone who could break the monotony of a long trip, if he weren't hungry. But no matter how she tried, she could detect no living beast and concluded that the aroma must be only the territorial splash of a stray. Beyond the cat smell she could only fnast wooden crates, and off in the corner below the roaches was the lumpy, canvas-and-paper smell of a sack of mail.

There was nothing more. Nothing else alive except those poor insects. She listened to the moans of the cockroach tribe as they lived their nightmares. That whimpering was too awful, because now they had all joined in. She remembered that her teacher, U Vayu, had once told her that insects often had communal dreams. "They must all be sharing the young one's nightmare now," Sherahi thought.

She listened for a moment and then, like a fisherman twirling a cast net out in an ever-widening circle over a still lagoon, she sent a good dream to quiet them: a cornucopia of slops and swills, coffee grounds, potato parings, rotten fruit, all bestowed by the hand of a slatternly housewife. Their moans were soon replaced by trills of pleasure and then by deep sleep. Sherahi listened to the air washing in and out of their breathing pores and envied their contented rest. She wished she had someone with whom to share a dream, or even a nightmare.

She thought of the hours of confinement ahead and fretted, "At least Ruthie could've said goodbye. I'd've gotten in all by myself—she didn't have to be so rough." Then this thought came into Sherahi's mind: "Is she sending me away—all by myself?"

The snake pressed her chin against one side of the traveling case so that her jawbones could conduct vibrations to the earbones buried deep within her skull. Hearing was her poorest sense and she used it only as a last resort. She was surprised to hear human voices outside. Maybe Ruthie had come to free her. The big python lifted her chin and drummed her tail against the floor of the box. If Ruthie were in earshot Sherahi wanted her to know that she was angry.

Sherahi put her chin back against the wood and heard a familiar, almost hypersonic voice and recognized a few words: ". . . water . . . morning . . . too hot . . ." Then a heavy door slammed shut and the voice was gone. For a long time Sherahi listened, hoping to hear it again; instead she heard the keening that warned that the train was going to move. Even though she'd heard it before, the sound was so like the cry made by a mother python forced to abandon her nest of unhatched children that Sherahi shuddered.

Then came the shriek of metal upon metal and her traveling box began to rattle against the floor. The sounds made her teeth ache and to escape the vibrations she settled her collie-sized head against her coils. "Why did Ruthie do this to me? She could have kept me with her—she knows I hate to be locked up. She knows I'd have climbed into this trunk willingly if she'd asked me to."

Sherahi sighed. "Humans are so strange. Their behavior is . . ." The pythoness didn't have the proper word and concluded, ". . . so unserpentlike." Sherahi remembered the times when she'd gone hungry because Ruthie had forgotten to bring her a chicken or a rabbit or even a scrawny rat. Yet, other times Ruthie would supply more food than she could eat. Humans were always like that: unpredictable, unreliable, unmanageable— exasperatingly unlike snakes. Even the best sort of human, like Ruthie, needed to be taught a lesson from time to time.

Sherahi sent her mind's eye backward in the train, searching for reptilian intelligence. It flicked quickly past rows of unremarkable human travelers and finally fastened on the minds of the two little boas that Ruthie had kept with her. Sherahi was actually seeking Ruthie and could have scanned for her characteristic thought patterns but, because there were probably no other reptiles on this train, finding the boas was the quickest way to find Ruthie. Sherahi saw that the little snakes were out of their pillowcase and were so excited by the novelty of this trip that for once they weren't bickering.

Carla, the younger boa, was coiled in a spot of sunlight on Ruthie's lap. Sherahi scanned her mind and wasn't surprised to find it filled with thoughts of rats: fuzzy, baby rats—warm nestlings with skin like ripe peaches. Carla was perpetually hungry. Through Carla's eyes Sherahi saw that her sister, Rosita, was perched on top of Ruthie's shoulders, looking out the window. Sherahi hated to see the youngster in her old guard post and wondered, "Has Ruthie forgotten about me?" Sherahi turned to Ruthie's mind. She thoroughly scryed it, turning it inside out and shaking it, searching for some evidence that Ruthie cared about her, examining the girl's mind as a pickpocket in an alley might ransack a stolen purse.

After the directness and order of the mind of the boa, it was a shock for Sherahi to be immersed in the mess of a human mind. Thoughts were jumbled on top of each other like abandoned plumbing rusting in a junk-yard. Sherahi found thoughts about the way the sunlight splintered into rainbows as it glanced off Carla's body, then felt a shiver of distaste as Ruthie's fingers explored the slick velvet of a worn armrest. This was cou-pled with a memory of her mother warning her never to put her head on the back of a seat at the movies: she'd surely get lice that way. There was the recollection of how coolly Marlene Dietrich sold her cigarettes to Gary Coo-per in *Morocco,* the last movie Ruthie had seen. There was the thought of copying Marlene and adding cigarette smoke and a feather boa to the act, flirting with both, toying with the audience as Dietrich had played with Coo-per. There were thoughts about the grimy windowsill, and a wish that she'd brought a spare handkerchief, impressions of a lingering smell of cigar smoke, and an idea that the man in the seat across the aisle had a nose like Uncle Pete's. There was a whole fugue about the swing he'd made for her in the backyard when she was a child. Sherahi became nauseated as she felt Ruthie swing up and down, up and down, and quickly resumed her search. Tucked into one corner of Ruthie's mind was the scrap of a song she liked to sing and a plan to cook Bernie's favorite meal of shepherd's pie once they had settled down. She'd serve it with homemade cherry cobbler and Bernie would whip the cream. Ruthie imagined him with his collar off, one of her hand-embroidered tea towels tied around his waist, smiling to her across the kitchen. There was the dream of buying her own house someday and having a real electric icebox. Ruthie wanted the kind that came with a thick china butter dish and its own trays for making cubes of ice. "No more ice pick for me," she thought. There'd be a mailbox out in front of her house and morning glories that encirlced the name "Weinstein." There'd be a rose garden and a wicker chair where she could drink afternoon tea from bone china cups in perfumed shade. But no matter how Sherahi searched, beneath memory, idea, impression, plan or dream, she could find no immediate thought about herself. It seemed incredible after all these years, but Ruthie seemed to have wiped Sherahi the pythoness completely out of her mind.

Sherahi decided to remind Ruthie of her existence and, after tensing her mind the way a sprinter tenses his back muscles just before the starting gun, she sent a stab of nasty, heart-searing guilt into the center of Ruthie's brain. She was pleased to see it lodge and drip dread all over the wind-whipped undulation of a growing field of wheat that had caught Ruthie's eye. Sherahi watched the guilt obliterate the prickly itch of the heat rash around Ruthie's waist and was delighted to see worries begin to cloud the girl's mind. "Is my big snake okay? Will the three-day trip in the baggage car be too hot for her? Should I have gotten a sleeping compartment instead? Should I have made Bernie drive us? Would my Big Girl . . ."

Sherahi saw the words "Big Girl" and hissed indignantly, even though there was no one to hear. " 'Big Girl,' indeed," she thought. "How can she call me that? I was strangling full-grown stags in the forest when she was still puking Pablum onto her mother's shoulder." Sherahi lashed back and forth within her prison, crawling up its walls and arching back across its ceiling in fury. All the while she thought, "Ugggh. By the eye of the Great Kali, by the fangs of the Mighty Nagas, I hate that name. 'Big Girl.' 'Big Baby.' 'Big Anything.' Why is she so thick-headed? Doesn't she see that size is the least important thing about me? It's the mind that's important. The *mind*. Can't that soft-skinned, hairy-eyed, thoughtless, legged creature understand anything?"

It was some time before Sherahi became calm enough to concentrate and when she returned to Ruthie's mind she saw that all her effort to create useful guilt had been wasted. While she'd had her tantrum and had turned her attention away from the thunderhead of guilt she had been creating, Ruthie's focus had shifted to the baby boas.

She was salving her conscience by giving them water to drink from a paper cup. Sherahi saw the beautiful stain of guilt that she'd created in Ruthie's mind grow smaller and smaller as the boas began to drink. She realized that she'd lost the momentum needed to make Ruthie rush to the baggage car and free her and, to make matters worse, she'd almost exhausted her own mental reserves. All the energy had been wasted for nothing.

Jealously Sherahi watched the littlest boa delicately draw water into her mouth. These spoiled South American mongrels were barely five feet long and not even thicker than Ruthie's wrist, yet she pampered them and catered to them as if they were the most precious snake flesh on earth.

"And they're so ugly," thought Sherahi. It was inexplicable.

She compared the profile of the boa constrictor with that of the Burmese python or the reticulated python or any of the python brethren and concluded that boas were obviously inferior. They had a rough, unfinished look—as if the Creator had mislaid his original pattern and had made them from memory. Details of their anatomy were flawed.

For one thing, their heat-sensitive labial pits were lodged between their lip scales, when any respectable python knew that lip pits belonged right in the center of lip scales—not haphazardly poked in between. "Makes them look like their pits were an afterthought—stuck in, any old way," sniffed Sherahi.

If that weren't enough, all boas lacked the bone above the eye that hoods and shadows the eyes of pythons. "They're as pop-eyed as pug dogs," thought Sherahi and added, as she watched one little boa snap at Ruthie's fingers, "and they've got tempers to match." The little boas were so irascible that, if Sherahi hadn't controlled and directed them during the rituals, Ruthie would never have been able to dance with them.

But missing teeth and bones and misplaced lip pits were minor physical deformities—any generous-minded python could have overlooked these shortcomings if the boas had otherwise behaved in a decent fashion. But boas didn't even have the grace to make a pretty nest and allow their young to hatch in the ancient, dignified, reptilian way. Instead their hordes of young were born alive, squirming on a wave of slime from the mother's body. The thought made Sherahi shudder with repulsion. "Disgusting," she said. "Humans may have given them pretty names like rainbow boa and emerald tree boa, but it doesn't disguise their filthy habits. Disgusting," she concluded; "all of them are disgusting. I'm ashamed to call them 'cousin.' "

Carla, the littler boa, was still drinking, pumping water down her throat. Sherahi sent her a message that said, "Mongoose . . . long, skinny, bloodthirsty mongoose . . . bright teeth bite, shake you back and forth and you're dead meat. Look out. Mongoose. MONGOOSE RIGHT BEHIND YOU!"

She was pleased to see the little boa gag on the water and writhe on Ruthie's lap, hiccoughing and sick. That would teach her to be so greedy.

The pythoness turned her mind to the other boa, balanced on Ruthie's shoulders. She toyed with the idea of sending her a command to bite Ruthie hard on the neck, where it would leave a bruise that no amount of makeup could conceal. That would show Ruthie that she had no special power over these two lizard-faces.

But before she did this, Sherahi reconsidered. "It won't do any good," she thought. "It won't get me out of this trunk and now nothing will ever convince Ruthie that she isn't the world's greatest snake trainer. I should never have taught these toadbrains how to perform their parts of the ritual."

Too late Sherahi realized that it had been a mistake to do everything that Ruthie wanted. But she loved Ruthie and owed her life to the girl. At first it had been a small thing to scry her thoughts and make the serpentine undulations that Ruthie imagined. Sherahi's reward had been the pleasure it gave Ruthie and for a while it had been enough. When the little snakes had arrived it had seemed natural for Sherahi to direct their movements in the ritual, too.

The boas were only babies. It would be years before they'd be able to read a human mind and by python standards they'd never be brighter than worm snakes. Without Sherahi's guidance the little boas would have wandered away—slithering to and fro, wherever they pleased. They would never have been able to participate in the rituals Ruthie imagined. So, Sherahi directed her two little cousins and allowed Ruthie to take all the credit. "I suppose I've just got a special way with snakes," Ruthie'd explain. "Some people are just gifted that way." She actually seemed to believe this.

Even though Sherahi knew that Ruthie was a human and somewhat limited, it still rankled her that Ruthie didn't realize who was responsible for the success of the rituals. "Ruthie doesn't know it," she thought, "but she's imprisoned the brains that direct her whole operation. She doesn't really care about me. It would serve her right if I died of boredom, or loneliness, or heat prostration before this trip is over."

For a long while the snake nosed along the locked lid of her traveling trunk, pushing against it, still seeking a way out. "Essence of toadstool and ratcrap," thought Sherahi and slumped to the floor of the dark trunk. "What's the use? Nothing will get me out of here now. I'll just have to get used to being locked up here in the dark, with no air, no water. Tomorrow I'll be sitting in my own excrement, taking the shine off my new skin. This *must* be the awful thing that I dreamed about. Being in a cage—it's the worst thing of all."

A while later Sherahi was calmer. Once more she sent out her thoughts and found the little snakes and Ruthie. This time she watched the boas sun themselves through Ruthie's eyes. They were only common, limited boas, but nevertheless they were serpents and made a pretty show as they braided themselves through Ruthie's fingers. It was reminiscent of the way they danced in the ritual and Sherahi suddenly realized that her own comfort was trivial. The ritual and the ceremony were the important things. They must go on. Countless generations of pythons had bequeathed this task to her and she had to ensure that the ritual was done and done correctly. She would not disappoint her ancestors, even if she had to travel as baggage.

Sherahi regretted her burst of evil temper and sent a message of well-being and contentment into Ruthie's mind. She saw it blossom there and color every corner of that mental shambles. For no apparent reason Ruthie felt inexplicably happy and started to hum her favorite tune. Sherahi also forgave the two little boas and sent them affectionate greetings. They couldn't help it if Ruthie liked them best.

The sound of the train seemed to make Ruthie sleepy and Sherahi watched her put the snakes back into their sack and knot it securely. Sherahi saw her two little cousins yawn and curl up in separate corners within the pillowcase. Their drowsiness was contagious and Sherahi herself was yawning, musing and nearly dreaming when she noticed that the peculiar uneasy feeling had not disappeared. Even though what she thought was the worst thing had happened to her, the heavy feeling was still within her chest; she still pictured that dim corridor filled with sadness.

Sherahi knew that she was gifted with remarkable mental powers and she focused them on this knot of unease, willing it to vanish or to show itself. With all the mystic charms of her kind she tried to exorcise the spot of dark feeling, but when she had finished every charm and incantation, it was still there. It lodged just below her heart and she could feel it stirring like the maggot of a parasitic fly—mouthparts scissoring bits of flesh. But it was no living parasite and Sherahi knew that it might not be soon, but something very bad was going to happen.

Iowa City, Iowa
October, 1931

AFTER THAT FIRST experience with her reinforced traveling trunk, Sherahi stopped fighting against it. She still didn't like being locked inside it, but she was resigned to the situation and when she saw the thoughts begin to form in Ruthie's mind, the big snake crawled into the trunk of her own volition. "They'll never force me into it again," she thought proudly.

Now as Sherahi traveled by train from Iowa City to Omaha, she was once again inside her trunk, curled around a hot-water bottle and nestled beneath a cast-off down quilt. Within this cocoon she had retreated, as only some reptiles can, into the furthest passages of her labyrinthine mind. There she was busy with the long thoughts peculiar to her race—thoughts that would astonish whole universities of comparative anatomists and neurophysiologists, who believed they had thoroughly charted the serpent brain with microelectrode, perfusing dye and microtome—thoughts that would fascinate gurus, saints and philosophers of every stripe.

Sometimes the pythoness pondered the shape of desert wind, or the feel of cold, green water, or the taste of ancient stones. But these were simple thoughts. Kindergarten stuff. Nothing special. All snakes and even her distant relatives the legless glass lizards, who liked to pretend that they were serpents, could do as well. "Tight-scaled copycats" the Elder Race called them. Sherahi's real genius was different. It involved combinations of her special sense organs and mental processes.

Although some vipers, such as rattlesnakes, have a heat-sensitive pit beneath each eye, only giant snakes have a row of heat sensors on their lip scales. In some boas these organs lodge between lip scales, but one of the marks of the Elder Race is that their labial pits are found in the center of each lip scale. Wherever they are located, these special organs are used for wurping; for judging the direction and distance to a warm-blooded prey animal. Wurping helps pythons strike with accuracy. It augments sight and the reptilian sense of taste-smell, or fnast. Pythons see poorly in the dark. Without these infrared sensors they might go hungry on the moonless nights when they glide among tangled branches, the quopping, the tingling of their labial pits alerting them to the hunched and silent forms of sleeping birds. Before her capture the pythoness had wurped in this mundane way, but since she no longer had to hunt for food, she had found that her lip pits could be used for a different purpose.

Sherahi had found that she could combine wurping with fnasting to produce inwitting, an eighth sense which bridged time and space. Inwitting was more than just a vivid kind of memory, because when she used it the pythoness could actually think herself back in time or translate her mind to a distant place. If she wanted to, she could inwit to the riverbank near the Shudong Pagoda, back to the time when she had been semidivine, to the time before she was captured and sold into captivity. Or she could inwit into the minds of other snakes, living or dead. This was difficult and tiring but the pythoness could do it if she concentrated.

Humans cannot even begin to think in the same way. Not only do they lack the specialized sensory receptors that mediate fnasting and wurping but, even if they had Jacobson's organs or labial pits, their constant body temperature would prevent it. Warm-blooded thoughts whirr as rapidly as the wing beats of hummingbirds, while the thoughts of cold-blooded creatures are leisurely and sustained—more like the slow, powerful wing beats of migrating storks or pelicans or herons. As a result, even though humans have great intelligence they cannot retain thoughts as cold-blooded creatures can. And although other cold-blooded vertebrates, like sharks, turtles and goldfish, can hold a thought as long as the giant snakes, the mental abilities of the great pythons far surpass those of all other creatures. Only they have developed the eighth sense of inwitting.

Thus, if a human had observed Sherahi while she was deep into inwit, he might have thought her dead. Her huge body would be motionless and cool to the touch; her pupils would be mere black slivers within her amber, velvet eyes; her restless tongue would be still. If she moved at all it would be slowly, deliberately, as if her mind were off on holiday while her body functioned via dimly remembered instinct.

If asked to explain this torpidity, a zoologist might say that it was the usual reaction of a cold-blooded animal to lower air temperature: all metabolic processes diminished and if the snake did not warm itself in some way, they would stop and the snake would perish.

Sherahi knew better, of course, and if she had heard this facile explanation, she would have laughed the silent, mirthless snake laugh that has never been heard by humankind. She might have sighed, "Count on those hairy bipeds to get everything wrong. They're in such a hurry that they always miss the point. If they'd only slow down—even a little—they might begin to understand."

However, as Sherahi lay coiled within her traveling trunk in that chilly baggage car en route to Omaha, she wasn't musing on the mental frailties of *Homo sapiens*. Rather, she had transcended space and time and had inwitted to an old python in a pagoda half a world away. There, in the shadows of a candle-lit shrine, she watched streams of bats flit over the head and shoulders of a ghostly image of Buddha and waited for her teacher, U Vayu, to notice and greet her. One of the statue's hands drooped earthward and U Vayu lay coiled beneath it—as still as a ring of watered jade that had slipped from one of Buddha's golden fingers.

U Vayu had continued to be Sherahi's teacher and mentor ever since she had discovered how to inwit. She knew that he was a traditional, old-fashioned serpent who cherished correct form above all else and it would have been rude to break in upon his thoughts. He had taught her better than that and, besides, it had been at least nine human years since Sherahi had been one of his regular pupils. U Vayu wasn't expecting her.

Because she needed his advice, Sherahi wanted to behave especially well, so she waited in the gloom while a ragged ribbon of bats patrolled overhead and the candles on the altar sputtered and guttered one by one until the shrine was illuminated only by moonlight glinting off the Buddha's golden brow. Sherahi fnasted the air and thought with longing, "Home. This is my home." For a moment the claustrophobia of confinement seized her and threatened to destroy her mental projection. She heard the advice U Vayu had given to her long ago when she had complained of her captivity, "Adjust, little serpent. Learn to bend." She put the yearning for home and freedom aside and concentrated on the task at hand.

Hoping to attract her old teacher's attention without offending him, the pythoness breathed a long, gentle hiss. If she'd been able to touch him she would have had his attention instantly, but even though her mental projection showed her in complete detail, down to the last scute and belly plate, it was only an illusion created by her mind. The Sherahi that crouched beneath the altar of U Vayu's pagoda was as insubstantial as a soap bubble filled with smoke.

If U Vayu kept her waiting too long she would run out of time. All too soon the train would reach Omaha and Ruthie would unlock the traveling trunk, touch her and end this inwit. Because snakes have so many enemies and such delicate bodies they have a reflex that short-circuits the process of inwitting if they are physically disturbed. This would be Sherahi's last opportunity to visit U Vayu until she traveled again and had the security of solitary confinement once more. She'd learned that, although traveling in the baggage car was demeaning and uncomfortable, it was good for one thing: undisturbed inwitting. She wanted U Vayu's advice about the feeling of dread that haunted her. Maybe he could help.

Her hiss produced no visible reaction from U Vayu and the py-thoness grew impatient. U Vayu couldn't be hurried. Time was a bottomless pool to him and he did everything painfully slowly, probably because his every need was met by this pagoda. Food was plentiful here and U Vayu gorged on the rats that squabbled on the altar, fighting over offerings of rice and fruit. Occasionally he would grab one of the pariah dogs that skulked in the gloom, competing with the rats for the largesse of the faithful. The monks who flitted in the gloomy archways of the pagoda like earthbound saffron moths revered the old python and did not object when his embrace ruptured the heart of a dog or smothered a rat—he freed these souls for yet another turn on the Cosmic Wheel. To the monks, U Vayu was merely an-other implacable instrument of fate, a swift although not painless form of death.

Whether he was an instrument of fate or merely a glutton, U Vayu was keeping Sherahi waiting and she was restless. He had taught her the etiquette for this as well as a hundred other situations. The only correct thing she could do was wait until he formally invited her to share his thoughts. Sherahi reasoned that politeness was fine when you had the rest of your life to lurk in a temple and inwit at your leisure, but she had respon-sibilities to Ruthie and to the ritual. She sighed again, this time much more forcefully.

Above her head she was startled to hear a small, hoarse voice em-phatically whisper, "Sh. Sh. SSSSSHHHHHHHH. Stop making so much noise. You'll wake him up if you don't stop and then, oh, it's too awful to think about, but then he'll take it out on me and my family. You'll be long gone, ladysnake, and we'll be the ones who'll suffer.

"Please, ladysnake, have pity. You don't know what he's like when he's angry. He'll hold a grudge, ladysnake, and he won't stop until he's got-ten even.

"He's the quietest thing that there is, ladysnake. He's quieter than owl wing or cat paw or mouse breath—and he'll sneak up and grab us, one by one. And all together we're not even a toothful for him—he'll swallow us whole just for spite—he won't even bother to put us out of our misery. So, please, ladysnake, nice ladysnake, just be quiet and we'll all bless you for-ever."

Sherahi was surprised by this torrent of words and immediately felt sorry for this poor rat and his family. "All right," she whispered toward the unseen speaker. "I'll be quiet, but I've come a long way and I need to talk with him. I'll be quiet, but I can't wait forever."

"Well," the voice rasped on, "you don't have much choice—once he starts one of these trances he's sometimes gone for days." The voice became hopeful: "Maybe you'll just have to go back to where you came from?"

Then he continued, "Where *did* you come from, anyway? You

33

couldn't have come through one of the doors. I watch and I know you didn't come that way."

Sherahi said nothing. She wanted this little voice to go away and let her decide what to do.

"So, where? Where did you come from?" he persisted.

"Iowa," she said flatly. "I came from Iowa."

"Oh."

The talk trailed away and Sherahi was pleased that the guardian had finally left her alone. She was still anxious to speak with U Vayu. Perhaps the guardian could be used. . . . She sent out a thought message that said, "Are you still here?"

"Of course I'm here. I'm always here. Where'd you think I'd be? In Iowa? I live here."

"What sort of rat are you?" Sherahi asked. "A bandicoot?"

The voice became indignant. "RAT?" it shrieked. Then, as if it had remembered U Vayu, it whispered fiercely, "I'm *not* a rat. How could you think such a thing? Rats are nasty, with long, dirty tails and buck teeth."

"Well, what are you, then?" asked Sherahi.

"Look up, ladysnake," said the voice. "Can't you see me? I can see you."

Sherahi scanned the tops of all of the arches and arcades, but all she could see were the bats that patrolled in the gloom. She saw no guardian peering down at her. "I can't see you," she said. "Show yourself."

A shadow detached itself from the corner of Buddha's right eye and fluttered down, to swoop back and forth before the altar, making velvet arabesques in the gloom. "Can't miss me now, can you, ladysnake?" the voice whispered close to Sherahi's head first on the right, then on the left. She whirled to see the bat more clearly. It was gone, but not before its silky wings brushed her cheek.

"A bat," she said to herself. "I've never spoken to a bat. . . ." And then she thought, "Maybe there's a way to use him to wake U Vayu. If he'll only cooperate. . . ."

In an imperious voice she said, "I've watched bats but I've never spoken with one. Since this may be my only opportunity, tell me, are you really as good at flying as you're supposed to be?"

The bat continued swooping in front of Sherahi's face and answered, "Ladysnake, in all honesty and humility I must say that bats are Deluxe Flying Vertebrates—the Crème de la Crème of living flying machines. Nothing with wings is better."

"Surely your judgment can hardly be called unprejudiced."

"I assure you, ladysnake: nothing can outfly a bat."

"How about a pterodactyl?" Sherahi asked.

"I don't know what that is," said the bat. "But I'm sure I can do better."

"It doesn't matter," said Sherahi. "It's extinct. What about a dragonfly? I've heard that they're marvelous fliers."

"Those things," the bat said disdainfully, "nothing but one big flying mouth. Grab and stuff. Grab and stuff. Grab and stuff. Their table manners are repulsive and their flying—well, it's strictly amateur. No zigs and zags. Or curvettes and belly rolls. . . ." To illustrate his words the bat performed a series of aerial maneuvers that were too complicated for Sherahi's eyes to follow. He continued whispering, panting a little from exertion. "No Immelmanns . . . or dead stalls. . . . Compared to bats," he gasped, "dragonflies can hardly get off the ground. That's why we can catch 'em so easily." He swooped very close to her head and added conspiratorially, "You know, they don't even fly at night anymore."

"No, I didn't know that," answered Sherahi, pretending to be interested.

"Sure," said the bat, puffing out his scrawny chest. "And you know why, don't you?" There was no answer and he continued, "It's because they're scared of us—they know they're no match for us—the Winged Terror of the Night—Flying Fangs!" In a burst of enthusiasm the bat spiraled off to the ceiling and then swooped low over Sherahi, dive-bombing her.

"No, I didn't know that," she said, all the while thinking to herself, "And now, little *Fledermaus,* you're flying right into my trap."

"I know one animal that can outfly even you," she said.

"What's that?" the bat asked pugnaciously.

"Hummingbirds. *They* can hover, and anyone knows that a bat can't do that."

"Who told you that?" demanded the bat.

"I don't know," said Sherahi vaguely. "I guess I learned it when I was little."

"Well, you learned wrong, ladysnake. Dead wrong."

"I'm sure . . . no, I'm positive that I learned that bats can't hover the way hummingbirds can. Oh, I'll grant that you're wonderfully acrobatic, but wing control like that of a hummingbird isn't evolved every day, you know."

"Ladysnake, I don't know about evolved, but I can tell you that I can hover like nobody's business."

"Show me," said Sherahi.

"If I do, will you go away and leave us in peace?" asked the bat.

"Yes, I suppose so," said Sherahi. "But you've got to prove it to me."

"Okay, but remember," warned the bat, "you won't do anything to wake him up, will you?"

"No," lied Sherahi. "I won't do anything to wake him up. Now, if you can hover as you say you can, go over to where U Vayu is sleeping and count the number of scales on his lower lip."

"One side, or both?" asked the bat.

"One side will do."

"Nothing to it," said the bat and flew off.

When Sherahi saw that he was hovering in front of U Vayu's face she hissed very loudly. The sound didn't waken her teacher, but it so startled the bat that his wing brushed the inwitting serpent's face. It was a touch as delicate as a single strand of spider silk brushing across your cheek, but it was enough to instantly shatter U Vayu's trance. Sherahi saw him stagger back to full consciousness. He looked up at the ceiling, seeking his guardian, and she could tell that he was furious.

Sherahi hissed again, to make sure that U Vayu would direct his anger at her, not at the bat. To the flier who had disappeared into the crowd that flitted near the ceiling she sent a message that said, "I know that wasn't fair, but you must understand that I couldn't wait much longer. My time is nearly gone. Forgive me."

There was no hoarse-whispered reply and Sherahi knew that U Vayu's bat would never trust a snake again. "And," she reflected, "he's probably better off that way."

U Vayu was a deep thinker, even by python standards, and when he broke his mental silence his tone made it clear that he was not pleased to have been interrupted. "I wonder," he said in a cranky hiss, "if you would have better manners if you'd stayed here in this country where you belong, rather than going off to fall under the influence of barbarian humans."

He gathered his body into a tighter coil and glared at Sherahi, his hooded eyes daring her to breach his rules just once more. She knew that a single word from her would send him running away to brood in his lair beneath the altar. Now she'd have to wait until he was ready.

After a long time he flicked his tongue into the air in a peculiar arcing motion, as if to fnast her mental projection. Finally, this was the sign that she was invited to share his thoughts. He said, "Tell me, anxious one, what is so important? What petty concern of yours could possibly be as important as my conversation with the greatest serpent nat of all, the one who holds the world in his embrace? Why are you here?"

The pythoness knew she had made a serious mistake. Interrupting any serpent's thoughts was rude; interrupting a conversation between her teacher and one of the most powerful spirits, those that U Vayu called serpent nats, was unforgivable. She didn't know what to say and considered going back to the traveling trunk. But then she would have wasted all this time and energy. She said, "U Vayu, I'm sorry . . . I thought . . . you see . . . well, it seemed to take you so long and I was afraid that I might not have enough time. . . ." She hoped she sounded contrite; she certainly felt foolish. But the moment that these words were out of her thoughts she regretted them: she'd said exactly the wrong thing.

U Vayu snapped, "Not enough time? Did I understand you correctly? How often have I told you that constraints of time have nothing to do with us?" He waited for a reply and the pythoness sighed inwardly, "Slime of salamander, I've done it again."

"Hear me now and remember," U Vayu commanded. "Time cannot run out for a serpent. Indeed, even mouthing that phrase is distasteful to me. Time is one of our gifts. We alone can ride the back of time as eagles soar on the wind, as giant turtles navigate the ocean currents, as water scorpions stalk their jungles of pondweed. Only we can skip in and out of age and aeon as easily as butterflies flit from blossom to blossom. We alone can . . ."

The pythoness stopped listening. No matter what U Vayu said, *she* could feel time slipping away. She realized that her innocent remark had launched U Vayu into one of his all-too-frequent panegyrics on the unique powers of serpents. He could go on like this indefinitely if she didn't stop him. Knowing that any interruption was rude, she broke in with, "U Vayu, tell me of the Midgard Serpent. Does he often inwit with you?"

Her question stopped U Vayu in mid-sentence. She could see his surprised thoughts writhe deliciously around her oblique flattery. The pythoness had intimated that the Great Serpent Nat had wanted U Vayu's company, when the reverse was actually true. U Vayu wouldn't have admitted it to his pupil but, although he had tried many times, he had never been able to actually find the holiest serpent nat of all, the Great Worm. He hid this thought deep in his inmost mind, however, in a place that was inaccessible even to Sherahi's scrying. He wanted her to continue to believe that he had unlimited mental power as well as illustrious friends.

Haughtily he said, "It is not yet time for you to know of the Great Serpent Nats. You're just a baby—you have barely shed your egg tooth; you can hardly close your mind to me, much less think of protecting it from the Great Serpent Nats. It will be many years before you are ready to learn about them. Many years indeed."

The pythoness closed her inner mind like a fist around the idea that U Vayu prided himself on being the most ill-tempered snake in the world. She was certain that he could not pry this out of her thoughts.

U Vayu scryed her mind and saw that a portion of it was shut tight. What could she be hiding? He laughed and said, "How transparent you are, Sherahi. Right now you're thinking unkind things about your old teacher, aren't you?"

Sherahi didn't suspect that he was only guessing and wondered, "How could he have seen that?" She relaxed her guard on her hidden thoughts for a moment and in less time than it takes to say it, the nimble mind of U Vayu had read the thought that she was shielding.

"Hmph," he sniffed. "I'm not the most ill-tempered snake in the world, my dear. Wait till you meet Lachesis the Measurer; then you'll see what a bad temper really is. And when you do, you'll feel very sorry that you thought so ill of old U Vayu, who only tried to show you the right way to do things. Old U Vayu, who only tried to help you."

The pythoness could think of no reply, so she let him continue and wondered, "How could he have wormed past my shield?"

"Take my advice, young one," U Vayu droned. "It will be many years before your mental powers are subtle enough to seek the Great Ones. Even a preliminary encounter with the Bloody One would leave you witless—that is, if you were foolish enough to try. And the Great Worm would probably find you unexceptional—even boring. Remember, hatchling, he has been around since the beginning and we are only mortal serpents, even if we do have extraordinary gifts.

"All of this, of course, assuming that you do have the mental capacity to actually reach the Great Nats. Unfortunately, this is highly unlikely. You will no doubt spend much time on fruitless errands, inwitting to the wind. . . ."

Like a window crashing down without warning, U Vayu suddenly closed his mind to Sherahi. He glared at her and puffed up his body. He opened his mouth and hissed.

Sherahi had never seen him act in such a fashion and wondered, "What's wrong with the old fool now?" She quickly looked behind for some enemy. But there was no one else in sight.

"Is he having some kind of fit?" She had never seen a serpent die and wondered, "Is he dying?" She tried to read U Vayu's mind, but it was completely closed. All the avenues to it were blocked with rage. It was inexplicable. He'd never done this before.

"What did I do?" Sherahi wondered. She wanted to turn their conversation to her problems with Ruthie and the bad feeling that haunted her, but how could she do this with him behaving so oddly?

"Please, U Vayu," she begged in her smallest voice, "forgive me for whatever I've done. I didn't mean to make you angry."

The old python stopped hissing and gradually sank into a resting coil once again.

"Please, U Vayu, if you won't tell your worthless pupil about your conversation with the Great Worm, then be so good as to just tell her the names of the other Great Serpent Nats. You have said that there is little chance that I will ever be able to follow in your track, but if I knew their names, I could think of your brilliant conversations and take solace imagining them."

"How could I have ever had such a mule for a pupil?" U Vayu addressed the image of Buddha in an exasperated tone. Then he fastened his hooded eyes on Sherahi and said fiercely, "I've *told* you time and again, this is not for you."

Actually, U Vayu was sure that his pupil was more than ready to inwit to the Great Serpent Nats, and the knowledge that she would so easily succeed where he had continually failed made him furious with frustration. "It isn't fair," he hissed to himself. "She doesn't even realize what she can do. Oh, what I could do with those mental gifts. They're wasted on her. Wasted.

"Well," thought the crafty old python, "if I can't have them, I can at least try to control them."

Sherahi was still trying to calm her teacher. "Please, U Vayu," she begged again, "just tell me their names. This will be enough."

U Vayu was silent. Even though Sherahi didn't realize the extent of her mental powers, he knew it was wrong to deny her her birthright. The names of the Great Ones would give her the essential focus—something to fasten onto as she sent her mind spinning out to find the serpent nats. Without a name or an image she could do nothing.

The sound of a bronze bell reverberated against the gloomy arches of the shrine. In the distance men's voices began to intone a rapid chant accompanied by the pings and chimes of gongs and bells. A volley of squeaks and thumps issued from Buddha's lap as young rats jousted for dominance. The rats offended U Vayu and he rose slowly and majestically to his full striking stance to glare at the noise makers. They froze in postures of wide-eyed, silent dread.

Finally U Vayu spoke. "If I tell you the names of the Great Nats you must promise to always use the etiquette that I've taught you. I don't want the entire serpent world to think that U Vayu doesn't train his pupils properly."

"I promise, U Vayu," said Sherahi. Behind her mental barricade she thought, "How tedious this old worm is. Why is he making this so complicated? I'll promise him anything if only he'll get on with it. I've got other, more important, things to discuss with him."

But U Vayu wasn't finished yet. "Secondly, you must promise to always ask me before you inwit to one of the Great Nats."

"Yes, U Vayu. I promise," lied Sherahi. She knew that this was one promise that she would never keep. "It's none of the old busybody's business who I inwit to and he knows it. What a ridiculous thing to try to make me promise. U Vayu must be going senile."

"All right. The Midgard Serpent is the first of the Great Ones. Of course, he's a personal friend of mine and will be kind to you." U Vayu was lying but he reasoned that it would do small harm. There was only a slight chance that Sherahi would ever be able to inwit to the Great Worm and now that she'd promised to always seek his permission first, U Vayu felt certain that the mediocre level of his mental skills would never be revealed. "I'll always be able to think of something to stop her," he thought.

"Then there is Lachesis. As I've told you, she is the third of the Fates—the Measurer who determines the length of each life. As you can imagine, Lachesis is always very busy. Do not pester her with your tiresome questions. Incidentally, she deals with so many that she may not remember an insignificant teacher like me." U Vayu didn't mention that he had never successfully inwitted to Lachesis, although he had tried many times. U Vayu was morbidly interested in the length of his own life and since he had never been able to reach Lachesis he'd been forced to consult other, less reliable, fortune-tellers. It was actually one of these that he'd been talking to when the bat interrupted his inwit.

"Let's see, there are others. What are their names?" For a moment U Vayu's memory failed him and he tried to mask the confusion that suffused his orderly thoughts. But then the catechism from his earliest training came back to him. "Oh yes, I remember now," he continued, recalling how he had been taught to tick off the nats' names on the scales of his tail. "There are the Nagas, the Hindu water spirits. They are the keepers of lapis lazuli and are supposed to be great healers, although they're a bit frivolous for my tastes. Spend a lot of time splashing about. If you can get their attention they will guide you to Ananta, the many-headed serpent who carries the god Vishnu on his back. The Nagas and Ananta were around long before the other nats and will teach you a great deal if they are willing, but they like to poke fun." He hid from Sherahi the memory of the humiliating encounter he had had with them, thinking, "She'll find out for herself, soon enough."

"Last is Quetzalcoatl, the Feathered Serpent. He isn't called the Bloody One for nothing. Be careful of him."

"What do you mean, U Vayu? Why should I be careful?" Sherahi was suddenly fearful. She hadn't realized that the Great Serpent Nats were anything but benevolent.

"The serpent nats are different from other kinds of spirits," U Vayu said. "They have great wisdom and knowledge concealed by great cunning. One can never be quite sure of their motives; they play tricks with words. If you sense that they are unfriendly, immediately break off the inwit and try to escape."

"Even without the farewell ceremony?"

"If you want to keep your wits you will do as I say."

"U Vayu, how can I become strong enough to approach the Great Serpent Nats? I have so many questions and you are so often busy. . . . And I wanted to ask you about something else. It's the reason that I came to see you in the first place. . . ."

The pythoness could sense that her teacher made some response, but before she could fully perceive it someone touched her body, which lay in the locked trunk in Omaha, and ended this inwit. The pythoness's consciousness was jerked from the dark pagoda and the familiar hiss of U Vayu's voice into the confusion and glare of Ruthie's dressing room.

Something was wrong. Ruthie was yelling, "Now see what you've done, Bernie Weinstein. Oh, Jesus—I think she's dead. She's so cold. Poor thing. Hurry, help me lift her out of this trunk."

All in slow motion the snake felt hands lift her head and neck. She lazily swam upward into conscious control of her body and began to react to the flood of sensory impressions. The quopping of her labial pits told her that there was heat coming from the side of the room and by reflex she began to move toward it. As she crawled out of the trunk toward the heat, the snake listened to Ruthie rail at Bernie. The sound was faint and very far away, like the buzzing of a fly against a screen. She undulated forward, fnasting steaming metal, and realized that the surface was too hot to touch.

"If you'd been on time the Burmese wouldn't have gotten so cold," Ruthie complained. "She's almost frozen to death. If she gets pneumonia, it's your fault, Bernie Weinstein. I should know better than to believe anything that you say." Their conversation didn't have any immediate importance to her and Sherahi stopped listening. As she crawled toward the radiator the snake wondered, "Will I ever be able to get accustomed to the shock of an interrupted inwit? Or will it always be as wrenching as the sudden sight of a hideous, scaleless, bulbous human face?"

Sherahi immediately reproached herself. "That's an unkind way to think about Ruthie. The poor creature can't help it if she was born without scales. She would look much nicer, though, if her face weren't so flat. If only she had the suggestion of a muzzle or snout. And just think what a long, sinuous tail would do for her looks."

Sherahi undulated into a resting coil a safe distance from the hissing radiator and thought, "And tails are so useful—so expressive. But Ruthie doesn't even have the stump of one. Still, as humans go, Ruthie is better than some and at least as good as most. She's kind to me; except for her physical defects, the only really bad thing about her is that she doesn't understand about names. For some reason she thinks that she can name everything."

Sherahi shuddered at the memory of some of the names that Ruthie had tried to give her. Condescending, pedestrian names; names that totally lacked the authoritative sting and beauty of her true name: Sherahi. It had been a difficult battle but the pythoness was pleased to have finally broken Ruthie of the habit of calling her "Big Baby" or "Big Bertha."

The pythoness watched the two small Brazilian boas crawl out of their travel sack and sent them mental greetings. "Ruthie has horrid, unexpressive names for them, too: Rosita and Carla. Ugh," she thought.

The boas were only babies, just five feet long, and like most of their kind they were rather retarded. They hadn't associated themselves with Ruthie's names for them as yet. Like most juveniles they spent most of their time fighting and Sherahi wished that a mature boa was around to supervise them. They needed manners, for one thing. As the only adult serpent in residence she'd have to do something about their education sooner or later. But that could wait; the important thing now was to get warm. "Besides," Sherahi thought, "they're not of the Elder Race. I'm not really responsible for them."

The pythoness let the heat soak into her thick coils. It made her sleepy and as Ruthie and Bernie left the room they took their argument outside and it grew quiet. Part of Sherahi's mind was still kneading memories—reviewing and editing them. She was still thinking about names and her dignity as a python.

"Getting her to stop using 'Big Bertha,' that was the worst. Ruthie was so fond of that name. Sometime I'll have to tell the little snakes about it. It will be their first lesson in managing humans.

"In a way," thought Sherahi, "I was lucky to have a human who was so easy to train. If she hadn't been so manageable, I might still be hearing 'Big Bertha' all the time. I'll have to remember to tell those little South American mongrels to teach Ruthie not to call them obnoxious names. But, they're so barbaric in other ways, it wouldn't surprise me if boas don't care about names at all."

Sherahi concentrated on basking, but part of her slow, reptilian mind continued to consider the issue of names. She had detested "Big Bertha" from the start. It sounded bovine and lumpy. It was not an appropriate name for an incarnation of the Divine Spirit. Almost at once she had decided to do something about it.

She had begun to retrain Ruthie by using vehement tongue gestures. "Surely," she had thought, "Ruthie will understand." She had remembered seeing Ruthie defiantly stick out her tongue at Bernie once when they were having an argument. At the time the pythoness had thought it strange that reptiles and humans used an identical signal to express rejection. When she had mentioned this astonishing discovery to U Vayu she had loftily added, "We have so little else in common with them."

After that, whenever Ruthie called her "Big Bertha," the pythoness had put out her tongue and slowly waggled its shiny, black tips. Ruthie, however, didn't seem to notice the signal and the pythoness's tongue had grown dry and cramped. She had eventually abandoned tongue gestures, concluding that serpents and humans were even more different than she'd imagined.

Her next tactic had been to simply ignore the awful name. Given her superb mental abilities she had thought this would be easy, but Ruthie had made it difficult for her by crooning "Bertha, Big Bertha, look what Mummy's got for you" and such drivel whenever she had dangled a mouthwatering, ratty-smelling meal in front of the pythoness's nose. Even though rabbits were a better size for a bellyful, rats were Sherahi's favorite food and it had taken all of the snake's resolve not to snap and strike immediately. She had abstained, though, because she knew that if she ate in response to that name she would be "Big Bertha" forever. That thought had made her lose her appetite.

Ruthie had great patience with the eccentricities of her animals, but it was insignificant when compared to the patience of the pythoness. Thus, their encounters invariably had ended the same way: sooner or later Ruthie would give up, drop the rat and depart, leaving the big snake to feast in private and, what was more important to her, in anonymity. As her six movable jaws had inched slowly over the rat's fur she'd had the extra satisfaction of knowing that she'd won another round in her battle against being labeled "Big Bertha."

Although Sherahi didn't know it, Ruthie had a different view. When the python had not responded to "Big Bertha," Ruthie had thought that she was just a slow learner. She had persisted with the name, reasoning that sooner or later the snake would associate it with food. She had been disappointed when the animal abruptly went on a hunger strike in the early stages of her training. Later, when she had read that snakes are deaf to airborne sounds and only hear vibrations transmitted through a surface, the pythoness's behavior suddenly made sense to Ruthie: it had nothing to do with intelligence; rather, Big Bertha hadn't responded to her name simply because she hadn't heard it. This seemed to settle the issue and Ruthie had given up trying to teach the snake her name and had concentrated on training her for the act.

Years had passed and, now that the pythoness had become a giant snake, Ruthie had discarded Big Bertha as an inappropriate name for such a majestic beast. Except for occasional lapses she simply called her "the Burmese." The way in which Ruthie hissed that name gave it an exotic, forbidden flavor that appealed to the pythoness's sense of drama. At least this new name had some dignity. It was far better than Big Bertha, but it still was not her *real* name—her given python name.

The pythoness wished that she could tell Ruthie what her real name was, but years of trying had taught her that it was not possible for her to insert information into a human's mind. The pythoness could read human thoughts, but communication of ideas was beyond her. Because emotions originate in the most reptilian portion of the human brain, it was possible for the pythoness to hurl guilt, hatred, love, happiness or such things into Ruthie's mind. A clever manipulation of emotions was usually enough to control Ruthie. The process took its toll on Sherahi, though. It always left her mentally and physically exhausted. Yet, even though entering Ruthie's maelstrom of jumbled sensory impressions and whirling cogitations was draining, the pythoness would have dared it again and again just to tell Ruthie what her given python name was. The snake was justifiably proud of her name: she'd had it since she was a hatchling and it was her single possession. She would have liked to share it with Ruthie.

Even though Sherahi realized that Ruthie wouldn't understand the significance of her name, she wished that Ruthie could know her as Sherahi, not the Burmese, Big Bertha, Big Girl or any of those other demeaning names. She wished that she could speak to Ruthie in the way that U Vayu had once told her that people and serpents had conversed in the old days, before the members of the Elder Race had lost their voices. Whenever Sherahi had these thoughts she was ashamed and hoped no other python was scanning her mind. She ought to know better: she owed her life to Ruthie; it was not right to ask for more.

Ruthie had bought Sherahi when she was operating a shooting gallery in a carnival outside San Francisco. Business was slow that day and she had several hours before the first show of the evening. The carnival belonged to a magician billed as the Great Gaswell (behind his back Ruthie and his other assistant, Paula, called him the Great Gasbag). Ruthie had run away from her mean-mouthed, small-minded relatives to what she had imagined was a life of freedom and excitement. Now she often wished that she was back home on the gritty back porch, swatting flies and minding her younger brothers.

Ruthie was seventeen and in the two months since she'd run away she'd grown bored with her lot as a magician's assistant: being sawed in half, levitated or made to vanish had grown tedious. She also was tired of, as well as frightened by, the Great Gaswell, his quick hands and his intimate whisperings. Whenever he had placed her inside a cabinet, or behind a curtain, or sometimes when she was bound hand and foot, waiting for him to metamorphose her into a fluttering dove, Gaswell's hands would fly all over her body, patting and pinching her in an all-too-practiced sleight of hand. The first time it had happened she had been so shocked that she didn't know what to think. She hoped that maybe she'd misinterpreted an innocent, reassuring touch. But she discovered that it had been no accident, because Gaswell repeated this performance each night. It made her furious, but what could she do, with the audience right out front? Offstage Gaswell denied everything, but when no one was looking he'd leer at her and whisper things she didn't quite understand. Lately he'd gotten worse.

Ruthie knew that she had to get a new job, but she was far from her home in southern Illinois and the little money she'd saved had been spent on a copy of the soigné turban that Natacha Rambova had made so popular.

Ruthie had found the teal faille creation in a milliner's shop in San Francisco and hadn't been able to resist it. She had added a dashing pheasant feather that arced dramatically back from her brow. She kept her treasure in its round, candy-striped box and every night she would put it on and admire herself, imagining the chic daytime suit she'd eventually buy to wear with it. The pheasant plume had cost extra and because all of her savings were gone, she'd have to wait for a better job to come along before leaving Gaswell's carnival.

It was Gaswell's boa that had given Ruthie the idea of becoming a snake charmer. Gaswell expected his two assistants to sew their own costumes and take care of his props, as well as appear onstage. Growing up on a farm, Ruthie had had a lot of pets, even a big black snake that a neighbor boy had given her, and she had never been afraid of anything except her father when he got his temper up. So she had taken charge of the rabbits, doves, goldfish and the boa that Gaswell used in his illusions. One day she draped the boa over her shoulders and it occurred to her that this might be a way out of Gaswell's carnival.

She needed a costume and found an old piece of green velvet in the bottom of a trunk. She cut leaves from the velvet and tacked them onto a halter and shorts. She added her turban to this costume and began practicing to appear as Eve in the Garden of Eden. When she had what she thought was a routine she showed it to Paula, who assured her that with her looks and with the right music and the right lights she could be really big in vaudeville—really big, not nickel-and-dime stuff like Gaswell. What Ruthie needed, however, was a huge, scary-looking snake; Gaswell's boa ate too much and looked about as satanic as a caterpillar. Ruthie couldn't wait to start her new act. Then she'd thumb her nose at Gaswell and his sleazy tricks. If only there were a snake that she could use!

The early afternoon sun warmed the sides of the shooting gallery to produce a distinctive, not unpleasant, smell that mingled odors of straw, canvas, trampled grass and machine oil. At the back of the booth a row of bright-yellow ducks swam in an endlessly clicking single file attached to a rubber belt, and at the front of the booth the five pellet guns that Ruthie had just cleaned glinted their invitation as they waited for some yokel to try his skill. As Ruthie dusted the rows of plaster of Paris statuettes of red Indians (each of which eternally knelt on a stump with one brown hand raised above his war-painted brow while he searched a remote horizon), she imagined herself a rich and famous burlesque star. Men in silk top hats and tails offered her bouquets of yellow roses at the stage door; she didn't care that her ermine-edged cape trailed in the dirt (she had three nicer ones in her closet); real diamonds sparkled on her wrist and a huge five-pointed star glittered on her dressing-room door. As she dusted the fat bellies of each of the pink Kewpie dolls that faced the row of red Indians, in her imagination she swept out the stage door, past the yellow roses and the flappers and sheiks clamoring for her autograph. A ragged bum watched her from the edge of the crowd. His mouth fell open in astonishment. She recognized him as the Great Gasbag and their eyes met just before the chauffeur closed the door. She stared at him coolly and asked her maid for the gold compact from her purse. She did not give Gaswell the satisfaction of recognition and settled back onto the limousine's leather cushions, admiring the reflection of her finely arched brow.

Part of Ruthie's job in the shooting gallery was to lure customers in to try their luck. She had finished dusting and saw a likely-looking marksman coming down the midway. He stopped briefly before the Freak Show, gawking at the canvas advertisements that showed Major John the Frog Boy crouching on an enormous lily pad; Dickie the Penguin Boy with his legs fused from the calves up; Frieda the Lady Sword Swallower, who had six steak knives plunged into her uplifted, open mouth; and Serpentina, the half woman, half serpent whose bifid, scale-encrusted tail twined around a barre. The picture of Serpentina showed her nude from the waist up and her nipples were the livid pink of the bellies of the Kewpie dolls. "Positively Alive," the broadsides claimed, but the sign in the Fat Lady's lap said, "First Show 1 P.M." Clara, the Fat Lady, wasn't a bad soul. She fanned herself, looked inquisitively at the sailor and hitched up her petticoat to reroll a shell-pink silk stocking. "Clara has more stockings . . ." Ruthie thought, wondering how much those had cost. The sailor shook his head and continued walking down the midway toward the shooting gallery. Ruthie heard Clara call, "Come back, sailor. I've got something for you." Ruthie knew that she was going to spread her knees for him. She'd seen the trick a hundred times. At first she'd found it embarrassing, but now it was only Clara trying to earn a little extra money for the silk stockings that were her passion. The sailor hoisted his sea bag to his shoulder and waved, calling, "Maybe some other time."

"Here comes a sucker," thought Ruthie.

She called out, "Whattcha got in that bag, sailor?" in a voice that got his attention. He stopped, unslung the bag, untied it and, to Ruthie's surprise, he pulled a long, angry snake out into the dusty grass of the midway.

At this time Sherahi was seventeen feet long, as emaciated as a vine snake and furious because she couldn't see. The scales over her eyes hadn't shed properly and she'd made them worse by scratching them against the crate in which the sailor usually kept her. She'd hoped to restore her sight by rubbing her eyes in this way, but now each was covered with a puffy, opaque scale and she was as blind as a white cave salamander. With her head raised and her body inflated she opened her mouth and hissed a loud warning, making it clear that she was angry and that she would hurt anyone who got within striking distance.

Ruthie was fascinated. Here was a snake that could frighten an audience. A huge snake that could impersonate Satan in the Garden of Eden. If only it wasn't as dangerous as it looked.

"Is it poisonous?" she asked.

"Nope." The sailor was surprised that this carnival girl hadn't screamed yet. He liked it best when women jumped on top of tables or screamed and shrank away in horror at his strange pets. He kicked at the python's tail and then jumped back as the snake lunged at and missed his foot. He knew she couldn't strike with any accuracy. He looked slyly at the girl to see her gasp in surprise, but her eyes were only on the snake—not on him.

"Does it bite?"

"It's a she and right now she might. Mighty dangerous kind of snake," he said. "Enough snake right here to kill a water buffalo. I've heard of one that ate a full-grown leopard." He kicked at the snake again and jumped out of its reach.

The python struck again and her mouth closed on air. She hissed more loudly. Humans were stupid animals: they needed to be told more than twice.

"Don't kick her," Ruthie said. "It's mean."

"They don't mind—anyway, I'm not hurting her."

"Well, you're not doing her any good, and you're upsetting her for no reason."

The sailor made no reply, but felt slightly ashamed of himself.

"How do you know it's a girl?" Ruthie asked.

The sailor deftly grabbed Sherahi's head and tail ends and, holding the snake out at arm's length so that she couldn't get a purchase on his body, he walked toward the shooting gallery. The big snake writhed and reached for a strangle hold. The sailor waited for her to tire and then flipped her tail over to show Ruthie its belly side. He pointed to two tiny claws that protruded between scales near her tail.

"See those?" he asked.

"Yeah."

"Well, if she were a he they'd be big—like rooster spurs."

"Oh." There was a moment while Ruthie watched the big snake and while the sailor watched Ruthie and while Sherahi fnasted the almost scentless body of the strange but apparently friendly new human.

"Did she ever bite you?"

Sherahi hissed again through her nostrils. The sailor held her head too tightly and he was hurting her. But he was strong and she was too weak to struggle.

The sailor gestured with one elbow and said, "Pull up my sleeve. You'll see what she can do when she's mad."

Ruthie rolled up the right sleeve of the sailor's middy blouse. Just below his elbow was an ugly purple bruise flecked with many small slashes and puncture wounds. He continued, "She did that yesterday. She can be mean when she wants to, but sometimes, like now, she's as gentle and nice as a kitten."

The sailor was disappointed when the girl only glanced at his battle scar. He'd wanted a little more attention and decided to play his last card. He gathered up the heavy snake, lifted her over the girl's head, settled the snake's body onto her shoulders and waited for a reaction, thinking, "This usually gives them hysterics and conniption fits."

Ruthie ducked out from beneath the snake's body and said, "Here, I know how to hold a snake. Just let her get used to me for a minute."

By this time Sherahi was exhausted. She had stopped hissing and lay suspended between the sailor's hands like a tired piece of rope.

"Sure you're not afraid? A snake like this can kill you if you're not careful."

"I'll be careful. Just let her get used to me." Ruthie took the snake from the sailor's hands. "She's heavy," she said. Her fingers could feel backbones and ribs through the snake's loose skin. "Don't you ever feed her?" she asked.

"Not too often. I've tried, but it goes against my grain to see her kill those helpless, little mice. Besides, she doesn't seem to mind—I guess snakes like this don't need much. My buddies tried to feed her a couple of months ago. They caught a rat in the galley and gave it to her, but she wouldn't touch it. She drinks a lot of water, though."

Feeling the accusation in Ruthie's green eyes he added pompously, "Cold-blooded things don't need to eat as often as we do."

"How long have you had her?" Sherahi moved and Ruthie felt how she swam within her baggy skin.

"Oh, about three years now, I guess." The sailor hitched up his bell bottoms, straightened his middy blouse and resettled his cap.

"Three years!" Ruthie exclaimed. "That's awful. How'd you like to go hungry for three years? Look at this poor thing—she's nothing but skin and bones. You should be ashamed of yourself. You're killing her."

The sailor hadn't expected this. He started to defend himself. In a softer, apologetic voice he said, "I told you, sweetheart, she won't eat anything."

Ruthie snapped back, "You're probably not treating her right. Poor, skinny thing." After a moment she continued, "And where do you get off calling me sweetheart? I don't even know you." Ruthie was mad at the sailor, but directed her attention to the snake that lay calmly in her hands and trailed down onto the grass. "Poor, skinny snake," she thought. There was a pause and then Ruthie looked straight into the sailor's eyes and asked suddenly, "Why don't you let me have her?"

48

The sailor was quiet for a moment, returning her stare and thinking that her eyes were awfully green. Then he dropped his gaze and said, "Well, I couldn't just give her away to a stranger. I paid good money for her." He was secretly pleased to be free of the burden of the snake. The prospect of getting a little extra cash brightened his spirits considerably.

Ruthie thought a minute and said, "My name's Ruthie Notar and I'll give you two-fifty."

Twenty minutes later Ruthie was back huckstering for Gaswell's shooting gallery, inviting the public to try their luck and maybe win a prize. At the back of the booth the yellow wooden ducks swam in a jerky single file against the canvas drop and on either side the rows of red Indians searched the horizon, ignoring the bug-eyed Kewpie dolls on the opposite wall that stared at their blushing toes, eternally self-conscious and institutionally cute. The only difference in the shooting gallery was the addition of a big python draped around Ruthie's shoulders. She'd given the sailor a whole week's pay for this eerie, white-eyed snake and if she'd known much about snakes she'd never have done it. The sailor had said that he was letting the animal go so cheaply because she was sick and would surely die. He'd pointed to the starvation furrows that traveled the length of the snake's body and tried to convince Ruthie that this was a poor buy. He'd also tried to make a date with her.

But Ruthie was having none of it. She'd neatly side-stepped his offer of a date and had made up her mind that she wouldn't let this snake die. This big snake with the queer white eyes was her ticket out of the Great Gaswell's employ and now that she had it she wouldn't let go of it easily. "Besides," Ruthie said to herself as she sat on the stool, next to the row of pellet guns tethered to the front of the gallery, "who wouldn't gamble two-fifty on the chance to become a star?" It was no sure thing, but only a sucker wouldn't grab for this brass ring with both hands.

Some months later Ruthie left Gaswell's employ and metamorphosed into Naruda, Exotique Dancer and Snake Charmeuse, and Sherahi began her career in show business.

Omaha, Nebraska
November, 1931

RUTHIE SAT ASTRIDE a chair near the edge of the stage of the Club Istanbul and listened to the six musicians murder her music. It was the first time that she and the Girls had performed in this club and, even though the audience would probably not know any better, she wanted to make sure that everything went smoothly.

Bernie had fixed her lighting as best he could in this rat trap and he sat nearby at one of the small tables. Ruthie saw him wince as the saxophonist tortured the final chorus. This wasn't a perfect place in which to perform, but then, none of the places in which she worked was any great shakes. Even though this was the first time she'd appeared at this particular club, it seemed like familiar territory. Like the KitKatt Club in Louisville, or the Tornado in Wichita, or the Queen of Diamonds in Minneapolis, or any of the dozen little remodeled speak-easies across the Midwest where Bernie found work for her, the Club Istanbul had a down-at-the-heels appearance and smelled of stale beer, spilled liquor and cigar smoke.

The minuscule dance floor that doubled as a stage was surrounded by a sea of white-covered tables that were barely large enough to hold two highball glasses, one pair of elbows and an ashtray. The room was lit by red-shaded lamps that threw ruddy semicircles onto the stucco walls and the décor was some wheat farmer's concept of the Kasbah: arched doorways, beaded curtains and the obligatory silhouette of a mosque and a crescent moon painted on the wall behind the bandstand. A single fly-specked fan creaked against the ceiling. Ruthie would have given odds that tonight the waiters and the band would all wear short red jackets and tasseled fezzes. This must be *the* place to go in a certain section of Omaha. How in heaven's name did Bernie find these places?

Ruthie had learned that a rehearsal was always necessary with the Girls and a new band. In fact, the success of her act depended on it. It wasn't that the snakes needed practice; rather, the purpose of the rehearsal was to show the musicians that the Girls weren't dangerous. Without a rehearsal the musicians tended to gawk at the animals, forget their cues and generally louse things up like that drummer had in Louisville. She'd found that one run-through with the band usually took care of this problem.

The combo finished playing her music, "In Allah's Garden," and the clarinetist turned to her and asked, "You ready to try it, honey?"

"Sure," Ruthie said, removed her kimono and walked to the huge rattan basket that stood in the center of the stage. She lifted its lid and gave the basket three sharp kicks to alert the snakes inside that they were supposed to come out soon. When the actual performance was about to begin she would do this in a blackout, as the bandleader announced the appearance of Naruda, for the first time in Omaha at the Club Istanbul.

Ruthie parted the beaded curtain that separated off the backstage area and waited in semidarkness for the third bar and her entrance. As she waited she lifted one leg slowly to waist level and then to shoulder level, propped it against the opposite wall of the corridor and flexed her torso down onto her raised leg. She repeated the stretches over the other leg and then flexed her body forward until both hands were on the floor.

Her act was really very simple: a straightforward acrobatic striptease with the snakes used as props. They were her gimmick. At the beginning of her dance she was clad in many layers of sheer fabric and at the end she was down to a sequined bra and panties. The two small boas had been used to carry away floating layers of chiffon and she draped them around her shoulders or around her head as a turban. She then did some acrobatic turns while the Burmese crawled out of the basket. The audience usually gasped at the size of the snake and Ruthie—or, rather, Naruda—led her around the perimeter of the stage in a pretty semicircle, allowing the crowd to fully appreciate the immense size of the beast. In the finale the Burmese slowly crawled up Ruthie's leg, while one of the little boas crawled across her shoulders and then down her chest. A long time ago the little boas had learned the trick of burrowing beneath clothing and Ruthie had capitalized on that trick by letting them nose beneath the left side of her brassiere while she simultaneously unhooked it. It all happened so quickly that the audience was fooled into thinking that the dancer, with one snake wound around her head, another around her chest and the third, huge, one climbing around her leg, was actually being undressed by a serpent. Some members of the audience swore that she was naked above the waist, but Ruthie had fooled them: she was actually chastely clad in snake flesh.

Ruthie heard her cue and made her entrance, and the rehearsal went as planned. Carla and Rosita helped her off with the many layers of chiffon and all went as it had many times until the Burmese's part came. As Ruthie led the big snake around the stage she noticed that she was much bigger than she'd remembered. How could the snake have grown so much in the six months since they'd worked? Ruthie guessed that she must be over twenty feet long and, as she started to climb up onto her leg, Ruthie realized that the snake weighed more than ever before. Ruthie could hardly support her, much less dance seductively under the weight. Somehow they finished the act and Ruthie guided the big snake back into the basket, removed the others from her head and breast and put them on top of the Burmese and locked the lid into place.

Taking the kimono from Bernie she said, "Okay, boys?" to the band and reached for the towel that Bernie had over his shoulder.

"What's wrong, sweetheart?" he asked in a whisper.

"Couldn't you tell?" she panted.

"No, everything seemed okay. You'll knock 'em dead tonight—Omaha has never seen anything like this, for sure. But you seem winded. Are you feeling all right?"

"Yeah, I'm fine. It's the Burmese." Ruthie pushed the damp curls off her forehead. "She's so big. I can hardly manage her."

"You did look like you were working awfully hard out there," Bernie replied.

"Yeah, too hard," Ruthie agreed. "God, it's hot in here. Let's go get some air."

They sat on the steps leading to the stage door, while Ruthie tried to figure out what to do to salvage the act. She could use Carla or Rosita more and maybe only show the big snake, maybe have her rear up and hiss at the audience. The Burmese was such a reliable trouper that Ruthie hated to use her as just stage dressing, but there seemed to be no other choice. She told Bernie of her plan and he agreed that it would work just as well as the original. Ruthie could do wonders with those snakes. As far as he was concerned she was the best snake trainer in the business.

He had another question. "What're we going to do with that big snake? If you don't really need her in the act, there's no sense carting her all over the country. She costs a fortune to ship. And freight charges are going up all the time. The smart thing to do would be to sell her."

Ruthie was incredulous. "Sell my Burmese? Never."

"Well, baby," Bernie said, taking out a cigarette and tapping it against his thumbnail, "I think you should at least think about it. Next spring, when we go through New York, we could trade her at Leftrack's. You could get some smaller pythons or maybe a pine snake or that indigo snake you've been talking about for so long. You could probably get a whole bushel basket of snakes for her."

"The Burmese is worth more than twenty pine snakes, Bernie."

"Look, baby, don't get sore at me. It's not my fault that you take too good care of your snakes and they grow so fast. I'm not complaining. . . ." He reached over and brushed the curls at the nape of her neck and added, "You take good care of me, too."

Ruthie turned toward him and put her arms around his neck. "The Burmese has been with me for so long—even longer than you have. I couldn't sell her any more than I could sell you."

"Ruthie, I'm not forcing you to do anything—only think about it. She could go to a zoo, maybe. You'd like that, wouldn't you?"

"Yeah, but still. . . ."

Bernie could see that Ruthie was dropping into one of her depressions, so he decided to change the subject. He lifted her chin, looked into her eyes and said, "I'll tell you what—in honor of your return to show business, let's go have lunch."

"But what about the Burmese?"

"Forget it. Go put on your glad rags. Let's see the town."

"Big thrill," said Ruthie, knowing what Bernie's idea of a high time was. On the way to her dressing room she glanced onstage and saw the big basket that had been pushed back and off the dance floor. She knew it was mostly filled with the Burmese and felt sad. As she pushed open the dressing-room door she saw a bruise beginning to blossom on the back of her right calf. It had the imprint of the Big Girl's scales and Ruthie remembered the snake's chin pressing down uncomfortably into her skin. "Jesus," Ruthie thought and at that moment she decided that, even though the snake had been with her since the beginning, she would have to go.

Inside the wicker basket the three snakes moved around and around, intertwining as if braided by an invisible hand. It was always like this after a ritual: it took Sherahi and the two young boas some time to calm down from all the excitement.

As usual, Carla and Rosita were bickering. Rosita nosed her way along Sherahi's broad back, pressing her muzzle into Sherahi's scales to get attention. As the older of the two boas, Rosita always felt responsible for their part in the ritual.

"Well, Auntie," she demanded, "what did you think? Did we do it right? Do you think She was proud of us? Did They like us?"

Sherahi was about to answer that it didn't matter what "They" thought. After all, "They" were only humans who came to worship at this temple. It only mattered that the two boas performed their part of the ritual in the old ways, according to the correct patterns and following her directions. Sherahi knew that the rituals were very important and had tried to get the two South American mongrels to behave properly, even though they didn't quite understand the significance and mystery of the ritual they performed. But before the words could form in her mind, the younger boa added, "And what about *me,* Auntie? Was *I* good? Come on, Auntie, tell me. Did I do it right?"

"What Auntie is going to tell you, baby sister," said the older boa in the exasperated tone reserved for hatchlings and irresponsible amphibians, "is that you nearly ruined everything. Even from where I was, 'round Her waist—even from there I could see how you tried to show off. Serves you right that you nearly fell off of Ruthie's headdress at the end. I'll bet you'll be punished. She won't use you in the act. She must know that only Auntie and I do our parts right."

"She won't," the littler snake wailed. "Auntie, She won't take me out, will She? It was just an accident. It could have happened to anyone. Auntie, you saw it, didn't you?"

"Don't be a little fool," her sister snapped. "Auntie can read your mind as easily as she can see little fishes hiding on the bottom of a creek. She knows that you were just trying to act big. Imagine, Auntie, our little Carla pretending she's a cobra. Serves her right that she nearly fell."

"You're just jealous because I'm prettier than you and She likes me best," said the younger snake.

"Am not."

"Are too. Liar."

"Takes one to know one. Slug."

"Worm. Fat, ugly maggot."

Sherahi had decided to stay out of this one. They were old enough to fight it out between themselves and to escape she settled down into the bottom of the basket, hiding her head beneath her coils. She tried to block their quarrel from her mind. When she realized, however, that the two boas had reared up against each other and that each was struggling for a purchase on the other's neck, she had to intervene. A territorial squabble in such a small space would end with both snakes bitten and bleeding and, since the loser couldn't retreat to safety, she might die. Sherahi did the only thing she could. She lifted her huge head above their fracas and hissed a warning that she had lost patience with them. Then she drummed her tail against the wicker for silence.

"You two should be ashamed—serpents carrying on like chameleons fighting over a bug."

"But I'm right," interjected one little boa.

"No," said Sherahi. "You are both wrong. Little sister, you should only follow my directions. Do not try to improve on our ritual. Let it be pure, the way it has been danced by generations of serpents and women.

"Older sister, you worry too much about the appearances of things. Remember that in the ritual it is our intentions that must be correct. If they are, all else will follow in its own way and time."

"But, Auntie, did They like us? Ruthie thinks that's awfully important."

"Even Ruthie does not fully comprehend what we do. She sees this as an act—a performance. She is only a human and does not realize the importance of the ritual. All you must do is follow my commands and everything will be fine.

"Now, apologize to one another. Even though you are not of the Elder Race, you should behave better. If one of my relatives had scryed your minds just now I would have been ashamed to be held responsible for your behavior."

The littler boa was still troubled. "But, Auntie, did *They* like us?"

"We are not meant to please them, little one."

"Then why is Ruthie so worried about it, Auntie? All during the ritual she worries about it. I've seen it in her mind, Auntie. If you don't believe me, you scry her mind tonight. You'll see. I'm right."

"Rest now. You are much too young to read anyone's mind. You're only a baby."

The two boas drifted off into separate spheres of consciousness, lulled by Sherahi's voice. At the back of her mind, however, Sherahi was curious. Could the little boa have discovered something that she herself didn't know? Had she been so busy with the ritual all these years that she hadn't noticed that this wasn't a religious rite?

During a ceremony Sherahi had always concentrated on what Ruthie wanted her to do, so she'd never bothered with any of Ruthie's other thoughts. She would look into the matter tonight, though, just to show Carla that she was wrong. Carla had to be wrong. She was only a child and a boa at that. "She must have gotten it wrong," Sherahi thought. The little snakes settled down to rest and Sherahi did so too, but her mind milled the thought, "If this isn't a sacred ritual, then how will I explain it to U Vayu? What will the Great Worm think of me if I ever am able to inwit to him?"

Naruda's act was booked for a month at the Club Istanbul and the snakes settled into the familiar routine. They danced with Ruthie twice or three times each night and there was one day a week when Ruthie didn't appear. The day off always came after Ruthie fed them. To keep them from fighting over their food, the little snakes were always put into separate, knotted sacks with their prey while Sherahi was fed inside the huge basket. She knew that after she had fed there would be ample time to mull over what the baby boa had said. Although she never would have admitted it to the little snakes, she was upset by Carla's idea that Ruthie's ritual might not be either ancient or sacred. The thought that Ruthie might have subverted one of the essential ceremonial dances into a tawdry form of entertainment was abhorrent to Sherahi.

Even though she had now scryed Ruthie's mind during several dances the pythoness clung to her belief that Ruthie was a priestess. Sherahi remembered U Vayu as he danced in the ruddy firelight with a woman and thought, "Our dances are just like that, only Ruthie's much nicer than U Vayu's partner." Sherahi had assumed that Ruthie's rituals weren't performed in holy places simply because the ancient religions were just beginning to be introduced to Minneapolis, Iowa City and Omaha, places too primitive to have permanent shrines, pagodas or temples. She had always thought of Ruthie as a kind of missionary who brought the ancient ways to these outposts of civilization. Sherahi wasn't sure what would happen if Ruthie wasn't really celebrating the ancient rituals, but she knew that it wouldn't be anything good. U Vayu had told her so, many, many times.

Besides, Ruthie had saved Sherahi from starvation and the pythoness owed the girl her life. Sherahi remembered how Ruthie had worked a spell on her eyes that had made her see once more. "She fed me when I was starving," thought Sherahi. "Dancing with her in the rituals and making the two little snakes behave is small payment for what she's done for me."

U Vayu himself had once explained to Sherahi why the rituals between serpents and humans were necessary. In some mysterious way that Sherahi didn't even begin to comprehend the rituals kept the spirit of life moving in the world. U Vayu had said that the rituals encouraged the Life Spirit—rejuvenating it just as a snake grows young again when it sheds its worn, faded skin for a brilliant, new one. "Because of our control of time and space," U Vayu had hissed, "we serpents have a sacred duty to dance the old dances with humans. If the rituals cease then the Life Spirit will wither. We will all be diminished."

Whenever Sherahi did her part well, Ruthie rewarded her with extra attention and affection. Sherahi was usually so busy when they danced that she had never thought to scan the minds of the people in the room. She had to pay strict attention so that the postures, gestures and symbolic images were correct. And the two little boas were such featherbrains that they needed constant coaching. Those two were a trial and Sherahi often wished that Ruthie would substitute two bright, eager young pythons for these two doltish boas. Even if Sherahi hadn't been busy during the rituals, it would have been sacrilegious to question Ruthie's sincerity. Once Sherahi had seen something in Bernie's mind that had seemed out of place for a holy occasion. But then, Bernie's mind was usually filled with thoughts of money or sex and Sherahi only tolerated him because Ruthie seemed to like him so much. Bernie reminded Sherahi of the sailor who had taken her from her home; he was not one of her favorite humans.

Ruthie had finished feeding Carla and Rosita and had put the two little boas into separate sacks. Sherahi knew that she would be fed next and she lunged at the limp rabbit that Ruthie dangled before her nose. As she coiled about it, strangling the already-dead body out of habit more than enthusiasm, she saw Ruthie's smooth face at the opening of the basket above her. Then the weighted lid was lowered and locked into place. Sherahi slowly engulfed her warm-bodied prey and felt staccato vibrations as Ruthie's high-heeled shoes clattered to the door. The room darkened and Sherahi felt the door close behind Ruthie. She wouldn't be back for a long time and it occurred to Sherahi that this was a good opportunity to try to inwit to one of the Great Serpent Nats. Ordinarily she would have gone to U Vayu with her questions about Ruthie, but he had been unfriendly the last time she had sought his advice and she didn't want to waste her time talking to his bat guardian again. Besides, she already knew what U Vayu thought about Ruthie. If Sherahi mentioned her he would only start a diatribe against sneaky humans and how they always blamed all their misfortunes on snakes. "He's so tedious," Sherahi sighed as she felt the rabbit slide down her throat. Sherahi decided to try to inwit to one of the Great Serpent Nats and see whether one of them could help her. U Vayu hadn't been encouraging, so she doubted that she would be able to succeed, but it was worth a try.

"Both the Great Worm and Quetzalcoatl sound formidable—even dangerous," she thought. "It will be better if I start with a serpent nat who has less power." She remembered that U Vayu had mentioned Lachesis—the Measurer of all life. "Well," thought Sherahi, "Lachesis decides when each life should end, so she must know how to judge humans and their thoughts. She will be able to tell me if Ruthie thinks this is a religious ritual or not."

Sherahi swallowed again and a wave of muscular contraction propelled the rabbit four feet down her throat and into her stomach. Feeling comfortably full, she took a long drink of water and pushed each side of her face against the inside of the wicker basket, realigning her jaws. She yawned and stretched her independent jaws, making sure that each had returned to its proper position after having been loosened at the rear to accommodate the rabbit. There was nothing more she could do to prepare to meet Lachesis.

Half-doubting that she had the mental power to reach one of the Great Serpent Nats, Sherahi sent her mind spinning out of the wicker basket. She focused on the name "Lachesis." Like a gyroscope set twirling as its string is whipped away, her mind whirled and moved in an ever-widening arc, passing out of the wicker basket, out of the dressing room, out of the Club Istanbul, out over the dark city of Omaha, out into the night sky. Beneath the gibbous moon Sherahi's questing mind sought Lachesis as she repeated the name over and over and concentrated all her faculties on finding the supernatural serpent spirit.

The widening arcs of mental effort were suddenly concentrated into a single powerful beam and Sherahi found herself in a sunlit meadow surrounded by grasses and wildflowers. She lifted her scaly head to peer over the vegetation and was surprised to find herself completely alone. In one direction the meadow was bordered by a stand of trees while in the others Sherahi could see only sky. She seemed to be on a mountainside. "Where is Lachesis?" she wondered. "Why am I here?"

Sherahi fnasted the air but could detect no nearby reptiles. There wasn't even an earth snake munching worms beneath a stone or a skink sunning itself on one of the trees in the distance. She was sure that there were no reptiles at all for miles around and it made no sense.

"U Vayu must have been right," she thought. "I guess I don't have the power to inwit to one of the Great Serpent Nats."

Sherahi had expected to materialize inside a shadowy chamber, deep below the surface of the earth. She had visualized Lachesis enthroned and illuminated by the light of torches that blazed and burnished each of her scales and made them even more splendid. Like a cobra, Lachesis would hold her head and neck aloft, displaying the mystic hieroglyphs that decorated her turquoise belly scutes. Her forked tongue would lash ferociously and her vertically elliptic pupils would flash as she fulfilled her sacred duty. A lesser deity—perhaps vulture-headed Thoth or jackal-headed Anubis—would stand behind her throne, holding a pair of scales to assist her in judging the intrinsic value of each soul. Alongside her throne would be a tall vase that held dead twigs and a dozen of Lachesis' Rememberers. At least that was what Sherahi had been taught when she was a young python. These Rememberers were chameleons trained to listen to all that Lachesis said. They remembered the exact values she assigned to each life.

The elder pythons who had taught Sherahi so much serpent lore in the first winter of her life had told her about the Rememberers. They had ordered Sherahi never to eat a chameleon. These were Lachesis' sacred assistants. The python elders also had told Sherahi that when a chameleon's body was green it was learning information and when it had changed to brown it was reciting the information for Lachesis. Chameleons didn't have quick minds, but they were reliable and never forgot anything. Slow and deliberate in all of their motions, they had double minds to match their double vision. When chameleons teetered back and forth on their perches, with their turreted eyes searching in opposite directions, they might be searching for a bug to eat or, on the other hand, they might be remembering something for Lachesis. Sherahi had always thought it more likely that they were reminiscing how their remote ancestors had once remembered for Lachesis. Irrespective of this, Sherahi had had ample opportunity to eat chameleons and had never done so. Not only were they sacred, but they were also skinny and she'd heard that they had a bad taste.

But Sherahi saw no Rememberers here. There were no exotic lesser deities; moreover, there was no Lachesis. Sherahi saw only grasses, flowers and the bees that nuzzled into the frothy umbels of Queen Anne's lace. She started across the field, frightening phalanxes of grasshoppers. Their hind wings flashed lemon yellow and hot orange as they flew off and Sherahi noticed that the females were armed with curved scimitars at the tips of their abdomens: fierce tools that would dig cradles for young hoppers. Sherahi watched the spur-legged insects whirr away, only to be startled into flight repeatedly. "Silly, nervous insects," she said. "I'm not going to harm you."

Sherahi continued her sinuous path through the meadow, scattering waves of grasshoppers before her, but she saw no sign that a Great Serpent Nat lived here. She felt like an archer whose arrow had inexplicably veered off into space when she had been sure that she'd fired a bull's-eye. "I guess U Vayu was right," she said to herself. "I was so certain that I could find the serpent nats, but I guess I was wrong."

She lay at full length in the grass and thought of gathering herself into the necessary coil for returning to the wicker basket that held her physical body in Omaha, but there was no hurry. Ruthie would be gone for a whole day. Sherahi had never been in a meadow before and she enjoyed this high and windswept place. She'd spent her early life as a free serpent on the safe, shadowy edges of forests and waterways and if she had been here in the flesh instead of as a mental projection she would have been frightened by the expanse of sky above her. Open skies like this held hawks and eagles. But since an inwitted projection was immune to most kinds of physical harm, the snake luxuriated in the open meadow and the unfamiliar sense of freedom.

Lying with her chin against the grassy ground she heard a buzzing voice that seemed to be transmitted through it. It was a very small voice, speaking a language that Sherahi could only partially understand. She listened a while and, although it seemed unbelievable to the pythoness, she was sure that it was a garbled version of ancient saurian mindspeech.

"It can't be," she told herself. "Mindspeech is only for reptiles and it is mental, not audible." She listened again and was certain that she was hearing the distinctive cadence and queerly emphasized syllables of saurian mindspeech.

"But where is the speaker?" Sherahi wondered. She raised her head six feet in the air and peered about, whirling furiously to look behind her. Garbled or not, mindspeech meant that the nat must be here—somewhere.

With her head in the air she could no longer hear the voice, so Sherahi put her chin to the ground again. She heard the voice once more and was certain that it spoke a strange dialect built around saurian mindspeech. The language was so cluttered with burrs and clipped vowels that Sherahi had difficulty understanding it. She took a deep breath, concentrated and the meaning of the words became clearer.

"All right," the voice said. "Let's move on to lot seventy-five trillion, three hundred million, seventy-nine thousand, four hundred and five. Let's not waste any time and get the thing measured before the afternoon feeding must commence.

"Hurry up, Seventy-Five. Don't trip on Seventy-Four's line. Do try to be a little more careful.

"And, Number Eight, don't go gawking at that big snake. She's not in this lot. We're measuring flowers, not serpents, and she's no business of yours.

"Get along there, Twenty-Six, and do the job properly this time. And, Twenty-Six," the voice paused for breath, "you could try to take a bit of interest in the work. I don't want to have to always be checking up on you.

Bad enough that I have to do all the remembering by myself. Don't want to have to do all the measuring, too."

Sherahi looked toward the voice and saw blurry movements along a stem. She drew her head back into a striking coil and focused on a procession of what looked like hundreds of small, green worms that synchronously inched up the thick stem of a milkweed plant. They moved toward the flower in single file, each spinning a strand of silk and clinging to the silk line paid out by the worm ahead. For a moment Sherahi watched the mass of worms alternately hump their backs and straighten, climbing higher and higher. "Where is the one that is directing them?" she wondered.

Sherahi studied the ground below the plant, the grasses around it, its lavender flowers, but she could see no one who seemed responsible for the movements of these worms. She wearied of the search and said to herself, "I must be imagining this. There's no one here." She put her head down again and watched the worms methodically inch over the stem, leaves and flowers overhead.

"I resent that," said the voice. "Just because you don't know how to use the eyes in your head, don't go saying that there's no one here. I may be a shadow of what I once was, but I'm here. Oh yes, my serpentarian friend. I am most definitely and emphatically here.

"For those that have eyes to see, I have length, width, depth. I'm minute in comparison to you. But then, most beasts are, I'm sure. But I've met many rotifers and creeping amoebae in my day—they thought I was a *giant* amongst worms. A giant. A veritable giant. Most definitely and emphatically a colossus.

"Use your eyes, Sherahi." The voice was less brittle when it said her name. "I'm right under your nose. Maybe it'll help if I use a language you can hear better."

Sherahi pulled her head further back and carefully examined the milkweed plant. On one of the leaves, surrounded by moving inchworms, was a form that, more than anything else, looked like a minute bird dropping. Then the dollop of excrement moved and Sherahi saw that it was some sort of caterpillar or worm.

"That's better," said the voice inside her head, speaking perfectly understandable saurian mindspeech. "Now you're behaving like a proper serpent.

"Clever disguise, isn't it?" The caterpillar reared back and gaily waved its three pairs of legs at the startled snake. "And that's not my only trick," it said. "Watch."

Before Sherahi's eyes, orange horns sprouted from the caterpillar's head and a foul odor filled the air. Sherahi heard the caterpillar laugh.

"Pretty good, huh? You should see how wasps react to that one! It's my favorite trick. And it fools all of the birds. I wish I could say it was my own idea, but I must confess I stole it from a black swallowtail butterfly that I measured long ago. Let's see, I guess it was about a year before I retired."

"Then you are Lachesis the Measurer?" asked Sherahi.

"The very same," said the caterpillar. "Most emphatically and dramatically. Three-point-five centimeters long, zero-point-eight centimeters wide and just about the same depth. My legs are each four millimeters long, except for the rear left one, which, for some strange reason, is three-point-seven, not four. But then, my dear, even retired deities are imperfect.

"My eyes have a circumference of zero-point-ought-five millimeters and my horns, when fully extended, are each . . .

"But I can see that you're not interested in my dimensions. Perhaps I could interest you in something in mouse or rat measurements—or perhaps this: it may surprise you to know, at least it surprised me—this flower above my head has a petal arrangement that exactly obeys the Fibonacci numbers. In fact, you can predict the sum of the squares of any two real numbers by counting . . ."

The caterpillar stopped and seemed to cock its head at Sherahi, staring with one blind, multifaceted eye at a time. A small voice said, "You're disappointed, aren't you?"

Sherahi didn't want to hurt the creature's feelings and said, "Perhaps surprised. You see . . . I had expected . . ."

"Oh, I know what you expected," interrupted the caterpillar in an irritated tone. "I know what everyone expects: they think they're going to find one of the all-powerful serpent nats—Lachesis, the Third of the Fates. The Measurer of all lives, the one who determines where Atropos will cut the thread of life that has been woven by Clotho. I know just what you expected. Everyone does. Everyone wants lightning bolts and mystery and all of their problems solved in a puff of smoke."

There was a pause and the caterpillar added, "That was what you wanted, wasn't it?"

"I suppose so," said Sherahi.

"Well, you're exactly eight hundred seventy-three years, fifty-five days, twelve hours, three minutes and twenty seconds too late. I've retired, you see. The shop is closed and now I am only interested in measuring things and in mathematical relationships—my great and only love."

The caterpillar took a thoughtful bite of the edge of the milkweed leaf and spat it out. "It's nothing personal. It's just that we've all retired—all of us. Me, and both of my sisters, we're weary of the lives of others."

There was a pause in which the caterpillar regarded the snake and then it quietly added, "Actually, we were forced into it." The caterpillar's voice grew tremulous and she said, "It's a terrible thing when you start to dwindle. I had heard of it long ago from the Etruscan gods who were dwindling, but I never thought it would happen to us. Year by year each of us got smaller and smaller as fewer and fewer animals believed in us. Things got so bad that I could no longer inhabit the beautiful ophidian body that I cherished for ever so long. So, I became an earthworm. At first I was one of those giant ones from Australia. I must have been over nine feet long. Being a worm wasn't nearly as satisfying as being a snake, but it wasn't too bad. I adjusted to it. And then I dwindled even more, first becoming a night crawler and then a common red worm. I kept shrinking and I suppose I've been this size for about two hundred years now."

"I would have thought you'd know to the exact minute," said Sherahi.

"I don't like to think about it," said the caterpillar. "I think I'm at a minimal size. I haven't decreased in years."

"But you're still measuring things," said Sherahi. "That must mean that you have some of your former powers."

"Only enough to maintain my hobby. I can make these stupid inchworms obey me. But nothing more. No, the only measuring I do these days is for my own amusement and edification."

"I have a problem," said Sherahi. "I wanted your advice about a certain human. I had hoped that you might have measured her soul and might be able to tell me about her."

"I am no longer interested in humans, or in snakes, for that matter. I probably did measure her soul, but I had my Rememberers then. I couldn't recall my judgments about a particular human even if I wanted to. And I don't want to.

"Now, if you were interested in the number four-point-six-three, we might have something to talk about. But then, I don't suppose you are. Snakes are never good with numbers. Even before I retired I knew that. Snakes can't count. It's one of their failings. I was an exception to that rule, but then, I was the last of a breed. Most emphatically and dramatically the last of a breed."

"Can't you tell me anything that will help me?" asked Sherahi.

"If it has to do with humans, all I can tell you is what experience has taught me: expect the worst. Be grateful if it doesn't happen. Remember that."

The looping inchworms had begun to return from measuring the milkweed flowers and the air was filled with the numbers shouted at the caterpillar in the garbled dialect of ancient saurian mindspeech. The caterpillar became suddenly active and Sherahi saw that she was weaving a silken cocoon about herself and that there were numbers inscribed in the web. It was clear that Lachesis had nothing further to say to Sherahi and the snake withdrew her mental projection from the flower-dotted meadow.

Back in the dim wicker basket she repeated what Lachesis had said, "Expect the worst. Be grateful if it doesn't happen." If this were true then it was likely that Ruthie was using her and the two boas for her own selfish ends. It seemed probable that this was no holy ritual and that Ruthie was no priestess. Sherahi felt ill and began to gag on the rabbit that was undigested within her stomach. Within minutes she had vomited up a slimy mess that would lie beside her on the bottom of the wicker basket until Ruthie returned. Sherahi was too upset to be bothered by the stench.

She decided that there was no use in trying to scry Ruthie's mind and evaluate her motives. "If Lachesis is right, and this is only some shoddy kind of amusement, what can I do about it?" thought the snake. "I'm trapped. I can't escape from this place. I could strangle Ruthie, but then other humans would probably kill me. Besides, I couldn't do that. I owe my life to Ruthie. I can't hurt her, and I certainly can't abandon her. Even if I could escape, I wouldn't know how to get back to my own country. I'll just have to get used to the idea."

Even as she had these thoughts Sherahi knew that she would never accept this situation. Sherahi the pythoness was the proudest and most intelligent snake in the world. She could not allow herself to be merely a human possession. Again Sherahi faced the knot of dread within her chest; she saw herself slithering along the dim corridor once more. Sherahi was certain that something bad was going to happen. She resolved to be ready to snatch her chance to transform this awful thing into something good.

CHAPTER TWO

Leftrack's Pet Emporium and
Animals International, Ltd
New York City
June 17, 1932

OPEN, GODDAMMIT. OPEN." Ira Leftrack gave the door a final, exasperated shake and released both knob and key. If only he could take a brick and smash this goddamn door—but glass was expensive and that would be a big repair bill. And besides, the other warehouse owners would think he'd gone crazy. "Patience," he told himself, "patience. All good things come to those who wait."

Leftrack pushed his hat onto the back of his balding head and mopped his forehead with the rumpled plaid handkerchief he always kept in a back pocket. The starched white one in the breast pocket of his suit was only an edge of cloth glued to a pocket-sized piece of celluloid. It had a comb and a shoehorn attached and Leftrack couldn't have used the handkerchief if he'd wanted to. Irma had seen the idea in the back pages of *The Wednesday New York Woman,* that fancy magazine she was always reading. Leftrack didn't like it: it gave her ideas. "This'll save on ironing," she'd said, tucking the false handkerchief into his pocket. "Look, Ira," she'd said, "the monogram looks so nice." Leftrack had looked, but he'd always hated it. "You never know when you'll have an emergency," he'd thought. Every day he meant to throw the contraption away, but he kept forgetting. "I've got to get a decent handkerchief tomorrow," he said every morning when he caught sight of the tired fold of cloth in his breast pocket.

Leftrack folded his plaid handkerchief and crumpled it into his pants pocket. His hands were sticky from struggling with the doorknob and they smelled acrid, metallic; his shirt clung to his sides. He wanted to get inside to wash, to cool under the electric fan in his office and to make his coffee. Wrestling with this goddam lock was far from his ideal way to start the day.

This was all Sorensen's fault—another detail that Sorensen had ignored. What was he going to do with that old man? Only last week Leftrack had noticed that this lock was sticking and he'd asked his janitor and handyman, Birger Sorensen, to oil it. Obviously Sorensen had forgotten, or, if he had done anything about it, it was in that dreamy, half-assed, absent-minded way of his. No question, Sorensen was getting too old. "What am I going to do with that man?" Leftrack thought. "I can't be always checking up on him—and I can't just fire him. He's been with me since I started this business."

Leftrack wiped his hands on his trousers and once again grabbed the key and doorknob. As if he were prosecuting Sorensen in front of a jury, he repeated to himself, "No excuse for this, Sorensen. No excuse. No excuse at all." The doorknob felt warm against one palm and the rounded end of the key bit into the fingers of his other hand. He could feel a blister forming beneath the skin. "Open . . . open," he ordered and shook the door so that the glass rattled and the SORRY WE'RE CLOSED sign danced like a marionette against the torn window blind. Leftrack thought, "Another thing Sorensen forgot to fix." He gnawed his thin mustache and ground his back teeth as he forced the key to the left, but it would only go so far and he felt it begin to bend in his hand. He swore under his breath and kicked the bottom of the door. Behind him he heard the flat voice of Meyer, the owner of the wholesale meat-packing house, calling from the curb. Meyer's warehouse was directly across the street. In shirt sleeves and white apron he stood outside, supervising the men who unloaded stiff-legged sides of beef in the still June morning. "Need some help, Mr. Leftrack?" Meyer's voice slid up the scale at the end of the sentence. "So nice he sounds," thought Leftrack. "So nice and so phony."

"Go to hell, Meyer," Leftrack muttered and pretended not to have heard the butcher. The sweat was running freely down his back and the son-of-a-bitching lock was still stuck. He looked up and saw Meyer's reflection in the glass of the locked door. Meyer stood outside his warehouse with his hands clasped behind his back, rocking back and forth on his heels. Sawdust clung to his trousers and Leftrack saw that Meyer's apron was clean except for two ruddy smears where he'd wiped his hands on his big belly. Leftrack was suddenly reminded of the stretch marks on Irma's belly in her eighth month of carrying Ehrich, their only child. Night after night Leftrack had smoothed coconut butter onto the red welts and assured her that the doctor had promised that they'd go away. He remembered the circles his fingers had made and how he had hoped that something—anything—would make Irma happy. But Irma had hated everything that summer. She'd stayed cooped up in their fourth-floor tenement, her hair always in pin curls that were never unwound. Every other day Leftrack had had to remember to get a block of ice from the truck and had brought it up the stairs, leaving a dripping trail behind him. She was fretful and withdrawn and even her favorite strudel from the bakery hadn't pleased her—even before he was born Ehrich had demanded all of Irma's attention. Leftrack hadn't thought of that time in years and he especially didn't like being reminded of it now. "Why doesn't Meyer mind his own business?"

Over his shoulder Leftrack called out, "No, Mr. Meyer. I'll get it open. Must be this heat that makes it stick." Leftrack pretended to concentrate on the lock and surreptitiously watched Meyer shrug and waddle back into his shop. He passed a slab of beef and paused to pat it with a fat-fingered hand. "Butinsky," Leftrack muttered.

Meyer was always spying, waiting to stick his two cents in, hoping for a juicy tidbit to cackle over with Sam the greengrocer, his pal who specialized in out-of-season fruits and steamer baskets. He could just hear Meyer crowing, "Hey, Sam—did you hear what that crazy Leftrack did today?" Crazy Leftrack. He knew they called him that behind his back. Ever since he'd rented the warehouse and opened the store, they'd made it clear that his weird business wasn't welcome in this neighborhood. They liked him even less now that he was doing so well. The only friend that Leftrack had on the street was Peter Chan, who owned the Jade Parlor Chinese Restaurant on the corner. And that was because Leftrack always gave Mr. Chan the pick of each shipment of the lion-headed goldfish that he was so fond of. Still, he did make the best shrimp in lobster sauce that Leftrack had ever eaten.

"To hell with them," thought Leftrack and gave the door a kick. "To hell with all of them." The pane of glass rattled again and Leftrack felt the key turn within the lock as the door swung inward all by itself.

It happened so suddenly that for a moment Leftrack couldn't believe that his ordeal was over. He squatted down to examine the door plate and jamb, but could see nothing wrong with either. A mystery. A mystery had kept him sweating in the street. He was grateful for the cool aquamarine twilight of his shop and closed the door and sighed, relieved that the shades were drawn and he was free of Meyer's scrutiny. He'd have to call the locksmith . . . and then there'd be another bill. . . . Leftrack pulled up the torn window blind and thought, "Maybe Sorensen can fix the lock. He should at least take a look."

Another detail to be attended to. "Detail, always details," he thought, "that's what kills you in this business. Forget just one little detail and you pay, god-in-heaven do you pay." He opened the cash register, pleased with the sound of the brass bell. The cash drawer was empty except for the cigar box. Leftrack closed it, pleased that the clerks were following his orders.

"Maybe Ehrich can take over some of the details," Leftrack thought. He heard the muffled ding of the trolley bell and watched as the first group of workers straggled down the street, carrying lunch pails. "Maybe Ehrich can check on old Sorensen. I should talk it over with Irma, but the boy will have four months before medical school starts. Four whole months with nothing to do. For all I've done for him—for all the special tutors, French horn lessons, sleep-away camps and trips to the museum on my days off—

for all this he can give me a measly four months. For once he can afford to help his mother and me in the business."

Leftrack waited for a moment at the cash register, allowing his eyes to adjust to the gloom of the high-ceilinged store. There was no use turning on the electricity: it would only wake up all the birds and cause a commotion. Besides, the bills were high enough already and, what was more important, Leftrack didn't need electric light to find his way around: he knew the layout of the store like the back of his hand.

Leftrack pulled his watch from his pocket and compared it with the clock above the door. He was pleased to see that at least one thing was right today: at least the clock had the correct time. He found his time card and entered 7:22 in the IN column for Thursday, June 17, put his card away and began to make his way toward the rear of the store, fumbling for his watch pocket, conscious that many of the animals around him were asleep or else were drowsing in their cages.

He passed aquariums filled with two-for-a-nickel goldfish, and a tankful of lion-headed goldfish from China. They swam with graceless, jerking motions of their obese bodies. Their tail fins streamed like gossamer. Leftrack stopped to watch their round mouths repeatedly catch and spit out invisible bits of food. He thought they were ugly, but then, he hadn't bought them for their looks. They were so unusual that even the thrifty Chinese in the neighborhood would pay $2.00 apiece for them and consider it a bargain. They would all be sold in a few days. Leftrack failed to see the beauty that always enraptured Peter Chan and thought, "They swim like Meyer the butcher walks."

He went past tanks of guppies of every color and description: fancy, long-tailed, sword-tailed, shark-finned, as well as platyfishes that sold cheap (two for 29 cents); past shrouded cages of canaries ($2.75 for plain, $3.75 for fancy); and parakeets ($1.50 apiece); past many-tiered cages of guinea pigs ($1.75) and rabbits ($2.00 apiece).

There was a loud thump as he walked past one rabbit cage and Leftrack was startled. He peered inside and could see the eye of a Belgian hare gleaming moistly from a rear corner. Even in this light Leftrack could see that its sides were heaving. Either the hare had had a nightmare or else he had frightened it worse than it had frightened him. "Well, don't worry, *klein Hase*," thought Leftrack, "I'm not going to be the one who'll make you into hasenpfeffer."

There was a high bank of cages filled with howler monkeys and marmosets. They were awake and rampaging in their cages, leaping madly from perch to perch.

One squirrel monkey held onto the bars of her cage and filled the air with shrieks and screams. "Got to get that one out of here," Leftrack thought. "Not good for business. She might bite somebody."

Leftrack continued toward the rear of the store, past a large tank filled with baby turtles the size of silver dollars (59 cents apiece for plain, 75 cents for those with sunsets and palm trees painted on their shells) and another filled with larger American sliders and cooters ($1.50 apiece). Most of the big turtles were asleep, with only their nostrils sticking out of the water, but one old fellow was awake and swam toward Leftrack. His yellow-striped neck was extended and his eyes watched Leftrack expectantly. "No, *Schildkröte*," thought Leftrack. "Go back to sleep. I have nothing to feed you this morning."

There were tanks with clusters of garter snakes (75 cents apiece) and one tank that had baby boas. They were the remnant of a litter of twenty-eight babies that had been born in the shop three months ago. That $115.00 had been an unexpected boon, one of those things that happen all too infrequently in the pet trade. Leftrack thought, "Usually things die on you instead."

It was also unusual to get baby snakes that would eat in captivity. They usually starved to death. These boas were gray and pale tan with pinkish markings on their heads. When they'd been born their scales had been so fine that they seemed to be covered in thick velvet. "Does that give them some sort of camouflage?" Leftrack had wondered. Someday, if he remembered, he'd have to ask Ditmars or one of the reptile boys at the Bronx Zoo about it.

At the rear of the store Leftrack walked past shelves neatly stacked with the many varieties of the specially formulated Leftrack Pet Foods. There were also cages, tanks, water bottles, feeding dishes, perches, imported cuttlebones and toys, as well as an array of bedding materials and first-aid remedies. On the rear wall was the display that he was most proud of: a sign with letters two feet high stretched across the entire back wall, announcing

LEFTRACK'S EMPORIUM and ANIMALS INTERNATIONAL, LTD
—ANIMAL OF THE MONTH—

Below the sign was a six-by-eight-foot plate-glass window. Behind the plate glass (that had cost him plenty) was a special enclosure that held the most spectacular animal currently in the warehouse that adjoined this public store. Usually, however, it wasn't really the most exotic or spectacular animal in the warehouse; rather, it was the most spectacular animal on hand that could withstand the strain of the hordes of people who would flock in to see it and point their fingers and rap on the glass and make general nuisances of themselves.

So, even though the aviary cage filled with black-headed Lady Gouldian finches was probably the most awesome shipment in the warehouse at the moment—a living rainbow that continually flitted and shifted—Leftrack would never display them as his Animal of the Month. They were delicate and would collapse from the shock in an hour. Instead, an African golden tree cobra was on exhibit. It was en route to the San Diego Zoo and Leftrack was holding it while he assembled a larger West Coast shipment. Benny, his wife's nephew, would be sent off with it on the next Yankee Clipper Express. Even in this dim light Leftrack could see the big cobra coiled around a horizontal limb of a piece of driftwood that Sorensen had fixed to the floor of the enclosure. The snake hung there motionless and apparently inoffensive, but Leftrack knew that what he'd told the newspapermen was true: it was the fastest and most dangerous snake in all of Africa—so fast that it left even the most agile mamba in the shade.

Leftrack was pleased with the way he'd handled those reporters. He'd alerted them before he'd opened the display to the public and both the *Herald Tribune* and the *Brooklyn Star* had carried the story, as well as a picture of him holding the cobra and the rather small headline, "Deadliest Snake in Manhattan." The crowds had been substantial, and the store had gotten considerable good publicity; besides, Leftrack liked to think of himself as fostering knowledge of exotic animals, but the big dividend was the way that small-pet sales had increased. Irma had said that sales were up by 40 percent and, although he made it a habit to stay out of the store during business hours, Leftrack couldn't avoid some of the excitement that had been going on for the last week. He'd seen a number of mothers and fathers cave in to the incessant whining of their children and purchase containers of goldfish or pairs of baby turtles or a rabbit. Each animal was sold with a supply of Leftrack's specially formulated food. He'd trained his clerks to stress the need for correct diet and every kind of small pet had a basic food, a treat and a tonic that Leftrack claimed was essential for its health. For example, Leftrack's Turtle Gro was a big seller. It supposedly contained ant eggs, but Leftrack had substituted grains of cooked rice and nobody was the wiser. "Who the hell knows what an ant egg looks like, anyway?" Leftrack asked himself. Like all of his animal products, Turtle Gro was concocted and packaged in the warehouse and sold at 275 percent above cost.

Leftrack was delighted with the way the Animal of the Month had stimulated sales and was anticipating that they would skyrocket when he exhibited the baby gorillas next month. All the children in New York and New Jersey would want to see them. He'd ordered fresh shipments of his most popular small animals and in the warehouse his men were packaging pet foods to meet the expected extra demand. Every chance he got he stressed the need to sell pet accessories to his dozen clerks: that's where the real profits were in the small-animal business. The animals were intrinsically worthless—only a means to an end.

When Leftrack reached the rear of the store he turned past the lovebirds and the parrots that slept in covered cages. He noticed that droppings and seeds littered the floor beneath each cage and he thought he saw a big

American cockroach scuttle out of sight. He'd have to get Sorensen to enlarge the circular tray beneath each cage. Roaches were inevitable nuisances in a pet shop: food and water were everywhere. Nevertheless, customers were squeamish about roaches and it wasn't good to have them in the store. He'd have to get Sorensen to clean this up. Another detail.

Leftrack halted at a door marked PRIVATE: EMPLOYEES ONLY. He looked back toward the front of the shop. A shaft of sun was already streaming in through the glass door. He held up his key chain and found the proper key to the warehouse, where his importing and exporting business, Animals International, Ltd, had its headquarters. During working hours this door was always locked and Leftrack would only unlock it now for his employees. Before he actually opened the door, though, he was careful to flip a hidden light switch that was alongside it. There were strange creatures inside, some of them dangerous, some of them poisonous, all exotic and valuable. He'd had the electrician install this special light switch after he'd been surprised at being greeted one morning by a deadly gaboon viper that had escaped from its cage. Now he could enter the warehouse with confidence, without having to grope for the switch inside, all the time wondering what form of death lurked at his feet.

Another safety measure was the design of this specially fitted door that separated the warehouse from the store. It was flush with the doorjamb and with the floor and only the barest crack allowed it to open and close: a precaution against slithering and crawling escapees. He'd learned this trick from the Munich Zoo, where all the doors were like this, but especially the doors in the Reptile House.

As a final safety precaution there was a glass foyer enclosing a short flight of stairs beyond the door. A plate-glass door opened into the warehouse proper. Once Leftrack was on these stairs he could see whether anything had escaped during the night and immediately plan for its recapture. Leftrack hated waste almost as much as he hated surprises. He remembered the empyrean pheasants that he'd imported for some rich woman on Long Island. It had taken months to obtain the birds and when they'd finally arrived from Tibet one had mysteriously gotten loose in the warehouse late one night after everyone had gone home. The next morning Leftrack had spooked it as it slept in one of the aisles. The bird had risen like an iridescent blue skyrocket and crashed into a wall. By the time it was recaptured the bird had broken several bones and damaged its plumage. It had eventually died, but before that it had lingered on for weeks the way that injured birds often do and Leftrack hadn't put it out of its misery because he'd kept hoping that it would recover. He'd given it to Sorensen for medical attention but even Sorensen couldn't help it. The worst thing was that the pheasant fancier had informed him, rather haughtily, that she was only interested in pairs. The surviving empyrean was of no value to her. Leftrack was eventually able to sell its surviving mate, but at a loss—a big loss.

Now, with the outside light switch and the glass foyer around the stairs, Leftrack prided himself that he had circumvented his problems with nasty surprises from escaped animals. The front set of double doors had worked so well that he'd even installed a similar pair in the bay at the rear of the warehouse, where crates of animals were loaded. Leftrack had built this business with money borrowed from his wife's relatives (and they never let him forget it, although he'd paid them back with interest) and it was just beginning to turn a profit. He didn't want to take any chances of running aground of the Board of Health of the City of New York. Meyer and Sam Salomon the greengrocer would love to see him go bankrupt and leave their neighborhood, he knew that. They didn't think a business like this belonged here. Moreover, he didn't want to lose money through slipshod management or bad publicity. Thus, he'd paid special attention to details of security and in his nine years of business no animal had ever escaped from his premises. Considering the volume of creatures that passed through his warehouse, Leftrack was justifiably proud of his record. That's why the jammed front-door lock had made him so angry and frustrated. *His* locks were supposed to keep the animals in, not keep him out.

From his vantage point on the glass-enclosed stairs Leftrack scanned the floor beneath the work tables, between the rows of cages, aviaries and aquariums. He didn't see that anything was obviously loose, so he descended the short flight of stairs and opened the glass door that led to the warehouse proper, to his office and to coffee. Then the day's inspection could start—just as soon as he'd had that first cup.

He took the pot out of the icebox and set it on the stove in the small kitchen that adjoined his office. Helga, his secretary, had been preparing his morning coffee for years and did something strange with eggshells and coffee beans that she ground herself. Leftrack had a suspicion that her method might not be kosher, so he'd never bothered to ask too many questions. Every night she set up the percolator and all he had to do was take it out of the icebox and set it to perk. It was always good coffee and the familiarity of the routine was soothing.

This was Leftrack's favorite part of the day: the hour and a half before the shop opened. It was the only time he had completely to himself. From his office Leftrack could see into the warehouse. Birds were beginning to chatter and sing in the walk-in aviaries. The squirrel and the rhesus monkeys were making their chittering calls. Howler monkeys combined their hoots with the scream of a peacock. This set off a cascade of hoarse calls from the pair of black-maned lion cubs and these were superseded by the trumpeting of the baby elephant that was in quarantine for the Cincinnati Zoo.

All these calls became background noise as Leftrack thought about how good it felt to be sitting here, the owner of all of this. It had been years of scrimping, but finally he had money in the bank. His first good luck had come with the pair of cheetah cubs that he'd sold to Pola Negri. This had been followed by all those animals that MGM and Twentieth Century needed for their run of white-hunter jungle adventure films. Before that his business had been limited to selling large mammals to zoos: elephants, rhinos, hippos, leopards, lions and all the antelope, which were so difficult to transport. Then Pola Negri, or Madame Negri, as she preferred to be called, had ordered that pair of cheetahs. She had specified cubs as tame as house cats. Leftrack himself had spent hours with those two, bottle-feeding them, playing with them, and when he had thought they were ready he'd personally delivered them to Hollywood. He'd even traveled in the baggage car with them to make sure they were happy. Madame Negri had been thrilled with her babies and had put in a good word for him at Paramount and almost overnight he had more orders than he could handle. He'd expanded, bought this warehouse and eventually had hired Benny and three of his wife's other relatives to do the legwork and travel with shipments. One of Leftrack's maxims was that it was always best to use family: you could trust them better than strangers. Many animals died from poor care aboard ship and unless an experienced person traveled with them they had only a 50 percent chance of surviving an ocean voyage. He'd had to fire one of the cousins after the shipment of crocs that he was accompanying died en route from Alexandria. How that schlemiel had let those crocs die was beyond Leftrack's imagination. It was hard enough to kill one with a rifle bullet. *That* had been an expensive mistake.

He'd probably never have been sitting here in the boss' swivel chair if it hadn't been for the way they'd treated him at the Munich Zoo. If he'd been able to get ahead there, even just a little, he would never have thought of leaving Germany. If they'd only promoted him once, from Assistant to Keeper, he'd probably still be there, shoveling shit and mucking out stalls.

Every day Leftrack thanked his stars that Heff, the Keeper-in-Charge of the Primate House, had thought enough of him to set him straight. Heff had told him flatly that he should never expect a promotion. Not because he wasn't qualified to be promoted, but because he was a Jew and the administrative board of the zoo would never let a Jew be anything but an Assistant. That was the day that Leftrack had decided that Germany wasn't for him and soon after that he'd borrowed the money to come to America. It was long before Hitler or any of this Führer business. He'd sold everything, packed up Irma and Ehrich and come to New York. Ehrich had been only eleven at the time. They'd lived on Essex Street in a tenement and had had to use a privy in the backyard. Leftrack went to work right away: he'd started small and saved and schemed, planned and cheated, when it would do him good. Now he had all this to show for it.

The Munich Zoo had dealt with many animal traders in Germany's former colonial empire and Leftrack had cultivated these men. He'd noticed that they didn't mind dealing with a Jew who had cash. Leftrack had found that the old Munich system of sending an experienced keeper with each overseas shipment was the way to ensure that the animals arrived alive and healthy and when he was building the business he hadn't seen much of his family: he'd traveled ten months of the year. Now he seldom went out of the country or even out of New York, but cousins and uncles traveled overseas and cross-country as a matter of course. The last time that he'd gone with a shipment was with those lions for San Simeon just about a year ago.

Within the last three years the business had expanded to supply animals to circuses and, surprisingly, to medical research. There wasn't a huge demand as yet, but he received steady orders for rhesus monkeys and chimps. He could only hope that this demand would increase, just as the craze for house pets had. This last bit of business was a gold mine. Small, exotic housepets were easy for him to get from his suppliers and he made it a point to order in such huge quantities that he could undersell his competitors. The most lucrative part, however, was the pet supplies that could be loaded into the arms of the buyer who was anxious for his new pet to have the best of everything.

On Leftrack's desk was a new novelty item from China, a crude pottery pagoda with an attached arched bridge. It was intended to sit on the bottom of an aquarium or fish bowl so that the fishes could swim beneath the mustard-glazed bridge. It would cost him about three cents to import each one. Leftrack turned the big electric fan on and took off his jacket, then he sat down at his desk again and turned the pagoda over in his hand. "Would it be best to offer it as a free gift with each aquarium? Or would it be better to sell it outright for nineteen cents?" Leftrack decided to do both and made a mental note to have Helga place an order for five hundred of the things as soon as she came in.

He could smell the coffee perking in the kitchen and went in to pour himself a cup, careful to switch off the electric fan as he went out of his office. Electric bills were high enough already and Con Edison didn't give any discounts for cash.

Eldridge Street
New York City
June 17, 1932

THIS SLICE OF early morning was Ehrich Leftrack's favorite time of day, too—the half hour after his father left for the store, but before his mother began crashing around in the kitchen: advertising her housewifely virtues by clattering cutlery, bashing pots onto the stove, letting the oven door bang shut. Irma Leftrack was a good cook, but she was the noisiest, most heavy-handed woman on the Lower East Side. When he had been a boy in Germany, Ehrich had thought that his mother made so much noise in the kitchen because she wanted everyone on the block to know that she was a good wife and mother; now that he was an adult he knew that she really wanted his attention. In his psychology course he had learned about this kind of inferiority complex and her early morning din no longer exasperated him. Now he pitied her and thought it sad that a grown woman used such childish ploys to get the approval of her twenty-two-year-old son.

Ehrich would have liked to use these early hours to study, but he'd stopped asking his mother to be quiet when he was still in high school at Stuyvesant. That was as productive as asking the waves to stop rolling or begging the winds to stop blowing. At first she'd act hurt and sulk; the next morning she would be back to her old tricks as if he'd never asked her for a little quiet. "After all," Irma Leftrack would tell herself, making sure that her son overheard, "he's only a boy. What does he know about cooking?" But that was all in the past and today Ehrich had a quiet half hour before the noise from the kitchen told him that Mama would soon require his presence at the kitchen table.

Ehrich was grateful that Eldridge Street was quiet this hot morning. He liked the sun that burned low on the horizon, right into his window. He liked the heat that radiated from the walls of this tenement. Today he was even pleased by the rhythmic, rolling cooing of the pigeons on the fire escape. Ehrich hated pigeons and another morning he would have shooed them away, but today was different. His first real vacation as an adult began today and he luxuriated in the thought that he had four months to himself. He had no classes to attend, no tests to cram for, no worries about whether he would be accepted into medical school. He was one of the lucky few who'd been given a full scholarship to Cornell University Medical School. In the fall he'd move into the dorm and, for the first time in his life, would not be living with his parents. His future seemed so bright, so assured, so filled with free time and unexplored possibilities that it made him smile up at the patched plaster of his bedroom ceiling.

He had the whole day planned: he was going to stay in bed until the last possible second, then have breakfast and take his mother to the store; then he'd have lunch with his father, probably at the Jade Parlor, and then maybe he'd go to Cornell at 69th Street to see if the medical library would let him borrow books. He wanted to get a head start on the gross-anatomy course that was the bane of all first-year students. He intended to specialize as a neurosurgeon and figured that his medical career started today. All the worry about acceptance and all the cramming for bio and chem courses had paid off: in only four years Ehrich Leftrack, also known as Fatso, Tubs, Fat Track, Two-Ton, Chubby and a whole litany of other names that had trailed him since sixth grade, was going to be Dr. Ehrich Leftrack. Then it wouldn't matter that he was seventy pounds overweight. Besides, the life of a medical-school student was grueling; he'd probably drop forty pounds in the first month.

He lay listening to the electric fan that oscillated on his bureau and thought about how living at the dorm would change his life. For one thing, he wouldn't be awakened every morning except Sunday by the sounds his father made when he went to the bathroom. For as long as he could remember Ehrich had lain in this narrow bed that was so short that his heels hung over the edge and listened to his father shuffle down the hall to the bathroom. Ehrich's room was located between it and the front door of the apartment and he was a light sleeper. Every morning he'd hear the same progression of sounds: first the bathroom door would shut and then he'd hear the sound of his father pissing (it took so long that Ehrich wondered if his father might have some sort of bladder abnormality); then the toilet flushed and the faucet started running. Ehrich always imagined the Old Man standing in front of the sink, shaving. He always saw him from behind and noted how baggy the seat of his wrinkled blue-and-white cotton underdrawers were. Ehrich saw him twitch his mouth to the right and then to the left, pulling the skin taut as he shaved, careful not to damage his neat, pencil-thin mustache. That mustache would be the last thing the Old Man would inspect in the bathroom mirror. Then the door would open and the leather-soled slippers would pad back down the hall, retracing the familiar path. Ten minutes later Ehrich would hear quick, efficient footsteps down the hall and the front door would bang shut and shake the walls and floor of his room. The Old Man could always be counted on for an emphatic exit— no quiet creeping out of the house for him. Maybe that's why he and Irma were a couple: maybe noisiness had brought them together. God knows they didn't seem especially fond of each other; they slept in separate beds. Maybe the only things they had in common were himself, noisiness and the business.

Ehrich turned on his side, bunched his pillow beneath his head and wondered if all families were like this, or was it only his? Thank God that school would be starting soon. He'd lived at home through college and had envied the fellows who'd lived in fraternity houses or even in the shabbiest dorms. He'd never been popular and he was too heavy to play sports, so no fraternity had ever asked him to join. Besides, he rationalized, he didn't need to live in a college dorm: NYU was only a few subway stops away from Eldridge Street. But in September all that would change. All first-year medical-school students had to live in the dorm and although everyone said the rooms were small and the facilities primitive, Ehrich looked forward to being awakened by an alarm clock in a quiet room of his own.

"Yes," Ehrich thought, "this is going to be the best summer of my life, my first really free time." He thought of how he would prepare for school in the fall. He'd memorize the origins, insertions and functions of even the smallest of muscles, the names and locations of even the finest of arterioles and veins. He would be the best first-year medical student that Cornell had ever seen. Everyone would call him a "brain," a "phenomenon," and his friends, whom he'd tutor late at night so they'd be able to get C's, would call him "Ehrich" or maybe even "Professor." Fat Track Leftrack would be someone that he used to know.

A flat, familiar voice called from the kitchen, "Ehrich? Ehrich? Breakfast." He heard the iron skillet crash down onto one of the gas burners and knew that Mama wanted him. He could smell the bagels heating and heaved himself up into a sitting position. He wondered what she'd have for him this morning and hoped it would be a four-egg omelet filled with dollops of sour cream and slices of lox with a sprinkling of dill. Alternatively there might be potato pancakes and sour cream or maybe some of her blintzes.

The pigeons were still cooing on the fire escape and nervously treading circles about one another. Fresh droppings splotched his windowsill and the birds nervously cocked their little amber eyes at him. Ehrich twisted the sweat-soaked towel that covered his pillow into a rope and snapped it at those nervous little eyes. The birds exploded off the fire escape and disappeared in the light that filled Eldridge Street. As an afterthought Ehrich took aim and flicked the pigeon droppings off his windowsill and, wishing that he'd been able to actually sting one of the pigeons with his towel instead of just scaring them, draped the weapon around his neck. As he opened the door of his room he heard his mother call again, "Ehrich?" On purpose he didn't answer, but waited for her to call a third time, only louder and in a more exasperated tone. "Ehrich Leftrack, are you awake? This breakfast won't stay hot forever." Without a sound Ehrich went into the bathroom and then smiled as he slammed the door behind him as hard as he could. It was a reply in a language he knew his mother understood.

The portions of shrimp in lobster sauce, pork fried rice, beef with snow peas, chicken almond din, moo goo gai pan and roast pork egg foo yung had disappeared and Ehrich's chopsticks expertly speared the last jade-green snow-pea pod and savored its musky crunchiness. He rolled the last helping of rice in the sauce that remained in the beef serving dish and scooped it up, enjoying more than anything the feel of a mouthful of food.

He noticed that his father's rice bowl was still full and reached across the table to claim it.

His parents' talk centered on the business and it bored him. They droned on and Ehrich emptied his father's rice bowl and began to think about dessert: vanilla ice cream with a side order of litchi nuts would taste good now. Or maybe subgum fruit? Or coconut ice cream? He wavered between subgum fruit and litchi nuts and then heard his father say something that made him forget all about dessert.

"Well, then, that's settled. Ehrich, I'll expect you at the store this afternoon and every day that we're open this summer. Even though it's only temporary, you'll start at the bottom, just like I did. We'll give you a desk in Sorensen's workshop. I'll introduce you when we go back. By the end of the summer you'll be running the place. Just like a son." Mr. Leftrack beamed benevolently and added, "You'll probably lose a few pounds, too, because you won't be sitting on your keister all day with your nose in a book. Working in the warehouse will be the best thing in the world for you."

Ehrich looked blankly at his father. Between the egg foo yung and the fried rice he'd obviously missed something.

His father continued: "I can see that you're not overjoyed with the prospect, but your mother and I have decided that it's time you gave us a hand. You're a grown man now—have been for some time. You'll get a paycheck like everyone else but you'll have to earn it. No special favors just because you're one of the family, eh, Irma?"

His mother said, "Yes, Ira. He can help out, just like Myron, my brother Morrie's boy, does. Now, that boy," she looked piercingly at Ehrich, then shifted her gaze to her napkin, her fingers mechanically folding and refolding it, first making a neat rectangle, then a triangle, then an even smaller triangle, "is a go-getter. Morrie tells me he handles all of their sales now. And he's such a *nice* boy, always so polite. We should all be so lucky to have children like that Myron. *He's* been helping his father since he was in grammar school. Every day he's in the shop, regular as clockwork." She looked at Ehrich coolly, dropped the napkin and poured tea for the three of them. Ehrich knew she was getting even for the way he'd slammed the bathroom door this morning.

"Dad, can I say something?" Ehrich asked.

"What's to say? Your mother and I have decided—a decision is a decision. It's time you got a taste of the real world. You've had your nose in books so long that you're a grown man and you still don't know anything about our business. Am I right or am I right?" Leftrack didn't wait for an answer. He continued.

"We're not going to live forever, you know, and what will you do with the business when we're gone? Sell it? After all the years we've spent building it up so that now we're living good, would you sell it to a stranger?"

"Dad, I'm going to be a doctor, a neurosurgeon. I won't have time . . ."

"Fine, be a doctor. Be a neurosurgeon. Be anything you want. But learn our business. Believe me, if someone had given me this chance when I was your age I would have known what to do with it. It's good that you're going to medical school and your mother and I want you to finish your training before you take over from us."

Ehrich opened his mouth, but his father rushed on, saying, "Believe me, Ehrich, this business is a gold mine. As a doctor, even a neurosurgeon, you'll never make half as much. Besides, how much call is there for neurosurgery? Don't most of the patients die?" Mr. Leftrack laughed his nervous little laugh and said to his wife, "That's a good one, eh, Mama? He studies for twelve years to become a neurosurgeon and then his patients all croak."

Directing his attention to Ehrich again he continued, "Just because you go to medical college doesn't mean you'll be a rich man some day. Look at your mother's cousin Benny. Where did all his fancy-schmansy education get him?"

There was a pause, but Ehrich knew that his father didn't want any interruption.

"I'll tell you where it got him," continued Ira Leftrack. "It got him nowhere. Nowhere. In my book, education isn't worth a damn unless you can support yourself. With the way things are going these days, it doesn't make sense to put all your eggs in one basket. It won't hurt you to spend one measly summer of your life learning something besides doctoring."

"But I want to spend the summer studying, so that I can be at the top of my class in the fall."

"All right, if you want to study, study in the evenings, study in the morning. Study anytime you want except from eight to six each day, because then you'll be busy studying the pet-importing trade."

Ira Leftrack saw the crestfallen expression in his son's pea-sized blue eyes and the mixture of fury and disappointment that twisted his pouting lips. He also saw that Ehrich didn't have the guts to defy him. He might complain or have a tantrum; no doubt he would whine to Irma; but in the end Ehrich would do exactly what Mama and Daddy told him to.

"But, Dad . . ." Ehrich faltered. He wanted to tell his father that he hated the pet business, that he hated even the smell of the place. He wanted to say that it wasn't fair for them to make him waste his only free summer for the next eight years in that stinking warehouse. If he'd needed extra help he could have gotten one of Mama's cousins, who would do just as well or even better than he could. No, the Old Man was just throwing his weight around—you'd think he was another Hitler.

78

He looked down at the table, littered with the remnants of their Chinese meal, and helped himself to a fortune cookie. He imagined himself standing up, throwing down his napkin and denouncing the Old Man for the rotten son of a bitch that he was. His thick fingers crushed the brittle cookie and unfolded the pink slip of paper that fell into his palm. He read, "Rain will always fall downward; don't try to change the impossible." "What the hell does that mean?" thought Ehrich and carefully put it into his wallet. Tonight he would add it to the others that he kept in an old envelope in the back of his sock drawer. His summer vacation had evaporated in the space of one meal.

Irma Leftrack's whining voice broke the silence at their table. "My fortune says, 'If you want a thing well done, do it yourself.' What kind of a fortune is that?" she complained. "Who ever heard of a fortune like that? Where's Mr. Chan? I want another one." She looked around but Peter Chan was nowhere in sight. "What does yours say, Daddy?" she asked.

Ehrich winced inwardly to hear his mother call his father "Daddy." There was something not right about it. It made his skin crawl.

"Let's see," said Ira Leftrack, "what bit of Oriental wisdom has Mr. Chan given me today?" He read aloud, " 'Your golden opportunity is coming real soon.' Clever, these Chinese, eh, Ehrich?"

With a forced man-to-man heartiness he leaned across the table and put his hand on Ehrich's arm. "See, it was written in the stars, your coming to work at the shop. Believe me, boy, you'll never regret it. It'll be the best thing that ever happened to you—give you a taste of the real world."

Ehrich said nothing. He merely glared at a spot of gravy on the tablecloth and shrugged his arm out from beneath his father's hand. In the back of his mind a small voice shouted, "Drop dead, Dad."

Sorensen's Workshop
Leftrack's Pet Emporium and
Animals International, Ltd

MANU THE LANGUR sat hunched in one corner of his cage, his bony knees drawn up against his chest. One arm hung limply at his side while the other cradled the back of his head. From time to time he glanced furtively around, watching with his good right eye for the arrival of Sorensen and food. The black fingers of one hand moved ceaselessly and systematically over his scalp, hoping to pounce upon any flea that might stray from the gnarled and rotted growth that used to be his left ear. He wished he could reach inside this ear to the place where the fleas were biting, but that wasn't possible. From time to time he violently shook his head and rubbed what should have been his ear back and forth against the wire side of his cage. It didn't do any good, though; the ruins of Manu's left ear were a paradise for fleas. The normal auditory canal had been blocked with scar tissue and not even a slender black langur finger could slip inside. But every now and then a foolish flea would venture beyond the safety of this haven and then Manu's clever fingers would attack. This was a treat for Manu and he bit through the flea's crunchy chitin with a gusto not unlike that of a Baptist minister biting into a piece of crispy southern-fried chicken after delivering a foot-stomping sermon that had even the back-sliders in the back row joining in on the amen chorus. But Manu had no amen chorus and when he did capture a flea he had to savor it in solitude.

Perhaps the worst part of being alone was that there was no one to groom him. No other pair of relentless black hands to pursue and dispatch these murderous fleas; no reassuring touch of quick, delicate fingers; no other langur to snuggle next to at night; no pair of shiny black langur eyes to gaze into. No eyes, at all, in fact, except for Sorensen's, or perhaps those of the Duchess—but a human and that neurotic parrot didn't really count. There was Dervish, but the baby coati was too young to be real company and, besides, Manu didn't really want to get attached to him. There was no way of knowing when this newest Cull might die. Manu sighed and listened with his good ear, hoping to hear Sorensen's footsteps. He was used to being alone.

The fleas seemed to know that Manu was at their mercy and sometimes his ear itched so much that he rubbed his head against the wire mesh of his cage until it was raw and sore. This didn't discourage the fleas, but it usually got Sorensen's attention and he'd douse Manu with a liquid that smelled awful but killed the fleas. Manu liked to watch them leap from their hiding places in his silvery fur. He could feel them hopping madly inside his ruined ear, too; and he imagined with satisfaction that they were dying. Some would spring onto the floor of his cage and he'd watch them spin 'round and 'round, legs twitching, till they died and moved no more. Manu had hoped they might be good to eat but the poison gave them a bitter taste and he spat them out. Langur mothers taught their children to reject any food that tasted bitter—Manu hadn't been with his troop long enough to have been given a complete education but he knew enough not to eat anything that tasted bad, no matter how delicious it looked or smelled.

Manu was one of Leftrack's early mistakes. He'd been part of a troop of Hanuman langurs that Leftrack had captured for the San Diego Zoo. It had taken three months of work outside a village in northern India, and when Leftrack had finished, the San Diego Zoo had the only family group of langurs in captivity. That is, they had an entire family group minus those that were killed during trapping, minus those that perished in transport and minus Manu.

At that time he was a newly weaned and independent youngster with a beautiful silvery coat and a long tail that he carried in the most majestic drooping curve that he could manage. He could leap farther than any of his playmates and was a fearless climber. The sight of Manu turning handsprings atop the high rocks at the edge of the village made the adults of his troop smile at the exuberance of Brahman while the little children, both monkey and human, tried to imitate Manu as he capered and spun through the air, a twirling, shining monkey with fur gilded by morning light.

He was big for his age and all the mothers in his troop said he would be troop leader someday. Even though he was too young to be really interested in female langurs, he knew that his playmates thought him beautiful and he intended to mate with all of them one day and have many wives and many langur babies to play with. Leftrack, however, had changed all that.

The troop had been captured in several ways: in pit traps, in cannon nets, in snares. It took Leftrack and his native workers time, but after a while the entire group had been caged and carted aboard ship. After an initial period of panic the langurs had calmed down. They were somewhat used to people, since they lived on the outskirts of human habitations, and Leftrack was delighted with the success of his expedition until the day when he heard the sounds of one langur murdering another in the hold where the cages were kept.

Leftrack had caged Manu with Ura, a full-grown adult male who was notorious in the troop for his all-too-predictable violent temper. The langurs knew to run for cover when Ura started staring fixedly at someone. They knew that he would soon erupt into a snarling, biting rage and unless the object of Ura's anger could escape, he or she was sure to be injured. The mothers whispered that more than once Ura had killed newborn children and was so capricious that he would do so again.

For the first month of the voyage, Manu had cowered in one corner of the cage, submitting to all of this tyrant's wishes. He'd allowed Ura to take most of the food and spent his days pretending to be invisible. Unfortunately their cage was right next to that of a female langur and when she came into breeding condition, it made Ura crazy. He outweighed little Manu by fifteen pounds and when Leftrack was finally able to isolate Ura in half of the cage so that he could remove Manu's body, it seemed that the youngster was dead. His silver-blond fur was soaked with blood. The entire left side of his coal-black face had been lacerated; his left shoulder was torn down to the bone. His left ear was badly mangled and both his eyes were filled with blood. The tail that he'd been so proud of hung by only a few tendons. Ura had nearly bitten it off.

Leftrack was furious with himself for having made such a foolish and expensive blunder. This particular specimen had been the most perfect young male in the troop; his proportions and pelage were perfect. Leftrack hated to lose any specimen through his own ignorance or stupidity and he set out to save the life of this little male.

For the remainder of the voyage Manu convalesced in a cage in Leftrack's own cabin. Although the ship's doctor helped Leftrack sew Manu's shoulder back together, most of his tail had to be amputated. They dressed his facial wounds as best they could. Probably the most important thing they did was to keep Manu clean, warm and fed. The doctor improvised a stomach tube and they gave him beef tea and warm milk three times a day. Amazingly, the little langur survived. His shoulder healed, but for a long time he favored his left arm. He also worried the bandages off his head and reinfected his partially healed ear so that it had to be lanced several times. Eventually the ear healed, but the skin grew together in a lumpy knot of scar tissue. Manu's left eye healed, too, but one of Ura's canines had pierced the lens and it had turned an opaque blue. Manu was obviously blind in it.

The left side of his face healed, but in a strange way. Its coloration was all wrong: the skin was shiny pink where it should have been coal black. The left and right sides of his face contrasted obscenely and Manu, who had once been the perfection of langur grace, now looked like a nightmare harlequin.

Even though Manu was healthy, he was so disfigured that Leftrack knew that he couldn't sell him. No zoo would pay good money to exhibit such an ugly creature and Manu, who was perfectly tame by this time, had been in a three-by-five-foot cage in Leftrack's warehouse for the six years since his capture.

If he had lived in another place and a different time, Birger Sorensen wouldn't have just been Ira Leftrack's janitor and handyman and he wouldn't have spent his life mending broken tanks, tinkering with recalcitrant plumbing and scrubbing shit out of cages. When he wasn't distracted by other worries, Birger Sorensen had a sixth sense for animals. If he'd lived in some other time or place he would have been a great shaman, able to communicate with animal spirits; or, if he'd had the chance, he could have been a famous animal trainer. Although Sorensen understood animals on an instinctive level and they trusted him, he was the lowest man in the Leftrack pecking order. Except for Sorensen's care of the Culls (animals like Manu who were injured, deformed, sick or dying), Leftrack and his two dozen employees took no special notice of Sorensen's abilities. There always seemed to be some crisis or emergency in the warehouse; and, unlike the others, Sorensen worked alone.

So, instead of spending his working hours mending broken feathers, dressing infected sores, removing parasites or calming terrified and confused creatures, Sorensen mended broken locks. When there were no locks to mend and no plumbing to repair Leftrack set him to work scrubbing cages. Only on his lunch hour or when there were no more cages to scrub was Sorensen free to care for sick creatures. He had been with Leftrack from the beginning and soon would retire. In the beginning he'd thought that the warehouse would be a good place to work. He'd thought that maybe the Boss would appreciate someone who could help with sick animals. And in the beginning that had been true.

Since Leftrack had developed his "system," however, an amateur veterinarian was superfluous. Leftrack's policy was to ship animals immediately, before they got sick or died. He wasn't interested in improving the health of his specimens and reasoned that, for every day that he kept an animal in the warehouse, profits flew out the window. Food, space and salaries were all costly. In addition, Leftrack had learned that animals kept around the warehouse became Culls. Culls were unsalable—total losses—like the hideous langur and the crazy macaw in Sorensen's workshop.

If he'd been merely a cold-hearted businessman, Leftrack would have immediately killed the animals culled from each shipment but, like most entrepreneurs, Leftrack was a gambler. His optimism was fed by the fact that once in a while Sorensen did cure a sick creature—when he had the time and presence of mind to focus his attention on it. More often, though, the Culls had injuries or diseases that were beyond Sorensen's kitchen-cabinet brand of veterinary medicine. Thus, Leftrack's hopes kept many creatures lingering near death for weeks, with Sorensen trying every remedy he knew, feeling helpless and wishing that the Boss would either let him spend the proper amount of time or put the poor beast out of its misery.

This noon, as usual, Sorensen entered his workshop carrying his lunch pail in one hand and a paper sack in the other. He was greeted in different ways by the three Culls who were expecting him. Manu's good eye met and held Sorensen's gaze for one moment before the langur looked down at the floor of his cage, meditatively scratching his head and rubbing his ear against the wire cage. Manu knew that it wasn't polite to stare.

The Duchess, a scarlet macaw who had formed the neurotic habit of plucking out her feathers, was more demonstrative. She screamed, "Hello, hello," and bobbed up and down on her perch, clamoring for attention. Sorensen knew that she wanted to be on his shoulder but ignored her. He had to feed Dervish, a half-grown coati who was scratching at the side of the wooden box beneath his workbench, making it plain that he wanted to get out.

Sorensen put down his lunch pail and the bag of groceries; making soothing noises in his throat and muttering, "I'm coming, I'm coming. Hold your horses, little one," he took the top off Dervish's box and scooped up the animated handful of red-orange fur. Dervish was still a baby coati and it would be a few months until his stubby-legged body had grown into his oversized, wildly twitching snout and long tail. These features, combined with his white-tipped nose and bandit mask with white eye patches, made him look like a cross between a panda, a raccoon and a miniature, fuzzy elephant. Dervish was delighted to be freed from his box, and after chirping hello to Sorensen found his favorite perch, on Sorensen's shoulder, gripping with his handlike paws and strong claws while using his long black-and-white-ringed tail as a balancing rod. His hypersensitive, elongated snout twitched back and forth and informed him that Sorensen had brought his favorite combination of bananas, peaches and fish heads. With thoughts of the feast to come, Dervish allowed Sorensen to scratch his ears and played tug-of-war with Sorensen's fingers, grasping them with his front feet while he kicked at them with his hind feet, all the time growling fiercely and shaking the hand to and fro, imagining that he had the neck of a venomous enemy between his teeth. Sorensen spoke sharply, and Dervish realized that he was on the verge of breaking the man's skin with his baby teeth. He hadn't meant to play so rough and as an apology Dervish licked the salt from the man's fingers, grooming them.

To show the man how grown up he could be, Dervish abruptly turned his attention to grooming himself and, oblivious to all else, lost his balance and rolled over and over, landing softly on the workbench.

"Little clown," Sorensen said. "Come and eat your dinner." The man fed him a banana and Dervish made happy, grunting sounds in his throat.

Dervish's mother had died shortly after giving birth in the pet shop and Sorensen had taken her babies home to try to raise them. Although he'd bottle-fed them every four hours and kept them warm, the other two newborn coatis had died after a few days, but Dervish had been the largest of the litter. He had thrived and now he was Sorensen's secret. Leftrack company policy forbade personal pets in the warehouse: thus Sorensen hid Dervish by day and let him out only at lunchtime for a romp around the work room. The other workers thought that Sorensen was a little peculiar, maybe even soft in the head, but Sorensen didn't care. He often muttered to himself that it was no one's goddamn business if he preferred to share his lunch with a sick bird and a crazy monkey.

While Dervish was eating, Sorensen unlatched the Duchess' cage and waited for her to clamber out and onto his shoulder. "Hello . . . hello," the macaw said, stretching her neck toward Sorensen's ear to taste it with her thick, black tongue. She knew that Sorensen had treats somewhere and her scaly feet sidestepped down his arm, as she looked expectantly at the pocket that always held peanuts for her.

"Wait a minute," said Sorensen, transferring her to the back of his chair. Even though she looked like a pathetic plucked chicken from some exotic butcher shop, Sorensen was a little afraid of the Duchess. Not only could her bill snap a broomstick in two, but she also had a bad temper and often nonchalantly drew blood. In *Ripley's* Sorensen had read that Australian parrots kill sheep by landing on their backs and ripping through their fleece to gouge mouthfuls of fat. If the Duchess' temperament were typical of her kind, Sorensen believed it.

Her irascible nature was at odds with her bizarre appearance. She looked like a rubber chicken come to life. Although there were a few red feathers sprouting from the top of her head, she had plucked the rest of her body clean, except for her stout-shafted wing feathers, which would have been too painful even for the Duchess to pull out. Whenever new feathers sprouted, she scrupulously rooted them out of their follicles and ate them. Sorensen gave her plenty of protein in her food and he'd tried everything to make her stop. Nothing had worked and he'd decided that the bird was just plain crazy. He had made a wide, wooden collar that would keep her bill away from her feathers. If he could get it around her neck without losing a finger, it might allow her feathers to grow back. On the other hand, if the collar didn't work the Duchess would sooner or later develop a taste for her own flesh. Sorensen had read that feather pluckers often committed suicide.

The Duchess, however, wasn't thinking about her feathers or about her temperament. Rather, she was pleased to be out of her cage and wondered what Sorensen had in that paper sack. Hanging by her bill and reaching with her feet she clambered down from the back of the chair and up onto the workbench. She could have flown but she'd been in captivity so long that she had lost the habit of flying. She preferred to walk across the workbench with the rolling gait that threw her body from side to side. She ignored the little coati, who was grunting over his lunch, and made straight for the paper sack. Anchoring it with one foot she ripped it open with her beak and screamed the prelude to her usual exchange with Sorensen, phrases that she thought Sorensen enjoyed.

"Shut up. Shut up," she screamed. "Good girl. Good girl. *Best girl.* Hello, Hello." He always said these things to her when he scratched her head. It only seemed logical for the bird to conclude that he'd like to hear them again.

"Talk, don't scream," Sorensen said to the bird and opened his lunch pail. She was busy destroying the paper bag and ignored him.

Sorensen finished his sandwich, sharing it with the Duchess and Dervish. The Duchess had atrocious feeding habits and when she was no longer hungry she continued to bite off portions of the baloney sandwich and fling them left and right.

"Don't be so sloppy, you horrible bird," Sorensen said. He picked her up, walked back to her cage and put her on top of it.

In Sorensen's voice, the Duchess mimicked, "Horrible bird. Horrible bird," and bowed and ducked her head coquettishly. The Duchess knew that her time with Sorensen was over. He tried to shoo her back into her cage but she squawked and hissed a protest.

"Say words, don't scream," said Sorensen and secured a leash around one of her ankles. "Say words, don't scream, you horrible bird," the Duchess mimicked, settling onto the top of her cage. It was time for Sorensen to see about Manu and he didn't want the Duchess competing for his attention. Dervish was no problem; he was busily investigating some corner of the work room.

Manu saw the bolt on his cage door move and continued to sit in the rear corner of his cage, rubbing his ear against the mesh. The solid metal front of the cage opened, and, squinting against the light, Manu glanced up at Sorensen and then grimaced as he felt the man's hands grasping his body, pulling him out of his favorite safe corner. He was scared and made a show of fear by pulling his mouth back, exposing his teeth and gums. Sorensen figured that this was merely Manu's way of smiling and disentangled his small, black hands as they found new handholds on the wire of his cage.

"Time for some exercise, old man," said Sorensen, grasping Manu's hands and forcing him to stand on his skinny shanks and hind feet.

This happened every day and Manu hated it. What did it matter that his leg muscles were so weak that they could hardly support his weight? There were no trees to climb here; there were no other langurs to play with. He wished Sorensen would just let him sit in the safe corner of his quiet cage.

"Don't you want to play today?" said Sorensen and patted Manu's back reassuringly.

The monkey slid his ears beneath Sorensen's fingers, mutely begging to be scratched, and Sorensen had the satisfaction of watching the langur's good eye close in delight as he scratched around his ears. "If only you weren't so afraid of everything," thought Sorensen, "we might be able to give you to a zoo—for breeding, if not for exhibit. But you're such a 'fraidy cat, you'd die of fright before you got there." He continued scratching Manu's little head and then, realizing that his lunch hour was almost gone, attached a leash to Manu's collar and tied the leash to the doorknob. Now Manu couldn't run back into his cage and Sorensen could clean it quickly and give him fresh food and water before attending to the other Culls.

Manu sat down on the floor with his back to the door and worried.

He hugged his thin knees to his chest and rocked back and forth, back and forth, wishing he were back in his cage. It wasn't safe out here. He saw the Duchess standing on top of her cage, trying to get Sorensen's attention. As if to punish Sorensen for ignoring her, the Duchess located the sheath of a new pinfeather beneath her left wing and made a show of fiercely plucking it out and rolling it around in her beak before she ate it. She screeched triumphantly but Sorensen was too busy to pay her any attention.

Now that his favorite charges had been attended to, he was fussing with some newly arrived Culls: sick river turtles from South America, whose eyes streamed a filamentous, white fungus. Even though he knew it was useless, Sorensen was applying eye ointment and had set up a heat lamp for them. There were fourteen turtles and each had to have the ointment massaged into its eyes—a task that took all of Sorensen's dexterity as he grasped a turtle's head in one hand, applied the ointment with the other, all the while wrestling with the animal's clawed feet. The turtles weren't grateful for his attention and it was exasperating work.

"Idiot," he said as one turtle tried to jerk his head back into his carapace at a critical moment, "I know you hate this, but it wouldn't cost you anything to cooperate." Sorensen's fingers were slippery with ointment and he lost his grasp of the turtle's head as the animal jerked away. In a shorter time than it takes to tell, the sharp cutting edges of the turtle's toothless jaws had clamped down onto Sorensen's finger. The pain was intense.

"Son of a bitch," swore Sorensen and, as he ran to the slop sink to run hot water over the turtle's head to make him let go, he accidentally knocked the jar of ointment to the floor. It shattered and sent glass shards flying in Manu's direction. Dervish, who was on the floor behind the workbench, heard the crash and froze; while the Duchess, startled by the sound, jumped up off her cage in a short flight that was soon checked by the leg leash she wore. With her great wings beating furiously she hung suspended beneath her cage, squawking and batting at the air.

Ordinarily Sorensen would have heard the footsteps and voices outside his door, but his attention was on the pain and on the turtle that refused to release his finger. Above the noise of the hot water Sorensen heard the door open suddenly. There was a scream. Too late he realized that Manu had been hurt.

Ira Leftrack and his son, Ehrich, walked into pandemonium in the Culls' room. The Duchess hung upside down beneath her cage, beating her wings and shrieking. She reached with her bill and feet for something to climb onto, but could get no purchase. At the same time, Manu was crying, baring his teeth and snarling hideously at Ehrich Leftrack, who stood frozen in the doorway, calling to his father for help.

Ira Leftrack took charge of the situation immediately. He wanted

Ehrich to learn how to handle animals, so, before Sorensen could intervene, Leftrack bustled in and ordered Ehrich to help the Duchess. "That one makes a lot of noise," Leftrack said, "but she won't hurt you. She's as tame as a kitten. Go ahead, Ehrich. And have a little confidence, boy. Birds can smell fear. Give her your arm to climb onto. You'll never learn how to do this any younger."

If Sorensen were thinking clearly, he'd have warned Ehrich to leave the Duchess alone, but before he could intervene Ehrich had extended his hand toward the macaw. In a moment she climbed up onto it, regained her perch on the cage and, as a passing gesture, as if to show that no good deed would go unpunished, she had bitten Ehrich's index finger, slicing effortlessly through skin and flesh and bruising the bone. It happened so quickly that blood was dripping onto the floor before Ehrich realized what had happened. From her perch on top of her cage the Duchess bobbed her head and weaved like a maniacal boxer sent to a neutral corner after a knockout. She opened her mouth and hissed a warning to these intruders to leave her and Manu alone.

"Talk, don't scream, you horrible bird," she screeched in a dark baritone.

Manu, whose stump of a tail had been pinched beneath the door as it opened, ran around and around in circles, still crying piteously. He sounded like a dog that had been kicked. More than anything else Manu wanted to get back into his cage—back into his safe corner. Ehrich hadn't seen the langur on the other side of the door and, as he clutched his hand in pain, trying to get away from the bird, he backed into Manu. Manu saw a huge leg about to trample him and did the only thing he could do: he bit this human's leg and then ran to the farthest end of his leash, teeth bared, listening as Ehrich Leftrack's hysterical yelping drowned the screaming of the Duchess.

Ehrich Leftrack didn't think about it until his wounds had been stitched and bandaged in the emergency room of St. Vincent's Hospital, but somehow he would find a way to get even with that ugly monkey and the horrid creature that he couldn't really believe was a bird.

CHAPTER THREE

Leftrack's Pet Emporium and Animals International, Ltd
June 18, 1932

WEINSTEIN, THE NAME is Weinstein. And tell him that my client here, Miss Naruda, has important business with him."

Irma Leftrack didn't like to be bossed around, especially by a stranger. She looked up from her newspaper and said coldly, "Do you have an appointment?"

Bernie Weinstein took the stump of his cigar from the corner of his mouth and gestured with it. "Look, sister. We want to see Mr. Leftrack, and if you don't tell him, you'll be the one that gets the blame when someone else buys the largest python in captivity right out from under Leftrack's nose."

"I'll see if *Mr.* Leftrack can see you," Irma said and reached with her stockinged toes for the shoes that squeezed her bunions. She slid off the stool behind the cash register and walked to the warehouse door, thinking to herself, "Of all the obnoxious, pushy, nervy . . ." Irma realized that the couple was about to follow her into the warehouse and when the door was unlocked she said, "You can't come in here," and pointed to the sign that read "EMPLOYEES ONLY." She let the door slam in Weinstein's face and went in search of her husband.

Bernie yelled after her, "And make it snappy—we haven't got all day."

He went to the door, yelled out, "Okay, fellas," and opened both doors as wide as possible to allow the crew of five Italians to enter, wheeling a heavy sack on a hand truck. He pointed to a place near the cash register and the men struggled to lift the sack and put it on the floor. Bernie gave one of the men a five-dollar bill and they left, pushing the hand truck before them.

Bernie jingled the change in his pants pocket and winked at Ruthie as if to reassure her that everything was going to be all right. Her wide, green eyes held his glance for a moment and then she turned away without smiling. She'd seen him operate before and knew that he was being purposely abrasive: it was all part of his act; however, she didn't find it amusing today. Bernie's obsession with driving a tough bargain for the Burmese seemed absurd: her Burmese was worth more than money. In fact, there was no way to calculate how much that snake was worth. Ruthie had argued that it was wrong to sell her. "But, Bernie," she had said, "it's just like I'm selling my own child." Then Bernie had reminded her of her new responsibilities. She was about to become a film star and hadn't danced with her snakes in months. The Burmese now spent all of her time locked in a closet in a big cloth sack. "How'd you like to be in there all day, with no company?" She had to admit that Bernie was right: it would be best to sell the big snake, and yet Ruthie resented the way he was going about it. To him it was just another negotiation: another game to win. It made Ruthie angry and her sling-backed high heels slapped in double time as she paced to the back of the store and stared at the golden tree cobra without really seeing it. She wished this was over.

Bernie waited by the door marked "EMPLOYEES ONLY" and watched Ruthie. No question about it, she was a knockout: she was innocence mixed up with sensuality in such a way that a man didn't know whether to take her to bed or tell her a bedtime story. Her crisp, white gloves contrasted primly with the plunging neckline of the dark-green silk dress that clung to her body. The way that her eyes peeked out from beneath her veiled, wide-brimmed black hat made her look like an inexperienced but willing pupil in some wicked Sunday school. Bernie knew that Reinhardt had seen her special qualities, too. That was why he'd given her a long-term contract; that was why she was having the screen test next month. Ruthie hadn't realized it yet but, if she played it right, she would be a big star and they'd both be fixed for life. No more of this nickel-and-dime burlesque and no more dancing in two-bit joints with snakes. Bernie thought it was important for Ruthie to understand that her future as a movie star was bigger than her career as an exotic dancer ever could be. As a first step toward her new life Bernie wanted to unload that monster snake and get the hell out of this place. He and Ruthie didn't need any of this snake-charming business any longer.

Ruthie looked at Bernie's reflection in the wide plate-glass window, watched him jingle the change in his pocket and hated him for being so unconcerned with the fate of the Burmese. She didn't like this place or the dumpy woman behind the counter. She didn't like the way that all the animals had price tags on their cages and she didn't like the way that the Burmese was nosing against the bag that held her, trying to get out. Ruthie could tell that the snake was nervous; the Big Girl always hated being confined. Ruthie sighed. If only there had been more time, she might have been able to find a good home for the Burmese. But ever since Reinhardt had seen her act and signed her to tour with the Follies of 1932, there'd been no time for anything. He was even talking about a motion-picture contract and if that happened she would be busier than ever. The Burmese had grown so big that now she was a liability. Even her huge traveling trunk was too small and Ruthie had had to sew two bed sheets together to make a bag that was big enough to hold her. Ruthie hadn't used the Burmese onstage since Omaha and, although Ruthie loved the animal, she knew that it would be best to get rid of her.

Ira Leftrack was out of the warehouse door and shaking hands with her and with Bernie before Ruthie realized who he was.

"My wife tells me that you have a snake to sell," Leftrack said, toying with his mustache and trying to appear uninterested.

"Yes, she's in that bag over there," said Ruthie, gesturing toward the front of the store. "I'll be happy to show you . . ."

"No need," said Leftrack imperiously. "I've handled reptiles before and, incidentally," he added with a superior smirk, "I've found that most of the really gigantic ones shrink considerably when brought face to face with a tape measure." He smiled patronizingly at Ruthie and untied the sack that held Sherahi.

"Are you ready, boys? Miss, since she's your snake you hold her neck. I'll take her head. Ehrich, you're the biggest; you grab her body and hold on for dear life. Don't let her throw a coil around you. Above all, *don't* let go until *I* tell you to. Understand? The rest of you, grab whatever you can and hold on. You have no idea how strong a big one like this can be."

"Be careful of your hand, Ehrich," Irma Leftrack put in.

Leftrack glowered at his wife and continued in a martyred tone, "Try to not get bitten today, okay, sonny?" With an air of bemused tolerance he gestured to Ehrich's bandaged hand and explained to Ruthie, "We had a little accident yesterday. Even though he's going to be a brain surgeon someday, my boy still has lots to learn about the animal business."

Ehrich was embarrassed to be made the butt of his father's jokes in front of strangers, especially in front of this beautiful girl. He wanted to curse or to run away, but bit his lower lip instead and silently vowed to do exactly as he was told.

"Sorensen, you take her tail. Irma, you handle the tape. And be quick about it. We probably won't get a second chance to straighten her out."

"It's really not nec— " said Ruthie, but Leftrack had peered into the bag and grabbed the python's neck and head before Ruthie could say that none of these precautions was necessary: the Burmese was as tame as a puppy dog. She'd never bitten anyone as long as Ruthie had known her.

Leftrack couldn't quite believe his eyes. This snake's head was as big as that of a full-grown German shepherd and at its widest her body was as thick as a telephone pole. Her scales were glossy and smooth, her muscle tone was firm and she appeared to be in perfect health. "Got her," he said triumphantly and, using both hands, he began to pull her body up and out of the bag. She flowed upward like a rope of unresisting taffy. These people hadn't been lying: this snake *could* be the largest python in captivity. But whether it was the largest or not, one thing was immediately clear: the snake was very valuable and Leftrack decided there and then that somehow he would buy it. Ditmars at the Bronx Zoo would go crazy over it. He'd have to be careful, though; these two didn't seem to realize how much it was worth and if he appeared to be too eager it might drive the price up.

"Okay, everybody, grab hold. Irma: hurry up."

"Really, Mr. Leftrack, you don't need to—" said Ruthie.

Leftrack was intent on measuring the Burmese and curtly replied, "Lady, I've been in the pet business since before you were born. Don't tell me how to handle pythons, okay?"

"Jesus, this snake is heavy," said Ehrich, grunting beneath the burden of the animal's midsection.

"Sweetheart, be careful of your hand," warned Irma Leftrack, stretching the tape measure down the snake's backbone.

"Mother, *please,*" said Ehrich and tried not to think about the garter snake that had bitten him when he was a little boy. His leg muscles were dancing uncontrollably, his mouth was dry, yet even though he didn't like it, he held on to the snake with all his might. "Hurry up, Mother," he said irritably.

Ruthie didn't like Leftrack's patronizing attitude or the way he was holding the Burmese's head and had decided that she'd had enough of this whole thing. She had opened her mouth to tell Bernie that the deal was off when the pythoness began to jerk and coil like a watch spring gone berserk.

Sherahi hadn't been touched by strangers in years and she didn't like it a bit. Furthermore, she could sense that this nervous man with the ugly smear of bristles on his upper lip (where any self-respecting python would have had its labial pits) was making Ruthie unhappy. If that weren't bad enough, his fingers were holding her head too tightly, driving her jaws together and bruising her facial muscles. Sherahi had tried to control her anger. She told herself that if Ruthie were allowing this thing to happen then it must be all right. However, as this crowd of strangers continued rudely pulling and pinching at her, she decided that she couldn't endure this treatment any longer. They acted as if she were a rear-fanged false cobra: sneaky and untrustworthy. Well, if that's what they wanted to think she'd show them. After all, she wasn't named Sherahi for nothing.

With a flick of her thickly muscled neck, the snake twisted her head free. Opening her mouth and hissing ferociously Sherahi struck at the fat one who held her body. She saw him jump back and felt him release her. In a flash she bit the hand of the man who had been holding her head and encircled him in a strangling coil. As she did so she scattered the men who had been supporting her body and she fell heavily onto the floor.

Within her coil Sherahi could feel the man trying to jerk his hand free. She felt his scream of pain and fright reverberate in her chest and dug her teeth even more deeply into his hand. His other hand was still free and he alternately pulled and hammered at her head with his fist until she immobilized it with a second coil. Sherahi knew that he was no match for her and locked her jaws. Her brain hummed the sweet song of death that the elders had taught her so long ago. Her lidless, gold-flecked eyes stared into the oily face of her enemy and she willed him to die, willed him to gasp again and again for breath. She felt his rib cage strain outward and knew that it would be only moments before he would exhale. Then she could tighten her coils and feel his heart fluttering against his ribs. He would die soon.

Leftrack had been bitten by snakes before, he'd even wrestled with crocs, but he'd never been attacked by a giant snake and he hadn't been prepared for the swiftness, the pain or the horror of it. Every jerk of his hand seemed to impale it even more on the hundreds of teeth that he could feel slicing into his hand. Every breath that he was able to draw seemed to make her coil more tightly about him. He felt the blood surge into the veins of his neck until they seemed about to explode. "Help me. Somebody help me," was all that he could gasp before he grew dizzy. He heard a humming in his ears that sounded strangely hypnotic. He felt as if he were falling and black specks floated before his eyes.

With little effect Ehrich Leftrack tried to pull the monster snake off his father's body. Then he grabbed the broom from behind the fish tanks and repeatedly hit the snake, hoping to make it relinquish its hold. "Stop that. You're only making it worse," said Sorensen, who was still holding on to the python's tail. "Here, help me."

Ehrich grabbed hold of the snake's tail, alongside of Sorensen, and together they tried to pull the snake's body from around Leftrack, whose face had turned an alarming shade of purple. Sherahi sensed what the two men were doing and quicker than a whip crack her huge, legless body lashed out, sending Sorensen and Ehrich reeling back into the hamster cages. They crashed to the floor, scattering cedar chips and sending little rodents scurrying for freedom.

Leftrack gasped, "Do something. Do something, somebody," and sank to his knees. He wanted to say more, wanted to plead for help, but could only open his mouth and try to strain outward against the snake's coils.

"Oh my God, oh my God," Bernie said. Irma Leftrack was frozen against the cash register and watched in horror as the huge snake writhed and coiled around her husband. The tape measure dangled from her hand. She suddenly found her voice and screamed, "Help him! Help him, some- body!" as her husband's head flopped forward.

Sherahi's mind hummed the man's death song and revolved around a single thought: "Strangle. Strangle this man. Squeeze him tight. Squeeze his ribs. Make him gasp. Make his mouth open like a fish that is drowning. Strangle. Strangle this man."

She concentrated on Leftrack's death so completely that it was a while before she was aware of a familiar pair of warm hands pulling on her neck. The calm touch of these hands distracted her from Leftrack's death song and she relaxed her strangling coils. Above all the confusion in the pet shop she heard Ruthie's voice reverberating within Leftrack's chest. It said, "No. No. You mustn't do this. Let go. Let him go. Please. Please let him go."

Obediently, Sherahi relinquished her strangle hold on the man's chest and disengaged her teeth from his hand. He slumped to the floor, still breathing. She scryed Ruthie's mind and saw that Ruthie wanted her to crawl back into the sack. Sherahi looked at the inert body of her enemy and sent a final hiss and wave of hatred into his mind. Feeling very much that she had taught these strange humans a lesson, Sherahi slowly crawled into her bag and coiled up to relive her victory in solitude. U Vayu would be proud of her.

Leftrack was immediately surrounded by his family and employees. They propped him into a sitting position. Slapping his cheeks and chafing his wrists, Sorensen asked if he was all right. Leftrack's face resumed its normal pallor and Sorensen, looking for broken bones, felt his rib cage. In moments Leftrack waved them all away. He regained his senses as Irma began to wrap his hand in a handkerchief. Blood streamed onto the lap of her dress and, although he made a big show of catching his breath and trembling, Leftrack knew that by some miracle he was unharmed. He lowered his head between his knees, took a deep breath and planned how he could profit from this accident.

"Are you all right, Dad?" asked Ehrich, hoping that his father would have to be hospitalized.

"Should we call the ambulance, Ira? Do you want a doctor?" asked Irma.

Leftrack was irritated and snapped, *"Don't* go calling any ambulance or any doctors. I'm fine. Just leave me alone so I can catch my breath. You'd think that you people had never had any experience with snakes before."

Ruthie said, "I'm so sorry, Mr. Leftrack. I don't understand why she did that. She's never bitten anyone before."

Leftrack looked up scornfully at the girl and sneered, "Don't try to con me. I've got witnesses. I could sue you for what just happened. That snake almost killed me. She's a public menace."

Bernie interrupted, saying, "Now just a minute, Mr. Leftrack . . ." but the pet store owner continued, "That snake is a killer. You're lucky that she didn't attack someone before this. All of these big snakes are like that—unreliable. Never can tell when they're going to do something vicious right out of the blue—just like that."

"I'm sorry, Mr. Leftrack, but if you'd listened to me in the first place this never would have happened," said Ruthie. "You scared her. I don't think you understand anything about snakes and I wouldn't sell her to you on a bet."

Ruthie picked up an injured hamster as it limped past her feet and handed the animal to Sorensen. "Come on, Bernie," she said, "let's take the Burmese home. Mr. Leftrack can send us a bill for damages."

Leftrack didn't respond to anything that Ruthie said. Instead, he jerked his hand away from the ministrations of his wife, saying, "Goddammit, Irma, leave me alone."

Irma's lower lip trembled and obediently she went back to her habitual perch behind the cash register.

Leftrack's hand throbbed and his ribs ached, but he felt well enough to give orders: "Sorensen, get this mess cleaned up. Ehrich, I'm not paying you to stand around and gawk. Catch those goddamn hamsters. They'll be all over the place in a minute. And tell Leonard to bring our biggest galvanized tank from the back."

Ignoring Ruthie, Leftrack turned to Bernie, saying, "I'll offer you fifty dollars for that snake—take it or leave it—and I won't even charge you for damages or doctor bills."

Ruthie interrupted with, "Bernie, I don't think so. The Burmese won't be happy here."

"Ruthie, we've been all through this before. You agreed that we would sell her. Now, even after all he's been through, Mr. Leftrack is kind enough to offer us good money for the Burmese and I think we should take it." Bernie was thinking about lawyers and lawsuits and wanted to get the hell out of this place.

"I don't know, Bernie," Ruthie said. She saw the way the big snake was nosing against the knotted bag and found herself hoping that Bernie would urge her to take the snake out of here. That would be the right thing to do.

"Okay, Missy," said Leftrack. "I don't know why I'm being so generous, especially after all the trouble she's caused, but I'll make it seventy-five dollars and I'll throw in four of those little boas over there. They're worth another seventy-eighty dollars all by themselves.

"But that's my final offer. Take it or leave it."

"Done," said Bernie.

In a few minutes a huge galvanized tank with a weighted wire-mesh top was rolled into the pet shop and seven of Leftrack's men picked up the knotted bag. They groaned with effort as they lifted it into the tank. The bravest gingerly untied the bag and the others quickly slid the top into place before the snake could strike.

Sherahi saw that her bag was being opened and poured out to investigate. Through the wire-mesh top she saw the man that she had marked for death sitting alongside the tank, his hand wrapped in a white cloth. His face was gray and his skin was slick and she didn't like the shape of his thoughts. She inflated her body and hissed in his direction and had the satisfaction of seeing him jump back, his eyes wide with fear.

Sherahi reared up against the top of the tank and, looking across the room, she saw Ruthie making a fool of herself over some more mindless baby boas. She tried to scry Ruthie's mind and, although she could not concentrate very well amidst all the commotion, it was plain that something was very wrong. After all the trouble she had just caused, Ruthie was not even thinking of her a little bit. It suddenly occurred to Sherahi that Ruthie and Bernie intended to leave her behind. "Please, please don't leave me here," Sherahi begged, even though she knew that Ruthie could not understand. "It smells wrong. It feels dangerous. I don't like these humans. Please take me with you."

Sherahi pushed her bruised muzzle against the wire top, seeking a way out of this new prison, but the top wouldn't budge. She heard the oily man say, "You'll never get out of this tank, so don't try," and realized that he was talking to her.

Ruthie draped the two baby boas around her neck and held them up to let them slither down her arms. She was making foolish noises at them and Sherahi felt a pang of jealousy. The oily man gave Bernie a handful of paper money and Sherahi realized that, indeed, they were leaving her behind. With all the power of her mind she screamed to Ruthie for help, saying, "Please, please don't leave me here! Ruthiiiieee!"

The girl was about to go out of the pet-shop door but suddenly turned back. "What was that noise?" she asked Bernie.

"I didn't hear anything." Then he added, "C'mon, baby, let's get out of here before Leftrack changes his mind."

Ruthie cocked her head and listened for a moment but heard nothing, and then Bernie closed the door after them. Exhausted by her unsuccessful effort to send a message into a human mind, Sherahi slumped to the bottom of the tank that held her prisoner. She smelled the strange animals around her and felt the stares of the strange humans who stood above her tank and realized that this was the bad thing that she had been expecting for so long. Ruthie had abandoned her.

Leftrack listened to the door close behind the snake dancer and her boyfriend. Mentally he counted to ten before slowly opening the door and peering outside. He saw them get into a taxicab at the end of the block and waited until the taxi had disappeared from sight. Returning to the pet shop, Leftrack shut the door and capered over to the cash register. If his ribs hadn't been so sore he would have picked up Irma and danced around the room with her. "Irma," he said. "Irma, do you realize what has just happened, right before your very eyes?"

Irma watched her husband hopping excitedly from one foot to the other and thought that maybe the snake attack had affected his mind.

Leftrack looked at her astonished face and answered his own question. "No, I can see that you don't. But you will. I promise, you will—soon enough." He leaned across the front counter, planted a kiss on her cheek and hurried to his office in the warehouse, thinking, "A mink. I'll get her a beautiful ranch mink coat. Then she'll get the idea."

He raced down the inner flight of stairs and burst through the second glass door. "Helga! Helga, where are you?" he hollered. His yell panicked a pair of emperor penguins, who squawked in fright and tottered to the far end of the cage, their dignity offended. Leftrack paid them no attention and hollered again, "Helga! I need you." His secretary stuck her head out of her office and he ordered, "Get me Ditmars at the Bronx Zoo, immediately." Then he changed his mind and said, "No, forget Ditmars. Call those reporters from the *Sun* and the *Herald*. And get someone from the *Times*, too."

Leftrack perched on the edge of his desk, waiting for his phone to ring, congratulating himself on his cleverness and good fortune. He thought, "It's got to be the biggest snake in the world. I can sell it for eight hundred—maybe a thousand—maybe even two thousand. *And* it only cost me seventy-five dollars! Those two stupid schlemiels: they didn't have the faintest idea of what that snake is worth."

Leftrack cackled to himself and took a fresh handkerchief from his desk drawer, so absorbed with his triumph over those two rubes that he didn't notice the throbbing of his lacerated hand. Then he suddenly remembered: Ditmars from the Bronx Zoo had a standing offer of five thousand dollars for a python over thirty feet in length. The monster that he just bought must be at least that. "Wait till the Bronx Zoo hears about this," he thought in triumph.

It seemed to be taking Helga too long to get the reporters and Leftrack paced to her desk, heard her speaking to someone who seemed to be obviously uncooperative, grabbed the phone away from her and demanded, "Hello, who is this?"

There was a pause and then he continued, "Okay, City Desk, this is Leftrack. I've just survived a vicious, unprovoked attack from the biggest python ever seen by man. It's here in my shop under lock and key now and if you want an exclusive story you'll send a reporter and a photographer over here right away." There was a pause and then he said, "Yeah, Leftrack's Pet

Emporium—Broadway and Houston. And if they're not here in twenty minutes I'm calling the other papers."

Leftrack handed the phone to Helga and smiled, saying, "Now, call the other papers and tell them exactly the same thing. Except tell them that you're my wife. Tell them that the doctors are here now dressing my wounds, otherwise I'd be calling myself."

"But, Mr. Leftrack, you just told the *Times* that they had an exclusive."

"It's a dog-eat-dog world, Helga. Don't give me arguments, just get on that phone and do as I say."

Leftrack fetched a long pole with a noose attached and returned to the front of the store to wait for the press. With the noose pole in one hand he stood over Sherahi, thinking of the five thousand dollars and mentally measuring the hissing snake. "At least thirty feet," he assured himself. "That son of a bitch's got to be at least that long—maybe more."

That night Sherahi lay with her jaw pressed to the bottom of the escape-proof metal tub in which Leftrack had imprisoned her, listening for danger in the darkness. Her labial pits told her that there were many unfamiliar animals in this room and still others in rooms not far away. A scan for nearby reptilian intelligence had revealed the newly hatched boas that stared pop-eyed into the darkness, their minds filled with yolky baby talk and play. There was a tank of common garter snakes and a little farther away was a huge, sleeping golden tree cobra. Sherahi wanted to question this snake, but etiquette demanded that she wait until it awoke at midday. Cobras were widely known for their intelligence as well as their imperious ways. They considered themselves a cut above all other snakes and Sherahi had often thought that their delusions of superiority had been caused by humans. After all, the confused, bulbous-headed fools had worshiped cobras for centuries and, as anyone could have predicted, it had eventually turned the snakes' heads. They considered themselves so superior and celestial that even the average cobra guarding a rubbish heap in the slums of Karachi would hardly reply to a polite greeting from a fellow serpent. But Sherahi needed information from this cobra. She wanted to know what this place was, who these people were and what they were going to do with her. She'd never learn anything from a crabby cobra and, although it frustrated her, Sherahi knew that her questions would have to wait until tomorrow noon.

In a room beyond this one, far from the sleeping cobra, Sherahi sensed another group of reptiles. She could hear the faint moaning of turtles and saw that their minds were preoccupied by pain and the fright caused by their sudden blindness. They didn't respond to her scan and the sound of their anguish unnerved Sherahi. Summoning her nearly exhausted mental reserves she sent a balm spinning out to them. It webbed and enveloped their pain like glistening spider silk and Sherahi was gratified to hear their moans taper away into silence. She sensed that many of them were weak and about to die and knew that at least they would have good dreams for one night before they were engulfed by the black hand that takes all.

Sherahi could hear the scurrying and digging sounds of small mammals in cages all around her, and once or twice she heard birds chirping. Earlier in the day, when Leftrack had been measuring her, she had seen tanks of small fishes. She wasn't surprised that she couldn't detect any intelligent thought because even though fishes were cold-blooded and had long, sustained thoughts, the actions of their minds had been shaped by water instead of by air and wind. Thus, communication between fishes and reptiles, except by visual signs, was impossible.

The humans had left long ago, when it was still daylight. The door had slammed and then clicked behind them. The man Sherahi had marked for death was the last to leave. Even when he was outside the door she could hear him bragging, obviously pleased that she had failed in her second attempt to strangle him. She shouldn't have been surprised, though; he was only a human and she, better than anyone else, should have known that humans seldom played fair. He'd tricked her by sliding a noose around her neck and pulling it tight so that she couldn't bite again. It was a metal loop attached to a long pole and her neck hurt where the loop had dug into her flesh. The fat boy who'd beaten her with the broom had held the pole that was attached to the noose and no matter how Sherahi had twisted and pulled, the noose had held her neck fast. She had been humiliated that she was not able to get free and had wriggled like a fish hooked through the gills. The oily man, Leftrack was his name, had run about directing a small army of men who held her writhing body. It had taken eighteen of them to subdue her and from the way they touched her she knew that each of them was terrified. Hands had gripped her even more tightly than they had in the morning and Sherahi's body hurt in many places. Only one old, white-haired man had spoken calm words to her and had touched her like a friend.

Eventually they had been successful in stretching her out so that the mousy-haired woman could measure her. Photographers snapped pictures, creating the bright flashes that Sherahi remembered from her days with Ruthie. Leftrack had smiled broadly and gestured with his bandaged hand. He posed proprietarily with Sherahi again and again and had been so smug that Sherahi wished that she'd bitten him much more savagely. If only she hadn't listened to Ruthie, that man would be cold and stiff by now. While the fat boy held the noose-pole and the frightened men restrained her thrashing body, Leftrack had become quite bold and had actually brought his face right next to hers. Sherahi remembered Ruthie's smooth skin and sweet smell and was astonished to see that Leftrack's slick cheeks were covered with blue-black bristles. There was a rancid smell about him. In disgust she wondered how humans could look and smell so different.

Now Sherahi's mouth throbbed and her tongue found gaps where teeth had broken off. They must be embedded in Leftrack's wounds and Sherahi was pleased by the thought that these teeth would work inward farther and farther and cause him pain. She was happy to have at least this shred of extra vengeance, meager though it was. Her missing teeth would eventually be replaced by the embryonic teeth waiting below her gum line, but the knowledge that her bruises and minor injuries would heal quickly was small comfort to the pythoness. She wished that she'd killed Leftrack outright. She would rather have been mortally wounded in a battle that she had clearly won than be in this stand-off.

Lying in her new metal prison, Sherahi heard the pattering of cockroach feet across its wire-screen top. She felt their inscrutable compound eyes watching her and knew that if she concentrated she would be able to speak to them and get answers to her questions. But she didn't have the mental energy to converse with insects.

Sherahi thought about Ruthie and Bernie, Carla and Rosita and the new baby snakes and wondered if any of them thought of her. If she had felt stronger she would have scanned for them, but she really didn't want to. If only Ruthie had taken her home, Sherahi wouldn't have minded having lost the struggle with Leftrack. But for the first time in a decade Sherahi was alone. She had been betrayed by the only human she had ever completely trusted. Lying in the darkness with strange, caged animals all around her, Sherahi ignored the waving antennae of the cockroaches who stared at her and she vowed to never make that mistake again.

Leftrack's Pet Emporium and Animals International, Ltd September, 1932

THREE MONTHS LATER Sherahi was still in Leftrack's pet shop in the same galvanized iron tank but, except for her great length, no one would have guessed that she was the same snake who had caused so much commotion and whose picture had been splashed all over the New York City newspapers. (Leftrack claimed that she was thirty-one feet, three inches long; but no knowledgeable person believed him. It was a common practice for animal dealers to add 30 percent to the measured length of any giant snake.) Sherahi looked different because she was on a hunger strike: grieving for Ruthie and the old, familiar routine. In two months she had lost seventy-five pounds, her good looks and her health. Even though she would have severely reprimanded Ruthie if she were able; even though she'd sent Ruthie many a nightmare filled with roiling, writhing, attacking snakes; even though she'd tried her best to load Ruthie's mind with a heavy burden of guilt, Sherahi had only recently stopped hoping that Ruthie would rescue her.

For three months Sherahi had eaten nothing and had hardly touched water. A mouth infection had begun when Leftrack bruised her jaws. In two months they had swollen to twice their normal size and a cheesy white substance clotted her mouth. The condition had become so severe that it was painfully impossible for the snake to grasp and swallow prey. But in two months of hunger and sickness, Sherahi had not been idle. In the way of her kind she had vowed not to eat again until she had either escaped from Leftrack's pet shop or killed Ira Leftrack. Her hatred of the man had crystallized and now included all of the Leftrack family. She despised the fat boy and the drab woman almost as much as oily Leftrack himself. Whenever one of them came in sight she would raise her head as high as her cage would allow and would hiss, resonantly cursing them for her pain and misery.

Leftrack had been greatly disappointed when Ditmars, from the Bronx Zoo, refused to buy the huge Burmese. Shortly after Leftrack had purchased the snake Ditmars and his keepers came to the shop and measured her once again. After a careful inspection Ditmars had said that, because she wasn't actually thirty feet long, he'd save his money to buy a large male Burmese to mate with the twenty-two-foot female that the Bronx Zoo already owned. Ditmars had apologized, saying that in normal times he would have bought the python. Because of the Depression money was short. He had added that he was afraid that the Zoo might have to close its doors to the public, as the Brooklyn Botanic Garden had done a few months before.

Ditmars had examined Sherahi's mouth and had told Leftrack that she had the beginning of a serious mouth infection. After recommending a medicine to be applied twice a day, he had left the pet store, once again expressing his regrets. Leftrack was busy with a shipment of baby gorillas that had just arrived and he had assigned Ehrich the job of applying the medicine. Ehrich was terrified of the huge snake and too frightened to try to approach her, so he had poured the medicine down the drain when no one was looking. A few weeks later he had complained to his father that Ditmars didn't know what he was talking about. The medicine was just a waste of good money: the snake was plainly on a hunger strike.

Ira Leftrack was undaunted, reasoning that there were other zoos in the country—a valuable snake like this one wouldn't go begging. By this time he had mentioned the mink coat to Irma. She had protested that she really didn't want one—there were lots of other things they needed first. Ehrich needed a typewriter for medical school. But Leftrack could tell that she was just waiting for him to force her to take it.

Three months later, however, Leftrack's business had suffered a series of setbacks. The retail business was slow, actually losing money, and when the new Animals of the Month, those baby gorillas from Kenya, had suddenly died in spite of Sorensen's heroic efforts to save them, Leftrack's mood had changed. Irma's mink coat and Ehrich's typewriter were forgotten.

Early one morning Ira Leftrack came into the pet store as usual, worrying about bills he couldn't pay and the threat of bankruptcy. In the darkness he tripped over the huge tub that held the now-emaciated and febrile giant python. Infuriated at whoever had put it in the aisle, he kicked furiously at the tub, taking his anger out on the metal. The pythoness inside raised her head, hissing and threatening, and Leftrack saw how sick and sorry-looking she was. "She won't live for more than a month," he thought. "She's certainly not fit to be shown to the public."

He looked at the knobs of bone that traveled the length of her back and thought, "She's a loss—a total loss. No zoo will buy her now." He thought of the stack of bills that waited on his desk and the taxes that he could not pay and kicked the tub again.

When Sorensen came in that day he found the huge metal tank and the python in his work room, alongside Manu's cage. Sherahi, the largest and most majestic python in captivity; Sherahi, who was of an ancient lineage that could conquer time as effortlessly as a diving kingfisher cleaves still water; Sherahi—a snake fierce enough to grapple with tigers and win; this same regal beast had become a worthless and unwanted Cull.

CHAPTER FOUR

Leftrack's Pet Emporium and Animals International, Ltd

SHERAHI LISTENED TO the door close behind the men who had moved her tank. Their footsteps receded into the distance and when it was quiet the pythoness raised her head to peer beyond her prison's screen top. Her view was restricted to two sturdy metal cages. In the long-legged cage that was closest to her she fnasted a warm and furry lump and surmised that it was a sleeping mammal of some kind. The other cage was more of a puzzle: it was shrouded, and Sherahi had observed that only birds were kept in cages that were covered at night. She was puzzled, though, because she did not detect the usual hot-fusty aroma of feathers. Perhaps it wasn't a bird, after all. She was about to scan the minds of the inhabitants of these two cages when her jawbones transmitted the sound of heavy claws clicking rhythmically across the floor. Instantly her labial pits began to quop, informing her that something warm was coming toward her. She began to worry: if it were a rat it could slither like a weasel through the small, open drain in the floor of her cage. There was little room for her to maneuver and with her mouth the way it was she wouldn't be able to bite a rat anyway. She would have to grab and strangle it with her coils and hope that it suffocated before its teeth were able to puncture her skin and penetrate to her backbone. If it bit her behind the head . . . Sherahi stopped thinking and listened, all senses alert. Would a rat make so much noise? She took several breaths to inflate her body, so that she would seem more formidable to her enemy, and watched the drain hole, waiting for the gray hunchback to appear. But instead of running beneath her tank to sniff at the open drain, the creature leaped onto the screen top of Sherahi's tank and, as she whirled to face her attacker, she was greeted by a long, whiskery, twitching nose and the bright, curious gaze of a baby mammal. It made chirping noises in its throat, tentatively extended a front paw and patted at Sherahi's nose where it pressed against the screen.

Startled, Sherahi drew her head back into an S-shaped striking coil, flicking her tongue to and fro, fnasting this creature. It was clear that this youngster was curious, not dangerous, but what was it? Its mouth was open and to either side of a lolling tongue she could see a mouthful of sharp teeth. Its lower jaw was slung back beneath a nose that was too attenuated to be anything but a joke. Snakes cannot twitch their noses from side to side. Their faces are locked into a rigid, dispassionate and thus inscrutable expression. As a result, most snakes consider the nuances of facial expression available to mammals as excessive and overwrought—about as attractive as that old family friend who insists upon being kissed hello upon her hairy lip and cheek. So Sherahi, who expressed her emotions through elegant tail movements and body postures—not through facial movements—found the lateral undulations of this animal's nose most unattractive. She checked an impulse to tell it to stop twitching like that. She had to remember her position among these captive animals and she reminded herself that true nobility ignores ugliness. "Actually," she thought, "this youngster isn't ugly, merely ungainly—a pastiche of hand-me-down parts." Its flat feet had the strong claws of a badger but, unlike the earth diver's, its forelegs were half the length of its hind limbs and, instead of having the short tail of an animal that spends most of its time underground, it carried its long, white-ringed tail aloft like a vertical banner. Its fur was an intricate patchwork of red, orange, brown and black. Irregular white patches surrounded its shiny eyes. With that snout and all its other strange parts, this little creature reminded her of the mythical beasts that had watched godlings cavort on the old stone wall behind her pagoda.

Although this beast was a baby and had barely any scent, he was real enough and seemed intent on play. He fearlessly lunged again at her nose with his front paws, his small eyes twinkling and his head cocked to one side. Sherahi scryed his mind and found to her surprise that, unlike the other animals she had encountered in this place, he had no fear of her. No one had taught him that a snake like her might engulf him and his three brothers and sisters for a snack. It suddenly struck Sherahi that something was wrong. "Why is he free?" she thought. "Why isn't he caged like everyone else?" Sherahi looked into his mind for an answer, but his thoughts were only of playing tag, of chasing his tail and of crunching fish heads. She was trying to find a way to communicate with him, when a strange cool voice spoke inside her head.

"You're right, Pythoness, Dervish is a strange little fellow. But for all those queer looks he's remarkably bright, even by my standards, which, I venture, are quite as high as your own. Forgive me. I've been eavesdropping as you were trying to speak to him and I assure you that he's too young. Perhaps your powers are greater than mine, but I doubt whether you'll ever be able to communicate with him. His mind simply isn't shaped for it: his thoughts run too lightly and rapidly. The humans call him a coatimundi, or *téjon*, Pythoness. He comes from South America. Perhaps you know the place because, even though you hold them in such low esteem, your closest relatives, the boas and anacondas, come from there too."

The voice stopped as suddenly as it had begun and Sherahi re-scanned the room for reptilian intelligence. But there were only the not-quite-dead turtles that floated belly up in an aquarium across the room. Who could be speaking to her? Who could scry her mind so perfectly and converse with her in the manner of pythons? The voice startled Sherahi because, in the three months that she'd been in Leftrack's pet shop, the only animals that had spoken to her were the cockroaches, who carried news and gossip from cage to cage. They were fond of gambling and odds-making, and those mercenary collections of ganglia that they called minds had lost interest in her when she had failed in her most recent attempt to strangle Leftrack.

The coati saw that Sherahi was not about to play and he lay down on top of her cage and began to groom himself vigorously, first stretching out a leg and giving it a thorough going-over, and then delicately licking between his toes like a cat.

"Where are you?" Sherahi's thoughts asked. "I didn't know there was another serpent in the room."

"Don't jump to conclusions, my dear," chuckled the voice. "I'm right next to you. Up here." With her jawbones and the ears buried within her skull Sherahi heard the same voice chittering audibly. She saw the coati look up at the cage next to her tank and he seemed to listen, his left leg still stretched out, grooming temporarily forgotten.

A moment later he leaped onto the front of the cage and began to climb. He gripped the screening with all four paws, and his tail trailed as he moved up to the latch. One hand and that incredibly mobile nose and jaw worked together to slide the latch to one side. The coati clung to the door of the cage and his weight made it swing open. He hadn't expected this and a burred chirp made it clear that he was frightened. He looked down, released his hold on the door and fell, landing on all four feet, tail in the air. In a moment he had climbed back up and into the opened cage, chittering to Manu, greeting him and saying, "That was fun, Manu. Can we do it again?"

"Yes, Dervish, but later. We have to greet our new visitor."

"It's a big, ugly snake, Manu. It didn't say good morning and it doesn't know how to play. I don't like it very much."

"Ssh, Dervish," said Manu. "She might hear you."

"She can't hear," whispered the baby coati. "She hasn't got any ears."

"Snakes hear everything with their minds," said Manu, "and they are very sensitive. You don't want to hurt her feelings, do you?"

"No," said Dervish, in a distracted way. His attention was on the stump of Manu's tail, which waved faintly, beckoning him to play. Imagining that it was a playmate, Dervish pounced with both paws. He was about to bite and worry the furry snake with his teeth when he realized that it was attached to Manu. He was confused, released the tail and rolled over on his back, paws waving in the air over his fat, round stomach.

Manu was used to being mauled by his playful friend. He was trying to teach Dervish how to behave like a proper young langur, but Dervish's weasely mind resisted his tutelage. "Get up now," Manu said. "Shake that sawdust off your fur and come pay your respects to the pythoness. It's not often that Culls like us have such an honor."

"I already met that snake. Let's play with the door, instead," said Dervish, launching another attack at what remained of Manu's tail.

"All right, suit yourself," said Manu. He shook himself free of the youngster and, holding on to the door frame with one black hand, he swung himself out of the open door of his cage. The muscles that once had propelled him with ease to the top of the tallest mango tree were stiff with disuse; nevertheless, he climbed to the top of his cage and from this perch surveyed the room below.

Dervish lay in the sawdust on the floor of Manu's cage, batting at his own tail, that familiar enemy who always followed him just out of sight—and, most often, out of reach. "Gottcha this time," he gleefully thought and bit down hard on the banded, furry snake. The stab of pain from his needle-sharp teeth surprised him and with a squeak he sat up and shook the sawdust from his fur. He started to whimper, but then he wondered where Manu had gone. In a moment he pattered out of Manu's cage and began to clamber up after him.

When Dervish reached the top of the cage he found Manu looking down at the huge python in the tank below. The langur sat with his legs drawn up to his chest and, from his attitude of total concentration, Dervish knew that his friend did not want to play. He stretched out beside Manu, pillowed his head on his front paws and sighed. He shut his eyes and imagined the breakfast that Sorensen would be bringing: peaches and fish heads. Dervish's mouth watered at the thought and he licked his lips in anticipation.

Sherahi and Manu were exchanging thoughts. Sherahi found that this langur had learned mental communication in his long years of captivity. He'd developed the skill to keep from going insane like so many other monkeys had that he'd known in Leftrack's—monkeys who spent their days bounding from perch to perch, wasting their energy in a frenzy that would never set them free. Manu said that it had taken him a long time to learn how to control and slow his thought processes and immerse himself in concentration. An anaconda with pneumonia had been his first teacher and, after she had died, as Culls invariably did, there had been other teachers—pythons, boas, other anacondas. Eventually Manu had learned to communicate mentally with most kinds of animals—except for fishes. He was pleased that Sherahi had also found them unapproachably distant because of the barrier imposed by water. Either thoughts traveled differently through water or else the minds of fishes were very unlike those of land animals. "Small matter, though," said Manu. "Fishes never last long once they become Culls."

Hearing a word she didn't understand, Sherahi asked, "Culls, what are Culls?"

"You, me, Dervish, the Duchess—who won't wake up for a while yet; why, my dear Pythoness, we all are," answered Manu. "A Cull is an animal that Leftrack cannot sell. You can see why I will never be sold. I'm so deformed that, even if I weren't so old, no one would ever buy me. Sorensen once said that Leftrack couldn't even give me away. But I've cheated Leftrack; I haven't died yet. And if you know what's good for you, you'll try to cheat him too. Not like those poor turtles over there. They didn't last more than four days.

"Sorensen tries, but most Culls are beyond his help, except for me and Dervish here. We're healthy, but the Duchess—over there in the cage that's covered—well, I hate to say this, but it's only a matter of time for her. Between you and me, Pythoness: there's something wrong with her mind. She won't let her feathers grow in, but pulls them out and eats them instead. If you think that I'm ugly, wait till you see her. And I can tell that you're a little like our Duchess. If you don't mind my speaking frankly, Pythoness, you don't look very good yourself."

"What's wrong with me?" asked Sherahi, who knew that she was the most beautiful Burmese python in the world.

"Well, you may have once been the most handsome Burmese python in the world, but right now you're awfully thin and your mouth is swollen and puffy. You don't look good at all. In fact, Leftrack would have never sent you in here if he had thought that you had a chance of surviving. He expects all Culls to die.

"Now, Sorensen is a different sort of human. He'll try to help you, and you must let him, Pythoness. You must live and help me to cheat Leftrack. Then, when you are well, you can carry out your plan to strangle him."

"How did you know that?" asked Sherahi.

"Don't forget, Pythoness," chuckled Manu. "You're not the only one around here who can read thoughts." Then he spoke to the little coati in the chittering language that the beast understood. "Come, Dervish," he said. "Wake up and pay your respects to Sherahi. Take a careful look at her. She's a very powerful animal. If you ever get back to your jungle, *don't* ever try to play with a snake like that."

Before Dervish could reply, the langur heard a noise and said, "Quick, Dervish. Come and lock me in. Sorensen's coming." He leaped down the side of the cage and hurried inside, pulling the door behind him. It shut with a faint metallic clank and Dervish followed Manu's directions, sliding the latch into place. He dropped to the floor and, chittering, looked up at the langur. Then he ran to his box beneath the workbench to hide. Dervish liked this game.

In a few moments the door to the room opened and Sorensen and Ehrich and Ira Leftrack entered. Sherahi hadn't known Sorensen's name, but she remembered his kind hands and calm words from the measuring episodes. Of the three men who stood over her cage, looking at her, he was the only one she would not kill if given the opportunity.

"Well, Doctor Ehrich Leftrack," said his father, "there's your first patient. She's got mouth rot pretty bad. I want you to follow Sorensen's instructions, but you've got to take the responsibility for curing her."

"But Dad," whined Ehrich, "I already tried the mouthwash. I told you, whatever she's got can't be cured by the treatment that Ditmars recommended."

"Well, I'm sure that Sorensen here has some ideas of how you can help her. Maybe force-feeding. She hasn't eaten in three months. I know they can go for long periods without eating, but a good feed might help her throw off this infection."

"But Dad . . ."

"Don't 'but Dad' me, just do as I tell you, Ehrich. I still intend to get my money out of that snake, even if I have to sell her for shoe leather. Understand?"

"Yes, Dad."

"That's better. Sorensen, tell him what to do and *don't* do it for him. You've got your own work. Is that clear?"

"Yes, Mr. Leftrack."

"Ehrich, come with me; I have another matter to discuss with you. I want you to see the animals that are going to make my fortune."

"What are they, Dad?" asked Ehrich. "More thirty-foot-long pythons?"

"Don't be disrespectful, young man. For your information, they're chinchillas and ten pairs of them are going to make your mother and me enough money to retire from the pet business." Leftrack's voice diminished and, as the door closed, the Duchess began clamoring to be uncovered and Dervish poked his long nose out from his hiding place beneath Sorensen's workbench.

Sorensen called Dervish and smiled as the little fellow came out to have his small, round ears scratched. Straightening up with difficulty, Sorensen walked to the Duchess' cage and uncovered it. "Morning, Duchess," he said, but the macaw didn't reply. She fixed him with one cold, black eye, fluffed up the few feathers on her head, back and wings, shifted her weight from one clenched, scaly foot to the other and closed her feathered eyelids. In a clear tenor voice she said, "Go away." Unlike all normal birds, the Duchess loathed the morning. She liked to sleep till noon and was never fully alert until lunchtime.

Sorensen went to where the python's tank stood against the wall near the door that led to the bathrooms and the rest of the warehouse. Looking down at the emaciated snake he thought, "I'll have to keep that bumbler Ehrich away from this poor animal. Even if it costs me my job. I can't let him try to doctor her—even if he is going to be a brain surgeon. He has no feeling for animals—he can't even clip a parakeet's claws without making them bleed." Sorensen scratched his jaw and remembered how Ehrich had begged not to be given the job of taking care of the snake. "It won't take much to keep him away from her. He doesn't want to help her, anyway."

Sorensen felt sorry for the huge snake. There was little wonder that Leftrack had called her a Cull. The body that had been as thick as a telephone pole had shrunk to half that size. Her belly was concave and there were the beginnings of starvation furrows paralleling her backbone. This seemed strange, because pythons and boas can often go a year between meals with little apparent effect. No, something other than starvation was happening to this snake. Her condition clearly showed in her skin. Her scales, which only three months before had been iridescent in sunlight and plumply convex, were hollow and puckered at their edges. Her skin was dull and patchy. He wondered if she had fresh water and, unlatching the lid of her tank, he lifted its hinged top; he saw to his disgust that, of necessity, she was coiled in her own dried excrement. Her cage needed cleaning and her water trough was dirty. Ehrich had been in charge of her while she was in the store. Obviously he hadn't done his job in some weeks. Sorensen would make sure that from now on she would at least have clean bedding and fresh water.

With the screen out of the way, Sorensen could see more clearly the mouth infection that had made her a Cull. Her lower jaw was swollen. The left lower jaw bulged, exposing the white lining of her lower lip. It didn't look good. He'd have to begin by swabbing it with hydrogen peroxide. The important thing was to stop the mouth rot before infected tissue blocked her windpipe and plugged her lungs. How would he handle her, though? In her present condition she would tire easily, but those twenty-nine feet of python could do a lot of damage before they got tired. Three months ago she'd almost killed Leftrack—yet, that little girl who had sold her had said that she was as gentle as a kitten. Leftrack had been awfully rough with the snake. As Sorensen looked at her, it occurred to him that perhaps she would respond differently to him than she had to Leftrack.

Dervish was pouncing on Sorensen's shoelaces and Sorensen picked up the little coati. Against the animal's protests, he locked him in his wooden box, saying, "No, Dervish. You stay in there. I have enough on my mind. I don't need you poking around and making me even more nervous."

Sherahi had read Sorensen's mind and saw that he was about to do something that no one had done since Ruthie had abandoned her in this place: he was going to try to handle her—not measure her or sex her or force her to do something she didn't want to. He wanted to be kind to her. His mind was clouded with worry about her health. She saw herself through his eyes and was amazed that she could look so ugly. "Surely there must be some mistake," she thought. She also saw fear in Sorensen's mind. He had a vivid memory of her coils wrapped around Leftrack's chest, her muscles constricting, the texture of her variegated scales contrasting nicely (she thought) with the flat, gray fabric of Leftrack's suit. It had been a long time since any human had shown such regard for her and respect for her physical power and, against her better judgment, she began to like this man. When he had uncovered her tank she had brought her head back at the proper angle to deliver a stunning blow, but now she relaxed a bit. She would wait and see how he behaved; if he treated her kindly, she might not attack.

Sorensen set a chair next to the opened tank and sat down, looking at the python. He did some fast mental calculations and figured that she could strike about ten feet from a coil. He was sitting well within that distance. Very slowly he extended his hand toward the snake, letting it rest on the side of the metal tank, about three feet from her head. Thinking that it might calm her, he began to speak, the way he talked to all animals. He assured her that he wasn't going to hurt her, and said that she was a nice snake and that he was going to make her mouth better. He saw her begin to waggle her tongue at him. This was a sign that either she was going to attack or that she was curious. He wasn't sure which.

Sherahi watched the pictures in Sorensen's mind. She saw his fears that she might bite him or possibly kill him. She saw how dry his mouth felt and could fnast the moisture on his palm. She saw his fear that she might get loose and cause mayhem and his fear that she might attack Dervish. Mostly, though, she saw the worry that she would die before he'd had a chance to help her. She saw his regret that an entire shipment of turtles had died of neglect before he could help them. He didn't realize that the turtles' minds still lingered on the fringes of life, even though their bodies were starting to decay.

It seemed like a long time since Sherahi had sensed anything but revulsion, fear or awe from a human. She knew that Ira Leftrack hated and feared her and that his wife and son found her repulsive. The hordes of people who'd pointed their fingers at her in the pet shop had been in awe of her. Some of them thought she was ugly. A few would have killed her. "Humans are so strange," Sherahi thought. Even Ruthie, the one who had saved her life so long ago, had abandoned her with hardly a second thought. Here was this white-haired man in workmen's clothes sitting next to her and, for some inexplicable reason, he wanted her to live. She was important to him. He didn't want to make money from her; he didn't want to use her for anything; he simply wanted her to live. Sherahi decided that if he didn't make any false moves, she might not kill this man today. She moved forward so that her head was within inches of his hand, and her forked tongue moved across it, fnasting him.

Sorensen kept his hand still as the black tongue flickered over the back of his hand, tickling the hair that grew there. He continued talking to the snake, not realizing that his words were inaudible to her and that they really were calming him instead. Her head was actually resting on his hand now and he was amazed at its weight. He tried not to tremble. He didn't want to frighten her. Her yellow eyes, with their vertical black pupils, regarded him coolly. Her face was inscrutable. For the first time he noticed the pink lining of each of the pits that marched along her upper lip scales. This was a very different animal, indeed, from the hissing, snapping, thrashing beast who had given Ira Leftrack and all of metropolitan New York nightmares a few months ago. He wondered if she would let him touch her with his other hand. If he was going to treat her mouth, she'd have to cooperate.

In Sorensen's thoughts Sherahi saw that he intended to touch her with his other hand. She jabbed an enormous bolt of fear into his mind. She didn't want him getting too familiar just yet—there would be time for that later. She looked up at his face, noted the white-gray drooping mustache and bristly white eyebrows. His worn denim shirt smelled of frangipani blossoms and Sherahi could not imagine where he could have picked up that fragrance. She hadn't smelled those flowers since she had been captured and for a moment she was a baby three-footer hiding among the fuchsia blossoms of the frangipani tree behind her pagoda. With that rich fragrance in her nostrils she had pretended to be a limb, and had patiently waited for a naïve, fuzzy bandicoot to blunder within striking distance. Perhaps U Vayu could explain how this man could smell of frangipani here in this faraway, northern city. Then she felt a pang of guilt because she hadn't paid her respects to U Vayu since she'd been in Leftrack's pet shop. He would be angry with her—again.

Sherahi felt Sorensen's other hand lightly resting on her back. She couldn't believe that he had had the temerity to actually touch her when she had actively inserted so much fear into his mind. "Am I losing control?" she thought. She allowed him to stroke her back and scryed his mind once more. The fear that she had sent him was etched in bold relief against the rest of his thoughts, but its edges were obscured by concern for her well-being. "Manu was right, after all," Sherahi thought. "Sorensen is a unique human." She decided that she would let him handle her and cure her mouth sores. Without any further examination of Sorensen's mind, Sherahi removed her head from his hand and coiled into one corner of her tank, settling her head upon her body. She watched surreptitiously as he cleaned out the bottom of her tank and put down layers of fresh newspaper. Then he scrubbed her water trough with hot, soapy water and filled it with fresh, clean water.

When Sorensen had left the room, Sherahi moved her head to the water trough and drank deeply, carefully drawing mouthfuls down into her stomach. She knew that he'd eventually notice the difference in the water level and it would please him. Sherahi drank slowly and it occurred to her that she couldn't remember when she had last had a drink. She hadn't realized how thirsty she was.

With a martyred air Ehrich Leftrack stood before the cages that housed his father's prized colony of chinchillas and wondered how these little gray rodents could make such a stench. Close to the cages the smell of their ammoniacal urine was so strong that he could taste it, even though he was breathing through his mouth. Ehrich pulled one of the wide metal trays from beneath a cageful of silent, dark-eyed rats and scraped sawdust soaked with urine and spotted with turds into the fifty-gallon garbage can that stood in front of him. As he sprinkled fresh sawdust into the first of the twenty stinking trays that he had to clean, he spat into the can, hoping to rid his mouth of the foul taste. It wasn't fair that he had to do this disgusting job. One of the menial workers could do it better and more quickly than he could, but no, he had to sacrifice his morning to his father's pipe dream. Such a waste of time.

He scraped dirty sawdust from another tray and thought, "He's gone crazy this time. All of these chinchillas put together don't have enough fur to make a pair of socks. You'd have to have at least a thousand to make a coat."

Then he thought, "I wonder if he's told her about this get-rich-quick scheme?" and returned to his job, wishing that it was finished. His father had said that he would be learning the pet trade this summer, but instead all he had learned was how to clean cages. He'd also learned how to goldbrick, though, and had made a work space in Sorensen's back room, where he had spent many stolen hours dissecting Sorensen's dead Culls. Today he'd planned to learn about turtle anatomy and he'd have been able to do it, too, if his father's shitty chinchillas hadn't interfered. Ehrich groaned at the thought of cleaning these cages every day. He'd have to find some way of avoiding this job. There had to be a way of making Sorensen clean these cages. School would start in a month and Ehrich was far from prepared.

He still cherished his dream of being the brightest first-year medical student that Cornell had ever seen, but his father kept thwarting his plans by giving him extra work: these big-eared rats and that monster snake were only the latest in a string of projects that his father had assigned.

He decided to tell Sorensen that, starting tomorrow, Sorensen was to look after the chinchilla colony. The old man took orders without asking questions and he'd never suspect that he was doing Ehrich's work. As Ehrich sprinkled clean sawdust into the second tray and slid it back into place, he thought about his second problem: that python. He didn't intend to ever touch it. He still remembered the garter snake that had bitten him when he was a boy and thought that one snakebite was enough for a lifetime. It had happened when the whole family—uncles, aunts, everybody—had gone on a picnic to the Palisades. Ehrich was exploring what to him was a wilderness and to his delight he had captured a garter snake at the edge of a meadow. He vividly remembered its bright-yellow stripes and the black-edged flicker of its red tongue. The five-year-old was playing with it, letting it pour from hand to hand, when, without any provocation, the snake opened its mouth and bit one of his fingers. Ehrich was more surprised than hurt and tried to pull away, but the snake wouldn't let go. It stared back at Ehrich and for what seemed like hours it chewed at his finger, swallowing more of it with each movement of its jaw. Ehrich remembered that he had read how snakes could unhinge their jaws to open their mouths very wide and in his imagination he saw the snake expanding to engulf him. He had gotten dizzy and screamed for his mother, but she didn't come, and the only thing he could think of to do was to beat his hand against a rock until blood came from a corner of the snake's mouth and it released his hand. He remembered picking up a stone and hammering the snake's head into the dirt. Then, to make sure that it was dead, he beat it against the ground until blood came out of what had been its eyes. But the snake's body would not die. It kept jerking and twitching, and its mashed head end wriggled spasmodically, as if it were still searching for something to bite. Ehrich's mother had finally arrived to find him squatting over the dead snake and she had picked up a stick and thrashed what remained of it. Her face had gone terribly white and he remembered her eyes huge and staring and the sound of the stick crisply slicing the air. She had covered the snake with leaves and small stones and, hollering at Ehrich for wandering away, she had taken him by the collar and dragged him to the pump to wash his hand. Later that day, Ehrich had uncovered the snake and poked at it. To his surprise the bloody, mutilated body still shuddered and writhed and sent Ehrich running to burrow into the safety of his mother's skirts. That night he dreamed about a wall of writhing snakes and woke up to find that he had wet his bed. He wouldn't touch a snake after that and even though his father had just assigned him the task of curing the sick python, Ehrich knew that he would let her fester and die before he'd ever go near her.

If he did nothing for the snake, Sorensen would probably take care of her like he took care of all the other Culls. This meant that soon she would be dead and Ehrich could dissect her. It was really a perfect setup. Snakes were supposed to have only one lung and one ovary. Ehrich wanted to see if this were really true. Gruesome as a living animal, the python would make an interesting dissection specimen.

Ehrich put the third cleaned tray back into place and thought, "Old man Sorensen is such a sucker, all I have to do is keep out of his way. He'll do everything for that snake if I ignore her. And he can't do much. She'll be dead in a couple of weeks."

In the soiled sawdust of the next tray Ehrich saw four red, wriggling objects. Holding his breath against the stench he picked one of the worm-like bodies from the tray to examine it more closely. It was hot in his hand and he realized that it wasn't a worm, it was a baby chinchilla. There were three others beside it. All were so tiny that they'd fallen through the wire floor of the cage after being born. Ehrich looked up into the shadows of the cage he was cleaning and saw the mother crouching over the rest of the lit-ter. Blood dribbled from her vagina. The baby chinchilla in his hand had crumbs of sawdust adhering to its head and Ehrich brushed them away. As he did so the little creature let out a loud squeak and the mother in the cage above stiffened in alarm.

Ehrich had never seen a newly born rodent and examined this one closely. Its eyes were sealed shut by transparent pink eyelids. Fine, almost invisible whiskers sprouted from its blunt snout. As it lay in his palm its legs worked as though it were swimming and its mouth made suckling motions, like a goldfish blowing bubbles underwater. Ehrich decided to test its re-flexes and picked it from his palm by the scruff of its neck. He was gratified to see the four tiny legs curl beneath its belly the way the textbooks prom-ised and he wondered if the textbooks were also right about newborn mam-mals not being able to drown. "What would happen if I put it into water? How long can it swim?" he wondered and decided to experiment as soon as he had finished his chores. He dropped the little animal into his shirt pocket for safety. He also wanted to dissect one of those turtles today and, thinking of all the things he had to do, Ehrich vigorously scraped the tray where he had found the newborn chinchillas, filled it with clean sawdust and turned to the rest of his job with renewed energy.

He finished cleaning, feeding and watering the chinchilla colony, and then looked back into the cage containing the mother chinchilla, won-dering how many other babies she had. He was surprised to see only one and he realized that he had accidentally discarded the rest of her litter. He thought of them at the bottom of the garbage can wriggling beneath all of the stinking sawdust. For a moment Ehrich felt a pang of regret at having killed all those babies, but it would be a lot of trouble to root through that mess. He probably wouldn't find them and they were probably dead by now. His father need never know what had happened. Besides, it was getting near lunchtime. Ehrich smoothed out an empty feed bag and carefully covered the mound of sawdust. Then he wheeled the can to the rear of the warehouse and left it there. Sorensen or some other underling would empty it later.

"What difference do three baby chinchillas make?" he asked himself, remembering that his father had boasted that these rodents bred like rabbits. "In the long run, three less babies won't matter," he told himself and, after making sure that no one was watching, he hurried as fast as his fat feet would allow to the back of Sorensen's work room. With a sigh he settled behind his desk, which was hidden from view by a wall of forty-pound bags of bird seed. The lunch that his mother had given him was in the top drawer.

Five minutes later Ehrich began his first and last experiment with the newborn chinchilla. He dropped the protesting little animal into a glass of warm water and sat down to watch its reactions. The newborn squeaked loudly and for a while its red legs with their nearly transparent claws swam doggedly. Ehrich watched the purple and blue arteries and veins that showed through its delicate skin and imagined the red blood corpuscles lining up to be pushed single file through the capillaries that joined them. He could see the animal's raw umbilicus, and the milk in its intestine made a white splotch below its thin, red skin. He was fascinated and took a bite of a sandwich, hardly tasting the pastrami-on-rye that his mother had given him.

Abruptly, the baby's leg movements slowed and its head fell forward into the water. Ehrich thought of giving it something to crawl out onto, but decided against it. After all, the textbooks said that newborns cannot drown. They are supposed to hold their breath by instinct.

Ehrich dropped the crust of his first sandwich and automatically began to unwrap the waxed paper from the second. The newborn chinchilla had stopped swimming and floated on the surface of the water. Its head drooped like a broken crocus after a rainstorm. Between bites of his sandwich Ehrich noted the convulsive motions of the animal's belly. It attempted to lift its head, but wasn't strong enough to break the surface tension of the water. By the time Ehrich had discarded the second crust, the carcass had turned on its side. It was purplish-blue now and looked like a small, fresh bruise rather than an active, demanding newborn.

Ehrich wet his finger and thoughtfully picked fragments of pastrami from the waxed paper and transferred them to his mouth. He hadn't expected his subject to die quite so quickly and now wished that he had taken the rest of the litter. One isolated experiment was worthless: it proved nothing.

He sucked a shred of pastrami from between two back teeth and thought about fetching the rest of the newborns, but decided against it. He had enough on his hands with the turtle dissection. It would be absorbing work and he'd have to borrow Sorensen's coping saw to get through the plastron. He still felt hungry and, after counting the change in his pocket, found that he had $1.83: plenty for a soda and maybe a couple of hamburgers and French fries at the drugstore.

With thoughts of food uppermost in his mind, Ehrich unbuttoned the stained and yellowed laboratory coat that he habitually wore to protect his clothing and, after plucking the dead baby chinchilla from the glass of water, he rolled it in the waxed paper with the crusts from his sandwich. He flung the package into the garbage can as he waddled out of the room toward more lunch.

A few nights later Dervish freed himself to ramble through the darkened warehouse. He watched and listened, sniffing with his long, whiskery nose for something good to eat or something to play with. He would have preferred to play with Manu, but ever since Sherahi had become a Cull, Manu had spent most of his time with her, speaking in the soundless way that excluded everyone else. Dervish didn't mind too much; there was plenty to investigate in the warehouse and he was always busy. The Duchess, however, was more than a little jealous. She made a point of not speaking to Sherahi, whom she considered an interloper and a rival. "After all," as she had remarked several times to Manu, "why should you put yourself out for a snake—a creature that kills defenseless little birds as well as full-grown monkeys who don't watch their step. She's a killer, Manu, and you shouldn't encourage her. Everyone knows that making friends with a serpent is like putting your foot into a crocodile's mouth. Like my mother always used to say, 'A lion can't change his spots.' "

"You mean a leopard," said Manu gently.

"Leopard, lion—what difference does it make? Don't be a fool, Manu. A snake can never be a friend."

Once the Duchess got started it was hard to make her stop and Manu listened patiently as she told him again of the boa that had threatened her when she was a fledgling. The snake (it grew larger every time Manu heard the story) had stealthily crawled up to the nest in the crown of the strangler fig tree where the Duchess had been hatched and, before her terrified eyes, the boa had seized and swallowed her little sister. The Duchess's mother had flown at the boa, attacking it with talons and beak, but had not been able to drive it off. (The third time Manu had heard the story, the Duchess's father, who had been absent in the previous versions of the tale, had joined the attack. But even both parents hadn't been able to deter the bloodthirsty and gluttonous snake.)

The Duchess's mother had flown to a nearby tree, where she called hysterically to her young, urging them to fly for their lives. Summoning all her courage the Duchess had leaped from the nest and fluttered unsteadily to her mother's side, narrowly escaping the striking fangs that threatened to impale her. Her two small brothers weren't as fortunate. As the Duchess and her overwrought mother watched and scolded, the boa constrictor had engulfed them one after the other, barely pausing for breath between murders. The Duchess recalled the grotesque sight of the boa coiled up in the nest high in the strangler fig tree, maneuvering its jaw over the downy wing feathers of her youngest brother. When it had crawled down the bole of the tree she could see three distinct bulges in its slimy body.

The Duchess could not understand Manu's attraction to Sherahi and, after several unsuccessful attempts to explain their unorthodox friendship, Manu had stopped trying to convince the Duchess that Sherahi had any good qualities. Of course she was ruthless. Of course she was a murderess. But, she was also brilliant and witty and, for a snake, she had incredible empathy and warmth. He was fascinated by Sherahi's quick mind and her encyclopedic knowledge of the Oriental world. In short, they found much to share. For example, he hadn't realized that giant serpents could mentally transcend space and time and he wondered if it would be possible for him to learn, too. More than anything else he would like to travel to Sandeagozu and see his clan.

The Duchess felt very much excluded from this new friendship. To punish Manu she began to pull out her long, red primary feathers, even though she knew that if she damaged them she would not be able to fly. She hoped that Manu would notice her missing feathers and realize how unhappy he had made her. Unlike her smaller feathers, though, her wing feathers were too old and tough to taste good. When she had plucked one she would ostentatiously drop it and surreptitiously watch for Manu's reactions while she examined the feather's empty follicle with her sensitive black tongue, savoring the salty fluid that oozed from the place where the feather had grown. Soon the bottom of her cage looked like autumn had arrived in a red-maple grove; and, more than ever, the Duchess looked like an exotic chicken ready for the pot.

So, as Dervish prowled through the darkened warehouse, familiarizing himself with its smells and sounds, the Duchess sat in her cage, muttering to herself and clenching and unclenching her scaly feet while Manu and Sherahi became fast friends.

In the warehouse Dervish trotted past a tall block of cages that contained many strange, strong-smelling rodents. Somewhere above his head he heard the squealing of babies accompanied by a buzzing sound that was vaguely familiar, although he knew that he had never heard it before. The buzzing made Dervish pause and listen with his ears cocked forward and one paw motionless in midair. For once his questing nose was still.

Even though Dervish had never seen a South American rattlesnake, he instinctively knew that a cascabel, the most deadly snake in all of his world, was slaughtering newborn rats somewhere nearby. Dervish looked at the narrow space below each cage. If he held his breath he could slip in there to investigate, but he'd hate to meet a cascabel in such a vulnerable position. There would be no way he could win.

Torn between the desire to run and warn Manu and the others of the danger and the desire to attack and kill the rattler now, Dervish whimpered to himself. The snake was clearly too venomous to be allowed to live. It would be content with baby mice and rats for only a short time. Within a few months it might want to try the effects of its venom on coati or langur-sized prey.

Dervish imagined the cascabel sneaking up on Manu as he slept. Manu was so old and weak that he could hardly climb to the top of his cage without panting from exertion. He wouldn't have a chance against a full-grown rattlesnake. The Duchess was also defenseless because she had plucked the cushion of breast feathers that would normally have protected her from snakebite. Thinking about all of his vulnerable friends, Dervish bounded back to the Culls' room. First he must warn everyone. He would kill the cascabel later.

Sherahi was adamant. "He must not be killed," she said to Manu.

"But, Pythoness," said Manu. "Dervish, who has never even seen this snake, assures me that his instinct tells him that it is a threat to our lives. We must not disregard his warning."

"I tell you, that snake is more important than any of you know. It is a direct descendant of Quetzalcoatl, the Precious Snake, and must be allowed to live for that reason, if for no other."

The Duchess demanded an explanation and when Manu had supplied it she said, "Hmph. She only wants it to live so that it'll kill me." On the verge of hysteria she continued, "She's never liked me, ever since Leftrack brought her in here. Now that she doesn't seem about to die anymore she wants that rattlesnake friend of hers to kill me so that she can rule the perch."

"You mean rule the roost," said Manu, unable to keep himself from correcting the Duchess.

"Perch—roost. What does it matter? You know what I mean.

"Dervish, I'm with you, you've got to kill that rattler before it gets all of us. Just like that boa constrictor, it'll sneak up on me and this time I won't be able to fly away. Oooh, Manu, the thought of that snake loose in here gives me duckbumps."

"Goosebumps."

"I don't care what you call them. Look at me, I'm covered with them."

"If you'd stop pulling out your feathers you wouldn't be," said Sherahi, tired of the Duchess's complaints. She saw the puzzled expression on the bird's face and knew that her message had gone awry.

"Manu, you must translate for me," said Sherahi. She was only beginning to be able to converse mentally with the coati and the macaw.

"Now, listen, all of you," said Sherahi. "I am going to call the cascabel in here and speak with him."

When Manu explained what the pythoness planned to do, the Duchess shrieked at the thought of a rattlesnake so close by. Even though Sherahi said, "I assure you that I can control him and . . ."

"Hmmph," said the Duchess.

"If I find that he is malleable and willing to help us, you must all agree to let him live. On the other hand, if he turns out to be the incorrigible killer that you suspect all snakes are, Duchess, *then* and *only then* will Dervish attempt to dispatch him. I guarantee one thing: I will not allow this snake to harm any of you."

Manu related all of this and the Duchess merely repeated, "Hmmph." She was beginning to like the sound of this word. "I can imagine how you'd protect *me*, my dear. I *absolutely forbid* that snake to come into this room," she said and, as if to indicate that the matter was closed, she turned her naked back on the others and abruptly put her head beneath her denuded wing.

"What does she mean, 'help us'?" said Dervish. "Why should we need a rattlesnake's help? Seems like we're doing pretty good by ourselves."

"Yes, I agree," said the Duchess, nearly falling off her perch in an attempt to turn around and put in a final word. "What do we need a rattlesnake for? No one here, except for *one of us*—who shall remain nameless—eats the kinds of disgusting things that he is good at killing. If we don't need him to get extra food for us, I don't see any reason to have him around."

"The reason that we need him, my dear Duchess," said Sherahi, watching the images in the macaw's mind, "is because if he is cooperative, he just may be able to help us escape from this place."

Even Manu was surprised at this last statement and when he repeated it to the others his quizzical look joined their exclamations. Escape was something that they had often thought about but, as Manu had said many times to the Duchess, "If we escape, dear Duchess, then where will we go? Your rain forest and my lovely, dusty country are so far away that we'd never be able to get there. It is better to stay where we are. As Culls we may not be beautiful, but we are safe."

Sherahi hadn't completely formed her plan as yet but, as the Duchess squawked harshly in protest and Manu and Dervish gaped at her, the idea suddenly mushroomed in an unsuspected corner of her mind. "Sandeagozu," she thought. "Once we are out of here we will find Sandeagozu."

Manu saw the idea shimmering in her mind and whispered, "Sandeagozu. Do you really think we could find it? Oh, Pythoness, it would be wonderful. It's a brilliant idea.

"Everyone I know is there—all my old friends and relatives. I haven't seen them since I was little."

Manu turned to the Duchess and Dervish and said, "Sherahi wants to take us to Sandeagozu. It's a wonderful place. I've heard Sorensen and Leftrack talk about it many times. Only the luckiest, most beautiful animals get to go there. It's always warm in Sandeagozu and there's lots of food and sunshine, and . . ." he added, looking at Dervish, "lots of playmates and mates."

Dervish rubbed his face against Manu's knee, pleased to see his friend so excited, and thought, "If it'll make you happy like this, Manu, I'll do anything you say."

Manu turned to the Duchess and said, "You'd like to have a mate, wouldn't you, Duchess? A gorgeous bird like you would have lots of suitors to choose from and, Duchess, think of the lovely nests you'd make and all those pretty eggs and fluffy little babies."

The Duchess wistfully batted her feathered eyelids at Manu. She liked babies.

"But that's not the best thing about Sandeagozu," he continued. "If we can get there we'll be safe as we are as Culls, but we'll be free because in Sandeagozu there aren't any bars on the cages. It won't really be as good as being home, but it'll be a hundred times better than being here. If Sherahi can figure a way to get us out of this place and to Sandeagozu, and if this rattlesnake can help, then I think we ought to let her try."

The fanged killer had eaten his fill of newborn rodents and had found a snug and convenient crevice behind which to hide for a few days while he digested his meal. Like a lethal watch spring his ten-inch-long body formed a coil the size of a silver dollar and his triangular, rough-scaled head rested on the topmost coil. Making and eating his first kill had been exhilarating as well as exhausting and the month-old rattler was asleep.

He had been born in Leftrack's warehouse, only one of thirty offspring of a cat-eyed, heavy-bodied South American rattler. His mother had given birth shortly before Ira Leftrack made his early morning inspection and the little serpent, who had only recently caused such fear and sorrow in the chinchilla colony, had been one of three young who had escaped from their mother's cage. Like all female vipers, his mother had not deposited a clutch of shelled eggs in a shallow nest in the earth but instead had carried her shell-less eggs inside her body. After two months the embryos had metamorphosed from mere threads attached to golden balls of yolk into fully formed pit vipers. They had hatched within her and the mass of squirming young had surged into the world, wet and wriggling and completely venomous.

When he was born the little cascabel had been just nine inches long and slightly thicker than a pencil. His mother's cage had been built to restrain large serpents and there were openings in its floor. He and two litter mates had slithered away. While the others had lingered in splotches of sunlight on the warehouse floor he had found an attractive crevice beneath his mother's cage. The vibrations from Leftrack's footsteps had made him freeze motionless in this hiding place and Leftrack soon captured the others. Later that day the mother and her young were sent to the Philadelphia Zoo and the newborn cascabel was alone in an unfamiliar place. But it didn't occur to the cold-minded serpent to feel alone or afraid and in the independent way of his kind he was content. He didn't need companionship.

He had discovered that although this place was busy during the day, it was quiet at night. He had found that his eyes worked well in dim light and his facial pits augmented his vision. He could feel heat with them and, by combining their sensations with the olfactory information brought by his tongue, he had begun to explore the warehouse at night, never venturing far from the space behind a baseboard where he rested, comfortably surrounded by crumbling plaster and rough-hewn laths.

For the first two weeks of his life he neither ate nor drank, but instead had consumed the last of the yolk that remained within his stomach, a remnant of the supply that had nourished him while he had developed within his mother's body. When the yolk was gone he had shed his embryo's skin for the first time and had discovered that his vision improved. Now he could see everything quite clearly. He had also discovered hunger and thirst, and the emptiness in his belly compelled him to explore and search for food. It was only a matter of time before he had located the feast that was spread for him in the chinchilla colony.

In his week of exploration he had learned to control his muscles so that climbing up a vertical surface had presented little problem. He had angled up one metal leg of the tall block of cages. His large belly scales had located and gripped minute surface irregularities and he climbed upward, drawn by the sweet smell of suckling rats. Soon his arrow-shaped head and flicking tongue had appeared over the edge of the lowest tray and he had coiled in a corner, alert for danger. He had looked up and seen a metal grid above his head, the underside of a cage of rats. His twin facial pits had quopped insistently and he had known without being told that many warm, furry bodies were only inches away. He had fnasted the creatures, had seen their eyes glimmer in the darkness and here and there had caught a flash of bared, white teeth: the chinchillas knew that something was wrong. He had decided that the first rats that he had found were too big for him to eat and had moved on, leaving a sinuous trail in the sawdust.

He had climbed up to the next tier of cages, labial pits quopping and tongue flickering, and had found a small puddle of water beneath a bottle that had a leaky stopper. He had put his jaw down to drink and for the first time his deeply buried ears had heard the shrill whistle of alarm from the male chinchilla. For some reason the sound had irritated him and after he had drunk his fill his head had snaked right and left, looking for prey of appropriate size. His tail had vibrated soundlessly in the air.

In the second sawdust-covered tray he had found prey that was the right size. Guided by instinct, the serpent coiled into the shape of death. His head was drawn back into an S-shaped curve; his muscles were tense. His rattle-less tail stood straight up and vibrated soundlessly. His loreal pits and tongue told him exactly where to strike and in a moment his fangs were briefly embedded in the small, smooth body that lay in the sawdust only inches away. It made no attempt to run away, but instead lay on its back, limbs flailing. The cascabel's mouth tensed over the hot skin for only a moment and then his head flashed back as quickly as it had struck. The newborn chinchilla exploded into a nightmare of pain. For a few minutes it thrashed in the sawdust, screaming for its mother. But its agony was brief; the cascabel's venom was strong enough to kill an animal twenty times larger. In a few minutes the blunt nose of the serpent was nudging the still body of its prey and it wasn't long before the cascabel was maneuvering the dead newborn down his throat, past those wonderful fangs that were now carefully folded against the roof of his mouth. The serpent had enjoyed his first kill so much that he coiled again and elegantly repeated the process twice before he retired to his nest behind the baseboard.

The cascabel had found an endless supply of baby chinchillas and had returned time after time to slaughter the helpless ones and drink his fill. Then a strange thing happened: his vision became obscured, as if he were peering through heavy mist. Also, his labial pits became numb. He rubbed his face against the laths of his nest, but neither sense returned to its former acuity. The cascabel felt particularly irritable. His skin felt too tight and ached where the laths touched it. The next day this tenderness had disappeared and his vision had cleared somewhat, but his sight wasn't nearly as good as it had been. His mouth felt itchy and he rubbed it against the back of the baseboard. He was surprised to feel his outer skin catch on something and he pulled his head free of its old, thin casing. It was the second time he had shed and to his amazement he found that his vision was crystal clear and his labial pits were more sensitive than ever. It wasn't long before he crawled free of the transparent outer garment, leaving it snagged on the baseboard.

For the first time in days the cascabel felt hungry. He stretched and yawned, opening his mouth and stretching the teeth on each side of his jaw. He was pleased to feel first his left and then his right fang erect itself and he vibrated his tail in anticipation of the feast to come. The cascabel's ears were buried too deeply to hear airborne sounds well, but if his jaw had been in contact with the floorboards he would have noticed a faint buzzing coming from his tail. His second shedding had produced the first segment of the rattle that would grow throughout his lifetime. It was the buzzing of this rattle that had attracted Dervish's attention and warned him that a fanged killer was prowling in Leftrack's warehouse.

The cascabel was asleep when Sherahi began to probe his mind. If he had been awake he might have noticed an insistent sensation deep within his skull, a sensation akin to what a tightly closed oyster must sense when a carnivorous oyster-drilling snail glides over its thick shell and begins to bore through its defenses with a rough and relentless tongue. Just as the oyster cannot avoid its predator, the young cascabel could not have escaped Sherahi's scan. He felt a strange itching sensation in his brain, but it was an itch that he could not scratch. It didn't last long, though. Sherahi had thoroughly scryed brains that were much more complex than his and was finished soon after she had cast her questing mind into the darkened warehouse, searching all the nooks and crannies for his particular brand of reptilian intelligence.

What she saw in the cascabel's mind troubled her, though, and thinking that her mental talents might be rusty from disuse (after all, she had just spent weeks conversing with a primate and that was bound to alter her perceptions) she repeated the process, unwilling to believe that an infant serpent could originate such repellent thoughts.

Filled with grit and sharp stones, the cascabel's mind reflected the environment that had shaped it. Sherahi was surprised that there were no dreamy, yolky edges to any of the hatchling's ideas. Instead, a dream of killing blazed with the dazzle of fool's gold. All snakes imagine killing their prey and Sherahi had expected this hatchling's thoughts to be similar to those of the baby boas that she had known. Just as a cow does not apologize to the grass that it murders as it grazes in the field, a snake does not apologize for taking its normal prey. It is the natural order of things. But there was something unnatural about this small snake: he took inordinate pleasure in killing. He was thrilled by the thoughts of combat and fascinated by his power to deal out death. She had never encountered such a pugnacious, power-hungry creature.

In his mind she saw a dream in which the rattler, grown to enormous proportions, battled with a kingsnake. The bodies of the two snakes braided together in a single, writhing form. The rattler's rough tan-and-brown scales ground against the kingsnake's silky black-and-yellow ones and the rattler struck repeatedly without pausing to close his mouth. Sherahi felt the thrill of pleasure as his teeth raked the satiny skin of his enemy. Venom mingled with blood and lubricated the struggle. The kingsnake was stronger and maneuvered for a hold on the rattler's head, but the cascabel was too quick for him. In the lightning attack of an elegant killer he struck at the kingsnake's forehead. Holding fast with all six sets of teeth he loosened his jaws and began to swallow his enemy.

The pythoness had battled with cannibals like this kingsnake, but in real life. Not in dreams. Several times she had been ambushed by king cobras. She had been fortunate: she had remembered what the elders had taught her and had survived each encounter and had triumphed. But she had triumphed in the python way—using her mind and strength. This infant rattler was something very different: he dreamed of beating the kingsnake at its own game. The thought of actually eating a kingsnake—a snake swallower—repelled Sherahi. She was nauseated and broke off her probe of the small rattlesnake's mind.

Sherahi looked at the gray metal of her tank and thought of her brave words to the other Culls. "What have I done?" she wondered. "How can I protect them from this killer?" She had never thought that the cascabel or any serpent could be as fierce as this. "Should I have Manu tell Dervish to kill the cascabel? His kind has been doing it for years and this one is only a baby. Maybe . . ." Sherahi's thoughts faltered. She thought of Dervish's happy face and curious, patting paws and decided, "No, Dervish doesn't know anything about hunting and killing. He could never dodge those fangs. He'd be dead before he knew he'd been bitten.

"Sorensen has always fed him," Sherahi thought, "and Dervish is used to eating from a plate. The only prey that he's been quick enough to catch was that big American cockroach, and the clattering of its wings scared him so much that he let it get away.

"No." Sherahi was certain. "He can't kill this cascabel. Dervish is foolishly brave and very loyal, but he isn't a trained killer whose instincts have been honed by millennia of desert combat." If the Culls were to escape they would need someone who could protect them efficiently. Sherahi knew that she was a superlative killer and an extremely dangerous beast when she needed to be, but strangling enemies took time—envenomating them was much quicker. "Besides," she thought, "the Culls will be safer with two defenders. If only I could defuse some of the fury in that cascabel's mind, he would be a perfect assassin—a willing, enthusiastic killer who needs no training to perfect his skill. I've never done anything exactly like this," Sherahi thought, "but it's worth a try."

Sherahi sent her thoughts spinning back to the crevice behind the baseboard in the warehouse where the cascabel was dozing and dreaming of death. As he slept she began to insert and weave a fabric of new thoughts into his venomous brain. She webbed his flinty killer's instinct with the concept that somewhere nearby there was a wonderful friend—someone who would help him survive in a dangerous world. She entered the thought that he was a lonely orphan longing for the companionship and advice of someone older and wiser: someone whom he would obey without question. She also sent images of Dervish, Manu and the Duchess, picturing them not as enemies or potential prey but as helpless friends who needed the casca-bel's protection. He must never harm them but instead must cherish them. If necessary, he must kill or die for them.

Sherahi had never tried to color and control another serpent's thoughts in quite this way and she wondered if the ideas that she had placed in the cascabel's mind would be strong enough to thwart his inde-pendent killer's instinct. "There's only one way to find out," she thought and sent an image of herself and the impression of her scent into his con-sciousness, telling him that she was to be the teacher that he needed and the friend that he would gladly obey. "Come to me," she whispered into his thoughts. "I'm ready to see you. Come."

The cascabel woke suddenly, opened his mouth and stretched his fangs. He had had a strange dream about a huge and glittering snake that had talked to him and promised wonderful adventures. He wanted to find her and, folding his fangs twice to make sure that they were in perfect work-ing order, he slithered out from his nest behind the baseboard and began to search for someone called Sherahi.

"Manu," Sherahi whispered into the darkness. "Manu, wake up."

In his dream Manu was stretched out on a limb in the crown of a tall banyan tree, surrounded by twisted lianas and sprays of minute yellow and brown-speckled orchids. The white-blond fur of the other members of his troop, asleep on branches below, shone in silvery splotches as the moon came out from behind a cloud. The night was quiet, without wind, and he could hear the troop around him breathing gently as they slept, mothers and babies secure because Manu was on guard.

The rapid wings of a hawk moth buzzed beside his head and Manu's quick-fingered black hand flashed out. The fur on his arm glistened in the moonlight as he snatched the moth out of midair. Holding it by its furious wings he looked at its glowing, red eyes beneath the plumes of its antennae.

Its body was covered with maroon and chartreuse scales in intricate patterns. It looked delicious and Manu's mouth watered. While its furry legs clawed ineffectually at his face he quickly bit off the soft abdomen and crushed it against the roof of his mouth. He was surprised that it had no flavor. Moths were a langur delicacy and he bit off the thorax and head, hoping for the familiar fatty taste. But there was none and he spit out the moth's hard parts and then dropped the soft, uneaten wings. He watched them flutter down into the darkness, each marred by a round, bare spot where one of his fingers had rested. Manu sighed and thoughtfully licked his hand. Cleanliness was a langur obsession.

His left ear itched madly and he rubbed it against the rough bark of the tree and noticed that in the moonlight the tree bark had a curious cross-hatched pattern. Manu awoke with his eyes open, staring at the shadowy, wire-mesh side of his cage. He put up his hand to touch it and reassure himself that he was awake and in his familiar cage. The moonlight, the tree and the moth had all been a dream. Someone was calling him. For a moment he wasn't sure if he were hearing the voice with his ears or with his mind and he shook his head and listened.

"Manu. Manu, wake up." Sherahi's voice was insistent. She knew that soon the rattler would enter the Culls' room and she didn't want Manu or Dervish to be caught unawares. She knew that the Duchess was asleep in her cage, which was suspended from the ceiling. It wasn't likely that the cascabel could crawl that high and it would be better not to alarm the macaw. The Duchess was hysterical at the mere mention of the word "snake." If she realized that the cascabel was abroad and nearby she might die of shock, and if she didn't collapse she would make such a ruckus that everyone else would be hysterical, too. It would be better to let her sleep.

"Manu, are you awake? Can you hear me?" Sherahi was anxious. She needed Manu to warn Dervish. Sherahi could sense that the cascabel was approaching the corridor that led to the Culls' room. Soon it would slither under the closed door. She had to be ready.

"Yes, Sherahi," Manu yawned. "I can hear you, but you ruined a perfectly beautiful dream. What's wrong?"

"Manu, the cascabel is coming. He will be here any minute. He may already be in the room. I don't know yet. You must tell Dervish to let you out of your cage. In case something goes wrong, both of you should be free to escape. Then, if I fail to tame this little monster, you won't be defenseless."

"But, Sherahi . . ." Manu wanted more information.

"There's no time. Whatever you do, keep Dervish out of the way. He is no match for this snake."

Sherahi broke off abruptly and Manu chittered to Dervish. In a few minutes the two had climbed to the top of Manu's cage. Manu yawned and wished that Sherahi had picked a more civilized hour at which to interview her cold-blooded relative, while Dervish lay with his head hanging over the top of Manu's cage, intently watching the door. Manu had told him that the cascabel was coming and, if Manu hadn't forbidden it, Dervish would have been down there, ready to greet his enemy with teeth and claws. Dervish watched the crack below the door with his nose twitching. He didn't realize it, but the fur along his spine was standing on end.

Sherahi focused all of her attention on the hard, cold mind within the brain of the serpent whose head and flickering tongue had just been thrust around the corner of the corridor that led to the Culls' room. To her dismay she found that the fabric of ideas that she had so carefully woven around his flinty killer's instincts was tattered and even destroyed in places. He no longer remembered the images of the Culls that she had inserted or the instructions to protect them. Instead of thinking of Sherahi with happy anticipation he was annoyed because his sleep had been interrupted. Mere insertion of new ideas hadn't affected the rattler's instincts at all. She would have to use more drastic measures if he were to help them escape to Sandeagozu. Sherahi prayed that she would remember everything that U Vayu had taught her about mind control and prepared herself for the worst.

A moment later the cascabel's arrow-shaped head appeared below the door. It was raised aloft on his thin, striped neck and in a shorter time than it takes to tell, the cascabel's scaly body, marked by a bold pattern of diamonds, had slithered into the room. The serpent coiled just inside the door with his back to the wall. In the manner of its kind he lifted the first third of his body up off of the floor, holding his head and neck in a lateral S-shaped striking coil. He was ready to attack and rattled twice to announce his presence.

Sherahi's sight was blocked by the metal sides of her tank, and although she did not hear his rattle, she knew when the cascabel had arrived. For the first time since her visit to U Vayu, so many months ago, Sherahi took the precaution of hiding certain things within her mind. This had been unnecessary when she had conversed with Manu because the langur's mental powers, although exceptional for a warm-blooded creature, were rudimentary. He could only read surface thoughts. Sherahi had never encountered a rattlesnake and didn't know if he would be able to scry her mind. One thing was certain: she didn't want the little cascabel to know that, like the rest of the Culls, she too was susceptible to his venom. As if she were bolting shutters before a hurricane, Sherahi concealed this knowledge deep within her mind. Then she sent her thoughts spinning out to confront the cascabel.

Hollywood, California

"QUIET ON THE SET. Cameras? Lights? Action."

The clapper board that read "Naruda—#1" was snapped before the camera's lens and after the initial long shot the camera rolled in for a close-up of Ruthie Notar, dressed as Naruda, the snake dancer. Ruthie delivered the usual two sharp kicks to the snake basket and then retired to lean languorously and mysteriously against a column at the rear of the set, a turquoise chiffon veil drawn across her face. The camera moved back to record her dance.

Offscreen a pianist began to play "In an Oriental Garden" and Ruthie undulated through her old, familiar routine, thoroughly at ease in front of the camera. She already saw herself as a movie star and, even though she hadn't signed her contract yet, had begun to acquire the accouterments of stardom. She and Bernie had hired a liveried chauffeur and limousine and were looking at real estate next to Valentino's villa. Reinhardt, dear Reinhardt, her business manager and theatrical agent, had assured her that today's test was a mere formality. She was a sure-fire thing. Taking his cigar from between his stained teeth with a hand that flashed diamonds and semaphored "MONEY, WEALTH, POWER," he had said, "Just get out there and do your snake number, baby. The boss will love it. Then you and Bernie settle down in someplace nice—maybe even have a little rest—a vacation till I bring you the papers to sign. They're going to love you, baby. You've got *It*."

Dear, sweet Reinhardt. He would take care of everything. He wasn't at all like Bernie: he treated her like somebody. "I know I can depend on him," Ruthie thought, as she removed one veil and danced over to the snake basket.

She knew that something was wrong right away. When she told Bernie about it later she said, "I knew then that something was wrong with the Girls. I should have followed my instincts instead of trying to go on. Animals tell me things. I should have stopped right then."

But she didn't follow her instincts and instead of merely lifting a waiting snake from the top of the basket, she had to rummage around in the bottom and finally pulled out Carla, who had been napping and didn't like being disturbed.

Nothing seemed to go right after that and the two boas wouldn't obey her commands. Carla seemed to have forgotten her part and kept crawling up Ruthie's shoulder to investigate her hair while Rosita trailed down Ruthie's arm and slithered out of reach, causing a commotion behind the camera.

The director's assistant screamed and fled, dropping her clipboard and pencil with a clatter. In a tired voice the director said, "Cut." He turned a livid face upon Ruthie and his contemptuous voice said, "Will somebody *please* collect this animal."

Rosita was recaptured and the screen test began again, but this time was no better than the first. After the eighth unsuccessful take the director called to Reinhardt, took him by the arm and led him to the rear of the studio; the two men talked intently, rapidly and very quietly. Ruthie knew that it meant trouble. She sighed and turned away, pretending to examine her manicured, blood-red nails.

The director paused with his hand on the door to the sound stage and called back, "Okay, everybody. It's a wrap."

Reinhardt returned to Ruthie, who was waiting before the camera, ready to start again, and holding back the tears. "Sweetheart," he said, "they're going to use what we have. If Mr. Goldman likes you, they'll reschedule the test. And if that happens, I suggest that you have these snakes better trained." Reinhardt turned and walked off the set and Ruthie put the lid back onto the basket that contained her snakes and broke into tears. She didn't understand what had happened. The Girls had never disobeyed her commands before.

Culls' Room
Leftrack's Pet Emporium and
Animals International, Ltd

THE CASCABEL WAS ANNOYED. As he glided along the cement floor, searching for a snake called Sherahi, he wondered why he was bothering to do this. It had seemed like such an attractive idea only a half hour ago, when he had first left his nest behind the baseboard, but in traveling to find this creature he had changed his mind. His temper had grown shorter and shorter as he moved through the darkened warehouse toward Sherahi, whoever she was. With every foot that he traveled he became more furious. He had ignored several opportunities for dinner. He had smelled a nest of mice beneath a grain storage bin and had fnasted the warm shapes of fuzzy, suckling young. He knew that they would be so very easy to kill once the mother was out of the way. But, he'd passed them by because he was looking for a snake called Sherahi.

If that hadn't been bad enough, he had found a whole new source of food that promised a different sort of hunting. He had not known it, but on the other side of the chinchilla colony was an aviary filled with small, warm-smelling birds. He fnasted them, asleep and unaware on their perches—succulent, easy picking. "How does a bird die?" he wondered. "Will feathered creatures die faster than furred ones?" He paused in the shadows, looked up at the sleeping birds and asked, "What do feathers taste like?"

Something urged him past the sleeping birds and he slithered on, thinking, "Why am I searching for this creature called Sherahi? Seems to be a waste of time and, besides, visiting another snake is a queer idea. Especially when there's so much hunting to be done. If she doesn't get this nonsense over with quickly I just might bite her." Pleased with the prospect of biting a snake to hurry it up, he laughed a soundless laugh filled with the noise of icicles shattering on steel walkways. "My poison will hurry her up, all right. It'll hurry her up to death!"

The cascabel ducked his head beneath the door of the Culls' room and emerged on the other side, tongue flicking and head aloft, searching for Sherahi. He backed against a corner and lifted his body into the right-angled striking position that seemed to come so effortlessly, so elegantly. He flicked his tongue and discovered that the room in which he found himself also held warm-blooded creatures. He could fnast three of them and noted the heat coming from two furry shadows high on the top of a cage. They did not move and the cascabel decided that they were asleep. There was warmth coming from a cage suspended from the ceiling, but it was out of reach and the snake gave it no further thought. All of these animals were of little interest to him. They were too big to eat and too far away to be dangerous. He did have an academic interest in the strength of his venom, but that could wait until later. He wanted to get this stupid business with Sherahi over. Where was she? She had called to him before, he was sure of that. "Why doesn't she call me now?" he thought. "Why is she wasting my time?"

"So," an impersonal voice said inside his brain, "you've come."

"Yes," replied the cascabel, "I'm here. Although I have a thousand other more interesting and important things to do, I am here. And I hope that this doesn't take too long. I must hunt and eat before the morning comes and the heavyfoots return."

Sherahi was astonished that the infant cascabel sounded so crotchety. It was as if he had entirely skipped childhood and adolescence and had become a miniature and very cross adult viper.

"Let me look at you," said Sherahi. "I've never seen a rattlesnake, and especially not a cascabel, although I've heard that in your part of the world you are the most deadly snake. I can't get out of here to see you, so please climb up on top of my tank."

"Is that what you called me here for?" demanded the cascabel.

"It's only one thing I had in mind," said Sherahi. "I am old and sick," she lied. "I would like to die knowing what the deadliest snake in the New World looks like."

The cascabel sighed as he looked at the tank that held Sherahi. Its sides were smooth. There was nothing for his belly scales to grip. He slithered around to the other side of the big metal tank, looking for something to climb up on, and saw a wooden chair near the tank. In a few moments he had slithered up the chair leg and had extended his body out into space, bridging the gap between the chair and the wire-mesh top of Sherahi's cage. When he was on top he coiled into his striking stance and, alert for danger, he looked down. To his surprise he saw a snake that was larger than he ever could have imagined.

The infant pit viper had grown since his last shedding and was now about a foot long and as thick as an index finger. His jaws, bulging with venom glands and the musculature that operated them, were the largest part of his body, which tapered to his tail and ended in a minuscule rattle. Until now his mother had been the largest snake that he had ever seen and since he had seen her once he had only a hazy memory of what she had looked like. His mother had been a big snake, but this Sherahi was . . . gigantic! He had not known that there were snakes this big and at first he thought that there was something wrong with his eyes. Maybe they were going misty again or playing some new kind of trick. He realized that he was staring at the thickest part of her body and began to work forward, seeking the head of this snake.

When he located her head he was surprised to find that it was nearly as long as his entire body. Even in this dim light he could see her amber eyes and inscrutable, vertical pupils. Her expression was placid, even stupid. He was about to remark on this when he found that he could not speak. This made him nervous and he had a sudden foreboding of danger. He wanted to look behind him, but found that he could not shift his gaze. Those placid eyes had a strange hold upon his and it felt as though his head were held in a firm, but not unfriendly, grasp. Friendly or not, he didn't like it and he tried to stick out his tongue to fnast for danger, but found that he could not will his tongue to move. Neither could he turn his head to the side to see what was happening. He could not twist away from Sherahi's gaze and it felt as if his entire body were held in a rigid coil. He tried to wriggle free, kicking furiously with his back muscles, but to no avail. Within his mind he heard the voice of the pythoness saying, "Don't struggle, little killer. This won't hurt. I won't hurt you." And then as if to make a liar out of the pythoness, the coil grew even tighter, especially around his head. It felt as if his brain were being wrung out and his skull seemed as empty as a blown-out eggshell. His thoughts seemed to echo within a hollow space. Then the emptiness began to be slowly replaced by unfamiliar thoughts and bits of whirling color. At first the cascabel did not like this at all but then he began to fancy some of the jigging, kaleidoscopic patterns. The last thing that the pit viper remembered before he lost consciousness was one of Sherahi's glowing amber eyes, flecked with motes of bright gold. It whirled within his mind and Sherahi's voice echoed inside his head, urging, "Let go. Let it go."

Leftrack's Pet Emporium and
Animals International, Ltd
September 20, 1932

EHRICH LEFTRACK sat at his desk behind the hedge of forty-pound bags of bird seed. He had just returned from lunch at Chan's Jade Parlor and was looking forward to munching on the rugelach that his mother had baked yesterday night. Eating always helped him study. School would begin in two weeks and, after a summer of cramming, it was time to round out his theoretical knowledge with practical experience. In a few weeks he would be taking gross anatomy and he wanted to be prepared. He had convinced his father to let him work at Sorensen's workbench and had brought in his dissecting set. He was ready, and now all he needed was a specimen.

In college Ehrich had already examined rats, cats, fishes, fetal pigs, sharks and frogs, so, even though dissecting one of these would have been good practice, he didn't even consider it. What he needed was a human, or something close to it. Too bad he hadn't thought of it in time to get one of those gorillas that had died at the beginning of the summer. A small gorilla would have been perfect, but those corpses had been sent to the American Museum of Natural History. If there were only some other primate that he could use; if only scrawny, old Manu would die—he would be a perfect dissection specimen.

Ehrich got up from his desk, carrying his paper bag full of sweet rugelach, and walked over to Manu's cage, half hoping that the langur would be sick. But, as usual, the monkey was hunched on a shallow shelf at the back of the cage. He looked at Ehrich with fast, sidelong glances, brushing at his left ear and grinning feebly, showing those pointy canines that had bitten Ehrich at the beginning of the summer. Ehrich pushed a piece of rugelach through the mesh of the cage where Manu could reach it and walked back to his desk. Although the langur was disfigured, he looked bright-eyed and quite healthy. He wasn't about to die of natural causes.

When Ehrich got back to his desk he looked at the cage and noticed that the rugelach was gone. Manu sat on his perch, biting at the crunchy sweet pastry, evidently enjoying it. This gave Ehrich an idea. If Manu liked rugelach, maybe he would get sick if he ate too much of it—maybe he would get sick enough to die. "Then," Ehrich thought, "I could help him along by putting a little poison on the rugelach. Maybe Manu won't notice. Then he'll die even faster."

Ehrich had a clinical knowledge of poisons. For example, he knew that arsenic, the active ingredient in Sorensen's Rat Bait, was an additive poison. If a small, tasteless dose of Rat Bait were applied to grain, the rats would return time and again to feast. Eventually they would have consumed a lethal dose of arsenic and they would keel over dead. If he gave Manu rat poison—just a little at a time—he would die within a week. And, it would look as though he had died of old age. Ehrich thought, "Sorensen said that he didn't expect Manu to live much longer. Since it's obvious that that old monkey's going to die, anyway, what does it matter if I hurry it up a little bit? It's not such a horrible death: the monkey won't feel any pain. And, besides, he'll be dying for a good cause: I'm going to be a surgeon someday. I'll save people's lives."

Ehrich convinced himself that it would benefit everyone if he poisoned Manu and used him as a dissection specimen. Sorensen wouldn't have to care for the creature, his father wouldn't continue to lose money on a worthless Cull and the monkey would be put out of his misery. Most importantly, he would be able to hone his dissection skills and someday probably become an even greater neurosurgeon. Ehrich took one last piece of rugelach from the half-full bag and carefully twisted the top and put it into his bottom desk drawer. Walking back to the cage, he forced the bit of pastry through the bars and watched with satisfaction as the monkey slowly crept off his perch and in a flash grabbed the sweet pieces and fled back to the highest corner, crooning to himself and gobbling happily. Ehrich was pleased that the monkey liked his mother's cooking. It would make poisoning him so much easier.

Leftrack's Pet Emporium and
Animals International, Ltd
September 21, 1932

SHERAHI AWOKE feeling as though she had been drugged. Her head ached, she had a terrible thirst and, for the first time in months, she was hungry. Every day since her mouth had healed Sorensen had offered her a freshly killed rabbit. If she hadn't made the vow not to eat until she was free or had strangled Ira Leftrack, she would have snapped at the limp, warm body that Sorensen dangled before her nose. But, when he offered her the rabbit, she pretended not to see it and wished Sorensen would finish his early morning chores and be gone. She had business with Manu and Dervish.

But this morning Sorensen was in no mood to hurry. He stood looking down into Sherahi's tank, admiring the huge snake and wondering how long he could keep her recovery a secret from Leftrack. Sorensen had grown fond of her in the two weeks that she had been in residence in his work room. He often looked over at her as he worked at some bit of carpentry and wondered what was going on in that big brain. Her eyes were too quick and intelligent to belong to a creature that operated solely on instinct. Sorensen was sure that she was different, that she had thoughts, real thoughts, and he was pleased that her mouth was no longer badly infected. She certainly drank a lot, that was for sure. She still hadn't eaten, but that was no real concern. As long as her mouth was healing and she was drinking water she could fast for as long as a year—maybe two—without any harm.

Sorensen heard Ira Leftrack calling him and put Dervish's sardines into his dish. "Where is that animal?" he thought. Dervish hadn't greeted him this morning in his usual way, twining around his ankles and rubbing his bandit's face against Sorensen's knees. Sorensen hoped that the coati hadn't gotten into trouble and, absent-mindedly wiping sardine oil onto the leg of his trousers, he hurried out of the Culls' room and closed the door behind him.

"Manu. Manu. Where is Dervish?" Sherahi said, as soon as Sorensen had left the room.

"He's here," said Manu. "I think he's found something nice to eat in the fat boy's desk." Manu called to Dervish, and the coati looked up from the paper sack that he had found in a desk drawer. His body was halfway into the sack and if he hadn't loved Manu so much he would never have abandoned the sweets that the fat boy had hidden there.

"Manu, tell Dervish that I have an important job for him. He must find a way for all of us to get out of this place. Tell him that tonight, when all the humans have gone, he is to start searching. Tell him that it's important. He mustn't let Sorensen lock him in this room tonight."

It seemed to take Manu a long time to translate this message to Dervish. Spoken speech was cumbersome and tedious to listen to and Sherahi found herself growing very sleepy. She lowered her head onto her heavy body. Reforming the cascabel's mind had been more exhausting than she had realized. She would need all her mental strength tonight, when she would introduce the cascabel to the other Culls. In a few moments she was asleep.

That night Dervish made sure to hide outside the Culls' room so that Sorensen couldn't lock him in. Although he was a little afraid of the huge pythoness, Dervish knew that she represented an ancient and, in many ways, superior strain of animal intelligence. He might have been willing to try to find a way out of the pet shop just because Sherahi had asked him to. But Dervish attacked this job with special enthusiasm because Manu wanted so very much to get to Sandeagozu, wherever that was. Manu's whole family was there. Dervish would have done anything for Manu and the coati was secretly proud to have been given such an adult responsibility.

As he explored the corners of the darkened warehouse, looking for a way out, Dervish wondered what had become of the cascabel. After the rattler had crawled onto the lid of Sherahi's cage it had coiled and simply stared down at Sherahi. The two had stared at one another, without moving, for what seemed like hours and Dervish had gotten bored. He had fallen asleep on top of Manu's cage and Sorensen had surprised both of them in the morning. Although he had searched the Culls' room, Dervish hadn't been able to locate the rattlesnake and had concluded that Sherahi had killed and eaten it. He was relieved that Sherahi seemed to have abandoned the idea of taking the rattler along to Sandeagozu. "I'm glad he's dead," thought the coati. "He frightened me."

Dervish pattered through the huge, darkened warehouse, keeping close to one wall, seeking an escape route. The cement floor of the warehouse was separated from its brick walls by only a slight crack. Dervish knew that even his strong claws couldn't dig through cement and brick. He found that all the doors of the warehouse fitted so snugly against the floor that a cricket couldn't have crawled beneath them. But one wall of the warehouse was made of plaster instead of brick and there were places where the baseboard had pulled away. Dervish dug at one of these places and found that behind the smooth white plaster were rough boards and more bricks. He could never tunnel out that way and shook the plaster dust from his fur like a dog scattering bath water. "Sherahi said to find a way out," thought Dervish. "I must keep searching."

Dervish found that the covers of the floor drains could be lifted off to reveal black, foul-smelling holes. "I could fit in there," he thought, but then he imagined what the Duchess would say if she had to escape from the pet shop by crawling into that filth. He looked again and was glad that the holes were really too small to accommodate any of the Culls except himself.

There were no windows in the warehouse and, after an hour of searching, the only part of the warehouse that Dervish hadn't examined was the corridor that led out of the Culls' room. That was Dervish's home territory and he knew that those walls had no holes in them, either. He'd sniffed along them many times. He was trotting back to the Culls' room when he remembered the small room down the hall. It was his last hope.

The room smelled strongly of the fat boy's urine and, after sniffing around at all of the walls, Dervish was disappointed to find them intact. There wasn't even a hole in the plaster that he could widen to see what lay behind. Dervish took one last look around the small room and slowly went back to the door to the Culls' room, wishing that he didn't have to tell Manu and Sherahi that he hadn't been able to find a way out. Manu would be so disappointed. He really did want to go to Sandeagozu to see his relatives and friends. Last night, while they lay on top of his cage, Manu had said that Sherahi might even kill a human in order to escape. Manu had been so sad that Dervish had wished he could do something to keep this from happening. "Sherahi will never be able to beat the humans," Dervish thought. "Manu said they run in packs. They always help one another. Sherahi can kill Leftrack if she catches him alone, but sooner or later the other humans will get her and then they'll kill her, too. Humans are like that; Manu said so."

When Dervish reached the door to the Culls' room he found that he had forgotten how the humans manipulated the knob to make the door open. Dervish's hands were nimble and strong. He remembered how unhappy Sorensen had been the morning after he had spent the night learning how to unscrew the top of the ink bottle. Dervish knew that the door could be opened by moving the knob, but he couldn't remember if the humans pulled it or pushed it or turned it. He would have to try all three.

Dervish was stretching up to grasp the softly glinting doorknob with both paws when he saw a sudden movement of light on the floor at the end of the corridor just outside the small room that he had already investigated. The light glimmered in a rectangular shape, growing dimmer and then brighter. It reminded Dervish of the way that the light in the Culls' room could be dimmed if he wrapped his tail tightly around his eyes. Dervish was fascinated. He soundlessly returned to all fours and began to slink down the corridor toward the mysterious patch of light on the floor. When he was two feet from the light it was suddenly extinguished. Dervish waited quietly, barely daring to breathe, willing the light to shine again. In a moment it returned in all its radiance and in a flash the little coati pounced, clawing and growling, wrestling with a patch of moonlight. He was disappointed that he couldn't hold the luminous substance between his claws and teeth. He tried, but it seemed to be stuck to the floor and he looked up and realized that the light was coming from a glowing ball high on the wall of the toilet.

The light was very bright now. It dazzled Dervish and made him want to yip and yowl and roll over and chase his tail with high delight. He had never seen it before but there was something so familiar about it. He looked up, squinting at the white sphere hovering in one corner of the window. The longer he looked the more certain he was that this was the source of the light. It made his spine feel all shivery. The ball seemed to have no smell and it made no sound, but merely hung in the upper corner window. Dervish was strangely excited. He noticed that where the light touched his paws they had turned to silver. His long, shiny, black claws gleamed like polished, white metal. He wished Manu could be here and for a moment considered running to fetch him. Manu would take such joy in this light. Then Dervish thought, "No. I'll get it down from there and take it to Manu as a surprise. When he sees the beautiful light he won't be so disappointed that he can't go to Sandeagozu."

Dervish's eyes had become accustomed to the brightness and now he could see more clearly. The window was high on the wall of the toilet. Three of its four panes were painted the same green as the wall, but the fourth was different. It was black and the ball of light hovered within that black space.

Like a salmon leaping up a white-water river toward its natal stream, Dervish leaped from commode to washstand to top of medicine cabinet. He dislodged a container of scouring power and cringed as it crashed to the floor below, sending clouds of dust shooting up to curl and twist in the still air. Dervish paused for breath, hoping that no one would come to investigate the noise. Then he climbed onto a small shelf that held rolls of toilet paper. From there it was an easy leap onto the toilet tank high on the wall. His jump made the pull chain rattle and frightened the coati, nearly making him lose his grip on the varnished wood that enclosed the tank. His long, red tongue lolled out of his mouth. This was more difficult than he'd imagined it would be, but he was so close to the ball of light. He couldn't see it from below, but its light shone into the toilet room. From below it looked like a wide shaft of silver. Motes of scouring powder filtered upward and made it even more beautiful as they sparkled and swirled and eddied in the air currents that Dervish's leaping had created.

Now for the last part. Standing on his hind legs, Dervish stretched up very cautiously. He didn't want to knock down anything else. His paws found the windowsill. Scrabbling against the plaster with his hind feet, he lifted his body onto the sill and, cautiously, he stretched up toward the light, his paws and jaws ready to grab it for Manu.

But when he reached the place where the shining ball had been, he found that it had moved farther away. The crash of the scouring powder must have frightened it. He was disappointed and wanted to call to the light to ask it to come back, but contented himself with merely staring at it. He curled his paws against his chest and sighed, "Now it's so far away that I'll have to bring Manu here to see it for himself."

For the first time in his life Dervish looked at the night sky. The full moon outshone the few faint stars that were visible over New York City and again Dervish had the strange feeling that he had seen all of this before. He felt a breeze ruffle his whiskers and the ruff of fur around his neck. It tickled the tufts of fur in his ears and he rubbed his head against the window frame, shivering with a strange longing. The black sky, with its few stars and the luminous round moon trailed by wispy clouds, seemed incredibly high and far away. Until now Dervish's universe had been circumscribed by man-made ceilings, walls and floors, but here was a world constructed on an entirely different scale. He had never felt space overhead like this and it made him feel very small and unimportant. And alone. For the first time since he had met Manu he wished for a playmate—not a monkey, but a coati like himself. He didn't want to be all alone in this vast and echoing space, even if he could catch the beautiful light and keep it for his own.

He heard sounds that he couldn't identify: faint, intermittent rumblings and shriekings came from below the ground and then there was a sound that made him cringe—a high, moaning wail that began in the distance and increased in intensity until it seemed to fill everything. The wail even vibrated within his chest. Dervish hated this sound and just when he thought that he could bear it no longer, it diminished. It seemed to veer away into the distance and Dervish thought that the stricken animal had somehow been comforted. The wail grew fainter and fainter and finally Dervish couldn't hear it anymore. He drew a deep breath. He hadn't realized that his legs were trembling and it took some minutes before he was calm enough to notice anything else in this new world outside the window of the toilet.

There was a sour smell coming from below and Dervish looked down. In the shadows he recognized the shapes of garbage cans and the smell of rotting garbage. This was strange, because the cans in the warehouse had always smelled appetizing and sweet. Dervish didn't like this odor at all and exhaled hard to clear his nose of it. Across from Dervish's window was a featureless brick wall and he saw that the garbage cans sat in a passageway that was about twice as wide as the corridor that led to the toilet. The passageway was dark, but there was a bright light in the distance in either direction. Large, shiny objects occasionally whizzed by beneath these lights but they moved too fast for Dervish to see them clearly.

Without any warning the alleyway exploded into noise. There was a succession of metallic crashes accompanied by yowling, and it frightened the little coati so much that he pulled his head back inside and thought of running back to the safety of his nest box in the Culls' room. When it was quiet he cautiously peeked out again. The noise seemed to have frightened the shining ball in the sky, too. Now it was hidden by mist and it was easier for Dervish to see down to the ground. He heard another shrill squawl and a hiss and then the air was filled with a sharp odor that prickled his nostrils. Dervish had smelled lions and margays and ocelots in the warehouse and he knew immediately that some kind of cat was loose in the alley below. Then, in the shadows beside the mound of garbage, Dervish saw a pair of hot, green eyes. They were looking directly at him and Dervish was glad that the cat's claws couldn't reach him up here. When he was littler, Dervish had tried to make friends with a full-grown ocelot. It was just about the right size for a playmate and he had been so lonely. Manu, however, had put a stop to it. He had warned Dervish that cats were to be feared and respected. Their claws and teeth were like blades; they never grew tired of hunting; they often killed for pleasure. "Full-grown cats are dangerous and unsuitable playmates," Manu had said.

"What is this place?" Dervish asked the eyes, glad that their owner was so far below.

"What do you take me for?" an angry voice hissed. "A tour guide?" It turned its attention from Dervish to sniff the garbage that it had strewn all over the alleyway. In a barely audible voice it muttered, "Long-nosed fool. I've got better things to do than waste time with you." The animal yowled once again and the hot, green eyes winked out. A moment later Dervish heard a spitting sound and then more howling and the sound of tin cans rolling in noisy concentric circles and bottles clattering on the pavement. The din made his hair stand on end and Dervish leaped down the way he had come. At the door to the Culls' room he stretched up and, grasping the doorknob with both forepaws, pulled it a quarter turn around. The door swung open beneath his weight. Dervish entered the room holding his ringed tail proudly erect. He was sure that Manu and Sherahi would be pleased. He thought that, perhaps, he had found a way out of Leftrack's pet shop—a way to Sandeagozu.

CHAPTER FIVE

ERVISH COULDN'T BELIEVE his eyes. Manu was sitting in his cage, on his habitual perch, with the rattlesnake wound around his wrist. The rough scales of the rattler's body made a grotesque and lethal-looking bracelet and Manu stared intently at the rattler's head. "They must be mindspeaking," thought Dervish. Then he panicked and thought, "What if that snake has hypnotized Manu?" The longer he watched the two of them, the more he was convinced that Manu was in danger. Suddenly Dervish could bear it no longer. His fur stood on end. His lips curled back from his teeth in an ugly snarl. His ears were laid back and a low growl issued from his throat. In a moment he was inside Manu's cage, chittering with rage; ready to attack and kill the rattler.

"Don't do anything quick or anything rash, Dervish," said Manu in a low, controlled voice. Dervish noticed that Manu was speaking in a strange way. He hardly moved his mouth and he didn't look at Dervish at all but stared steadfastly into the eyes of the deadly serpent that twined around his wrist and traveled from one hand to the other like a living, scaly rope.

"Junior and I are just getting acquainted," Manu said in a voice that was flat and calm. "We don't want to startle him just now."

Dervish froze, unsure of what to do. Growls still issued from his throat. One thing was certain: he didn't want to be in this enclosed space with the cascabel. As he worried about what to do, Manu spoke again in the same, slow-motion way.

"Don't worry, Dervish," he said. "This snake is perfectly safe. He tells me that he has promised that he will never hurt me, or you, or the Duchess, for that matter."

"But, Manu," said the coati, "that's a deadly snake. How can you believe anything that he might promise? Even a retarded toad knows that snakes will always lie to get what they want." The words were out of his thoughts before he realized what he'd said. If Sherahi had heard him it might have hurt her feelings.

"You must understand, Junior is no longer a cascabel; he only looks like one. And, what is even better, he will fight like one if provoked. But Sherahi has removed the vicious streak from his mind and now he's as harmless as a smooth green snake. They eat only insects and are too sweet-tempered and mild-mannered to ever think of attacking anything bigger than a beetle unless they have been seriously threatened."

Dervish growled again.

"I assure you, Dervish," Manu continued in his calm voice, "Junior—we're calling him Junior because Sherahi says he doesn't know what his real name is yet and she says that it's only polite to call all baby snakes Junior—I assure you that he's perfectly safe. Why, he's been sleeping in here with me all day and half the night. Poor little thing, the transformation has exhausted him. He will have to sleep again soon. But first, you must make friends with him."

Sherahi couldn't understand every word that Manu said to Dervish but she saw the effect that Manu's words had upon the coati. His fur bristled again. His eyes grew wide with fright. He was about to run and hide in his nest box. Manu must have seen it, too, because in his calmest voice he continued, "Now stay perfectly still and don't make any sudden movements. You mustn't frighten him. Just think friendly, happy thoughts. He is only learning to mindspeak. We've been practicing and I think you're going to be pleasantly surprised. He's a smart little thing, but then, Sherahi tells me that all vipers are extremely quick-minded and very intelligent."

Manu turned all of his attention to the cascabel, staring at it intently. This seemed to have a marked effect upon the little rattler. From his perch on Manu's arm the serpent raised his lethal-looking, pitted face and turned it right and left. His black, forked tongue lashed in and out. Then his head turned in Dervish's direction. Dervish knew that the cascabel was coming and he was terrified. He didn't want that snake near him and thought of jumping out of Manu's cage. But he heard Manu saying, "Steady, Dervish. Trust me. He won't hurt you. Now hold still. Let him come to you."

The cascabel unwrapped itself from Manu's arm and slithered toward Dervish. The coati could not have imagined a snake could crawl so rapidly. Its head was held aloft and steady while its body slithered beneath it in complicated undulations. Soon it was coiled between Dervish's front paws. For one horrid moment Dervish thought it was going to strike and then, instead, the cascabel rubbed the side of its face against one of Dervish's ankles. Its eyes, with their slitlike vertical pupils, peered upward, trying to locate Dervish's eyes. Like a cat welcoming a beloved friend, the cascabel ecstatically rubbed against Dervish and, to his surprise, Dervish heard a small, cold voice inside his mind. "Hello, Dervish," it hissed. "I'm so glad you've come. Sherahi said you would be my best friend." And the serpent glided up and around Dervish's front paw and angled across his collarbone to encircle his neck. Inside his head Dervish heard the voice say something about being so nice and warm and comfortable and suddenly Dervish felt claustrophobic.

With one swift snap of his jaws Dervish could have bitten the cascabel in two. With a quick, raking movement of his claws he could have disemboweled it. But both Manu's voice in his ears and a soothing humming in his mind reassured him that the rattlesnake meant him no harm. "He's only a baby," Manu said. "He's never had a friend and he needs one very badly. Imagine, Dervish, Junior has always been completely alone. Even though each of us has been knocked around a bit, at least we've known friends and relatives. And now we have each other. Little Junior has never had anybody. We must take good care of him, Dervish. He trusts us."

Dervish was still edgy. While the cascabel seemed harmless and hadn't bitten him, he wasn't sure that he liked having it coiled around his neck. "What if it suddenly gets mad?" he thought. "Is Manu right?" To Manu he said, "How do we know that Sherahi is telling the truth? You know how snakes are."

"Trust me," said Manu.

Dervish felt the little snake curl deeper into the fur of his neck and didn't know what to do. He was almost afraid to move. "He could bite me any second," Dervish thought.

The small snake stopped hissing to himself about how nice and warm he felt and snuggled his head very close to Dervish's ear. There was the sound of yawning and a sleepy, hissing voice spoke in Dervish's mind, saying, "I'm so tired."

"There, Dervish," said Manu. "He's dropped off to sleep. Just as we thought he would.

"You're very brave, Dervish. Most coatis wouldn't have had the nerve to let that snake come near them." Manu beamed at Dervish. It was the first time that Dervish had felt admiration from anyone. Walking very carefully so as not to disturb the sleeping cascabel, he touched Manu's hand with his black, wet nose and sighed.

Inside his mind the odd humming sound that had been there since he entered the room intensified and braided into three harmonic tones. They wove into a pattern and Dervish could see each sound glowing and moving. They sounded like moonlight and starlight and cloud. He was comforted and knew without being told that it was Sherahi's way of saying thank you.

—————————————

Birger Sorensen trudged into his work room, put down his lunch pail and collapsed into the chair at his workbench. He rested his head on his hands. He felt so tired. And his back was acting up. He felt the pressure of Dervish's paws on his thigh and Dervish's cold, wet nose explored his ear.

The coati sniffed at Sorensen briefly, rubbed once against his ankle and then pattered back to his nest beneath the workbench. He turned in a circle three times before lying down, making himself comfortable in his wooden box. Dervish put his head upon his paws and sighed. It was plain that Sorensen didn't want to play.

Junior was asleep in Dervish's box. He had burrowed beneath the layers of newspaper and coiled into one corner. Dervish knew that he wouldn't wake until the humans were gone. Sherahi had asked Dervish to protect the rattler from the humans and tonight he and Junior were to find a place for the Culls to hide once they had escaped from the pet shop. At first Dervish had been frightened of the little serpent, but now he was unafraid. He was excited by the prospect of actually going outside into the world beyond the broken window. His adventure last night had shown him how ignorant of the world he really was and he was eager to explore and see what lay outside of the pet shop and warehouse. "Maybe there are other coatis out there," he thought and wished that the day would be over and the humans would go home.

The door banged open to announce Ehrich Leftrack's entrance. His habit of kicking at the bottom of the door as he turned the knob disturbed all of the Culls, but it especially infuriated the Duchess, who began swearing within her covered cage. As Ehrich passed he tore off the cover and put his florid, perspiring face next to the bars. The macaw erected the few feathers on her crown and opened her beak. She hissed and sputtered in anger and reached for his cheek, hoping to slash it. But the bars of her cage interfered and all she could do was bite them, swear at him and bob up and down on her perch. The pupils of her eyes alternately dilated and constricted with rage.

"So's your old man," said Ehrich contemptuously, his face still next to the bars. "You know what, you stupid bird? You give me a pain in the ass. A royal pain." He turned his back on the shrieking parrot. Today, when he would begin to dose the monkey with Rat Bait, he just might put some in the Duchess's water, too. That would be good for business. It would rid his father of another of these worthless Culls that no one had had the guts to kill. Until now, that is.

The Duchess bobbed and weaved on her perch, furious that she'd failed to hurt the fat boy. When she was a fledgling she'd heard a story about a vile giant who was tortured forever by a vulture that gnawed at his liver. Her mother had said that his torment was continual, because, as fast as the vulture consumed his liver, a new one would grow to replace it. The Duchess pictured the fat boy bound to a rock with heavy chains while a vulture with hard, red plumage plucked out dripping beakfuls of his innards. She heard the fat boy scream and felt happy. Then she thought a minute and changed the vulture's beak to one more closely resembling her own. She was sure that a vulture's beak couldn't slice through that layer of blubber on the fat boy's belly. In her imagination she saw the parrot gobbling the fat boy's intestines and the thought made her even more agitated. "If only I could get at him, I'd teach him a lesson," she thought. "Even for a human, the fat boy is incredibly stupid. Only a short while ago I slashed open his finger. I saw him bleed. Obviously he needs to be reminded who rules this perch."

"Duchess, Duchess, please stop screaming," said Sorensen in a tired voice. "Ehrich, do you *have* to antagonize her?" Ehrich made no reply and Sorensen gave him a stern look as Ehrich disappeared behind the wall of sacks of bird feed. "Good riddance," thought Sorensen. He walked over to the Duchess's cage, making soothing sounds. The bird began to quiet and he gave her a handful of peanuts. As she expertly shelled each nut, he looked at her denuded, fragile body and felt guilty that he had procrastinated so long. "Today," he said, "I'm going to do something for you, Duchess. If I do nothing else I'm going to get that collar on around your neck." He saw that she had plucked out most of her long, red primary feathers. An angry sore festered on one of her bare shoulders and he knew that she couldn't fly at all—even if she wanted to.

He put out fresh food for Dervish, Manu and the Duchess and gave Sherahi clean water. Sorensen couldn't bear listening to Ehrich brag about medical school this morning and left the Culls' room without speaking to him. His morning round of chores awaited: the chinchilla colony had to be cleaned; the aviary had to be disinfected so that it would be ready for a new shipment; the garbage cans had to be scrubbed and brought in from the alley. Then he suddenly remembered that the light above Helga's desk and the window in the bathroom had to be fixed. And those were only the jobs that he could remember. No doubt Leftrack would add others and somehow he'd still have to find time to get that collar on the Duchess. Sorensen straightened up with a groan. If only his back didn't hurt so. He'd strained it carrying pails of water to the tree ferns. "Damn those hooligans who stole the forty-foot hose. It's bad enough that the conservatory is closed to the public and that they can't pay me for being night watchman. But I've got to get Dr. Crotty to buy me a new hose. I have to water those plants somehow. I can't just let them die."

Wishing that he could simply lie down and rest, Sorensen put his lunch pail into the file drawer of his desk and went out into the warehouse. Leftrack was already hollering for him and Sorensen could tell that today was going to be a doozy.

As soon as Sorensen had left the room, Ehrich stealthily went over to the small store of remedies that Sorensen kept on the shelf above his workbench. He located the bottle of Rat Bait, with the skull and crossbones on the label, and hurried back to his desk. His father poked his head in the door, yelling, "Ehrich, new shipment of rhesus monkeys arriving in a few minutes. You and Sorensen are going to uncrate them and remove any Culls." His father's head disappeared as quickly as it had popped around the door frame and as Ehrich hid the bottle in the bottom drawer of his desk, he hoped that maybe one of the monkeys had died en route. Then he'd have his dissection specimen for sure.

Hollywood, California

TRYING TO SIT without wrinkling her new taffeta dress and willing herself not to perspire, Ruthie perched on the edge of a cranberry velvet armchair. Bernie sat on one side of her and Reinhardt was on the other. As usual Reinhardt puffed on a cigar, spewing a plume of smoke into the light from the projection booth behind them. Across the room, in an emerald velvet wing chair, sat Mr. Max Goldman himself, surrounded by a constellation of advisers, secretaries, accountants and assistants. Mervyn LeMarr, the director of Ruthie's screen test, sat on Mr. Goldman's right, adjusting his silk cravat, smoothing his brilliantined hair back from a temple and turning his famous profile to Ruthie, Bernie and Reinhardt. He made it clear that they weren't important—hardly in his universe at all.

Mr. Max Goldman was a small, overweight man who wore dark-blue suits and heavy horn-rimmed glasses and favored loud ties and loose women. He'd made his money importing gemstones from the Far East and he liked to invest in sure things. He bragged that he could spot a flaw in an emerald or a winner in a chorus line a mile away. His feet did not quite reach the floor as he settled in the wing chair in his private screening room and his chauffeur rushed up to slide a footstool beneath the immaculate pair of hand-sewn Italian shoes. The delicate pink tea roses petit pointed on the cushion of the footstool clashed with Mr. Goldman's red silk socks—his trademark and personal talisman. He believed in luck the way others believed in the Virgin Mary or marriage or even gambling: luck was Max Goldman's religion.

After what seemed like a million years, Mr. Goldman smiled grimly at Ruthie. She smiled back, too brightly, and then regretted it. She saw that behind his heavy glasses his eyes were set in the way a surgeon's eyes might be fixed before he began a difficult operation. Only his mouth smiled. Then he turned toward the screen that occupied one wall of the room and said, "Roll 'em," in a voice that expected obedience.

Ruthie shut her eyes and crossed all her fingers on both hands. She sent a silent prayer to the god that makes movie stars and held her breath as a twenty-foot-tall image of herself danced across the screen dressed as Naruda, Exotique Dancer and Snake Charmeuse.

"Please let him like me," she prayed to the gods of Paramount, the Roxy, Radio City Music Hall and the Bijou. "Please let him like me," she prayed to the gods of popcorn and jujubes, Milk Duds and Holloway bars.

She saw a flickering black-and-white image of herself lounging seductively against a pillar. A nearby harem light threw a filigreed shadow onto one side of her face and reflected mysteriously in the eyes that vamped from beneath a fringe of eyelashes made of genuine mink. Ruthie was enthralled. Somehow the film made her look prettier, better—larger than life. She liked what she saw and was starting to enjoy her own performance. Then everything went wrong. Her film image came to the bit where she was supposed to pick up the snakes and everything fell apart. Ruthie couldn't watch any longer. She saw her timing fall to pieces and the camera mercilessly recorded consternation and dismay on her face when the boas refused to obey her commands. Ruthie looked away and listened to the mechanical clicking from the projection booth.

After a few of the retakes had been shown, Mr. Goldman made a sign to one of his assistants and the lights went on again. Ruthie braced herself for the brush-off that she knew was coming.

In a voice that rasped from the effects of too much whiskey Max Goldman said, "I want her."

Ruthie gasped and felt Bernie's hand squeeze hers. She hardly heard the rest. She began to smile and wanted to throw her arms around Bernie and Reinhardt. The gods of the Roxy and the Bijou were forgotten as she bit her lower lip to keep from crying from happiness. It would ruin her makeup.

Mr. Goldman continued: "Reinhardt, we're planning a remake of *Crown of Thorns* and I think we've got a part for . . . what did you say her name was?"

"Naruda—Ruthann Notar," said Bernie.

"We'll have to see about that," said Goldman. "Anyhow, a name isn't important just yet. Let me tell you about this picture. I think we could work that snake-charming number in a couple of ways. Don't you think so, Harold?"

There was a pause and then a voice said slowly, "Yes . . . I hadn't thought of it, but I suppose . . ."

"But she's going to have to really put those snakes through their paces. We'll need a real show. Not anything like that . . . that . . ." He couldn't find the proper word and returned to his narration.

"I can see it all now." Goldman's chubby hands gestured with his cigar. "It's a big party at Judah Ben-Salam's villa. He's the hero and everyone is there: Nero, Venus, Apollo, King Tut, Pharaoh, Caesar, Cleopatra— all of 'em. Lots of slave girls carrying trays of food. A fountain with wine. The floor show begins: dancing girls, maybe an African number—leopard skins and greased coloreds dancing around. Then she makes her entrance rolled in a carpet. She dances around Judah, runs her fingers through his hair, through his toga, weaves her snakes around him. Very sexy. Very sexy. He is nuts about her. This happens just before the chariot race." Mr. Goldman paused to puff his cigar. The room was quiet. He continued, "Then, in the end, she gets leprosy and dies with his mother and sister.

"Can you do it, Harold?" Mr. Goldman didn't wait for the writer's answer but instead turned to Mervyn LeMarr, asking, "What do you think, Merv? Is she right for the part or am I a monkey's uncle?"

Mervyn LeMarr removed the ivory-inlaid cigarette holder from his teeth and regarded Mr. Goldman thoughtfully. "Yes," he lisped archly, "she *could be* right, but I'm not sure if those snakes will cooperate." His tone became intimate and he confided, "It was an *absolute shambles* during that test. My script girl went *completely hysterical*. I had to *practically beg* her to come to the set the next day. It's given her an *awful complex*. She's having dreams and *everything*. Those snakes actually came *at* her. She was so frightened she practically ran all the way to Encino! And the unions are complaining, asking for hazard pay. If she can't control those *disgusting* beasts, *I*, for one, doubt if she's worth it."

Max Goldman turned to Ruthie, acknowledging her presence for the first time. "Well, can you make the snakes behave?" he asked.

"Of course, Mr. Goldman. They'll do whatever I tell them. They were just nervous because of the lights and all. I know I can do it."

"Good." Mr. Goldman smiled genuinely for the first time, displaying his stained teeth. He walked over to Ruthie's chair and, extending his hand in a courtly gesture, said, "Let's have a little dinner together tonight to get acquainted. Just the two of us."

To Reinhardt he said, "I'll send the papers over tomorrow." He ignored Bernie and, tucking Ruthie's arm beneath his, he led her toward his waiting limousine. He said, "Tell me, my dear, how did a pretty girl like you ever get interested in snakes?" Without waiting for an answer he continued, "You know, I had a garter snake once. I got it in camp in the Poconos when I was seven or eight. . . ."

As she left the room Ruthie looked back to see Bernie frowning at her and Goldman and at Reinhardt.

Culls' Room
Leftrack's Pet Emporium and
Animals International, Ltd

SHERAHI HADN'T MOVED in hours and to all outward appearances she was asleep. But outward appearances, as any snake can tell you, are deceiving; and although Sherahi was physically inert, mentally she was more active than she'd been in months.

Sherahi hadn't confided it to Manu, but the alterations she had made in Junior's psyche needed constant monitoring. Only this morning she had found that his new, gentle disposition had worn thin in one spot, as if the severed edges of the cascabel's vicious nature were working below its surface, abrading and unraveling all her hard work. She had rewoven the breach but knew that if her plan were to succeed, she would have to constantly survey and repair her work. In addition, she had to encourage Dervish and, although her mindspeech with mammals was improving, it was still impossible for her to speak directly to his mind. She could, however, send a stream of positive, glowing thoughts to the little coati. If she stopped this barrage of confidence, the fears that were his evolutionary legacy might overwhelm him and he might kill the cascabel. "If that happens," Sherahi thought, "we have even less chance to escape successfully."

So, as Sherahi lay immobile in her tank, she was as active as a juggler in the center ring. One portion of her mind sent comforting thoughts to Dervish, whirling colors and hypnotic tones to soothe his fears. Another portion of her mind regularly patrolled Junior's psyche, scrying it for damage to the placid disposition that she had superimposed on his dark and bloody nature. And, if that weren't enough, she kept reviewing her plan for escape, turning it inside out, reconsidering and rethinking every move. There might be no time for this later.

Dervish and Junior would search for an entrance to the tunnels of the Holy White Crocodiles tonight. The crocodiles were the key to the entire plan, because if anyone could tell the Culls how to find Sandeagozu, they could. They weren't just ordinary crocs. On the contrary, the white crocodiles were highly specialized and frighteningly intelligent descendants of the ordinary Nile crocodiles who had entered the underground water supply of this city by chance, evolving there in isolation for hundreds of years.

One of the original Dutch settlers of the city had found that his little pet "pebbleworms" had grown at an astonishing rate. When one had eaten his prize spaniel he couldn't bring himself to kill these intelligent animals, who had learned to follow him around like a trio of puppies, and he had released them north of the settlement, in the swampy area near the Village of

Greenwich. Descendants of the original three crocs had taken refuge in the warm underground springs that perforated the area. Cut off from external influences, the population had become inbred and specialized for subterranean life. A chance mutation had produced the mightiest minds known in the animal kingdom and the fame of the white crocs had spread. Sherahi had first heard of them from the garden-variety crocodiles that used to bask on the riverbank below her pagoda.

The crocs had sunned themselves there, sometimes propping open their mouths and inviting bold tooth thrushes to remove the leeches that parasitized their gums. While the birds had stepped nervously over leviathan lip and tongue, feasting on bloodsuckers, the crocs had gossiped and Sherahi had eavesdropped. In this way she had learned of the white crocodiles. "If they're even one tenth as wise as their reputation," she thought, "they'll be able to help us." On the other hand, they lived in a strange environment and, although they might be very wise, they might also have insatiable appetites. The Culls might run the risk of being crocodile lunch before they'd get a chance to learn about Sandeagozu. They would have to be very cautious. Sherahi could leave nothing to chance.

That night, before Dervish and Junior made their first foray into the city, Sherahi would explain her plan to all of the Culls. In case Dervish and Junior found a suitable hiding place for them or the entrance to the tunnels of the white crocodiles, each Cull would have to be ready to leave—perhaps even tonight.

She explained that Dervish would carry Junior around his neck and that she would advise Dervish through Junior.

"Seems a waste of time to me," said the Duchess. "It's all very well for them to go larking about exploring things, but we're still stuck here. I think we should all go together. Sorensen may fix that window today. Then we'll never get out of here."

"We will just have to take that chance," said Sherahi through Manu. "It may take some time to find the tunnels of the white crocodiles. If they have survived in this city their tunnels must be inaccessible and well hidden. We must be prepared to hide where no one will be able to find us. A deep underground nest—something like a rock-bound hibernaculum—would be best. Whatever else, we don't want to escape from this place only to be captured by another set of humans."

None of the Culls said anything and Dervish, with Junior coiled around his neck, was anxious to be off. "Good luck, Dervish," said Manu and watched as the coati trotted to the door, stretched up as far as he could reach and let himself out of the Culls' room. Full of excitement and anticipation he bounded down the hall to the toilet. In a series of graceful bounds he leaped to commode, to washstand, to highest shelf, to top of toilet tank.

Above him was the broken window and, as he paused there with his front paws resting on the wooden frame, he saw that no moon shone tonight. He knew the name for that fascinating globe of light now. Manu had told him all about it. Dervish was disappointed that the sky was dark, with only one bright star. He would have liked to see the moon again. The alley below was in shadow and there were no cats in sight.

"Good," thought Dervish. "It'll make this just a little easier."

Gathering all four legs beneath him, he leaped out of the window. Junior, who was around his neck, saw the twelve-foot drop below and, as the coati jumped, he heard a cold voice hiss in fright and felt the snake encircle his neck even more tightly.

The coati landed soundlessly on all fours and raced to the deep shadow on one side of the alley. He crouched next to the building for a moment, his sides heaving more from excitement than from exertion, allowing his eyes to adjust to the darkness and hoping that no one had seen him. The alley was quiet and Dervish thought, "I did it. I'm out!"

A small voice rasped in his mind: "You mean *we're* out, Dervish," Junior hissed, a bit surprised to have been forgotten so quickly.

"Yes, of course," Dervish chittered excitedly. "We're out." He couldn't believe that he was actually free. Then an awful thought occurred to him: how would he get back inside?

His eyes were accustomed to the gloom now and he saw that the brickwork of the rear wall of the warehouse was rough with many crevices and projections. When he returned tonight he would just climb up onto the garbage cans, scale the wall and go back in the broken window. It would be simple.

Junior's voice hissed within his mind, "Are you all right, Dervish? Sherahi wants to know."

"Yes, I'm fine. Tell her what this place looks like and that we're going toward the light."

There was a pause and the little snake spoke again, "She says to keep low and move like a shadow."

"Okay," said Dervish. "Tell her not to worry. Coatis know how to slink in the shadows as well as any cat."

"She says to look out for cats."

"I will. I will," said Dervish, wishing that Sherahi would mind her own business and let them get on with it. Keeping to the shadows, Dervish trotted down the alley, nose twitching, tail aloft. He was alert for danger. "No cat'll ambush us," he thought. Dervish was free for the first time in his life and didn't intend to make any foolish mistakes.

The alley led to a side street that had rows of darkened buildings on either side. The darkness was punctuated by pools of light in the middle as well as at either end of each street. There was a distant rumble of sounds that Dervish couldn't identify and in the distance came the wail that had frightened him before. This time it was far away and it didn't make him feel like howling an accompaniment. Before leaving the alley he paused and urinated on the pavement, leaving a scent mark that would make the alley that led to the pet shop easy to find.

"Which way do you think we should go, Junior?"

"I don't think it matters. Look, Dervish, over there. There's a hole. Let's go see that."

In the middle of the black pavement was a large metal plate with a small hole cut out of one edge. The plate was round and its surface was raised in an intricate pattern. Steam was coming from the small hole and Dervish sniffed at it. His nose wrinkled in disgust. It smelled worse than rotten garbage.

From his vantage point around Dervish's neck, Junior fnasted the smoke coming from the hole in the street and sent the information to Sherahi. Her reply came swift and fast. "That smells all wrong. Remember, Junior, these are holy, sacred creatures. They wouldn't live in putrid tunnels." Junior relayed this information to Dervish. Dervish listened and added, "It was too small for us to squeeze into, anyway." He returned to the shadows on one side of the street and trotted rapidly down the block. All senses alert for danger, he watched for a hole that might be an entrance to the tunnels of the white crocodiles.

Hours later the coati was discouraged. He hadn't realized that the world outside the pet shop was so large and that this would be such a tiresome job. They had traveled countless blocks and had investigated and rejected many additional manhole covers and street drains. Dervish had become accustomed to the smell of cat, dog and garbage as well as to the fine black dirt that sifted down into his fur and nostrils. It would take hours to get clean again tonight. Covering all the other odors was the smell of people—too many people. They weren't here now, but he could tell they had been here recently. The thought of so many humans made Dervish nervous and he glanced over his shoulder and became aware of the long shadows that jumped ahead and then behind him as he moved from one pool of light to the next. Except for Sorensen, Dervish was afraid of humans and he was glad that none seemed to be about. Junior had grown quiet, and Dervish had his thoughts all to himself. He wondered if Sherahi had been wrong. She had been so certain that there were entrances to these mysterious tunnels, but Dervish saw nothing except the same monotonous dark buildings, the silent streetlights and the hard pavement. He didn't know what crocodiles smelled like, but expected to be able to sense them long before he located an entrance to their tunnels. But the dark and silent city blocks were filled with smells of cats, dogs, garbage and people. There was no smell of reptiles.

Dervish stopped at an intersection. "What should we do, Junior?" he chittered to the cascabel, who had been silent for a long time. "I'm getting tired. And we haven't found anything."

The snake unwound himself from Dervish's neck and lifted the first third of his body straight up. Looking like the Hindu rope trick come to life, the little snake fnasted the air in all directions. "I could be wrong," he said, "but I think there's a different smell coming from up there." He indicated a fence that surrounded something across the street.

"Well, let's have a look," said Dervish and the pair crossed the street to examine what lay inside the fence.

"If it doesn't turn out to be interesting, I think you should ask Sherahi if we can go back. We can try again tomorrow." Dervish was footsore and his tail drooped. The sky was getting light; he knew that they would have to go back to the pet shop soon.

Across the street was a metal fence surrounding a flight of stairs that led down into the darkness. The dank smell of rat urine filled the air. Dervish hesitated. He noticed that currents of air rushed at them from the bottom of the stairwell and thought, "If something's alive down there, at least it won't smell us coming." Keeping to the shadows, he moved cautiously down the staircase. If he hadn't had such sensitive whiskers he might have run smack into the barricade that blocked the staircase, but he avoided it and neatly poked his long nose between two strips of wood and sniffed. Dervish sensed that there was a large open space beyond the barricade. Without waiting for Junior's prompting he began to work at the bottom of one of the battens. In five minutes his strong claws and teeth had made a hole large enough to crawl through. Before he did so he lifted his leg and marked this spot. It was pitch black inside and he didn't want to risk getting lost.

Unlike Dervish the cascabel didn't need light to be able to see. His cat's eyes were made for slithering in the dark and the infrared sensors on his face told him that there were many warm bodies beyond this gate. He uncoiled from Dervish's neck to investigate on his own. Dervish heard his rasping voice say, "I'll be back soon," and then he was gone. Dervish's neck felt suddenly bare.

Dervish crawled through the hole he had made in the barricade and, keeping close to one hard, smooth wall, he moved slowly forward, wishing that his eyes worked better in the dark. All that he could tell was that he was in a large, dry space. It was evidently unused because he could feel a cushion of dust and soot beneath his paws. Some of the dust got into his nostrils and he sneezed and froze as the sound echoed and reechoed in the space above him. Dervish cautiously moved forward, conscious of the listening blackness all around.

Then the passage widened, and Dervish found himself traveling down another staircase similar to the one that led from the street. He paused again to mark the spot. If there were cats or dogs inside, he wanted to be able to make a quick exit. Air was still blowing into his face and it made him feel invisible and secure. Patting with his paws, Dervish carefully made his way down the staircase, wishing that that little snake hadn't decided to be so independent all of a sudden. "Just when I need him, he disappears," thought Dervish.

At the bottom of the staircase Dervish bumped into a concrete wall, and inadvertently yelped in pain. Immediately he regretted the sound, because rustling noises stopped. "They're all listening now," thought Dervish. "They know I'm here." Soundlessly he marked the spot and turned to the right, licking his bruised nose and vowing to be more cautious. After the blackness of the staircase he was surprised to see faint light filtering down from above. He saw that he was in a long, high corridor, on a wide, cement platform that dropped off into blackness on either end. Obviously this place had been made by humans. He could smell them, even though the scent was old and overlaid by the smell of rats. Dervish did not see any rats, but he knew they must be all around, smelling him—watching him. He thought he heard the high-pitched squeal of newborns begging to be suckled and a rustle and scratch in the darkness beyond this dim pool of light. "Well," thought Dervish, "it may be full of rats, but at least we've found some place underground. Some sort of cavern." He had a sudden thought: "Maybe the white crocodiles live here. I wish I could ask Sherahi. Where is Junior when I need him? Fine time for him to disappear."

Junior's answer came almost immediately into Dervish's mind. "I'm down here, Dervish," he hissed. "Just having a look around." The rattler climbed up from below the platform where Dervish stood and slithered toward him. In a moment he was back around his neck, saying, "In the pit below there are shiny metal strips that are vibrating. They are shaking as if something heavy is pounding them. I think we should get away from here, because something big is coming down that tunnel. It may know we are here in its nest. It may be hunting for us."

Dervish looked toward either end of the platform but could see nothing. Then, in the distance at one end of the platform he saw two large, shining eyes. They looked like the alleycat's eyes, and as he watched they grew larger and brighter and the animal started to growl. If this were a cat, it was an enormous one.

Dervish ran back to the darkness at the foot of the stairs and stood motionless, peering out into the cavern. The growling grew louder until it rumbled and echoed from wall to wall. Then, incredibly, the rumble increased until it thundered and resounded and the cavern was illuminated by the searching eyes of the beast. Without warning there was a heart-stopping rumbleclatterclash screechclack and a huge, glowing serpent sped straight through the cavern. It passed with a rushing wind that buffeted Dervish and made him narrow his eyes. Grit blew into his face, but he could see that the serpent had lights inside of its body, too. Shadows jumped all over the walls and ceiling of the cavern. From below the serpent sent up sprays of blue-white sparks to mark its path. It didn't look left or right and didn't seem to notice Dervish and Junior crouched in the shadows at the foot of the stairs.

The serpent arrived and passed in such a fury that Dervish stared at it for a long time, listening to it roar and screech and watching the red glow of the stinger on its retreating tail. When he closed his eyes the image of the glowing beast was imprinted upon the inside of his eyelids. Dervish crouched in the darkness, listening to the fire snake's retreating bellow. He was too awestruck to move and was surprised to hear Junior's small, incredulous voice say, "Did you see them, Dervish? There were people inside that thing!"

Dervish was too stunned to say anything and only wanted to be back in his nest box beneath Sorensen's workbench. The Culls' room seemed like a safe haven compared to this place. Sniffing for his scent marks he hurried up the staircase and, with only a few wrong turnings, he found his way beneath the wooden barricade. In the darkness he heard the scufflings of rats, but in his haste to get to the surface he dismissed them. "What do a few rats matter, anyway," Dervish thought as he bounded up to street level. "The important thing now is to get back so that all the Culls can escape."

_____

The glistening, beady eyes of the south perimeter guard watched as the strange-smelling, red-furred stranger ran up the stairs and out of sight. "What was that?" he wondered. "Some kind of cat?"

He reexamined the smell that lingered in the air and decided, "No, it smells too clean. Maybe it's an odd breed of dog." He remembered the long, banded tail and thought, "Maybe it was a 'coon dog!"

The guard had been stationed at this post for many weeks now and was accustomed to sounding the alarm for marauding cats. With their silent feet, quick claws and dark-seeing vision, cats were a real danger in these tunnels and one shrill whistle from the guard would bring troops of Norse soldiers to defend the perimeter. But the guard hadn't known what to do about this most recent interloper and he had merely watched him from the shadows, waiting for him to make a false move. He'd been ready to pounce upon the stranger and sever his spinal cord with one deep puncture. As he watched from the darkness the guard had ground his long upper and lower incisors together, making sure that their cutting edges were razor sharp.

As the long-nosed creature stumbled about in the darkness, however, the guard had decided that this animal was no threat to the people of the Norse, who owned the tunnels on the north side of the cavern. The stranger had been terrified by the sight and sound of the uptown local and had cowered in fear. It had scared him so much that he had run off shortly after it had passed and the guard could still smell his fear in the air. "He'll never come back," the guard chuckled and remembered how the clumsy-looking animal had shut his eyes and tucked his tail between his legs. "Any of our Norse children would have stared down the rushing train. They'd have kept their noses in the air and their ears cocked and at the ready." The tribe of Blacks, who lived nearby, often attacked when trains were passing and generations of Norse had learned that the real threat came from their territorial enemies, not from the subway.

Although it seemed clear to the guard that this stranger would never return, he had left his scent behind. "That'll never do," thought the guard, sucking on his yellowed incisors. Looking left and right to make sure none of the Black swine were lurking about, he loped from mark to mark, covering the nasty smell of the ring-tailed creature with the sturdy scent of the Norse. This task completed, he returned to his post in a drain hole at the bottom of the second staircase. As he settled down to another monotonous stretch of duty, it occurred to him that he might be able to use this incident to bring himself to the attention of the Chief. Perhaps the Chief would reward his good judgment with a promotion.

The guard hoped that one day he would belong to the elite Chieftain's Bodyguards. As things were, that would be the only way that he'd ever have a chance to mate, even though it would be with a female that the Chief had discarded. Moreover, if he could get a promotion, he would not have to spend all of his nights in isolation out here on the perimeter, watching for cats and Black raiding parties. "I'd be in the nest itself and everyone knows that the Chieftain's Bodyguards get the best of everything—food, even females."

The guard spent the rest of his watch revising his report to the Chief until he arrived at a version that stressed his bravery and sober judgment. When he was relieved by the day guard he scurried down the unused train platform, heading eagerly for Norse headquarters, which were just beyond the south end of the station. He imagined his promotion to Bodyguard and could almost feel the haunches of a willing female within his forepaws. As he hunched along toward the Norse nest, he didn't realize that a dangerous predator had escaped his notice that night. But then, the guard had spent all of his short life in subway tunnels. He'd never have known a rattlesnake, not even if it had bitten him.

LEAVING A TRAIL of wet footprints on the hot, smooth terrazzo and wrapping a towel around his waist, Bernie entered the bar that was off the patio of the mansion they had rented. It took a moment for his eyes to adjust to the gloom and, to his surprise, he found Ruthie next to the window, scowling out at the turquoise swimming pool that glinted beyond the hedge of yellow crotons. "What's the matter, baby?" he asked. Ever since Ruthie had become a hot studio property, Bernie had been particularly solicitous. He could feel her slipping away. She had very little time for him these days—even in bed. He put his hands on her shoulders and tried to pull her close, but she shrugged out of his grasp, saying, "Don't. You're wet."

He went over to the bar and was about to make himself a drink when she said, "Give me a cigarette, will you," while she continued to frown out the window. She inhaled deeply and blew out the smoke in an irritated fashion. She'd worked all morning with the snakes and he could tell that things hadn't gone well at all.

"It's no use, Bernie. They won't do what I tell them to."

"What's wrong? Are they sick or just out of practice?"

"No, they eat like horses. There's nothing wrong with them. It's just that they're so . . . I can't exactly put my finger on it, but they're so . . . remote. It's like they don't hear me or see their cues. They always used to respond before. I don't understand it. In the old days it used to be so easy. The Burmese understood everything, but those boas are acting so strange. I can't control them."

She sighed and turned away from the window and impatiently stubbed out her cigarette in an ashtray that was fashioned from an elephant's foot. "Oh, Bernie," she said, "what am I going to do? Everything's riding on this. Mr. Goldman expects me to do a real snake act. If only I had the Burmese. She always did everything right. I just knew that we shouldn't have sold her."

"Ruthie, we've been over this a million times. You know we couldn't have kept her."

"Yes, I know. But that was a mistake. I should never have let her go."

"Well, why don't we try to get her back? We've got the money now. If you wanted to you could build a special wing just for her."

Ruthie turned to Bernie, her face suddenly hopeful. "Do you think we could?" It was the first time in weeks that she had looked at him in the old, confiding way; the first time that he felt he had her complete attention in months.

"Sure, baby. Consider it done. I'll have the Burmese for you just as soon as I can."

Ruthie jumped up and ran over to Bernie. She threw her arms around his neck and hugged him. "That would be wonderful, darling," she purred. "How soon can you get her?"

"Well," Bernie asked, beginning to nuzzle the curve of the side of her neck, "how long before you begin rehearsals?"

"Oh, not for another month at least."

"Well, then, there's no problem. I'll call Leftrack's first thing tomorrow morning. They're closed now. It's after six in New York."

Ruthie stretched languorously against him as if a weight had been lifted from her shoulders. "Thanks, darling," she said. "I knew I could depend on you." As if she had just remembered something important, she looked at the clock on the mantel and exclaimed, "How did it get so late?" She kissed him perfunctorily on the cheek, picked up the sweeping skirt of her peach satin dressing gown and raced from the room in a flurry of marabou.

Bernie looked after her for a long minute before pouring himself a neat whiskey and tossing it down. He lit another cigarette and stood looking out at the water in the pool as it danced in the late afternoon sunlight. It was going to be a long night: as usual, he hadn't been invited to the party at Goldman's estate.

New York City

THE CASCABEL LOCKED his tail around his neck and held on as tightly as he could without choking Dervish. Then he closed his pupils to the narrowest of slits and tried to endure the shaking ride around the coati's neck as he hurried from scent mark to scent mark, retracing the route back to the alley that led to the pet shop. It seemed to be a very long journey and several times Junior felt Sherahi's questing mind probe his. He knew that the huge pythoness was worrying, like a broody hen who has suddenly realized that there were two fluffy bodies missing from her string of chicks. "Hurry, Junior," she said into his thoughts, using the ancient language of their kind. Whenever she called to him, Junior listened proudly. Those elegantly simple and direct mental images were the heritage of millions of years of reptilian intelligence. They carried with them the leathery flap of pterodactyl wing, the rumble of grazing herds of hadrosaurs, the slither of the first lizard to slash free of its eggshell, the hiss of the viper who invented hypodermic fangs.

"Day is coming," Sherahi said, "and you must be careful. Neither you nor Dervish has ever actually felt the light of day, and you will want to stop and look at the sun. But this isn't the time for sightseeing and you must help Dervish to remember his responsibilities. Soon the sky will grow lighter and the night that has hidden you will vanish. Meddling humans come out with the light and you have only a little time before they swarm into these streets. You must make Dervish hurry. He is curious and everything distracts him. Even now he's sniffing at that garbage can. Tell him to stop it, Junior. Help him to concentrate and return quickly to us."

Junior obeyed Sherahi's directives and coaxed Dervish away from the garbage. Soon he was trotting along, stopping every now and then to mechanically locate and reinforce his scent marks. Junior read Dervish's mind and learned that this was important because these marks would later guide the Culls back to the cavern. Nevertheless, he hissed in Dervish's thoughts, reminding him to hurry. From his lookout between Dervish's shoulder blades the cascabel watched and worried as the streetlights above were extinguished one by one and the sky had turned ashy gray. The day that Sherahi had warned about was here. "We'll have to wait until tonight to make our escape," Junior thought.

"At last," rasped Junior's voice as he saw that they had finally entered the alley that led to the rear of the warehouse. "Soon we'll be safe inside, telling Sherahi, Manu and the Duchess all about it." Using reptilian mindspeech he told Sherahi that they were nearly home. Junior was proud that he had helped Dervish to find the underground hiding place that Sherahi thought was so necessary. Everything had worked perfectly. He could not read Sherahi's thoughts completely, but he saw her plan and knew that the Culls would escape tonight.

Junior felt Dervish's neck muscles tense and bunch as the coati leaped to the top of a garbage can. He realized that Dervish was getting distracted by the high deliciousness of the aroma of fresh garbage and spoke in his mind, saying, "Not now, Dervish. You can rummage in this cess pit later. Now you must climb back the way we planned."

Where the cascabel's jawbone pressed against Dervish's shoulder blade, he heard the faint clatter of the garbage-can lid as the coati's back claws sent it sailing to the cobblestones below. Beneath his belly scutes Junior felt the coati's muscles strain as he struggled to climb up the rough wall. The broken window was a small, dark spot high above them. It seemed impossibly far away. Junior realized that scaling the wall was more difficult than Dervish had anticipated and he had a sudden wave of fear that they might not be able to get back inside. "Sherahi is depending upon me to bring Dervish back to her," he thought and he willed the little weasel to climb. The cascabel tried to do as Sherahi had explained and concentrated all of his mental strength and urged those furry, long-clawed hind feet to dig into the rotten mortar; he cheered as Dervish's clever forefeet fought for niches that would support their weight.

The cascabel never knew whether his thoughts actually helped Dervish to climb the wall but, in a matter of minutes, the coati reached the broken window and rested there for a moment, regaining his breath. Then, eager to see Manu and Sherahi and the Duchess; realizing for the first time that the Culls were nearly free; and without any thought that there might be danger inside, the coati leaped back into the pet shop. He'd been so busy with his happy thoughts that he didn't hear Junior's voice hissing within his mind. Too late he realized that Junior was saying, "Look out. Someone's coming!"

The coati landed in the hallway just beyond the toilet, nearly at the feet of Ira Leftrack, who had just finished his ritual morning inspection of the warehouse. Dervish had never actually seen this bald man with the thin mustache, but his voice was all-too-familiar and Dervish knew his reputation. He was no friend. The coati darted down the hall and into the Culls' room. He heard Manu's voice chittering, "Hide, Dervish. Hide and don't move." In their panic, neither Manu nor Dervish paid any attention to Sherahi as she urged, "No, Dervish. Don't come in here. He'll trap you."

Sherahi heard Manu calling to Dervish and realized that both had ignored her warning. She would have to be better prepared for emergencies in the future, if their escape were to succeed. The pythoness didn't know when she would find the time, but after Dervish was safe, she would have to visit U Vayu and ask for his advice before the Culls left the pet shop. He would help her to find the flaws in her plan.

As Leftrack had walked to the toilet he had been immersed in worry about a shipment of orangutans from Mandalay that was two weeks overdue. One of Irma's idiot cousins was in charge and if those orangs died, there would be hell to pay. Leftrack caught only a glimpse of the coati as it leaped down at his feet. The animal had looked up for a moment and then had darted into Sorensen's dark workshop. It took Leftrack a moment to realize that, inexplicably, a more-than-half-grown coatimundi was loose in his warehouse. Leftrack knew that those hands could open all kinds of latches and locks and the animal would have to be captured before it got into mischief. Nothing would be safe until the coati was behind bars.

Leftrack stealthily walked back to the Culls' room and switched on the light, hoping to see the coati; but the only thing that moved was Manu, the disfigured langur. Leftrack closed the door, satisfied that he had trapped the coati. Sorensen could capture it later. Only after the door had been securely closed did it occur to Leftrack that it was strange for this animal to be running around loose. The only recent shipment of coatis had died shortly after delivery—about six months ago. Coatis were delicate; they almost never survived in captivity.

As Leftrack turned back toward the toilet he realized that something was wrong with this whole thing. That coati had run into Sorensen's work room as if it knew where it was going. "Does it belong to Sorensen?" he wondered. "He knows that personal pets aren't allowed," stormed Leftrack in a fury. He decided that he would get to the bottom of this and looked at his watch. Sorensen would be here in a half hour. In the meantime, Leftrack would call the mammal house at the Bronx Zoo and see if they wanted a coati. He knew that they were building their small mammal collection and, because no zoo had ever been successful with coatis, they'd probably offer a premium price for a healthy, semitame one. This could be a coup both for Leftrack's and for the Bronx Zoo.

Leftrack was in the toilet, unbuttoning his fly, when he noticed the broken window above him. "Goddamn it," he thought. "I told Sorensen to fix that two weeks ago. First the coati, and now this. Can't he do anything right?"

This had gone too far. Sorensen wasn't even able to repair a broken window. He'd outlived his usefulness and only sentimentality had kept Leftrack from firing him before. The sight of the broken window infuriated Leftrack so much that he forgot his urge to urinate and, buttoning his pants, he stomped back to his office. This was the last straw: Sorensen had to go. "I've been far too lenient with that man. I've given him every chance to make good, but this is too much. He's keeping pet animals against company policy and he's not doing his job. I'll have him turn over that coati and then I'll give him two weeks' pay and tell him to clear out. I can't afford men like Sorensen."

Dervish had hidden beneath the pallet that held the pile of forty-pound sacks of bird seed and Junior had slipped away to hide in some snug, inaccessible crevice. When Leftrack's footsteps faded into the distance, Manu chittered to Dervish again, telling him to stay hidden. "Even when Sorensen comes," Manu said urgently. "You must not let yourself be caught, Dervish. Even though he offers you wonderful treats. If they get you, our plan to escape to Sandeagozu is ruined."

More than ever, Sherahi realized that she needed to speak with her old teacher, U Vayu. Now that Dervish was in danger of being captured, she realized just how precarious the Culls' situation was. Without Dervish they would have difficulty in finding the tunnel that he and Junior had located. Their progress through the city's streets would be slow, laborious—even dangerous. She would have to create and maintain a continual barrage of confusion in the minds of any humans that might cross their paths. Sherahi thought of the energy needed to do that and simultaneously defend them from cats and dogs and humans and decided, "I'd never be able to do it without Dervish."

In addition, Manu and the Duchess were used to sedentary lives in their comfortable cages. They would tire quickly and she'd have to mentally support them—maybe even coerce them to keep moving. Sherahi knew that she couldn't do all of this, as well as concentrate on crawling as rapidly as her great bulk would allow. "Without Dervish to lead the way we will be crippled. We can't get there without him." Besides, although she would never have admitted it to anyone, Sherahi the pythoness, whose ancestors had always prided themselves on their solitary, self-sufficient lives, had grown fond of the curious, long-snouted little coati. In the back of her cold, proud mind she thought, "I won't allow him to be captured. It simply cannot happen."

She called to Manu and to Junior and told them of her plan to retire inward for a while to consult U Vayu. If anyone came near Dervish's hiding place, Manu and the Duchess were to distract him. If that failed, then Junior would set up a screen of confusion around the coati's hiding place as best he could. Then he was to hurry to her cage and touch her and she would instantly return to the here and now. She said that she did not intend to stay long at U Vayu's pagoda. She would probably be back before Sorensen arrived with their breakfast.

Sherahi sent a wave of confidence to each of the Culls, telling Junior, Manu, Dervish, and even the Duchess, who was still drowsing beneath her cage cover, that tonight they would escape. "Tonight we will be done with cages and human whims. Tonight we will be free." Then she formed a compact coil and, concentrating on her teacher's name, she sent her mind spinning out across half the globe, searching for U Vayu.

Ehrich Leftrack opened the door to the Culls' room and, looking over his shoulder to see that no one was coming, silently closed the door and hurried to his desk. He didn't bother to take off his jacket, but opened the bottom desk drawer and uncapped the Mason jar of rugelach that he had carefully hidden there. Using a pair of long-handled tongs, he gingerly removed one piece of pastry. Careful not to touch the inner lining of the lid of the jar, and wishing that he had thought to wear rubber gloves, he set the cap back in place on the jar and carried the rugelach to Manu's cage. He opened the small bottom door of the cage and placed the pastry inside.

From his perch high in a corner of the cage the monkey eyed Ehrich suspiciously and showed his canines as he gripped the wire mesh, ready to leap and scramble away if Ehrich came any closer.

Ehrich ignored the langur, closed the cage door and went to the sink. He dropped the tongs beneath the faucet and rinsed his hands. Then he dried his hands, removed his jacket and rolled up his shirt sleeves. He scrubbed the tongs with a bottle brush and then, using steaming water and thick, soapy lather, he thoroughly scrubbed his hands and forearms, thinking all the while, "This is the first of many times that I'll scrub up before an operation." He imagined a masked nurse holding up a sterile gown so that he could slip into it. "In a way, that monkey'll be my first patient." For a moment he wondered whether he should actually try to anesthetize the langur, but then dismissed the thought. "It would be too difficult to restrain that monster. And if he came to during the operation, he might bite me again."

Ehrich imagined the groggy, disemboweled monkey, trailing intestines and sinking his teeth into a rubber-gloved hand. Only after he had finished scrubbing and had donned his lab coat did he glance back at the langur's cage. The poisoned piece of Mama's rugelach was gone from the cage floor. Ehrich smiled and said to Manu as he passed the cage, "Good, isn't it?"

From the warehouse, Ehrich heard his father's muffled yell and hurried out of the Culls' room, careful to close the door behind him. Dad had said that he was going to can Sorensen today and Ehrich didn't want to do anything that would make him change his mind. His father was mad as hell at Sorensen and Ehrich was delighted. With Sorensen gone he'd have a free hand with the Culls.

In the warehouse Ehrich busied himself at the chinchilla colony just outside his father's office. Knowing that everyone was too busy to observe him, he scraped clean sawdust from the trays into a garbage bin and replaced it, meanwhile keeping a watchful eye on his father's office. It was the best vantage point from which to see the fireworks that Ehrich knew were about to start.

Sherahi found herself in the curved shadow of the gilded dome of U Vayu's pagoda as the sun rose and bloodied the lilac dawn. The quicksilver sun slipped upward and disappeared beneath clouds that swathed the horizon like dirty flannel. She saw the pagoda's golden dome turn to brass against a leaden sky and the plaza about her was washed with a flat, gray light. It was not a welcoming morning and Sherahi resisted the urge to find a snug hole and hide.

A herd of scraggly Brahma cattle had spent the night beneath the grove of fever trees adjacent to the plaza. The herd's hump-necked bull blinked in surprise when he realized that his old enemy, the giant serpent, had somehow materialized on the cobblestones only a few feet from his hooves. Swinging his upswept horns left and right he assured himself that his cows and calves were safely behind him. The motion of his head upset the clusters of flies that lodged in the corners of his eyes and they buzzed and jostled one another as they resettled in their moist paradise. A string of saliva dangled from the bull's wet muzzle as he lowered his horns and pawed the earth, ready to destroy this killer of innocents.

His cows looked up from their breakfast in surprise. In preparation for the festival the cowherd had daubed their halters with red ocher and wound them around the base of their horns so that each wore a prim, crimson tiara. The cows were preoccupied with the business of eating and, although they did not see Sherahi, they were awed by the bull's unexpected change of mood. Sherahi, however, paid him no heed. She had to find U Vayu. She uncoiled and slithered across the plaza, wondering, "Why did I inwit out here instead of inside? Seems strange."

She felt the vibrations of the bull's heavy hooves as they gathered speed with his charge. He was prepared to meet considerable resistance and was thrown off balance when his furious horns impaled thin air instead of a heavy, writhing snake. He looked about for the enemy that had been right in front of him only moments ago and saw it moving away at top speed. His charge had sent it packing. "That'll teach you," he snorted and tore the grass from between the cobblestones and shook his horns left and right in triumph. His cows looked on in admiration and his winged contingent busily reassorted themselves at the corners of his eyes.

Sherahi had no patience for his mammalian clowning but couldn't resist twitting him a bit. She sent the message "stupid cow" into his mind and had the satisfaction of seeing him charge again and again at the cobblestones where she had coiled briefly. As his hooves clattered in the gray dawn, he was the quintessential picture of bovine machismo. Sherahi watched his territorial display with faint disgust and was once again proud that she was a reptile and relatively free of these automatonlike, territorial performances. "They're such a waste of energy," she sniffed, "so intellectually stifling.

"Now, where is U Vayu?" she thought, annoyed that once again she was wasting precious time playing hide-and-seek with him. Sherahi slithered toward the pagoda and noticed that the plaza was decorated in an odd way. Some kind of festival must be in progress. She was thankful that she hadn't inwitted into the midst of a crowd of people. If they didn't go berserk with fear and trample one another as they fled from her, there was the risk that humans might interpret an inwitting materialization as a supernatural event. She'd heard that entire religions had been founded as a result of hapless inwitting serpents and while Sherahi thought that serpents were worthy of worship, she didn't fancy the responsibilities of a deity. She had enough to do to shepherd the Culls to freedom and Sandeagozu.

Like most snakes, Sherahi was somewhat nearsighted and her eyes were best at seeing moving objects at close range. As she crawled closer to the pagoda, the festival grounds came into sharper focus. She saw a tall pole silhouetted against the gray sky. Ropes were tied to the top of it and they radiated down all around. Their free ends were staked firmly into the ground, forming the skeleton of a tent above objects that had no significance for Sherahi. The ropes were strung with multicolored flags that hung limply in the gray dawn. Beneath this tent of ropes was a high arch that had been driven into the ground at either end. It had some kind of intricate spiral carving and it was also festooned with pennants. Beneath the arch were three tall posts painted with colorful, intertwined serpents. Sherahi strained to see to the tops of the posts and thought she could make out golden snake heads painted on their tops. As she drew closer she saw that there was a ring of stakes around either end of the arch. Each stake was decorated with long, scraggly streamers and a terminal blob.

"Not very pretty," thought Sherahi. The blobs were rough and dull-colored—a sharp contrast to the brightly painted posts and the ribboned arch. Then one of the blobs moved and the pythoness saw that a live monitor lizard had been pinioned to the pole. What she had thought was a long streamer was the animal's tail. Its head had been splashed with red paint and the cords that bound it were green and gold. Sherahi could see that they cut into the animal's belly skin and knew that he must be in pain. The lizard's tail whipped back and forth, cutting the still air. Its skinny toes flexed in grotesque silhouette and its snaky neck arced to and fro as the animal struggled to get free. But the cords were knotted too securely and after a few minutes of animation the creature grew limp again and its long tail streamed flaccidly down the pole. Once more it looked like a misshapen blob on the top of a rough stake.

Sherahi could not bear the creature's agony and to calm it until she could rescue it she sent a wave of compassion into its mind. Then, to her horror, she realized that there was a monitor lizard at the top of each stake and she repeated the mind balm eleven times, grateful that U Vayu had taught her to use the ancient saurian mindspeech. Atop the stakes the lizards no longer struggled and Sherahi knew that each now felt as if it were dropping down into a tranquil, velvety, black well. Pain and panic were forgotten.

"This is an outrage," thought Sherahi. "Monitor lizards—the closest living relatives to snakes—stuck up on poles and left to die like scaly lollipops. How can U Vayu let this happen outside his own pagoda? Where is that coward? Where is that slimy, syphilitic toadspawn?"

None of this made sense to Sherahi. Even if U Vayu had abandoned the place and no longer protected the pagoda, the humans here revered and worshiped all living things. They even strained their soup so they wouldn't inadvertently swallow gnats. They wouldn't think of killing an animal. "How could this happen here?" Sherahi wondered.

Then, from far above, she heard a faint whisper of beautiful and archaic serpent mindspeech and recognized U Vayu's voice. "But where are you?" she said angrily. Above her were only the tall posts with serpents painted on them, the carved arch and the central pole with the ropes. She looked carefully at each, but she didn't see U Vayu.

"Come on," she said in an exasperated voice. "Stop playing, U Vayu. I haven't got all day. I don't like your ugly game."

The words were barely out of her mind before she regretted them. She saw the arch above her shudder as U Vayu's rib cage deflated and realized that the arch wasn't carved in a spiral pattern; rather, the old python was tied to it. Somehow, his heavy body had been straightened out, wound around the arch and secured in a hundred places with the same cruel green and golden cords that held the monitor lizards. "U Vayu is a strong, old python," Sherahi thought. "It must have taken twenty men to subdue and humiliate him in this fashion. I hope he killed some of them before they did this to him."

Then she saw something that made her heart thud with horror. The lizards were merely tied to their stakes, bound at armpit and groin, but whoever had tied U Vayu to the arch had taken extra precautions to make sure that the snake couldn't escape: four stakes pierced his body, forming cross-pieces with the arch. One stake was behind his head, a second was just below his heart, a third was in his belly, and the last was at the tip of his tail. U Vayu was so securely pinned to the arch that he couldn't even lift his head. The cross-pieces were decorated with gilt and emerald-colored tassels, as if to disguise their sinister function.

Sherahi scryed U Vayu's mind and found that he was still alive, but only barely. To shield himself from pain U Vayu had inwitted away, relying on a protective mechanism that serpents use only as a last resort. This special trance slows down all body functions and postpones death while it obliterates pain. Other animals, including humans, have always misunderstood this death trance and it is the source of the widely held superstition that snakes cannot die before sundown.

Sherahi did not touch U Vayu's body, but instead sent a message of hope and courage into her teacher's mind. "I'm going to help you, U Vayu. I'll get you down from there somehow."

"These ropes and cords are the main problem," Sherahi thought. "If I had a real body instead of this flimsy inwitted apparition I could slash the ropes with my cheek teeth. Then I could push over the arch and bite through the cords that are around his body. I could free U Vayu and all those poor monitor lizards as well. But I can't do anything like this. I'll have to get someone to help.

"If I had chisel teeth like a rat it would be easy," Sherahi thought, slithering back and forth nervously. Then she remembered that U Vayu's pagoda was full of rats. "Will they be willing to help the serpent who has feasted upon their grandmothers, cousins and aunts for generations?" Sherahi knew the answer to this question and quickly decided that she didn't need their cooperation. "If I concentrate," she thought, "I can compel the rats to help."

Sherahi sent her mind into the gloomy pagoda, searching for the nervous, scaly-tailed thoughts of rats. She settled upon two dozen burly males and, using all of the power in her mind, forced them to hurry out to the plaza and gnaw at the cords that bound U Vayu and the monitor lizards. She overrode their repugnance and fear and instead made them think that wonderful, sweet treats awaited them in the plaza. If they hurried out, they could feast to their hearts' content.

Only moments later the rats flooded out of the arched doorways of the pagoda and swarmed to the plaza. Following Sherahi's orders they climbed up the rough posts and gnawed the cords that bound the monitor lizards at armpit and groin. Sherahi saw the lizards land with soft plops onto the cobblestones of the plaza. They were unharmed by their experience and slowly came into full control of their faculties. They flicked out their thick, forked ribbons of tongues, fnasted Sherahi and the rats and then suddenly scattered in all directions. Sherahi broadcast a message in saurian mind-speech, warning the lizards to stay away from human places for a long, long time. None of the monitor lizards stopped to thank Sherahi, but she didn't expect them to and didn't feel slighted. "Now," she thought, "I must free U Vayu."

Sherahi instructed the rats to climb up either side of the arch that held U Vayu. At her command, teams of rats began to pull and finally to jerk out the four cross-pieces that pierced his body. As they did so, Sherahi instructed one rat to carefully lick and clean each wound. If these places became infected, her teacher would surely die. Then the rats gnawed through the cords that bound U Vayu to the arch. Sherahi ordered the rats to gnaw the cords at either end of U Vayu's body. When they got to the fetters around his midsection, he began to slip down the arch. The weight of his body broke the last bonds and U Vayu crumpled into a heap on the ground below the arch. The rats scuttled back to the pagoda, feeling full of sugary food. They licked their chops as they ran and later they would brag to their fellows of the wonderful feast they had had in the plaza at dawn.

Sherahi gathered her courage and slithered over to U Vayu. His stately head was upside down and his lips had been forced back over his teeth as one side of his jaw had been ground into the earth by the force of his downward-sliding body. Dirt plugged his labial pits and covered his eyes. His glossy, black tongue lolled limply from his mouth and blood oozed from the wound in his neck. "He's gone," Sherahi realized. "I can't help him." As she looked at the dirt-covered serpent who had once been her teacher, she knew that he would give her no more lessons. She could never turn to him for advice. He'd never hear her plan to escape to Sandeagozu. "I'm on my own now," Sherahi thought sadly.

Sherahi shut her eyes and was about to utter the ancient serpent howl of anguish and loss, when something unexpected happened. Someone touched her physical body, which lay within the tank in the Culls' room in Leftrack's Pet Emporium in New York City. As her mind caromed back across space and time, her mourning cry for U Vayu echoed and reechoed across the plaza. It startled a flock of pigeons that had roosted in the fever tree near the plaza and sent them clapping into the dismal morning while U Vayu lay crumpled and motionless, like a bundle of dirty laundry. It wasn't long before the flies found him and began to deposit eggs on the open wounds in his sides.

Sherahi braced herself for disaster. Nothing short of that could have made Junior call her back to the pet shop before her inwit was over. As she adjusted to the discomfort of an interrupted inwit, she was surprised to find that the Culls' room was quiet. She had expected bedlam, with Manu and the Duchess screeching in their cages, but both animals sat quietly on their perches, looking expectantly at her. She could sense Dervish's hot mind as he crouched beneath the sacks of feed. Junior was beside her in her tank. There were no humans about and the warehouse was quiet.

"Why did you call me back?" she demanded. "I told you to touch me only if there was an emergency and obviously there's no emergency here."

"It's just that you were gone for so long, Pythoness," said Junior. "The day is over and all of the humans have gone home. Dervish says that it is dark outside and if we are going to escape, we must leave at once. You were gone so long. . . ." Junior's mind, using the ancient serpent mind-speech, made Sherahi remember U Vayu and she said gently, "I understand, Junior. Forgive me."

"This can't be true," thought Sherahi. "I was at U Vayu's pagoda only for a few moments—long enough to see him. . . ." The image of her teacher, impaled and lifeless, rose before her eyes. Once more she saw his imperious head broken and covered with dirt. There would be no one to guard his body until all of his intelligence had died. The carrion crows and vultures were probably gathering above him even now. The thought made her angry and more than anything she wanted to get away from this place that reeked of humans. Humans were all the same, whether they were here or at U Vayu's pagoda. All were killers—torturers. The only difference was in degree. She looked across the room and Manu's disfigured face silently condemned humans. "Well," she thought, "there will be five fewer victims in this place after tonight."

Realizing that Junior was waiting for her to continue, she said, "I must have lost track of time, Junior. Dervish and Manu are right. We must go as quickly as possible. We may never get another chance.

"Manu, tell Dervish to open your cage and the Duchess's, too. It's time we were going."

Sherahi tried not to think about U Vayu. There was no time for grief now. She must manage the minds of these bedraggled creatures and give them the courage to leave their cages and this familiar world. She knew it would be difficult for Manu and the Duchess. Dervish and Junior were younger and more adventurous. But then, they hadn't spent most of their lives in captivity. They didn't really know what it was to see the world from behind cage bars.

She watched the coati scramble up to the door first of Manu's and then of the Duchess's cage. His clever fingers opened the latches in minutes. Sherahi sent waves of courage flooding into the minds of the macaw and the langur. She encouraged them to step outside and was surprised to see Manu leap nimbly from his perch. The Duchess came out more slowly and cautiously and Sherahi saw that there was a strange collar around her neck. Sorensen had finally made good his promise, but the Duchess wasn't grateful and she walked nervously about the bottom of her cage, with her rolling gait, swearing and muttering. The Duchess hated the collar and had begged Manu to make Dervish remove it. Manu had examined the collar and had lied to her, saying that it was fastened so strongly that even Dervish's clever fingers couldn't budge it. She'd just have to wait until it fell off all by itself.

Manu knew that Sorensen had fastened the collar around the Duchess's neck to keep her from plucking what remained of her plumage. No matter how much the Duchess hated it, the collar should remain in place.

With the ridiculous collar around her neck, the Duchess walked to the door of her cage and turned her head from side to side, examining the room with first her left and then her right eye. Then she grabbed the bar closest to the door with her bill and slid down as far as it would allow. She hung limply for a moment beneath her cage and then opened her beak and released the bar. She landed with a bump on the floor and found that the collar allowed her to walk freely, although she couldn't see her feet or what was behind her. She paced back and forth beneath her cage, nervously picking up and flinging away hulls of sunflower seeds. From time to time she cocked an eye back up at her cage, as if she were considering returning to it.

"Now, Manu," said Sherahi. "You and Dervish come over here and help me get out of this tank."

When the two animals were alongside her tank the pythoness instructed them to push as hard as they could against one edge of the top that fit over the sides of her tank as securely as a lid fits onto a saucepan. If they pushed with all their might from the outside, and if she pushed up from the inside, it just might be possible for them to lift the weighted top. All they had to do was dislodge it from the lip and slide it a few inches. Sherahi could do the rest alone.

The three animals drew deep breaths and pushed. Dervish stood on his hind legs and braced his long-clawed forepaws against the lid. Manu did the same, but in a few minutes they were exhausted and it was still firmly in place. Sherahi began to despair, thinking that all of the other Culls would escape to Sandeagozu, leaving her behind, when she thought of a plan. She sent a message into Dervish's mind that he was no coati with puny forearms made for digging grubs out of rotting logs: instead, he was a wolverine. He was so strong that no cage or trap could hold him and no walls could keep him out. She heard the vibrations as Dervish growled and snarled outside her metal tank.

She sent Manu the message that he was not a langur, adapted for a life in the treetops, with graceful, attenuated limbs. Instead, he was a huge, silver-backed gorilla, with forearms like railroad ties. And, he was angry. There was a territorial rival within this tank. She heard Manu make deep hooting sounds and pound his thin chest with cupped palms and knew that he now believed himself to be the mountain king.

"Now," she commanded the newly transformed wolverine and gorilla, "push up, as hard as you can. Push."

She heard the two entranced animals growl and snarl alongside her tank and saw the lid begin to move. She planted her huge coil against the inside of the lid and joined her strength with theirs. Miraculously, the lid moved again. It shifted up and over from the locked position. It was ajar. Sherahi knew that in moments she would be free and she thanked Ra for allowing this to happen. Then she moved her coil laterally and felt the lid of the tank slide. She allowed it to resettle and looked up to see a half moon of clear space between the gridwork of the lid and the side of the tank. In a moment her massive muzzle had poked up into this space. She pushed with all of her might and widened the hole. Now her head was outside the tank and her neck followed rapidly.

She was resting with her head above the tank, in cobra fashion, when she remembered that she had left Manu and Dervish in slightly altered mental states. She saw Dervish leering at the Duchess, his head lowered, growling fiercely, and sent a message into his mind that he was no longer the terror of the north but a lovable, half-grown coati. He stopped growling, shook his head and looked sheepishly at the frightened bird, lolling out his tongue and giving the coati version of a smile.

Manu was sitting hunched up in a corner. Somehow he had emerged from the trance on his own. He had a distracted look, as if he were totally absorbed by some internal process. "Manu," said Sherahi. "Look. I'm almost free."

"Yes, I see," said the langur listlessly.

"Is there something wrong, Manu?" asked Sherahi as she drew deep breaths and inflated her body to twice the diameter of a telephone pole. She could feel the lid slide aside with each breath.

"No," said Manu quietly. "Everything's just fine."

The last third of Sherahi's body flowed easily through the space she had made between lid and tank and in moments she was free. For the first time in months she was able to stretch out to her full length and did so, luxuriating in the free movement. She was four times as long as her bathtub-sized tank. She hadn't realized how cramped she had been.

Manu and the Duchess eyed the pythoness with the same thought: neither had realized how big she actually was. Both were frozen in fear of the huge snake and didn't respond when she said, "Come on, all of you, we must go."

She saw their frightened thoughts and laughed, saying, "No, I'm not going to hurt you. You'll just have to get used to the size of me. Now stop being silly, you two.

"Dervish, take Junior around your neck as you did yesterday and show us the way out."

"I think we ought to tell her, Duchess," whispered Manu, thinking that Sherahi could not hear him.

"Oh, Manu, don't be so tiresome. There'll be time for that later."

"No," said Manu. "It's not fair. We must tell her now. It might change her mind entirely."

"I assure you, you literal-minded ape, it won't matter at all to her. Besides, if you tell her she might not take us out of here and how are we going to defend ourselves without her and the little trained killer?"

"It isn't fair that she doesn't know," said Manu and then, at Sherahi's touch, whirled around to see that she had been listening to their whispers. Her hearing was better than he had suspected.

"What isn't fair?" demanded Sherahi, who had just begun to pay attention to their spoken conversation.

"There, Manu," whined the Duchess. "You've gone and done it now. Now she won't help us get to Sandeagozu. Now we'll be eaten by rats and cats and we'll all die." The macaw reached behind her to where she could feel a succulent new pinfeather sprouting. But the collar impeded her reach. Because she couldn't pluck out the pinfeather she nervously ground her upper and lower bills together. "Damn that Sorensen and this horrible collar."

"What's all this?" said Sherahi. "What are you hiding from me?"

"Well," said the Duchess, "I thought it could wait till later, but since the cat's out of the sack, so to speak, we'll just have to tell you. Go ahead, Manu. Tell her."

"She's coming for you tomorrow," said Dervish, hoping to be helpful.

"Who?"

"Your human," said Manu. "The one you're always wishing for. That snake dancer. She's coming to get you and take you away to Hollywood. Leftrack said so today, just before he fired Sorensen."

"Fired Sorensen!" said Sherahi. "Why didn't you tell me any of this?"

"Well, there hasn't been any time, Sherahi. Don't be angry," said Manu. "We were just trying to do what was best."

"So," thought Sherahi. "Ruthie's decided to come back and get me. She's finally realized that she needs me for the act to be successful. By now she must know that she has no special talent for training animals. Her only talent was that I thought I owed her something.

"Now she wants me to go back to being her puppet. She'll lock me into a closet or into that basket and let me out only once every two weeks."

"Let's go," she said grimly. "We're wasting time here."

"You mean that you still want to go with us?" said the Duchess.

"More than ever," said Sherahi. "I'm done with humans. Forever.

"Now, Dervish, how about showing us that moon that you've been bragging about?"

Dervish capered on his hind legs in excitement and bounded down the hall to the toilet. In a flash he leaped up to the broken window and there was his moon, shining as it had the night he had first discovered it. It beckoned to the Culls, showing them the way to Sandeagozu.

"Manu, help the Duchess climb up there. I have an old score to settle. I'll be back soon," said Sherahi. She slithered as quickly as she could into the darkened warehouse. Now that she was free, she would eat. She prowled through the rows of cages, looking for a possible meal. Then it occurred to her that there were lots of rats to be had quite easily: round-eared, gray rats with silky, curly fur. She didn't want to eat too much, but one or two of them would give her strength. Besides, she had heard Leftrack brag about them. The rats were going to breed and make his fortune.

Sherahi approached the chinchilla colony and braced her body against the rows of cages. With one shove she sent the whole thing toppling to the floor. There was a screech of metal and then a crash as the cages fell, spilling water bottles, feed, sawdust and chinchillas everywhere. Sherahi saw the rats scuttling in panic and, guided by his strong smell, located the stud male. In a split second she struck, grabbing him with her rows of recurved teeth. She stopped his heartbeat with one snap of her jaws. It was as if the chinchilla had been flattened by a two-hundred-pound weight: he was dead before he'd had time to be afraid. Sherahi quickly swallowed him and then hurried away from the panicked females and their young. Sherahi knew she had struck Leftrack in the place where it would hurt him the most: in the pocketbook. Leftrack could get another male, but it would cost plenty. "The new male will kill all of the old one's young and the females will be so upset that they'll stop breeding. Rats are like that," she thought gleefully.

When she returned to the window she saw that the others were gone. She knew that they were waiting outside in the alley and slithered upward, climbing the wall with a dexterity that belied her great bulk. She extended her head outside the window, feeling cool autumn air and the light of Dervish's moon on her back. When she was halfway through the window frame, she felt it give beneath her and heard the pane below it crack and shatter, but the wooden frame did not break. Sherahi slithered down to the cobblestones and became another shadow in the alleyway outside the pet shop. "We're free," she thought. "Now all we have to do is find the caverns that Junior and Dervish told us about."

It took a moment for her dark-adapted vision to be fully operant, and in the meantime she was surprised that her labial pits told her that only two warm-bodied animals waited for her in the shadows of the garbage cans. When her vision augmented her labial pits she affirmed this and said, "Who's missing?"

She was greeted only by sniffles and muffled sobs.

"Now what?" she asked in an irritated tone.

"He wouldn't come," said Dervish.

"What do you mean, 'He wouldn't come.' Where is Manu?"

"At the last minute he said that he didn't feel well enough to go out of his cage and ran back inside."

"Go and fetch him, Dervish. Make him come."

"Yes, Sherahi," said Dervish and clambered back up the rough brick wall and disappeared into the dark pet shop.

"Manu," Sherahi said into the langur's mind. "You can't do this. We need you. The Duchess is in tears and Dervish is so frightened without you that I don't think he can go on. And I need you, too, Manu. Don't desert us now. Please."

"I cannot come, Pythoness," said Manu. "I am too old and set in my ways. All that space out there—it frightens me. I got dizzy and had to throw up when I looked out the window. I'll come another day. I'm too sick now."

"There may be no other day, Manu. This may be the last chance you ever have to be free."

"I know, Sherahi. I'll just have to take that consequence. Please understand. I'm not well, Pythoness. I guess I'm showing my age. All I want to do is stay here in my cage and be quiet."

Sherahi tried to coerce the langur to come with them, but she found that he had set up stubborn barriers in his mind. "He must have learned to do this recently," she thought. "He's never been able to do it before."

Through Junior's eyes she watched Manu sitting on his highest, most inaccessible perch, clutching his knees to his chest in the old, withdrawn way. She saw that the pain in his stomach was intense and real and sent a balm to calm and heal it. If she couldn't make him come to Sandeagozu, then she certainly could take away his pain.

"Dervish," she heard him say, "close my door and lock it."

"No, Manu," said the coati. "Don't stay here. Come with us—please, please come with us. We'll take care of you. I promise."

Manu looked at the coati and said, not unkindly, "Can you stave off death, little friend?"

"Please, Manu, I'm scared without you," the coati whimpered.

"No, Dervish. You and the others must go. Be good and lock me in now."

The coati gave the langur a wistful look and said nothing. Obediently he locked the door to Manu's cage. Taking one last look at Manu's twisted, wrinkled face, Dervish said, "I'll be back, Manu," in a small voice that stifled a whimper. "I'm not leaving you here."

In a few moments the coati reappeared outside the window and leaped to the alleyway. His banded tail sagged, but his twitching nose was firmly resolute. As he led the way to his first scent mark he was alert for danger and he vowed that somehow he would make Manu come. Not tonight, maybe, but soon—another night. "I'll go back all by myself if no one else will help and I'll carry Manu out of there by the scruff of his neck if he still won't come."

Junior saw Dervish's sad plan and hissed into his mind. "Don't worry, Dervish. We'll get him out. Another night."

Sherahi slithered in the shadows down the alley and watched the little coati and realized that he was leaving behind his mother, his father, his playmate and his teacher. "Good, loyal beast," she thought. "Junior, we must help Dervish," she said and did her best to comfort the coati as she crawled behind the sniveling Duchess in the shadows outside Leftrack's Pet Emporium.

CHAPTER SIX

THIS ISN'T IT," said the Duchess as she walked along the abandoned subway platform, her beady eyes busily searching for something to eat. "This isn't what I had in mind at all. This isn't being free. This is just another kind of prison and I don't like it."

The macaw had been in captivity for all of her adult life. As a juvenile she had blundered into a tangle-foot trap set by Colombian villagers. Years of captivity had compressed distance for the Duchess and she'd forgotten how long her journey inside that wooden crate to Leftrack's Pet Emporium had taken. When Sherahi had suggested escaping, the macaw had agreed, thinking that her own jungle was somewhere nearby. Once they were free she'd planned to fly away toward the distant green blur of treetops that she felt certain was just outside the brick walls of the pet shop.

She'd imagined that other macaws would be there to greet her. Fierce scarlet and blue plumage would shine brilliantly and their raucous welcoming cries would fill the day with joyful noise. The Duchess had rehearsed the scene of her homecoming so often that she could almost hear the garrulous voices and feel the sun on the delicately puckered, bare skin of her face. How wonderful it would be to sunbathe in a swaying treetop. She'd be with her own kind and she'd be home once more.

She'd anticipated taking a bath in a mountain stream and feasting on Brazil nuts and the fruits of the Maracaibo palm and the strangler fig. She would find a snug perch shaded by soft banana leaves and would drowse through the afternoon, lulled by the soft rustling of leaves and the faraway sounds of the sleepy forest below.

Somehow she'd convinced herself that her rain forest was only a short flight away from the pet shop and had thought that, even with her plumage in this sorry condition, she'd be able to fly there quite easily. She'd been stunned to see what really was outside Leftrack's pet shop: the hard pavement had seemed to stretch on endlessly and tall metal poles that the others called streetlights grew straight up in regular files. "Where are the trees?" she had wondered. It was all so frightening and ugly that, even though she couldn't see jungle on any horizon, she wanted to fly off immediately. She would have done so, too, but she had found that too many of her wing feathers were missing to allow her the effortless, arrow-quick flight that she'd dreamed of so often in her covered cage. She'd imagined herself a blur streaking through the night sky—the moonlight shining on her tail feathers. To make matters worse, she had found that the collar that Sorensen had fastened around her neck interfered with the forward stroke of each wing beat. She had attempted a short flight in the alley behind Leftrack's and had crash-landed, bruising the bare skin above her breast bone as she belly-flopped onto the pavement. The crash had brought tears to her eyes and, feeling very sorry for herself and even more upset to learn that Manu had abandoned her, she had cried and sniffled the whole way to this horrid cave. She had waddled behind Dervish and Junior and the march had been especially humiliating for an animal that once had been able to fly. As her claws had scraped across the pavement with each step, the Duchess had cursed the split tongue of the feathered goddess who had allowed her to be captured so very long ago.

Unable to fly, the Duchess was no different from any other beast and for the first time in her life she regretted that she'd torn out all those beautiful feathers. But it had been so boring in her cage and they had tasted so good. "Tasted so good," she said in a shrill tenor and was amazed at how muffled her voice sounded in this cavernous subterranean nest that Dervish had found.

The Culls had arrived hours ago and now the others were drowsing in a corner at the bottom of one staircase. They were safely away from the platform where the Duchess paced. They had made sure to be far away from the fire serpents that roared through the cavern every so often. The first few times that the fire serpent had shown itself, the Duchess had cowered in fear, just like the other Culls. But she'd observed that the ferocious animal didn't seem to care about her. She'd discovered that she could even insult its ancestors at the top of her lungs as it roared past and it wouldn't react at all. She had grown so accustomed to it now that she hardly looked up when it roared by, sending grotesque shadows jumping all over the walls. But its noise was annoying. It interrupted her thoughts and hurt her ears and she'd tried to hide her head beneath one wing to block the sound, but Sorensen's damned collar got in the way. The fire serpent was gone as quickly as it had appeared and the cavern was quiet except for a distant rumble as the monster retreated down the tunnel.

"I hate this place," muttered the Duchess as she walked, rolling heavily from side to side with each step of her four-toed feet. She remembered how she'd used those long claws to hold Sorensen's peanuts. One of those would taste so good right now. Even a nice, juicy pinfeather would be delicious. The Duchess was used to having plenty of food and she hadn't known hunger in a long time. Even though the light that reached down into the tunnel was dimmer than that from a jarful of exhausted lightning bugs, the Duchess's internal sense of time told her that if she were back at Leftrack's, Sorensen would be sharing his baloney sandwich with her right about now. Thoughts of the delicious beakfuls of baloney that she had once carelessly tossed aside in hopes of more exotic treats made her groan. Now she'd be happy to settle for just a crust of one of Sorensen's sandwiches, even if it were smeared with that hateful, yellow cream that he liked so much.

The Duchess had grown used to talking to herself in her cage, so it was only natural to do so as she paced along the dim platform, thinking of the food that Sorensen might have given her—if only she'd stayed in the pet shop. "Horrible," she said in a harsh contralto. "This place is horrible. How could they have brought me to this hole in the ground? Do they think that I'm an owl? Do they think I can see in the dark? Maybe they think that parrots are related to petrels, and that we fancy dark, underground burrows."

No one answered and she continued speaking in the cacophony of squawks and shrill screams that she thought sounded exactly like Sorensen's strange human speech. "And where am I supposed to rest? There isn't even a decent perch in the whole place, except maybe way up there." The Duchess cocked one eye at the shadowy ceiling, where she could see the outlines of heavy buttresses, angled struts and the beams that supported the ceiling. "But they might as well be perches on the mountains of the moon. I can't get up there." She clenched one foot against her naked breast to ease her tired claws and then continued walking, squawking, "I'm so hungry. Those others don't care but the few feathers that I have are so dirty that they'll probably never come clean—even if I preen them until they're frayed and useless. I'll starve down here in the dark. My feathers will never grow back now and I'll never be pretty again."

The Duchess crooked her neck and tried to look behind to see her bedraggled tail feathers but the collar blocked her view. "If only I could get this thing off, I'd feel better," she muttered. "But Manu says that that stupid Dervish can't undo it. He was smart enough to open drawers and locked cages, but he can't manage a simple thing like this—the only thing that really matters to me. Long-nosed twit. And he was the one who thought that this was such a fine place. Fat lot he knows."

There was a distant rumble and the Duchess stopped squawking and cocked her head to listen. A few moments later she resumed her pacing and talking to herself. "That's what you get for associating with mammals and snakes," she said. "Creatures like that are happy in dark, disgusting holes. Come to think of it: this would be a good home for a mole or a bat or even a whole army of rats. But a refined and sensitive creature like a hummingbird or a scarlet macaw can't endure these barbaric conditions for long." She sniffed and batted her eyes delicately.

"Manu did the right thing," she squawked in a mournful baritone. "I should have stayed in my cage, too. Culls like me don't have any business trying to be free. I've lost the knack of freedom—I'm no good at it anymore."

Behind her the Duchess heard another distant growl, followed this time by a steadily increasing roar as yet another fire serpent announced itself. It roared through the station, sending up a surf of blue-white sparks, and the Duchess screeched at it in frustration. "Get out," she screamed, but her cry was drowned by the roar and clatter of the uptown-local train that had skipped this station for years. Her scream was plainly audible to the guard of the people of the Norse. He had been silently and intently observing the group of odd animals who had arrived before dawn in this outpost of Norse territory. Looking over his shoulder to see that the fierce bird with the hooked bill didn't see him, and sniffing nervously for any sign of Black invaders, the guard scuttled toward Norse headquarters. He wondered how the Chief would deal with these trespassers and worried that he might be punished for abandoning his post. He hoped that perhaps the Chief might reward him in the usual way for a job well done: it had been a long time since he had mated and the bone in his penis ached with desire.

The guard was nearly out of the station. He was down in the rail bed and was tiptoeing across a railroad tie that marked the uptown boundary of Norse territory. He thought he was safe and had allowed his mind to wander to the reward that might await him. He was no longer alert for the scent of Black thugs who might lurk to ambush him. Instead he was anticipating the feel of the soft, welcoming flanks of a female in estrus when he stepped on something unfamiliar. It felt strangely soft. Simultaneously he heard an angry buzzing near his head. He looked around in confusion for the source of this noise. "Is a work train coming down the tracks?" he wondered.

The next thing he felt was a pinprick in his neck as Junior's fangs drove their poison home. The guard was so surprised by the instant explosion of pain that he didn't think to cry out. He felt his leg muscles go into inexplicable spasms and then he found that, no matter how hard he inhaled, he couldn't catch his breath. It felt as if his chest had suddenly been squashed flat. He died without having seen his murderer, who was coiled in the shadows, ready—willing and even hoping—to strike again.

The guard of the people of the Norse suffocated in moments. Hours later, when the relief watch found his stiff-legged body, he noticed that his mouth was drawn back in a horrible grimace, revealing his teeth and gums and a swollen, purple tongue. The relief guard sniffed at one stiff paw and at the guard's firmly erect penis. He heard the sizzle of the electricity that sparked nearby and decided, "The stupid fool. After all these years you'd think he'd know better than to electrocute himself."

Sherahi lay in the dusty darkness with Dervish curled within her mound of coils and tried to ignore the pervading stench of rat all around her. The coati's furry body rested just below her long, slowly beating heart and his warmth radiated deep into her muscles. The sleeping coati made her feel contented and strangely at peace, as if she were stretched out on a safe, warm rock ledge, absorbing heat and listening to the spirit of the rock whispering its memories of sun-splashed days and brittle, cold nights. When she was free she had spent a good deal of time basking on rocks, and Sherahi had found that, if she listened long and slowly enough, all rocks had something to say. A few were very ancient and could tell the entire history of the earth. Rocks had long memories and could recall every event and creature that they had ever known. Some whispered the story of the chemical brew that melded them and gave them birth far below the crust of the earth. Some spoke of their sulphurous, explosive emergence as boiling lava and their gradual metamorphosis into solid rock. A lucky few cherished memories of long, slow cooling in a simmering atmosphere and the happy knowledge that this patient cooling would foster the growth of huge, sparkling crystals within their rocky bowels. Crystals of any kind—ruby, garnet, amethyst, tourmaline, pegmatite, quartz or even humble mica—are the glory of stones and their sole, cherished possessions. Rocks are usually close-mouthed about their crystals and tend to hide them beneath shabby, weatherworn surfaces, but U Vayu had taught Sherahi how to be silent and listen to rocks. Over the years she had overheard many a slab crooning over the beauty of its hidden gems. On the other hand, sedimentary rocks, especially those that held fossilized plants or animal, spoke with many voices. The cement below Sherahi's chin felt like sandstone, but it was silent. Sherahi wondered if it were dumb because of the racket that the fire serpent made or whether it had no voice because humans had fabricated it. "It would be nice to lie here in the dark and listen to slow, nattering rock speech," she thought. "It would make me feel free—or close to it." But the cement beneath her chin had no tales to tell and Sherahi knew that the Culls had many anxious days ahead of them before she would be free enough to hear the slow speech of stones.

One part of her mind was alert to the noises in the darkness. She heard the fire serpent roar through its tunnel and clatter off into the distance. She'd seen it enough now to know that Junior was right: it was no animal, but some kind of human device. There *were* humans inside of it. The serpent usually hurried too quickly for her to see, but one had slowed somewhat as it barreled through the tunnel and in its belly she had seen ordinary-looking humans reading newspapers. In the midst of that moving uproar one man was actually asleep and once the fire serpent had actually stopped and she'd seen a young couple. They sat quite close together, holding hands, and the girl's head had rested on the boy's shoulder. None of the humans seemed frightened by the fire serpent, so Sherahi had dismissed it as a potential danger, but warned the other Culls to stay out of its path.

This tunnel must have had something to do with the fire serpent, because, as Junior had observed, the creature slid along shiny metal rails and, although the fire serpent avoided them, there were rails in the tunnel alongside the platform. Although Junior seemed fascinated by the fire serpent and had gone off to investigate the darkness closest to the tracks, Sherahi was only peripherally interested. She had other things to think about. Dervish had been exhausted after guiding them to this place and almost immediately he had curled into a corner and tried to sleep. The coati was nervous by nature and Sherahi had feared that his resources were stretched to the breaking point. She'd spun him a healing, comforting dream and had coiled protectively around him. The Duchess was too agitated to rest, and Sherahi sensed that she, too, was mentally and physically drained by the journey. But Sherahi had little sympathy for the macaw. "Most of that bird's troubles come because she's torn out her feathers and she did that only because she felt sorry for herself and was bored. It serves her right."

When Sherahi had emerged from Leftrack's and found the Duchess and Dervish both weeping in the alleyway, she had immediately thought that the macaw was upset because Manu had refused to accompany them. Later, Sherahi had learned that the Duchess was only remotely concerned with Manu. She had been weeping out of self-pity. Sherahi had scryed the bird's thoughts and discovered that the damnable parrot had planned to fly away as soon as she was free. Sherahi had been enraged at her selfishness. To punish her, Sherahi had immediately retracted the macaw's share of the comfort she had been projecting to the newly freed and frightened Culls and had ignored the Duchess.

Sherahi listened to the bird's angry voice screeching in the adjacent tunnel and thought, "It won't harm her to fuss and fume. She's the most spoiled, self-indulgent nonhuman that I've ever encountered. And I'll never trust her again. That's for sure."

As the next fire serpent raged through the adjacent cavern, Sherahi heard the macaw scream in fury and stubbornly refused to comfort her. "Let her scream her head off," thought Sherahi. "It just might teach her something."

The Cull that Sherahi was worried about was Manu. She hadn't been able to keep in constant mental contact with him as they were traveling to Dervish's cavern. He hadn't responded to her last call and Sherahi had assumed that he was asleep. The langur had been ill and Sherahi hadn't wanted to disturb his rest. "It must be afternoon now," she thought. "Surely he will be awake." Sherahi wanted to reassure herself and so sent her mind spinning out of the dark cavern, casting her thoughts like a shining spider web revolving around the thought, "Manu."

She materialized in the Culls' room, outside Manu's cage. One quick look told her that something was very wrong with the langur. He lay face down on the bottom of his cage. His limbs were sprawled in an unnatural way and it looked as if he had fallen from his high perch. His grotesque face was turned toward her and she could see his single good eye moving mechanically back and forth beneath the silver-furred eyelid. Then his limbs contorted and his head arched back, his single eyelid opened wide and his mouth froze in a rictus that was a mockery of the primate fear display. Sherahi watched her friend agonize for only one moment. Then, without quite knowing what she did or how she did it, Sherahi sprang into what little remained of Manu's conscious mind. She knew the langur well enough to recognize normal from abnormal patterns and, by furiously striking left and right, reorganizing his thoughts and nerve impulses, she was able to restore some order and remove the hallucinations that were convulsing Manu's body.

This close to him she could fnast that Manu smelled wrong. His thought patterns were unrecognizable as belonging to the Manu she knew so well. Bit by bit she restored order in his mind and body and after a while the serpent knew that the langur's convulsions had passed. He breathed normally once more.

Sherahi knew that, even while he was unconscious, she could hypnotize Manu and so she prepared his mind to receive and follow her instructions. Later tonight she would send Dervish to fetch him and guide him to the caverns where the others waited. "It'll have to be tonight," she thought, "because if we wait any longer, Dervish's scent marks will have vanished and he won't be able to relocate Leftrack's."

Sherahi didn't know what was wrong with Manu. Maybe old age or some strange disease was claiming him, but if he were to die, she and the other Culls must see that he died free, not as a human pawn inside a cage. Sherahi continued her hypnotic therapy and was pleased to see the langur's tongue wet his lips and his eye open. She knew that in time it would focus and decided that now she could let him sleep. Manu's crisis had passed and he no longer needed her beside him. It might even upset him to see her. She decided to return to Dervish's cavern.

Sherahi was retreating toward her physical body in the depths of Dervish's cavern, when she saw the door to the Culls' room open and

Ehrich Leftrack enter, his arms clasping a paper sack full of containers of Chinese take-out food. Sherahi's materialization was fading and Ehrich did not see her, but she saw him walk over to Manu's cage. He looked at Manu, who by now was sitting up and scratching his head, and Sherahi heard Ehrich say, "Shit. He's not dead yet." She returned to the cavern knowing just how urgent it was that Dervish fetch Manu from the Culls' room to-night.

Hollywood, California

"LISTEN, LEFTRACK," Bernie said angrily into the telephone. "I haven't got time to play footsie with you. I'm coming east tomorrow and I want that snake."

There was a pause and then Bernie said, "I don't care what it costs. Look, can you deliver the goddamn snake, or not?

"Two days—three at the most. And, Leftrack, if I don't have it by then, the deal's off. Now, can you deliver, or do I look elsewhere?"

Bernie took an agitated drag of his cigarette and listened to Leftrack dither on the other end of the phone.

"What do you mean, you're not sure? Yesterday you said you had it right there. What're you trying to pull, Leftrack?

"Well, catch it."

There was a pause as Bernie listened and then said, "Sure, sure. I'll call you back tomorrow—same time. But I want that snake.

"Yeah . . . yeah . . ." he said. Bernie didn't bother to say goodbye and crashed the receiver back onto its ornate ivory and brass cradle. Ruthie had insisted that every room have one of these fancy French telephones. She said that all the stars had them. The telephone made Bernie feel like a pansy and, thinking that Leftrack was pulling some trick, he lit another cigarette. He could hear Ruthie humming in the adjoining pink satin boudoir and wondered where she was going tonight. As usual, he hadn't been invited to join Goldman's party and another long evening stretched ahead of him. "Things will straighten themselves out as soon as I get that snake that she's mooning over," he thought and stubbed out his cigarette in a heavy, pink glass ashtray that sat on the frail, bowlegged desk next to the telephone. "I'll just have to lean on that weasel, Leftrack. He's trying to pull a fast one, but he doesn't know that he's dealing with an expert. A real expert."

SHERAHI WILLED the night to come and prepared for Manu's rescue. Dervish was still asleep, but Sherahi introduced a dream into his quicksilver mind. In this dream he saw himself hurry back to Leftrack's, running more rapidly than a water shrew darting along a familiar trail.

Dervish saw himself streak into the alley in back of Leftrack's and, with the liquid strength of a leopard bounding into the twisted branches of an acacia tree, he leapt onto the familiar window ledge. There was no awkward struggling up the wall, scrabbling for toeholds and gasping for breath. Dervish saw himself claw at the window and in his dream his dexterous front paws, which looked so much like Manu's hands, were transformed into the forelimbs of a giant anteater. They were covered with coarse, gray fur. He could tell from the way his shoulder muscles flexed that these unfamiliar appendages were very strong. Instead of having fingers, each arm ended in a three-inch-long recurved claw and when Dervish hooked these into the corners of the newly repaired window, it immediately came loose from the frame and fell onto the cobblestones below. In Dervish's dream the glass shattered without making a sound. He gave it no further thought and poised for a moment on the window ledge before he leapt down to the floor of the toilet. There he noticed that his front paws were his own again. Without wondering where those anteater arms had gone he raced to the Culls' room and scrambled up the front of Manu's cage. He opened the door and saw Manu hunched over in one corner. Pulling Manu by the wrist, he led him to the broken window and, like a collie with a reluctant ewe, nipped at Manu's heels and forced him to climb up and out. Then the two of them hurried back to the cavern, keeping to the shadows of the deserted streets. From around his neck, Dervish heard Junior threaten to kill anyone who interfered with them.

After she had inserted this dream in the sleeping coati's mind, Sherahi felt his leg muscles twitch as he replayed it over and over. It would be several hours until Dervish would be needed and, fearing that he might exhaust himself and wake up tired, Sherahi sent him the image of hypnotically waving ribbons of color. The dream began with vivid reds and oranges, which tapered into pale washes of violet and indigo. Soon Dervish was breathing calmly once again and Sherahi turned her mind to other matters.

She hadn't had much opportunity to think about the way in which U Vayu had been killed, and had had no time to mourn him. The anguish that she had felt at the time had hardened into a clot of hatred of humans and a dislike for all things made by them. Sorensen had been the only genuinely kind human that she had ever known and she knew that he, too, had been badly used by the Leftracks. "Just like a Cull," Sherahi thought. Although Ruthie had never been cruel to her, the snake now realized that she had misinterpreted most of the things that Ruthie had done. Now that she knew the truth, Sherahi was embarrassed to have believed that a tawdry dance was a mystic religious rite. "She just used me to help her titillate and divert men as they drank their way into a comforting stupor. Leftrack tried to use me too, just like Ruthie, but he was different. At least she had tried to take good care of her 'Girls.' That slime, Leftrack, didn't care if all the beasts in the warehouse died as long as he got a fat profit.

"The dumpy woman is bad, too, but the son, Ehrich, is the worst of the lot," Sherahi thought furiously. "From his father he got a legacy of contempt for animals. Ehrich believes that we are nothing more than intricate, living machines—flesh-and-blood mechanisms to be taken apart and examined and then thrown away." She thought of the pathetic turtles that he had sawn apart—and some of them weren't even dead. She remembered Ehrich's thrill when he had seen the slow, convulsive contractions of the turtle's heart. "Yes, he sees us as mechanisms, but unlike boys who tinker with clocks to see what makes them go, Ehrich will never have the skill to put animals back together again—or humans either." Sherahi had scryed his mind and had seen his intellectual limits: he had the capacity to learn only a litany of facts. She suspected that his studies would generate nothing more than a vocabulary of ponderous four- and five-syllable words. She envisioned Ehrich diligently memorizing words and facts, impressing his schoolmates and professors but never glimpsing the significance of a whole animal. "Mastery of minutiae will never expand his mental horizons," she thought.

Sherahi remembered the silvery gleam of the set of small knives and scissors that Ehrich had sharpened as he had sat at his desk. The thought of Manu's belly skin being slit open ever so cleanly by one of those silvery knives made her shudder. It was clear that Ehrich intended to kill Manu. She decided that, even though it would exhaust her, she would have to do something further to protect the langur. "All I need is one day," she thought. "In only one day Manu will be safe."

She sent her mind spinning back to the Culls' room in Leftrack's Pet Emporium, seeking Ehrich Leftrack. She found him seated at Sorensen's workbench, with the open containers of Chinese food arrayed before him. He had just finished his appetizers: barbecued spareribs and two egg rolls with dollops of duck sauce. His chopsticks flew from container to container, conveying choice morsels that he hardly paused to chew.

Sherahi saw that Manu was sitting up in his cage, rubbing his head against the screen in his habitual way. "Someday I'll have to do something about those fleas in Manu's ear." But she set that task aside. "There's no time now." Sherahi was relieved to see that Manu had survived his bout of convulsions and that her mental support seemed to be working. He looked normal and she concluded that he would be able to get to the caverns when Dervish and Junior came for him tonight.

Sherahi also saw that the Culls' room looked different. Ehrich had arranged his dissecting tools on one end of Sorensen's workbench. The huge tank that she had lived in for months had been removed and the Duchess's cage was also gone. For a moment Sherahi thought of scrying Ira Leftrack's mind to see how upset he was that the Culls were missing, but decided to leave well enough alone. Although she would have liked to see Leftrack fuss and fume, Sherahi decided to forgo that pleasure. He would be frantic and would blame everyone but himself for the loss of such a large investment. But it didn't really matter whether Leftrack was upset or not: by midnight tonight all of the Culls would be beyond his reach.

Ehrich seemed very much in command at Sorensen's workbench and Sherahi could find no trace of the old man who had treated the Culls so kindly. Sherahi had avoided it as long as she could but, with a shudder of distaste, as if she were forced to crawl through another creature's excrement, she began to scry Ehrich Leftrack's mind.

His thoughts were so occupied with food that it was like trying to read a menu through a murk of spattered grease and oyster sauce. Ignoring the nausea produced by Ehrich's relentlessly chomping jaws, Sherahi saw his plan to poison Manu. As she watched Ehrich's mind fill with sensations of pea pods bursting against the roof of his mouth and the slither of warm tree-ear fungus along his tongue and down his throat, Sherahi saw at once that U Vayu had been right: serpents had no business dealing with humans. They *were* an alien species. Sherahi could tell that Ehrich was no longer hungry and that, unlike snakes, he was eating just because he liked to. His thoughts were of the taste and feel of the partially masticated food that filled his mouth, while his belly swelled against the waistband of his trousers and some part of his mind gluttonously called for more.

"Still hungry, Ehrich?" thought Sherahi. "Well, I've got just the thing for you." She dug down below his thoughts of the feel of the half-chewed food in his mouth and found his fondness for sweets. Sherahi inflated the idea of an insatiable hunger for sugar and set it spinning in Ehrich's mind. Like sticky fibers of cotton candy spun onto a paper cone, the idea grew. She saw the image of a banana split topped with hot-fudge sauce that dripped and puddled, mingling deliciously with hot butterscotch sauce and carrying hints of melted pistachio and butter-pecan ice cream. It mushroomed in his mind like a fragrant fungus and was accompanied by the thought, "I *need* ice cream. Lots of ice cream."

Even while his chopsticks flew between the containers of beef with snow peas and roast pork egg foo yung, seizing limp bean sprouts and scooping up mounds of slivered, sautéed beef, she saw the idea catch and grow. When the containers were empty she saw him decide: "I want a Gut Buster." She saw him imagine the huge vat of ice cream compounded of every flavor that the corner drugstore carried. It was topped with peaks of whipped cream and marshmallow sauce, as well as dribbles of hot fudge, chocolate sauce, strawberry goo and butterscotch, strewn with pecan halves and studded with maraschino cherries. Two tiny paper parasols and four wafer cookies surrounded an American flag that waved stiffly from the peak of the Gut Buster. She saw Ehrich remember to insist that the soda jerk leave out the nuts. "They're not good for the digestion—at least, that's what Mama always says."

Ehrich finished his Chinese meal and loosened his belt. He threw out the empty containers and washed his chopsticks. Then he sighed and drew in his belly so that he could fish his wallet out of his pants pocket. He had a two-dollar bill; Nickerson's charged $1.65 for a Gut Buster. With a strange, intense expression, as if possessed, Ehrich licked his bottom lip, grabbed his jacket and waddled out of the room.

Back in the darkness of Dervish's cavern, Sherahi laughed. She knew that Manu would be safe for the rest of the day.

As usual, the introduction of images into a human mind had exhausted Sherahi and she wished that U Vayu were still coiled beneath the golden statue of Buddha, in his pagoda on the other side of the world. It wouldn't have mattered to her if he were mentally present or if he were remote and unresponsive to her as he hobnobbed with the Great Worm or one of the other celestial serpent nats. Sherahi would have been happy just to sit in his pagoda, waiting for him to recognize her, listening to the thin chant of priests who enumerated the thousand virtues of Buddha. Sherahi longed for the company of her own kind and she wished that U Vayu were alive. There was so much that she needed to know. For example, why did humans hate serpents? U Vayu might have known, but now he would never be able to tell her. Besides, if he had understood people, why had he allowed himself to be tortured and killed? U Vayu had been a venerable, perhaps even a holy, serpent. Perhaps he himself was a nat by now. Sherahi was unclear as to what happened to serpents when they died. U Vayu had never discussed this matter with her.

As Sherahi lay coiled around Dervish's sleeping body, it occurred to her that, since she knew the names of the Great Serpent Nats, maybe she might try to contact one of them. Maybe a spirit more powerful than Lachesis could tell her how to find U Vayu or perhaps help her to understand humans. She looked at the dim light that filtered into the tunnel of the fire serpent and saw that it was still daylight in the city above. "It'll be hours before I can send Dervish on his way." Mentally she called to Junior and asked him to rouse her at midnight. She noted that Junior responded in a snappish fashion, but gave it little further thought. A quick scan of Junior's mind showed that her mental surgery was holding firm. He was still trustworthy and she knew that he would make sure that she returned from her inwit in time to send him and Dervish out to rescue Manu.

Sherahi assumed that the procedure for inwitting to one of the most powerful serpent nats would be the same as that she followed when she inwitted to a lesser snake. She concentrated on the name of the Midgard Serpent. She imagined a huge serpent with its tail in its mouth, girdling the earth, and focused on the name "Oroborous." Instinctively she melded the sensations of her Jacobson's organs with those of her labial pits, concentrating upon the Worm Oroborous, and spun her thoughts into a luminous spiral, seeking U Vayu's friend, the Great Worm.

Sherahi found herself on a shelf of rock above a canyon in a landscape that looked unfinished. Rough-hewn pillars of layered rock towered all around, as if a sculptor had put down his mallet and chisel and stopped for lunch. The bases of the pillars were joined to a solid rock wall that sloped away into shadow. A shaft of sunlight penetrated to the bottom of the canyon and there Sherahi saw a pair of what she thought were cockroaches, grazing by the riverside. As she strained to see, it occurred to the pythoness that the animals couldn't be insects. With a shock she realized that they were antelope, drinking from shallow pools beside the thick-looking, brown river. This ledge was much higher than she had expected and she drew back from the edge and instinctively gripped the rock outcrop with her belly scutes. Sherahi didn't like heights.

"Why am I here?" she wondered. "U Vayu said that the Great Worm lay at the bottom of the ocean, encircling the earth. Did I make a mistake? Something seems wrong."

A shadow passed above and Sherahi looked up to see a vulture hanging above the canyon rim. Its rusty-black wings were stretched taut by the rising air currents and its naked crimson head moved left and right before it fixed on Sherahi.

The bird soared up and out of sight, only to reappear in a few minutes, alighting on a gloomy ledge that was across from her. A vertical drop of thousands of feet separated them.

"Greetings, cousin," said the vulture, settling its rag bag of feathers with a rustle and fixing a small, inquisitive eye on this stranger.

"Greetings," replied Sherahi politely and raised her regal head aloft to show the vulture that she was not dead meat—not a potential meal.

"Oh," said the vulture in a disappointed voice, "you're alive. Too bad."

Realizing that she had made a faux pas the bird hastily continued, "No, that didn't come out right. I'm always saying the wrong thing. Let's start again. You see, I had hoped that you might have—now, this isn't anything against you personally, but I had hoped that you might have—how shall I say it: kicked the bucket? bought the farm? become crow bait? No, too folksy for a fancy one like you. Let's see, what would be more appropriate? Passed away? Departed? Deceased? Not quite it. Slipped your cable? Gone to the last roundup or to the happy hunting ground? Given up the ghost? Breathed your last? No, no. None of those is right."

The vulture thought for a moment and then in a burst of enthusiasm said, "How about—made your final exit?"

"How about just plain dead?" suggested Sherahi.

"Sounds a little, forgive the expression, cold-blooded, don't you think?"

"Considering your line of work," Sherahi said, "it seems natural."

"Well, you'd be surprised at how few creatures see it that way." The vulture's tone was strangely intimate. "It's my reputation, I suppose. Most beasts think of me as the right arm of the Grim Reaper. They're afraid of me. My mate's the only friend I have—if you want to call him a friend.

"You can't count on nestlings, you know. Even after you've gone without and starved yourself to feed them day after day, they have no gratitude. Once they're fledged—pouf!—out of the nest forever. They only stay around to beg for handouts.

"And once the young are gone then *he* goes, too. A nestful of babies once a year to carry on his line—that's all he thinks of. I tell you, cousin, it's a rough life. No friends. No one to gossip with. No one to share lunch—to say nothing of all those stinking corpses heaving with maggots." The vulture shook her feathers again and exclaimed delicately, "I don't think I'll ever get rid of that smell. I tell you, if I didn't have Jordy, I think I'd go out of my mind."

"Jordy?" asked the pythoness. The name was somehow familiar.

"Short for Jormungand, or some fancy name like that. Can't you see him, cousin? He's sealed up in the rock right there." The vulture motioned to the canyon wall behind her.

"Old as the hills, Jordy is—maybe older. Only bones left of him now. But he must have really been something in his day. Much, much bigger than those monster lizards whose bones are weathering out of the rock about a thousand feet down. Jordy was the biggest of 'em all. No doubt of that."

The bird hunched its shoulders and gave a backward glance and whispered across the space that separated them. "And as old as he is, he's not dead yet. He talks. For them that's got ears to hear, that is. When the sun hits him and he warms up a bit then he likes a bit of company—even if it's that of a poor, lonesome scavenger.

"And the stories he tells. . . . He's seen it all, or at least he says so. Don't really know how much of what he says is true, but he does love to go on and on. He's the one that told me we were cousins. Given me quite an education, Jordy has."

Sherahi looked at the crumbling rock wall behind the vulture. "Where is this friend of yours?" she asked. "I don't see anyone."

"Hold your horses, cousin of mine," said the vulture. "It's just about time for the sun to wake him up. Then you'll see. . . ."

Sherahi noticed that the sun had moved higher in the sky now. Its rays inched down the canyon wall and in a few moments they struck the rock ledge where the vulture perched. The bird blinked in the bright sun and Sherahi flinched as Jormungand spoke in a voice that boomed with the sound of boulders smashed like gigantic dice tossed by a flood-swollen river.

"What do you want, little serpent?" The voice was so loud that it rattled the ear bones buried within Sherahi's skull.

Sherahi hadn't been called "little serpent" since she was a hatchling and she looked for the source of the voice. But there was no one else in sight and, feeling a bit foolish, she faltered. "I was looking for the Midgard Serpent. I wanted to ask his advice, but I seem to be in the wrong place. I was told that the Midgard Serpent lives at the bottom of the ocean, holding the earth together."

"Used to," interrupted the voice.

"Pardon me, but to whom am I speaking?" said Sherahi, not knowing where to look. "I feel silly speaking to a cliff."

"You're not speaking to a cliff. You're speaking to Jormungand—I am the one you are seeking."

"But, where are you?"

"Don't be so literal-minded, little serpent. Open your eyes. Look here."

Sherahi saw an outcrop of crystals winking in the sunlight and realized that they filled the bony eye socket of a rusty-red skull that protruded from the rock wall. The crystals dazzled her and Sherahi found herself yawning. She felt so sleepy. "It must be the sun," she thought and shook herself alert. She saw more of the creature's enormous bones in the tan rock matrix. "Oh my," thought Sherahi as she began to understand the size of this beast. His vertebrae were bigger than bathtubs and were lined up along the rock face as if the ancient creature were lying on its side. These backbones marched along the rock layer and wound around the sides of the canyon and out of sight. Sherahi couldn't see any end to them. She saw that what she had thought were runnels in the rock were actually gigantic ribs lying next to each vertebra. Whatever this creature was, he was certainly enormous. "Much larger than anything that's alive today," Sherahi thought. "His skull is so long that it wouldn't have fit into the Culls' room at Leftrack's." The teeth that fringed his upper jaw were ten inches long. He was far bigger than any of the ancient thunder lizards that U Vayu had told her about and Sherahi was glad that she was seeing only his stony skeleton. A live serpent of this size would have been nightmarish.

A second wave of fatigue swept over her. She kept imagining a nice, dark hole. Her bones ached for a nap, but she forced herself to stay awake. "What's wrong with me?" she wondered. "I shouldn't be tired at a time like this." She was being impolite to this ancient monster and U Vayu had told her to always be polite to the Great Serpent Nats.

"I don't understand," she said, suppressing a yawn. The crystals in the creature's eye socket kept winking at her and, even though her pupils were shut tightly, the twinkling seemed to interfere with her thoughts. For once in her life Sherahi wished that she could completely close her eyes in the way that Dervish could. She tried to look away from the winking crystals and said slowly and with effort, "I thought you were one of the Great Serpent Nats—supernatural and eternal. U Vayu said that, with your tail in your mouth, you held the world together and kept it from spinning to pieces. He said that you . . ." Sherahi opened her mouth in a wide yawn and said, "Excuse me. I don't know why I'm so sleepy. Where was I?"

"Something about someone called U Vayu." The booming voice was soothing now.

"Oh yes, he said that you lived at the bottom of the ocean and when you moved, you made the earth quake."

"U Vayu was a very limited serpent," the voice said, sounding like rain pattering on a tin roof. "Some might even say that he was a fraud, but he did have a few sad, little tricks."

"Did you keep the world from flying to pieces?" asked Sherahi.

"In a manner of speaking I still do," said Jormungand.

"But why aren't we on the bottom of the ocean?" asked Sherahi.

"Look around you, little serpent. We are at the bottom of the ocean—millions of years ago."

Sherahi looked at the rock layer behind her and with an effort focused her eyes on small, fossilized shells. She put her chin to the rock and instantly heard small voices whispering, but she didn't listen long enough to understand what they were saying. The serpent nat was right. This rock had once been at the bottom of the ocean. "But why aren't you holding the earth together?" she asked.

"The earth is older now. Different. I am no longer needed. Most of the old gods are dead—just like me. In fact, the only one of us that is still active is Quetzalcoatl or his black twin. I'm not sure—they're so hard to tell apart. I guess there'll always be room in the world for his kind of nastiness, but the rest of us—Lachesis and Ananta and the Nagas—our day is past. We're all finished—retired. There are new gods now."

"But you're still powerful," said Sherahi.

"Oh yes, there are a few tricks, a few illusions, that I can still manage. But mostly I spend my time now just lying in the sun, letting my bones weather out of this rock. Soon they will work their way loose and one by one they will fall to the canyon floor. They'll break into a million pieces and I, who have lived on the earth for uncountable years; I, who fought Thor to a stand-off and killed him in the process; I, who was worshiped and revered by generations of humans; I, Jormungand, the Midgard Serpent, will be no more."

With her black vertical pupils a mere slit in her amber eyes, Sherahi found herself nearly asleep. His voice was so melodic and gently rhythmic. She wished that she were back in Dervish's cavern, but was too sleepy to excuse herself. She would have a little rest now. The nat would understand. He was a kind spirit.

His voice droned on. "But there was a time when I held the earth within my coils, a time before Thor and his silly little hammer—a time before all of them. Those were the days, little serpent. Those were the days."

Within Sherahi's lulled mind his rusty, fossil bones grew flesh and, as if a chiffon scarf had been snatched from a magician's fist, she could see the Midgard Serpent quite clearly now. His muscles were encased in an armor of scales that were as big as tabletops. The serpent was huge—far bigger than anything that Sherahi could comprehend. He stretched around the rock face as far as she could see and his bulk filled the canyon as he writhed and hissed in delight. Sherahi felt her will evaporating as he began to feed on her mind and grow.

"Believe," he commanded. "Believe." His voice boomed like a cataract. Now his body was banded with yellow, red and black rings and his tail was a flat paddle. Sherahi saw the colors that warned of his venomous nature and was suddenly afraid of this huge beast. She remembered what U Vayu had said about the Great Serpent Nats. They could be dangerous—deadly. "They may do you great harm," U Vayu had warned. Sherahi felt light-headed and giddy.

With the sound of a whip cutting the air, the serpent's long, forked tongue lashed to and fro, searching for her. The huge head that had been lifted high in the air above the canyon moved down in sinuous curves, seeking Sherahi on her ledge. When there were still thirty feet separating them, the animal's enormous eyes, slashed by half moons of vertical pupils, fixed on her. The eyes gleamed with recognition and the serpent opened his jaws. "Believe. Believe. Behold me and believe," he commanded as two jets of venom hissed from his array of ivory tusks.

Somehow Sherahi twisted out of the strangle hold that Jormungand had on her mind. Although she knew that his venom could not damage her inwitted apparition, instinctively she ducked and the venom splashed against the rock wall behind her, sending up a cloud of smoke. With the sound of a mountain exploding, the serpent hissed and sent a second volley of venom directly at Sherahi's forehead. But before the venom could hit home and make her his creature, Sherahi realized that this cannibal had been spinning a spell so that he could feast upon her mind. As quickly as possible she sent her mind funneling back to her body, which waited in Dervish's cavern. As she fled the canyon and the lair of the Midgard Serpent, she heard his voice booming furiously. "Come back," he ordered. "I'm hungry. Come back. We can be together forever, little serpent. Don't be afraid. It'll only hurt a little. You'll be immortal—you'll become a part of me." Mixed with his voice was the harsh scream of the vulture. With a shock Sherahi realized that he had nearly engulfed her with all his talk of pottering retirement and old bones rotting in the sun. She shuddered at her close escape and wondered, "What would have happened to Manu and Dervish then? Would Junior have taken care of them? And what about the poor Duchess?" With real annoyance she remembered U Vayu's bragging about inwitting to the Midgard Serpent. "U Vayu lied again," Sherahi thought. "If he'd met Jormungand he might have lost his mind too. Surely he'd have warned me if he'd known how deadly that serpent nat is.

"Yet," Sherahi sighed, "he lied to me. Isn't there anyone that I can trust?"

Sherahi found herself back in Dervish's cavern, coiled about the sleeping coati. She was trembling, and as her senses readjusted to the blackness of the cavern, she heard the rumble of an approaching fire serpent, the screeching of the Duchess and the unmistakable scrape and rustle of many pairs of rat feet. Her questions about humans and the whereabouts of the white crocodiles would have to wait. She hissed a warning into the darkness around her and called to Junior. It would soon be time for them to go after Manu.

Leftrack's Pet Emporium and
Animals International, Ltd

IRA LEFTRACK was so agitated that he paced around his desk talking to himself. "Dogs," he said. "What we need are snake-finding dogs. Maybe bloodhounds. Snakes never go far. That python may still be in the warehouse, though how a snake that size could hide is beyond me."

He called to his secretary in the outer office, "Helga, tell Ehrich to get in here. With all that college education I paid for he should be able to locate a pair of bloodhounds to track this snake."

"Yes, Mr. Leftrack," said Helga and hurried toward the back of the warehouse and the room that now belonged to Ehrich.

It seemed to take Ehrich a long time to appear and Leftrack went out of the office to the chinchilla colony, which the men had finally put to rights. He yanked out a cage. The mother flinched and cowered in one corner while her babies lay dead and blue in another. He pushed the cage back in place violently, not noticing that his action made all of the gray South American rats stiffen in fear. It was the same in all of the cages he examined.

"Damn," thought Leftrack. "They've been scared by all this commotion. Probably won't calm down for months now. The shock may even kill them all." He saw his retirement nest egg going down the drain. "Now Irma will never get that mink coat." Chinchillas were hypersensitive to any sort of disturbance. That's why he'd put their colony in the quietest part of the warehouse—outside his office where he could watch it.

"Damn hooligans," he thought. "If I get my hands on whoever did this, I'll . . . I'll . . . I don't know what I'll do."

And half of the colony was missing—mostly the young ones, as well as the special pedigreed stud that he'd earmarked as the father to his fortune. Leftrack had set a dozen box traps and hoped that tonight he'd recapture the male.

Whoever had gotten into the warehouse last night had done incredible damage: the chinchilla colony all busted open; the window in the toilet broken; animals stolen. The police figured that the culprit entered and escaped through the broken window. The strange thing was that no cash was missing from the strongbox in his desk. Must have been some sort of animal fancier, because only chinchillas, the macaw and the big python from the Culls' room had been taken.

If Leftrack hadn't known Sorensen better, he might have accused him of the robbery. Sorensen was the only one who had a motive for stealing the macaw and the snake. They were his pets and to Leftrack it looked as if the old man had come back, stolen the animals and pushed over the chinchilla colony just for spite. The only real mystery was how Sorensen could have gotten that monster snake out the window. If Sorensen had done it, he must have had accomplices, because the snake weighed at least five hundred pounds. It would have taken a dozen men to control her. The more Leftrack thought about it, the more far-fetched the idea of Sorensen masterminding a burglary became; nevertheless, the detectives from the Fourteenth Precinct were investigating Sorensen's whereabouts at the time of the robbery. Leftrack doubted that it would come to anything. "Still," he told himself, "you never know."

It was just barely possible that the snake was still in the warehouse. They had torn the whole place apart this morning, searching for it and for the macaw. The police had asked Leftrack if it were possible for the snake to have escaped all by itself, followed by the bird. Leftrack had said that although it was highly unlikely, it was possible. If so, the snake would be still lurking in the neighborhood and dogs could find it. Leftrack pleaded with the police not to alert the papers until he was certain that the snake was not still on the premises or nearby. "Escaped snakes never go far," he'd said. "All we need are those dogs. If the snake has escaped, they'll find it."

"Where's my goddamn son?"

Helga returned to find her boss staring grimly at the decimated chinchilla colony. "I can't find Ehrich anywhere," she said.

"Great," said Leftrack. "Just great. I'll have to do it myself—like always. Get me the detectives at the Fourteenth Precinct. We've got to start while the trail is still hot."

In the commotion over the robbery, Leftrack had forgotten all about the coati that had been loose in the warehouse the previous day. But he hadn't forgotten about the man from Hollywood who wanted that big snake. If the dogs didn't find the python, Leftrack would have to tell him that it had died.

Muttering, "Got to keep the lid on this," and visualizing headlines that screamed "MAN-KILLING PYTHON LOOSE"; worrying that the Board of Health might close him down and wondering exactly how much money he had in the bank, Ira Leftrack sighed, "Orchard five-five-eight-seven-eight," in response to the operator's voice, which asked, "Number, please?"

Dervish's Cavern

THE LIGHT HAD GONE from the tunnels of the fire serpent and the Duchess had ceased her pacing. Now she crouched at the bottom of the stairs near Sherahi. "Isn't it time yet?" she nagged. "It's been dark for hours. Are you going to let him sleep all night?"

Sherahi sighed. The Duchess was getting on her nerves. She would have liked to still the bird's endless string of complaints. It would have been so easy: one coil wrapped around that skinny, knobby throat and a single, brief squeeze. Then there would be no more moaning about food and cold and no place to perch. "It would be so very easy. . . ." Sherahi found herself stalking the bird who sat so trustfully in the darkness nearby. Realizing that she was estimating the distance for a strike that would impale, stun and kill the bird, Sherahi shook her head to clear these bloodthirsty ideas. She was angry at herself for letting the Duchess annoy her. The bird seemed to trust her now and it wasn't the macaw's fault that she was so bossy and selfish. If she were still in that jungle that she dreamed of so often, she'd probably be a well-respected member of her flock, not a scrawny caricature of a Thanksgiving dinner come to life. "Humans taught her to behave like this," thought Sherahi. "Perhaps if we ignore her, she'll understand. It might work and, if not, we'll have plenty of time to teach the Duchess better manners."

Using ancient saurian mindspeech, Sherahi called to Junior, telling him to come and be her eyes and ears. It was time for him and Dervish to rescue Manu. Junior's reply came quickly. "I'll be there in a few minutes. I'm busy now."

"This is more important. You must come," insisted Sherahi.

"But, Auntie . . ."

"Now," Sherahi ordered. She didn't like the tone of Junior's voice: self-important and callous. Once he and Dervish were safely on their way to the pet shop, she would inspect his mind again. The changes she had made in his temperament probably needed repairs.

"Wake up, Dervish," she thought, trying to remember the way Manu's mind had formed the chittering language that Dervish understood. She was gratified to feel the warm little animal stir and stretch all four legs out straight. At least he was reliable. She felt him yawn and in a moment he had leaped out of her coils; as she heard him chitter to Junior she knew that the pit viper was encircling his neck. "Junior, make sure that Dervish knows what he's supposed to do," she said to the cascabel.

"All right, all right," said Junior. "Don't be so bossy."

Sherahi definitely did not like the pit viper's tone. In a few moments the answer she had been waiting for came into her mind.

"Dummy here says that he will bring Manu; that he will run with the speed of a spotted cat and the strength of ten antbears. Funny. Huh, Sherahi? I wonder where he got such stupid ideas?"

"Good," said Sherahi, ignoring Junior's remarks. "Go. Be quick and be safe. And Junior," she said, gripping his jagged thoughts in hers, "don't *ever* call Dervish 'dummy' again."

There was no reply from the cascabel and Sherahi sent the message, "Did you hear what I said?"

"Yes, Auntie," came his sulky reply. The pythoness and macaw listened to Dervish patter away and settled down to wait. Through Junior's eyes Sherahi followed the progress of the two animals along the shadowy streets and simultaneously examined Junior's mind.

A light rain had begun to fall and she watched both animals react to it. Neither had ever known rain and Dervish couldn't resist splashing in shallow puddles, leaping into them with both forefeet. The rain was cold and made Junior burrow deeper into Dervish's fur. He hissed in annoyance when Dervish plunged off a curb into one deep puddle and Sherahi had to check his impulse to fang Dervish. As she had expected, his vicious, independent nature was working free. She was thinking about the quickest way to repair her psychological surgery when there was an astonished squawk in the darkness. Instantly her labial pits began quopping, warning her that she and the Duchess were surrounded by a circle of rats.

Not knowing if the Duchess would understand, Sherahi commanded her, "Duchess, get behind me. And be quick about it." She wasn't sure that she'd be able to communicate directly with the macaw and had never tried to do it without Manu's help, but she knew that, without the protection of her feathers or the ability to fly, the Duchess would be an easy mark for these rats. She felt the macaw's scaly claws clamber quickly over her coils and then Sherahi forgot the bird that cowered behind her.

Sherahi knew that the rats could see much better than she could in the dark. After all, that was one of the hallmarks of the mammals. Once, this attribute had enabled them to carve a nighttime niche for themselves in a world that belonged to reptiles. Of course, they couldn't see colors but then, they didn't need to: they lived in a twilight world of dim, subterranean burrows and only emerged at night. So, the rats that formed an intense, furry ring around Sherahi had this advantage over her. And that wasn't all. They were also on home territory and there were a lot of them. The only numbers that Sherahi knew were "one, two, three, many" and she knew that she was surrounded by many, many rats. "How many is unimportant," she thought. "They'll all be dead soon."

Although she couldn't actually see them, her labial pits and Jacobson's organs easily located the rats for her. She could sense the warmest parts of their bodies as well as their approximate ages and even their sex. From what her special sense organs told her, it was as if she actually saw their coarsely furred bodies trembling with excitement as they stood around her, waiting for the fight to begin. She saw them pause, hunchbacked and scaly-tailed. Their whiskers were erect and their neck fur bristled. They rattled their incisors, ready to pounce. Ready to bite.

Sherahi knew the ways of the rat tribe and didn't wait for one brave and foolish would-be hero to spring and try to straddle her neck and sever her backbone. Like any rodent his tactic would be to try to immobilize her in this way. Sherahi had seen giant snakes that had been attacked by hordes of rats and she knew that once she was powerless they would taunt and torture her at their leisure. It was a slow death, dealt by their razorlike incisors. If Sherahi had never encountered rats, she might have been frightened—

might have tried to confuse them—but she had fought off many packs of bandicoots in her days at the pagoda and now her heart swelled with excitement. By the time this was over this rat tribe would know what an angry python could do.

All these thoughts flashed through Sherahi's mind and then, without thinking about what she did, she attacked. She seized the rat closest to her and snapped his body between her jaws. She stunned, crushed and dropped him in almost the same movement. Pain and death caught the rat by surprise and he died with his hind legs kicking frantically. Once she had dropped him, he kicked once or twice more and then stopped. His demise had no effect on the other rats: their minds were fixed on attacking the giant serpent.

A second rat dashed in to challenge Sherahi and she dealt him the same fatal blow. Then rats came faster, sometimes two at a time, squealing to one another in high excitement. Soon Sherahi lost count of how many she snap-stunned and dropped. No one had ever taught her how to battle with rats; she was guided by ancient instinct. It was as if she had discovered a suit of dusty armor in an attic, donned the breastplate and reforged links to fierce, forgotten ancestors.

The Duchess was terrified. She cowered behind the great snake, put her head beneath her wing and listened fearfully to the thumps and squeals of the rats as Sherahi fought soundlessly and furiously, sometimes grabbing an opponent and hurling him against the wall, sometimes down onto the floor. The bodies made a solid plopping sound and the Duchess heard the knock of bone against cement and knew that brains and blood spilled in the dust. Other rats were squeezed in Sherahi's expert coils, their long incisors gnawing impotently as they gasped for air. One suffocated just after the pressure of Sherahi's deadly embrace made his eyeballs start from their sockets. The Duchess imagined all of this and more and prayed that Sherahi would win or that the rats would go away, and hoped that, once it was over, Sherahi wouldn't kill her, too.

Sherahi whirled to grab the last rat and felt his tail slip through her mouth as he ran away. She thought of going after him, but then decided not to. The survivor would carry news back to the rest of his tribe—news that a monster now lurked in this tunnel. The Culls would be safe until the rats forgot what happened here tonight. Then they would be back.

The exercise had made Sherahi hungry and she nosed against the limp, warm bodies of the rats that littered the floor and began to eat one of them. She would eat her fill and leave the rest for Dervish. He liked rat flesh. Her mouth was half full of fur when she heard the Duchess say, "Can I come out now? Are they all gone?"

"It's safe," Sherahi's thoughts hissed in the Duchess's mind, and Sherahi returned to her meal.

She felt the Duchess's toes gripping her coils as she edged out of the corner. From the unsteady way that the bird walked, Sherahi knew that she was in shock.

"Come on, Duchess," Sherahi's thoughts said to the bird. "It's all over now. They won't be back for a long while." There was no reply from the bird and Sherahi wondered if she'd understood. Feeling guilty of depriving her of psychological support for so long, Sherahi sent the macaw a wave of comfort. As she alternately inched the teeth on each side of her jaw over the rat's body, she scryed the bird's quick-moving mind and saw the shapes of fear and of hunger. "How stupid of me," thought Sherahi. "The Duchess is almost dead of starvation. No wonder she is so bad-tempered. She must eat.

"But what can she eat?" Sherahi asked herself. "There aren't any of the seeds or fruits that she likes. There are only rats here. Maybe someday Dervish can find other food for her, but that will be risky. He might be seen and followed or even killed. And besides—she's hungry now. If only I could convince her that rats are delicious. After all, they are the food of the gods. Maybe I can fool her into thinking that she likes them."

Sherahi spun the image of a soft-feathered, yellow-eyed, hook-billed bird into the Duchess's mind. She also sent the memory of nights spent hunting in the dark for warm-blooded prey. Delicious, musky-smelling prey. She made the Duchess remember dropping out of a starry sky and silently striking, feet first, into the back muscles of a careless young muskrat.

The Duchess felt her talons grip and stifle the rodent's breath and, screaming fiercely, she killed him without effort. Then she rose, carrying her burden back to the rocky shelter high on the cliff face that was her winter home. The Duchess imagined the warm body of her kill in her talons and when Sherahi picked up one of the dead rats and dropped it at the Duchess's feet, she had the satisfaction of seeing the entranced bird spread her thinly feathered wings and mantle her prey. With wide-open beak she hissed at Sherahi and said coldly, "Get away from me, serpent. This is *my* kill."

Sherahi hadn't expected the bird's mind to be quite so malleable and she was startled by the fierce predator that spoke to her out of the darkness. Suddenly Sherahi found the situation funny and, as she withdrew to engulf a second rat, she chuckled over the macaw-turned-huntress. If she would continue to feed on rats, it would certainly simplify things. Sherahi was pleased with her success. Normally the Duchess would have recoiled from the touch of the unfamiliar, warm, limp body. She would have stalked away, her claws scraping the cement, and in the dark tunnel would have shrieked and squawked, cherishing her anger, half afraid that Sherahi might turn and attack her. Now that the Duchess was convinced that she, too, was a killer she might feel more at ease in these caverns. "She probably won't be quite so afraid of me," thought Sherahi. "Maybe she'll even fight if the rats come again."

The bird was certainly hungry and Sherahi could hear the snapping of leg bones as the transformed macaw devoured her dinner. This deception would do her no harm. She had to eat something or she would die and rats were the only food around here. Besides, a change of diet might even improve her temperament and make her feathers grow back more quickly. Then she could fly back to her jungle and leave the other Culls to find their way to Sandeagozu. Sherahi hoped that her spell had been strong enough to make the Duchess hoot like an owl and, as the second rat slid down her throat, she chuckled at the thought in her silent, mirthless fashion.

In the excitement, Sherahi had forgotten the rescue party and after the second rat was comfortably within her stomach she called to Junior. She was surprised to hear him very nearby. The fight with the rats must have taken longer than she had thought, because the three animals were already descending the outer steps to the cavern. In a few moments Dervish, Manu, and Junior were at the top of the stairs above Sherahi and the Duchess.

"They're right down here, Manu," chittered Dervish. "Isn't this a great place? We'll be safe and dry. Come on, Manu, shake all that rain out of your fur. You'll get sick if you don't dry yourself."

Sherahi heard Junior sigh and mutter, "Come on, stupid. Can't you hurry it up? All this bother about a little rain and a sick monkey. I've got things to do." She was relieved to find that Manu and Dervish had not been harmed by the cascabel. Now she could make him more tractable at her leisure.

The wet langur was half-pulled down the stairs by Dervish. His eyes hadn't quite adjusted to the blackness and he felt confused and suddenly very dizzy and unwell. "Not so fast, Dervish," he said, and then felt something soft give beneath his foot. Manu slipped on one of the rat carcasses, lost his balance and fell down the dark staircase. When the other Culls reached him he did not respond. Sherahi knew that, although the spell that she had woven had gotten him out of the warehouse under his own power and allowed him to reach these tunnels, it had failed at the last moment. But Manu was safe from Ehrich Leftrack's silver knives. If he lived, he would at least be free and on the way to Sandeagozu.

Leftrack's Pet Emporium and
Animals International, Ltd

"HURRY UP, CAN'T YOU?" asked Ira Leftrack.

The blue-uniformed dog handler was used to people who thought they knew his job better than he did. He regarded the nervous man with the pencil-thin mustache for a moment, while he held the leads of the three, patiently sniffing dogs.

"The dogs do things in their own good time," he said, regarding them with affection. "You can't hurry 'em. They've got to get the scent up into their brains. Once they know what they're looking for, we can take them outside.

"Now, why don't you let us do our job? If this rain has left any sort of trail at all, the dogs'll find it."

Leftrack watched the three sober-looking dogs sniffing at Manu's cage in the Culls' room and hoped that somehow they might find something—anything. They had searched everywhere, after having been introduced to the smell of the python and the macaw, and had trailed each animal to the toilet. But there the trail seemed to end and Leftrack had watched the methodical trainer go outside with the dogs several times. The result was always the same, though. The trails dwindled in the alley behind the pet shop.

Last night the warehouse had been robbed again, even though Leftrack had had the window repaired. Now the old langur was missing from his cage. Nothing else in the warehouse had been touched and all of the circumstantial evidence seemed to point to Birger Sorensen. But the man had a tight alibi: he had been at a card game in Staten Island all night. Three relatives swore that Sorensen had spent the evening with them, losing at canasta. Although the police believed them, Leftrack suspected they were lying. Without any other evidence, their testimonies would stand. The detectives had looked for fingerprints around the alley window, but they could find only strange scratches on and below the windowsill. If Sorensen had stolen the animals, he was hiding them in some secret place. The police had searched his home in Staten Island and found nothing. It seemed to be a dead end and the police admitted that they were baffled.

Twenty minutes later the dogs were in the alley, sniffing around the garbage cans again. It was a cold, raw day and the drenching rain that had started last night had continued through the morning. Leftrack watched for a while, hoping to hear the dogs bay with excitement, telling their handler that they had located the trail. They worked their way down to the side street in one direction, but there was no smell of langur. The officer and his three dogs disappeared down the side street and searched diligently on both sides of the street for blocks. Leftrack followed behind, watching the dogs strain at their leashes, hoping for the sign of a trail. He wanted to be there if they found something, because he didn't want the dogs to harm his animals. But there was nothing except gray sky, cold wind and rain that soaked his feet. Thoroughly wet, with their senses partially numbed, the dogs returned to the garbage cans below the warehouse window and searched in the opposite direction, but after three hours of walking in the cold rain, the officer decided that the dogs had had enough. He told Leftrack that there didn't seem to be any sort of trail. If there had been one, these dogs would have found it. Whoever stole the animals must have taken them away in a car. "Sorry, Mr. Leftrack. I'll have to report this to headquarters."

Ira Leftrack offered the officer a cup of hot coffee and tried to ingratiate himself. "What happens now?" he asked.

"Well, I make my report to headquarters and, unless one of the detectives has a bright idea or unless the property in question turns up somewhere, there isn't anything else that we can do. Of course, it is possible that the animals are still at large. With the cold and the rain and all, their trail could have been washed away. I'll have to make a report to headquarters and the public will have to be warned. That's a dangerous snake that might be loose. I've thought plenty about it while I was out with the dogs. It's over thirty feet long and mighty strong. What if it grabs a little kid or an old lady?"

"Officer," said Leftrack, suddenly very serious. "Let's not be hasty. It could cause a panic in this city if people thought that a man-eating python were loose."

"That's not my worry, Mr. Leftrack. I've got to go by regulations and make my report to headquarters."

"But don't you see what the press will do with that kind of story? Think of the headlines. People will be scared to go into the streets. It wouldn't be sensible to scare everyone like that. You yourself said that the animals were probably taken away by car. Wasn't that your explanation for not finding a trail?"

The officer nodded over his cup of coffee.

"Well, that must mean that someone has them under lock and key. They're not running about loose."

"That's only one possibility. They could have escaped. I admit that it seems unlikely, but I'll have to include it in my report."

"But how far could they have gotten? Wouldn't your dogs have found them? Do you want the people to think that the New York City Police Department, with their specially trained bloodhounds, have been unable to find a thirty-foot python, a scarlet macaw and a monkey? It seems to me, Officer, that you and I have a common interest in keeping that information just between us. Besides," Leftrack looked meaningfully at the policeman, "you wouldn't find me ungrateful for your interest in the public good."

The officer patted the neck of one of the dogs that sat at his feet, and regarded Leftrack. He took another sip of coffee while Leftrack continued, "Times are difficult for all of us. Believe you me, I know how hard it is for a man to raise a family."

"Well, we do have a scholarship fund at the Precinct House. Contributions to that are always welcome."

Ira Leftrack took out his checkbook and said, "To whom shall I make this out—cash?"

"That'll be fine," said the officer.

"Let this be my contribution to your fund," said Leftrack, tearing off the check and handing it to the policeman. "I've got a boy in school myself. I know how expensive that is. And I'm glad, Officer, that we've reached an understanding about how we'll handle this." He smiled and reached into his wallet and took out two twenty-dollar bills. "And this is just a little something for the dogs there. They've certainly done a fine job today. Maybe you can get them an extra-special dinner." He patted the dogs and said, "Pleasure doing business with you, Officer."

When the man and his dogs had gone, Leftrack sat down at his desk. He'd done everything that he could to make sure that the press didn't learn anything. This afternoon he'd have bars installed on that bathroom window. Now, all he had to do was tell that maniac in Hollywood that the snake had died and the entire matter would be closed.

Dervish's Cavern

IT TOOK A LONG time for Manu to recover. For many days he hardly moved at all. After he regained consciousness it was a long time before he was strong enough to eat anything more than the nutritious paste of minced rat flesh that the Duchess painstakingly prepared for him. In those months the Culls noticed that the tunnels had grown cooler and now it was cold all the time. They huddled together at night for warmth and in the daytime Junior hunted, bringing down huge Norse or Black rats for the others, and killing baby rats for his own meals.

Under the Duchess's ministrations, Manu regained strength and the day eventually came when he was well enough to scramble hand over hand up onto the supports of the fire serpent's tunnel. Except for the grime of the tunnels, which turned his silver fur a streaky gray, he looked better than he had in years. Younger. Stronger. The months also brought a transformation to the Duchess. She no longer looked quite like a butchered chicken, but was covered with soft, scarlet feathers. She had been so concerned with Manu's recovery that she hadn't thought of plucking out her feathers in weeks and she had grown so used to the collar that she no longer fussed with it. It had become a part of her new plumage. The spell that Sherahi had cast over the macaw had lasted only a few weeks, but in that time it had taught the Duchess that rat flesh was edible and she was no longer the whining bird that had walked away from Leftrack's Pet Emporium.

As the months in the cavern passed, Dervish reached his full adult size but retained his cheery, inquisitive nature. He was still devoted to Manu and while the langur convalesced he had lain at his side, hoping to be asked to do a favor. He would have done anything to make the langur feel better and none of the Culls was happier than Dervish when Manu began to recover from the effects of Ehrich Leftrack's poison. Sherahi explained what Ehrich Leftrack had tried to do and they all agreed that, no matter what happened, they would never go back to Leftrack's pet shop.

The months had also produced changes in Junior. Fed on a steady diet of suckling rats, he was now more than two feet long. He had shed several times and now had four segments attached to the button at the tip of his tail. He could produce an audible rattle that frightened Dervish so much that instinctively he froze in his tracks whenever he heard it. Junior was a loner and spent most of his time prowling in the tunnel of the fire serpent, looking for rats' nests to plunder. He was plainly jealous of the way that the others favored Dervish, and Sherahi had found that, as the cascabel grew, she needed to repair her psychic transformations nearly every day to keep him tractable. But she had little else to do and the process had become routine.

Sherahi had spent most of the time worrying about the white crocodiles. She had been disappointed to find that the holy reptiles were not nearby. Even though she had thought it unlikely, she had hoped that these tunnels belonged to them. Now she was certain that they were some sort of underground road for humans and had nothing to do with the white crocodiles. Once Manu had regained his health, she had withdrawn more and more from the daily pursuits of the Culls. Except for mastering the art of mindspeaking with Dervish and the Duchess, Sherahi spent all her mental energy on locating the beasts that would have the secret to the whereabouts of Sandeagozu.

Every day Sherahi lay apart from the rest of the group, scanning for these elusive reptiles. She had had no luck for many weeks and had begun to doubt that she would ever be able to find them. They certainly hid themselves well, or perhaps they had erected barriers to any penetration, friendly or otherwise. At one point in her search she had grown so frustrated that she had begun to doubt the reality of the white crocodiles. "Is it possible that I made them up in a daydream?" she wondered. She scanned for the nearest crocodilian intelligence and found that a Nile crocodile at the Bronx Zoo confirmed that the white crocodiles did, indeed, exist beneath this city and that they were the wisest and most holy of all beasts. "They do not reveal themselves to all," the captive croc had said.

So, Sherahi began her scans again, knowing that the Culls could not stay in these tunnels forever. For one thing, the supply of Norse and of Black rats had begun to dwindle. One day Junior reported that he had seen the Blacks moving en masse away from this place. He had chuckled over the thought that he had scared them off, but Sherahi worried and hoped that there would be enough of the larger, Norse rat tribe to feed the Culls until she had found the white crocodiles. The temperature was another source of concern. It was very cold in the tunnels now and one day snow filtered down onto the platform of the fire serpent from the grating above. It was clear that the Culls needed a warmer shelter. They would have to move soon.

The Culls had lived in the caverns of the fire serpent for three months when Sherahi received the first faint signal from what she thought might be a white crocodile. It sounded like a sort of lullaby. And, though Sherahi wasn't quite sure of its meaning, she caught a glimpse of a mysterious singer lying gaunt and phosphorescently white in a steamy, wet place deep below the city. Something told Sherahi that the singer was a female and very happy. She seemed to be alone and, when the lullaby stopped, Sherahi guessed that she was outside the mental barriers that the rest of the white crocodiles had erected to guard their territory.

The next night Sherahi sent Junior and Dervish out to try to find an entrance to a different sort of tunnel. "There's got to be another tunnel nearby," Sherahi told them. "Please try to find it."

Although he acted standoffish, Junior coiled obediently about Dervish's neck and the two went into the upper world. Dervish found that it had snowed outside and slid down snowbanks with delight, much to the disgust of Junior, who coiled even more tightly around the coati's neck and ordered, "Quit the clowning, Dervish. I don't like this cold."

In a short time the two animals found an entrance to a tunnel that was below a grate set in the street. Dervish was able to slither between the bars of the grate and found that the tunnel below was both dry and big enough to allow even Sherahi to enter. A short distance from the place where the two animals had entered, the tunnel fed into a larger one; using Junior's labial pits, Sherahi found that faint heat was coming from the tunnel that branched to the right. The new tunnel was large enough for Dervish to walk with his tail fully erect and, although there was a trickle of water running along the bottom of the pit, there was a shallow shelf along one wall. The animals would be able to travel without getting wet.

But best of all, Sherahi found that the song of the female white crocodile was stronger within this tunnel. "That must mean that it will lead us to the nests of the white crocodiles," Sherahi thought. Elated, Sherahi told Junior to bring Dervish back. She was careful to include Junior in her praise and said, "You have both done well. We will leave tomorrow night and find the white crocodiles."

CHAPTER SEVEN

T HE CULLS LEFT the caverns of the fire serpent the next night. In the months since they had been in their subterranean hiding place they had seldom gone to the upper level, preferring instead the platform at the bottom of the second set of stairs, where Sherahi had battled the rats. That platform had become their home and, except for Junior, who hunted for rats all through the adjacent tunnels, they had confined themselves to this small portion of the abandoned subway stop. Thus, they were on guard as they crept in single file up the stairs to the upper world and the tunnel that Sherahi was certain led to the white crocodiles.

Sherahi had warned the others of what might await them on their journey to the storm sewer. Even though it was relatively nearby, they might encounter rats, cats, dogs, and humans. "We've come too far," she said, "to be stopped now." It might be dangerous, but they could no longer waste time in the tunnels of the fire serpent. It was getting cold and, besides, all were anxious to get to Sandeagozu and to do that the Culls had to get to the tunnels that would lead them to the white crocodiles. Sherahi had found it impossible to contact these odd beasts in the normal reptilian manner, so the Culls would have to travel to them.

Guided by Dervish's scent marks, they easily located the second set of stairs, which led to the entrance and its worn, wooden barricade. Dervish and Junior were in the lead and, since Dervish knew the way, he wriggled beneath the barricade and waited on the other side for the others. It had snowed all through the day and the stairs were covered with a deep drift. From around his neck he heard the serpent hiss and complain, "Oh Dervish, don't start playing in that white stuff again. It makes me so cold." The coati checked his impulse to roll on his back in the drift and wondered why Junior was always so crabby now.

"Come on, you two," Dervish said to Manu and the Duchess and, remembering what Sherahi had said about rats, cats and humans, he cautiously made a trail through the drift that led up to the street.

Manu and the Duchess had been in the darkness for so long that both were dazzled by the light that spilled into the cavern entrance from the streetlight above. When they could see without squinting, first Manu and then the Duchess wriggled beneath the wooden barricade. "I don't know how I'm going to get up there," she said, looking at the flight of snow-covered stairs that stretched up almost as high as she could see.

"Don't worry, my dear," said Manu. "We won't go fast, but we'll get there."

Sherahi waited behind the barricade, watching the langur and macaw toil up the stairs. Manu climbed up easily and then, bracing himself as well as he could against the slippery snow, he held onto a ledge as the bird grasped the stump of his tail in her bill. Scrabbling with both feet, she climbed up to join Manu on the stairstep above. Shortly, the two animals had joined Dervish and Junior in the snow at the top of the stairs and after checking to see that no enemies were about, first Dervish with Junior, then the Duchess and finally Manu raced to the storm drain that opened in the curb across the street.

Dervish had been there before and leaped down through the hole at the rear of the drain. He knew that he would land in a round, dry cement chamber and that a dark tunnel branched off from this. Manu was next to arrive. With effort he lowered himself below the grate. Looking down, he saw Dervish and Junior waiting below and released his grasp on the bars of the grate. The Duchess was more cautious. She didn't like the thought of going underground again and wished she could fly off into the snowy night but, again, she could see no jungle on any horizon. Streetlights and dark buildings crowded all around. Her feet were cold and that decided her more than anything. Hunching to make herself as small as possible, she ducked below the grate and, holding on with her bill, hesitantly lowered herself into the darkness, feeling with her claws for support. Manu's hands grabbed her and she released her hold on the bar. Now the four of them waited for Sherahi.

The pythoness had decided that she should be the last up the stairs and had urged the others to follow Dervish and to get into the new tunnel as quickly as possible. This was partially because she feared that their luck might not last. "Only one human has to see us and then we'll be pursued and hunted and perhaps even recaptured," she worried. Sherahi did not intend to ever let this happen. She had decided that if humans interfered, she would kill them as a last resort. She had insisted on being the last up the stairs because she knew that she was the slowest and she would be a danger for the others. If they had to wait for her, all of the Culls might be seen. So, she had sent the others ahead and watched them clamber up the snowy stairs while she thought about the cold.

Exposure to the snow and the freezing temperature would slow all of her body processes and she would only have a short time before each movement became difficult. Her thoughts would slow, too, and if she remained cold too long, it would kill her.

There was one way that she could keep warm, though. She could twitch her deep body muscles in the way that female Burmese pythons did when they were brooding and incubating a clutch of eggs. This continual muscular twitching would make her almost as warm-blooded as a hummingbird—and as active as a coffin-headed mamba that had basked in the sun for hours. In a sheltered place, Sherahi would have been able to keep her body temperature elevated for two or three months—the time it takes for a clutch of eggs to hatch. Ordinarily she would never have considered using this special method of temperature control, because it required too much energy. Rather, she would have relied upon the mundane saurian method of alternately basking in and hiding from the sun. It would have warmed her enough to easily hunt for food, escape her enemies and digest her meals. Sherahi didn't like wasting her fat reserves on temperature control but, unless she did, she would be trapped in the fire serpent's cavern until spring came.

So, as she waited for the other Culls to climb the stairs and hurry across the street, she coiled in a tight mound, keeping as much of her length off the cold cement as possible, and began to twitch muscles deep within her body.

She watched the Duchess's ragged red tail feathers disappear from the topmost step and knew that the bird was walking awkwardly toward the street drain. Then Sherahi scanned for Junior, who was already safely within it. Through his eyes she saw Manu and then the Duchess enter the chamber below the grate. Satisfied that the others were safe and feeling a little light-headed from the surge of body heat, Sherahi began to climb the snow-covered stairs.

Her giant coils heaved up each step and Sherahi methodically climbed and twitched, climbed and twitched. The falling snow melted upon her sleek, warm scales and she watched the streetlamp light glisten on the snow all around. It looked as if some heavenly fish had shaken its skin, scattering clouds of small scales that twinkled in the lamplight. They seemed to invite Sherahi to pause and wonder as the light played upon them. She stopped and stared.

Sherahi was in the middle of the staircase when she came to her senses. She discovered that, although it was the last thing she had wanted to do, she had stopped moving and was lying in the snowdrift that trailed down the stairs. She had stopped twitching and for some reason had become fixated on the patterns of individual snowflakes. "This will never do," she said to herself and, contracting her deep muscles again and again, the snake resumed her climb. "I must get to the tunnel. The others are waiting," she thought. "I can't stop here."

Ignoring the finely detailed snow crystals that danced around her, Sherahi concentrated on climbing the stairs. She climbed and twitched and thanked elephant-headed Ganesha for the well-fed rats that had lived in the fire serpent's tunnel. Their bodies were giving her the strength to fight upward and their fat helped insulate her from the cold that was only now beginning to numb her broad belly plates. She climbed and twitched and tried not to think about the cold, but it needled into her mind and she thought, "Once we are in Sandeagozu, none of us will ever be cold again. We'll always be warm. And there'll be lots of food . . . and there'll be lots of friends . . . and there won't be any bars on the cages. It'll be like being free, only . . . better." She found that she had stopped moving again, this time only momentarily, but even that was dangerous. She shook her big head and tried to concentrate. "The cold must be doing queer things to my mind," she thought and repeated, "warmth, food, friends . . . warmth, food, friends . . . warmth, food, friends," over and over until her head finally reached the top of the staircase and she paused for breath.

To her alarm she found that she couldn't pull her length up the stairs and form the loose mound that was her characteristic resting posture. She could feel her backbones trying to move, but her yards of thick muscle did not budge. She could no longer feel the hard-packed snow beneath her belly. If she could have formed a coil, it would have gotten some of her body off the cold snow, but as it was, she was forced to stop stretched out with half of her length still trailing down the stairs. It was getting more difficult to twitch her deep body muscles and Sherahi noticed that her breathing was slower. She felt sleepy and the streetlamp light was doing strange things with the snow again. Now it spread a carpet of crystal shards over the drifts. Sherahi looked at her body as it trailed down the subway stairs, and saw that she, too, was covered with snow. The flakes no longer melted on her flanks, and she fancied that she had been transformed into a snow serpent with crystalline scales and fangs that held the light, chill touch of death.

The street drain was only a body length away, on the other side of the street, but it might as well have been on the other side of the world. Sherahi could see the snow partially melted around the dark hole that the others had entered and knew that they were waiting for her. She wanted to hurry and join them, but the cold had drained her of energy. She would have never left the caverns of the fire serpent if she had known that this would be so tiring. She felt limp, like a piece of wet rope—very cold, heavy, sodden rope. "This will never do," she told herself. "I've got to get over there." But the part of her brain that thought those words no longer controlled her body and she had the sensation of splitting into two minds: one hovered above and calmly watched the snow serpent try to contract her muscles and raise her temperature again; the other was cold and so sleepy that she didn't realize that the thuds that her jawbones passed to the ears inside her skull were footsteps until it was almost too late. Surprised, she looked up and saw two humans hurrying across the street. "How did they get so close?" she thought. Sherahi looked for a place to hide, but everything was covered with snow. She couldn't go back down the stairs. They'd surely see her and then she'd never be able to climb up again. She was so tired. If only she were warmer, she could surround herself with a shield of confusion that would hide her from the two humans, or she could call to Junior for help. But both took a supple, active mind and hers was as stiff as frozen leather. She couldn't even manage to send emotions into the minds of these humans. Like a fawn left by its mother in a sun-dappled forest, or a bronzed frog who freezes in shallow water, hoping to fool the stalking heron's eye, Sherahi did the only thing that she could do. It was also the single thing she did not want to do. She lay motionless in the snow and prayed that the humans would quickly pass and not see her.

The couple stopped at the abandoned subway station and the girl whined, "See. See, I told you, Morris. Why don't you ever listen to me? This station's closed—it's been closed for years. We've come all this way for nothing and now the next nearest one's way over on Canal. My suede pumps are ruined and my feet are frozen. I can't even feel my toes anymore. We should have called a cab. *That* would have been the smart thing to do."

Cold and miserable, the girl looked down at the barricade that blocked the stairs and then up at her companion. She hugged her thin coat tighter and wished that she'd worn galoshes instead of these thin-soled pumps. But galoshes made you look as if you'd just come in from the barn and she'd wanted to impress the other girls at the social-club dance. If only Morris' car hadn't gone dead, her feet would be warm and dry. If only he hadn't insisted upon taking her home. If only she'd gone with that swell Jimmy McAndrews instead of stupid Morris Weiner. This was all his fault. It was the last time she'd ever see him, that was for sure.

Snowflakes had frozen onto his spectacles and Morris couldn't see very well. She waited for an answer, while Morris dithered in his eggheaded way. "Such an Einstein," Shirley Hagenbloom thought. "Jimmy McAndrews would have known what to do *and* would have done it in a minute. I'm sure of that. Morris Weiner will be buried in ten feet of snow while I freeze to death on the corner of Eighteenth and Seventh. Why do I always get these weak sisters?" she asked herself.

To bring some sensation to her numbed feet, the girl stomped against the snowy pavement. One high heel crashed down next to Sherahi's head and without thinking about it, without knowing where the energy came from, the giant snake hissed and raised her head from the snowdrift where she had been hiding. She opened her mouth and, as the snow sparkled in the lamplight all about her, she warned the girl to be more careful about where she put her feet and those spikes she had on her shoes. As soon as she'd reared up, Sherahi regretted it, but by then it was too late. The cold had dulled her brain and only instinct guided her now.

The two humans heard a hissing behind them and turned to see a huge serpent only inches away. Its mouth was open and it flashed rows of white teeth; its vermilion tongue lashed at them. It was poised to attack.

The girl forgot her frozen feet and screamed.

"Oh, my God!" said her companion and grabbed her arm. He pulled her behind him as he ran down the street. For once in his life Morris Weiner made a decision and yelled, "Run! Goddamn it, Shirley. Come on. Stop screaming and run!"

When they reached the middle of the block he looked back, saw that the snake was not following and stopped. The girl collapsed into his arms, sobbing hysterically and tugging his lapels. "It isn't going to get us, is it, Morris?"

"No," Morris panted. "It's still at the corner." He could see the enormous serpent still standing erect in the lamplight. He watched as it lowered its head and disappeared into a shadow at the curb.

"Morris, I think I'm going to be sick or faint or something."

"Not now, Shirley. Just wait till we can find a drugstore. Can you hold on till then?"

"I don't know. Oh God, I wish I were home."

He put his arm around her and half-carried her toward the lights of a neighborhood bar, which shone blue and red through the falling snow. While he trudged through the snow he thought out loud, saying, "That thing could have killed us. It was trying to kill us. What was it? Snakes don't get that big, do they? Its head was a foot long and its body was like a telephone pole. God only knows how long it was. It almost got you, didn't it, Shirley?"

She replied and he wondered to himself, "What could I have done if it had bitten her?" The thought of the enormous coils strangling poor, thin Shirley was too awful and Morris pushed it from his mind. He put his arm around her and concentrated on hurrying toward the bar.

They were a half block away when Shirley said, "Morris, don't you think we'd better tell the police? That snake could kill somebody."

"Yeah, we'll tell them. We'll tell everybody, but nobody's ever going to believe us. They'll think we're crazy or something."

After the excitement Sherahi felt strong enough to cross the street. She entered the storm drain as quickly as she could. She was relieved that the round subterranean chamber below the iron grate was much warmer than the street above. Now she had the strength to form a resting coil and, after twitching her deep muscles repeatedly, she was able to raise her temperature to a tolerable level. She was thinking more clearly and began to respond to the others' questions. "Humans have seen me," she said. "I think they may even know that I came down here. We must leave this place and travel deep within these tunnels to a place where they can't find us. I frightened those two humans, but others may come looking for us."

"I could make sure that they never tell anyone what they saw," Junior hissed in a sly, quiet voice.

"No, Junior," she said. "That isn't necessary. Perhaps sometime we will have to rely upon your talents, but now we must find somewhere safe to hide. We can't kill all the humans. There are too many of them. The white crocodiles have lived beneath this city for many, many years and in all that time they have never been seen by humans. If we can get to them we will be safe. But we must start now. Our enemies will be looking for us soon and by the time those two recover from their fright and tell someone about us, we must be far away from here."

Sherahi was quiet for a moment, listening, and then she said in her elegant mindspeech, "I'll go first and listen for the song that I told you about." She undulated away from the group a short distance and said into their minds, "It *is* much stronger here and the singer can't be too far away. Manu, you follow me; and Duchess, hold onto Manu's tail. Dervish, you and Junior will be last. Junior, your part is especially important. You must be our rear guard and watch for anyone who might follow. No matter what comes, human or animal, you must cover us with a screen of confusion—the way I taught you. You could use a bad smell, or noise, or fear of the walls closing in, but you must make the screen strong enough to hide us.

"And remember: from now on we must be silent. We don't know what kind of enemies are down here. If humans come, we'll have plenty of notice: they always make lots of noise. They've forgotten how to move without a sound."

For a moment the Culls looked at each other and then the Duchess said in a soft contralto cheep, "I'm scared."

"Don't be, Duchess," said Sherahi. "Look at how well we've done. We're out of the pet shop; we've been free and living on our own for months. We're all healthy. Look at you, Duchess, you even look like a bird again. And look at Manu—has he ever been stronger? We're closer to Sandeagozu than we've ever been before. We don't have the time to be scared; we're going to find the white crocodiles."

"Couldn't you do something to make us braver?" said the Duchess.

"No, Duchess. I don't think so. I could fool you into thinking you're some other kind of animal, but you don't need my charades. You've got your own kind of courage now."

Sherahi was warm and she slithered rapidly down the dark tunnel that led away from the storm drain. Her labial pits received queer, warm air currents from someplace far ahead and from time to time she heard the song the female white crocodile sang to the embryos that grew within the dozen large eggs that she guarded.

Sherahi slithered as rapidly as she could through the tunnel that sloped down and away from the street drain. Before she had traveled three body lengths the tunnel abruptly joined a much larger one and if Sherahi had been a smaller snake she would have tumbled five feet to the bottom of this next, larger tunnel. She sent a silent mental warning to Manu to grab hold of the tip of her tail and, feeling his small, warm hand respond, she turned into the larger tunnel. She found that it was even darker, but the space felt different—not nearly as enclosed as the tunnel that led from the street drain.

Sherahi told the others to wait while she investigated. She discovered that this new tunnel was about three times larger—"big enough for a human to walk upright in," she thought, "while one could only slither on his belly through the tunnel from the storm drain." Although the first tunnel had been dry, there was a trickle of foul-smelling water in the bottom of the new, larger tunnel. Curiously, this new tunnel sloped upward ever so slightly.

Sherahi didn't fancy the thought of traveling through the putrid water in the bottom of the tunnel and knew that it would give the Duchess a fit. She was happy to find a narrow shelf carved into the left-hand wall. The shelf was high up on the wall where the storm-drain tunnel entered and Sherahi realized that the Culls could walk along it and avoid wading in the foul-smelling trickle in the pit of the tunnel. Sherahi wriggled the tip of her tail, which was still in Manu's hand, giving the signal to move ahead.

The Culls traveled for hours along the shelf of the black tunnel, each holding on to the animal in front. Having spent three months in the fire serpent's caverns, they were accustomed to darkness and none of them was particularly bothered by it. Once or twice Dervish stepped on the Duchess's tail feathers and received a sharp peck on the skull. He whined an apology and was more careful where he put his feet after that. Other than this incident, their passage through the large tunnel was unremarkable. It was very dark and the water that flowed in the pit below smelled bad, but they soon became used to it. At regular intervals the large tunnel was joined by smaller tributaries and the Culls soon realized that the tunnel from the storm drain had been like these. Each of the tributary tunnels must have had a round chamber at the end and a gate above that led to the street. The Duchess and Manu didn't like being underground and felt slightly claustrophobic, especially when the Duchess thought about how far beneath the earth they were. The thought of the ceiling collapsing frightened her and she began gasping for breath. Manu felt his tail being pinched in her beak and said gently, "Duchess, why are you biting me?"

She stopped and said, "I don't like this place. What if the ceiling falls in on us?"

The next time that they passed a tributary drain Manu pointed upward and the Duchess saw light in the chamber at the end of it. She realized that they could escape from this place any time they wanted to and thought, "Maybe it's not exactly like being buried alive."

"That's number twenty-one," said Manu. "Count them as we pass. It'll show you that we're getting somewhere."

As they continued along the narrow shelf of the large tunnel, Sherahi saw that all of the tributary tunnels seemed to be lit from above. "It must be daylight now," she thought. Faint rumblings and clatterings reached them from the street drains. Once they heard a newsboy crying, "Papers, get your morning papers. Killer snake on the loose—python terrifies city," and the Culls hurried away toward the next tributary drain. "If we're going to be followed," Sherahi thought as she slithered in the darkness, "it will happen soon." She increased her pace and the Culls hurried toward the white crocodiles even faster.

The animals kept shuffling along, anxiously listening to the noises from the upper world and peering behind every now and then, but nothing happened. No dogs came baying and slavering at them. No poison gas suffocated them. No parties of men came with lamps and clubs to kill Sherahi. At one place the Culls cringed as a familiar roaring filled the air and the ceiling trembled.

Manu's face was upturned toward the sound and a fine curtain of dirt sifted into his eyes and open mouth. "Phtah," he said as he spat it out. "Sounds like another fire serpent," he whispered, hoping that the tunnel wouldn't collapse.

"You all right, Manu?" asked Dervish.

"Just a little dirtier," said the langur.

"Sshhh," Sherahi hissed. They all cringed as another fire serpent roared overhead, in the opposite direction. This large tunnel must be directly beneath those of the fire serpent. The noise retreated and disappeared, replaced by the less-threatening rumble of traffic above. Then, in the distance, came the wail of yet another fire serpent and the Culls hurried away from the spot.

Sherahi could see the opening of the next tributary tunnel and she wondered how far they had come. "We've been running since midnight. It's day now and the humans must be looking for us by now."

She slithered even faster and thought, "They could send dogs down here—the kinds of dogs that chase foxes and weasels from their burrows. It would be bad to fight them down here—enclosed. But," thought Sherahi, "the humans think they are dealing only with a giant snake. They don't know that there is a cascabel to be reckoned with. They probably don't even know what a cascabel is."

Sherahi imagined a fierce fox terrier or a short-legged dachshund sniffing excitedly down a tributary tunnel and meeting up with Junior. How surprised the dog would be to feel Junior's fangs inject hot poison into his neck. Sherahi had never liked dogs and the thought made her smile in the inscrutable way that serpents use to express amusement. But that wasn't her only worry: the main tunnel was big enough for men to walk through. If men came, Sherahi couldn't let Junior kill them. She knew that if some men died, others would surely follow, and the Culls could never kill all of the humans. "I can confuse them for a while," Sherahi thought, "but we must find someplace to hide." That thought kept Sherahi moving forward, questing for the spot where the white crocodile crooned to her eggs.

She heard the Duchess counting behind her. The bird's tenor voice said, "Forty-five," when they passed one dimly lit tributary tunnel.

"What are you counting?" Sherahi asked mentally. She didn't really understand numbers, but the Duchess didn't have to know that.

"Number of tunnels that we've passed since we started," the Duchess replied in soft bird squawk. "That was forty-five and I'm wondering when we're going to stop. I'm tired." The Duchess wasn't exactly complaining in her old way. She'd outgrown that, but Sherahi knew that all of them were fatigued by the strain of trudging in the darkness without any visible goal.

"Let's rest here," said Sherahi. "Dervish, you take the first watch and I'll relieve you in a while. I'm going ahead for a bit."

As the Culls traveled, Sherahi had listened carefully to the song that the brooding female white crocodile sang to her unhatched young. It grew louder and stronger within her mind and now the singer seemed to be very close. Sherahi thought that she could actually hear the song reverberate in the walls of the tunnel. With her chin against one brick wall, Sherahi listened to the song and it occurred to her that if it weren't being sung in the ancient saurian tongue, the song could have been any mother singing to her babies. It could have been the song of a mother spider as she guarded her eggs wrapped in homemade silk. Or it could have been the song of a mother penguin hunched against the Arctic wind, communicating with the embryos floating within the egg worlds clutched between her warm, webbed feet. Or it could have been the song of a mother python—the song that twists sunshine with leaf shade and hot dust with dew as the mother tells her unhatched children of the world that awaits them. Python tradition holds that the song encourages the snakelets to feast on the yolk that the mother has provided and prepare for the day when they will slash their way toward the light and the singer that they will never see.

Sherahi listened and crawled toward the song. After experimenting she found a spot where it seemed to be loudest. Something was wrong, though, because she could find no difference between this and any other part of the tunnel. All the bricks seemed identical; nothing led toward the singer. Sherahi was disappointed. This was not what she had expected.

"Please, Holy Ones," she prayed, "please give us shelter. Our enemies are coming. Please let us find you."

There was no response to her prayer and Sherahi sighed and pressed her chin against the spot again. There was no doubt that the singer seemed to be on the opposite side of this wall and Sherahi inched across the face of the curving bricks again and again, looking for a loose place or a depression, for some sign of an entrance. But she could feel nothing to indicate that one of the Holy White Crocodiles had a nest only a few feet away. Indeed, if Sherahi hadn't been able to hear the song, she would never have suspected that this portion of the tunnel was any different from the rest. Sherahi thought of sending a mental message to the mind of the brooding female, but decided against it: that might frighten her away.

Sherahi lay in the dark tunnel with her chin pressed to the spot where the song was loudest. When the others had rested, she'd have to get them to help her search. "Maybe one of them can find something that I have overlooked. There must be an entrance," Sherahi thought. "We've come too far to be trapped by humans in this endless tunnel. The Holy White Crocodiles will help us. I know it."

Then she thought, "They've done this for a reason. It isn't just by chance. These are clever creatures. They may be the most intelligent beings in the world. Of course it's going to be hard to find them: they've camouflaged the entrance to their nests. Just like spider-hunting wasps, who provision their nurseries with paralyzed spiders, the crocodiles have disguised and sealed the entrance to their nursery so that nobody can find it. How stupid of me not to have realized it before.

"But they're here. I know they're here. Somehow they've found a place that's warmer than the rest of the tunnel we've come through. They must be here—only a few feet away."

The place where Sherahi's head and the first third of her body were coiled was as snug as a cliff face at noontime. For a moment the big snake allowed herself the luxury of pressing close to the warmth that seeped through the wall of the storm drain. Then she yawned and returned to the others to relieve Dervish and allow him to sleep.

"Find anything, Sherahi?" he chittered at her.

She couldn't really hear what he said, but from the way his quick mind worked she knew he was asking her something. As a reward for being such a good and loyal beast she sent him a wave of sleepy comfort. In a few minutes he had curled up beside Manu and was asleep.

With her labial pits Sherahi surveyed the sleeping animals: Manu and Dervish were curled side by side and the Duchess hunched near them. Junior had coiled a bit apart and Sherahi knew that he had intercepted the mental reward that she had sent to Dervish. He was jealous again, but since a quick scan of his mind showed no damage to his remodeled personality, she merely said "Good night" to him in ancient saurian mindspeech. In a shielded part of her mind she thought, "Teenagers are so difficult."

Feeling a bit like the mother crocodile that sang to her babies so close to where the Culls slept, Sherahi sent a dream into their sleeping minds. The dream was all about Sandeagozu and how wonderful it would be. "Maybe the dream will give them the courage to actually get there. To-morrow, when we've rested, we will find the white crocodiles. And the holy reptiles will tell us how to get to Sandeagozu."

Sherahi stopped thinking and, although she had planned to guard the others in case men came, she fell asleep.

The newspapers carried the story the next day, with the headline "PYTHON LOOSE IN SEWERS." There was a double-page spread of pho-tographs of the abandoned subway station, where police investigators found evidence that the python had hidden for months. It showed pictures of the snake's trail up the subway stairs and through the snowdrifts to the storm drain. There was an artist's sketch of what the monster snake looked like and interviews with the couple it had terrified. There was a long, scholarly interview with Raymond Ditmars, Curator of Reptiles at the Bronx Zoo, who said that none of his snakes was missing and that, from the description, it sounded like a snake that Leftrack's Pet Emporium once had offered for sale.

The reporters questioned the police officer who had searched for the snake outside Leftrack's shop. He said that, although his dogs had lost the trail, it was possible that the animal could have eluded them. He said that, because there was no trail, he and the owner, Ira Leftrack, had concluded that the snake had been stolen. There had seemed to be no reason to alarm the public. The policeman had no reply to the question, "Why didn't you report the matter to your superiors? You knew that the missing snake had once nearly strangled Mr. Leftrack, didn't you?"

It wasn't long before the reporters began to call Ira Leftrack. He told his secretary, Helga, that he wasn't taking any phone calls and put on his hat and coat. He would take Irma to the Jersey shore for a few days. Ehrich was away at medical school and the business could run itself for a while. When they came back, the whole thing about the escaped snake would be forgotten.

A reporter met Leftrack as he was leaving the pet shop.

"Going somewhere, Mr. Leftrack?" the reporter said. "Cliff Jones of the *Tribune;* I want to ask you a few questions about the python of yours that's got this whole town scared to death."

"Can it crawl down into a drain?" asked another reporter, who appeared behind Jones, note pad in hand.

"How did it escape from your store?"

"Don't you think it's irresponsible to bring dangerous animals into a city like this? Isn't it some kind of health hazard?"

Leftrack answered none of these questions, but instead hailed a cab and hurried home. He telephoned to the store to tell Irma, Helga and the others to close up early. First the line was busy and when he finally got through, his wife answered the phone.

"Irma, send everyone home and lock up as fast as you can."

"It's too late, Ira," his wife's voice said. "The man from the Board of Health was just here. They've shut down the warehouse and confiscated everything. They're going to send all the animals to the Bronx Zoo. There are policemen here now. They say that the pet shop can go on but, unless the city changes its mind, we can't import or export animals here anymore.

"Where are you, Ira?"

"I'm at home."

"Well, stay there. I'll be home in a while and we'll talk."

There was silence on the other end of the line and Irma said, "It's not so bad, Ira. Maybe we can still move to the country and raise chinchillas. You said that was a sure-fire thing. In a few years Ehrich will be a doctor and then we'll be on Easy Street."

There was no response and she added, "Ira, did you hear me? Ira?"

Her husband's voice said softly, "You're dreaming, Irma," and he hung up the phone.

The next day was worse for Ira Leftrack. The papers carried the news that the snake had been traced to Leftrack's Pet Emporium and that the store had been closed by the Board of Health, acting under the mayor's special direction. There was also the quote from Leftrack that the python had been stolen from his shop, and the paper said that "Leftrack refused to say whether or not the python was a danger to the public."

There were further interviews with the couple who had seen the python, with their respective families and friends. Again and again Shirley Hagenbloom and Morris Weiner recounted their narrow escape and with fascinated horror New Yorkers read again and again of how the gigantic snake (it was at least forty-five feet long now) had threatened them on the night of the blizzard. Several papers reprinted the account of Leftrack's snake attack. A woman in Brooklyn set off a second wave of terror by calling in a snake alarm. What she reported as the killer python turned out to be a milk snake that was hibernating in her basement. Without a second thought the police smashed the serpent's head with a coal scuttle.

People imagined that they saw snakes everywhere. City Hall was besieged with calls from people who were frightened to use the subways, frightened to walk down streets at night, frightened to use the plumbing in their own homes. The mayor saw his chance to be a hero. Not wanting to have a lawsuit on his hands, he closed down all of the other animal importers who handled exotic snakes and then organized a special crew of workers who would search the storm-drain system for the python. Donning hip boots and miner's helmet, he joined the crew of maintenance workers, police riflemen and dogs that assembled at the storm drain adjacent to the abandoned subway station at 18th Street.

"It's here," Sherahi called to the others. "Junior, if you put your chin to this brick, you can hear how much louder the song is, can't you?"

The cascabel slithered from around Dervish's neck and pressed his chin to the spot Sherahi indicated. "The bossy old lady is right again. Someone is singing on the opposite side of this wall," he hissed in a scree-filled snag of his mind. "She's right," he said into Dervish's mind and crawled away to brood.

"Have a look here, Dervish," Manu chittered to Dervish. "Is there anything different about these bricks?"

Dervish had spent the time since they had awakened scratching at bricks. His claws were dull from digging at rocklike, hard-fired bricks, and dust and powdered mortar filled his nostrils. The place that Manu indicated seemed to be no different from all of the other bricks that he'd tried to destroy, but Dervish wanted to do his job well. Digging in one more place didn't matter now. He wasn't surprised when he found that this one was as hard as all of the rest.

"Just the same," he chittered softly to Manu. "All hard as rocks. Ask Sherahi if she's got any other ideas." Dervish flopped down onto the ledge above where the others worked in the tunnel and rested his chin on his paws. He sighed and wondered, "Are we ever going to get out of this place? What if men and dogs come while we're here? We'll be captured. Or worse."

The coati rolled restlessly on his back, with his hind feet braced against the curved wall of the tunnel. Absent-mindedly he scratched at it with his powerfully clawed feet. If he'd been a wild coati he would have spent hours ripping open fallen trees, searching for fat, white grubs. He would have used his back feet and claws just like this (he raked them strongly against the brick wall) to dig a comfortable burrow beneath the roots of a strangler fig tree. There would be a chamber that he would sleep in (he raked his claws furiously), and there would be a chamber for his first wife and her babies (one more furious burst of scrabbling at the wall), and there would be another for his second wife (more furious digging). He'd have to find some way to keep them from fighting. Manu said that females always fought. And there would be a chamber for storing food and a second and a third tunnel that led to other parts of the forest. Each of these would have to be carefully plugged with hard-packed earth so that no predators could sneak in during the daytime when all the family was asleep and silently grab his first wife by the neck. . . .

"Dervish, what in hell are you doing?" asked Manu in a very annoyed tone. "You're throwing dirt all over everyone." There was a pause and Manu rushed to where Dervish lay, nearly covered with soft dirt and small stones. He felt the soil on the coati's fur and then felt the wall where the animal's feet had opened a hole. It was directly opposite where the snakes were listening to the song of the white crocodile and it was very high up on the wall. "Sherahi. Junior," Manu called in the mindspeech they understood. "Come here. See what Dervish has found."

In moments the other Culls clustered around Dervish, who had shaken the dirt from his fur and was trying not to feel too proud.

"Dervish," Sherahi said into his mind, "dig a little more. Right here." She indicated a place where the hole that Dervish had made was deepest. "But be gentle."

Using his favorite front paw, Dervish tentatively clawed at the hole he'd made. He stopped from time to time to allow Sherahi to press her muzzle against the hole. "A little more," she said. "I think we're almost through."

Dervish dug a bit more and the wall gave way. Warm, spicy-smelling air flowed through the hole to Dervish's nostrils and, incredibly, a pale light emanated from the hole.

"Junior," Sherahi ordered. "Quickly go in and have a look." She saw thunderheads of objections cloud his brain and commanded, "No—don't argue, just go."

The cascabel slithered through the hole. In moments he was back and put his head through the opening. "There is a strange-looking crocodile here, Auntie. She's not quite like you said she would be, but she says that we can come in. She's been expecting us. But we'll have to hurry because she says that men and dogs are coming. And she says to not make any noise and to throw all of the dirt in here so the men won't find us."

Sherahi looked either way down the black tunnel. There was no sign that people were coming, but if a Holy White Crocodile had said so, it must be true.

"Hurry," she said to the others. "Do as Junior says. Since I'm the slowest, I'll go first. The rest of you clean up this mess as best you can and come in quickly."

Sherahi widened the hole that Junior's head had so recently occupied and then slowly crawled through it.

The Duchess, Dervish and Manu swept the dirt from the wall into a neat pile. When Sherahi's body had cleared the opening they threw as much of it as possible inside. The Duchess clambered up with beakfuls of the stuff and, once most of it was inside, she opened her wings and beat them powerfully, sending any stray crumbs into the pit of the tunnel where no one would see them. Manu climbed through the hole in the wall that led to the white crocodiles, followed by the Duchess.

As she jumped from her perch on Dervish's back to the breach high in the tunnel wall, she heard the coati whine. In the dim light that spilled down into the black tunnel from the crocodile's chamber she saw him staring at distant points of light that bobbed up and down. "Get out of the way, Duchess," he said. "I'm coming."

Dervish sprang onto the wall that separated the chamber of the white crocodiles from the tunnel, hoping that the dogs wouldn't be able to find them and that there would be some place inside where they'd be safe.

None of the Culls was prepared for the first sight of the famous Holy White Crocodile. It was a small, twisted animal, with thick legs and a spindly body. Huge, bottomless eyes stared coldly from the pale head that mechanically turned to watch as one animal after another entered the dimly lit chamber through the breach in the wall. With its glowing, pale skin and rows of long, sharp teeth it didn't look friendly. Once all of the Culls were inside, the beast seemed to lose interest in them and ran back and forth on the nearly vertical wall like an overgrown ant or termite soldier, carrying mouthfuls of the dirt that the Culls had excavated mixed with a black, tarry substance that they knew was crocodile dung. The creature quickly plastered the break that the Culls had made and, once the gap was filled, it did not relax but continued pacing and plastering until the wall showed no sign that it had been recently broken.

Sherahi was as surprised as the others at the dexterity with which the crocodile mended the wall. But then she recognized that the wall-building was just an amplification of the nest construction which crocodiles had perfected over more than a hundred million years.

Manu was closest to the wall and touched the mended place with one finger. He was amazed to find the surface dry, hard and as smooth as the brickwork of the tunnel had been. The glimmering animal had even sculpted details, such as edges of bricks and lines of mortar between bricks. Manu turned to congratulate the mason, when the spindly crocodile turned from its work, opened its mouth and hissed at the Culls. It lunged for the Duchess and snapped her up crosswise in its horrible mouth. Manu thought he heard it hiss something that sounded like "Birdflesh for breakfast." The Duchess squawked once and then her head flopped to one side. A milky nictitating membrane filmed her eyes and her black tongue protruded from her open bill.

The other Culls were stunned. Sherahi had expected that this otherworldly creature, who sang so sweetly to her unborn young, would be a gentle and indulgently maternal reptile. She had expected to find a refuge in the chambers of the white crocodiles, not a nest of voracious predators. She watched in horror as the Duchess's neck, with its cheerful froth of red feathers, bobbled limply in the crocodile's jaws.

"The Duchess can't be dead," thought Sherahi. "She's only fainted."

The white crocodile stared intently at the huge snake coiled within her nesting chamber. "This is the dangerous one," she thought. "The others are helpless without her." The crocodile knew at once that the serpent controlled the others and concentrated on immobilizing her—preventing her from speaking to them and preventing her from attacking.

"We've got to do something, Manu," said Dervish in a low, chittering voice. "Look at Sherahi. Something's wrong with her."

Manu saw that the pythoness lay with her head resting on her coiled body—immobile and inert. "This animal has done something to her," he thought. He saw that the white crocodile was about to give the Duchess the violent shake that would snap her neck and kill her. Without thinking, Manu began scolding the crocodile and ran to her nest.

The white crocodile whirled to see what the monkey was doing and found him sitting on top of the steaming mound that held her eggs. He dug into the pile of loose earth and one by one brought the warm, white eggs to the surface. A moan came from the crocodile's throat.

"Sherahi," said Manu, "are you all right?"

"Yes," said the pythoness, in a voice that sounded strangely mechanical and distant.

"Sherahi, do something. Tell that white monster to put the Duchess down and be quick about it. Tell her that, if she doesn't, we're going to kill all of her babies." Manu had six eggs out of the mound now. He stood over them and, in the steamy underground chamber, lit by globs of phosphorescence that gave off a pale light similar to the color of the crocodile's skin, he held one egg high above his head and gestured to the crocodile that he was going to hurl it against the floor.

Sherahi felt as if she were under water. She heard Manu's voice very faint in the distance. She saw the fury in the bottomless eyes of the glimmering beast, heard her growl and knew that the crocodile understood Manu's threat.

"I mean it," said Manu to the crocodile. "Put the bird down. And, if you've hurt her, we'll kill your children before we decide what to do with you."

The white crocodile looked from Manu and Dervish to the huge py-thon near the outer wall and slowly opened her mouth. Delicately she depos-ited the Duchess on the ground. Then she breathed on her and the bird's eyelids fluttered. Soon the Duchess had righted herself, shaken her feathers and was walking about as if nothing had happened. Actually, she felt freer than she had in months because the jaws of the white crocodile had snapped her collar. It lay in pieces on the ground between her and the white beast.

"Fine way to treat visitors," she said to the female crocodile. "What's the big idea, anyway, grabbing me like that? After all Sherahi said about you being so holy and so smart, who'd have thought you'd be just a common thug with no manners at all? If you hadn't caught me by surprise, you'd have had quite a fight on your hands. I'd have ripped your nose off, you scaly white wart. Lucky for you that I fainted."

The Duchess walked haughtily over to the white crocodile and, with a motion that was too quick for the eye to follow, bit the animal as hard as she could on the tip of its scrawny, phosphorescent tail. It bellowed and whirled around, hissing and biting at the bird who had half-flown, half-walked away. The crocodile snapped at thin air instead of red tail feathers and bellowed again.

Bobbing and weaving from her refuge behind Sherahi's coils the Duchess said, "Go on, yell all you want to. I hope I've hurt you. The very idea of treating strangers like that. And we've come so far just to see you and you try a vicious trick like that. I never . . ."

Manu was still on top of the crocodile's nest, with her clutch of eggs around him.

"Get off them," the mother crocodile hissed. Her eyes glittered like obsidian. She lifted her spindly white body high off the ground and began to run at him. "Give me my eggs," she hissed. "Give me my babies—all of them—or I'll call the others. If the soldiers come they'll take you to the meat rack and you'll be sorry that you threatened Annahe's babies."

"Manu—Dervish," said Sherahi, "do as she says. She kept her part of the bargain. We must keep ours."

"But Sherahi," said the langur, "as soon as I give up her eggs, then we're completely within her power. We can't trust her. I don't care what you say, I'm keeping one egg as insurance." The white crocodile's charge had brought her to the nest mound now and the two Culls scrambled away to safety. Manu carried an egg as he retreated.

Annahe, the female crocodile, was busy at her nest. She made birdlike chirping sounds and gently buried the remaining eggs. Sherahi was responding more normally now and noticed that the crocodile's nest was near a large, rusty pipe that traveled the length of this low chamber. Even at this distance from the pipe and the nest mound, her labial pits told her that the pipe was hot and the crocodile's nest steamed slightly.

The Culls watched as the female crocodile hurried over to a pool beneath the pipe and drank. Then she quickly returned to the nest and, conscious that the strangers were staring, she opened her jaws and allowed the water to dribble down onto the nest. "Poor tiny ones," she said, "don't be frightened. Everything's all right. Mother's here now."

The creature noticed that the newcomers were staring and, as if she felt a need to explain her behavior, she said, "Have to keep them damp—otherwise they'll die of the heat."

The Culls said nothing and she continued in a mournful voice, "That's what's going to happen to the one in your hand. It'll dry out and die in a few hours."

Her round, black eyes seemed to grow larger in her eerie, pale skull and it seemed as if a huge dirty tear rolled from each eye and dropped onto the steaming nest below her.

"And I had such hopes for that one. She was the only one that wasn't reverted. And now you're going to kill her. I should have never let you in here. I should have let the men and dogs get you. They're outside right now. Can't you hear them?"

Sherahi put her chin to the floor of the chamber and listened to a party of men and snuffling dogs moving down the adjacent tunnel. When the sounds had disappeared she said, "We thank you, less-than-holy one, for saving us from them."

"You have to understand," said Annahe, trying to make herself look as small and as pitiful as possible, "the eggs won't hatch for a while yet, and I haven't eaten anything but the ambrosia in half a year. I'm sorry if I hurt you, but it wouldn't have been a bad death—at least it would have been quick. And in one sense you would not really have been dying at all. White crocodiles don't die, you know, and parts of you would have been incorporated into my body and would have lived forever. You would have become bone of my bone and flesh of my flesh. . . ."

"I've heard that before somewhere," thought Sherahi, remembering the parting words of the Midgard Serpent.

Annahe's hypnotic words didn't fool the Duchess at all. She had only recently been inside those pale jaws and she interrupted the crocodile in mid-sentence.

"Get off it," she snapped, surprised that she could understand anything that a reptile had said. "You're about as helpless as a striking cobra—forgive the expression, Pythoness."

"Nevertheless," said the crocodile, "our eggs can't just hatch anywhere. And you're killing the only baby that would have survived. Give her back. Please."

Sherahi could tell that Manu believed the crocodile's pseudosincerity. "Wait, Manu," she cautioned. "Don't do anything rash. She's hypnotizing you, just like she hypnotized me. But I don't think she can hypnotize all of us at once. She's clever, but not as clever as she thinks.

"Tell me, Annahe, tender mother of crocodiles," Sherahi said, "what is a reversion?"

"It'll take too much time to tell. Give me my egg."

"We have lots of time, Annahe, although the baby in Manu's hand doesn't seem to have too much. . . ."

"All right. Have it your way. I'll tell you. You're going to the meat rack anyway. It won't make any difference. You see," said the pale saurian, settling down into a comfortable position atop her mound of eggs, "white crocodiles are quite unlike our grotesque relatives that live in the sunlit world. You can see for yourselves that we are exceptionally beautiful, but you probably don't realize that we are also perfectly suited to life in these underground chambers. With your poor, stunted senses you cannot possibly appreciate it, but our eyes and ears are much different from those of terrestrial animals—much improved. For example, even if we don't have to, because of the lightning slime"—the creature gestured with the tip of her tail toward a phosphorescent glob that glowed like a wet stalactite near her nest mound—"we can see perfectly well in complete darkness. And, we have the finest hearing of any creatures above or below ground. Did I not warn you that the men were coming long before any of you heard or saw them?

"When our ancestors first found the subterranean spring and began to excavate the ancient chambers, they were terrestrial crocodiles. Three hundred years of living down here has produced the finest animal minds on this planet and has also changed our appearance. We've abandoned many of the terrestrial crocodilian features because they became an unnecessary encumbrance down here. I have very little body armor—a diet of ambrosia does not require all of that heavy protection—and, of course, we've lost the dark skin color of our relatives in the sunlit world. After a few months of life a white crocodile acquires a symbiotic colony of lightning slime and that enhances our paleness and allows for territorial marking.

"You can see how perfectly adapted my body is for life in these tunnels. I have special hold-fast organs that are essential in the flood times"—she lifted her chin to show a pair of peculiar, oval suckers that extended from her throat on a stout stalk—"and, you would think that with all this physical perfection, life would be easy down here. But it isn't. Oh no, ungrateful visitors, it isn't easy at all."

Annahe interrupted her story with a bout of sobbing, and even the Duchess was beginning to feel sorry for her. Then Sherahi silently reminded the Culls that the crocodile was trying to trick them again.

224

"Come on," hissed Junior from around Dervish's neck. "Stop bawling and get on with it. We have better things to do than to listen to you feeling sorry for yourself."

"Junior," said Sherahi, "don't be so rude." For once she was delighted at his irascible nature. "Yes, go on, Annahe, tell us the rest."

"It's our babies," sobbed the crocodile. "Most of them are throwbacks to the ancestral type—or else the heat deforms them. Luckily we can scry their minds while they are still embryos and encourage them to hatch as perfect white crocodiles. And we can monitor their development and prepare ourselves to kill the deformed ones. The egg that's in your hand, ugly, gray monkey, holds the only perfect baby white crocodile. It is the only one of this clutch that isn't a reversion."

"What will happen to the others when they hatch?" asked Manu.

"I will help them out of their shells and allow them to swim briefly. Then they will crawl into my open mouth, as all newborn crocodiles do, and one by one I will eat them."

Sherahi could feel the Duchess stiffen in horror. Before she could protest, Manu slowly walked over to the mother crocodile and, keeping a wary eye on her phosphorescent jaws, placed the egg at the foot of the mound.

"Manu," Sherahi said, "that was a mistake. Now we are completely in her power."

"I know, Pythoness," said the langur sadly. "But it was the right thing to do. I couldn't help myself."

Triumph gleamed in her yellow eyes as the female crocodile picked up the egg and gently nuzzled it beneath the top of the faintly steaming mound. Then she opened her jaws and cackled triumphantly. "Fools that don't understand how to survive. Soft-headed, soft-skinned idiots. You have done just what I expected." She laughed and hissed from her mound of steaming earth and continued, "Since you are so interested in our ways, I will arrange for you to meet all of the others. And you will become intimately acquainted with the Holy White Crocodiles. Oh yes, you'll become *very intimately* acquainted with our ways."

The animal opened her snaggle-toothed jaw and called in a peculiar way. It sounded like bones snapping and flesh ripping, but was more resonant. In moments the Culls saw other white crocodiles swim into the chamber, following the sluggish stream that wound toward Annahe's nest. Soon the Culls were surrounded by phosphorescent giants who looked like Annahe, but were larger. The leader gestured for the Culls to follow them and, looking at one another, the animals saw that they had no choice. They walked into the shallow pool and began to wade in the thick, warm, spicy-smelling liquid toward a band of lights on a distant shore.

"Stupid monkey," said Junior, "now see what you've done."

"Stop complaining," said Sherahi. "Concentrate on what I'm saying, and stop wasting your anger on Manu. We'll get out of here yet. Trust me. We've come too far to be stopped now."

The mayor of New York City and his crew of police and sanitation men trailed the escaped python from the abandoned subway station at 18th Street to the place where it entered the storm-drain system. The dogs bayed enthusiastically and from 18th Street to 45th Street it seemed that they would discover the python any minute. But then, inexplicably, the trail went cold and the dogs stopped barking. It took the crew two days to completely traverse the main sewer that drained runoff from New York City's streets. When they found nothing the search was abandoned. Somehow the snake had eluded them.

At a public conference on what was being called the "Python Problem," it was decided that, even if the snake were alive and lurking below the city within the storm drains, it posed little threat to the populace. The mayor appeared on a special radio broadcast and was interviewed, along with Ditmars. They agreed that the cold within the sewers would kill the huge snake—and if it didn't, the animal still had little chance of survival. The snows would be melting soon and nothing could hide within those storm sewers: water coursed through them like flash floods through arroyos. The raging water flushed out everything that was in its path. Every year stray cats and rats by the hundreds were found floating in the East River after the first spring rains. The experts agreed that the python would become immobilized by the cold, and would fall prey to these same killing waters. There was really nothing to worry about.

"You see," said the mayor, hoping to put the best face on the matter, "the snake has really signed her own death warrant by entering those tunnels. She'll be dead before long. New York City has nothing to fear from this snake, even if she is on the loose in the sewers.

"Just as my administration has made an all-out effort to shut down illegal drinking parlors, so we have cracked down on the snake dealers that infest this city. We have closed them down and I assure the citizens of New York that this can never happen again. Not while I'm mayor.

"Any further questions, gentlemen?"

CHAPTER EIGHT

Leftrack's Pet Emporium and
Animals International, Ltd
December 17, 1932

I RMA HAD BEGGED him to stay home. She warned him that the city had confiscated all of the animals. There was no point in his going back. There was nothing to see there. "Please, Ira," she had said, "stay home with me tonight. We'll see the lawyers in the morning. No good can come of going tonight. There's nothing there anymore. Believe me, Ira. There's nothing there."

He sat across the room from her, staring intently at the teapots and blue roses on the faded wallpaper behind her left shoulder. She said, "Ira, did you hear me? Are you listening?"

Leftrack made no reply and Irma shrugged. "I might as well be talking to a stone," she said to herself and went into the kitchen. Sighing and banging her mixing bowls down onto the counter, she began to assemble the ingredients for the potato latkes that she would take to Ehrich's dormitory tomorrow. He was hardly eating these days—getting so thin. Her hands were covered with the minced potatoes that she molded into patties and she was busy thinking about how Ehrich would be a doctor someday when she heard the front door slam.

"Ira?" she called. "Ira?" The living room was empty. "Well," Irma said to herself, "he's used to being the boss. Once he's made up his mind, there's no stopping him. Best to let him alone."

It was past midnight when Ira Leftrack returned to his pet shop and warehouse. Except for a light behind the blinds of the office of Meyer's meat-packing house, all of the warehouses on the block were dark. Leftrack fumbled for his keys and thought of that tub-of-guts, Meyer, behind his counter, grinding meat for sausages. "Meyer must be happy with what has happened," thought Leftrack. "I'll bet he and his pal, Sam the greengrocer, are having a big laugh over this." Leftrack thought of the butcher's fingers pressing meat into the maw of the meat grinder. He imagined sharp knives and heavy cleavers lying nearby and suddenly thought, "Maybe Meyer'll have an accident. Maybe he'll cut himself a little."

Leftrack saw that a notice was nailed across the front door of the shop. It read, "CLOSED BY ORDER OF THE BOARD OF HEALTH OF THE CITY OF NEW YORK. KEEP OUT." There were official-looking signatures across the bottom and Leftrack ripped it from the door and cast it onto the snow-covered street. "No city officials are going to keep me out of my own shop," Leftrack thought. "They can't do that to me. I'm in business here. My lawyers will make mincemeat of them in the morning." Leftrack wouldn't let himself think about what he would do if it were really all over and if he really couldn't import animals anymore. That wasn't possible.

Leftrack slammed the door behind him, and in his shop across the street Meyer the butcher heard the noise and looked up from his paperwork. Out of habit Meyer wiped his fingers on his blood-stained apron and pulled down one slat of the Venetian blind. He saw the Board of Health notice lying crumpled and discarded at Leftrack's shop door and, like any conscientious neighbor, Meyer telephoned the police and warned them that a prowler had broken into the warehouse across the street. Meyer went back to his accounts, but glanced up from time to time, and listened for the arrival of the police.

Inside his shop Leftrack was at first dismayed and then became infuriated when he saw what the city had done. "What right do they have?" he kept asking himself. "This is a free country. They can't just shut me down—just like that. Just because one snake gets out. They can't keep me from earning a living. This isn't Germany. This is a free country. They can't do this to me."

But they had. In the public part of the shop there was one empty row of cages after another. White mice, guinea pigs, turtles, rabbits, parakeets, canaries, mynah birds, frogs, snakes—everything was gone. Irma had said that the city had confiscated everything, but he hadn't expected this desolation. He saw that the Animal of the Month exhibit was empty. They'd even taken the ocelot that had been promised to the San Diego Zoo.

On his way to the warehouse door, Leftrack saw a flash of color and movement and found that the hundred-gallon tropical fish tank still had three neon tetras in it. "The city probably couldn't catch them," he thought ruefully and noticed that whoever had cleaned out the place had not disconnected the motor that ran the tank's pump and filter. "Three tetras aren't worth all of that electricity," he thought and quickly pulled the plug. "Do they think I'm made of money?" he thought.

Within the tank, bubbles stopped streaming up from the helmet of a deep-sea diver and the three iridescent fish darted off in opposite directions. Now that the motor had stopped chugging, there was no sound in the pet shop, except for Leftrack's footsteps, and he began to wish that he'd stayed home with Irma. She'd been right. There was nothing to see here. Nothing at all.

"Maybe they left the chinchilla colony," he suddenly thought. "The

228

bastards took everything else, but Irma must have told them that the chinchillas weren't for sale. They were our old-age insurance. They couldn't have confiscated them. Those poor chinchillas'll die if they're upset again."

Before he entered the warehouse, Leftrack looked at the three little tetras that hovered near the top of the nearly empty aquarium. "It would be kinder to kill them," he muttered. Without an air pump they'd die soon, anyway, and before long the water would go foul and start to stink. He took an aquarium net from beside the tank, captured the fish with one expert scoop and folded the net so that the three fish were trapped inside. He laid the net alongside the tank. As he unlocked the warehouse door he heard their fins flipping wetly against the net. They would suffocate in a few minutes. "Not a bad death, all things considered," he thought. "Besides, there's no use keeping them alive. They're worthless now."

Leftrack found that Irma had been right: the warehouse had been completely cleaned out. The chinchilla colony was empty. The aviary cages held no finches. All of the rare South American river turtles were gone, as well as the new shipment of colobus monkeys and the dozen scarlet ibises that he'd gotten on speculation. He found the only animals in the whole warehouse in a wooden crate that was on top of his desk: a shipment of nonpoisonous snakes that had been returned in the late afternoon. The crate was marked "REFUSED."

"They must have arrived after the cops had gone," thought Leftrack. "Well, they're worthless now, too. Just like all the rest. Worthless."

On impulse, Leftrack opened the crate and untied one bag after another. He found a red, black, and yellow scarlet kingsnake; a brick-red blotched eastern milk snake; a big garter snake; two lovely, smooth green snakes, and a big black-and-yellow chain kingsnake. Leftrack poured the snakes out onto his desk and watched them slither beneath the pile of papers that needed attention. For a moment he forgot all of the trouble. He forgot that the city had closed down his business. He forgot his debts and his worries and watched the liquid movements of the animals. The garter snake found the edge of the desk and slithered down toward the floor. Leftrack watched it and thought, "Let it go wherever it wants. It really doesn't matter, now." Leftrack liked the idea of freeing these snakes to surprise the cops and the officials from the Board of Health. A little joke, Ira Leftrack style.

He realized his mistake too late. The cannibalistic snakes smelled their prey and almost simultaneously the milk snake, scarlet kingsnake and chain kingsnake began to attack the others and one another. Their ferocity caught Leftrack by surprise and for a moment he watched the intense, silent ball of snakes that writhed and coiled about one another.

When he began to try to separate the cannibals from their prey the snakes turned their fury on Leftrack. Kingsnake, scarlet king, garter and milk snakes all struck at and held on to his hands and wrists. Their excitement seemed to reinforce one another's attacks and strikes. Leftrack made things worse by jerking back and pulling snake teeth through his flesh. He saw that he was bleeding, but since they were nonpoisonous snakes, the bites didn't really bother Leftrack. Instead, his sense of order was outraged. The snakes weren't supposed to attack one another. He meant for them to scare the city officials. "I can't even control a handful of stupid, harmless snakes," he fumed and *that* made him angry.

With the quick, none-too-gentle hands of an expert, Leftrack disengaged one kingsnake's jaws from his wrist. The snake rattled its tail against the papers on Leftrack's desk and before it could turn and strike at him he grabbed it by the tail and snapped its body through the air like a whip. He cracked it a second time and felt it begin to jerk and twist and pull, like a fish hooked through the gills. The snake's glossy, black head hung limply and its tongue lolled from its mouth. Blood spurted from its broken neck.

Suddenly this seemed like a very good thing to do and Leftrack whipped each of the snakes through the air. He had the satisfaction of seeing the milk snake's head shoot off across the room. It left a bloody smear on the wall below the clock. The long snakes snapped and died more easily than did the smaller ones and Leftrack had to kill the baby green snakes by beating them against the edge of his desk.

When the police found Leftrack his hands and face were spattered with blood. He was examining the blood splatters minutely and the sight of the writhing, coiling bodies of not-quite-dead snakes struck him as terribly funny. It was all a great joke and he laughed hysterically and pointed at the dead snakes. The police took him away and he didn't understand why they weren't laughing. It was funny—so terribly, terribly funny.

When they walked by the empty hundred-gallon tank, he pointed at the net with the dead neon tetras inside and started laughing again. He took the net with him and sat cackling in the back of the paddy wagon. He wouldn't relinquish the net until the doctors at Bellevue took it away from him.

Meyer the butcher came outside to watch as the police put Leftrack into the paddy wagon. He heard the pet-store owner's cackle echo in the deserted, snow-covered street and knew that something had gone wrong with him. The next day he told Sam the greengrocer, "I always knew he was crazy. Only a crazy person would run a business like that in this neighborhood. The cops said that they found him in his office, with dead snakes all around him." Meyer paused and put his hand on Sam's forearm and said with horror, "Sam—there was blood in his hair and he was laughing to beat the band." Meyer pointed to his head and made a circle in the air with his index finger. "Such a sad thing. His wife told me this morning that he tried to kill himself in Bellevue. I never liked Crazy Leftrack, but I didn't wish for this to happen. Crazy Leftrack. Too bad."

"Too bad," echoed Sam the greengrocer, shaking his head. "We always knew he was a strange one, but who would have expected something like this? I'll tell you, Meyer. Such a shame. You never know. You just never know."

Tunnels
of the White Crocodiles

THE CULLS SOON LOST track of time. The white crocodiles marked only the seasons. Days, weeks, and months meant little to them. Winter had just begun, a time in which the crocodilians prepared for the year to come. The tunnels had to be cleaned, repaired and enlarged. Every scrap of refuse and excrement had to be carried to the sludge ponds and carefully mixed with the tepid, glowing water. The pond reeked like a fetid bear den, but the crocodiles didn't care. Their sense of smell had always been feeble and their olfactory lobes had now regressed to mere nubbins. In the hundreds of years that these animals had inhabited their tunnels they had learned to foster the growth of spherical, jelly-coated algal colonies. They had discovered that the algae grew fastest in tepid water that held a suspension of night soil and phosphorescent bacteria. The pools where they cultured the algae stank, but the crocs who patrolled them, continually stirring their contents with their sinuous swimming movements, did not seem to mind. They knew that their actions were necessary to keep the sludge from settling and putrefying.

Once the algal blobs had grown to the size of a human head they were scooped from the reeking water and set to dry upon the hissing steam pipes that perforated and warmed the chambers. After a few weeks the algae had dried to the flat cakes that fed the entire population of white crocodiles. This staple was supplemented by meat only at the annual Spring Glut. At that time the captives that had wandered into the tunnels were slaughtered in a gory ritual in which the crocodiles reenacted the lives of their terrestrial ancestors. The largest share of their flesh went to the crocs that had been chosen to mate. It was believed that the extra protein would foster the development of highly evolved and unreverted young.

Even though they had been assured that they would not be killed until the spring rains had flooded the mucky underground ponds, the Culls were aware that the eyes of the pale crocs watched them hungrily. Only tradition restrained the crocs from making an immediate kill and they lavished hungry, yellow glances on all of the Culls, but especially on Sherahi. She was a brilliant reptile and whoever ate her flesh would gain a share of that intelligence. Moreover, Sherahi was fat from feasting on unlimited rats. The crocs imagined the yellow fat hanging from her heart and crammed between her intestines. The saliva dripped from their jaws. The white crocodiles craved fat; there was none in their vegetarian diet.

The Culls were welcome in the tunnels of the white crocodiles not only because they would be part of the menu at the Spring Glut, but also because they could be pressed into service as workers. During the day all of the Culls except for Sherahi worked for the white crocs. Manu and Dervish helped with masonry repairs, while the Duchess did a different sort of work in the brightly lit chambers of the oligarchy that governed the crocodilians. These huge and oldest white crocodiles seemed to find a talking bird an excruciatingly funny evolutionary joke. It had something to do with lineage, as birds were direct descendants of crocodiles, and the holiest and whitest of the white crocodiles demanded that this novelty be present to entertain them every day.

Junior had eluded the crocodiles and had refused to be frightened by their threats. He had hidden in an inaccessible crevice and the crocs couldn't pry him from it. They were too large to follow him into his hiding place and, because they planned to mentally compel him to sacrifice himself in the Spring Glut, they had decided to ignore the small snake for the immediate future. They knew he couldn't escape and would eventually starve. "We'll find his desiccated body someday," the white crocs hissed and, instead of hunting for Junior, they concentrated their mental efforts upon subduing Sherahi.

The crocodiles had immobilized Sherahi's mind, erecting mental walls that did not allow her to communicate with the others. Believing that the pythoness was the most dangerous of the strangers, they focused all of their psychic constraints upon her and left Manu, Junior, Dervish and the Duchess mentally unfettered. They seldom even bothered to listen to their thoughts. At first Manu had been affronted at being thought to be so unimportant, but then he realized that the crocs had made a mistake that might be turned against them.

"We're safe for a time," he thought as he dumped a load of mud beside the snaggle-toothed crocs that were busy echo-locating weak spots in the chamber wall. Manu watched them alternately grunt, squeal and then pause to listen intently to the echoes of these sounds. The two moved over the walls and sides of the low chamber like huge, white insects, searching for places where the nest was not secure. From time to time their process was interrupted by exchanges of inscrutable glances and Manu heard them converse in mindspeech.

They didn't know that Manu could read their thoughts and Manu hadn't told them of his skill. Remembering how Sherahi had done it, he shielded his mind and covertly watched their thoughts. Eventually one of them would manually signal to Manu. The monkey would clamber up to them and deposit his load of mud. Manu had found that the crocs didn't like to be kept waiting and he was alert for the wave of a front claw that meant, "Here. And be quick about it."

He'd found that the crocs had short tempers as well as incredibly fast reflexes. Early in his captivity one had leapt out of the water, grabbed and twisted the monkey's tail and disappeared below the surface of the pool before Manu had even felt the pain. The crocs liked to do things quickly and efficiently and if Manu didn't pay attention they would club him with their heavy tails or do something worse.

The two showed no sign of needing him and, as he watched them, he thought of Sherahi. Maybe she would talk to him in mindspeech and he sent the message, "They're not going to kill us yet, Sherahi. Maybe we can still get away."

As usual, Manu got no reply from the pythoness. It had been that way ever since they had been captured, and he sent a message to Junior, who was usually lurking in his crevice near the helpless snake. "Has Sherahi said anything?"

"No. Nothing's changed. Sometimes it seems as if she's trying to speak but those white buggers have done something awful to her mind. It's like she's dead. She doesn't hear what we say and I've been scrying her mind. As far as I can tell she hasn't had a single thought in days. She might as well be dead."

"It can't be that bad, Junior. They must be terribly afraid of her to go to all this trouble. It must be costing them a lot of energy to control her so completely. You must stay by her, Junior, and be on guard. She's always helped all of us; now we must help her. We've got to figure out a way to get out of here. That's what she would do."

"Fat chance of that," said Junior. "We can't even help ourselves. How can we do anything for her? Face it, Manu, we're all going to be croc bait when spring comes. At least the four of you are, for sure. They'll never take me alive. I'll fry myself on one of those pipes before I let them tie me to that meat rack the way the Duchess says they're going to."

"Junior, you've got time to explore and to watch over Sherahi, too. *You've* got to find some way to get us out of here."

"What can I do?" asked the cascabel. For the first time there was a plaintive note to his voice and it sounded to Manu as if the little serpent might be worried. "These white slugs are immune to my venom. Don't think I didn't try to kill that cow Annahe when she sat on her stupid eggs, singing to them. I snuck up on her and stabbed her in the soft flesh of her

233

neck. I thought I'd killed her, but I couldn't even puncture the skin. And I broke a fang trying. I don't see what I can do, Manu. Without Dervish I can't cover much ground and these tunnels stretch on forever. I can't do it alone."

"If I can get Dervish free will you try to find a way out? Can I tell Sherahi that I can count on you?"

"I suppose so," said Junior. "But make sure you and the others keep out of my way when I'm angry. I can't promise that I won't bite one of you by mistake when I'm in a passion."

"So, you'll help us?"

"All right," hissed the cascabel. "But don't expect me to be able to work wonders like Sherahi did. I'm no pythoness, you know. There's only one like her in all the world."

Manu thought that the rattler sounded as if he were about to sob and their mental communication was abruptly broken. Manu was pleased that the poisonous youngster did seem to have some feelings for Sherahi and the rest of the Culls, after all. Maybe Sherahi had put something into his mind to soften the sharp stones and grit that she had discovered there so long ago.

Manu heard a bellow and found that both of the white crocs were staring malevolently at him. One was growling and had raised itself up on its legs. It was about to charge. Knowing that he hadn't been paying attention and that they were angry, Manu made all of the submissive gestures that he knew and even improvised some. He hurried to drop the load of mud where they indicated. He backed away and grimaced in fright, showing white teeth in his mud-covered face. He hurried to the sludge pond for another load, expecting to feel the whip of a tail.

Instead, he was relieved to hear the long tails of the crocs slapping the mud into position on the wall. As he scooped out more handfuls of reeking mud he thought about Junior and Dervish and felt inexplicably hopeful. Even though the Culls were buried beneath a human city in subterranean tunnels that no one would ever rescue them from, even though they were being held captive by nightmare creatures that meant to eat them to ensure the continuance of their twisted species, Manu began to think that there was hope. The Culls might be able to get out of here yet. He would have to make a plan. He would talk with the others, but now that Junior was willing to help, anything was still possible. This might not be a dead end. They might get to Sandeagozu yet.

That thought made Manu jubilant. Before he gathered up his new load of mud he turned a handspring in the glow of the phosphorescent bacteria that the crocs had smeared into the walls in the decades that they had inhabited these tunnels. Manu looked at his filthy fur and laughed at himself. What a picture he must make: a mud-covered monkey cavorting at the

234

edge of a hole that smelled like a fetid-spicy cess pit. He was glad that the others couldn't see him. "They'd think that I've gone mad," he laughed. Nevertheless, for the first time since he had been captured by Leftrack's men, Manu felt as if he were still the same silver-furred youngster who had spun cartwheels and dazzled the morning sun.

For the first time in his short life, Junior was frightened. Ever since he had learned that he possessed deadly venom and had learned how to accurately deliver it with a stab of his long front fangs, Junior had thought himself better than all other creatures. He knew that he had the power of life and death and there were no animals, not even humans, that he was afraid of. He'd even dreamed of vanquishing kingsnakes and indigo snakes: the fiercest predators of the serpent realm. Junior knew that his venom was strong enough to drop a hawk or owl within two heartbeats and he'd hoped for the day when one of those razor-clawed hotshots would hurtle at him from the sky. Junior had been ready for anything. He knew he was a superior killing machine. Meeting the white crocodiles, however, had changed all that.

He'd told Manu that he had broken a fang while attacking Annahe. What he didn't tell the langur was that he'd bitten the female croc in the neck after he'd embedded his fangs between the scales of her armpit: the place where a crocodile's skin is thinnest and softest. He was sure that he'd hit her with enough poison to make her writhe and die. He'd slithered away in triumph, waiting for his venom to take effect. He'd always enjoyed observing the reactions of various animals to his poison and he'd expected the usual trembling, the convulsions, the choking; but nothing had happened. Annahe had merely continued sitting on her nest, singing the same stupid song that had lured Sherahi and the other Culls. It had angered Junior so much that he'd gone back and in a rage had bitten her again, in the neck this time. That was when he'd broken his fang. Annahe paid him no more attention than she did the gray sow bugs that scuttled about the nursery chamber. She was immersed in motherhood and seemed impervious to everything except the cheeping of her eggs.

Junior sat within the inaccessible crevice that he had found on top of the steam pipe that traversed the ceiling of Sherahi's cell. The hole was just above the place where the pipe entered the chamber and it was too high for the crocs to reach. They had threatened that they would compel him to emerge when the Spring Glut was near and Junior had retreated to the back of his hiding place and rattled. He'd been confident then that he had nothing to fear from these beasts, but all that had happened before Sherahi had been frozen and before he'd discovered that his venom was ineffective against the crocs.

Twice a day steam hissed and banged through these pipes and Junior's hiding place would have been deadly if he hadn't insulated it with a pad of dried algae. The heat made him restless, though, and he arced back over the ceiling of the crevice, wishing that he were free to slither about and explore. But crocs were everywhere.

"Manu wanted me to find a way out of here, but how can I?" he hissed to himself. "If only Dervish were free, then maybe we might be able to do something, but that's not possible. The crocs are always on guard."

Early in their captivity the coati had run away and the white crocodiles had caught him. Dervish said it felt as if they had bound him with invisible ropes. Then they'd beaten him until he cried. It was awful to watch. "Poor Dervish," Junior thought, "if Sherahi had been herself she would have done something." He knew that she would have given him a mind balm to make him forget his pain, and Junior felt helpless because he didn't have any of her unique, pythonine wisdom. While the huge pythoness lay motionless in her cell the other Culls had helplessly listened to Dervish's cries.

As Junior lashed back and forth in his crevice above the steam pipe he dislodged a small stone, and fine dirt sifted from the ceiling. He shook it from his scales and wondered, "Can I dig out of here? The others would really think I was something if I could do that."

The crocs hadn't repaired this wall in years, if ever, and he could see soft earth and small stones beneath a thin coat of croc plaster. Junior knew that some snakes were good diggers. Sherahi had said that they had special, hard snouts and tails that were like augers. The cascabel pushed at the loose earth, but he seemed only to be able to pack it more firmly. "If only Dervish were here," he thought. "He could dig us out of this place in seconds."

Junior wondered, "Could Dervish fit in here?" The entrance looked barely large enough, but he thought that, if the coati were to hold his breath and twist his shoulders, his head and paws just might fit. He could stand on the steam pipe with his head in the hole and dig. If he put the pad of algae beneath his hind feet they might not get burned. It would be risky—not only because of the crocs. Junior felt the hot metal of the steam pipe. He remembered the clouds of steam that rose whenever the crocs slapped new wads of algae on the pipe to dry. The metal was now as cool as it ever got, but it was still too hot to touch.

"If I can get Dervish here, and if he will let me climb around his neck, and if he can stand on the algae, and dig fast enough; if he doesn't get caught and doesn't get burned, then maybe he can dig out of here. Once he's made this crevice big enough, he can dig up higher. If I can make a screen the way Sherahi taught me, the crocs won't be able to get us." Junior sighed, making a soft, hissing sound, and thought, "There are so many 'ifs,' but it might work.

"But how long will it take for him to make this crevice big enough? And if he can escape, how long before they're able to stop us?"

Hoping that the crocs weren't listening, Junior whispered to Dervish in mindspeech, saying, "Can you hear me?"

The coati heard Junior's whisper as he sat alongside the main waterway that connected all of the cells of the white crocodiles. He looked at the pair of huge, pale reptiles in his work party to see if they had intercepted Junior's message. They seemed to be intent upon their repair work and Dervish whispered, "What do you want?" He was annoyed with the cascabel and thought, "That nasty, little snake has been safe up in that hole in the ceiling while Manu and I have been working like slaves. He didn't do anything to help when the crocs attacked me. He's not a friend. Any friend who had his kind of power would have tried to help. He could have done something to help me. Sherahi would have."

"Can you get away from them?" asked Junior. "I've found some soft earth. It may be a way out. Manu said to ask . . ." Junior faltered and was still.

He knew that he owed Dervish an apology. The two hadn't been such close friends since their sojourn in the caverns of the fire serpent. At that time Dervish had infuriated the cascabel because he had always wanted to play. The serpent had made it clear that he preferred not to associate with Dervish. He had deliberately disobeyed Sherahi and had called the coati "Dummy" and "Stupid" whenever he could. Although Dervish hadn't understood these names at first, eventually his feelings had been hurt and he had stopped thinking of Junior as a friend or playmate. He'd allowed the snake to travel to the white crocodiles around his neck only because Manu and Sherahi had wanted it. More than once he'd regretted that he hadn't followed his instinct and killed Junior when he was still small.

Dervish's reply was cautious. He wasn't used to Junior being so nice. "Soft earth. I hope you're sure, because if they catch me again, they'll surely kill me. Besides, I've dug everywhere and the only soft earth in these tunnels is in the stream bed. The crocs have lined every inch of this place with croc plaster and you know how that stuff turns to stone when it dries."

"There's soft earth here, I promise," said Junior.

"Where are you?"

"In my hole above Sherahi's cell. Oh, Dervish, don't worry about details—I'll tell you all of that when you're here. Will you come?"

"Do you really think there's a way out?"

"I don't know—I'm not Sherahi. I can't see the future. All I can tell you is that there's soft dirt here. I thought you might be interested. Sorry that I bothered you." The cascabel broke off their communication and didn't respond when the coati tried to speak to him.

Dervish deposited a load of mud next to his growling, pale masters and eavesdropped on their conversation. He heard that once again Annahe had been chosen to mate in the Spring Glut. Each of these males claimed to have been the father of her surviving hatchling, which now swam beside her in the nursery pool. As she had predicted, the other hatchlings had been reverted and she had eaten them shortly after they'd struggled free of their eggshells.

"Nasty things they were, too, those reversions," hissed one reptilian mason. "Bodies like little turtles, with all those bones beneath their scales. And those awful colors—black and olive green and those yellow bands. Garish." The croc shuddered.

"Quite archaic," replied his partner. "And don't forget how fat they were."

"Amazing how grotesque reversions can be."

The second croc agreed and added, "But the New One is a different matter. Quite distinguished—don't you think?"

The first croc grunted in agreement and the other continued, "You know, I hadn't realized how satisfying it would be to see myself in a new generation. I guess I never thought about fatherhood. It's caught me by surprise."

"What are you talking about?" said his partner, looking up sharply from the wall repairs. "That's my baby, not yours. I mated with her last."

"I hate to be the one to tell you, friend," said the other croc, looking up slyly from the wall he was mending, "but you're mistaken. She lifted her tail for me *long after* you and all the rest were snoring on the bank. The New One is mine. Can't you tell?"

"That's ridiculous," hissed the first croc. "It's the spit'n image of me. It's mine. I'm sure of it."

The second croc laughed and opened his mouth to roar in triumph.

The first croc pounded his tail, bellowed and lunged at the other's throat. They forgot wall repairs and echo location as they grappled and tussled in the mire. When the second croc finally surrendered, they both stood panting and staring balefully at one another. The victor signaled with his front claw and waited for the coati to drop the next load of mud that they needed. He panted and thought, "Nice little creature, this one is. Helpful and cheery. Almost like one of us. He's learned his lesson for sure. Not one bit of trouble with him ever since we punished him. Put the fear of his betters into him, that's for sure. Too bad he'll be taken in the Glut. We could use more helpers like him."

The croc was thinking about finding a way to prolong the little mammal's life in the tunnels of the white crocodiles when he slowly looked around to see what was delaying the coati. The croc growled in surprise to see that the stream bank behind him was empty. The coati had vanished.

238

Kicking furiously with his back muscles, Dervish swam under water, watching for and avoiding all of the crocs that patrolled the waterway. Silently he surfaced in the room where Sherahi was kept prisoner. All was quiet. The big snake did not stir and the pair of crocs that guarded her had their backs to him. In a moment the coati had climbed up to the steam pipe, where Junior waited. Water streamed from his fur onto the pipe and sizzled beneath his paws. Clouds of steam rose around him, but the crocs guarding Sherahi did not notice.

"Quick, get this beneath your feet before they get burned," the cascabel hissed at Dervish. "Stand on it and let me get out of the way." Junior coiled around the wet fur of the coati's belly and said into his mind, "There. Now hurry. I think your head and paws can fit inside."

Without making a sound the coati wriggled his head and shoulders into the narrow opening above the steam pipe and began to dig furiously at the back of the crevice. He was surprised to find that it was soft earth, just as Junior had said. His fur dripped water onto the hot pipe and more clouds of steam engulfed them. Dirt flew out of the crevice and fell to the pool below, but the two crocs seemed inert. Perhaps they couldn't hear over the clanging and hissing of the pipes. Perhaps they were asleep. But Junior was nervous. "Do you have to make such a mess?" he complained. "They'll get us."

"Do you want me to dig or not?" came Dervish's reply. "The dirt's got to go somewhere."

"But they'll see."

"I can't help it," said the coati. "Do something to confuse them."

A keening sound penetrated into the chamber—the sound of the alarm of the white crocodiles. Simultaneously, Junior heard the alarm being called in ancient saurian mindspeech. Dervish heard it, too, and said, "If you don't do something, they'll get both of us this time."

"I'll try," Junior said, "but I told Manu that I'm not Sherahi. I can't do the things she can."

"Stop being stupid," said Dervish without stopping his frantic work. "Nobody expects you to be Sherahi. Do what you can. I know you can keep them from catching us if you try."

Dervish was no longer standing completely outside the crevice. He had crawled deeper into the excavation and now only his ringed tail protruded. It jerked madly as he dug.

"Can't you pull in your tail?" whined Junior. "They'll see it."

"Not and dig, too. Stop giving me orders and do something to help. They'll be here any minute."

Junior folded his fangs even more tightly within his mouth and focused his thoughts upon the minds of the crocodiles. He could sense that eight of them were nearby. Sherahi's two guards were alert and staring up at the coati's tail. They knew that he and Dervish were above and were ready to tell the others when they arrived. They couldn't do anything themselves, though, because they had to control Sherahi. If they took their minds off her, even for a moment, she would be able to erect mental shields to thwart their control. So, Junior concentrated on the eight muggers that swam toward the chamber, making a pale chevron formation in the phosphorescent water. He saw how quickly their bodies undulated, like snakes swimming across a rock face. "How can I stop them? What can I do?" he thought. Then the idea came to him.

"Cold," he thought. "That'll stop any reptile. I must make them cold."

The cascabel remembered the snowstorm that the Culls had passed through. He remembered how cold the snow had felt upon his ridged scales. He remembered how the white, sparkly flakes had whirled and shifted before his eyes, drifting into powdery mountains, needling and stabbing at him as he coiled deeper into Dervish's warm fur. He shivered and sent the idea of cold: the idea of shards of ice, of icicles, of stalactites of snow, of glaciers calving icebergs in a frozen green ocean, of cold wind piercing, of numbed skin. The crocs had always lived in a subterranean tropical swamp. They had never known cold. They had never felt wind. He sent blasts of ice and snow sleeting into their minds and buffeted them with frigid headwinds as they swam. He was concentrating so hard that he barely heard Dervish say, "We're through."

Junior felt the coati's body leap and struggle forward. Cold, dry air rushed into his facial pits and he fnasted a wholly different odor—something unpleasant. Junior sent his mind back to the crocs in the chamber below and saw that his thoughts had chilled them. They were still swimming, but only very slowly and laboriously. They were cold and would never catch him and Dervish now. He had done it. He rattled his tail in triumph and the sound echoed loudly in the shadowy space around them.

"Shut up," said Dervish.

Junior was surprised at Dervish's fierce tone and he stopped rattling his tail.

"You know better than that," said the coati severely. "There's no telling what's in here." He silently pushed dirt back into the passage behind them and tamped the earth down firmly with his back legs. As he did so the pale light from the chamber below grew dimmer and soon the blackness was complete. Not wasting a moment, the coati marked the place with urine and stood panting over the hole. His head hung and his tongue lolled out.

While Dervish regained his breath and waited for his eyes to adjust to this new darkness, Junior fnasted the air and said in mindspeech, "We're in a tunnel."

240

"Gee," said Dervish. "Aren't you the perceptive one! I'd never have known."

"It dead-ends in a few paces, so I think we'd better go up, following the pipe."

Dervish was silent and the cascabel listened to him pant before he said, "Dervish, I'm sorry for calling you 'Stupid.' You're not stupid, you're smart—way smarter than me. Can't we be friends?"

"We'll see," said the coati. "Maybe we can talk about it after we've found a way out of here. Let's go." With the cascabel around his neck, the coati started off to cautiously explore this new tunnel, which climbed around the steam pipe that heated the tunnels of the white crocodiles.

Inside Dervish's mind a small voice said, "Be careful of rats, Dervish."

The coati sighed and replied, "I will."

Sherahi lay stretched out at full length on the muddy bank of the stream that ran through the tunnels of the white crocodiles, her steady eyes locked in the glittering gaze of her pale captors. For the first few days after they had seized the Culls, Sherahi had actively struggled against the net that bound her agile mind. It had seemed that no matter how she squirmed or twisted, no matter how hard she shoved against the fetters around her thoughts, she could not escape their control. She had tried to inwit away, but even that small pleasure had been denied. She lay calmly now and had long since ceased to fight. She could sense that, little by little, the white crocodiles from remote parts of the nest had withdrawn their attention and control. She hadn't dared to think, but her mind now felt much lighter. It now seemed to Sherahi that only the two big males who lay on the bank facing her still actively monitored and regulated her thoughts.

There was a disturbance in the pool beyond her guards and, although Sherahi saw it, she was careful to keep her mind as still as a mirror. She recognized Dervish and saw him leap out of the shallow water and onto a huge, rusty pipe. Quite inadvertently the thought issued from her mind, "Good, faithful Dervish," and she felt a wrenching between her eyes as her crocodilian guards realized that their captive was thinking once again. With their superior mind control they squeezed and wiped her brain clear of thought.

They weren't quite quick enough or completely scrupulous and their wrenching squeeze didn't reach into one small corner of Sherahi's mind. Quicker than a deer mouse leaping into its hole Sherahi erected a formidable, cleverly disguised barrier that was impervious to their control and invisible to their scans. Behind this wall a tiny portion of her unique pythonine intelligence coiled and stretched, delighted to be free again. In this bastion, deep within her mind, Sherahi hissed, "You have taught me well, Holy White Frauds. And, if there's time, I can turn it all against you. The Culls will get out of here—somehow. We won't be fodder for your Spring Glut."

The Duchess was in the brightly lit chamber of the Holiest of the Holy White Crocodiles when the news came that Dervish and Junior had escaped. Although Manu and Dervish had been forced to do manual labor for their captors, the Duchess had been given a different sort of task: entertaining the leader of the white crocodiles. The mere idea of a talking bird had sent this Holiest of the Holy White Crocodiles into hysterics and he had summoned the marvel to his chambers. Even though he knew that she did not speak perfect English, her mispronunciations and garbled phrases delighted him and she had become his favorite diversion, a sort of feathered court jester. Every day one of his acolytes appeared and ferried her to the distant chamber. As her living barge floated through the phosphorescent waters, the crocs resting on the banks and swimming around her gawked at her in wonder and nodded to one another. The Duchess preened her new breast feathers and tried to seem not to notice their admiration. She found her celebrity gratifying, but more than anything else she thought that it was well deserved.

"It's the least they can do," she had said to Manu one night in the Culls' cell. "Even though they are our distant relatives, birds are, you realize, a far superior breed. As anyone can see, we are infinitely more beautiful than they and of course there is no match anywhere for our cleverness." She had waited for the langur to reply, but he was too tired from his muddy labor. His bones ached—especially the arm that had been broken long ago. Besides, sometimes even Manu found the Duchess hard to bear. Before their capture she had shown signs of becoming a reasonable animal; now that the crocs had made such a fuss over her, the stupid fool thought she was some sort of avian Cleopatra. Manu sighed and looked at the macaw for one long, silent minute. She was busily rubbing oil onto her face from the gland above her tail. She was humming. Then he turned his back to her and closed his eyes, listening to the Duchess talk to herself and wishing that she'd shut up.

But the bird continued. "Of course it's preposterous, but they want me to teach the New One to speak. Can you believe that, Manu? All these crocs are agog over that baby and *I'm* supposed to take charge of his education. I'm to start as soon as he's able to swim properly." There was a silence, in which Manu began to relax, when her sharp soprano voice cut into his sleep. "Manu, are you listening?"

"Ummm," came the langur's sleepy reply and the Duchess continued preening her belly feathers.

"They say that eventually I'll have a whole class of youngsters. They expect many unreverted ones in the next hatch. So much protein, you know. And they want some sort of entertainment for the Spring Glut. I know I never should have sung for His Holiness, but then, we're not supposed to bury our talents under a basket."

The Duchess looked coquettishly at Manu, but the langur made no reply. She hadn't realized that he was quite so dirty. "Why can't he clean himself like he used to?" she wondered and edged a few paces away.

"Now, what can I do in the Spring Glut? The rabble," she sighed, "all they want is cake and carnivals."

"So," interrupted Manu, "they're going to keep you alive. I thought they might. Well, I hope you'll have fun living down here with these monsters. Personally, I'd rather face the meat rack. But I guess it doesn't matter to you. You'll be terribly busy with much more important matters—essential things like teaching a mixed chorus of crocs to sing in four-part harmony. Who knows, maybe you can do madrigals someday?" He glared at her and turned on his side again.

The Duchess looked at the monkey's back. Not only was he filthy, but large, gray insects moved in the fur along his spine. The sight of lice made her shudder and she moved a few more steps away. She hadn't told Manu that the crocs were building her very own chamber for her. It would have a real perch—a branch sculpted out of croc plaster. How restful it would be to sit on a perch again. That's where she'd conduct her classes. And they'd promised to make glow globes of lightning slime for her so that the new chamber would be almost like the sunlit world. The Spring Glut would come, bringing the other Culls ugly but brief deaths. The Holy One had assured her that they wouldn't suffer too much. "Painless," he'd hissed. "It'll be over before they know it's started."

"Besides," she said to the langur's back, "we never could have gotten to the San Diego Zoo." She pronounced each syllable distinctly. "It's much too far."

"What do you mean?" Manu suddenly demanded. "What have you learned about Sandeagozu?" Somehow hearing the Duchess say the word with such precision enraged him.

"Nothing much." The Duchess was nonchalant. She didn't like disappointing Manu, but it was better that he learn the truth from her. "Only that it's impossibly far away—across a whole continent, I think they said. The Holy One said that it would take even a fast flier like me two weeks to get there. And even *I* might be killed crossing the mountains.

"Sherahi was taking us on a fool's errand. Even she wasn't powerful enough to get us there.

"And it's worse than that, Manu. Sandeagozu doesn't exist. There's only a place called San Diego Zoo. And it's a zoo—a place where people come to stare at creatures like us. Apparently Sherahi got it all wrong. There is no such place as Sandeagozu. The mere word now strikes me as terribly funny."

"Well, that's your opinion, Duchess, but tell me one thing: if Sherahi isn't more powerful than they are, then why are your new friends so afraid of her? Why don't they let her loose?" He glared at the macaw and added, "Ask your Holy One to explain that. Watch him slither in the mud as he flounders for an answer."

"But the Holy One . . ."

"Don't tell me anything more," said Manu. "I'm sick of him and of you. While you've spent the day reciting limericks, I've been grubbing in the mud. Or maybe you haven't noticed the delightful activities your pals invent to keep me amused. My back aches and I'm tired. If you don't mind, I'd like to spend what remains of my life in peace."

"But, Manu . . ."

"Peace!" screamed the monkey. "Do you know what that means?" He suddenly turned on her and bared his canines. If their crocodile guard hadn't rushed up to drag him away, Manu might have torn the red feathers from her throat.

"Well, I never," said the Duchess. Feeling betrayed by her only friend, she fluttered off to the farthest corner of the chamber. "That's gratitude for you," she said. Her guard heard her speak and stopped shaking Manu, distracted by the sound of her voice. The crocodile chuckled and it infuriated the Duchess. "Shut up, you ugly, overgrown lizard," she said. This only made him laugh all the more and the hissing sound filled the chamber.

The next morning the Holiest One heard that Manu had tried to attack the Duchess. His soldiers appeared in the Culls' chamber and four of them held Manu down while a fifth delivered blows with his heavy tail. The Duchess tried to pretend that she was happy with this treatment, but when Manu fell unconscious beneath the first blow she begged the soldier crocs to stop.

Later that day she moved to her splendid new chamber. She spent the next few days imperiously directing the activities of the crocodile masons from her long-anticipated perch. When they were finished there was a network of perches and feeding platforms over the phosphorescent bathing pool. She flew from perch to perch, admiring her reflection. The bird that looked back at her had violet feathers and a blue bill. "I look absolutely gorgeous," she thought and began to wonder if she should change the color of her plumage now that she had a new, flamboyant vocation. "After all, I must think of my public."

The lessons of the baby croc began and the Duchess found that she learned more than her student. Even young crocs had an encyclopedic knowledge of their surroundings, as well as a way of speaking into the Duchess's mind that seemed to make it grow larger. She felt excited, flushed with her success. From the New One the Duchess learned the geography of the tunnels. She also learned that the only way out of the chambers was through the underground spring that supplied water to the main channel. This was impossible, though, because the strong current was against the swimmer. The Duchess also learned that, even if an animal could swim through the current, when he surfaced he would find himself within a busy city, surrounded by people. Capture or death would be certain.

She learned that above the tunnels of the white crocodiles was one of the largest buildings in this city. Although she couldn't quite believe it, they said it was a barnlike place where fire serpents arrived and departed, carrying hundreds of thousands of humans. The steam pipes that warmed the crocodiles' tunnels were a part of the heating system of this huge building. They had been driven so deeply into the earth because the ground above them was perforated by train tunnels, by sewers, as well as by the underground spring. The tunnel that the Culls had been in before they'd been lured to the nursery chamber was a storm sewer. They'd been fortunate that it was snowing at the time and that the sewer was dry. When the snow melted or when the spring rains came, the Culls would have been washed out of the storm sewer and drowned in the East River.

In the weeks that followed, the Holiest One still had frequent, long talks with the Duchess. He tried to make her realize how lucky she was that fate had brought her to the chambers of the white crocodiles—the Chosen Ones. With the improvements they were making in her thought processes she would soon be able to speak real English, not the parrot pidgin that she now realized was at her command. Then, she would teach unhatched generations to speak. With speech and their ability to control minds the white crocodiles could lure many more animals and humans into their tunnels. Their numbers would increase and eventually they'd emerge from these tunnels and enslave the humans who lived above. "They're so greedy," rasped the Holiest of the Holy White Crocodiles into the Duchess's mind. "They'll be easier to control than centipedes."

He explained the plan to flood the city streets and herd the humans into breeding pens. "Then all of our females can breed," he had exulted. "Just think of all the nests and eggs and unreverted young. Think of the civilization we will build." The Holiest of the Holy Ones had been intoxicated with the idea.

"Don't you see, my dear?" he wheezed. "With the mastery of human speech there is no limit to what we can do. You will become a heroine to unborn generations of white crocodiles. Perhaps we will have shrines to the Scarlet Bird that brought us speech. It will be a wonderful symbiosis: we will improve your mind and you will teach this New One and all future New Ones to speak and they, in turn, will teach others. You will remain with us as a revered and respected teacher. We will be forever indebted to you and when you die your body will be carefully preserved and only your brightest, most promising students will be permitted to eat from it in the Spring Glut.

"And, until then," the Holy One added, "you can teach our youngsters in your beautiful new chambers. I might point out that, unlike your human masters, we have given you a cage without bars."

The phrase "cage without bars" set the Duchess thinking. The idea of the white crocodiles actually leaving their tunnels and dominating all other creatures frightened her. She knew how powerful they were: she had seen what they had done with her mind. "But they're so cruel," she thought. She remembered Manu, shriveled from his diet of dried algae and hard labor. He couldn't last much longer.

"I'll do it on the condition that you let Manu and the others live out their lives with me," she said.

The Holy One opened his pale jaws and laughed. "Impossible, my dear," he hissed. "Quite out of the question. Now that the other two are gone the monkey and the python are necessary for the Spring Glut to be successful. We have no other choice. There are no other victims, unless, of course, you'd like to volunteer." He laughed again at his small joke.

The Duchess imagined Manu torn asunder on that horrid meat rack. Something in the Holiest One's eyes was too eager—too sly. "I'll have to think about it," she said. "Perhaps you've heard the old proverb, 'Act in haste, repeat it later'?"

The Holiest One looked at her blankly. "The meaning escapes me, Scarlet Bird, but I am not familiar with human idioms, although I trust that my successor will understand completely because of your tutelage.

"Think about my offer. As you have already seen, there are obvious advantages to being our friend."

The Duchess was carried back to her chamber and soon settled onto her luxurious sleeping perch. She was tired and ordered her servants to darken the glow globes. They curled obediently about the phosphorescent orbs and the Duchess put her head beneath her wing. She was standing on one foot, relaxed and nearly asleep, when she heard one servant whisper to the other, "I've heard that they're going to let the Scarlet Bird live."

"Don't be a simpleton," said the other. "The Holiest One is using her just like the others."

"What do you mean?"

"He'll get her to teach our young ones all she knows and when that's done, she'll be ripped to pieces, just like the others. It's common gossip that she doesn't know half of what she thinks she does. He's just having his little bit of fun with her. You have to admit she *is* funny. And fun is in short supply around here."

The Duchess couldn't believe what she'd heard. How could the Holiest One be so devious? "Has he been laughing at me all the time that I've been teaching the New One? It can't be true. I don't believe it. He said that they loved me because I was related to them—but then . . ." Her thoughts faltered and then she asked herself, "Why didn't I think of it before? It can't be true that they love me because we're related—Sherahi is a reptile and they hate her."

The Duchess roused her feathers and shifted her weight to the other foot, but she couldn't sleep. She felt the pale, malevolent stares of the servants coiled around the glow globes and decided that she wouldn't be their jester anymore. She decided that she would do the only thing she could to thwart their plans.

When the Holiest One requested her presence she feigned sickness. After a few days of sickness, he realized that the Scarlet Bird had decided not to teach human speech to the New One anymore. He knew that he could not force her to teach unborn generations and the Holiest One whipped his tail against the glowing water of his chamber in frustration.

"Put her with the others," he ordered. "Destroy her chamber. She will be shredded in the Glut. Until that time she will replace the escapee. Put her to work carrying mud for the masons. Perhaps that will change her mind."

Sherahi gazed at the part of the ceiling where Dervish's banded tail had disappeared a short while ago. She felt the fetters threaten to seize her mind again and purposely kept it as blank as she could to fool her guards. Meanwhile, behind her cunning mindscreen she imagined a perfectly round, white-shelled egg and, floating within it, a perfectly formed and very determined green baby sea turtle.

She felt his firmly clenched, toothless jaw and saw the wrinkled old-man's eyelids that protected his large, round eyes. She saw his soft shell and the four, claw-fringed flippers that swam, even though he still floated within the shell his mother had made for him. He was not yet ready to hatch. "Soon, little turtle," thought Sherahi. "Your time will come soon and you will swim and fly free in an ocean that's bigger than you can possibly imagine."

Sherahi lay on the muddy bank, with a fraction of her mind actively undermining the psychic control of the white crocodiles. Like an earthworm poking an inquisitive nose out of its burrow on a misty night to sniff for succulent leaves, Sherahi gently peered out from behind her mental screen. Surreptitiously she rearranged her mindscreen to reclaim a greater portion of her thoughts. In the wheezing snores of her sleeping guards she imagined she could hear the beckoning roar of surf.

"I think we'd better go back," said Junior. "There's nothing here. It's just another tunnel going nowhere."

"Don't be simple, Junior," snapped Dervish. "Why would humans build a tunnel leading nowhere? Those creatures always have a purpose. We'll look a little longer. Besides, what's there to go back for?"

"The others. We have to help them," said Junior. "We can't just leave them. It's been days now. Maybe the Spring Glut has started. We must help them."

"Why?" said Dervish. "We're free. Why do we have to worry about them?"

"I can't believe that you're actually saying that, Dervish. It just doesn't sound like you at all."

"That's because you're used to your former friend—Dervish the Dummy. But he's gone now and I'm looking out for myself. To hell with the rest of you.

"I could have escaped long ago. I could probably be safe in some nice, warm place with lots of food and no white crocodiles. But *no*, that was too simple. I had to be the hero. 'Find a way out, Dervish,' she said. 'Go back and get Manu,' she said. Do this. Do that. Fine mess it turned out, too.

"I've made up my mind. I won't do anybody's bidding anymore. This time it's me first."

"You'd actually leave Sherahi and Manu and the Duchess in there with those creatures?" The cascabel was incredulous.

There was a long period in which the coati paced along without saying anything. He eventually broke the silence. "No," he chittered, sounding more like the Dervish that Junior knew. "I guess I couldn't really do that. I'd want to—at least part of me would. I promise you, though, if we ever get out of here, I'm watching out for me first."

"Hush," the cascabel said. "Something just moved. Up there."

The coati stopped and sniffed the air. There was a strong smell ahead. A human smell—not sweet-human like Sorensen, but a sour, rancid human stench. The odor was more like a white crocodile's than a human's. But it didn't make sense to Dervish: what was a human doing here? He felt the cascabel around his neck stiffen into a striking coil. Without making a sound the coati moved forward.

The smell grew stronger but Dervish still couldn't see anything. Then a match flared and shadows jumped on the walls. Dervish flattened like a cat stalking a cottontail. There was light for an instant and then it was suddenly extinguished and a gravelly voice swore, "Summofabitchin' match. Where's that candle?"

There was a rustling sound in the tunnel and another match was struck. Dervish's eyes squinted against the sudden light. He saw a figure crouching in a heap of rags and paper. It blocked the tunnel fifteen feet from where he and Junior watched. The person's hand shook violently and she had difficulty lighting the stub of a candle that she held in one hand. Three stained front teeth gnawed at her slack lower lip as she concentrated on lighting and setting it into a pool of melted wax on top of the steam pipe that formed the perimeter of her hovel in this subterranean tunnel.

When the candle was fixed in place, the woman stared at it as if transfixed; rubbing her hands convulsively and rocking to and fro, she suddenly began to laugh. Her hair hung in strings and rags fluttered when her arms moved. Her face was as creased as a worn, brown paper bag and when she stopped cackling her mouth twitched ceaselessly, forming words without making sounds. Her whitened eyebrows danced above her eyes and to Dervish it looked as if she were enacting the whole range of human emotions. With her eyes fixed on the candle's flame, the rag woman's face registered glee, fury, sorrow, even hope. From time to time she muttered phrases that Dervish did not understand, rubbed her hands together and rocked herself to and fro.

As suddenly as this began, the woman ceased her mad performance and, with a businesslike sigh, she began to empty two paper sacks that lay beside her on the discarded mattress that was her home in the tunnel. She took each object out, examined it and carefully set it on top of the steam pipe alongside the candle. She pried the top from a small, round tin and took a sip. She pursed her lips against the taste and then scrubbed at her mouth with the back of one scrawny hand, exhaling forcefully. It was as if she were trying to eradicate the memory of what she drank. Her grimace reminded Dervish of Manu. He made a face like that when he was scared.

She took another drink and her cracked voice said, "Bad. He must've put iodine or som'thin' in it." She placed the tin on top of the steam pipe, along with a man's left oxford shoe, the want ads from the *New York Herald*, a maroon mitten with a hole in the thumb, a stale bagel and half of a hot dog bun. She had spent the whole night rummaging upstairs in Grand Central and this was all she had to show for her effort.

She took another drink and thought about the cold and the numbness in her feet and hands. She'd been trying to ignore the spots before her eyes for a long time. "Can't think about that. Think about Ben. Got to trust him. He's my friend."

The woman took another sip from the tin and, after a short spell of hand-wringing and muttering to the flame, returned to her sorting. She smoothed the newspapers and stacked them neatly on top of those that already covered her mattress. She put the bagel into her food bag, along with the sandwich crusts that were left over from yesterday. She looked at the shoe and saw that the sole was whole. "Maybe Ben will want it," she said, thinking that maybe tomorrow night, if she was lucky, she could sneak into the Ladies' Room when the matron was asleep. Maybe she could clean herself up a little—maybe even take a bath in one of the toilets. "Ben has always had eyes for me—I know that." She smiled and pushed the lank hair out of her eyes, cackling in maniacal glee, "Maybe he will give me some more. Have to get some soon. This won't last long, not with these bums down here." She reached for the tin again and held it protectively against her chest, looking suddenly over her shoulder and scrutinizing the darkness behind.

There was a sound of arguing in the distance and the woman quickly reached for the club that she kept beneath her mattress. She got to her feet and crouched down, ready to defend herself. The voices died and she settled herself once more. As she did so, she looked toward the dead end of the tunnel and saw a pair of green eyes. She stared at them and mechanically reached for the tin and took another sip. "You're watching," she said softly. Then she began to whimper and said, "Someone's always watching." She rubbed her hands together and scratched her head. Then in a very calm voice a different persona said kindly, "Effie, now don't get excited. If you're calm, *They* won't come any closer. It's probably just a cat."

She blinked back at the eyes and her voice grated, "Used to have a cat. Sophie. That was her name. One day she run off and never came back. Maybe this's Sophie." She reached out a gnarled hand, crooning, "Here, Sophie, nice pussycat." The calm voice said again, "Yes, Effie, that's Sophie out there. Not one of *Them*."

She rummaged in her food bag for a crust to offer to the eyes and called out in a high voice that reverberated in the tunnel and made the hair on Dervish's spine stand on end, "Here, kitty. Nice kitty. Kittykittykitty."

But the eyes didn't move and her arm grew tired. She tossed the crust into the darkness and watched as the green eyes blinked out.

The crust landed near Dervish and he snatched it up and growled delightedly. It was the first real food that he'd had in a long time. The woman continued talking, saying, "Nice kitty. Pretty kitty. Come, kitty."

With the bread in his mouth Dervish watched her take another swig from the tin. Then she set it down and crashed her club onto the floor, yelling, "All right. Don't come. Be that way. Jus' like all of 'em. No one wants to be with Effie. Not even an alleycat." She made a gesture with both arms as if to push the eyes away and hugged herself again.

She looked at the walls that seemed to waver in the light. "Now you, cockroaches, you're pals. You like Effie. You'd like to crawl all over me, just like Them. This is for you." She tore off a small piece of bagel and threw it against the wall and had another drink. "Go slow," she said to herself and carefully set the tin beneath her mattress and turned on her side, staring at the candle and wishing it would never go out. Effie had liked to sleep with the light on, ever since she had been a little girl. That way if any of Them came while you were asleep, They couldn't sneak up on you. Dervish saw shadows move on the wall as huge roaches smelled the food and drew closer, antennae waving.

The woman was muttering as she lay on her mattress. "Tomorrow'll be better. If I lock myself in they can't make me come out. . . . Maybe that fat cow'll be asleep."

She felt something run over her leg and sat up suddenly, beating at the roaches that tried to feed at the sores on her ankles.

"OOhh, Jesus," she shrieked. "Please, Jesus, I'll be good. Please get 'em away. Don't let 'em get me. Get away. Get away! Please."

Her plea ended in a series of shrieks and howls and she pulled the mattress on top of her as she tried to get away from the demons that materialized out of the darkness. She upset the candle and the light went out. In the blackness Junior and Dervish listened to the woman wrestle with her invisible fiends.

Her cries turned to whimpers and when she'd been quiet for a time, Dervish crept forward. He located the bag that held her food, grabbed the hot dog bun and dashed back to where Junior coiled, waiting for him. "She's asleep," said Junior. "I'm going ahead to hunt for food. You stay here."

The snake slithered away, his scales making a slight scrape against the tunnel floor. Dervish chewed at the hard bread, using his cheek and rear teeth on one side. The smell and taste of the mustard made him think of Sorensen, the man who used to play with him and give him treats. Dervish wondered where Sorensen was now. He shivered and remembered the snug nest box under Sorensen's work bench. It had grown colder in the tunnel and Dervish was used to the warmth of the chambers of the white crocodiles. "They must have done something to make these same pipes give off so much heat in their chambers," Dervish thought. He curled up, nose to tail, and tried to shiver himself warm. When that didn't work, he crawled beneath an edge of the mattress. The woman smelled putrid, but she seemed harmless and at least she was warm. Dervish curled next to her and slept.

When Junior returned he found Dervish beneath the woman's mattress. The snake had seen others like her in the tunnel ahead. All were dressed in rags and had the same sour stench. Some were asleep. Others muttered to themselves. Junior saw a few by candlelight, but most were only malodorous lumps in the darkness. Eventually he had fnasted a rat's runway and had positioned himself to await his prey. Before long a half-grown female blundered into his jaws. The struggle was brief but satisfying and the cascabel had slithered back to Dervish with an idea. He knew how they would save the others.

He coiled apart from Dervish and concentrated on the idea that he would send into the coati's mind—the thought of play. He sent the image of the tin can rolling along the tunnel, jerking forward and then stopping suddenly, shining and mutely begging Dervish to slap it again to see what would happen.

"Dervish," the cascabel wheedled, "this is a good, new game. And it's been such a long time since you've been able to play the way you used to. Wouldn't it be fun to have someone chase you the way that Sorensen used to?

"She'll play with you, Dervish. But first you have to fetch her round box. The one with the lid on it. The one that's by her hand. It's her favorite thing in *all* the world. Careful. Take it from her slowly. You don't want to wake her. Not yet. That's a good boy."

Dervish cautiously crept up to the woman's hand and stealthily grabbed the tin by its edge. He found that he could carry it in the side of his mouth. "A toy," thought the entranced coati. "This'll be fun. A game. Just like Sorensen and I used to play."

He ran a few steps from the woman and began to bat the can with a paw. He found that if he set it on edge the can would roll. That was fun. He chased it back and forth, guided by its scent. The can was easy to locate in the darkness because it smelled like one of Sorensen's medicines. It made a nice plonking noise when he hit it. It seemed to ask for him to hit it again and again.

The woman awoke to a strange clatter. Her first impulse was to grab for her club. The usual morning headache was bad and she felt sick. She retched over the edge of her mattress and when the nausea had passed she felt for her tin. Some of Ben's special mixture would make her feel better. Where was it? Then there was that banging again, very close to her. "What the hell . . ." she said. The noise stopped. "Where's that damn candle?" Her fumbling hands located it and the matches in her pocket, but she had some trouble bringing the match to the wick. Her eyes didn't seem to be working right.

When she finally got the candle lit she lifted it high above her head. Just at the edge of the circle of light she saw a little cat with a long, banded tail. He looked up, startled. Between his paws was a tin can—her precious can.

"How did you get that?" she growled. She saw the animal's ears flatten and realized that it was about to run away with her booze. Not moving from her mattress she stretched out her hand and in a soft, wheedling voice said, "Bring it here, nice kitty. Pretty kitty, bring it to Effie."

The animal cocked its head and watched. As if he understood, he picked up the can in his teeth and walked a few paces toward her. Then he reared on his hind legs, waggled his front paws in the air and scampered away. After a few yards he stopped, put the can down and his eyes glowed at her in the gloom.

"Oh, you want to play, eh?" she said. "Effie'll show you how to play right and proper." She grabbed her billy club and stuffed the stale bagel into her pocket, along with her other candle. Standing up made her sick again and her eyes weren't focusing—everything looked wavy.

Supporting herself against one wall she staggered after the cat, calling in a soft voice, "Come, kittykittykitty. Don't be scared. Look what Effie's got for you." She was sick and too intent upon regaining her hard-bought liquor to notice the attenuated shadow that slithered down the tunnel behind her.

The water had begun to rise in the chamber where the white crocodiles had imprisoned the Culls. "It won't be long now," thought Sherahi. "Soon it'll all be over and none of us will have to worry anymore." Then her brief thought was detected by one of the crocodiles that guarded her. With a glimmer in his pale eyes he extinguished even this and Sherahi surrendered to the immobility and nothingness that had suspended her for so long.

Behind her mindscreen the baby turtle that she'd thought of so often was jostled within his egg by the swimming movements of the other hatchlings who surrounded him in the egg chamber, dug long ago by the mother he had never seen. The hatchlings practiced swimming, their movements exciting one another into flurries of paddling. Impatient to join them, the miniature leviathan rubbed the egg tooth on his snout against the inside of his eggshell. His egg tooth was sharp. It pierced the shell and he felt the pool around him drain and the shell collapse inward. Above him a hatchling practiced swimming and its flipper deflated the soft, unresisting ceiling above his head. Angrily, the baby sea turtle poked his head out of the opening he'd slashed to find scores of nest mates who were instinctively scrabbling upward in the sand.

He could hear the roar of the ocean and knew that in minutes they would climb higher in the soft sand. He heard someone calling him, singing in a lovely siren song, and yearned to frantically crawl out of this crowded, sandy hole and cross the short stretch of tide-pounded beach that separated him from the welcoming tide.

In the portion of her mind that Sherahi allowed the crocs to see she resigned herself to death and saw that they didn't mind if she thought, "I will die. They have ensnared my mind so efficiently that I can never escape. All of us will die."

The freed portion of her mind watched the clever act that she put on for the benefit of her guards, thinking, "We can't die. We will get away from these monsters." In his subterranean nest, surrounded by brothers and sisters, the baby green turtle rested and thought about the sea.

She saw that Manu and the Duchess were in the middle of the waterway, tied to the meat rack, a stilt-legged lattice constructed of croc plaster. Manu was ill and hung limply from his bonds. Death would be a blessing for him. The Duchess, however, was healthy and furious. Her scarlet feathers were streaked with mud and the delicate white skin of her face was filthy, but she looked balefully at her captors and returned every hiss and glare. They taunted her, saying, "It won't be long, Talking Bird, before you squawk your last. Then you'll wish you'd found your tongue in time."

The fog that engulfed her mind lifted and Sherahi was able to read her guard's mind. She saw that the crocs weren't going to pin her to the meat rack. They were afraid that she was too heavy and would break it, and that would be a poor omen for the Glut. Instead, she would be guarded until the last minute and when the entire crocodile population had surrounded her, the mind fetters would be removed and she would be slaughtered in the shallow water of this chamber. Sherahi didn't have time to reflect upon this news. Her guard let her know that much and then clamped down his control again—he'd only let her see his mind to torture her a bit more, yet in that short time Sherahi had reclaimed still more of her mind and moved her camouflaged mindscreens once again.

"Run, Dervish." Junior's orders were explicit. "Run. Don't let her catch you."

The coati held the tin between his paws and batted it ahead of him. The can clattered merrily down the sloping tunnel and the woman hurried after the coati as quickly as she could without extinguishing her candle or hitting her head. From time to time she would stop for breath and Dervish would approach within feet of her outstretched hand—a hand that offered food. He would seem to teeter on the edge of letting her touch him and then Junior's voice would hiss again within his mind, saying, "No. Don't go near her. She'll hurt you. Where's that lovely can? Go hit it again."

Soon they were back to the dead end of the tunnel, quite near the place where it ended. Dervish sat panting in the candlelight as the woman drew slowly closer. "Nice kitty," she said. "Pretty kitty." She put down the candle. "See, we can't go any farther. It's a dead end." She advanced slowly, thinking, "Funny-looking cat you are—but then, my eyes aren't too good today." In a soothing voice she said, "I'm not going to hurt you." She spoke calmly and Dervish watched her, his tongue hanging out, his head to one side. Slowly the woman lifted the club above her head. The can was on the ground next to Dervish and she could have taken it easily but she seemed to have lost all interest in it. Something made Dervish stare at her haggard face in fascination.

When she was only three feet away the woman brought her club down at Dervish, with a short, murderous, chopping motion. She used it expertly and would have broken his back if Junior's rattle hadn't sounded in the tunnel and startled her. Her aim was off by a foot and the club crashed down onto the tin, smashing it flat. The woman saw her precious liquor drain out onto the tunnel floor and simultaneously felt something hit her calf. The pain was immediate and intense. It felt as if a hot spike had been driven into her leg. "What the . . . ," she said and looked down to see blood welling up in two punctures on her leg. They were surrounded by a delicate tracery of blood-filled pinpricks. She put her hand down to touch the place and make the pain go away and fell on her side, knees clasped to her chest. Junior struck again. This time he delivered a double dose of venom directly into the woman's neck. She felt the stab—it was as if a branch had snapped against her neck. The pain in her leg disappeared, but she could not move.

She saw the candle before her and the light in the tunnel grow stronger, as if all the candles in the world had been lit. The flame grew brighter and bigger and Effie died with a happy but puzzled expression on her tired face. She'd never be afraid of the dark again.

"Quick, Dervish," said Junior. "Dig. Open the hole that you made to get us away from the white crocodiles."

"But you've killed a person. And she was going to be my friend."

"Come out of it, Dervish. *I* gave you that thought. Does a friend try to club you to death? That was me fooling you. Now, come on. Hurry up. We've got to get in there and save the others."

The coati growled at the cascabel. He regarded him for a long moment and said, "I don't like being used in that way." The hair bristled along his spine.

"So help me, Dervish, I'm at the end of my patience," threatened the snake. "If you won't do what I say, I swear I'll kill you, too." The cascabel coiled into an oblique striking coil and the coati realized that he had no chance against the snake. "That's better," said Junior. "Now, hurry up and dig a hole that's big enough for her to fit through. And be careful not to let any dirt fall into that room. If the crocs are in there, and I'm sure they are, I don't want them to suspect anything until it's too late. If they repaired the place the way they always do, they made a mistake that's going to fit into our plans just perfectly."

The coati gave Junior a hate-filled look and began to dig at the floor of the tunnel, guided by the scent mark that he had left there days ago. He knew that the Culls were below, but what could Junior do to save them? "Whatever happens," he decided, "I'm not going back down there. He can kill me if he likes, but I won't do it."

The Spring Glut was in full swing in the chambers of the white croc-odiles. The entire population was assembled in or outside the Culls' cham-ber, awaiting the penultimate ceremony—the ritual feeding. The males and the single female that would breed this year were assembled around the meat rack, which held Manu and the Duchess, while Sherahi lay in the shallows. She was reserved for the final ceremony of the Glut. There was special excitement this year because no croc could remember when there had ever been so much meat to share. Often the crocs reenacted their cere-mony with only a scrawny rat for the entire population. In those years most members of the community got only a scrap of skin and a sniff of the sacri-fice. Even those that would mate were usually rewarded with just a sliver of rat leg. This year, however, the ancient ritual would be celebrated with plenty of meat, and every croc looked forward to cruising into the shallow water and wrestling a mouthful of python flesh from Sherahi's living body. Best of all, she was a reptile and her flesh would be slow to die. It would still be alive when it reached their stomachs. And she was so fat. The crocs could hardly wait for the mating dances to be over. A diet of dried algae was nour-ishing, but no one would call it toothsome or satisfying.

Led by Annahe, a circle of the females of breeding age performed a water dance in which the crocs expressed their gratitude for the bountiful spring rains. All had agreed that the rains were especially plentiful this year; the wall repairs had been finished none too soon.

As the female chosen to mate for the second year in a row, Annahe was the Princess of the Glut and was to be awarded a special treat. She would be the first to taste living flesh and had decided that monkey meat was what she wanted. She'd already had a mouthful of feathers and found them tasteless. Fur might be nicer. She was closing in on the meat rack, her black eyes nearly level with those of Manu, when he lifted his arm and pointed to the ceiling. Something was happening to the croc plaster there. It was caving in, and among chunks of it and a shower of dirt something big and heavy dropped into the midst of the dancing females. The crocs screamed and bellowed in alarm and fled to the farthest corners of the pool. The object bobbed, and one brave male swam up and nudged it with his snout. The croc's mindspeech was astonished. "A human woman—a dead human woman," he gasped.

Pandemonium broke loose as the entire croc population rushed forward to try to see this miracle. They had never seen a human, except with their minds, and a fight broke out over ownership of this wonder. The Holiest of the Holy White Crocodiles tried to restore order, sending in his mugger and soldier crocs to threaten and bellow and beat with their tails, sending up fountains of water.

The air was filled with saurian mindspeech.

"Let me see."

"Get out of the way. Get back where you belong."

"She's mine. I saw her first."

"You there, get out of the way."

"I was here first. I outrank you."

"She's mine."

"No. She's mine."

"Mine."

"Mine."

Over all of this the Holiest One bellowed, "Get back to your positions. We must have a proper ceremony. The Glut must continue."

But no crocs listened to him. Even his own guards and soldiers joined in the melee around the floating corpse. It was only a matter of time before one croc pulled off an arm or a leg and cruised out of the Culls' chamber, trailed by others that coveted his prize. On the edges of the churning pool, even the New One whimpered for his share.

The crocs were so preoccupied with the bounty that had literally fallen into their midst that they forgot the Culls tied to the meat rack. Sherahi's guards saw the other crocs battling over their share and leaped into the water. They wanted to get some before it all disappeared down a score of croc gullets.

When Sherahi's guards abandoned her she immediately took charge of her mind. First she erected ramshackle shelters around the thoughts of each of the Culls. "They'll never enslave us again," she thought, amazed at how quickly and efficiently she'd regained her powers. Then she looked up into the hole above where the corpse had fallen and saw Dervish's long-snouted face peering down at the melee. Junior coiled around his neck and stood erect, like a little cobra, between Dervish's ears.

"Hurry, you two. Get down here and untie Manu and the Duchess and then follow me to the nest chamber. Quick, Dervish. Junior, help him," she ordered, gliding into the waterway, careful to strengthen the temporary barriers that would protect each of the Culls from the crocodiles that were busy churning blood and hair and rags into the phosphorescent water. She thought of the baby sea turtles who, in concert, would burst up out of the sand and simultaneously paddle frantically across the beach to the tide and said into the minds of all of the Culls, "Hurry. We're digging out of here."

With strong, sinuous motions she swam faster than any crocodile and pleaded with the coati, "Please, Dervish, one last favor. We need you more than ever. You must dig for us again. We've got to get back to the tunnel that brought us here. It is our only hope."

The coati forgot his resolve to never go back into that awful tunnel and leaped into the water. With Junior hissing about his neck he landed at the foot of the meat rack and quickly severed the Duchess's bonds and then Manu's. "Quick, Duchess," he said. "Get to the nursery chamber. Run or fly if you can." Pulling the comatose langur by the scruff of the neck, Dervish started for the nursery. "Good, Dervish," hissed Junior, wishing that he could do something to help. But there was nothing to do except hiss open-mouthed at the crocs in the water all around them. He saw that the crocs did not respond to his threat and felt impervious to their control. "Sherahi has done this," the cascabel thought. When the coati and cascabel hauled out on the slimy bank they found Sherahi and the Duchess there. Junior knew from the intense look of concentration on her face that Sherahi was doing something to keep the crocs away.

Then she turned her mind toward them and seemed to grow larger, filling Junior's mind with her presence. "What has happened to Sherahi?" he wondered. "She's different."

Dervish didn't seem to notice the change in the pythoness. "Help him," he said, dragging Manu up the bank and dumping him next to the Duchess.

"Did you see, Dervish?" the macaw said, dancing up and down, her eyes kaleidoscoping with excitement. "I flew. I flew! It's the first time in years. And it was a really long flight! I'd forgotten how wonderful it was.

"I flew, Dervish, I actually flew." She batted her scarlet wings as if to embrace them all and suddenly focused on Manu, who slumped in the mud. She bustled up to him, squawking in her parrot speech, which had been markedly improved by contact with the white crocodiles. "Now, Manu, what's wrong with you?" There was no response and she prodded him with her bill, saying, "Perk up, Manu, and listen to my news: I flew. I flew!" The macaw rolled Manu onto his back and her thick tongue cleaned the mud from his closed eyes. In a soft voice she crooned, "I'm sorry, Manu. I'm sorry for all they did to you. Come on, now. Please, please don't die. I can fly again. You've never seen me fly. Please don't die now!"

The macaw looked across Manu's inert body to Sherahi, mutely begging the pythoness to do something to help the langur. Dervish knew what he had to do and began to dig at the nursery wall, working more frantically than ever before. He had trouble locating the exact place—all the walls had been reinforced with croc plaster, and he began to worry that they might never get out. He worried that the guards would come swimming into the chamber any moment and looked behind nervously, thinking, "Can Sherahi really shield all of us from *all* of those white crocodiles? What if I can't find a soft place? How long can she hold them off?"

"Hurry, Dervish," said the Duchess, trying to encourage him, and was surprised that she could speak into his mind. It seemed only natural to speak to the coati, who dug wildly at the rock-hard walls. "You can find it, Dervish. But do hurry. I think they're coming."

Dervish panted and tried yet another spot, this time higher on the wall, and felt the earth give beneath his madly treading claws. "I've got it," he said. "We're going to get out of here."

"Won't they follow us?" said Manu, who had recovered conscious- ness—because Sherahi had entered his mind and convinced him that he wasn't really sick or exhausted.

"No," said Junior from around Dervish's neck, rearing his head and flinching as Dervish sent dirt flying in all directions. "They'll never dare to leave these tunnels. Once we get out of here we're safe."

"And I know how to get us to San Diego Zoo," said the Duchess, flapping her wings and making a joke.

"I thought it was impossibly far," said Manu.

"It is, but who wants to go there anyway?" the Duchess said slyly. "We're on our way to someplace better. Sherahi's taking us to Sandeagozu! The Holiest One said we'd never be able to escape. He said we'd be dead meat by now. I figure that if we try, we've at least got a chance. Besides, Manu, I can *fly* again. I can fly and you're sitting up and taking notice of things. We've gotten away from them. Looks like the impossible is happen- ing with some regularity and just you watch—I'm going to *fly* out of this tunnel. I'll meet you at the other end."

"What do you think you are," said Sherahi, "an owl or something?"

It was the closest that Sherahi had ever come to a joke and it was not lost on the Duchess. "If you say so, Sherahi. Okay. I'm an owl—I'm a tawny frogmouth—I'm a double-breasted spouse and I'm flying out of here. Here I go." The red tail feathers of the macaw disappeared through the hole that Dervish had made into the storm sewer.

Dervish said, "You're next, Sherahi. You take the longest."

"No, Dervish. I'll be rear guard this time. Hurry up, get in there. You and Junior lead for a while."

First Dervish, with Junior encircling his neck, and then Manu climbed up the mound of dirt that Dervish had piled below the hole. Each took a last look at Sherahi, at the glowing chamber, and disappeared into the storm drain. The sounds of the feeding frenzy were drowned in a keening alarm wail that told Sherahi that the crocs had discovered that the captives had escaped.

"Too late, too late, you ingrown abortions that have the nerve to call yourselves reptiles," she said and followed the others through the hole in the nursery wall.

She took a deep breath and concentrated to reinforce the mental barriers that shielded each Cull from the white crocs. "You'll never get us now," she said. "Starve, you maggots."

It was black on the other side and she had climbed fifteen feet out into the tunnel before she realized that she was alone. The tunnel below was filled with rushing water. "It must have swept the others away," she thought in panic. "I must find them."

Holding onto the wall with her tail, Sherahi clung to the side of the storm sewer and sent her mind spinning down the length of the tunnel, searching for the Culls. She found Dervish with Junior coiled around his neck. He was madly dog-paddling, lifting his long-snouted head out of moonlit water. "Swim, Dervish," she said. "Save your strength. Swim only enough to keep afloat. Let the current take you to the opposite bank. Don't fight. We will be safe. All rivers have two banks. Think of your relatives the otters, the beavers. Think of porpoises, of great whales. You can swim as well as they can, but you must not fight. Be brave. Like baby sea turtles we can do the impossible."

To Junior she said in the ancient speech that only he would understand, "Little brother, you must help Dervish. He thinks he is tired. Give him courage. Make him feel as confident as a cobra killing a mongoose. Help him. You know how. Protect him until we meet again."

The cascabel sent the message, "What about you, Sherahi?"

"I am not afraid of water," the pythoness said. "I was born on the water. I can hold my breath for a month. Help Dervish make for the opposite shore, little brother. Do not fear. We are going to Sandeagozu. Remind Dervish."

She sent her mind spinning out over the rushing water to the langur. She found him outside the storm drain, floating with his arms clasped around a piece of timber. He was in a warm current in a wide river and about to lose consciousness.

"Breathe, Manu," the python said. "Lift your head up out of the water and breathe. Use that cunning that your tribe is famous for. Look around you, see the moonlight shining on your silver fur. You are Manu, the most marvelous langur that ever lived. You outlasted the white crocodiles, you outlasted the humans, you will outlast this river. Now we are *finally* free, Manu. We are going to find Sandeagozu and all of your tribe. It's over there on the opposite shore. Near those rocks. The current will take you. Help the current, Manu. Steer. Swing through the water as if you were in the treetops. Swim, Manu. Swim to Sandeagozu."

"Now for the Duchess," thought Sherahi. She sent her mind spinning out a fourth time, seeking the macaw. Back and forth she searched, over the dark river that glinted in the moonlight, through the length of the storm sewer, even on the opposite shore. But she could find no flying scarlet bird—only white, stout-billed birds standing on one foot on rocks and on the river's banks.

One of two things had happened: either the macaw was dead or she was unconscious. Sherahi sent the message out into the night: "Be strong, Scarlet Bird. Live. Breathe. Be free. We are going to Sandeagozu and you must go with us."

Sherahi inflated both of her lungs, drawing gallons of air down into the long, tubular sacks that reached back to her kidneys. She usually used only the front portion of one lung for breathing and the surplus air made her feel giddy and light. She let go of the wall and slipped down into the black, rushing stream, thinking of herself as a feather—a long, tan, gold and black plume floating downstream to Sandeagozu.

BOOK

CHAPTER NINE

The East River, New York City
April, 1933

MANU'S WET HEAD emerged from the street drain. Confused and dazed, he clung to the side of the culvert long enough to shake the water from his eyes and peer out. He saw a span of lights flung across the river and for a moment he wondered if he were seeing a tree full of fireflies. Then something heavy bumped him from behind and the rushing water ripped his numb fingers from their hold. Panic seized him as he fell, flailing through the night to splash into the water below. Only moments after Manu fell there was no blemish on the river's surface to show that he had survived.

The splash sounded like a basketful of wet wash had been dumped into a tub. It was loud enough to alert a great black-backed gull who stood a one-legged watch for the colony that roosted nearby. The guard made a mental note to search between the boulders on the rocky shore for a drowned animal. He'd seen cats and dogs taken by the river and knew from the way that the creature splashed that, whatever it was, it couldn't swim. "Not to save its life," the guard remarked to himself and chuckled grimly, amused by what passed for wit among his tribe, the Coffin Bearers.

Then the sentinel closed one eye and returned to thoughts of food and slaughter. He thought of the shining sand lances that he would spear in shallow water and of the cringing cherrystone clams that he would drop from midair. Even in his reverie their descending wails writhed deliciously in his feather-covered ears, whetting his appetite. He was mentally ambushing month-old tern fledglings, kidnapping them as they practiced their first clumsy fishing dives, when a second splash broke the quiet night. There was a third muffled splash on the far side of the water, near the shore, but the guard watched for the emergence of the second swimmer and paid no attention to the faraway splash. It could have been any sort of flotsam or jetsam falling into the river, but whatever it was it didn't matter because it was out of the territory of his tribe. The black-backs behind him were light sleepers. They groaned and complained.

"It's not my fault," the guard protested. He sighed and muttered,

"They act as if I could do something about it." To his fretful tribe he said, "It's nothing. Go back to sleep." He heard feathers rustle and roused himself, shaking his own plumage into order. He didn't want to be accused of sleeping on duty.

From his perch the sentinel could see the length of the river as it rolled, flexing and rippling all the way to the horizon. He saw a second swimmer's head break water and thought, "Now, he's luckier than that other one—at least he can swim."

He watched the animal bob up and down in the braid of the currents as it worked doggedly toward the opposite shore and thought, "Not likely he'll make it." He decided to look for this one in the morning, too. "He'll give out before the river does," the guard thought and stretched his webbed toes. "They all get tired and go under. Too bad so few of them can float like the Coffin Bearers."

For a long while it was quiet and the guard resumed his thoughts of feasts to come. Soon it would be summer and he would attack the horseshoe crabs who swarmed ashore with thoughts of mating uppermost in their hunched, hard-shelled minds. The crabs were stupid and defenseless and the guard had learned to flip them over on their armored backs and scoop beakfuls of flesh from their succulent underbellies. He imagined bristly legs beating weakly against his forehead while he glutted himself on horseshoe crab roe. He closed both eyes and imagined pale green eggs sliding down his throat and thus he neither saw nor heard Sherahi slide from the street drain.

Unlike the other Culls, Sherahi was a water creature. She plunged into the river silently and swam as surely as a hawk kettling on a tower of rising air. The next time the guard scanned the watery expanse he saw a large head trailed by a thick, undulating body. "What's that?" he wondered, opening both eyes and straining forward. To his amazement the thing moved across the river's surface like a dust devil twirling down the face of a dune, buffeting clumps of dune grass in its path. He'd never seen anything like it.

"Hens and chicks," he thought and blinked the nictitating membrane across each eye to clear the sleep away. Standing at attention on both legs, he watched the huge, elongated animal dive and frolic in the current. The guard couldn't quite believe it. He thought, "It's stronger than the river. But it can't be—nothing's stronger than the river."

The creature abruptly disappeared and the guard checked his impulse to alert the sleepers around him. "They'd never believe me, anyway," he thought and curled one leg back against his breast.

Downstream from the guard and the roosting tribe of great blackbacked gulls, Manu struggled against the current. It tumbled him head over tail and pulled him down into the river's depths. He fought against the current, flailing his arms and legs as if he were being chased by a tiger; but this river was no striped and whiskered, slit-eyed foe. If it were, the odds would have been more equal because Manu knew how to run and hide from a tiger. Like all properly educated langurs from the hill country of India, he had always been warned about deep water. Crocodiles lurked there, ready to snatch an unlucky langur. Like all his kind, Manu had been taught to be afraid of water; he had never learned how to swim.

Abruptly the current shifted and Manu was pushed toward the surface just as strongly as he had been pulled down. He heard Sherahi's hypnotic command within his mind: "Swim, Manu. Swim." The words were repeated over and over and Manu forgot his fear. He forgot that his lungs ached for air; he forgot the crocodile teeth that lurked in the depths waiting to seize and slash him; he forgot everything except Sherahi's voice and Sandeagozu. Her voice gave strength to his frantic struggles, and his flailings became regular swimming movements. Manu remembered the times he had raced, hand over hand, to the top of his cage in the Culls' room. And he remembered how once he'd run, much faster than any of the young langurs, to the top of Lookout Rock at the center of his tribe's territory. Right foreleg and left hind leg stroked together; down and back, down and back, against the water.

In what seemed to be slow motion, Manu stopped tumbling down and established a direction in the water. With tail streaming behind, he angled up to the surface and his head broke water. He grabbed a single breath and in the next instant he was swirled down again. Manu listened to Sherahi's voice and fought his way to the surface once more.

He snatched another breath and thought with surprise, "I'm swimming. I didn't know I could." He forgot to be afraid. Time and again the langur was pulled down by the shifting currents that made the East River one of the most treacherous rivers in the world. Soon he was tired and so exhausted that he could barely lift his head for breath. His arms and legs felt heavy, like wet ropes. "I can't go on much longer," Manu thought. "If the crocodiles are here, I wish they'd take me soon."

Manu struggled to the surface for what he thought must be the last time and something heavy bumped his shoulder. He was glad that the monster had finally come and knew that any moment its jaws would snap him in half. But before the croc's mouth opened, Manu grabbed its snout and tried to climb onto its back. To his surprise, the beast rolled over in the water, pitching the langur upside down. He spluttered and choked as he surfaced and tried to get an arm around this slippery "croc," which he now realized was a waterlogged tree trunk. Slick with slime, it was four times his length and too sodden to support his weight, but it floated and it would keep him from being seized by the currents. Coughing and wondering if he would ever catch his breath, Manu rested his cheek against the barely floating wood and said, "Thank you. Thank you," to whoever had sent him this log. Then another vicious current took the log and for one awful moment Manu thought it would be swirled away. He finally got both arms around it and clung with the tenacious grip of a baby langur buried in its mother's belly fur. "I'm safe now," thought Manu and held his breath as yet another current swirled the log about.

Manu's log floated into a warm, upwelling current and he felt the temperature of the water change. The moonlight danced around him as the lights on the right-hand shore slid by. "More fireflies," Manu thought, panting. The river was carrying him into a wide, dark expanse and he wondered how he'd ever get to shore.

Manu heard Sherahi's voice in his mind once more. "Swim, Manu," she commanded. "Don't stop. We are free now and we're going to Sandeagozu. It's over there, on the other bank, away from all the lights. You can't rest yet, Manu. Steer. Steer to Sandeagozu." Sherahi's voice suddenly exclaimed, "Oh!" and then she was silent.

The langur listened, hoping for more encouragement, but all he could hear was his own hoarse breathing and the water lapping against the bank. Following Sherahi's last command, he steered toward the darker shore, holding the log with his hands and kicking with his hind legs. His progress was slow. Several times the current carried him away from the shore and back to the center of the river. When he eventually felt rocks beneath his feet Manu was so grateful that he didn't care how slimy they felt. Sliding between two boulders, he scraped his palms and knees on barnacles and dragged himself ashore. The log that had helped him across the river submerged once more and bobbed off in the current. For a long time it could be seen skimming beneath the surface, but Manu didn't watch it go. He collapsed without even bothering to shake his fur dry.

With the cascabel that he had grown to hate coiled around his neck, Dervish had plunged from the street drain and splashed into the East River. Ever since they had left the nest of the white crocodiles he had heard Junior's voice rasp in the part of his brain that was directly between his eyes and had stubbornly refused to answer. Dervish was angry. He growled as he dog-paddled against the cold crosscurrents in the river and his thoughts raged. "Mind your own business, Junior. Leave me alone."

Dervish shook his head madly, as if to free himself from the little cascabel, but he found he could not dislodge the snake. "Why do I always have to be the one to carry him around?" the coati fussed. "Him and Sherahi and all their brainy ideas—they treat me like a slave. 'Do this, Dervish; do that, Dervish.' As if they're the only ones that matter. But not any more. Once Manu and I are together again things are going to be different. If they don't change, I'm going on all by myself—that's for sure."

Junior felt the cold water surge about his scales and burrowed deeper into the thick ruff of fur about Dervish's neck. "It's so cold," he thought. "If I lose Dervish now I'll never be able to swim to the other shore." He knotted his rattled tail around his own neck and tried to climb up between the coati's ears, hoping that it might be drier and warmer there. To his dismay he found that even the top of Dervish's head was thoroughly soaked and for the first time he noticed that the coati wasn't swimming quite as buoyantly as he had at first.

"You must help Dervish," Sherahi had commanded as he and the coati had leaped out of the tunnels of the white crocodiles. Obediently, the cascabel scryed Dervish's quick mind, hoping to encourage him and help him to swim. Overlaid by a patina of transitory, shivering thoughts about the cold, black water was the image of a spiteful, rough-scaled serpent. Junior was amazed at how nasty the little snake looked and thought, "I'm not like that. I'm sweet—not like that snake at all." Junior was sad to see the change in Dervish's thought patterns. This determined creature was very unlike the happy, entranced coati who had capered on his hind legs, luring Effie to her death at the end of the tunnel. Junior saw Dervish's deep resentment of the mental trickery that Junior had used, as well as his resolve to rid himself of the nasty serpent that encircled his neck.

Junior felt a pang of guilt and thought, "I shouldn't have tricked him like that, but it was the quickest way. What else could I do? The crocs had already started their disgusting Glut; they were about to kill Manu and the Duchess. I'm sure that Sherahi would have done exactly the same thing and Dervish would have loved her for it. He doesn't like me—that's all there is to it. He's never liked me and so all the clever things that I do to help us are wrong." Junior hissed in annoyance and then thought sadly, "I'll make it up to him—if he'll let me."

Junior looked away from Dervish's thoughts and realized that the coati's nose was barely skimming the surface of the water. He could feel Dervish's body swimming ever more slowly and felt the labored movements of his numbed paws. Worse yet, they weren't any closer to the far shore. "We've got to get there," Junior thought. "Sherahi said that's where Sandeagozu is." On the fringes of Dervish's consciousness Junior had seen the specters of shock and fatigue waiting to engulf the coati and knew that they must have taken hold. "I must help him," Junior thought. "Sherahi made me promise that I would. Dervish doesn't have to like it. I've got to trick him again if we're ever going to get across this river.

"Dervish," the cascabel hissed into the coati's mind. "I'm going to help you. I'm . . ."

"No, you're not," panted the stubborn coati. Unable to chitter, he barely managed a low growl. "I don't need your help. I won't let you."

Junior watched as the coati struggled to erect the semblance of a barrier over his quick mind. The cascabel recognized it as a pathetic imitation of the poor sort of mindscreen that Manu could make. "The white crocodiles taught Dervish something, too," Junior hissed to himself. "Too bad he wasn't a more apt pupil.

"Okay, Dervish," Junior rasped. "If that's the way you want it, you can keep me out of your thoughts. But when we drown, and we're surely going to drown, don't say that I didn't warn you."

The cascabel lapsed into silence, feeling the coati struggle with the current, watching the impotent mindscreen wilt until it draped limply over his thoughts. Fifteen minutes later, when they were still in deep water and swirled about by currents far from shore, Junior knew that the coati was near the end of his strength. He saw the coati's impulse to rest and let the current take them. "Dervish doesn't care anymore. He's given up."

Surreptitiously, using the special brand of subtlety that serpents had invented, the cascabel swept aside the puny mindscreen that webbed Dervish's thoughts. It was as if a tattered cobweb was whisked away from the corner of an attic window and Junior now directed Dervish's swimming movements. He hypnotized Dervish, making him forget his exhaustion and giving him renewed strength. He also convinced Dervish that his mental shield was intact and that he was guided by his own desires. He felt the coati's head lift from the river's surface and felt him move purposefully toward the shore. Junior looked back to see a V-shaped wake trailing them and his silent serpentine laughter snaggled within his mind. Junior resurrected and strengthened Dervish's inept mindscreen and thought, "Poor Dervish, you should stick to what you know best."

When the coati finally reached the rocky shore, he shook the water from his thick fur and shivered. "Get away from me," he growled at Junior. "I promised to carry you around, but that's only until we find Sherahi and the others. Whatever else, I didn't promise to let you sleep near me." Junior knew that he couldn't use his fangs to defend himself if Dervish turned nasty and he was suddenly fearful of the coati's teeth and claws. Obediently he slithered from around Dervish's neck, even though he would have preferred to stay in his warm traveling perch. Dervish disappeared beneath a boulder and curled head to tail. Just before he fell asleep Junior heard him chitter softly, "I told him I could do it and I did. I got here all by myself, with no help from him. No help from him at all."

The cascabel kept a nervous watch as he coiled beneath a nearby boulder. His cat-eyed pupils were open wide and he wasn't sleepy. Through much of the night he thought about Dervish and wondered how he would ever make friends with the coati again.

The Duchess was excited to be flying, even though it was only in a tunnel. The air rushed at her and she narrowed her eyelids, arrowing straight at the half moon of dim light that was ahead.

Her wings cleared the rounded walls of the storm drain by a foot on either side and she thought, "No room for a mistake. I've got to concentrate." She flapped her pointed primaries and panted as she labored low over the rushing water, delighted to be flying free again and for a moment ignoring the danger ahead. By the time she could clearly see the end of the tunnel, she found that she was flying much too fast and that the tunnel's opening was much narrower than she'd thought. "I'll have to fly very low over the water to fit through," she thought. She saw the rapids foaming in the storm drain below and thought of stalling to settle so that she could walk out of the drain, but there was no perch in sight. The Duchess's feathers were not waterproof and she knew that if she got wet she would get water-logged and drown. Macaws were fastidious bathers, but they never swam. "It's simply not done," the Duchess thought and shuddered at the idea of getting her fine feathers wet. She looked below for the ledge where the Culls had once walked in single file, but it was submerged. "The water is too deep. I can't walk." She looked again at the semicircle of light, which grew larger with each wing stroke, and saw that she had only one choice. "I'll just have to try to fly out."

If the Duchess had been a smaller bird she could easily have darted through the opening of the storm drain. If she'd been a stronger flier she could have done it easily, but by the time she was nearly there her wings ached from the unaccustomed effort and her chest and neck muscles trembled from exertion. Her wing beats were erratic and, as she neared the opening, the twilight spilling into the black storm drain dazzled her. She narrowed her eyelids even further and closed her wings. She clenched her claws and dove at the half moon of twilight, hoping for the best.

Moments later she flew out of the storm drain. She opened her eyes and was amazed to find herself free of the restricting tunnel. A crescent moon was overhead and a wide, black river rolled below. She opened her wings again and the feeling of unbounded space made her giddy. For a moment she forgot to beat her wings. Like a stone thrown across a pond, the macaw arced out of the storm drain, falling in a graceful curve toward the water below. She caught herself a few feet over its braided surface and began to flap as best she could, thinking, "I'm going to crash." She struggled to lift her heavy body once more and had almost reached the rock-studded shore when muscle cramps seized her chest. With a squawk, to tell the other Culls where she was, her flapping body splashed into the water on the far side of the river. She lost consciousness as the cold currents seized her and swirled her around in the shallows.

The next morning the great black-backed gull found Manu's crumpled body and alighted to investigate.

"Must be the one that couldn't swim," he thought, stretching his neck and peering first with his right and then with his left eye to produce a three-dimensional view. "Looks sort of human, but whatever it is, it's nearly dead." The gull's yellow eyes glittered, urging the man-animal to die as he watched the skin stretched across the rib cage. It moved ever so slightly. "Not much meat there," he thought, "but at least it'll be fresh. And it is all mine."

Suddenly the air was filled with wings and loud, ragged cries, as others of his tribe descended. There were adult Coffin Bearers who wore crisp, white body feathers and had capes of dead-black feathers on the skyward surface of their wings. They were accompanied by a mass of young birds who had feathers that were streaked and spotted with varying amounts of dirty gray. The one-to-three-year-olds looked as if they had forgotten to bathe after a mud wallow; Coffin Bearers had to wait until their fourth spring for the immaculate white and black adult feathers to grow in.

Two adults and two large three-year-olds alighted on the sand near Manu and began to eye the carcass. They craned their necks and edged forward, black pupils dilated with excitement. It was clear that thoughts of breakfast and of battle were uppermost in their minds.

However, this creature was strange—sort of an undersized human, and the Coffin Bearers were unsure of exactly where to make the incision that would most efficiently disembowel him. If he had been a common prey animal—a cinnamon teal, for instance—they'd have immediately ripped open his abdomen, using their lower mandibles like scalpels. If he had been a rat or a kitten, they'd have swallowed it whole, choking the carcass back and using its own weight to force it down into the safety of their gullets. But Manu was the largest animal that these Coffin Bearers had ever found washed ashore, and his resemblance to a human bothered them. They knew that the langur was a feast spread before them, but they didn't know where to begin.

The younger birds and less dominant adults found perches on the rocks lining the shore. Settling themselves comfortably with their necks tucked back against their shoulder blades, they waited for the inevitable squabble between the guard and these four contenders. As the youngsters were smaller than the adults, their only chance to snatch a mouthful would come after all of their elders and the more aggressive young Coffin Bearers had eaten their fill. Still, the fight would be exciting to watch.

The guard considered Manu his private property. He jumped purposively into the air and glided down in front of the langur's body. "Don't try anything funny," he warned the four Coffin Bearers that were eagerly converging on Manu. "This is mine. I found it and if you don't clear out, you'll be sorry." He picked up a beakful of dry bladder wrack and shook it just the way he'd shake prey or one of them if they challenged him. Scornfully he tossed the seaweed into their midst and watched them flap and flinch. "Cowards," he taunted. He lowered his black-mantled wings, holding them slightly away from his sides, ready to buffet an opponent. He lifted his neck high, pointing his murderous bill down at a sharp angle and making it clear that he was ready to pounce onto the back of any competitor and peck a bloody hole in immaculate feathers.

"Come on, Stanley, sweetheart," one female wheedled. She lowered her head and opened her bill, exposing her red tongue and the pulsing lining of her throat. She slyly sidled up to him as if she hadn't seen his threat display. "There's plenty here for all of us, dear one."

The guard stared at her. Who was this female Coffin Bearer? She seemed vaguely familiar, but he just couldn't place her. She didn't seem to respect his threat and it enraged him to see her approach in such a trusting, familiar manner. She behaved in such an openly sexual manner that he was angered. Hadn't he just shown them what he would do to anyone who tried to monopolize his kill?

The female was speaking again, paddling even closer. He could see the tiny feathers around her yellow bill. "Don't you remember, Stanley, sweetheart, how you and I used to share meals, last year on the breeding grounds? You're such a dear, darling thing. So masterful." She reached up with her bill and softly pecked at the bright-red spot on the guard's lower mandible: a sexual signal as universal to Coffin Bearers as a languid wink or pouting lips are to humans.

But the guard was having none of it. He didn't know who she was and was annoyed that she didn't recognize his rights to this carcass. He gave her a fierce peck on the crown. She squawked in pain and the two juveniles behind her, as well as all the birds on the rocks, joined and amplified her cries. Stanley ignored their noise and was gratified to see these challengers fly up to join the others on the rocks.

But the female wasn't quite finished. From a safe distance she called, "You didn't have to hit me like that. I've got a lump the size of a hummer's egg on my head. I'll have a scar for sure. You always were a mean bastard, Stanley. I don't know what I ever saw in you. Mother said that you'd have a short memory . . . and after all the eggs I've laid and all the babies I've brooded for you these are the thanks I get."

She turned on the two squawking juveniles from last year's brood who still followed her everywhere, begging for handouts. "Fine father you've got," she screamed and pecked one ferociously on the nape of its extended neck. His brother instantly pulled back his head and tried to become invisible, but the mother pecked him just the same. Soon all of the Coffin

Bearers on the rocks echoed the cries of the two juveniles. Their chorus condemned the guard as selfish.

"Shut up, all of you," he said ineffectually and resumed his threat posture, facing the lone adult male who was still interested in wresting a share of Manu's innards.

"You've always been a bully, Stanley," this male said. "Now you're going to get what's coming to you." He calmly assumed the ritual combat posture and strutted toward the guard. With necks held high, beaks angled down, wings folded and held down and slightly away from their bodies, the two males faced one another like twin samurai with drawn blades. Confidently, the challenger advanced. When he was a foot from his opponent he reached down and picked up a beakful of bladder wrack, wrenching it from its holdfast on a piece of driftwood. Holding the plant aloft he shook it ferociously, scattering sand over himself, his opponent and Manu.

The guard's unblinking yellow eyes locked on those of the challenger and, amidst cries of "Cummon, Jonathan, get him," "Murder the bum," "He doesn't know how to share," "Kill the bastard," "Peck him," the guard grabbed the free end of the bladder wrack and began to pull.

For one moment both birds were motionless white and black mirror images that fought silently. Each pulled with all his strength, intent on intimidating the other. But the guard was stronger and pulled the bladder wrack from his opponent's grasp. Quickly tossing it aside, he deftly grasped the challenger's bill in his own and, facing him, began to deliver blow after blow with his wings. It sounded like waves slapping a rock face. Then he released his hold on the bird's bill and, biting at his thinly feathered neck, leaped on his back. Feathers flew and the guard was about to peck his opponent's crown, perhaps drawing blood and finishing him off for good, when he heard the Coffin Bearers on the rocks switch from their chorus of hostile cries to the alarm call. That meant danger. He looked up to see the tribe hurrying into the air. Something had happened. They were frightened.

The guard gave his opponent one half-hearted peck on the head and rose to safety in the air after the flock, screaming, "Next time you won't get away so easy."

The challenger could barely drag himself aloft and settled on the river, apart from the rest of the tribe. It would be a long while before he challenged the guard's or anyone else's supremacy.

The victorious gull hovered thirty feet above the carcass. He saw the other Coffin Bearers land in the middle of the river. That was a sure sign that some four-footed danger was on shore. If it had been a human they'd have flown a short distance down the beach. But no cat, fox or even a human was in sight. He could see no reason to abandon the property that he'd just defended. He landed quickly and hurried over, thinking, "Nervous, stupid Coffin Bearers. You'll do anything to trick me out of my prize. That's the last time I'll listen to fools."

274

He smoothed his rumpled feathers and lifted his bill and wings into the air, trumpeting his victory. Without hesitation he turned to the breakfast that lay before him. The easiest thing to do would be to find the tenderest morsel: the eye. He walked to Manu's head and saw that one twisted socket held a lifeless, bluish-white orb. "Ants must've gotten it," he thought. "Must've been here longer than I thought." He nudged Manu's head and it rolled over to the other side. "That looks nice."

The guard's stout, yellow beak was about to grasp and peck out Manu's remaining eye and swallow it like a limp sea grape when he saw a sudden movement behind him. Too late he realized that a striped, sleeked-down cat was stalking him. He wasn't sure, but there seemed to be a rope braided about its neck. With a short run and one forceful downstroke of his wings he hurried into the air again, but his takeoff was a moment too late. He was six feet off the ground, beating his wings like a giant hummingbird and hovering to scold his attacker. The gull thought he was safe and shrieked the alarm cry at the cat. In the flick of an eye the striped animal jumped and, although the gull couldn't quite believe it, he felt hot fingers close around his neck. The cat's teeth were buried in his breast feathers and only their denseness prevented them from slashing the skin. The cat growled and snarled like nothing the gull had ever heard. He beat at his attacker with his wings. He tried to peck open the animal's skull but didn't have the proper leverage. He battered the animal with his wings and felt the cat's hands (thinking back on the attack later, the gull thought it was strange that the cat didn't use its claws) lose their grip. But before the animal fell away, the gull felt teeth rake his foot. He looked down to see the webbing between the claws of his right foot hanging in bloody, painful tatters.

What was this animal? No cat he'd ever seen could jump so high and almost wrestle a full-grown Coffin Bearer from the sky. He looked down and saw the animal's face distorted in a lip-curling snarl. Frightened and shaken by the thought that he'd nearly lost this battle, the gull didn't wait to see more. In a few moments he joined the other Coffin Bearers in the middle of the river.

Still jumping into the air and snapping at the retreating large, white bird, Dervish suddenly remembered Manu. He ran to the langur and licked his face, cleaning crumbs of sand from the useless eye socket. "Wake up, Manu," he chirped at his friend, rubbing his long-snouted face against the langur's rounded jaw. Manu made no response and Dervish prodded him over onto his side. He whined into his ear, "Manu, wake up. Manu, it's me, Dervish. I've found you." But Manu did not hear him. Finally, Dervish rolled the langur over onto his back and sat down beside him, looking at the inert body and wondering what to do. He snapped at two blowflies that were trying to lay eggs in Manu's fur.

"Stupid bugs," Dervish said as his incisors smashed their fatty bodies. "You'd think they'd know better than to lay eggs on someone who's still alive. That's a waste."

The coati blinked and thought for a moment and it occurred to him that the carrion-eating birds and blowflies might know something that he didn't. They usually didn't make those kinds of mistakes. "Is Manu going to die?" he wondered.

"Junior," Dervish said to the cascabel that was coiled around his neck. "I hate to impose on you," he said stiffly, "but speak into Manu's mind for me. Tell him to wake up. Something's very wrong with him. Tell him that it isn't safe here. We've got to hide."

The cascabel glided down from Dervish's neck and undulated over to the langur. Like scaly death coiled in a spot of morning sunshine, he fixed the coati with a basilisk's gaze and said coldly, "Before I do that, I'd just like to say that the next time you decide to attack something, it would be nice if you thought to give me, perhaps, just a little warning. Nothing special, just a simple 'Look out' or 'Heads up' would do.

"You could have killed the both of us, you know. That bird nearly stabbed me. It meant to kill us both."

Dervish wanted to reply, "Both? He didn't even know that you were there, you cowardly bit of baggage. You could have killed him for me, if you'd had half the brain that you're supposed to." But he said nothing. Dervish had vowed not to speak to the cascabel again until he made it clear that he was sorry for having used him like a mindless puppet in their escape from the white crocodiles.

The cascabel wasn't surprised that the coati didn't reply. They hadn't spoken all morning. He knew that the coati was still angry with him and wished that Sherahi hadn't made him responsible for Dervish and Manu. With a sigh the cascabel hissed a greeting into Manu's mind.

Manu was, indeed, very far away. His mental reply to the little serpent was slow and deliberate, as if it cost him great effort. "Leave me alone, Junior," said Manu. "I'm tired. I must rest now."

The cascabel relayed the message to Dervish, who said, "We'll let him rest, but tell him that he's not allowed to die. Not after all we've been through. Tell him we'll wait till tonight. Then he's got to come around."

The langur sighed in his sleep and showed no sign of having understood the cascabel's second message. Dervish felt exposed in the daylight and grabbed Manu by the scruff of the neck and pulled him out of sight into a hollow in the sand beneath one of the larger boulders. He lay down beside him and rested his head on Manu's chest. From time to time he licked the langur's chin, hoping that he would awaken. Now that he had found Manu again, Dervish planned to guard him until the langur awakened—forever if necessary.

276

"I'm going to find something to eat," hissed the cascabel as he slithered away.

Dervish didn't bother to answer, knowing that the rattler could read his mind. "That's all you think about," he growled as he watched the cascabel leave. Then he chittered audibly, "Remember, if Manu's awake, we're leaving here after dark. Don't keep us waiting."

The snake made no reply and Dervish said to himself, "All right. Be late. Better still, don't come at all. Manu and I don't need you or anybody else. We'll find Sherahi and Sandeagozu without you."

The two animals who had saved the Culls from the white crocodiles were still not friends. It would take more than proximity to heal Dervish's hurt feelings. The coati licked Manu's chin and whined. "Wake up, Manu. Please. I don't know where Sandeagozu is. I can't even find Sherahi without you. Please, Manu."

Propelled by the running stream within the storm sewer, Sherahi had feared only that the current might trap her against an obstacle and snap her backbone. A hatchling's memory of a banded krait thumping its life out in the dusty wake of a bullock cart made her wary of dangers that might lie in her path. Even though her body was marvelously strong, her backbone was fragile. An accident could happen without warning and Sherahi knew that, after hours of pain, she would lie twisted and still, just like the black-and-yellow-ringed krait had. She could have traveled to the outlet of this tunnel completely submerged, with her head below the stream's turbulent surface. If she had done so, though, the pythoness couldn't have watched the water ahead, looking for submerged rocks or other dangers. Unfortunately, her labial pits were of little use in this situation and, as she anxiously peered into the darkness, she watched for sticks that might be wedged crosswise to trap her in the current. But nothing barred her path and, after what seemed like a long, dark journey, the snake saw chains of lights winking in the distance. Their reflections grew larger and she knew that this travel in the flooded storm drain would soon be over. She saw the mouth of the drain, black with a semicircular view of the lighter sky outside. The lights grew bigger and, with the help of their reflections, Sherahi saw that her path to the outside world was clear. She would not be smashed and broken like the banded krait. Just before she reached the mouth of the pipe the quopping of her labial pits told her that the air was cool, but not cold. It was a lovely night for swimming.

The giant python slid into the river's depths and felt delicious bubbles bounce and tickle down her body. The water was colder than she'd expected, but after all her years in captivity swimming was such a treat that she gave no thought to the water's temperature. None of her captors had ever given her enough water to bathe in. Even her drinking trough at Lef-track's was only big enough for her to immerse her head and neck. So, this was the first time since she'd lived behind her pagoda that Sherahi was free to swim as she chose.

The braid of river currents caressed the length of her body and she allowed one and then another to swirl her along, feeling as light as a puff of milkweed down borne aloft on a child's wishes. The water supported her and Sherahi forgot how her belly scutes dragged when she crawled on land in her normal serpentine fashion. In the river she could move at will, now actively swimming, now diving, lashing from side to side to elude a whirl-pool, spiraling down to investigate the muddy bottom and, finding it not to her liking, languidly relocating the crescent moon that played on the sur-face, creating a shifting mosaic of silver facets. She swam with the ancient lateral undulations that her ancestors had stolen from the mosasaurs. It was so easy, so effortless, that it felt as if she were actually flying, cleaving the water with the freedom of a pterosaur piercing an ancient sky, soaring aloft just for the fun of it.

In the water, Sherahi was grateful that she had been born a serpent. Swimming was a pleasure for her, merely a continuation of the undulations that moved her huge body across any surface. And, unlike all other animals, she didn't have to worry about getting water into her eyes or ears. Like those of a fish, her ears were hidden deep within her skull; there was no canal to become filled with water and she could actually hear better in water than in air. Her eyes were protected by special optic scales that were a part of the scaly fabric that encased her body. In water these spectacles worked like diving goggles and on land they kept dirt out of her eyes. Breathing while swimming was also not a problem for Sherahi. She had two lungs, an unusual feature in snakes, and she prided herself on this special heritage, which marked her as the most ancient kind of serpent. One of these lungs was enormous and extended for two thirds of the length of her body. Thus, she was never out of breath, because her slow, cold-blooded metab-olism used this enormous reservoir of air very slowly. It would be nearly impossible for her to use the entire supply and she would never know the chest-constricting panic of a drowning bird or mammal. In all, Sherahi was as drown-proofed as a duckling; she swam with the skill of a seal and the delight of an otter. Her only problem was temperature control.

Sherahi was in the middle of the river when she felt an especially cold current grip her body. For the first time since she'd plunged into the water, she noticed that she was colder than she ought to be. The heat pro-duced by her muscles was rapidly lost to the water and, with extraordinary effort, Sherahi drove toward shore. The river behind her pagoda had always been warm and she hadn't known how quickly cold water would bleed her body heat away. Close to the rock-strewn bank, Sherahi had to struggle to overcome the drag of an offshore current. She wriggled ashore and the warmth of the sand beneath her belly scutes was a comforting contrast to the cold river water. She coiled yard after yard of her body into a loose mound that would absorb heat from the ground. Surprised at how tired she was, Sherahi lowered her head onto the topmost coil and rested with no thought of the other Culls or of their journey to Sandeagozu.

Sherahi woke with the feeling that something was watching her. Without moving her massive head or shifting her coils she flicked her tongue to fnast the predawn beach. An undefined sense of unease told her that many eyes followed her movements from the shadows beneath the nearby boulders, but Sherahi could detect no smell that she recognized and her labial pits did not register warmth. "Whatever it is," she thought, "it's as cold as I am." She would have liked to stay where she was and return to the dreamless sleep that had engulfed her but, even though she closed her cat-eyed pupils as much as possible, those multitudinous eyes made her uncomfortable. "It's not safe here," she decided and warily abandoned her resting place near the riverbank.

She flowed inland, not knowing where she was going but seeking shelter and food for herself so she would be strong enough to inwit to the other Culls. As the snake moved through the stunted beach grass and disappeared beneath the dense growth of bayberry bushes, she frightened the squad of fiddler crabs that had watched her through the night.

The male fiddlers broke ranks and scuttled sidewards to safety, each holding his single, oversized claw horizontally. Stalked eyes jerked nervously and multijointed mouthparts worked mechanically, tasting the sand that Sherahi had traversed. "What is this monster?" they called to one another.

The female fiddlers watched from their burrows in the sand, swiveling their eyes to watch the disaster that had come ashore in the night. With one sweep of its body the Monster had crushed and compacted dozens of tunnels, destroying the fiddler crab village that had stood for generations. Some of the fiddlers were buried alive. They'd die without understanding what had happened.

On the periphery of her inwitting consciousness Sherahi thought she heard tiny, hoarse voices screaming, "Look out! The Monster's coming!" as the minute crabs fled before her like timid bathers scampering from an incoming tide. One particularly bold fellow ran up to the big snake's tail and threatened it with his claw as it lay in the sand, waiting to slither away.

His rash action made his fellow fiddlers scream in terror.

"Don't. Don't be foolish," his mate pleaded. But the bold fiddler would have his way. It was as if the diminutive warrior were attacking an armor-plated wall that was twelve times his height. Lifting his claw and pinching with all his strength, he made his gesture of defiance and scuttled sideways into his burrow. Only his eyestalks protruded. All of his fellow fiddlers watched in horror, wondering, "What will the Monster do?" Some said, "Now you've done it, Jack. It'll kill us all."

But the Monster did not turn to attack and for the remaining seasons of his life this particular fiddler was given special treatment by his fellows as well as credit for having vanquished the Monster that had come ashore to wreak havoc and destroy burrows that had existed as long as anyone could remember. The Monster had not only damaged the fiddlers' fortifications and crushed a few of them, it had also frightened the entire population. Later that year, which, as a result of their scare in the early spring, became known as the Year of the Sea Monster, the males were fretful. Many were too nervous to remember all of the intricate and essential rituals of courtship. A few attacked their partners instead of cradling them in a ten-legged embrace. The females were affected too. They fed nervously, keeping a watchful eye on the shoreline; at any moment another Monster might rise from the tide. As a result they produced fewer eggs. The once-burgeoning colony dwindled and before long the fiddler crabs abandoned their ancient tunnels and deserted the salt marsh on the Brooklyn side of the East River.

––––––––––––––––––––

The wind flattened the spike grass all around her and Sherahi lowered her head, cringing against the black silt of the salt marsh, wishing she were invisible. The tide was out and Sherahi felt conspicuous in the sparse vegetation. "I won't move," she thought, "and perhaps I'll be mistaken for a dead log." The snake lay with her chin flat against the black ooze. Her jawbones conducted faint whispers of foreign speech and clicking sounds, as all around her clusters of ribbed mussels sealed their shells and settled down to wait out the dry hours till the tide flooded the marsh once more. Muddy-shelled marsh periwinkles traveled down the stems of the spike grass to graze on the algae that furred the marsh floor. Sherahi scryed the mind of the largest snail as she watched it unfurl its zebra-striped foot and glide away on a carpet of slime that it spread for itself.

The snail's thoughts coiled around images of small male periwinkles and of the sensation of her soft mantle being pierced by an aphrodisiac dart. Sherahi felt her belly muscles begin to twitch in sympathetic courting movements and realized that this female snail was searching for a mate. The pythoness scryed through the spiral convolutions of the snail's mind for any information about Sandeagozu, but found only thoughts of embracing a small, virile male in her ample, pliant mantle. In the amorous periwinkle's mind Sherahi saw an elaborate clock that chronicled tidal rhythms, as well as a calendar that charted the phases of the moon. She found a fondness for the filamentous algae that grew on mussel shells and a concern that the teeth of her rasping radula were dulled from continuous scraping, but Sherahi could find no knowledge of the human world that was beyond the margins of the salt marsh. "Those stalked eyes can't even see the grass stems very well," thought Sherahi. "She doesn't know how to get to Sandeagozu any better than I do."

The pythoness felt strangely jealous of the simplicity of the life that this marsh periwinkle lived. "She doesn't know that humans or even serpents exist. All she thinks about is food, mating and the movement of the tide." The pythoness withdrew her scan, thinking, "I can't spend all day here. I've got to find a safe place where I can inwit to Junior, Manu and the Duchess. I wonder if she did finally decide to fly south to that jungle that she was always looking for. I've got to find them before they wander away. I wish this wind would stop. It makes me cold."

Raising her neck and head above the grass once again, Sherahi peered ahead and flicked her long, black tongue left and right. The marsh smelled of the long ears and strong hind legs of rabbit: a full-grown buck had passed this way not long ago. "He's probably in his burrow now," she thought and wished that she were inside a dark, snug, comforting den instead of lurking in this wind-buffeted marsh. "I don't belong here," she thought, eyeing the wide expanse of gray sky. "And I'd better get moving because it's about to rain."

She fnasted the gusts of wind that tousled the marsh grasses and detected a sweet, familiar smell. "Frangipani," she thought, recognizing the scent at once. "But it can't be." She remembered the frangipani trees where she used to hide behind her pagoda. The image of Sorensen's thick-knuckled fingers rose in her mind, too, and she remembered him stretching out his hand so that she could smell it. "That's odd," she thought and then it struck her: "Sorensen used to smell of frangipani blossoms sometimes."

The gusts of wind were followed by sheets of rain and, although it chilled her even more, she welcomed the downpour. She wound through the grass with her head and neck erect. As she moved the hint of frangipani became more pronounced—as if the cold had intensified the fragrance. She found herself following the scent across the wide marsh toward a stand of trees that was ahead. "If I can just get to those trees, I can hide and inwit to the others. Maybe there's a frangipani there. They give good shade." The rain dripped from her scaly chin and coursed down her neck in cold streams and she thought, "This rain's good for one thing—it'll keep every sensible animal at home." The snake steadily and slowly crawled toward the trees that she'd glimpsed before the rain began.

When she'd crawled beneath the rocks along the riverbank, Sherahi had planned to sleep through the day and move only at night. She knew that it was stupid for a thirty-five-foot python to be crawling about in the daytime—especially in an unfamiliar landscape. But the scrutiny of fiddler crabs had awakened her and Sherahi had seen large, white predatory birds hanging in the air above. Their clear, yellow eyes had followed her hungrily. She had fnasted humans all around and fled inland, crawling as fast as she could across the marsh toward a dark blur on the horizon that she sensed was a stand of trees. She thought she could see shadows there; even leafless bushes would give some cover. Sherahi was a forest creature and the open sky intimidated her. She wound through the tawny, winter-killed grass, leaving a wide, flat track in her wake and hoping that she would find shelter soon.

The chill had made Sherahi forget that she was hungry. It would take hours of drowsy basking in the hot sun before she could lunge in a single, crisp movement, making a sure, swift strike. Sherahi felt cold, but she could not shiver to make herself warmer. At this temperature she reckoned that she would be able to travel for about another hour before the cold penetrated to the core of her immense body and slowed her heart and brain. Chilly weather could not kill the giant python, but it taxed all of her reserves. "I've got to move faster," she thought and kicked with her back muscles, driving the sides of her body deeper into the marsh ooze.

"I'll never be cold again once we've found Sandeagozu," she said as she moved toward higher ground. "Even that fraud, the Holiest of the Holy White Crocodiles, told the Duchess that it was always warm there. I don't think he was lying, even though that ingrown maggot didn't deserve to call himself a reptile. When I think of what they tried to do to us . . ." Sherahi's next thought startled her into silence. "They were reptiles and they treated us worse than humans did." She remembered Manu's scrawny body, spattered with mud, his knees raw with sores that would not heal. She remembered how the Culls had been lured into the foul, subterranean chambers of the pale, stunted crocodiles. "They were supposed to help us find Sandeagozu. That's a joke. We're no closer than we were when we left the pet shop. All we know is that Sandeagozu exists and that it is very far off in the western part of this country. They said it was impossibly far—even for a flier like the Duchess. And the others are depending on me to get them there." She crawled beneath small, leafless trees that were on the border of the forest ahead and, remembering the uncomplicated life of the periwinkle, wondered, "We're free, but what good is it if we die out here?" The same worry stabbed like a heron impaling a green frog: "Where is Sandeagozu? How will we ever get there?

"You can't think about that now," said Sherahi to herself in a businesslike tone. "First of all, it's too cold to be out here worrying about Sandeagozu. Any local snake worth her scales is still hibernating. You've got to hurry up, while you can still move at all."

282

The ground rose beneath her and the saplings were replaced by larger trees. She was nearly at the fringe of trees she had seen from the marsh and stopped to investigate a likely-looking hole between the buttressed roots of a spreading beech tree. She fnasted rabbit again and if she'd been warmer she might have followed its trail. She thought of the powerful hind feet of a rabbit and of its long incisors and sighed, "Even if I were fast enough to strangle it before it slashed me, I couldn't digest it anyway. I'm so cold that it would rot in my belly."

She was crawling beneath large trees now, but the sky seemed awfully bright. "Forests are supposed to be full of shadows," she thought. The cold was making her lose muscle control and her neck wavered unsteadily in the air as she peered upward and tried to bring the tops of the trees into focus. "What's happened to all of their leaves?" she wondered. In the forests at home the trees shed their leaves all year 'round, but there were always more leaves on the branches to shade the forest floor. Sherahi had expected a dim, green-shadowed forest, not a faint tracing of leafless branches. "Perhaps it'll be darker ahead," she thought, and moved on, nosing through the wet leaves, amazed that the scent of frangipani was stronger here. It was now too tiring to hold her head up.

Sherahi fnasted the scent of humans long before she saw the street lined with rows of small houses. "Toadslime," she cursed. "These must be the nests of humans." Sherahi lay still, not daring to breathe. She watched the quiet, rain-drenched street for a long time. There was no movement and, although the scent of humans was very strong, she decided, "These nests must be abandoned. There's no one here."

This observation had kept her motionless in the driving rain. She was very cold now and it was hard for her to raise her head to see a dark stand of conifers and the leafless branches of many other trees at the end of this block of houses. The gusts of wind made the overarching branches of the trees whip to and fro with a soughing sound. Sherahi looked at the ashy sky and felt exposed. Once again she saw the darkness below the conifers and thought, "I have to get there. I'll be safe there." She thought of a large, dry fallen log or of a rocky cave that might be behind that grove of trees—just a stretch of houses away—and decided she would have to risk being seen by humans to find shelter.

For the first time since she'd watched them leap one after the other through the wall into the storm drain, Sherahi missed her traveling companions. She wished she could inwit to them, but that required solitude and utter concentration, because the process of sending her thoughts to the mind of another creature rendered her oblivious of her surroundings. Her old teacher, U Vayu, had warned her never to be foolish and try to inwit in an unprotected place. So, Sherahi could not call to Dervish and Manu for help. "I'll have to do this myself," she decided. "I have to get to those trees.

"It's lucky that there don't seem to be any humans lurking about,"

Sherahi thought and, following the scent of frangipani, she nosed off the curb and down onto the rain-swept street.

Rain beaded and dribbled down the sides of automobiles that were parked all along the curb and Sherahi discovered that it was drier and slightly warmer beneath them. She undulated as rapidly as her cold body would allow beneath the wheels of two Nashes, an Oldsmobile, a Packard, three Fords, a Hudson and a Stutz Bearcat. Sherahi didn't like the oily smell of the machines but, as she crawled nearer to the thick stand of trees that grew on the opposite corner, she looked to the left and to her amazement saw that a whole forest began just across the street. It extended down the block as far as she could see, and Sherahi knew that she had done the right thing. As she slowly crawled beneath the automobiles she smelled the frangipani once again and it encouraged her.

She could see the dense shade beneath the dripping boughs of hemlock and hoped that the ground beneath them would be dry. "I'm almost there," thought Sherahi and laboriously gathered her length into a resting coil. She lay with her thick body stretched beneath two automobiles, her head forward, fnasting the open street ahead. The odd scent of frangipani came to her questing tongue and made her feel strangely at home on this windswept, quiet street that was so far from her own jungle. "Home," thought Sherahi, remembering the broken wall where she and U Vayu used to bask and watch the colors of the sky glow and ruin and fade into twilight. "I wonder if I'll ever see home again."

Sherahi saw that a final open stretch lay between her and the shade of the conifers. "I wish I were warmer," the snake's chilled mind thought slowly. "I can't move as quickly as I'd like to, but I must go on."

Sherahi looked carefully down the block and fnasted in all directions, alert for movement. She pulled her head back when she felt the thuds that she recognized as human footsteps. Something heavy slammed in the machine above her head. There was a thin, insistent sound, as if a metal pig were gagging, and then a roar. Sherahi flattened against an oily puddle as the car above pulled straight ahead and disappeared around the corner. The blue cloud of exhaust hung in the air and Sherahi watched the wheels disappear and shook her labial pits to rid them of the smell of hot fumes. She looked at the house from which the humans had come and saw a hand drop a white curtain that continued to tremble slightly for a long time. "There are more humans in there," Sherahi thought. "These nests are not deserted. I can't stay here." Sherahi bolted straight ahead, slithering as fast as her cold-chilled muscles would allow, into the intersection ahead.

Her head and neck flowed up and over the opposite curb and her long body trailed across the street, undulating as rapidly as her cold-slowed muscles would allow. "I'm going to make it," Sherahi thought, fnasting ahead in all directions, alert for movement that would mean danger. She fnasted the quick tail-flicking of a gray squirrel many feet above and saw him peer out from a snug leaf nest. With his head protected by an upcurled, furry tail he watched Sherahi and scolded and spat at her. "Get away. Get away," he chirred. Sherahi ignored him and tried to hurry her long body across the street, afraid that the squirrel's alarm would attract other animals to the place.

She put her head down onto the ground beneath the conifers and heard a blue jay shriek his warning, "They're coming—they're coming." The sound frightened Sherahi and she tried to urge her hind coils ahead to the safe haven where her head and neck rested. Then, a movement down the block caught her eye and she saw that something large was moving toward her. Her eyes had never been good at distance vision and now she used her special senses to see that a boy was slowly pedaling a bicycle down the street. A cap was pulled low over his eyes and his collar was turned up against the rain. Every now and then Sherahi heard a squeak of brakes as the boy stopped the bicycle. Standing in the street with the bicycle between his legs the boy would reach into the sack slung over one shoulder. Sherahi saw that one of his thick socks was wadded around his ankle. She could see the pale skin between the knee of his knickerbockers and the laces of his high-topped shoes. He took a roll of paper from the sack and hurled it at the front door of a nearby house. Then he would remount the bicycle and, after a few steps to get rolling, pedal to the next house. The progression of sounds that Sherahi could hear was whirr-whirr-whirr, squeak, thud, step—step; whirr-whirr-whirr, squeak, thud, step—step. He was three quarters of a block away.

Sherahi saw that her long body had still not completely crossed the street and kicked as hard as she could with her back muscles. "I'll never make it," Sherahi thought. "He'll see me." The thudding noises sounded closer now.

In panic and without really knowing where the thought came from, Sherahi reached into a dark pocket of her mind and sent a bolt of confusion and doubt into the boy's mind. She'd never tried anything quite like this before and wasn't sure whether it would work. As her midsection climbed the near curb she saw the boy's bicycle skid on the rain-slick pavement. He fell, and the sack spilled newspapers into the gutter. By the time he had picked up everything and fastened his sock with a bicycle clip, Sherahi was safe beneath the tall hemlocks that grew at the corner.

She watched the boy push his bicycle past her hiding place and rested there for a long time. As she peered out she saw the file of cars depart from the curb one by one. A door of one of the houses opened and a large black-and-white collie ran down the steps. He put his nose to the ground and ran to the tree that stood in front of his house. Balancing on three legs he quickly urinated and then busily nosed to the curb. Sherahi watched as the dog found her scent and lifted his head to sniff left and right. Suddenly the fur along his spine rose and he looked intently at the place where she lay. The dog crouched low, moving in a stealthy, slow-motion stalk. He had advanced three feet when the door of the house opened once again. Sherahi saw the dog quickly look at the door as if to say, "Leave me. I've got important business." Then he looked again and Sherahi saw his ears perk up and he stopped stalking toward the hemlocks and ran happily into his house, wagging his tail. The door closed and the block was quiet again.

"I can't stay here," Sherahi thought. "There's no place to hide and if that dog comes back . . ." Sherahi didn't want to think about having to fight a dog when she was this cold. It would be a very one-sided battle. "I must find someplace warm."

She noticed that her labial pits were faintly quopping, throbbing to tell her that something warm was in the vicinity. But Sherahi was cold and disoriented. She felt like a bruised ribbon of syrup poured from an overturned pitcher and lay helpless for a long time, listening to the rain beat against her skull, before she perceived that her heat-sensitive lip pits were trying to tell her something.

Her mind revolved around the sensations from her special sense organs, and if she could have compelled the muscles of her tongue to fnast the air, she would have, but she had gotten much too cold to move anything easily, much less her tongue. "I'm dying from the cold," she thought and wondered why she felt so calm about the prospect. "I'm having hallucinations," she decided. "U Vayu once told me that dying snakes often imagine things."

She looked at the grass beyond the hedge that bordered the hemlocks and noticed that it was covered with pink, soft scales. She saw that these scales were beneath her chin, too, and like everything else that she could see the large, strange scales were beaded with rain. "A mirage," Sherahi decided. "This can't be really happening." Her labial pits were quopping insistently and Sherahi could no longer ignore their signals. It was clear that something was giving off a great deal of heat ahead, just beyond the grove of conifers. Summoning all of her remaining energy, the pythoness raised her head and forced her body forward. She reached another, nearby knot of conifers but the sensation of heat lured her on. She undulated up a broad flight of concentric marble stairs and found herself in a round, white marble basin filled with wet, rotting leaves. With poor control over her muscles she nosed ahead and, from the height of the basin, fnasted frangipani once again. "Now I know I'm dying," she thought as she looked down into the valley that was on the far side of the fountain and saw what appeared to be a house made of crystal. "This can't be true." Sherahi could barely manage the thought.

She lay draped over the side of the basin with her labial pits insisting that this crystal house was warm—wonderfully warm—even hot inside. It was the only warm place in the chilly, rain-swept landscape. "This must be what it's like to die," she thought, crawling slowly toward this queer source of heat. "Maybe I am dying. Maybe U Vayu is inside that place." Slowly, laboriously, feeling giddy and light-headed, Sherahi undulated down the slope toward the glass house. Too tired to travel with her head held aloft, she nosed her way through the blanket of pink scales that covered the grass.

For only a short while after the pythoness had passed, a wide, green stripe remained in the carpet of fallen cherry-blossom petals. Then rain shook the orchard and buried her sinuous trail.

"There's no point in telling them," thought Junior as he lashed back and forth in the sand, making a shallow trench that was twice as long as his body. "It'll be better if they think that she's just flown away. Seeing her like this will only make them sad."

He continued digging in the soft, powdery sand and before long the trench was ready. "That's about right," the serpent said, measuring depth by standing on his ribs and stretching up a third of his body length. "She'll be safe here and at least the cats and the flies won't find her so easily, though I can't see how that matters much now. But Sherahi would want me to do this. I'm sure of it."

He put his head beside the dead bird's wing and pushed. The trench had been dug alongside it and the corpse rolled easily into the grave. Her eyes were half closed. A filmy nictitating membrane covered each pupil. Junior saw that sand adhered to the macaw's moist eye, but he could do nothing to remove it. Her freshly washed plumage shone brilliant scarlet, yellow and blue, but all of her feathers were awry, bedraggled. She needed grooming, and had the Duchess been alive she would have used her beak and tongue to reset the minute hooks and barbs that interlocked the filaments of each feather. Junior was intent upon hiding the corpse before the others found her. He didn't like the feel of the macaw's stiff feathers and hurried to cover her, working as efficiently and quickly as any red-spotted necrophorous beetle. Anyone watching might have thought that he'd spent a lifetime burying dead animals.

Using side-winding motions, he pushed the excavated sand into the hollow around the dead bird. Soon only one scarlet epaulette marked her grave. "Goodbye, Duchess," the rattler thought and spread sand over this last sign that the scarlet macaw wasn't squawking her way south toward the jungle she'd always longed for.

It was late afternoon when the cascabel returned to Dervish and Manu. The rattler was surprised to find the langur awake and intently sucking at something that he held in one hand. A heap of shells lay at his feet. Junior was pleased to see Manu alert and active. He was about to greet the langur but left the words unuttered when he saw Manu close his black-fingered hands around a slim clam shell and hurl it against a rock. Even though Junior couldn't understand the soft blur of words, the cry of pain that issued from the shellfish's exposed body was unmistakable. Junior knew that Manu heard the scream, too, and that the langur had chosen to ignore it. Junior had never seen an animal eat another creature without first bothering to stun or kill it. Both the act and the idea disturbed him. Even Sherahi strangled her prey. Only water snakes were such gluttons that they didn't kill frogs before they swallowed them whole. Sherahi had told him how water snakes would lurk around ponds, hoping to snatch their victims. She'd said that you could hear the frogs croaking within the bloated snakes as they slithered off to digest their meal. All serpents considered water snakes a contemptible, sneaky lot—"very unevolved," Sherahi always called them. "How can Manu do this?" thought Junior and looked away. Until now he'd always admired the langur.

Dervish was not far down the beach, digging in the sand just below the tide line. As Junior watched, Manu continued cracking clam shells and slurping their contents. His pleasure was obvious and Junior thought, "Manu should know better. No civilized animal eats another alive. It's cruel. Against the rules."

He was repulsed by the sight of Manu licking scraps of clam flesh from his furry chin and announced himself, saying, "You could at least put them out of their misery first." He made his mental message grate into Manu's mind like the sound of shells splattering against rock, but Manu didn't seem to notice. Junior coiled below the boulder and constricted his pupils to thin, vertical slits against the strong afternoon sun.

"Hello, Junior. Nice to see you again," Manu said between gulps. He watched the cascabel luxuriate in the warm spot of sun and added, "Feels good after all that rain, huh?"

Junior tightened his coil, making a slight scraping noise to show his annoyance. He made no direct reply into the langur's mind.

With his banded tail erect and his eyes shining brightly, Dervish bounded up and dropped another razor clam at Manu's feet. He chirped something to Manu and then stiffened into silence when he saw that Junior had returned. He gave the snake one long glance, hesitated as if he were about to say something and then changed his mind and trotted away on stiff legs.

"Here, Junior," said Manu, tossing an opened razor clam toward the rattler. "You ought to try one. They're delicious."

Junior was startled by the sudden movement of the langur's arm and drew his head back obliquely into a striking coil. He inflated his neck and the sound of his rattle buzzed ominously from the hollow beneath the boulder.

"All right. Don't get so excited," said the langur. "Nobody's insisting." Manu swiveled his head so that he could see the threatening rattler with his good eye. Cautiously he retrieved the clam, adding, "But then, you're probably not hungry. You've had plenty of time to hunt. Dervish said you'd been out since morning."

"No, I'm still hungry," said the rattlesnake into Manu's mind. "But I couldn't eat something that's alive, Manu. I can hear those clams screaming and you can, too." There was a silence and he hissed, "It's not right."

The langur said nothing. He lifted the next freshly opened clam to his mouth and chewed it loose from its shell with his side teeth. He avoided the rattler's fixed stare.

Dervish dug furiously in the sand and brought up another clam. He cracked its thin shell with his back teeth and dropped it before Manu. "I'm going down the beach to see what else I can find." Before he trotted away he chittered, adding archly, "Seems strange that the Great Hunter is still hungry. This one's for him." The coatimundi's tail disappeared around the boulder and Junior settled back against the warm rock face. It was clear that Dervish was upset, but the rattler didn't know what to do or say to heal the breach between them.

"I think," said Manu, speaking into Junior's mind, "that Dervish is ready to be friends again."

"He certainly doesn't act like it."

"He's trying. Give him a chance. He'll come around. Only a few minutes ago he was telling me how *you* were the one who really saved us from the white crocodiles. I think he feels guilty for wanting to abandon us. Don't give up on him, Junior. Even though he's almost full grown, he's only a youngster. He may not sound like it, but he wants to be your friend again. He just doesn't know how to tell you that he's sorry."

Junior's reply was drowned by a howl and Manu dropped the clam that he was chewing. "That's Dervish," he said and raced toward the sound. Junior knew without being told that Dervish had found the Duchess. "Damn," thought the cascabel, "now they'll blame it all on me." He thought of slithering away to hide and wavered for a moment, fnasting the air and scanning the minds of the two animals that had disappeared from sight. "If only Sherahi hadn't made me responsible for them." With a soft hiss of annoyance he undulated after Manu.

No longer hungry, and satisfied that Manu had eaten his fill, Dervish had found a new game for himself: chasing the ghost crabs that flitted from their holes in the sand to scrounge a meal from the tidal wrack. The slanting afternoon sun cast long shadows behind the wary crabs, exaggerating all of their movements. The inoffensive creatures moved with a clockwork jerkiness that mesmerized Dervish. Instinctively he flattened against the sand, lowered his banded tail and began to stalk one particular victim.

He waited motionless for the crab to resume its feeding. "You can't see me," Dervish crooned to his prey. "I'm a rock. I'm a dead log. There's nothing here." As if he had heard the coati, the crab swiveled his stalked eyes and tentatively edged up and out of his hole. His pale carapace blended so perfectly with the gray sand that Dervish could hardly see him when he was still. If he hadn't cast a hunched shadow, the crab would have been invisible.

Dervish remained motionless, muscles tensed and ready to pounce. "Just come a little farther from that hole, little swift-footed crab," wheedled Dervish. The crab flitted forward suddenly, dancing across the sand on white-tipped claws, running like a sandpiper at high tide. Now six inches separated him from his home in the sand. "Just a little farther, my light-footed friend," urged Dervish. Abruptly the crab started sideward again, his eight walking legs a blur that moved. In the next instant Dervish leaped. He grabbed with both paws and felt the crab's shell slide between his fingers. Then the chase was on and Dervish felt sure that he would win: he'd deliberately blocked the crab's path to his hole. What he didn't realize, however, is that ghost crabs can hide almost anywhere. Out of the corner of his eye he caught the motion as his prey scurried down another hole in the sand that was three feet away.

"How could he have gotten there so quickly?" thought Dervish. With his tongue lolling out from his underslung jaw he padded over to investigate. Using one paw he dug tentatively for a moment and then put his nose to the sand to smell the way that the tunnel retreated into the powdery sand. Then he began to dig, flinging jets of sand out between his hind legs. Abruptly he stopped and watched for movement in the pit he'd made. Pale, multijointed legs scrabbled deeper into the sand and Dervish pounced again, grabbing with both paws.

"Now I've got you," he purred, feeling something tickling his palm. He'd eaten other ghost crabs this morning and liked their delicate, salty taste. He hardly noticed the pinching of their small claws. Sitting back on his haunches, he brought both paws close to his chest and slowly uncurled each long-clawed finger, expecting the crab to erupt from his fist at any minute. He was certain he'd caught it. But when he opened his favorite hand he saw four tattered, scarlet feathers instead of the ten-legged, sideward-scuttling snack that he'd expected.

Dervish didn't see colors in the way that the other Culls did, but he recognized this particular shade of gray as what Manu called "scarlet." In a moment Dervish had forgotten his ghost crab and was widening the pit he'd dug. Soon he uncovered the scarlet back and bright blue tail of a large bird that looked familiar. Much too familiar. "This could be the Duchess's cousin," he thought. "Or it could be the Duchess herself, if she weren't flying toward the jungle now."

He unearthed the bird's head and, taking care not to damage her delicate skin with his teeth, Dervish pulled her body from the sand. A few neck feathers came off in his mouth and he saw that a wide, yellowed callus encircled this bird's neck. Dervish remembered how the Duchess had complained that the collar that Sorensen had forced her to wear made her neck sore. He looked at the bare, finely puckered skin surrounding her beak and at the familiar topknot of tiny red feathers. There was no mistaking it. This bird wasn't some cousin of the Duchess—it was the Duchess herself.

Sand and feathers filled Dervish's mouth and he spat them out. He touched the bird's face with his wet nose. She felt warm; maybe she wasn't dead. "Wake up, Duchess," he chittered. Half afraid that the bird would suddenly shake herself alert and bite him with that cruel beak, he carefully washed the sand from her half-closed eyes and watched for a reaction. For a moment he thought he detected a shallow breathing movement, but then she was still once again. Her scaly, gray toes were firmly clenched, as if gripping an invisible perch. He prodded her with his nose again and whined in her ear, but the Duchess didn't move. Her plumage made a dark blot of color against the sand. Dervish suddenly realized that the Duchess wasn't flying to her jungle at all. She was dead. Now she'd never see Sandeagozu or complain about not being an owl. Now she'd never say the wrong thing at the wrong time again or hatch a nestful of baby macaws. Something terrible had happened to her last night when she'd flown down the flooded storm drain and whoever had killed her had buried her to hide it.

Dervish sat on his haunches and howled.

With the length of her huge body pressed against the warm glass, Sherahi absorbed the heat radiating from the crystal house. As she warmed she felt muscular control return and her giddy, light-headed feeling disappeared. She was hidden behind shrubbery, but she felt exposed stretched out like this. She needed a coil to launch a strike and it would be difficult to defend herself from this position. When she reached a temperature that allowed her complete muscular control, she gathered her coils into a careless skein. Feeling more confident, she began to investigate. "This is obviously a human place," she thought. "But no one seems to be here." Fnasting in all directions she could detect a faint trace of the rancid smell that clung to all human habitations. "People don't come here often," she concluded. "I wonder what's inside?"

Guided by her quopping labial pits she nosed her way up the glass panes at one corner of the structure and, stretched to a quarter of her length, cautiously peered inside a high window that was propped open. It was much warmer inside and instinctively she inched through the vent, alert for danger. It was twilight outside, and even dimmer inside, but she could see the silhouettes of tall palm trees against an arched glass dome. Plants grew everywhere. She fnasted the odor of tomcat and the damp smell of mossy stone and pools of water. More than anything else the smells inside the crystal house reminded her of the forest that grew behind her pagoda and of home.

Stretching from the open window, Sherahi reached across a twelve-foot drop to the branch of a gnarled tree that grew near the corner of the building. She carefully nosed beneath bouquets of smooth leaves and clusters of blossoms. She didn't dare to put her full weight upon the branch until she'd coiled twice around the tree's trunk. Once she had a firm grasp she slowly relaxed onto the branch. She was relieved that it sagged only a little beneath her weight. Slowly she pulled yard after yard of her body behind her. By the time her tail released its hold on the open window frame, her head and most of her length had spiraled into the crown of the tree. Her tail swung precariously through space and the branches swayed beneath her. For a moment the big snake was afraid that she might slip. A fall from this height might not kill her, but it would certainly hurt. Her days of lashing through treetops after lizards and birds, and of falling harmlessly from canopy to understory to continue the chase, were over. Now she was ponderous and such a drop would surely break her ribs. In a moment, though, she had regained her balance in the tree and had distributed her weight along the topmost branches.

It was dark, warm and humid in the crystal house and silent, except for the sound of leaves rustling as Sherahi hid in the bare-branched interior of the tree. She was completely screened by the bouquets of leaves and flowers that grew at the tips of each branch. For a while she allowed herself to luxuriate in the feeling of being in a tree again and then she remembered the Culls.

"I must gather the others," she thought. "We could be safe here." Just before she sent her mind spinning out to Junior and to Manu, she fnasted the air, to double-check that no enemies were about. All she could smell was the penetrating perfume of the clusters of white blossoms that studded the screen of foliage around her. Deep within the maze of shadowy, naked branches, Sherahi recognized the fragrance as frangipani. Such a tree had grown outside her pagoda. Its blossoms had been orange, not white, and their throats had been tinged with fuchsia, but the perfume was unmistakable and it made Sherahi feel secure. Even before she scanned the glass house around her, from curved dome to brick floor, she knew that, except for gray colonies of pill bugs that clustered beneath stones and bright-eyed jumping spiders who crouched in crevices, she was alone. She was certain that she and the Culls had found a safe haven.

From her lair beneath the creamy-white and yellow blossoms and broad green leaves of the frangipani tree, Sherahi sent her mind spinning out toward the other Culls. She sent the image of the full moon bleeding a golden streak onto still water and the smell of the frangipani in full flower—things that meant home to the pythoness. She told the others to waste no time in getting to the crystal house. "Hurry, Junior," she said. "Gather them and come here. I think I've found Sandeagozu."

It was as if the Culls on the beach never heard Sherahi at all. Manu sat next to the dead bird, distractedly patting her sandy feathers. Occasionally he peered into her face with his good eye, looking intently for some sign that she lived. From time to time he brought his good ear to her beak and listened. But the result was always the same. The langur rocked back on his haunches and hugged himself, staring with wide eyes at what had once been a raucous bird screeching for Sorensen's attention—a wisecracking parrot who had learned to eat dead rats and to trust a giant pythoness. "Duchess," Manu kept repeating, "you can't be dead. I won't let this happen. Please wake up."

But there was no response from the still bird and his delicate fingers plucked individual grains of sand from the corners of her half-closed eyes, moving as lightly as a stilt-legged spider through the sticky maze of its web. Manu wished for Sherahi's power to scry any animal's mind. "This doesn't make sense," he thought. "How can it be? She feels warm. Sometimes she seems to breathe. She doesn't look dead, but she's so still. If only Sherahi were here. She'd know what to do."

Manu rocked back and forth and resisted the impulse to violently shake the Duchess. Something told him that this was forbidden. It violated an ancient taboo of his tribe. Hanuman langurs didn't touch dead things. Manu realized that he'd been touching the face of a dead creature and the thought revolted him. With a shudder he drew back from the corpse and wiped his hand against his furry thigh. "How could I have done that?" Manu thought. Oblivious to all around him Manu tried to content himself with watching the Duchess, comforting her in an inarticulate way and hoping that she might suddenly shake herself alive. He was so absorbed that he didn't see the cascabel arrive. Dervish did, though. The coati had been sitting near Manu. When he saw Junior he stood up, erected the hairs along his spine into stiff bristles and lost no time in confronting the serpent. "Why did you kill her?" he demanded.

"Don't be ridiculous, Dervish. I didn't do any such thing," Junior replied. "I found her lying here."

"Why didn't you tell us?" Dervish's lips curled back, exposing the yellowed bases of his canine teeth and an alarming flash of blood-red gum. "I know you buried her, Junior. So don't pretend to be innocent. It just makes me mad."

"Why are you so sure that I buried her?" the cascabel asked. "There are a million animals that could have done that." Immediately after Junior sent these words into Dervish's mind he regretted them: he had said exactly the wrong thing.

"Stop lying, Junior. We both know that you did it. It's as plain as those pockmarks on your face."

Dervish motioned with his head toward the beach, where the Duchess lay. "Just look around. Your tracks are everywhere. You think that you're so smart, but if you used your eyes and nose instead of those stupid snake senses, you'd know that you've dropped your calling cards everywhere. Even a mole could tell that you were here." The coati laughed grimly and added, "Whoever said that bats are blind didn't know anything about snakes. That's for sure, eh Manu?" The coati made an exasperated sound when he saw that the langur wasn't listening. Manu crooned softly to the dead bird. Dervish watched him for a minute and thought, "What a waste of time. She'll never hear you now, Manu."

The sight of the langur and the dead macaw infuriated Dervish even more. He remembered that Junior often fanged animals just for the fun of it—just to keep in practice or to see how they died. He had convinced himself that the snake had killed the Duchess. The bird had always been frightened of the cascabel and without Sherahi around to control him there was no telling what this vicious rattler might do. Dervish imagined the macaw lying wet and disoriented on the beach. Maybe she couldn't fly; maybe her wing was broken. He saw the prowling rattler coil and strike. The Duchess might have flapped her wet wings once or twice but she had never had a chance.

Dervish continued his cross-examination. "Answer me, Junior, why did you hide her? Was it an accident? Or were you suddenly struck by a hunger for bird flesh?" When Junior's small, cold voice did not reply, Dervish chittered, "What's the matter? Couldn't you open that mouth wide enough to actually swallow your kill once she was dead?

"Tell me, Junior, was it fun to kill a helpless bird—someone that trusted you? Did you do it out of curiosity? Are you sorry now that the Duchess is dead?"

Dervish shook with fury. His erect fur made him look twice his size. His snout seemed to elongate even more as his lips curled above his incisors once again. His forehead was furrowed with animosity. His ears were slicked back against his skull and if Junior hadn't known him so well he would have thought that Dervish was hatred incarnate. He punctuated every word with low, rolling growls.

Junior realized that the coati would attack at any moment and drew his head back into the high, oblique striking coil that was the trademark of the cascabel. He grated his saw-toothed scales against each other and rattled a warning. "Don't press your luck, Dervish," he hissed calmly into the coati's mind. "You know I can kill you before you realize that I've even struck. So don't threaten me, my friend, unless you want to die, too. You'll never win against me. Listen before you make me do something that we'll both regret. I didn't kill the Duchess. I found her like that." The cascabel held his tail erect and rattled another warning, but this only further infuriated the coati.

"Don't wave your stupid rattle at me," Dervish fumed. "I'm sick of listening to it. I never want to hear it again." Dervish leaped at the cascabel and the snake felt teeth rake across his skin and fasten deep into his back muscles. He heard bones grind and break as the coati crushed a mouthful of his ribs. Like Medusa's hair come alive, the serpent writhed between the coati's jaws. Before his cold-blooded brain registered pain and before the coati could do any more damage the snake delivered three rapid strikes. On the last he erected a single fang and injected a small fraction of the venom necessary to kill a meadow mouse. Pain gripped him and he couldn't think clearly, but even so he knew that he didn't want to kill Dervish. "I must just control him," the snake gasped. He fought the waves of nausea from his crushed rib cage and, as is the habit of venomous snakes, he stabbed a message of fear and panic into his victim's mind. For the cascabel this message was as instinctive as crouching motionless when the shadow of a hawk passed overhead.

"Stupid coatimundi," his icy voice said. "I thought you had more sense than the other fur-footed ones, but you're worse than a rabid weasel. Now you've killed yourself. In the time it took you to take a single breath I've bitten you three times. Right now there's enough poison flooding through your bloodstream to kill a hippopotamus."

Watching Dervish's thoughts carefully he added, "No—don't go blaming me. You started this. It's all your fault."

He saw fear begin to blossom in Dervish's mind and hissed in exultation, "Feel numb yet? No? Well, just wait a moment. Concentrate on that tingling place just above your left shoulder blade. Good. It's numb now. Soon your whole body will feel like that.

"It's that way with all my victims. Soon your gums will start to bleed. Then you'll drool blood. It will embarrass you but you won't be able to help yourself. Then you won't be able to catch your breath. After that you'll be as dead as the Duchess, and Manu will have another Cull to mourn.

"But you know something, Dervish? I won't bother to bury *you*. The Coffin Bearers can rip you to pieces for all I care."

The cascabel's greatest fear was that Dervish would shake him and snap his spine in just the way that a cat kills a mouse. One shake would injure him; two or three would kill him. He couldn't stop tormenting Dervish until he'd fooled the coati into releasing him. Junior was pleased that his voice had a hypnotic effect: Dervish's jaws slackened their grip.

"You're getting very tired, Dervish," he insisted. "Now drop me, before I bite you again. You never had a chance against my venom. The very idea of you attacking me is ridiculous. You were brave but foolish, Dervish. Very foolish." Junior laughed, making a creaking sound. "You should have known that you couldn't kill me anyway: even worms know that snakes don't die until sundown." Still bluffing, he added, "Don't ruin your last moments, weak-minded fur-foot. It's time for you to prepare to die. Drop me, Dervish. Drop me *now*."

Miraculously, the coati's mouth opened and the bloody rattlesnake fell to the sand. He retreated a few feet and turned to watch as Dervish began to frantically bite at his back as if killing a flea. Then the coati rolled in the sand, hitching from side to side as if trying to scrub away the venom. He panted and whined as he staggered to his feet, trying to crawl to Manu and the Duchess. But his energy faded after he'd taken a few steps. A blue-white membrane flicked across his black eyes and he fell on his side, his legs twitching convulsively.

Manu was stunned. He had watched the end of the fight between the rattler and coati, helpless to control either animal. He saw Dervish collapse and spoke into the cascabel's mind. "I can't believe this, Junior. That wasn't necessary. Couldn't you see that he was beside himself? He thought you'd killed the Duchess and buried her to hide it. The Duchess is dead; now Dervish is dead and Sherahi is lost. Why don't you go ahead and kill me, too?"

"Don't be a fool, Manu," said the cascabel. "Dervish isn't dead. I injected only enough poison to make him sleep. He was actually going to kill me. Didn't you see that? Besides, what kind of a monster do you think I am? Do you honestly think I could kill Dervish after all we've been through? I promised Sherahi. Don't you know me at all?"

Manu regarded the bloody reptile. More calmly, he spoke into his mind, saying, "I'm sorry, Junior. I shouldn't have doubted you. I don't know what's wrong with me—with all of us."

There was a silence in which the waves slapped against the rocks and then Junior said, "And Sherahi's not lost. She's been calling us. Surely you've heard her."

Manu looked blank. "No," he faltered. "I've been thinking about the Duchess. Where is Sherahi? We must find her." Manu looked from the dead macaw to the coati, who lay on the sand, breathing shallowly. "But what about Dervish?" Manu asked. "We can't just leave him here. He's helpless."

"Do you think you could carry him?"

"I can try. If he doesn't weigh too much, I think I can carry him. I won't be able to go very fast, though."

The cascabel watched Manu struggle to pick up the unconscious coati. The langur staggered a little beneath the weight, but signaled Junior to move on.

With the coati over his shoulder Manu asked, "Are you sure that Dervish'll be all right?"

"Yes. I'm sure. He'll be fine in a little while—even able to walk. I, however, may be seriously wounded." He added to himself, "But then, that would hardly interest you."

Junior rasped into the langur's mind, "Come on, Manu. Sherahi isn't far from here." Wincing as the sharp edges of his broken ribs worked against torn muscles, the cascabel led the way toward the salt marsh, following Sherahi's directions. After a while the pain eased and he was grateful that Dervish's teeth hadn't done more damage. As he crawled, fnasting the twilight for danger, he wished that Manu had shown a little interest in his injuries. "But then, he thinks of me only as a snake—and he's afraid of snakes. Once Sherahi told me that they all liked me, even though they were frightened. But now I know different. Not one of them likes me at all."

The cascabel paused at the seaward edge of the bayberry thicket and waited for the langur to catch up. He saw the crimson blot that was the Duchess lying forgotten on the beach and decided not to remind Manu that she was an easy mark for carrion eaters. "Let the Coffin Bearers have her," he thought. "I'm not going to be punished for another good deed."

CHAPTER TEN

Hollywood, California

PLEASE HOLD STILL, Miss Naruda," Allie whined. "It won't be much longer now."

With a sigh Ruthie rolled her eyes toward the ceiling and thought, "If you weren't such a klutz, Allison Shaw, this would have been over an hour ago." The makeup woman had been fluttering around her for nearly two hours, applying and then removing color after color, smudging highlights and shadows, trying for just the right "effect." Ruthie was sick of the word. She could have done her own makeup in fifteen minutes, but that was out of the question: not even extras did their own makeup in a Goldman production. Even though Ruthie was Mr. G's favorite, as a novice starlet she didn't merit the attention of the head makeup artist. As a result she had to endure the inept ministrations of Allie Shaw.

Ruthie had had ample time to observe Allie and she hoped that, whatever else happened, she wouldn't end her career the way this haggard veteran of silent films had. Allie's face was heavily powdered and, as the morning had progressed, she'd bitten the center out of her carmine lip color. She had a vivid slash of rouge beneath each eye: a memorial to long-vanished cheekbones. "They always used to compliment me on my bone structure," she'd say to Ruthie, stretching her corded neck and sucking in withered cheeks. Her cap of frizzled, auburn hair had dirty, gray roots and up close she smelled of stale cigarette smoke and caked makeup. Ruthie doubted that her hands were clean. The tooth-marked mouthpiece of a cigarette holder protruded from the pocket of her smock and through the thin lavender material Ruthie could see the outline of a package of "ciggies," as Allie called them, and the Lucky Strike bull's-eye.

"Just the eyeliner and we're finished," Allie said. She unscrewed a small bottle, dipped a long-handled brush into it and carefully wiped away the excess black liquid. "Bend your head back and look up," she ordered. There was the smell of unwashed clothing mixed with cigarette smoke and Ruthie breathed through her mouth to avoid it. By the time Allie was ready to apply the eyeliner she found that it had dried on the brush. Allie was tired and her feet hurt. She wanted a smoke. Annoyed, she plunged the brush back into the bottle and brought it out dripping. As she moved the brush to Ruthie's eye, her hand trembled and she saw a bead of eyeliner bleed onto the white of the girl's uprolled eye. Too late she dropped the brush and reached for a tissue.

Ruthie cried out and jerked her head away. Holding her burning eye with one hand she pushed Allie aside and raced to the sink to splash cold water on her eye. When it had stopped burning she hissed, "Idiot. You nearly blinded me. Just look at what you've done, you stupid shit." Ruthie examined her inflamed eye in the mirror. "It's all bloodshot," she wailed. "How can I go on like this? I'll look awful in the close-ups."

Allie hovered behind her, clucking and making apologetic sounds. A clean towel trembled in her outstretched hands. "It was an accident," she said. "I'm sorry, Miss. Keep it under the cold water. That'll help." Allie Shaw knew that she might lose her job and repeated her apology again and again, as if it were an incantation guaranteed to ward off the evil eye.

Ruthie lifted her dripping face from the sink and Allie gasped to see the blurred and ruined makeup. "Stop it," said Ruthie, knowing what the woman was really upset about. "It's only makeup. *I'm* all right now—no thanks to you."

"Don't hold this against me, Miss Naruda. Please don't. It was an accident. Come back to the chair. I'll be more careful this time. You'll see." Once again she offered the towel, hoping that this imperious creature wouldn't have her fired. "I'll be more careful, Miss Naruda. Just relax. Let me help you. Like I helped Miss Swanson in the old days."

Ruthie took the towel and sat before the mirror again. She dried her face and skeptically eyed the woman who stood behind her, wringing her hands. "All right," she said, but her tone made it clear that this was Allie's last chance.

Allie smeared a thick layer of cold cream over Ruthie's cheeks, eyelids and throat, cleaning away the smeared makeup with circular movements. "I used to do this for Miss Swanson all the time," she said in a confidential tone. "Now, there was a star—a real one. She and I were the best friends—the very best. Started out together." Allie's tone was resigned. "Just goes to show what can happen if you have the right contacts. Things were different then," she said, pausing to look at Ruthie in the mirror. With a clean face and those calculating, green eyes closed, the girl looked barely nineteen years old. Allie had seen hundreds of starlets and knew that this one was no innocent—this Naruda wasn't Goldman's new favorite only by chance. Allie looked at her own face, reflected above that of the girl. There was a time when she, too, had had smooth, full cheeks and a firm chin line. Once, Allie Shaw had been the producer's darling, too—just like this one. Her memory made her feel protective and Allie thought, "She doesn't know what can happen—what they can do to her if she's not careful. She's got no idea at all." To Ruthie she said briskly, "We'll be done in no time. Now look up, please, just like before."

Ruthie sighed and obeyed. She hated the feel of Allie's fingers and the soft sponges and brushes on her face. Everything about the woman was third rate. "Mr. G'll have to get rid of her when I tell him about this," Ruthie thought. "Besides nearly blinding me, she's wasted all this time. He always says that time is money and Mr. G likes money better than anything." She remembered his eyes, magnified and watery behind the thick lenses of his horn-rimmed glasses. She'd seen those eyes grow bright and attentive whenever he wanted something real bad—something that, she fancied, only she could supply. She smiled to herself and thought, "No. That's not quite right. Mr. G likes money better than *almost* anything."

She found the familiar crack in the dressing-room wall. It zigzagged from the door frame to the ceiling and she fixed her eyes on it, holding her breath and wishing that she'd turned on the radio. Music would have made this more bearable. The crack moved from the corner of the door frame and struck across the ceiling, pointing like an arthritic finger at the empty sockets of the light fixture. "The decorator will have to do something about that," she thought, as firm strokes of Allie's sponge removed smeared mascara from beneath each eye.

That crack in her dressing-room wall was Bernie's parting shot: a memento of their last argument. She remembered how she'd sent him packing after he couldn't get the Burmese after all of his promises. Ruthie pushed Bernie Weinstein's name and face from her thoughts. "He's in the past," she thought, and was glad to be living alone—independent at last. Now that she was going to be a star, she'd resolved not to dwell on unpleasant people. Mr. G said that worries would show up in her face. "Let me do the worrying for you, baby," he'd said. Besides, Bernie was gone now—probably sponging on someone else. Making himself essential and then unable to deliver. "How tedious," she thought, looking at the crack that he'd made by slamming the dressing-room door. She'd forgotten his exact words, but the spidery crack pointed an accusing finger, like he had when he called her all those ugly names. She looked away. As far as she was concerned, Bernie Weinstein was as good as dead.

"Hold still, now, Miss Naruda," Allie said. "These lashes are ruined. They'll have to come off." Ruthie felt a puckering sensation as Allie pulled a strip of mink fur from each eyelid. "You can relax a minute," she said. Ruthie bent forward to snap on the radio and looked at herself in the mirror. She gasped to see the slick-skinned, red-eyed creature that sat before the dressing-room mirror and reached for a towel to wipe her face and rub color into her cheeks.

"Now, let's try it again," Allie said. "Close." With swift strokes she applied the layer of bronze makeup that transformed Ruthie Notar into Naruda, the golden-skinned Etruscan dancer who would tempt Judah Ben-Salam.

After a while Allie asked the starlet to look up once more and added, "Now, take a deep breath." She wanted to add, "And let's get this over with," but restrained herself. Makeup women didn't speak that way to Mr. Goldman's special girls. Not makeup women who wanted to keep their jobs.

Before Ruthie could react, Allie had whisked a teal-blue pencil along the pink inner border of each eye. "There," she said triumphantly, "that's the hard part." Minutes later a fresh pair of false eyelashes had been glued into place and she had rouged Ruthie's cheeks and sculpted hollows beneath her cheekbones. "Now, look at me." Allie wanted a cigarette and no longer cared if her work was perfect. This one didn't appreciate the miracles that Allie Shaw could work with makeup, anyway. "Pearls and swine," she thought.

Ruthie saw the admiration in Allie's eyes and knew that now she was beautiful again. It pleased her to see the effect she had upon Allie Shaw. Maybe she wouldn't have Mr. G fire her, after all. How many mornings had Allie appeared in this dressing room? Was this the second or third week of shooting? It was all a blur. Ruthie had been on the set ever since Mr. Goldman and Mervyn LeMarr had begun shooting *Crown of Thorns*. With only a little prompting from Ruthie during their quiet dinners at his estate, Mr. Goldman, sweet angel that he was, had expanded her part. Now, instead of just dancing with snakes, she was to have real love scenes with the great Thurston P. Topping, who was making his comeback in *Crown of Thorns*. Of course, she hadn't actually met the legendary star of silent films yet, but she knew that being on the same screen with him could only help her career. It was her big break. "If only he stays sober," she thought and smiled at Allie without really seeing her.

"Just a bit more." Allie rummaged in her pockets for a smoky-gray pencil to emphasize Ruthie's eyes. "Don't blink," she warned and Ruthie felt the pencil whisk just beneath the edge of each lower lid. It felt like the quick, intimate pressure that Larry had used to trace secret words onto her forearms when they had played "Mystery Messages": one of the homemade games that she had invented to control her little brother on those long summer afternoons before she had run away from her father's house. Larry had small, delicate fingers and she still remembered how they had felt. The letters would slowly become visible, emerging like slow-swimming goldfishes at the surface of a pond. At first, each mark appeared white against her tanned skin. Almost immediately the white mark disappeared and minutes later the letter would blush red. The words were visible for a long time.

The game was for her to guess what the words were before they became legible. It would continue until her forearms were completely covered with overlapping letters. Once Larry had begged to write letters on her legs, too. Ruthie had known that he would throw a tantrum and wake the baby if he weren't given his way and she'd given in, but his quick fingers moving over the skin of her thighs had disturbed her and she'd ended the game long before he was satisfied. As expected, Larry had thrown a fit and Ruthie had eventually relented and let him write messages wherever he wanted, even though it had made her feel uncomfortable.

With finality Allie said, "Good. Now look at me." Ruthie obeyed. She felt strangely embarrassed by the woman's cool appraisal and shifted her gaze from one of the woman's eyes to the other, not knowing where to look. For an inexplicable reason Ruthie suddenly thought, "Can she read my thoughts?"

Allie took a step back, cocked her head on one side and examined Ruthie's face. "Just one thing more." She took a long pencil from another pocket, sharpened it and commanded, "Close." The heavy mink eyelashes brushed Ruthie's cheekbones. There was the same intimate pressure and the same queasy feeling as Allie's pencil traced a line from the inner corner of each eye to each temple. Ruthie knew that this would enlarge her eyes, making them even more mysterious.

"Open." There was more scrutiny and Allie sighed and said, "That's it. We're done." She looked at her handiwork as she fitted a Lucky Strike into her mother-of-pearl cigarette holder, a relic of grander days. She took a long drag and began to sweep her array of cosmetics into a black leather satchel, saying, "It's a much better job than before. Take a look. You're beautiful, Miss Naruda. Really beautiful."

Allie left the room without another word, leaving Ruthie to stare at the exotic creature reflected in her mirror. "I *am* beautiful," she thought. She pouted and imagined that her eyes were as deep and inscrutable as Theda Bara's. She turned three quarters to the mirror and arched one finely penciled brow, mimicking Myrna Loy's publicity stills. She sucked in her cheeks and deep hollows appeared. "'Do I have a bone structure like Garbo's?" she wondered. "Max says I can be the next Garbo if Mr. G likes me enough." A frown formed between her brows and she speculated, "I wonder how I'd look as a blonde."

She was studying her reflection when a knock on the door announced the arrival of her dresser. *"Entrez,"* she said to the mirror, rolling the "r" in the way that she imagined the French did. Later, after she had donned the wig, headpiece and costume of the slave dancer, she dismissed the dresser and was alone with her mirror once again.

A brassiere of entwined gold lamé serpents wound around her neck and encircled each breast. Around her hips was a glittering skirt that had hundreds of knife-edged pleats. Its weighted hem allowed the skirt to fan open, magnifying her slightest movements. It was as if she were wearing a coiling whip. The skirt was designed to be easily ripped from her waist to reveal the gilt serpent that twined up and around her left leg. Her pubic hair had been shaved and she wore a flesh-colored brief. From a distance it looked as if she were clad in a handful of beautiful but deadly golden serpents. Ruthie wriggled her hips and watched the skirt shimmer, exposing and then hiding the snake that climbed her leg. Satisfied with the effect, she fastened a heavy, jeweled belt below her waist and surveyed her image in the three-way mirror.

Behind the facade of Naruda, the Exotique Dancer and Snake Charmeuse, she saw the eyes of Ruthie Notar. She pulled in her stomach to emphasize her bust and, wishing she had more cleavage, she slipped her hand inside one side of her brassiere. She lifted her breast and replaced it as high as possible, imagining that this gave the illusion that the serpents struggled to contain her bosom. For a moment she lifted a shoulder and, turning three quarters to the mirror, struck a sultry pose against the door of her dressing room. That was it. She smiled mysteriously at her reflection, knowing that Mr. G was right: she had It. And It would make them all grovel at her feet: the cameramen, the light crew, the gaffers, that drunkard Thurston Topping, but most of all Mr. G.

There was a knock at her door and the stage manager called, "Five minutes, Miss Naruda." Ruthie looked at her reflection one last time and then laughed, making a light, happy sound. Her sandals clicked against the floor and the strings of tiny bells on her anklets jingled as she moved to the door and paused once more to look over her shoulder at the three-way mirror. She smiled one last time at her reflection and left the room thinking, "Being a movie star is going to be a lot of fun. Bernie was wrong. I can get along without him just fine."

Brooklyn, New York

IT WAS DAWN when the three Culls straggled through the open window and entered Sherahi's crystal house. Junior was eager to be rid of Manu and Dervish and abandoned them without a backward glance. He scaled the wall easily. His broad belly scutes gripped wooden window frames, allowing him to quickly angle across the opaque panes of glass that formed the wall of the crystal house. Manu and Dervish waited below and saw the small rattlesnake move up the wall like an attenuated cloud writhing across the face of the moon. He slithered through the open window and disappeared.

Inside the glass house, Junior fnasted the moist, still air, investigating this new place and getting his bearings. From the window ledge he could see the shadowy forms of trees and smaller vegetation on the floor below. The roof arched above him, accommodating tall plants, and their feathery tops were silhouetted against the glass roof. All of the house was warm, much warmer than outside, but it was damp and Junior didn't like the smell of moldering earth and slime-covered brickwork. He was loath to leave the window ledge and descend into the dampness below. A metal rod ran below the dome and, rather than enter the wet place below, the rattler dropped down onto this pipe. Undulating along its rusty surface, he surveyed the glass house, alert for movements of prey and waiting for Sherahi to speak to him, as was the custom of all polite reptiles.

Junior made his way around the dome and located the pythoness, cradled in the twisted branches of a tree. His heat-sensitive labial pits augmented his night vision and he could just make out her position high above him. He perceived Sherahi as a lump that was only slightly warmer than the surrounding branches. "Where are the others?" she asked and made him glad to have shed the burden of guiding Dervish and Manu. Junior's rattles buzzed once, disturbing the quiet gloom of the greenhouse, and he slithered away without speaking to Sherahi. It would be weeks before he spoke to anyone and longer than that before any of the Culls actually saw anything of him except his track winding through the sand in the desert portion of the greenhouse.

Manu was next to climb up the rows of windows. He grasped each frame with strong fingers and toes and tried to peer inside. When he reached the open vent he paused a moment to catch his breath and allow his eyes to adjust to the darker world within. He could smell trees and flowers and damp earth, and for a moment believed that the pythoness had actually found Sandeagozu. It smelled like home—just as he imagined Sandeagozu would. Overcome by nostalgia, Manu leaped from the window ledge and landed in the top of a tall palm tree. The fronds splayed out in all directions and he nearly lost his balance before he pulled himself, hand over hand, into the crown of the tree and safety.

Once Dervish had scaled the side of the building and found the window ledge he was reluctant to follow Manu inside. The building was dark and he wasn't sure where either Sherahi or Junior was coiled. He didn't want to encounter either snake in the dark. He'd wait till morning, when he could see exactly where he was putting his paws. Junior had been acting angry and so strange that the coati didn't trust him in an enclosed space. "I know he killed the Duchess," thought Dervish. "No matter what he says or what Manu says. There's no telling what he'll do. He could kill any of us—just like that."

So, Dervish crouched on the narrow window ledge and pillowed his long-snouted head on his paws. From this perch he could see down into the shadowy crystal house as well as watch the tree-lined path that led to it. He felt lonely and chittered to Manu, begging the langur to return so that they could wait through the long, dark hours together. But Manu was almost asleep, exhausted from the effort of carrying Dervish to this place. Even though the half-grown coati weighed only fifteen pounds, he had been a heavy load for the old langur. Just on the edge of sleep, Manu heard Dervish's cry and decided to remain silent. "Dervish is growing up," the langur thought. "He doesn't really need me. He only thinks he does. It'll do him good to be alone for a change."

It was quiet inside the crystal house. Sherahi slept in the frangipani tree, Manu slept in the palm and Junior silently prowled through the darkened greenhouse below, fnasting this new place and nurturing his hatred of all nonreptilian life. He located the trail of a shrew and settled down to wait. "Mammals," he thought scornfully. "So predictable. No imagination. This shrew has used the same dirty path for months. It reeks of him."

He heard the minute pattering of shrew feet with his jawbones long before his labial pits gave him any information. Junior readied himself for a swift strike in the dark.

Junior could tell that this shrew was a male because it smelled worse than the stinking little things ordinarily did. Moments later his labial pits began to quop, telling him that the shrew was nearer now. He could feel it run and hesitate. Run and hesitate. Now it was two feet away. Junior's forked tongue brought the rank taste-smell of the male shrew to him so that even in the darkness he could visualize the smell and shape of his prey. His jawbones said that the shrew was a foot and a half away now. He felt it run and hesitate, run and hesitate.

The shrew pattered forward and stopped only a body length away— well within Junior's striking distance. He could feel its whiskers pulse with each beat of its trip-hammer heart. Junior could wait no longer and lunged open-mouthed into the darkness. He closed his jaws over the shrew's hot fur and made two tense pierces before he snapped his head and neck back into the safety of his striking coil. His rattles buzzed in anger as the shrew's poisonous, red-tipped teeth tried in vain to snag him.

"Too late, velvet stinker," he said into the shrew's mind, exultant with the success of this kill. "Now die; and be quick about it or I'll make your end even worse."

The shrew stumbled off, trying to escape from the numb and burning sensation in his side. It was as if he were chased by all the nightmares he'd ever had. His last thought, courtesy of Junior, was of a whirring, red maw that snapped him in two. Then everything in his mind went dark and the shrew fell unconscious alongside the lotus pool.

Junior felt the vibrations of the shrew's death agony with his belly scales. He was amused when he felt them falter and stop. "Dead," he thought triumphantly. In moments his labial pits and questing tongue had found the dead animal. Trying not to taste the musky little mammal, Junior worked his jaws over it and soon only a tail protruded from the corner of his mouth. Pleased with his prowess, the rattler continued slithering through the dark, hoping for more small, furry things to kill.

Outside, on the window ledge, Dervish watched the night sky and remembered the ball of light that he had once tried to capture for Manu. "That was what started this whole business," Dervish thought, "that ball of light and Sherahi." For a moment he wondered whether Sherahi had something to do with the glowing orb, but the question was too complicated for him and it slipped from his mind.

The ball of light that had lured him out of Leftrack's pet shop— Manu had told him its name, but Dervish had forgotten it—wasn't in the sky tonight and the coati wondered where it had gone. He remembered how he'd climbed to the open window to reach for it and how surprised he had been when his claws had closed over air. "That was the first time I'd ever seen the sky," Dervish sighed. It seemed so long ago now. So many things were different then: the Duchess didn't know how to fly then. She still wore the collar that Sorensen had made for her and her feathers hadn't even begun to grow back. Dervish thought of her scraggly, wet carcass and wondered what had happened to her after he and Junior had fought. Had Manu buried her so that carrion eaters wouldn't get her? "I'll have to find out," thought Dervish. "Poor Duchess. She was so afraid of everything that she made the rest of us seem brave."

For a while Dervish watched the lights that Manu called stars move overhead and when he grew sleepy he dug his long claws into the wooden window frame to make sure that he didn't fall. His long tail trailed down the side of the crystal house like a furry, banded banner and for the second time in his life Dervish slept beneath an open sky.

By firing him from his job as janitor and handyman at the warehouse, Ira Leftrack had unwittingly done Birger Sorensen an enormous favor. Unemployment had freed Sorensen to devote himself full time to the care of the derelict conservatory in Fort Washington Park that belonged to the Brooklyn Botanic Garden. He had plenty of time to tend the vegetable garden that fed him and his neighbors in Staten Island, plenty of time to care for the flock of egg-and-meat chickens that inhabited an empty greenhouse adjacent to what Sorensen considered his conservatory and plenty of time to water, prune and nurture the collection of rare plants housed in the old building. The boiler and pipes that warmed this pre-Civil War glass and wrought-iron confection were idiosyncratic: only Sorensen's skill kept them functioning and the tropical plants alive. Sorensen had never had time for a second wife after his Marina had died in the influenza epidemic of 1917. He was the kind of man who needed living things to look after and his cycads, palms and orchids had replaced the Culls who had once shared his work room at Leftrack's.

Sorensen often thought of poor old Manu, the crazy Duchess and little Dervish and wondered what had happened to them after they'd been stolen from Leftrack's. The police had questioned him after the robbery and he had the feeling that they'd actually suspected him of being the burglar. Luckily, Sorensen had witnesses to prove that he'd been losing at canasta on the night in question. Sorensen was outraged that Leftrack would have suspected him. "After all those years," he remarked to an Engelmann spruce at the edge of the ravine that led to his greenhouse. "That Leftrack must've been crazy long before they finally took him away to the funny farm."

Sorensen hoped that the animals had found a kind owner and was grateful that they were out of reach of Leftrack's disgusting son, Ehrich. "He's in medical school now," Sorensen thought. "I wouldn't like to put my life in his hands." He remembered how Ehrich used to slyly take advantage of him, making him do a double share of work at the pet shop while Ehrich sulked at his desk. Sorensen felt the angry pressure build within his chest and kicked a stone out of his way and tried to think of something else.

"The world is full of Leftracks," he said to the tamaracks that were just beginning to show rosettes of tiny needles. "Can't change that. No sense in even thinking 'bout it. All it does is make you mad."

Every morning Sorensen walked from the trolley stop and unlocked the high gate that led past the pinetorium. He angled down the ravine, crossed the daffodil meadow and walked through the cherry orchard to his greenhouse. Every morning he watched the beautiful, domed roof of his building appear out of the trees, glinting like the old rose-cut diamond that used to sparkle first on his grandmother's and then on Marina's hand. Now it was in a worn, blue velvet box in his dresser drawer. He thought of the old days, when he and Marina had been weekend workers at the Garden. She'd taught him to love and care for plants. He remembered the throngs of careless New Yorkers who'd crowded these paths; the lovers who carved their initials into the smooth bark of the beech trees, not caring that the scars they made would never heal; the visitors who trampled the grass and stole blossoms and cuttings from his plants. In short, Sorensen wasn't one bit sad that the Society had gone bankrupt and that his conservatory was now protected from the public.

"Overextended themselves—and a good thing, too," he said to the aged copper beech, planted over a century ago, which was one of the oldest specimens in the whole park. Its russet foliage and gnarled branches seemed to nod in agreement, but the tree made no audible reply. The only response to Sorensen's voice was the panicky scream of a blue jay, who cried, "Jay! Jay!" and disrupted the quiet.

"Oh, shut up," Sorensen said angrily as the bird's shadow flew across his path. He entered the daffodil meadow and noted that the jonquils and grape hyacinths were up. Then the path forked and he turned toward his conservatory. He thought of the squat concrete and glass structure with which the "experts" had intended to replace his building—his outmoded, fanciful antique that had once been the wonder of the borough of Brooklyn. Now Sorensen felt as if he were the only one who really appreciated it and he knew that if it weren't for him the structure would have moldered and collapsed in disrepair.

"Overextended. Tsk, tsk, tsk," he repeated and took the fork of the path that led toward the cherry orchard.

The Society had prided itself on being up to date. In its zeal to modernize it had built a whole new set of buildings in Prospect Park. A staff of professional horticulturists had been hired; they were university men in thick glasses and starched collars, men who spouted streams of Latin names and spent their days scrutinizing dried specimens glued to big pieces of paper. "Scientists," thought Sorensen with disapproval. Like all scientists they were all thumbs in a potting shed and didn't know which was the business end of a rake. "Scientists," muttered Sorensen. "They nearly ruined the place with scientists."

Since the Depression most of the book men had disappeared because the Society could no longer afford to support research into nonsense like the relationships of the Euphorbiaceae or the location of stomata of obligate halophytes. The Society was so bad off that it couldn't even pay salaries for the guards and had gone begging to the City for money.

But the City was worried about the homeless and hungry. There were no funds for fripperies like the Botanic Garden when thousands of people had no supper. Eventually the Society had closed the Garden in Prospect Park and, of course, it had closed the Fort Washington conservatory.

The head botanist, old Dr. Crotty himself, had given Sorensen the responsibility for the tropical and desert plants that were still housed in the ramshackle conservatory. The most important specimens had long since been moved to the modern building which Sorensen detested, but those plants which remained in the old building were also too valuable to be allowed to die; and too numerous to be moved to new quarters. Sorensen was a welcome, even an essential, worker. So, every day he took the ferry to Brooklyn and then the trolley to the Garden. He kept his charges healthy and the old greenhouse in working order. In turn, he raised vegetables and chickens on Garden property and considered the proposition more than a fair exchange.

Although his route to the conservatory was the same every day, Sorensen noticed different things. The day before yesterday, for example, the cherry trees had been in full blossom; today most of their petals had been beaten off by the heavy rain. From the orchard Sorensen had a clear view of the front of his building. As was his habit, he paused to check its glass walls—vandalism was one of his chief worries. Sorensen scanned the dome and the right front wall. All seemed intact. He started down the path toward the building, still examining the glass of the left front wall, when he saw something that made him catch his breath and stop. A raccoon's tail hung down from the front vent that was always open to allow air circulation in the tropical rain forest room.

"That's how you got in, you bastard," thought Sorensen. He quietly dropped his lunch pail and reached for the slingshot that he always carried in his rear pocket. He picked a smooth pebble from the path and thought of the fluffy hatchlings that had been killed by the raccoon that had mysteriously invaded the henhouse. It had left hand prints and footprints all over the place. "I'll get you this time, you chicken killer," he muttered.

Sorensen crept onto the lawn that bordered the gravel path so that he made no sound. When he was directly below the vent he pulled back the sling and took careful aim at the animal's head. It hadn't stirred. "Still asleep," thought Sorensen and pulled the sling taut. He wanted to kill the animal but would be content to merely stun it and knock it down. Then he could whack it with the shovel that rested by the side of the building.

"Can't afford to keep you around here," he thought and lined up the animal's head with his thumbnail. Then Sorensen held his breath and fired.

The pebble hit Dervish behind one ear. Dazed, he tumbled from the window ledge and landed unhurt in the hedge below. For some reason he felt disoriented, confused. He lay blinking in the sunlight, wondering what that loud noise had been. Why was his head ringing and why did one of his ears sting? "What am I doing here?" he thought, peering at the thorny branches all around him. He tried to sit up and flinched as his backside was stabbed in a dozen places. "This is no place to sleep. Where is the crystal house and Manu and Sherahi?" He tried to get his feet beneath him so that he could lift his nose and smell and find the others, but as he moved he fell through the flat, clipped surface of the hedge and lay tangled in the thorns below. "What's wrong with me?" he wondered. "Why won't my legs behave?"

When he'd seen the raccoon fall Sorensen had hurried to grab the spade from the corner of the building. He wanted to finish the animal off as quickly and humanely as possible before the chicken killer gathered its wits and ran off. Returning to the hedge, Sorensen saw that it was no longer in such an exposed position. There was no way to deliver a killing blow while it was hidden, half protected by prickly barberry bushes. In one quick movement he scooped up the animal and dumped it onto the gravel path. He heaved the spade overhead and thought, "One whack and that coon'll never know what happened." While Sorensen positioned the spade the animal lifted its head and looked about groggily.

"Funny-looking raccoon," thought Sorensen. "He's got a white mask instead of a black one." He lowered the spade to his shoulder. "And, come to think of it, what's the matter with his nose? It's way too long.

"Wait a minute," he said out loud. "That's no raccoon. It's a coatimundi." Sorensen stepped up for a better look and lost his only chance to kill Dervish with one blow.

Like bats funneling into a cave at dawn, the coati's senses were rapidly returning. He began to notice things: it was a human that blocked the sunlight and there was no place to run—the hedge grew thickly on either side of the path. He reacted as any sensible coati who found himself in this situation would have—especially a coati who had been trained to fight by a wise monkey and a snake who dispatched her prey with an efficiency that bordered upon grace.

He remembered Sherahi's voice saying, "Down. You must get down, Dervish. Get your head close to the ground and always slash up with those long teeth. Leap and snap like a shark, Dervish." He remembered that Manu had counseled, "Always attack from a position of strength," and widened his stance, firmly planting his miniature bear's paws against the gravel. "Give your enemy a fair warning," was another of Manu's maxims—one that Sherahi had countermanded. "Surprise them," she had said, "catch them off guard." Although the snake preferred to kill by stealth, Dervish thought Manu's way was more fair. He growled and lashed his tail back and forth, signaling that he would attack at any moment. Then he pulled his tail flat against his back and lowered his head to the ground, tilting it so that his bared canines on one side were uppermost—ready for the slashing charge that could come at any moment, depending upon what this human did.

Sorensen saw the animal's fur bristle, making it look twice its size. He saw its lips curl back from its canines and heard gravel flung backward. He thought of the pain that this animal could inflict and felt his back pocket for his slingshot. "Damn," he said, realizing that he'd dropped it when he'd grabbed the spade. Holding the tool horizontally in both hands, Sorensen began to slowly back away from the furious coati. He also began to talk softly to it, hoping to calm it.

"Okay, boy," he said. "It's all right. I made a mistake. Don't be so upset. I'm not going to hurt you. I thought you were a chicken killer. I like coatis. Really, I do. Now, calm down. No one's going to hurt you." He spoke in a soft voice, pretending that this snarling beast was little Dervish, the coati that he'd raised from a pup after its mother had died in Leftrack's pet shop.

Still walking backward, moving as slowly as possible so as not to alarm the beast and provoke a charge, he said, "You even look a little like Dervish. But you're much larger. I wonder if Dervish . . ." Sorensen never finished that sentence.

Dervish saw the man retreat and realized that he might not be forced to attack him, after all. To show that he wasn't going to be pushed around, though, he changed his snarl to a cascade of loud, coughing grunts and, like a cat stalking a butterfly, he slowly crept forward, looking for any opportunity to escape yet still prepared to leap and slash if the human forced him to do it. He stopped and listened when he heard the man's voice. It sounded familiar. He listened and thought, "I wonder if this is some kind of trick?" Once or twice the coati thought he heard something that sounded like his name. He listened even more carefully, but kept moving slowly forward, growling all the time.

Sorensen was five feet down the path and was even more alarmed now because he realized that the beast was stalking him. Its black eyes seemed to measure him with a concentration that was unnerving. Armed only with the shovel he felt naked and wished that there was someone he could call for help, but the patrol wouldn't make their rounds until late in the afternoon. The only thing left for him to do was to get out of this creature's way. Soon he had put ten feet between himself and the coati.

As Dervish saw the man retreat he relaxed even more. He lifted his head from its low position and changed his coughs to staccato grunts. For the first time since he'd fallen from the window ledge he took the time to carefully smell his surroundings. For the first time he examined the smell of this particular human.

"That's strange," thought Dervish. The man's scent evoked a vision of the snug nest box that had once been his nursery. It had been lined with one of Sorensen's old shirts and had smelled like the man. Dervish vividly remembered the grain of the wooden box that had been his landscape before his eyes were fully opened and he'd discovered that there was a world outside his box. "This can't be Sorensen," thought Dervish. He was so surprised that he sat back on his haunches with the forepart of his body erect, looking like a miniature dancing bear begging for marshmallows. With his nose in the air he rotated its sensitive, mobile tip like a periscope, checking and double-checking to make sure. Then he leaped to his feet and sent his banded tail straight up. He lifted his ears from close to his skull and gave a trill of friendly chirps. Dervish capered in glee and bounded forward, certain that he'd recognized an old friend. He was ashamed that he'd almost attacked the man who used to feed him peaches and fish heads, the man who had been his mother and father and playmate until he had discovered

Manu. Arching his back and wriggling like a puppy, Dervish rushed at the man and leaped.

"Christ, it's rabid," thought Sorensen when he saw the coati's contorted face and body. "It's having a fit." He dropped the spade and turned to run. For a moment he thought he might outdistance it, but then he felt something ram the back of his knees. To his horror Sorensen toppled onto the path. He landed hard on the gravel and covered his face with his arms. Before he could scramble to his feet he felt something cold poke into his ear. He wasn't expecting anything this gentle and froze, praying, "Please, God. Don't let it bite me." He knew that there was no cure for rabies. As he cowered, not knowing what to do, he heard the same kind of trills and chirps that Dervish used to make. He glanced up into the bright eyes and whiskers of his long-snouted adversary. The animal's mouth was open and its tongue lolled out of its underslung jaw. More than anything else it looked like a collie puppy that hadn't quite grown into its overly long nose yet. It clearly wanted to play.

Dervish poked his nose into Sorensen's warm ear, chirping, "It's me. It's me. Don't you remember?" But all he could sense from the human was confusion and fear. He sat back and cocked his head to one side. "Don't be afraid," he purred. "We're friends. Don't you remember?"

Astonished at the change in the animal's demeanor, Sorensen slowly extended his hand. He felt whiskers tickle as Dervish pressed his nose into his palm and sniffed. Then the animal nudged his hand over and Sorensen felt small front teeth nip and pull on the hairs that grew on the back of his hand. "He's grooming me. Just like Dervish used to. That's funny," he muttered. "I'd forgotten all about that."

The coati paused and looked up when he thought he heard his name again, but the man didn't notice, and Dervish continued his show of affection, wondering how long it would take the human to recognize him.

It was some time before Sorensen understood that this coati was not just an animal who behaved like Dervish. It seemed impossible, but this was Dervish himself. "Can you actually be Dervish, boy?" he asked, tentatively petting the animal with both hands. The coati wriggled with excitement and licked the man's chin.

Sorensen experimented with the coati's reaction to different names. It only responded to "Dervish" and Sorensen thought, "I guess you're Dervish, all right, but how in God's name did you get here? Irma Leftrack told me that you'd disappeared along with Manu, the Duchess and that big python."

Hearing his name gave the coati much satisfaction. "Finally he remembers me," he thought. "Humans aren't as dull as Sherahi said. You just have to be patient with them." Dervish saw his old enemies, Sorensen's shoelaces, and pounced on them, making knots and impossible snarls.

Sorensen wondered at the animal playing at his feet and watched him race around in circles and finally leap into his lap, begging to be petted.

"I wonder if you still like sardines?" the man said. With Dervish prancing around he located his lunch pail. Dervish could have recognized the smell fifty feet away and knew that a treat was coming. He stretched up on his hind legs and consumed the sardines greedily, making contented grunts. Only after the coati had cleaned the last drop of oil from the tin and was chirping for more, did Sorensen remember that he had a full day of chores ahead of him.

"You'll live with me now," he said to Dervish. "But you can't have any of my chickens. They're off-limits to you, my nosy friend. And just to make sure . . ." Sorensen took the belt from around his waist and fastened it around the coati's neck.

Dervish jerked back and forth, trying to free himself, but the noose only grew tighter. He snarled and begged Sorensen to remove it, but the man didn't understand anything he said and merely patted him. In a while Dervish realized that he couldn't pull himself free and stopped leaping like a suffocating fish. Sorensen fastened a bit of string to the end of the belt and led Dervish to the conservatory, saying, "Well, I don't know how you got here, but we'll always be together now. You and me. Okay, boy? And I'll take good care of you. From now on you're on Easy Street."

Sorensen bent down and scratched between the coati's shoulder blades. Dervish didn't understand what the man said, but he chirped back happily and twined the leash around and around the man's legs, nearly tripping him again. "Wait till Manu and Sherahi see Sorensen," he thought. "I know that they'll say that this place is better than Sandeagozu could ever, ever be."

Sherahi was adamant. She lay coiled in the dense shade beneath the frangipani's leaves and insisted, "No, Manu. That can't be right. I am certain that the Duchess isn't dead."

Without making a sound, the langur spoke into her mind, using the reptilian mindspeech that he'd been taught early in his captivity. "But, Pythoness," he said, "I saw her. I sat right next to her. I am ashamed to admit that I did it, but I even touched her and I am telling you that there is no mistake. She is dead.

"Dervish saw her, too. Ask him. Or ask Junior, if you won't believe us."

"Don't be angry, Manu," said Sherahi.

"I'm not angry," said Manu, ripping an unripe date from the fruiting branch over his head and hurling it to the floor below. "What makes you think I'm angry?"

"I don't doubt that you believe that she is dead, Manu. But you must trust my judgment. Appearances are often deceiving."

"But, Sherahi," said the exasperated langur, "you didn't see her. I did. How can you say that I am wrong?"

"I just have a feeling," said the serpent.

"Hmph," said the langur, annoyed with Sherahi. He thought, "She's always having these mysterious hunches and feelings. Makes such a fuss over them." He knew that the pythoness could read his mind, but didn't care. "I'm tired of being bossed around and contradicted by snakes," he sulked.

There was a silence which was broken by a muffled thud outside the building. It sounded as if a coconut had fallen and Manu dismissed it as unimportant.

Sherahi continued, "Where is Junior? Did he see the Duchess, too?"

"Junior was the one who discovered her in the first place. He found her lying on the beach and buried her. He claims to have buried her to keep us from finding her and being sad. At least, that's his story.

"Dervish nearly got himself killed because he suspected that Junior was lying and said as much. Junior claimed that he injected only a little venom but he fanged Dervish three times. I saw the bites bleed. A bit much, don't you think?"

Sherahi chose not to respond and Manu continued, "I had to carry poor Dervish almost the whole way here from the beach. On the way I got to thinking that maybe Junior's fangs aren't working so well. What do you think, Pythoness?"

Sherahi refused to take sides and this annoyed the langur even more. "Where is Junior now?" asked Sherahi, deliberately ignoring Manu's state. She did hate it when mammals got so worked up. It was such a waste of energy. "And it's my fault," she thought. "If I hadn't gotten separated from them for so long, none of this would have happened."

Manu noticed her reserve and thought, "Sherahi used to trust me. I wonder why she's changed. Become so remote—so . . . superior." But he answered her question, saying contemptuously, "Oh, he's probably skulking somewhere, trying to fang something helpless.

"Go ahead and ask him. He'll tell you the same story about the Duchess. Of course, who knows what he'll make up to explain the rest, though."

Manu didn't want to speak any longer and broke off their mental conversation. He found he was angrier than he'd thought. "Snakes," he fumed and shredded the leaves of a frond above his head. "They always trust their own first."

A flash of light at the far end of the building attracted his attention and made him freeze. A door opened and Manu peered down from the crown of the date palm—afraid to make any movement that would rustle the telltale fronds and make him conspicuous.

A man entered and Manu was surprised to see him pull an animal behind him on a leash. "Dervish," Manu gasped and the coati looked up, sniffed and chirped a greeting. "Hello, Manu," he said. Dervish trotted in happy circles around the man. From above he looked like a moon magnetically drawn to its master planet, oblivious to everything else.

Manu was stupefied. He watched the coati and his human companion wind along the path below and disappear into an adjoining room. "What's gotten into that thickheaded coati now?" he wondered. "You would have thought that he'd know enough to keep away from humans by this time. I thought he was brighter than that."

"It's no ordinary human," Sherahi spoke into his mind. "Dervish has found Sorensen. Try to help him, Manu. I am going to scan for Junior and after we've spoken I'll find out what actually happened to the Duchess. I'll be gone for a while."

"Inwitting again?" asked the langur, a bit jealous that Sherahi could abandon her corporeal body so effortlessly to go on mysterious and romantic-sounding mental journeys. But then he thought of the price the serpent paid: of that long, sluggish, scaly body, of the inscrutable face that could never smile, of her cold-blooded disposition. He decided that he really didn't envy the giant reptile after all. "Who cares," he thought. "Let her inwit to her heart's content." She did not reply when Manu bid her goodbye and he knew that Sherahi was already far away from the crystal house.

The pythoness lost no time in making contact with Junior. She remembered how unmanageable the rattler's mind had been when she had first encountered it in Leftrack's warehouse. Junior was dangerous, a deadly ally, but necessary if the Culls were ever to reach Sandeagozu. As surely as she knew that whorls of embryonic teeth waited behind each tooth in the four rows of her upper jaw, Sherahi knew that a journey across an entire continent was impossible for a naïve coati, an elderly langur and a cumbersome snake such as herself. But her extraordinary mental powers, coupled with Junior's venom, were secret weapons that moved the Culls' journey from the realm of the fantastic to the fringes of the possible. Junior could efficiently kill any enemy that threatened them—large or small, human or animal. And he'd already proved his loyalty by rescuing the Culls from the white crocodiles when she lay bound by the mind control of those slimy, ingrown maggots that had the effrontery to call themselves reptiles. The manner in which the white crocodiles had twisted the heritage of saurian mind control made Sherahi furious. It reminded her of how Ruthie

Notar had defiled the ancient rituals that serpents had always performed with women—the spiral dance that encouraged the mysterious procession of seasons, tides and moons, of life from death. When Sherahi considered how the snake dancer had bastardized those ceremonies, subverting them into tawdry entertainments designed to titillate the sexual palates of beer-bloated human males, she felt warm blood rush to her brain. It sickened her, and she knew that it was imperative that she make peace with Junior. "We must get to Sandeagozu," she thought. "Then none of us will ever be used by humans again. And Junior will help us get there.

"If it hadn't been for him, Dervish would have left us there to die. And he would have become a feral beast—just an alley cat of another stripe hiding in those filthy tunnels beneath the city, scavenging offal from de-mented, drugged humans. By now Manu, the Duchess and I would all have been processed into yolk: yolk to nourish a new generation of those crea-tures."

An image of a snaggle-toothed, hoary Holiest of the Holy White Croc-odiles hissed unbidden into her mind. Sherahi watched entranced as the croc and his acolytes slowly circled a cairn of small stones deep in their sub-terranean caverns. "Strange," thought Sherahi, "they're moving against the Great Circle. That's forbidden. All reptiles know that it's unlucky to walk or coil in that direction." She thought of all the serpents she'd ever known: pythons, cobras, earth snakes, sea snakes—all of them coiled in ac-cord with the Great Circle, their bodies mimicking the measured progression of the stars, sun and moon.

Looking closer she saw that there were five oddly shaped stones in the center of the crocs' circle. Two were long and slender, one much bigger than the other. A third stone had what looked like wings and the other two had four legs and long tails. "Those are us," thought Sherahi. "What are those monsters doing?" She knew that she couldn't delay finding the Duch-ess and Junior, but the saurian spectacle held her fascinated.

A small and particularly twisted crocodile, one of the acolytes, ap-proached the center of the circle. Delicately he picked up the winged stone and, after bowing to the cardinal points, he bit the stone. As he slithered back to his place in the moving circle she saw that the bird's wings had been sheared from its body. The crocodiles that were assembled in the phospho-rescent chamber roared their approval, sounding like the rumble of a thou-sand stomachs that were so starved as to never be satiated.

A second croc approached the central stones. He chose one of the tailed, four-legged effigies and deliberately broke all its legs. His eyes glittered malevolently as he heard the roared approval of the other crocodiles.

A third croc smashed the remaining tailed effigy with his tail. Things were moving faster now. A fourth and fifth croc slithered simultaneously to the hub of the circle and, churning the ground into quicksand, made the bits of broken effigies and the two crudely fashioned serpents sink into the mud. From the circle the crocs began to chant and Sherahi knew that they were cursing the Culls—individually and collectively.

She tried to send out a charm to counter their curse and saw the Holiest Croc pause a second and toss his head as if flies were biting his eyelids.

"It'll take something more than that," she thought.

Then he slowly and deliberately wormed his way through to the place where the head of the larger snake effigy had worked back up to the surface. It protruded like a broken tooth. "That's me," she gasped as he bellowed and pushed it below the surface with his glowing, scaly foot.

Water slowly began to accumulate in the middle of the circle and Sherahi saw it wheel in the mire as the crocs began to swim in the forbidden direction. "They are cursing us," Sherahi said and, although she knew that the white crocodiles' power was weak this far from their stronghold, their curse still made her nervous.

The crocs chanted: "Snarl and hiss. Bite and strangle. Hate, hate, hate. Rip and tear. Slash and kill. Hate. Hate. Hate."

"Hardly original," thought Sherahi. "A two-day-old python could come up with a more resonant curse." But she was frightened and knew that no python could match these beasts for malevolence. Once again Sherahi saw the Holiest of the Holy White Crocodiles writhe back to the center of the circle. Slowly and deliberately he pressed the head of her effigy back down into the mire again and roared in triumph.

Sherahi knew something of magical saurian arcana. She coiled mind and body into the Great Spiral and slitted her eyes. Feeling very old and sensing the weight of the ancient ritual she reached into the back corners of her mind and spun a protective spiral around the entire conservatory, flinging it up over the arched dome. Concentrating even more, she flung it in a wide, sheltering arc to encompass the forest beyond the conservatory. Finally she hurled the spiral to enclose the entire near shore. For a moment she saw the spiral glisten taut in the early light and then it faded.

"Well, it may temporarily retard the curse of the white crocodiles," she thought. "With enemies like those it's more important than ever to have Junior on our side." Then she laughed at herself, half-believing that what she did was foolish superstition.

"No need to get so upset about a bunch of overgrown lizards sloshing in the mud. What does it matter if those things that call themselves crocodiles have cursed us? We've outsmarted them. That's the important thing.

"But still," an older, deeper part of her mind insisted, "a curse should not be taken lightly."

"I've got to find Junior," Sherahi thought. "I wonder if our young pit viper knows how essential he is to us. If he doesn't, it's time we told him. The Culls can't afford to lose him now. Who knows how far we are from Sandeagozu?"

Sherahi thought of the pattern of diminishing diamonds that ran down the length of Junior's body. Each diamond merged imperceptibly into the next and, like a snake with its tail in its mouth, the pattern had neither end nor beginning. She thought of the jagged lines that radiated from his inscrutable, pitted face, warning all who could read signs that here was an animal to be feared. Last, she thought of the sound of Junior's rattle—like a treeful of venomous bees who could kill with a single sting. The sound filled her questing mind and as she concentrated upon it, she struck out into the conservatory below, searching for the flinty-minded little serpent.

To her surprise Sherahi found that there were many more rooms to this place than she had realized. She searched the tropical rain forest, scrying from the dome to the gallery of rat holes below the brick walks. She swam around and through the lotus ponds and searched forests of shrubbery. Her mind darted into the desert conservatory and scanned thorny shrubs and cacti. She even dug through the sand below the cacti and bearded Joshua trees, but the only reptilian intelligence she encountered was a terrified female blue-tailed skink.

"Maybe she's seen Junior," thought Sherahi. She paused to scry the lizard's mind. Indeed, the little female had seen Junior and she was still shocked by the experience.

Sherahi saw that Junior had chased her this morning. To escape, the skink had snapped off her bright-blue tail and, while this bit of trickery had saved her life, the little lizard now wished that she hadn't survived. The absent cerulean tail had been her most prized possession.

The lizard moped, head downward, below an orange plume of ocatillo flowers. "What will become of me?" she moaned, looking at the raw stump of her tail. "What male will want a freak like me, with no tail?" She allowed a curious fly to alight within millimeters of her face and didn't even think about eating him when he crawled over her glassy-scaled back.

"Foolish lizard," said Sherahi. "Your tail will grow back. By next year you'll be just as beautiful as you were."

"But that's a year away," the lizard replied, thinking she was talking to herself. "And I've spent all winter planning for this season. Now that the killer has come I may not live till next year. I don't have another tail to break off. The deathstalker may be smarter next time.

"My life is over," the lizard moaned hysterically. "I'll never have a mate and my eggs will rot inside of me. The only thing I'll ever have is bad dreams about that snake eating my poor tail. I'll have nightmares forever—I know it. I'll dream of my tail jumping like a grasshopper with broken legs;

my beautiful blue tail bleeding onto the sand. And then that horrid snake will come. I'll see him push it with his snout and he'll open his throat and swallow it. My tail. My beautiful, blue tail, the tail I've been growing since I was a hatchling. It stuck out of his mouth like he'd grown a blue tongue. And it's all because of him that I'll be alone. Forever. All alone. My life is over. That's all there is to it."

The lizard moaned again and drooped from the ocatillo branch and Sherahi's scan moved on. But the lizard's lament echoed through her mind, distracting her. "I won't be able to handle Junior with that racket going on," Sherahi thought. She concentrated for a moment and then sent the skink the idea that she had miraculously grown a new tail. Sherahi built it of minute, interlocking vertebrae and added a stronger complement of tail-wagging muscles than the lizard had previously possessed. "It's longer and more luxurious than the tail that Junior ate," Sherahi thought. "Now she can wave her tail like an angry tiger."

She colored the apparition an iridescent blue and was gratified to see the female brighten as she stared at the vision that gradually materialized before her eyes. Sherahi saw the skink tentatively waggle just the tip of her new appendage and then she skittered down from the ocatillo branch and onto the floor of the desert conservatory. With her mirage tail held off the ground she ran across the sand, looking behind her like a child running with a new kite. Sherahi smiled as she saw a big-headed male ponderously approach the stump-tailed female. The female began a rapid series of stiff-armed push-ups, bobbing her head to indicate that she was sexually excited. The male bobbed, giving a sober response.

Soon the pair of lizards were locked in a mating embrace. The male tenderly grasped the nape of the female's neck in his jaws and pinned her to the sand. The female lifted the stump of her tail and allowed the male a clear path to her cloacal vent. Sherahi had never mated and the sight of these intertwined reptiles stirred vague, unidentified feelings in the big snake. She could see the pink base of the male's hemipenis where it was firmly extended into the female's cloaca. Both lizards were wide-eyed with passion and the female's side stripes flushed alternately indigo and pastel blue. It seemed that the two skinks enjoyed their intense love-making, but Sherahi didn't want to intrude upon them any more. "Is that what it would be like?" Sherahi wondered. Unobtrusively she watched the pair for a while and then remembered that she had to find Junior. When her scan moved on, the skinks were still intertwined in their fish-hook embrace.

The conservatory was dark when she returned to the body that lay coiled in the branches of the frangipani tree. Although it was clear that Junior was somewhere in the desert portion of the conservatory, she had been unable to find him. She'd met a mourning family of shrews and a motherless nestful of fuzzy field mice, who, like the female blue-tailed skink, had been terrorized by a predator they could describe only as horrible.

Beneath a piece of dry cactus wood Sherahi had found a curious, murky shadow that was impervious to her scan. She had probed it in several ways and had found that it was no real shadow—no mere absence of light. Instead, it was a finely crafted reptilian mindscreen. "It's strange, though," thought Sherahi, when she saw that this mental screen had briars woven into its murky surface. They snagged Sherahi's mind and she recognized them as the hallmark of Junior's thorny personality. "He'd do something like that," she thought.

When the thorns had pricked her she had thought she'd heard a rustling sound that could have been Junior's laugh. She had called out to him in her most compelling voice, but there had been no reply. Nevertheless, she had told the cascabel, just in case he was listening, that the Culls needed him and that she trusted him. "You must forgive the others," Sherahi had said. "They're only mammals and have all the weaknesses of their kind." Junior had made no sign that he'd heard, but Sherahi had felt the thorns edging his mindscreen grow longer, curving upward as if they were reaching for her. Carefully she had extricated her scan from beneath the cactus wood.

Sherahi was surprised that the cascabel could construct a mental screen that even she could not penetrate. As far as she knew, he'd tried to make a mental smoke screen only a few times in the caverns of the white crocs. These had been flimsy, awkwardly constructed shields that had lasted for only a few crucial moments. The amateurish quality of Junior's mind-screens hadn't surprised Sherahi; this skill was usually the exclusive property of pythons. She had never heard of another kind of serpent even attempting to weave a mental screen. "But he's seen me protect us many times with screens," she thought. "He must have watched much more closely than I'd thought possible."

Most reptiles learned only from direct experience and this kind of learning was new to the pythoness. As far as she knew, her kin were unique among serpents in actually passing knowledge from older to younger generations. This ordinarily occurred once a year in communal hibernating dens. Except for those special times, experience was the only teacher that most snakes ever knew. Sherahi had been unusual in that she'd been tutored by U Vayu. "That is, until he was killed to death in some barbaric human festival," she thought bitterly. Sherahi wished that U Vayu were alive so that she could ask his advice about Junior, but since his death she had been unable to contact him and had assumed that it was no longer possible.

Sherahi tried once again to extend her mind into the desert conservatory and pierce the mental screen that Junior had erected around his hiding place, but again the screen was impenetrable. "There's only one thing to do," she thought. "If he won't let me speak to him, then I must do something to protect us from him. There's no telling what he might do." If the mutual trust between the Culls and the deadly pit viper could not be reestablished, she would weave strong and resilient screens around herself, Dervish and Manu to protect them from the cascabel in case an accident happened while she was away, inwitting to the Duchess or on some other errand. Sherahi couldn't bear the thought that Junior might actually attack one of his fellow Culls. "But you never know when you are dealing with something like a cascabel. You can't be too careful."

Sherahi set about constructing a mental shroud around each Cull—a cocoon blended of mindspeech, shadow and confusion that would baffle Junior, no matter how agile his mind had grown.

By noon she finished the final shroud, around herself, and knew that no matter how hard Junior or anyone else looked, it would hold. If the light were right she might even be so well camouflaged as to blend invisibly with the frangipani branches that surrounded her.

"Now," thought the pythoness, "I must find the Duchess and see what's happened to her. I know that she's not dead. I'm certain that I would have known long ago. And I'm just as sure that Junior would never have killed her. He never really liked the Duchess; he thought she was a selfish whiner and a weakling, but she was one of us. She was with us from the beginning and he'd promised to protect her, as well as Manu and Dervish. He wouldn't break that promise. Serpents don't take such things lightly."

Like a child inserting a thumbnail between layers of mica, Sherahi peeled her mind and body apart. In a moment she found herself floating above the crystal house and saw that, from above, the frames around the panes of glass made an enormous crystal-paned web. It was beautiful until Sherahi thought, "We're all of us caught inside that web." She didn't like the idea much. "Webs are made by spiders and all spiders are dangerous," Sherahi thought. But she could do nothing more to protect the Culls and tried to think of other things. She said to herself, "It may look like a web, but a web can be a good hiding place. And we're free." Like a hatchling learning how to swallow a cricket frog, she forced the premonition about the crystal house to the back of her mind and concentrated on the Duchess. She imagined a long, tapering, scarlet wing feather and remembered the way the bird's eye dilated when she was excited. In a moment Sherahi saw the bird lying on the sand near the river the Culls had crossed.

With a menacing hiss Sherahi banished the squadron of crabs that was cautiously converging upon this feathered boon. She could see Manu's and Dervish's footprints all around the bird's body, as well as the shallow trench alongside her. As Sherahi stared at the inert bird, it became apparent to her slow-motion senses that the Duchess was alive. She breathed, but the motion was so slight as to be almost imperceptible. "No wonder they all thought her dead," Sherahi thought.

"Duchess," the snake commanded.

There was no reply and Sherahi gathered herself and spoke into the bird's unconscious mind. "Wake up, Duchess," she commanded.

"Go 'way, Sherahi," the bird replied in a typically crabby voice. "I'm having the nicest dream. All about a lovely nest of sticks and four of the whitest, most perfect eggs. And they feel so nice and cool. And I'm so hot, Sherahi." The bird's voice trailed off. "So very hot."

"Wake up, Duchess."

"Go away, Pythoness, and leave me with my eggs."

"You must rouse yourself, Duchess. You are in terrible trouble. Something is wrong with one of your wings and if you don't get help soon you will surely die. Then those eggs will only have been a dream."

"Why do you always have to be so bossy, Sherahi? I don't want to wake up. I'm comfortable here."

"Leave them," said Sherahi in the voice that could not be ignored.

The Duchess sighed and, with great effort, opened one gluey eyelid. To her surprise, the huge snake wasn't in sight. She'd expected her to be coiled up nearby. "Fine thing," she complained. "Wake me from my nice dream and then run away. Well, what do you expect from a snake?"

Only then did she notice the gulls.

They stood around her in a silent circle. She grew nervous when she saw how they looked at her. She said, "Shooo. Get away from here," and tried to raise her wings, but found that her left wing hung limp and immobile at her side.

"I can't fly," she thought in a panic.

The yellow-eyed scavengers stared at her with a predatory intensity and the Duchess wondered how Sherahi could be so cruel as to have wakened her for this.

Then she forgot all about Sherahi as the gulls edged even closer.

Clarence Lester Hatch crouched between boulders on the Brooklyn shore of the East River, waiting for dawn and methodically listing all the birds he could hear. He got a special sort of pleasure whenever he used the pocket-sized, leather-covered book: it made him feel like a professional ornithologist—not just a bird-watcher.

He'd already noted all the common things—"junkbirds," according to some of his rivals at the Linnaean Society. Although they weren't exciting, the redwing blackbird, herring gull, great black-backed gull and mallard duck each counted as a species and that was what Clarence Lester Hatch was after this morning. Seeing a record number of species for the

Linnaean Society's annual Spring Count would give him the notice and respect of all the other birders at the American Museum of Natural History. Although he'd been attending the Linnaean Society meetings there for years, this was the first Spring Count in which he'd been treated as an adult. They'd given him his own birding territory, which included the Brooklyn side of the East River from the Bridge to the ocean. He intended to walk from sunup to sundown, counting numbers of birds.

Bird-watching gave the seventeen-year-old a talent—one thing that he could do better than anyone else his age. But the Linnaean Society was the big league of birders and so far they seemed unimpressed with the eye, ear and judgment of the pale, gangling, often tongue-tied novice. "I can do it," Clarence Lester thought. "At the least I'll get a decent number of species. And if the winds were right last night I could get migrants blown off course. Maybe even something rare."

As he listened to the sounds of the tidal marsh and waited for the sun to rise, he imagined how he would stand up in the next Linnaean meeting and recite his list. He'd have to be ready to defend and justify every unusual bird. The old guard of Linnaean members took the Spring Count seriously and were as feisty as broody owls about what was included. A "maybe" was not allowed.

Clarence Lester counted it as a tentative mark of respect that they'd given him his own territory this year instead of assigning him to tag along at the heels of some ladies' group. He knew that the experts would keep a careful eye on the results of his day in the field. He'd seen other volunteers cross-examined and made to look foolish. "I'll have to be sure—really sure—of each identification," the boy thought, pushing his wire-rimmed glasses up the bridge of his nose. "If I get anything extraordinary—like an early redstart or a late junco or an Arctic tern—I'll have to get all the field marks right or they'll think I'm a bungler."

So, Clarence Lester Hatch, who would someday be an ornithologist at a third-rate teacher's college in western Pennsylvania, a man who would never outgrow his shyness and would always be a bachelor, passionate only about birds—the future Dr. Hatch, who would explain his surname by saying that his parents had used only the future imperative—peered at the nearby stand of spartina grass through a borrowed pair of field glasses and tried to identify a series of insistent clucks.

"Is that a purple gallinule?" he wondered. "Is it going 'kek-kek-kek'? Or is it a Florida gallinule going 'kik-kik-kik'?" He listened more intently and looked for some sign of movement, but the birds were still. "Is it only a coot saying 'kuk-kuk-kuk'? If only they'd fly. Then I'd know for sure."

The unidentified calls continued and Clarence Lester was still unsure of which member of the coot family he was hearing. "I'm losing time," he thought. "It's not worth it for just a coot."

Clarence Lester took a stone from his pocket and threw it in the direction of the clucking sounds. With flapping commotion and much complaining, four birds jumped into the air. He followed them with his field glasses, noting plumage and bill color.

"Gray body . . ." he whispered. "Can't see the bill. Turn around, you stupid birds. What color are your legs?

"Hooray!" he wanted to cheer, but had already disturbed the marsh enough. Besides, Clarence Lester Hatch would never actually cheer right out loud for anything in his life. "The legs are yellow!" he exulted and abruptly jotted these observations in his memorandum book. He didn't bother to watch the birds disappear from sight. Triumphantly he added "purple gallinule" to his list.

"Betcha that'll be rare. There can't be too many of those around. Hope no one else sees one. Then all those fuddy-duddies at the Linnaean will really sit up and take notice."

Finding the purple gallinule had made him hungry and he began to stroll down the beach, taking quick, nervous bites from one of his sandwiches. He didn't really taste the peanut butter and mayonnaise, but kept alert for movements that could be birds at the water's edge. There was just enough light to see any "peeps" that were about. He'd listed spotted sandpiper, greater and lesser yellowlegs and sanderlings and had finished half of his sandwich when he saw the red-feathered bird struggling within a circle of black-backs.

"Oh, my God," he whispered. "A scarlet macaw!" He hurried to add it to his list, making careful note of the colors of its plumage, bill and feet. When he saw what he'd done he realized that he would be the laughingstock of the Linnaean. No one would believe him; worse yet, if he reported it, all of his observations would be questioned. He could imagine the predatory gleam in old Mrs. Harrison's eye and hear her querulous voice ask, "And just what was this scarlet macaw doing when you encountered it, Mr. Hatch? Eating a cracker?" No, it would never do. Clarence Lester crossed it off his list and glumly watched as the circle of great black-backs edged closer to the macaw. "If only I had a camera," he thought. "Then they'd have to believe me. But without some way to prove the existence of this bird I might as well put down kiwi or bee hummingbird.

"If only I had a net. Maybe I could catch it. There must be some way of getting proof."

The intensity of the gulls' squabble increased and Clarence Lester momentarily forgot that the Linnaean Society would never believe him. "What's going on?" he wondered and began to watch more carefully. "Something's wrong with that macaw," he thought. "I don't think it can fly. Its wing's busted."

The macaw hissed at its tormentors and panted. Its head drooped on bedraggled breast feathers. "Maybe it'll die," thought Clarence Lester, brightening. "Then I'll have the specimen." For a moment he imagined himself wrapping the dead bird in his jacket and carrying it home on the subway. Suddenly he knew exactly what to do.

Clarence Lester Hatch was not an impulsive sort of boy. Cautious by nature, he seldom did anything without careful planning and forethought. Later, when he would be questioned by reporters about how he had known how to safely capture the macaw, he would find that he had no explanation. Lamely he would stammer, "I . . . I don't know. Something just told me what to do."

He slung his haversack to the sand and rewrapped the remaining portion of his sandwich in waxed paper. He put the sandwich in the outer pocket and removed his binoculars from around his neck. Then he carefully stowed them inside his pack and hurried out of his jacket. He hitched up the long socks that continually threatened to slide down his calves and he rolled up his sleeves. He didn't want anything to distract him at the last minute.

His preparations complete, he crept forward, holding his jacket before him like a matador's cape. The gulls abandoned the macaw when he was twelve feet away. The bird hissed at him from the sand. When she saw that the human was not intimidated, the Duchess opened her one good wing and tried to fly. All she succeeded in doing was scattering sand and, as a last resort, she tried to scuttle overland out of reach.

Although he had doctored robins with broken wings and raised sparrows and blue jays that had fallen out of nests, Clarence Lester had never been so close to a big bird, especially a parrot. Somehow he knew just what to do. With his hands protected by his jacket he made one grab and swaddled the bird. The jacket pinned her wings to her sides and the bird reached around wildly with her huge bill. He turned the macaw on her back and cradled her in the crook of his arm. Her long tail feathers trailed down, reaching almost to his knees. The bird struggled for a moment, shuddered and suddenly was quiet. Clarence Lester was alarmed at how hot and light she felt. She gave him one glare before a filmy nictitating membrane descended over each eye.

"You can't die," Clarence Lester Hatch said to the still macaw. With the bird clutched to his chest he raced back to his haversack and found his canteen. Something told him to dribble water into the bird's bill. He stroked her throat and watched for her to swallow. "Don't drown, macaw. Please swallow."

Meanwhile, the Duchess listened to Sherahi's voice spinning a hypnotic melody that sounded like the shush and rattle of palm fronds and she heard the serpent singing of life in the jungle. Dew glittered on the leaves around her and the Duchess put her bill to a cup-shaped leaf and pushed it down. Cool water gushed into her throat. She was exhausted from her injuries and from battling the gulls. The shock of being touched by a human had drained her last bit of strength and the Duchess fainted.

Much later she opened her eyes to find Clarence Lester Hatch sitting on the beach, looking down at her. She could feel a finger gently scratching her head, ruffling the tiny feathers on her crown. It felt soothing and delicious and the Duchess tilted her head, begging for more. Clarence Lester Hatch felt the macaw's head shift in response to his touch and said, "Awfully tame, aren't you? I wonder if you're hungry."

After she'd eaten his second sandwich and drunk more water, the Duchess began to feel stronger. She cleaned the sticky goo from her tongue with one scaly foot, looked at Clarence Lester Hatch and, in a clear baritone voice, said, "Take me to Sandeagozu." Then she lapsed into a stream of parrot squawk and repeated, clearly enunciating each word, "Take me to Sandeagozu."

Clarence Lester blinked and sat down hard against a rock, staring incredulously at the self-possessed macaw, who suddenly grew coquettish and batted her eyes at him before repeating her command.

In the greenhouse Sherahi writhed in pleasure and, if she could have smiled like Dervish, she would have. Her plan had worked perfectly and she returned to her body in the conservatory knowing that the Duchess would completely bamboozle Clarence Lester Hatch. "She'll nag that poor boy until he takes her to Sandeagozu. If any of us has a chance to get there, courtesy of humans," she chuckled, "it's that parrot." The look of amazement on the bird-watcher's face when the macaw began to speak was still before Sherahi's eyes and she giggled, making a sound like carefree mice dancing across withered leaves.

Manu heard the noise and called to her, but Sherahi was busy with her own thoughts and for the moment they didn't include Manu, Dervish or any of the others. She thought back on how she had been able to make Clarence Lester Hatch do exactly what she wanted. "I made him find the Duchess," she exulted. "That's the first time I've put ideas into a human mind." Sherahi was stunned with her accomplishment.

"I completely controlled him." She remembered how he'd followed her mental directives, doing exactly as she wanted, like a minnow mesmerized by the wriggling lure on the tongue of an alligator snapper. "I couldn't do that with Ruthie or Bernie or even with Leftrack," she thought. "I could give them emotions and feelings, but not ideas." Then she remembered the white crocodiles swimming malevolently in their phosphorescent channels and wondered how they had changed her. "They certainly taught the Duchess how to speak better and the other Culls learned things, too. But I never expected anything like this."

For a long while Sherahi wondered how the white crocodiles would have given her the power to insert ideas into human minds. She concentrated so hard that she was oblivious to all about her. The silence in the conservatory was broken only by Manu rustling impatiently in the top of his palm tree. Sherahi knew that he wanted her attention but continued to ignore him. "Strange," the snake thought, "it's as if I've suddenly opened a door in my mind that I never knew existed and behind it are new and wonderful rooms. Places that I never knew about." Sherahi thought her long, cold, slow thoughts. She was conscious of shadows lengthening on the floor of the conservatory. When she finally released these ideas it was late afternoon.

"Well," she reasoned, "it doesn't really matter how I did it. The important thing is that the Duchess is safe. Clarence Lester Hatch will doctor her wounds and take her to Sandeagozu. I can't do any more for her. Even if I could control humans as easily as mindless toads, I don't like dealing with them. They're so messy. And it does make me tired. Strange that humans think so much of their intellect, when their thoughts are such a morass of scraps of ideas, fragmented memories and a welter of words. I guess they have no way of comparing theirs with other kinds of minds.

"I'm glad that's done," Sherahi sighed. "Long-distance control of humans is easier than it was, but it still is exhausting. The Duchess will have to help herself now."

Sherahi stretched luxuriously and resettled herself in the nest she'd made in the frangipani tree. For the first time since she'd taken responsibility for the safety of the Culls, everything seemed orderly and under control. Sherahi realized that she had nothing to worry about. The Duchess would get to Sandeagozu, and Manu and Dervish had Sorensen to care for them. Junior certainly didn't want or need any help: he'd always been more independent than any of the other Culls. And Sherahi had a whole rain forest to explore. "Well, not really a whole rain forest," she thought. "But it's almost the real thing. This place is sort of like Sandeagozu. There are no cages and no bars. It's warm and there's plenty of food. If only there were some other pythons or langurs or coatis it would be perfect."

Sherahi saw the reflection of long-stemmed lotus blossoms and the shadowy undersides of their ruffled leaves. Fat, orange fishes undulated in the shade at the far side of the pool. "There's even a pool that's big enough for swimming and those fishes will be fun to chase." One by one, the fishes languidly faded into deeper water. "We've got food, shelter, company. It's almost too good to be true."

A sudden movement caught her eye as a banded argiope spider with a body as thick as a child's thumb hurried from the hub of her web to a sticky corner. Sherahi saw that a flesh fly struggled to free himself. The spider grasped her prey with a front pair of legs and briefly plunged her fangs into the unfortunate fly, piercing his waterproof skin and injecting venom. The fly's multifaceted eyes turned dull as the spider ejected twin streams of liquid silk from her spinnerets and turned the unresisting insect over and over, wrapping it for future use. Sherahi saw that she planned to feast tonight, reinserting those fangs to suck up the muscle and innards that her venom had liquefied. Moments later, the small, white package festooned a corner of the web and the black-and-yellow spider had returned to her sentinel post, hanging head downward at the center of her concentric web. Sherahi scryed the spider's mind and listened to the dirge that she sang for her prey. Sherahi thought that the dissonant and atonal song was like wind whistling in hollow reeds—cold comfort for the fly whose body was slowly turning to mush within his bristly jacket.

The dirge reminded Sherahi of the song that Annahe, the female white crocodile, had sung to her embryos as they grew and revolved about the golden yolks of their watery egg worlds. "What an awful mistake," thought Sherahi. "How eager I was to be fooled. But once I had heard her song, we were trapped. We had no more chance to escape than that fly did; no more chance than a male mantid in the embrace of his ravenous lover; no more chance than a cobra facing a mongoose or a flea once Manu has it between his fingernails. Why didn't I know better? I should have sensed the trap." Sherahi listened to the dirge whistle and wail and realized, "I wanted to believe too much. I let them fool me."

She remembered her relief when, after weeks of mental questing through the maze of tunnels that lay beneath the city, she had suddenly heard Annahe's clear, sweet song. Sherahi listened to the argiope's song and wondered, "Could this place that seems so wonderful be just another sort of trap?"

Sherahi surveyed the lush foliage that seemed so welcoming, so much like home. "It's beautiful here, but I'd better have a more careful look. I was cold and tired when I scryed this place last night. I may have missed something important."

She fixed her mind on the smooth bole of the tree and coordinated the impressions from the Jacobson's organs in the roof of her mouth with the quopping sensations of her labial pits, throttling both with the methodical, slow-motion working of her icy mind. Once more, Sherahi began to scry the derelict conservatory.

There were a few surprises: today the resident tomcat dozed on the smoothest flagstone in the desert section of the conservatory, and in the henhouse she saw Sorensen's chickens. Their combs quivered a blood-red obbligato to their nervous clucks and occasional squawks. There were many insects stirring in the various rooms of the greenhouse, as well as the skinks that she'd already met in the desert conservatory. Deep within the well of a bromeliad she found a male tree frog brooding his tadpoles in a trembling throat pouch. Huge, hissing roaches slept among the leaves of the Madagascar compass palms and Sorensen plucked spent blossoms from vanda orchids in the epiphyte room. Sherahi saw that Dervish lay at his feet. She entered his hot, quick mind and saw his dream of sardines and peanut butter. To make sure that the Culls were safe from unfriendly humans she quickly scanned Sorensen's mind, too. She saw his proprietary pride in his conservatory and his pleasure that it was closed to the public. "It looks like we're as safe here as anywhere," she decided. "Everyone needs a rest. We can't try to get to Sandeagozu until each of us is strong again."

Satisfied that the Culls had no immediate need for her protection and confident that her mental screen would give her undisturbed sleep, Sherahi narrowed her pupils and began to count the spokes in the argiope's web. She fell asleep between "three and many."

"Sherahi?" Manu whispered. But the pythoness' cold voice did not speak inside his mind and the conservatory remained quiet. "I must be imagining things," thought the old langur, "but I could swear that I heard Sherahi laugh a little while ago. I wish she'd come back, or that Dervish would show up. I'm bored." He tried to fall asleep again but the quiet made him edgy. There was a splash and Manu started, nearly losing his balance. He looked down to see concentric rings on the smooth surface of the pool below. "Not surprising that I'm nervous enough to imagine that I hear things," he thought. "All day I've been as cautious as a soft-shelled crab, waiting in this tree just like Sherahi told me to. But how long does she expect me to sit here with no one to talk to and nothing to eat? I'm starving and those bananas over there are ripe." Manu looked at them and thought, "What does a ripe banana taste like?" He found that he couldn't remember. The only taste that came clearly to mind was that of the prickly pads of dried algae that the white crocodiles had given him to eat. The algae had just barely kept him alive. "If we hadn't escaped I would have died of malnutrition and hunger," Manu thought, feeling the bones poking through the skin of his thighs. Earlier in the day Manu had eaten all of the ripe dates from the cluster above his head. They had made him thirsty, but he had heeded Sherahi's order to stay hidden. He could smell the bananas that curled invitingly, beckoning him to come and feast. He watched the fruit intently and saw a cloud of fruit flies moving across the yellow peels. "They must be ripe," Manu thought and shifted his position in the crown of the date palm. "I wish I had just one, or even just a bite of one. Why doesn't Sherahi come back? Where can she be?" Manu didn't want to disobey the pythoness' orders. That had always gotten him into trouble in the past. "I should never have given that white crocodile back her eggs," Manu thought. "I should have obeyed the pythoness. If I had, they never would've been able to capture us."

"Sherahi?" Manu asked a while later. There was still no answer and the langur decided that he'd waited long enough. Moving as silently as possible he descended the trunk of the date palm. His heart thudded in his throat as he slipped from plant to plant, moving closer to the banana tree. The fruit looked more luscious with every step. He reached the trunk of Sherahi's frangipani tree and peered up into the branches, but it was too dim to see even the outline of the huge snake that he knew was coiled in the gloom. Something warned him not to investigate any further. "Funny that I can't see Sherahi," he thought. "I'm sure she's up there. But you just never know with snakes," he sighed. "They're so queer sometimes. Probably because they're so different from everyone else." The langur's neck began to ache from straining up and once more he thought of the dwarf bananas. Moments later he'd forgotten all about the pythoness and her orders. He pulled himself up into the banana tree and when Dervish reappeared, the langur was savoring his fifth banana, peel and all.

Dervish ran circles around the base of the tree. "Manu," he panted. "Did you see him? Sorensen is here and he has food for us. Come down, Manu. He'll be here in a moment. I told him about you and Sherahi, but he doesn't understand what I say. You can make him understand, can't you, Manu? Please?"

The langur saw the collar around Dervish's neck and immediately was alarmed. "What's that around your neck, Dervish?" He didn't wait for the coati to reply but continued, "How could you let any human do that to you, Dervish? After all we've been through, haven't you learned that humans mean us harm? We can't trust them."

"Manu, don't be cross," said Dervish. "This old thing isn't important. I can take it off anytime I want to. I only let him put it on me because it seemed to make him happy. He was so pleased, Manu. Sorensen isn't like the other humans. He's our friend. You remember how kind he used to be to us; it's a little thing to do and it pleases him. And, Manu, he's got food— wonderful food—peaches and green grapes and baloney sandwiches and salami. And peanut butter, Manu—wait till you taste it! Don't be cross, Manu. Come down. He'll be here soon."

Manu was suddenly very serious. His tone frightened Dervish into listening carefully. "Dervish, you must do exactly as I say, with no questions. Sorensen may be a decent human, but he's still a human. No matter how nice he seems, we cannot trust him. Sherahi said so. We have our own plans now and they don't include being Sorensen's pets. Don't you want to be free? Don't you want to find Sandeagozu?"

"Yes," said Dervish with his head cocked to one side. "But I don't . . ."

"Shush," said Manu. "Climb up here and be quick about it. Sorensen will get us and before we know it we'll be back in cages. I don't want to die in a cage, Dervish. We've got to hide. It's the only way."

"But, Manu—"

"Do as I say. Quick. Come up here."

Sorensen entered the conservatory only moments after the coati had scrambled to the top of the banana tree. "Come here, fella," he called, letting the glass door bang shut behind him.

Manu felt the coati's back muscles quiver. "Don't whine, Dervish," he ordered and held his breath. "Please don't let him find us," Manu silently begged and thought, "Sherahi, where are you when we need you?"

Dervish didn't move and Manu encouraged him to be silent, saying, "Good. Now he'll go away."

Sorensen scanned the plantings inside the tropical rain forest room. He remembered how Dervish had once loved to play hide-and-seek. His eyes caught the motion of a piece of twine that hung from one of the dwarf banana trees. Recognizing the string that he'd attached to his belt to lengthen Dervish's leash he thought, "I've got you now." Holding a ripe peach in one hand and a stronger piece of rope in the other, he stealthily moved beneath the tree and took hold of the dangling string. He looked up and was surprised to see not only Dervish's white-rimmed eyes blinking back at him, but also the single black eye that stared from Manu's half bright-pink, half sooty-black face. The langur's silver fur, mangled arm and distorted face were unmistakable. Sorensen held out the peach and reached up with both arms, saying, "Come, Manu." He never had any doubt that the old langur would recognize him.

Even though Manu had just vowed to shun all humans, the kindness in Sorensen's voice obliterated the langur's better judgment. Moments later Manu snuggled into Sorensen's arms. The ripe peach was in the langur's long-fingered hand and sweet juice dripped onto the rope that Sorensen had knotted around his waist.

CHAPTER ELEVEN

May, 1933

OILED HIGH IN the crown of the frangipani tree and confident that her shroud of confusion would baffle and discourage even the most relentless observer, Sherahi concentrated her unique pythonine mental talents and separated mind and body, seeking a way for the Culls to travel to Sandeagozu.

With the persistence of a rat gnawing out of a lead pipe, her cold-minded, slow-motion reptilian intelligence spun a glistening cable of concentration and hurled it westward. Like a limbless lamprey wriggling upstream, homing in on the blood scent of its living prey, she watched the barbed head of the cable anchor on what she was certain must be Sandeagozu. Concentrating on Sandeagozu, Sherahi's mind spiraled around her rope of thought and for the first time actually saw the garden full of animals that lived in cages without bars. She sighed, with relief, "Sandeagozu actually does exist." The Culls had talked and dreamed about this place so much that it had become mythical—a part of their liturgy. Sherahi thought, "Now we don't have to worry about not being able to get home again. All we have to do is get to Sandeagozu. Then Manu will be with his tribe, Dervish will find himself a mate and Junior and I will be free—or very nearly so."

Sherahi scryed the minds of many of the animals she saw and was surprised to find that, unlike the captive animals at Leftrack's warehouse, those at Sandeagozu were contented—even happy. "It's as if they were actually free," she thought as she watched a mother hippopotamus teach her infant how to float in a mud hole. Only two pairs of eyes, ears and nostrils protruded from the blanket of duckweed that covered their miry wallow. In a nearby meadow pairs of Japanese cranes bewitched one another with trembling throats, outstretched wings and stilt-legged leaps and pirouettes. Flaps and flashes of black-on-white plumage semaphored desire and Sherahi found herself embarrassed by this blatant sexual display of her distant relatives. "Fools," she thought, "your heads are as hollow as your bones." She turned away to see a spotted lion cub snarl and leap upon the tip of his mother's tail, biting it with needle teeth and disemboweling it with kicks of his floppy hind feet. A sweep of the lioness's paw rolled the baby backward and he blinked and shook himself before he pounced once again upon that irresistible, twitching appendage.

Sherahi saw drowsing hummingbirds brood bee-sized chicks in nests they'd made of spider webs and festooned with crumbs of lichen. Like flights of shrill, green arrows, whole flocks of parrots shrieked overhead, slicing the morning sky, while below a clan of ring-tailed lemurs sat on their haunches, grooming one another and basking like light-eyed lap cats. Sherahi saw schools of fish wheel in one silver movement, roosting fruit bats that shifted leathery wings like a tree full of nervous umbrellas and river otters who splashed rooster tails of water at one another just for the fun of it.

She saw that there were people in Sandeagozu, too, but they were well separated from the animals. Sherahi was amazed to see that the animals paid little attention to the humans. Instead of inspiring fear and suffering, the humans were as insignificant as a faraway frieze: a shifting bas-relief that was as unimportant to the animals as a monument to forgotten heroes of an obscure war, hieroglyphs that chronicled the genealogy of the petty nobility of a lost civilization or the recipe for chazlebdet. "That's the way it should be," thought the delighted pythoness. "The animals shouldn't even know that the people are here. After all, this is Sandeagozu and it's nearly perfect. It can be our home forever. We can be happy here, if only we can get to it."

Satisfied with what she'd seen, Sherahi began to trace her rope of thought back to the crystal house. To better survey the terrain she projected her mind high into the air. Peering below the clouds she saw Sandeagozu far below: a miniature garden dotted with giraffes the size of long-necked ants and elephants the size of flap-eared beetles. It was within a sprawling city and to the west an ocean stretched to the horizon. A range of snow-topped mountains was to the east of the city and Sherahi could see her cable of concentration travel up and over the mountain range and disappear.

"I must find my way home again," she thought and flicked her licorice-black tongue toward the unseen east face of the mountain range below. In a way that she only vaguely understood, but following the lessons that U Vayu had given her so very long ago as they communed beneath the shadow of the Buddha that glinted in the light of a hundred flickering candles, Sherahi wove an arrow of concentration and tempered it within her mind. Realizing that the Culls were depending upon her to find Sandeagozu, she released the arrow into the desert below and followed, streaming toward the east flank of the mountain like the tail of a kite snatched by a powerful downdraft.

She found herself coiled in the shade of a spiny bush and from the prickling sensation on the nape of her neck knew that someone was intently watching her. Sherahi forced the blush of life into her materialization, giving gloss and color to each scale, and drew her head back into the defensive posture that always terrified her prey. She needed information and hoped to mesmerize and frighten whoever was watching her. Moments went by and still she had not found any living creature. She noticed that it was midday on the desert. The sky was white with heat and the tops of the mountains were visible in the glare.

"Frog's blood," she cursed, "where is it? What is it? Why can't I find it?"

She quickly fnasted right and left and seconds later, after visual scrutiny had failed, her heat-sensitive labial pits located the motionless rabbit only a few feet away from her coil. The rabbit's fur matched the sandy soil and from the way that it crouched, with no twitch of ears or whiskers, and from its glazed stare she knew that this jackrabbit was witless with fear. Rabbits always lost their heads in tight situations and Sherahi wondered, "Why do lagomorphs insist on doing that? They're supposed to be resourceful, brave—even clever. But they spend most of their lives scared stiff. It's a wonder that any of them survive."

Sherahi sent a wave of comfort to the frozen jackrabbit and was pleased to see him come to his senses and blink. But before she could speak into his mind he leaped high in the air, gave a flash of white fur and disappeared. Sherahi could hear him thump and rustle in the bushes for a long time after he'd gone. "That's gratitude," the serpent thought and looked about, fnasting for another informant. Sherahi found herself alone in the desert at midday and even though she was only a materialization she could sense the hostility of this place. She thought, "This heat will kill us. We'll be able to travel only at night and what will we do about water? None of us can go without that for very long." Sherahi thought about the garden of animals that was on the far side of the mountains and thought, "It may be impossibly far." Sherahi saw that even the plants in this desert were protected with recurved claws and prickles and knew that food would be scarce. "We'll all have to be in top condition before we try to get to Sandeagozu this way."

Through the midday glare she could barely see the mountain range in the distance and decided, "It's too far. We could never get there. Even if we did, would we be able to cross the mountains? There's got to be another way."

Disappointed, but glad to escape the heat, the pythoness returned to her body, which lay in the upper branches of the frangipani tree. "There must be an easier way to get to Sandeagozu," she thought. "If I have more time I can figure it out. I'm sure I can find a way."

In the next month Sherahi repeatedly tried to find a more practical route for the Culls to follow to Sandeagozu. But it was always the same: Sandeagozu was too far away; the mountains and the desert would be insurmountable barriers to the Culls. Sherahi was so stymied in her efforts that sometimes she wondered if the curses of the circling white crocodiles blocked her path or if Junior's flinty mind was against her. Eventually she gave up, deciding that this wasn't the right time for the Culls to think about traveling west.

It was early spring when Sherahi had begun her mental quest for a way to get to Sandeagozu. By the time she abandoned the search the leaves of the trees that surrounded the crystal house hung in green tatters, thanks to hungry caterpillars and industrious leaf miners. The leaves had turned color, been scattered by the wind and gathered in scarlet, yellow and orange drifts when the idea of leaving the crystal house finally faded from Sherahi's mind. Thus, two thirds of a year had passed while four of the five animals who had escaped from Leftrack's pet shop had remained happily marooned within the derelict Victorian conservatory. When the wind shook the last leaves from the frozen branches, Sherahi's only thought of Sandeagozu was, "We can't get there. It's just too far."

Feeding was her chief preoccupation now and as she prowled around the lotus pool, alert for a telltale wriggle of the fat goldfish that was about to gobble a mouthful of air, she thought, "Why should we bother to go to Sandeagozu? We've got everything we need right here." She did not listen to the voice within that contradicted and warned, "Everything except others of our own kinds." Sherahi knew that the voice was right, but chose to ignore it.

The pythoness was accustomed to a reptile's solitary life. She had never had a mate and knew that the pangs of longing and waves of loneliness that overwhelmed her every spring would eventually fade and not pester her for another year. Sherahi had her emotions under control—a simple task for a reptile who had been schooled in mind control since she'd slashed free of her eggshell. Mammals, however, were at the mercy of hormone-controlled emotions. She had been surprised that Manu and Dervish had never suffered from loneliness or lack of mates. Sherahi watched the two chase and tumble about on the floor of the rain forest, marveling at how young and strong Manu seemed and at how big Dervish had grown. "He's nearly as big as a fox," she thought, "and he has no idea of what will happen to him next spring. Manu's been through it many times, though. He's been alone for many seasons." She paused to watch the langur leap effortlessly to a limb that was twelve feet above his head. From this safe perch he teased the coati into a frenzy and laughed as the two chased through the canopy of the rain forest, leaving a zigzag wake of waving branches and broken boughs. "Manu's never been this healthy, though," thought Sherahi. "It's the food that Sorensen gives him and all this exercise. I'll bet that he's never been strong enough to mate until now. Maybe he's never actually come into breeding condition before. He's always been weak and sick, but it looks as though he'll be ready for a harem next spring. I wonder how he'll treat his long-nosed playmate then?" Sherahi knew that male langurs often killed their competitors and that an opposing need, for companionship, was firmly woven into the fabric of the coati's mind. "I can't worry about that, though. I can't always be responsible for everyone. I found this place. I got them out of Leftrack's. I've done enough. Besides, I'm hungry."

Sherahi decided that it would be nice to have something different to eat. For a moment she thought about ambushing the tomcat that prowled outside the glass house, pouncing upon voles and mice, but then she remembered how much Sorensen liked that tomcat. "Sorensen has been so good to Dervish and Manu," she thought. "It wouldn't be kind to kill his pet." Thinking about Sorensen reminded her of the flock of chickens that he kept. "I wonder," thought Sherahi, "could I make him give one of them to me?" She had found that her control of human behavior wasn't perfect. Humans were unpredictable and she'd found that she was able to control them only when her purpose and theirs coincided.

She coiled in her nest in the frangipani tree, thinking, and then the plan unrolled in her pythonine mind. "Sorensen," she hissed to herself and thought about the old man's hands. They were thick-fingered and calloused from work and were seldom still. Sorensen was always puttering about, re-potting plants, repairing windows, patting Dervish or tinkering with machinery in the basement. Sherahi focused on these hands and sent her mind out to find Sorensen's.

The man was outside the conservatory, wrapping burlap over the rose bushes. As he worked she examined his thoughts, searching for the segment of his brain that stored his memories of food. Half hidden by the taste of his mother's pot roast was Sorensen's fondness for roast chicken. She saw that, although he took eggs home every night, he hadn't butchered one of his flock in weeks. It was easy for Sherahi to knead his fondness for succulent roast chicken into a hunger pang and to insert the idea of slaughtering one of his hens who had stopped laying.

Sorensen finished mulching the rose bushes and thought, "Fried chicken for dinner. Tonight's not Sunday, but it's canasta night. It would surprise the others."

Later that afternoon Sorensen selected a hen in the henhouse. In one quick grab he had her by the feet. Her strong, white wings beat the air, scattering feathers everywhere and sending the other chickens into a nervous frenzy. Sorensen hurried from the henhouse, making sure to carefully lock the door behind him. He didn't want to panic the other birds unnecessarily.

Carrying his hatchet in one hand he went to the stump of an old chestnut tree that he used as a chopping block. The hen hung quietly now, her white wings spread open. Sorensen flopped her body onto the dark-stained stump and, before she'd thought to struggle, brought down the hatchet and chopped off her head. In a second quick motion he threw the headless carcass into the air and wiped away the blood that had spattered onto his forehead. The chicken flapped and tried to rise in the air, but she fell and her headless body righted itelf and ran furiously around and around in wide circles. Streams of blood spurted from her neck and steamed faintly in the crisp air. Soon the bird keeled over on her side and Sorensen took the carcass, the head and the ax into the conservatory.

Sherahi had watched all of this with satisfaction. "It's working just as I had hoped," she thought. "Now, for the last part."

Summoning all of her thoughts Sherahi directed one sentence into Sorensen's thoughts. "The ax is dull," she said.

She saw the white-haired man stop and gently put the bird down onto the brickwork beside a clump of ferns that grew at the base of the frangipani tree. Their arching fronds screened the dead body and hid it from Sorensen's sight. Sorensen held the cutting edge of the bloody ax up to the light and made tsking sounds as he scrutinized the rusty, dull blade. Sherahi saw him drop the chicken head next to the body and walk away toward the toolshed.

As he stroked the edge of the ax with a whetstone she wiped away the memory of the dead chicken from his mind. He would remember the carcass days later, after she had disposed of the bird. "I'll have chicken tonight," Sherahi thought, proud of her control of the old man and wishing that nightfall would come so that she could slither down out of the tree and claim her prize.

Because their life in the crystal house was so easy and so idyllic, the Culls might have accommodated to it, and their original plan to travel to Sandeagozu might have been forgotten if it hadn't been for Junior. As the months had passed, the cascabel had made the desert conservatory his private preserve. He never ventured beyond the glass doors that separated it from the adjoining rooms of the conservatory and he habitually shunned the other Culls. He viewed himself as an outcast, a loner—misunderstood, unloved, unappreciated. "I don't need any of them" was a constant refrain as he nursed his bruised feelings and added more brambles to the screen of confusion that hid his lair.

Although Sherahi continued to try to contact him mentally, the rattler always retreated behind his barbed mental shield. He'd vowed to have nothing further to do with the other Culls and spent most of his time in the hole he'd excavated beneath a dead limb of saguaro cactus. He emerged infrequently to hunt for mice, rats and an occasional lizard.

Junior was active only after dusk, when his infra-red-sensing loreal pits and cat-eyed pupils gave him an advantage over his hot-blooded, quick-minded prey. He rarely saw Birger Sorensen, because the man usually left the conservatory an hour before dark. Sorensen didn't fancy encountering the hobos that congregated in the park at night. He was nearly seventy years old, suffered from angina pains and didn't want to court trouble.

Although Sorensen had a free hand in the abandoned Victorian conservatory, one of the few requests that Dr. Crotty, the head botanist, had made was that Sorensen collect seed from the cacti as they flowered. To Sorensen's annoyance, however, he found that mice were always ahead of him, harvesting the seeds even before they ripened. Sorensen had great respect for the way that Dr. Crotty had held on, despite lack of financial support from the Society, and he didn't want to disappoint the old man. Thus, to preserve a few seeds of the rarest cacti, he had decided to trap the mice that infested the desert conservatory before they took the next crop of cactus seeds.

Sorensen had locked the building for the night and was on his way home, thinking of breaded pork chops smothered in limp fried onions. He was nearly to the cherry orchard when he remembered that he hadn't set the traps. It had been a tiring day. The boiler was acting up again: he'd had to dismantle it and would have to spend the next two days putting it back together. "Cold weather'll be here soon," he thought, buttoning his collar against the wind. "The traps can wait till tomorrow. I've done enough for one day." As he ducked beneath the weeping cherry trees he thought of the destruction that Manu and Dervish had caused as they rampaged through the rain forest. "If they don't mind what I say, I'll have to put them into cages. I've told them not to do that, but they won't listen. I can't let them destroy everything."

The idea of the traps nagged at his mind and he trudged on, saying, "It'll wait another day." He had nearly reached the gnarled copper beech when he remembered how wistful Dr. Crotty's voice had sounded when he'd made his request. "It won't take long," he thought, looking at his watch. "If I hurry I can set all of them and still catch the 6:15 ferry." With the handle of his lunch pail rattling hollowly in one hand, Sorensen turned back to the conservatory.

It was dark when he unlocked the front door but he knew the floor plan of the building by heart and didn't bother to turn on the lights. He hurried through the rain forest room and pushed open the glass door to the hot, dry desert enclosure. Earlier in the day he'd placed a dozen snap traps among the display of cacti and sagebrush. He finished baiting and setting nine of them and was crouched near a creosote bush when he heard an unfamiliar buzzing noise. "What's that?" he wondered. It sounded as if a huge fly were trapped between panes of glass, buzzing for freedom. For some reason a cold sweat broke out on his forehead. "Don't get spooked," he said to himself and unbuttoned his collar. "There's nothing in here but too many mice."

Sorensen had never heard the warning rattle of a cascabel, the most deadly of all American rattlesnakes, but something cautioned, "Watch out." He reached for the tenth trap, which was beneath a piece of dry cactus wood.

As Sorensen moved closer and crouched down, he inadvertently planted his feet so that one was upon Junior's midsection. Junior rattled more intently, but there was no relief from the pressure. He tried to wriggle free, but found himself firmly held beneath a great weight. Annoyed that his warning had been disobeyed, and bruised by Sorensen's heavy boot, the rattler felt the heat of the man's body coming closer and launched himself into the dark, striking open-mouthed and with both fangs erect. He wanted to get free before he was hurt even more. The sensitive lining of his mouth registered the rough stubble on the old man's whiskery throat and just as Junior identified his victim as Sorensen, Manu and Dervish's friend, his hollow fangs injected a huge volume of venom into the warmest part of the man's neck.

Sorensen jerked back and lifted his foot. He felt as though a sapling had snapped across his neck, just above his collar. "What was that?" he wondered and stood up and felt his throat. He held his hand up to the moonlight and was surprised to see it glisten darkly. There was no time to wonder about the liquid on his throat, though, because he grew suddenly dizzy. His eyelids were unaccountably heavy. "What's happening?" he thought. His heart pounded and he felt the familiar pains of angina encircle his ribs. "What's wrong with my eyes?" He felt woozy and faint and clutched the edge of the cactus display for support. "My head . . . so heavy." He tried to steady his neck, which insisted upon flopping forward, and found that even his hands couldn't hold his head upright. He felt like a rag doll that had lost all of the stuffing from its neck and then he collapsed onto the sandy floor beneath the display of cacti. As he fell he jarred two nearby mousetraps and they snapped in unison. Sorensen didn't hear them. The venom had reached his diaphragm and he had stopped breathing. It reached his heart and stopped the convulsions of a heart attack. But before either of those things happened, Birger Sorensen lost consciousness.

Junior wriggled out from under the man's foot and flicked his tongue to and fro, trying to assess the condition of his victim. "I didn't mean to kill you," he said into the man's mind. "You shouldn't have been here. You shouldn't have stepped on me." He could see consciousness ebbing. Color was draining from the man's mind and Junior knew that he didn't hear him at all as he said, "I didn't mean to kill you. Why did you hurt me?"

Frightened by what he had done, and feeling the heat flood from

Sorensen's body, Junior suddenly thought, "Sherahi. Maybe she can bring him back. Sherahi can do anything."

The little rattler sent a frightened cry to the pythoness and in seconds a misty cloud appeared near Sorensen's body and condensed into the giant snake. Silently she coiled next to the man's inert form, her mind intertwined with his. Junior knew she was trying to rouse Sorensen and he watched anxiously.

In a few minutes the door of the desert conservatory opened and first Dervish and then Manu entered, cautiously trying to locate the cascabel. The two mammals hurried to Sorensen and Dervish poked his long, cold nose into Sorensen's cheek and eye socket and whimpered while Manu kept a wary eye on the little rattlesnake. The conservatory was silent except for the chittering sounds Dervish made as he licked Sorensen's neck and face clean of blood. Finally the pythoness said, "He's beyond my help. I can do nothing for him. Nothing at all."

CHAPTER TWELVE

I T WASN'T LONG before Sorensen was missed. His body was discovered and taken away in an ambulance. The police found no signs of a struggle and concluded that he had suffered a heart attack. A coroner's examination confirmed this supposition. The coroner who examined the dead man didn't notice the paired pinpricks above the great arteries on Sorensen's neck. An internal examination showed coronary occlusion and the diagnosis of heart attack seemed inescapable. Sorensen's brother and canasta partners were not surprised, because Birger had complained of chest pains for years. He'd always been meaning to go to the doctor for some pills but had been too busy to get around to it. No one suspected that Sorensen's death had actually been caused by the bite of a two-foot-long South American rattlesnake. Sorensen hadn't told his brother of the langur and coati that lived at the conservatory and he never would have been allowed to keep the animals there if officials of the Botanic Garden had known about them.

With Sorensen gone the Culls retreated to the safety of the screened upper branches of Sherahi's frangipani tree. At first Manu and Dervish didn't want Junior to be allowed to have Sherahi's protection.

"Why does he have to be here?" Dervish fumed at Sherahi. "He's a murderer. How many times do I have to tell you that before you'll believe me? Who does he have to kill before you'll realize that? Now he's killed Sorensen—just like he killed the Duchess. And Sorensen was our friend. He used to bring me treats. He used to play with me. It isn't right, Sherahi. He's not one of us anymore. He's a murderer."

"Dervish," said Sherahi as calmly as she could, "Junior did not kill the Duchess. I told you. He found her lying there unconscious on the beach and was only trying to bury her. He did bite Sorensen, but it was an accident."

"Sure," growled Dervish, refusing to listen. "That's what you say. Go ahead—defend him. Why do I even bother talking to you—another snake—just like him. You've forgotten that he tried to kill me, too."

"Manu," said Sherahi, "can't you explain it so that Dervish will understand? He won't listen to me."

Sherahi saw the coati catch sight of the cascabel, who had climbed to the uppermost reaches of the frangipani tree to avoid the other Culls. Junior hadn't had time to reweave his mindscreen and Sherahi now observed that he couldn't do it as easily as she had imagined. Dervish's lips curled back from his teeth and he slicked back his ears. He lowered his head and in slow motion began to climb through the branches, stalking the cascabel. "He means to kill Junior," Sherahi thought.

"Manu," her mindspeech insisted. "You must do something. He won't listen to me."

Manu put out one of his slender-fingered black hands toward Dervish and touched him lightly on the shoulder. At once the coati whirled and leaped onto the langur. There was a struggle and withered frangipani leaves fluttered to the ground. Sherahi saw Dervish snarl and look for a place to bite Manu. She saw his mouth open and knew that he meant to sink his teeth into the monkey's neck. Without further thought she sent an angry, cold hiss into Dervish's overheated, bloodthirsty brain. It froze his attack and locked his jaws in a half-open position: he found that he could not close them and growled even more furiously, shaking his head from side to side. In the next instant Manu freed himself from the coati's frothing mouth and fled, hand over hand, to the crown of the tree. He clambered behind Sherahi's coils, rubbing his bruised neck and shoulder and scolding Dervish with angry coughs. Sherahi had never heard Manu speak so harshly in his own langur dialect and she saw that it had a marked effect on the coati.

Sherahi heard Dervish whine as he looked up guiltily at Manu, who said to him, "Dervish? What is wrong with you? We are supposed to be friends."

Sherahi watched Dervish slink away to the lower branches of the frangipani. Still growling, he found a crotch of the tree and lay down with his head on his paws, morosely staring into space. Some hours later Sherahi heard him chitter into the quiet conservatory. "I'm sorry, Manu," he said. "I hope I didn't hurt you too badly. I guess I was wrong about Junior. I'm sorry."

Manu didn't get a chance to reply because the cascabel's hiss came from the topmost branches: "It was an accident. I never meant to kill him. His foot was crushing my ribs. He was killing me."

"We believe you, Junior," said Manu in saurian mindspeech.

"And I didn't kill the Duchess, either," the cascabel said. "Why didn't you believe Sherahi when she said that the Duchess was already on her way to Sandeagozu?"

"Is this true, Sherahi?" Manu spoke into the pythoness' mind. "Why didn't you tell us?"

342

"I thought I did. I guess I forgot," she replied. "But it hardly seemed important. You and Dervish were with Sorensen all the time and there was so much else to do. . . ." She knew it was a lame excuse, but the truth was that all of the Culls had led separate lives in the derelict conservatory. Sorensen, Manu and Dervish had spent most of their time together, Junior had sequestered himself in the desert room and Sherahi had coiled in her frangipani tree, thinking her long, slow pythonine thoughts. More than anything else she had been pleased to be free of the responsibility for all of the Culls.

"Now that Sorensen isn't here," said Sherahi, "things will have to be different. For one thing, we don't know what new humans will come. We must be very careful not to be seen by them. I will reinforce my screen of confusion about this tree, but we may not be able to stay here."

"You're right," said Manu. "This tree is a little small for all of us."

"I don't mean that," said Sherahi. "We may have to leave this glass house."

"But where will we go?" asked Dervish. "You said that Sandeagozu was too far away."

"I don't know," replied the pythoness. "Let us hope for the best. We'll just have to see."

By the end of the week Dervish and Junior were fast friends once again. More often than not Junior could be found wound around Dervish's neck in the way that they had traveled when they were both youngsters. Slowly the old alliance of Culls, led by Sherahi, the Burmese python, and advised by Manu, the Hanuman langur, was reforged.

Manu and Dervish missed Sorensen for a while, but Sherahi gradually made them realize that, if Sorensen had lived, they might have been back in cages again. "That thought was in his mind," said the pythoness. "You two were being too rough on his plants and these plants were like children to him. I think he loved them more than you. It had something to do with a woman—I'm not sure—but I'm certain that if you'd kept breaking off limbs and scattering flowers, he would have been bound to capture you and lock you up."

That thought made Manu and Dervish very quiet. Each soberly vowed to have nothing to do with humans again. "We can't trust them," said Dervish one night when Sherahi and Junior were off hunting. "Even the best humans, like Sorensen, seem compelled to try to control us. It doesn't occur to them that we might have other plans. Strange creatures and very dangerous."

"But some of them are nice," said Dervish. "Remember the peaches and the sardines, Manu? Remember how he used to play with us?"

"Yes," said Manu sadly, "but those peaches had a price, Dervish. We would have had to pay it sooner or later."

Sherahi assumed the role of leader of the Culls again as if there had been no break in their confederacy. Her most immediate concern was cold. From her explorations of the conservatory she knew that as long as the sun was shining the crystal house would be warm—even hot—and comfortable. There was one problem, though; the day that Sorensen was bitten he had dismantled the heating system. She had seen that thought fade from the hodgepodge of miscellany in his dying mind. Sherahi prowled the basement boiler room and was dismayed to fnast oily metal parts scattered about on the floor. "Something's wrong," she thought. "It was never like this before."

What Sherahi didn't know was that maintaining the heating plant of the Victorian conservatory was one of Sorensen's major jobs. She did realize the effects of his death more acutely, though, when a week of rainy, cold days made the conservatory chilly and dank. "This will never do," the pythoness thought and sent a silent command into Dr. Crotty's mind. "Check the temperature of the old conservatory," she implored.

Later that morning the head botanist and his young assistant, Paul, appeared at the door of the crystal house. Secure behind the improved mental screen that Sherahi and Junior had collaborated upon, the Culls watched the two men shake the sleet from their hats and coats and stamp their feet at the entrance to the conservatory.

"Something's wrong," said the old botanist. "The leaves of this *Platycerium madagascariense* are turning black. And that *Ficus benjamina* doesn't look at all well."

"Oh, my God," said his assistant, "look at the temperature. Why hasn't the boiler kicked on?"

A few minutes later the two stood in the basement. Parts of the eviscerated furnace and boiler littered the floor.

"Sorensen didn't get it overhauled in time. Paul, get a mechanic immediately. We're going to lose everything upstairs if we don't get some heat in this place."

The single mechanic left on the Garden's staff arrived that afternoon and began tinkering. Although he succeeded in reassembling the machine, he couldn't make it work. Dressed in his overcoat and scarf, Dr. Crotty watched morosely as the temperature fell another half a degree in the tropical rain forest room. "Get smudge pots," he commanded.

By the afternoon the air was thick with warm smoke, but Dr. Crotty found that heat from the smudge fires didn't warm the conservatory sufficiently. He looked at the stubborn, antiquated boiler and ordered the mechanic to get the wood stove from the main office building and vent it through one of the panes of glass. "A wood stove may work," Crotty thought. "It'll cause hot spots, but maybe we won't lose everything." At the same time he and other workers began transplanting the smaller plants to

344

the already crowded, newer greenhouses in Prospect Park. "They don't have the romance of this old place," he thought, looking up at the way the gnarled frangipani was silhouetted against the arching, intricate roof, "but at least they're the right temperature."

The conservatory resisted every attempt to equalize the temperature within the rain forest room. "If only Sorensen had taught someone how this place works," fumed Dr. Crotty as he paced from room to room, peering at thermometers and frowning. "Well, perhaps if we seal all the drafts we can last through the winter. Perhaps we can afford a new boiler in the next fiscal year."

The most valuable small plant specimens were uprooted and transplanted to the new conservatory building, leaving the larger trees and plantings behind. While this was going on, the Culls remained within the frangipani tree, anxiously watching the workmen below and holding their breath whenever the crew with shovels approached their hiding place. But Sherahi's mental screen and the shroud of confusion that she had draped around the frangipani repelled the men. For some vague and inexpressible reason there always seemed to be other jobs more important than digging up the deep-rooted frangipani. "We'll leave that for last," the foreman decided.

Little by little the rain forest conservatory was stripped of all but the largest plants. "What am I going to eat?" thought Manu as he saw the dwarf banana tree being swathed in layers of burlap, covered with a windproof tarpaulin and wheeled out the conservatory door. He remembered the treats that Sorensen used to bring every day and his stomach growled.

"How long before they find us?" wondered Dervish. "Without Sorensen to protect us, those men'll probably kill us. We're trapped in here. It's too cold to go outside."

"Don't worry," the langur silently told the coati. "Sherahi will think of something."

"I hope it's soon," Dervish whimpered, tucking his cold nose beneath his belly fur. "I don't like this cold one bit."

It soon became apparent to Dr. Crotty that the plants that remained in the conservatory were dying from exposure. The snow was eight inches thick when he and Paul trudged over from the main building to check the temperature in the sealed conservatory building. "It isn't working," he said, looking at the withered, brown fronds of the compass palms. A few leaves fluttered from the frangipani tree, exposing the twisted lower branches, and he thought, "Even that old one's suffering." To Paul he said, "We can't just stand by and let these plants die. There must be some way to save them."

In their overcoats and winter hats the two men paced below the Culls' hiding place and silently Sherahi grasped the glimmerings of a plan. Even though she found Crotty's mind a green-tinged tangle of tendrils and suckers, with worry sprouting from odd corners like a leprous dead man's fingers, she concentrated all of her skill at mind control and willed the botanist to find a solution to his problem—a solution that would take the animals to Sandeagozu. She remembered that lush garden filled with animals and sent the image of warmth and sun and an even climate into the jungly overgrowth of Dr. Crotty's thoughts.

Sherahi watched him pace back and forth along the path below, clucking and exclaiming over frost damage to his specimens. "Come on," she thought. "Make a decision." Relying upon the mental skills she had practiced on Sorensen, Sherahi concentrated all of her mental powers and said desperately into Dr. Crotty's mind, "These plants are dying. Do something."

Finally, Dr. Crotty began to speak. "These plants are dying," he said. "We must do something. If only someone would take them off our hands. We can't just let them freeze—they're a part of New York history. Some of them have been here since the turn of the century. I grew that *Ficus annularia* from a seedling presented to the Society by the Raja of Banjitpur and this lovely old *Auracaria* was given to Gentleman Jimmy Walker by the King of Siam. These plants are history. It's criminal to let them die.

"If only someone would give them a good home, I'd be willing to sell them—even give them away."

The old botanist sighed as he looked at the shriveled cacti, at the film of ice that skinned the drained lotus pool. "Paul," he said, "we can't wait any longer. Get on the telephone, and tell the newspapers that we will give these plants to whoever will bring a truck and a work crew to haul them away to someplace warm. As a matter of fact, call the West Coast papers. Tell them that the new owner will be expected to make his own arrangements for moving the plants and will have to make a donation to the Society."

"But, Dr. Crotty," said the assistant, "the Board of Governors won't be happy when they find out that we've sold part of the collection. You know how touchy they are about publicity."

"I don't care. If they're so concerned, they could have come up with a new boiler for this place, instead of going off to Boca Raton and Hobe Sound and Havana to even their tans and play golf. I'm in charge and I'm not going to stand by and watch these wonderful old specimens die of exposure just because we haven't the money to replace Birger Sorensen, God rest his soul. If the Society doesn't like it," said the white-haired man, wrapping his scarf tighter around his neck, "then they can find someone else to manage this place. I want these plants on their way to someplace warm within a week."

Dr. Crotty's scheme worked. In a few days trucks and a crew of men arrived to begin the removal of the large plants that remained in the conservatory. The Los Angeles financier who would be their new owner had made a fortune in the stock market and gotten out before the Crash. He now was retired on the West Coast and was adding the finishing touches to the grotto that formed a backdrop to his indoor swimming pool.

One of the friendlier trustees had called him from Hobe Sound and explained the problem that the Society was having with these special, large trees.

"Just the thing I need," the financier had said as he watched one of his guests leap off the diving board into the pool. "It is a bit empty in here. Besides, trees with a bit of history will add a certain special—*je ne sais quoi*—to the place, don't you think?

"I'll have my men take care of everything. Glad you told me about it, Dudley.

"Yes, they'll be there before the week is out. And, do tell Charlesworth just exactly how much the Society will think is right. Wouldn't want to take advantage. You understand, Dudley?"

The gardeners from the West Coast arrived at the end of the week and carefully uprooted and packed the remaining trees and plants into five specially heated trucks. Soon the frangipani tree stood alone in the derelict conservatory. Even though the workmen knew it would be easy to uproot, they had avoided it. There always seemed to be other plants that would fit into the truck better than it.

"That'll be the last one," the foreman thought as he looked at the tree. "We'll dig it out tomorrow and then the last driver can set off across country."

When the workmen had left for the night, Sherahi sent Dervish and Junior to investigate the truck. They found it parked outside and reported that it was warm inside. Better yet, the door was ajar and the Culls could easily get inside.

"Good," said Sherahi as she laboriously unwound her coils from the frangipani branches. The cold had penetrated her muscles and joints and each movement was a struggle. "Now listen, each of you," she said into the minds of the other Culls. "We're going into that truck to hide. Those plants are going west and that's where Sandeagozu is. Some way—don't ask me how—frankly, I don't know just yet, but somehow we're going to get there."

"But what'll we eat?" asked Dervish.

"We'll have to go without," said Sherahi. "And take a long drink, because there won't any water for a while, either."

Sherahi suspected that it might be colder in the back of the truck than in the conservatory and so decided to wait until the last minute to join Manu, Dervish, and Junior around his neck, in their hiding places beneath the leaves of the last truckload of plants.

"Aren't you coming, Sherahi?" Dervish chittered as he leaped up onto the apron of the truck. "It's going to be morning soon. The men will be coming."

"Yes, Dervish, I'm coming," Sherahi answered. "But not just yet." For some reason she didn't fancy being shut up inside the truck until the last moment. Through Junior's eyes Sherahi watched Manu and Dervish shiver as they sniffed the corners of the plant-filled truck. Soon she saw only the truck door that was slightly ajar and she saw Dervish's breath steam in the chill air. "It's much warmer in here than out there," Sherahi thought. "I'll wait a while. No use getting cold until I have to." She heard Dervish chitter to Manu and grew sleepy as their conversation tapered off into occasional murmurs.

The next thing Sherahi heard was a sharp clatter. "What was that?" she wondered and lifted her huge head off her coils to peer down to the floor of the empty conservatory. She saw two workmen standing below the frangipani tree. Four shovels lay on the brick walk that wound through the conservatory and Sherahi saw that the men had just deposited their tools. "It's morning," she thought. "They've come to take this tree."

"Where is Mahoney with the coffee?" one man said to the other. "I want to get on the road before traffic gets heavy. That guy is always late. I'm going to see if he's coming." He walked across the empty conservatory and Sherahi saw him open the far door and leave.

"I've got to get into the truck," Sherahi thought in panic. "I'll have to go now. Maybe he won't notice me."

Sherahi was halfway down the trunk of the tree when the swaying movement of her big head and neck caught the attention of the workman who sat on an upturned crate nearby.

"Toadslime," Sherahi cursed as she saw him freeze and then turn white with fear. Sherahi continued to uncoil from the tree, keeping her eyes on his. "I must not show fear," she thought.

"Holy shit," the workman muttered as he watched the yards of snake coming toward him. He thought of running way, but knew that it could run faster than he could. "There's only one thing to do," he thought and slowly got up off the crate and began to slowly reach for the shovel that lay three feet away. "Don't do anything fast," he said to himself. "Don't want to make that thing attack."

Sherahi scryed his mind and saw what the man planned to do with the shovel. She held onto the upper branches of the frangipani tree with her hind coils and concentrated. "There isn't much time," she thought. "This'll have to be quick." Her mind whipped through his, erasing the fears and thoughts of a giant snake that were uppermost in his mind. She ignored the lower layers of thoughts that had to do with snakes. They would take longer to expunge. Her amber gaze locked with his and she intoned hypnotically in his mind, "There is no snake here. You do not see a snake. You have never seen a snake today. Snakes do not grow this big. You are imagining things. There is no snake here."

She saw the man drop the shovel back onto the brick walk and sit down again on the upturned crate. "You do not see me," Sherahi continued to intone as she slithered across the floor of the empty conservatory. "You have never seen me. You have imagined this." As quickly as she could, she found the door near where the truck was parked. Still keeping most of her attention locked around the man's mind she opened the door with her prehensile tail and hissed to Junior. "Is it safe?"

The cascabel replied in an excited bolt of mindspeech. "Hurry, Sherahi. No humans are here," the little cascabel hissed.

Sherahi lifted her regal head, towering above the man who sat with his chin in his hands, staring at her, his face drained of color. "You are tired now," she said calmly. "Your friends will not be back for a while. Go to sleep. Have a nap." She saw the man's eyes close and took one last look in his mind. Although the rest was the typical jumbled maze of miscellaneous thoughts, the portion that had held thoughts about her was as clear as a windswept beach. Sherahi saw that the man was really asleep and smiled in her inscrutable fashion and lowered her head and neck and crawled out of the conservatory into the waiting truck.

The other men arrived at the conservatory in half an hour. "Have a nice nap, Santucci?"

"Yeah, you guys took your sweet time getting the coffee," the man replied, standing up and stretching. "I should nap more often. I feel great."

Later that morning the crew dug up the frangipani tree, wrapped its soil-covered roots with burlap and carted it into the rear of the remaining plant-filled truck. Carefully, they laid it on its side and roped it down.

The driver closed and locked the rear door and set the thermostat for seventy-five degrees. Soon he was driving past the wrought-iron gates of Fort Washington Park, heading west toward Pennsylvania.

From their hiding places within the truck the Culls felt the truck sway and lurch around them. "Get some sleep," Sherahi said to the others. "I'll take the first watch and will wake you if anything happens."

It grew comfortably warm in the truck and Sherahi smiled to herself in the darkness. Although she didn't really want to, she thanked the white crocodiles for the unexpected gift they had given her.

Even though she'd admonished them to rest and had volunteered to take the first watch, Sherahi was not surprised to find that Manu, Dervish and Junior were too nervous to sleep. The first hour of their journey passed in tense silence, each animal starting at the unfamiliar noises of the moving truck, afraid that the wide back door would be suddenly thrown open and they would be discovered. When Junior explained that the truck could be opened only when it was still, the two mammals were somewhat relieved and began to make themselves more comfortable on the uprooted trees. Manu pulled burlap coverings from the balls of soil that protected the roots and bunched them into a padded nest that insulated him from the vibrations of the truck's floor. Dervish followed his example and soon the two were more comfortably arranged in the hollows between root balls and waving branches.

But they were still edgy. Dervish chittered to Junior in the dark, requesting that the rattler scry the driver's mind. "Tell us what he sees," pleaded the coati. "It's too dark in here. I had enough of that when we were cooped up in the tunnels of the fire serpents and with the white crocodiles. Please, Junior, look into his mind and tell us what's going on outside."

"Is that all right with you, Pythoness?" Junior asked.

"It's fine," replied Sherahi in silent, reptilian mindspeech. "I had hoped they would fall asleep, but, until they can, it would be kind of you to show them what's outside. And since the three of you are so wide-awake, I'll rest instead. Wake me when you get tired."

For a while Sherahi listened to Junior's sibilant hiss describe the view of the road as seen through the driver's eyes. He noted houses and signs, farms and cow pastures, laundry flapping stiffly in a backyard, fields of stubble covered with thin, drifted snow, a cock pheasant poised at the edge of a fence row. He described the inside of the cab of the truck and recited the thoughts that ran on the surface of the driver's mind, thoughts that skittered over the man's consciousness but did not register—just as a water strider's splayed pair of legs dimple but do not penetrate the elastic film that separates air and water.

Junior's voice rasped, " 'EATS,' 'Philadelphia 150, Baltimore 325,' 'Coca-Cola—the Pause that Refreshes,' 'I'd Walk a Mile for a Camel,' 'HE HAD THE RING' . . . 'HE HAD THE FLAT' . . . 'BUT SHE FELT HIS CHIN' . . . 'AND THAT' . . . 'WAS THAT' . . . 'BURMA SHAVE.' "

There was a silence and Dervish's sleepy voice asked, "What's a Burma Shave, Manu?"

"How should I know?" replied the langur. "Ask Sherahi. She's the authority on humans, not me."

"Don't bother her right now, Dervish," Junior interjected. "She's tired. I don't know what a Burma is, but I can tell you what a shave is. I saw it in the driver's mind." He explained the human custom of shaving to the two mammals, who were amazed that a human male would cut off a portion of his facial fur every day.

At the edge of sleep, Sherahi smiled. She hadn't realized how much Junior's mental abilities had grown. "Shave," she thought, "it is a strange idea. I didn't know what that word meant. But then, so much about the hairy bipeds is irrational—even perverse."

She found that she, too, was curious about this custom of shaving and, since Manu expected her to know everything, she decided to learn more. "I have my reputation to protect," she thought. Languidly the serpent ransacked the driver's mind, slithering through his rags of thoughts and crumbs of ideas until she saw the idea of shaving half hidden by the smell of bay rum. The idea of shaving was coupled with the impression of a bright spot of light above the washstand mirror and the memory of his father's shaving brush. Sherahi saw that the worn hog bristles were tinged with green where they fitted into the wooden handle. She heard the soft, slopping sound of the driver's father mixing lather in his shaving cup and through four-year-old eyes saw a tall man looking at his reflection in the mirror. To her surprise Sherahi saw the driver stroke his chin in exactly the same way that his father had so many years before. The two-day-old stubble rasped against his fingertips. She felt the raw spot where his razor always cut too close and realized that he was pleased not to have to shave for the next five days—the length of time it would take to drive to the West Coast.

The number "five" had little meaning for Sherahi, but she stored the information, thinking, "I'll tell Manu later. He'll know what it means."

His dislike of shaving was uppermost in the driver's mind as he began to unwind a memory of an especially bad cut that he'd once given himself. Water-thinned blood coursed down his cheek and dripped onto the white porcelain sink below, turning islands of shaving cream pink. He cursed as he cut himself a second time and grew nauseated from the sight of blood spilling from the second wound.

"That's odd," thought Sherahi. "Humans should be used to the sight of blood. In comparison with other creatures, their lives are drenched in it. They're born in blood. They eat other creatures. They reek of it. Yet this man feels sick when he sees his own. You'd think that humans would be tougher than that."

Sherahi was nearly asleep. The truck wheels drummed dully against the highway. The truck vibrated with a hypnotic roar that lulled her into a trance. She saw thick drops of blood puddling on the washstand and thought, "Bloody—they're covered in blood." She felt the thought coalescing into a pinpoint of consciousness. Very small and faraway she heard herself repeating the words and too late realized that it was the name of the one whom U Vayu had called the greatest and most powerful of all the serpent nats: Quetzalcoatl, the Bloody One. U Vayu had cautioned her against approaching him with anything except the greatest care, but that warning was forgotten as the pythoness's thoughts arced out of the westward-traveling truck and sought the mind of the Bloody One.

Moments later the drumming roar of truck wheels had vanished and Sherahi found herself gazing up at a star-filled sky. Smooth stones radiated a cozy warmth into her belly scales. She stretched to her full length, luxuriating in the heat that invigorated her and made her mind and body work faster than normal. She raised her head and rapidly flicked her tongue into the night air, fnasting her surroundings, looking for something familiar.

"Where can I be?" she wondered. "What is this place?" She remembered the other times that she'd talked with serpent nats. The Worm Oroborous had wanted to consume her; Lachesis had shriveled to insignificance. "I must be careful," she thought. "Serpent nats aren't anything like U Vayu described. He said that the Bloody One is the most dangerous and even though he was wrong about the others, I'll still have to be on guard. Manu and Dervish are depending upon me. Junior could probably get them to Sandeagozu, but he's so hotheaded. I'm not sure what he'd do if he got angry at them. Besides, I'd like to see if there are any male pythons at Sandeagozu. Spring is coming and it would be nice to have some little ones. Sooner or later I must perpetuate my line or . . ."

The moon slid from beneath a scarf of trailing clouds and Sherahi saw that she lay in a plaza within the shadow cast by a pyramid that was so tall that, even though she reared up a third of her body length, she could not see its pointed top. The pyramid blocked the sky and a wide stairway seemed to stretch up to the stars. "Should I climb up there?" she wondered. "It's awfully high. If Quetzalcoatl isn't there, it'll take hours to get back down. . . ." Instead, she decided to explore the plaza and slithered around the corner. A second flight of stairs stretched up to the sky and at the foot of the stairway was the head of an enormous serpent. Sherahi immediately sent her mind toward it, thinking, "This must be him. Quetzalcoatl."

A moment later she was embarrassed to find that she had been trying to communicate with a limestone carving. In her confusion Sherahi hurried forward and found that the heads of two enormous serpents guarded the pyramid. Their mouths gaped and their fangs were erect. "They look exactly like Junior would if he had a plumed headdress," Sherahi thought. "At least they can't hurt me," she thought and with her mind sheathed in layers of protection, she slithered over for a closer look.

Enormous though she was, Sherahi could have coiled comfortably within the maw of one of these serpents. She watched the shadows and moonlight engrave imbricate scales upon their stone snouts and temples. She examined the empty sockets beneath their hooded brows and called, "Quetzalcoatl," in the politest reptilian mindspeech that she knew. The open-mouthed serpents were silent. Their eyes were lifeless. Sherahi saw that someone had battered their snouts, leaving blunted stumps where there should have been scimitarlike fangs.

"If the Bloody One is here," she thought, "I won't learn about it from these two."

Sherahi had returned to her explorations, wishing that the moon would rise above the clouds that obscured it, when she fnasted a draft of cold air. It came from an opening in the pyramid behind the yawning serpent heads. Without being told, Sherahi knew that this was the way to the Bloody One. She slithered cautiously into the darkness, wishing that her infrared sensors worked more efficiently on cold-blooded vertebrates. "That's what comes of specializing in killing mammals," she thought and trained all of her mental powers upon whatever might lie within the pyramid.

The space inside smelled of an amalgam of damp earth, human urine, rodents and bat droppings. Sherahi fnasted bats flitting in the gloom above her head and thought about scrying their little minds for information, but they had darted out of the doorway before she could contact them. "Careful," she said to herself, somehow feeling that she was about to enter a trap. There was a flash of light behind her and she hissed and whirled, but the light was gone and she saw nothing. She moved back to the doorway and peered out. The paved plaza was white in the light of the full moon. "Maybe it was just heat lightning," the serpent thought.

She turned back toward the corridor that paralleled the face of the pyramid, lifted her head and inflated her neck, wanting to appear as formidable as possible to the serpent nat. Holding her head level and continuously sampling with her split tongue, Sherahi slithered over smooth blocks of stone and into the blackness. The corridor turned right at the corner of the pyramid. Sherahi detected the difference in air flow and moved along the second side of the pyramid. She tried to keep her mind open and receptive for any signal from the Bloody One, but heard nothing from deeper within the ancient structure. Cool air rushed up toward the apex of the inner pyramid and her labial pits detected another solid wall as the corridor made a second right turn. Sherahi slithered along in the dark and knew that she was now traveling parallel to the passage that lay behind the stone serpent heads.

The light from the arched doorway had long since disappeared and the corridor was utterly black. "Quetzalcoatl," she called impatiently, only half-expecting an answer. "Where is Quetzalcoatl? Where is Kukulcan, the Feathered Serpent, the mightiest of all serpent nats? Why does he hide from his small, helpless cousin Sherahi?"

The pythoness held her breath and waited, but no answer came from the depths of the pyramid. She repeated her question, using the archaic phrases and formal greetings of the reptilian mindspeech that U Vayu had taught her, but still no answer came. She thought of returning to the body that lay in the truck traveling toward Sandeagozu and attributing this failure to another of U Vayu's fabrications when the black corridor was gashed by light. With her pupils closed against the sudden brilliance she saw the sign that she'd hoped for: reflected upon the stone wall of the inner pyramid were seven triangles that formed a huge but unmistakable serpentine shape. The triangles of light and shadow began high on the inner wall and undulated down to where Sherahi crouched. The light serpent moved upon the stone wall and as it came close she ducked out of its path and hissed. A wheezy cackle echoed up the hollow pyramid and faded against the pointed ceiling. Sherahi recognized the laugh of an ancient serpent—a souvenir of those first days when serpents still had the gift of audible speech. She heard the slither of scales upon stone and the voice laughed again and commanded, "Come down, little serpent. Follow if you can."

Then the image of the serpent of light faded. Sherahi peered up at the wall of the outer pyramid and saw that the moon had moved from the zenith. "That was only a trick—just moonlight shining through openings in the staircase," she thought. Then the trailing clouds enveloped the moon and Sherahi was left in the dark again. She knew that she had been summoned by someone out of the ordinary and checked and readjusted her mental defenses. As she did so she realized that this was probably an unnecessary precaution. "If he's as omnipotent as they say, I'll never be able to match wits with him. I can only hope he's kind as well as powerful."

Then she concentrated on the serpentine cackle that had summoned her and linked the words "Come down" with "Bloody One." "U Vayu would be proud of me," she thought as his method for forging a mental link that would draw her inwitting mind to the source of power began to work. Sherahi whirled into the vortex of a black pool and lost conscious control as lightless waters closed over her head. The power drew her below the stone foundation of the inner pyramid, past the scores of sacrificial victims whose grinning skulls guarded its foundation, down into an unknown realm.

Sherahi awoke to utter blackness. Cold crosscurrents of sea water gripped her from all sides. The pressure on her ribs and skull was unbearable and for a moment she forgot that her actual body was in a truck on a highway traveling west to Sandeagozu. "Don't be silly," she told herself. "This isn't real. The skin and flesh of a mental projection cannot register pain or discomfort—just like a severed tail cannot be pinched. If I concentrate I can ignore it all." With all the skill that U Vayu had given her, the pythoness denied the cold and pressure. Slowly, the weight lifted from the length of her rib cage and the sensation of numbing cold subsided.

"That's better," she sighed. "Now, if only I had some light I might be able to see where I am. This is the blackest place—even the sewers had more light than this."

Sherahi felt something brush against her and as if wishing had made it so, the water about her was suddenly filled with sparks of light. Wincing against the sudden brightness she found that she was in the midst of a cloud of phosphorescent particles that churned and eddied, expanding outward until they disappeared like sparks arcing from a spent skyrocket. By the light of this transient cloud Sherahi saw that the water was filled with spidery shadows that chased one another. At first she thought they might be playing, but as Sherahi watched she saw that if this was a game, it was a serious one, indeed.

The creatures that darted away from the phosphorescence they created were vermilion-colored prawns whose long antennae groped delicately in the darkness. Sherahi saw that a few of the nervous creatures were trapped within the cloud and seemed momentarily blinded. Others fled into the protective surrounding blackness, leaving a luminous wake to confuse whatever had frightened them. Sherahi was reminded of the way that many serpents extruded foul-smelling musk to distract predators at close range. "They can't have been frightened by me," she thought. "Something dangerous must be coming."

A school of small, silvery fishes flashed into the phosphorescent cloud. "Strange," thought Sherahi, "they've got too many teeth to fit into their mouths." The fishes had holes in their cheeks where their teeth protruded. They had enormous eyes, and rows of paired spots glowed on their fins, casting a greenish light into the water below. From a distance they looked like moving constellations, while up close they were mobile, slash-toothed mouths that restlessly patrolled the inky waters, driven by their hunger.

The saucer-eyed predators darted at the retreating crustaceans, pulling them into the cloud of light. Two or three would converge upon a prawn. Simultaneously their extensible jaws wrenched whatever flesh they could from the struggling, segmented creature. The phosphorescent cloud that had been intended to confuse predators was soon filled with bits of bright-red carapaces and broken antennae, which the fishes spat out before turning to attack again. Sherahi watched the detritus. It drifted out of sight, falling farther into the abyss.

"Something even worse than these fishes is coming," Sherahi thought as she saw two oval spots of light swoop out of the distant black. The headlights were followed by rows of luminous spots that shed a hot-orange glow into the water, but the outline of the creature's body was invisible. It had entered the phosphorescent cloud and was striking left and right, stabbing and engulfing prawns before Sherahi had time to collect her wits. Lured by the lighted feast spread at the bottom of the sea, the eel-like creature wriggled, frantic to get its share. It swam with jaw agape, displaying row upon row of grotesquely elongate fangs.

The silvery predators saw the newcomer. Simultaneously they extinguished their lights and darted away. Sherahi watched the nightmare fish turn upon his prey. With his jaws shut, long, white teeth overlapped on its upper and lower lips and contrasted with his pitch-black skin. With a shiver of recognition Sherahi thought, "Junior would look like that if he couldn't fold his fangs against the roof of his mouth." The viperfish paused a moment, alone in the swirling phosphorescent cloud. Then he darted to one side and snapped at the tails of the fleeing fishes. When he failed to catch any of them he turned his attention to the much slower prawns. Hoping to blind or distract him, the prawns spewed out fresh clouds of phosphorescence and darted away. Sherahi saw the viperfish snag and impale three prawns. It hardly paused to swallow them before striking again. More often than not its jaws closed on empty water. As it expelled undigestible bits of shell a second, larger viperfish dashed up and there was an open-mouthed confrontation in the midst of the phosphorescent cloud before the two murderers wheeled to pursue their terrified victims.

Seconds later the light-bearing creatures were gone and the astonished pythoness was alone on the sea floor, with the phosphorescent spoor fading in the black water all around her. Sherahi watched the lighted carnage retreat into the distance and felt compelled to follow. She knew that this slaughter had been sent to guide her to the Bloody One.

As Sherahi swam through the abyss with her mind fastened upon Quetzalcoatl, she found that she could control the luminous emissions of the vermilion prawns by merely thinking about light. "All I have to do is wish for light," she thought, "and they spew it out. But it costs some of them their lives." The hungry-eyed silver predators and grotesque viperfishes were never far behind. They fell upon the prawns so voraciously that Sherahi felt the grip of the Bloody One in this weird realm. She remembered the tales of the human sacrifices that he had demanded. Floods of human blood would gush down his steep-sided pyramids as hearts were torn from the chests of his victims. His priests were spattered with gouts of blood. They were never able to clean it from beneath their fingernails. Surely the slaughter in the water all around her was a sign that the serpent nat beckoned to her.

Sherahi began to feel sorry for the prawns and forced herself not to think about how dark the water was. Their luminous emissions faded. As her vision readapted to the abyssal blackness she saw that hordes of even more ghoulish fishes also chased the prawns. These strange forms hovered at a respectful distance from the viperfish but they also were marked with constellations of luminous markings. From their emaciated bodies and huge mouths equipped with oversize teeth she knew that they roamed the depths with a hunger for flesh that was seldom satisfied. They were gulper eels, who could engulf prey five times their size. Their distensible bellies shivered flaccidly as they attacked the other fishes drawn to the swarm of prawns. Shy but deadly wallflowers, lantern fish cruised the fringes of the deep-sea assemblage. Luminous lures dangled innocently above their black jaws. Curious fishes would approach these lights to investigate and the mouths of the lantern fishes would suddenly open, drawing the luckless smaller fishes between sharp, pitiless teeth. Snipe eels, with jaws like elongated pincers, slithered through the darkness, hoping to spear a few of the silvery hatchet fishes that lit the water about them just enough to keep their school intact. The wary hatchet fishes knew the danger of the lights they carried. Each school would simultaneously extinguish all lights and scatter when one of its implacable predators approached.

The most efficient hunters seemed to be the luminous squid, who traveled in packs. Sherahi was amazed to see that, unlike the viperfish, gulper eels, lantern fish and snipe eels, the squid never bothered to extinguish the batteries of lights that spangled their pale tentacles. Unlike the other dwellers in the deep they seemed to disregard the protection of darkness and flaunted their phosphorescence, completely unafraid of attracting the attention of larger predators. Sherahi was reminded of the poison frogs who wore gaudy colors and stalked the rain forest floor in the daytime, relying upon their bright pigments to remind all that they had a deadly poison in their skin. Merely touching these fearless frogs could be fatal.

"Can squid be poisonous, too?" Sherahi could see no other evidence of the kind of warning coloration that was used on land. "Either the rules of the sunlit world don't apply here, or else the squid are relying upon their numbers for protection," she decided as she saw three of the big-eyed, tentacled creatures corner a bright-red prawn. Signals that Sherahi didn't completely understand were exchanged by the squid, and the prawn was awarded to one of the hunters. Soon all but the tail had disappeared into the maw of the squid. Even as two of its tentacles held the struggling prawn, its free arms groped for another victim and it followed the pack of luminous, deep-sea arrows, helping to subdue another mouthful.

More than once Sherahi wanted to turn away from the scene of carnage but didn't have any idea of where to go to find the Bloody One. The water before her was filled with sudden shrieks as prawns were dismembered, and clouds of silvery scales glistened as they fluttered out of sight. The bottom of the ocean was a dark, lonely plain that rolled endlessly about ten feet below where Sherahi swam. She did have occasional glimpses of scuttling movements as she moved along. These welcome glimpses helped Sherahi to orient herself in this cold, dark wilderness in which there seemed to be no up or down and no horizons. In forcing the sensation of pressure from her mind, she had lost the reassuring tug of gravity, and the bottom of the ocean was so monotonous and sterile that Sherahi imagined that it might stretch ahead forever. She concluded that few creatures could inhabit it and was surprised to see the familiar, dark plain precipitously fall away.

Sherahi felt as if she were soaring over the edge of a deep canyon. A momentary sense of panic and vertigo seized her. Far below was a bizarre, otherworldly scene: shells of huge clams littered the canyon floor. They glowed with an inner phosphorescence. The clams looked as if they might have been boulders tumbled beneath a wild river. She saw movements in and around them and, looking closer, saw that olive-green crabs scuttled busily about, removing and eating detritus that fell from above. The clams opened to admit the cleaner crabs and Sherahi saw that the flesh inside their glowing shells was blood-red. Stranger still, the clams were on the periphery of a waving forest of algae that was arranged about a plume of dark-colored water that spewed turbulently from the ocean floor. Sherahi floated above this algae and saw that each frond was a white tube capped with a pair of blood-red, fleshy lips. The long, white fronds danced violently, whipped by the invisible current that flowed from the crack in the ocean floor.

Sherahi was eager to abandon the parade of murderers and victims that had led her to this place and she angled down toward the luminous clam bed, which washed the canyon walls with an eerie but welcome light. As she swam down Sherahi felt the water grow faintly warmer. When she remembered the parade of creatures that had led her here she looked behind to see a host of orange, chartreuse and lavender lights wink from the rim of the canyon. She saw that the prawns, viperfish, lantern fish and gulper eels had not followed, and the water above the canyon rim was as black as the bowels of a cave. One by one the lights of the fishes who hovered at the rim were extinguished and Sherahi turned her attention to the world below.

"He's here," she thought. "I feel it." She paused to readjust the mental screens that might protect her if Quetzalcoatl proved to be as deadly as the other serpent nats she had encountered. Sherahi took a more careful look at the crabs that tended the glowing clams and noticed that they had no eyes. It suddenly occurred to her that if the blood-red clams were like others of their kind, they were also blind. "I'm alone at the bottom of the sea," she thought. "If Quetzalcoatl traps my mind, no one will see or remember what happens. There's no one to turn to. If I don't get back, will Junior understand? Can he get Manu and Dervish to Sandeagozu?"

For the first time since U Vayu had taught her how to use her special pythonine senses to conquer space and time, Sherahi the pythoness was frightened of making a fatal mistake. Until this point inwitting had been a game for Sherahi—a special pleasure because it was a gift granted only to pythons and even more so because very few pythons had mental abilities that could match hers. Until now she'd thought that this gave her a kind of protection—an immunity similar to that which king cobras have to the venom of the vipers they feed upon. For the first time Sherahi realized that she might be as insignificant and dispensable as those vermilion prawns had been. The Bloody One had sacrificed scores of them merely to bring her to this place. For the first time it occurred to Sherahi that she might not live forever.

"I could go back right now," she thought. "It would be easy to return to the truck. The others would never know that I almost saw Quetzalcoatl. I don't have to lie; I don't even have to mention it. No one knows that I've even tried to come here.

"Yes," she thought as she watched the dark plume of mineral-laden water shower crystals into the cold, deep-sea water, "it would be safer to go back before I get into trouble." The crystals winked mockingly from the floor about the crack in the sea floor and Sherahi decided that she could not turn back now.

"If I did the safe thing, I'd never be able to ask Quetzalcoatl for advice. If I lose this opportunity to understand humans, I may never get another. How will I be able to guide the others to Sandeagozu if I don't understand why humans act so strangely and why they hate us so much? Besides, maybe Quetzalcoatl will be able to help us get across those mountains."

The serpent looked down at the white fronds of algae and decided, "I must speak to him. The others would be disappointed. They expect me to know everything. They must never know the truth."

Sherahi willed herself not to think about what might happen to her if the Bloody One trapped her, as the Worm Oroborous had tried to. She swam past the waving tubes of algae to the place where the superheated water met the frigid depths. She peered past the crystalline coating that frosted the opening in the sea floor, down into the furnace of liquid rock. Sherahi knew that high temperatures could not harm her materialization, yet she was cautious about entering the plume of boiling water. She was even less eager to seek Quetzalcoatl if he were lurking there, below the crust of the earth.

"Even if he is immortal, can he live in that?" she wondered as the bloodshot eye of the undersea volcano glared at her, sending a fresh spume hissing up to solidify, inches from her snout. A shower of clear, minute hexagonal crystals rained back to the sea floor and Sherahi called, "Quetzalcoatl?" in the boldest mindspeech she could manage.

Within her mind a withered voice croaked, "No, Sherahi. Don't parboil yourself in that chimney. Come here."

She looked around and saw the white tubes of algae wildly waving once more. Relieved that the Bloody One's lair wasn't within that seething mass of liquid rock, Sherahi swam back to the fronds of algae. She saw that each plant was tubular and firmly attached to the ocean floor. The fronds were of different lengths, but most of them were as long as or longer than Sherahi's body and about as thick around. Alongside these cables she felt tiny—even delicate. More phosphorescent clams grew at their bases and the blind attendant crabs busied themselves, plucking off sediments that would eventually smother the clams if they were not removed. Remembering that the first serpent nat she had ever encountered had dwindled into an inchworm, Sherahi meticulously scryed the minds of the crabs and clams, but found no trace of Quetzalcoatl. As she did so the huge fronds of algae waved violently, even though Sherahi could detect no current.

"That's odd," she thought. "Plants can't move like that. They don't have muscles." She contemplated the waving tubes and suddenly it occurred to her, "They can't be plants. Plants can't live without light and even if the clams do glow it can't be enough light to keep plants alive."

"Plants," the withered voice mocked. "Don't let appearances fool you, young python. Things are seldom what they seem."

Sherahi was surprised. Of course U Vayu had taught her that plants had a kind of intelligent consciousness. But he had emphasized that it was so far removed from the higher form of reptilian thought that mental contact between plants and reptiles was impossible. Not wanting to appear incredulous and thus offend the Bloody One, she circled the waving fronds, keeping her mind clear and watching for some clue that would betray his hiding place. She saw that the free end of each frond parted into lips that looked like thick petals. Using all the power she could manage she carefully chose a single frond and scryed it, seeking signs of intelligence. The frond was as free of thought as a block of ice. "There's no mind here," she concluded. "Or at least not the kind I can understand. Where can he be?"

Hovering above the waving algae, Sherahi watched the fronds undulate. "Am I imagining it?" she wondered. "Or are they saying something with movement?"

"A serpent," the fronds seemed to mime. "How lovely. How perfectly lovely to see a creature from the old days. Oh, I do adore serpents. Lovely, slithery things, they've always been my favorites. Such an efficient form. So pretty. And so faithful. I remember that when I had to leave the upper world I wove a raft of serpents and they brought me here."

The voice sighed and continued, "I used to take any shape I wished. But now I'm reduced to appearing like this. No brain. No ears. No eyes. No mouth. Not even a gut. I can only eat by absorbing tiny plants through the skin of these petals. I, who invented coffee and chocolate for the people's enjoyment—I am forced to subsist on the bacteria that swarm in this hot water. Ironic isn't it, little serpent? That I, who taught humans how to till the soil; I, who taught them which plants were poisonous and which were good to eat; I, who once mastered the sunlit world, am reduced to this poor remnant—a form which cannot even see food.

"You wouldn't happen to have any chocolate with you, would you, small friend? I would so love just one taste. . . ." The voice creaked with longing, wheezed and was silent.

Sherahi realized that Quetzalcoatl, the mightiest of the serpent nats, had been reduced to this strange, half-plant, half-worm colony that grew in darkness at the bottom of the sea. Then the voice began again, more matter-of-factly this time.

"I mustn't think of such things. I would dearly love one tiny chocolate drop or just a glimpse of the sun, but at least I am free of him. He doesn't bother me anymore now that I have nothing he wants."

"Him?" Sherahi questioned.

"My brother. My twin. I was everyone's favorite, you see, and he was always envious. He did have some talents, though. He was clever and good with jokes. He could always remember punch lines, while I was hopeless at that. The people liked his buffoonery well enough, but then, you know how people are. But I was the one that they worshiped. I was the one that they loved. And, if I do say so myself, I was an awfully good god. I deserved their worship—every bit of it. I deserved those monumental pyramids they built to honor me. After all, I could do anything—anything at all. I taught those people how to make clothes. I healed their sicknesses. Pythoness, you don't know the number of oozing pustules and crooked limbs that I cured. I even made their crops grow. They were so ignorant when I came to them that they didn't even know what corn was. Imagine: they'd never ever heard of a tortilla before I taught them how to grind corn and use fire. I taught them how to weave cloth and make earrings for themselves from gold and silver, too. Yes, I was a good god.

"Now I have nothing. He tricked me into shaming myself. I could not abide the shame and guilt of what he made me do with our sister. He was so cunning, so hateful. It was the beginning of the end for me.

"If only I hadn't expected to be perfect, Pythoness. If only I'd been a little more humble, I might have been able to salvage something." The nat's voice was filled with remorse. He stifled a sob and the fronds ceased to make pictures before her fascinated eyes.

Sherahi sensed that he would continue his narrative and quietly watched the fronds, hoping that the flow of images and mindspeech would continue.

The nat's voice spoke again, thick with emotion. "And now he isn't content with merely shaming me into exile so that he can be a high god. Now he spreads lies about me. Lies that frighten people and make me into a blood-hungry monster. But really, Pythoness, I was good—I tried to help."

Sherahi was incredulous that the serpent nat could be so deluded. She thought, "He's lying. U Vayu told me not to trust anything a nat said. I know that Quetzalcoatl was a horrid god." She remembered stories of piles of corpses that had been mutilated for his pleasure. She had seen clots of blood dried in the hair of his priests. She made no reply, but the nimble mind of Quetzalcoatl had read her thoughts.

"I was not a horrid god," he insisted petulantly. "It was him—my evil brother. He did all those things after he'd started to impersonate me. We're identical, you know—only he's left-handed. He forced me down here in the dark. He always did bad things when we were children and blamed them on me. Now that the universe is older he still is the same. Oh, little Pythoness," the nat's voice implored, "beware of him. He is evil itself. And now that I have no power the sunlit world is in his lap. The left-handed twin rules the sunlit world now."

Once again, Sherahi hid her thoughts behind her mindscreens and didn't reply.

The nat seemed to tire of his reminiscences. "But that isn't why you've come, little serpent. Speak quickly. Ask your questions. I cannot sustain this for long. The cold robs me of energy."

Sherahi could find no central spot at which to direct her flow of mindspeech and sent it at the entire cluster of waving fronds. She began, "I need your help, Quetzalcoatl. I am trying to get to . . ."

The nat demanded, "Are you sure you don't have some chocolate or maybe even just a single coffee bean? You could grind it up and maybe I could taste it. It used to be so different in the old days. Petitioners would first make me an offering and then begin to ask their favors. They brought me lovely chocolate and cacao leaves and jaguar skins and green parrot feathers and maize flour and carvings and flowers, whole armloads of beautiful flowers."

Sherahi was embarrassed. "I . . . I'm sorry. I didn't know . . . I have nothing," she said lamely.

"Oh, well." The nat's voice was small and dejected. "I suppose that it's the thought that counts. But still, maybe sometime you could come back again with just a little chocolate?"

"I can't promise, but I'll try."

"Well, don't forget. Now begin again."

Sherahi began again. "There are four of us traveling together. There used to be five but . . ."

Quetzalcoatl suddenly interrupted, "Look at me, Pythoness. You're the first creature to visit me in centuries. Centuries—you can't imagine how starved I've been for company. I wish I had something to offer you to make you feel more at home, but in my circumstances—I'm sure you understand.

"Of course you don't know what I was before, but just look what he has done to me. I was so beautiful. I was the Lord of the Four Winds. They called me the Eastern Light, the Morning Star, the Precious, the Feathered Serpent. Now I'm not even as intelligent as a worm. And my power dwindles all the time. Five hundred years ago I could still see what was going on in the sunlit world. But even that little power has dwindled. Now I can only see what happens in this blackness. See what his jealousy has done.

"He wouldn't leave me with even one thing. If only I had my beautiful scaly, feathery body, or my exquisite turquoise mask. It was decorated with fistfuls of quetzal plumes. You should have seen those feathers. They were more brilliant than the wing covers of dung beetles."

The nat began to sniffle again. "In the end there was nothing left. Everyone died. Even my clever dwarves and the poor hunchbacks who used to amuse me with puppet shows—they all caught the coughing disease. They were so cold and so feverish at the end. I had been the greatest of all healers. For millennia I had eased the birthing pains of all women who called my name. But my poor dwarves and hunchbacks—I had no power to help them. Just my touch chilled them and brought on fits of coughing and convulsions. He'd taken away everything: my power, my honor—I had nothing.

"Only the serpents were faithful. They stayed with me as I buried the others and eventually they brought me here. It isn't so awful, I guess. I'm nothing like I was but at least I am close to our mother, the earth, and I can watch her continuously renew herself. This is all that's left." The fronds seemed to undulate toward the crack in the sea floor and reached to caress the hot eye below.

The voice was resentful. "I must be content with this while he lords and struts up there. He's so vicious. And humans listen to his still, small voice now. They have become his creatures. They follow his orders now."

"Is that why they hate me so much?" Sherahi asked, hoping to turn the nat's thoughts back to her questions.

"Of course it is, Pythoness. They hate you because he eggs them on to it. Even though he's taken everything that was mine and banished me, his lust has never been satisfied. He makes his human puppets hate you because you remind him of me—and he hates me more than anything. You're caught in the middle, Pythoness.

"Humans are literal-minded creatures. Their minds are quite different—wonderful in their own way, but set apart from those of the Elder Race. Since they cannot understand your mental powers, you bother them. He likes it that way. Whenever a serpent is killed, my wretched brother is pleased. Even down here I can feel his twinges of wicked pleasure.

"He's made them jealous of you. He's told them that serpents have a secret that they will not share. He's told them, 'Serpents never wrinkle.

They never look old. Yet, even an aged serpent can kill in the flash of an eye.'

"Humans are queer creatures. They live their lives with the thought of death always before them and they fear it more than anything. Although they cannot understand how, humans sense that serpents have mastered time and space. Thus, in one devious way or another, my left-handed twin brother has ensured that humans will eventually kill and exterminate all of you. It's just a matter of time.

"When I ruled the sunlit world it was different, but now that he is in command, you must steer clear of all humans. They mean you no good. Even the best human is dangerous, Pythoness."

Sherahi was about to ask the serpent nat how to cross the mountains safely when she felt something touch the body that was in the truck moving west with the rest of the Culls. With a brain-splitting wrench her mind was pulled up through the black, lifeless waters toward the surface of the ocean. As she departed she heard the nat's voice in her mind: "You and three others seek a safe haven. Only one of you will succeed. Beware, Pythoness. Humans are the creatures of the left-handed twin. They mean you no good."

Against her will Sherahi was pulled from the dispersed remnant of consciousness that was Quetzalcoatl, the greatest of serpent nats, and forced to return to her own body.

CHAPTER THIRTEEN

Southwestern Arizona

JUNIOR RATTLED a warning as Sherahi's consciousness funneled back into the massive, finely scaled body that lay within the truck among the uprooted trees. Withered leaves of the frangipani crackled as she stretched her thick, cramped coils. "Why is it so bright in here?" she thought, wincing at the swath of sunlight that cut into the rear of the truck. The light etched each round-headed rivet and threw the overlapped seams of the metal compartment of the truck into sharp relief. As usual when an inwitting session was interrupted, Sherahi was disoriented. For a moment she wondered, "Is that really sunlight, or does it only seem bright here because I've been on the bottom of the ocean for so long?"

She was about to send a mental question to Junior when the scales of her belly touched the metal floor of the truck. She recoiled like a cracked whip as the searing heat sent her slithering up to a cooler perch upon tree branches. "Something's wrong," she thought as her movements rustled sere leaves and tree limbs snapped beneath her weight. "These trees are nearly dead." She peered at the desiccated vegetation around her. "Everything was green and alive when I left. What's happened? How long have I been away?

"Junior? Manu? Dervish? Is anyone here?" Sherahi began to look for the other Culls and saw Manu's face lift from the tangle of roots that lay on the floor of the truck. With effort Manu squinted in the bright sun, making his good eye more of a match for the empty, twisted socket on the scarred, bright-pink side of his face. The blond fur that framed it was incandescent and glinted in the light, making him look like a monkey made of beaten brass. He licked his lips and Sherahi saw that they were parched and cracked. Suddenly she missed the constant drumming that the truck's wheels had made against the highway. She felt waves of heat entering the metal box and knew that the truck was broken down by the side of the road. "What's happened, Junior?" she asked and heard the rattlesnake's reply in mindspeech that was too rapid to be understood.

"He's been that way for a long time, Sherahi." With effort the old langur spoke into her mind. "He tried to do too much. I think that was the problem. When the truck stopped for a day and it got so hot, he brought the driver back and forced him to open the back of the truck. The driver's been gone for five days now. He was drunk when Junior brought him back here from that little town. I don't think he'll ever come again."

"Why didn't you fetch me when the truck broke down?" asked Sherahi.

"Junior wouldn't let us. He didn't want to bother you. He said that you were doing something very important and that he could take care of everything."

"Where is Dervish?"

"Somewhere—out there," said the langur, gesturing toward the brilliant sunlight. "When Junior didn't come back, he went to search for him."

"But Junior's here," said Sherahi. "I heard him rattle. I'm sure of it."

"Yes, he's here. He came back a little while ago. I touched you and fetched you back because he was behaving so strangely. He frightened me, Sherahi. He's not right. Look at what he's doing. You'll see what I mean."

Using the intimate mode of reptilian mindspeech, and a tone that she might have used with favorite hatchlings, Sherahi called to the young rattlesnake. "Junior," she said. "Where are you? Why are you hiding from me?"

A meaningless clot of mindspeech shot into her mind. It was rapid and indistinct. Pronunciations were blurred. Thoughts were broken. It was not the normal, elegant fabric of images or the bold pattern of ideas that usually zigzagged from Junior's mind to hers.

"I can't understand what you're saying, little serpent," she said. She scryed the cascabel's mind as he slithered restlessly on the floor of the truck. She saw that shapeless monsters lurked in the withered foliage, threatening him. He rattled warnings at dead leaves and struck at branches that were in his path, but the monsters still loomed above him and cackled wickedly.

"He's raving," thought Sherahi. "There's no time to lose. Junior," she said, "you must get off the floor. It's too hot. It's affecting your mind."

The cascabel seemed not to hear her. He continued to slither rapidly upon the hot metal, hissing at clumps of soil, cringing from shadows. Sherahi realized that he was hysterical and on the verge of heat prostration.

In the forbidding, hypnotic tone that could not be disobeyed, Sherahi commanded, "CLIMB, Junior. NOW. OBEY and CLIMB."

She saw the rattler stiffen as if in the grip of a convulsive fit. For a moment his tongue lolled out of his mouth—a lifeless, black string that clung briefly to his chin scales. Then she saw his deadly, lance-shaped head begin to lift and his body flowed upward. With movements that were faster than her eye could follow the feverish little snake with the zigzagged diamonds on his back climbed to the highest branches. There he restlessly lashed to and fro.

"What's wrong with him?" asked Manu. "Is there anything I can do?"

"There's nothing you can do, Manu. He's sick from the heat. I taught him other things, but I never taught him about it; there was never time. He didn't know that it can kill us."

"But I thought that serpents loved to be warm," said Manu.

"We do," answered Sherahi. "The problem is that we don't sense heat as quickly as other animals. Something that's very hot, like the floor of this truck or the sand outside, can burn us before we realize the danger.

"We of the Elder Race sense temperature with our minds. Our scales are as insensitive to heat or cold as your fur is, Manu. We have to wait until our brains notice the temperature difference in our blood. As you can see from Junior's behavior, if we aren't careful we can be hurt. I suppose it's the price we pay for our mental powers. But if we had heat receptors in our skins, as you do, we'd be a lot safer."

"But I just saw you avoid the hot metal floor a few moments ago. You knew that it was hot enough to burn you," said Manu.

"Only from experience, Manu. I've been burned—never as badly as Junior, but I remember how that felt."

Junior had suspended himself between two adjoining branches, holding on with curves of neck and tail muscles.

"Good, Junior. Now try to rest," Sherahi said in soothing mind-speech. "Let the air cool you." She kept a watchful eye on the rapid ticking of his heart as it pulsed against his wide belly scutes. After a while his superheated metabolism slowed very gradually and the feverish flicking of his tongue ceased. She saw that his heart was beating slowly, but regularly. Gently Sherahi said, "We live by different rules in a place like this, Junior. You must never go out into the sun like that again."

"But I only wanted to help," protested the cascabel in a voice that sounded like pebbles scraped against glass.

"I know that, and you have done very well. But it nearly killed you. How do you feel?"

"My skin hurts, Sherahi. I think I'm going to throw up."

Immediately Sherahi sent a balm into Junior's mind to numb his pain. She saw the burned nerve endings and scalded flesh of his belly and was pleased to see her anaesthetic begin to take effect. In a wintry tone designed to calm the cascabel she spoke into his mind: "The sun is not necessarily the friend of the Elder Race, Junior. In the desert it has no pity for us or for any creature. That wide expanse of sky holds many enemies, but the worst is the sun.

"Once you are feeling better you will hunt again, but you must remember that here every creature has his hour. Yours is at night. Haven't you noticed that your eyes work best in the dark? That your lip pits are more sensitive then? Your kind have always lived in places like this, Junior. But you must abide by the old rules. From now on you are a creature of the night who hides from the hot hours and comes out only after dark. Even then you must be careful. When you're feeling better I will teach you about owls and mussuranas. They prowl at night, too. But that's a different lesson, for another time.

"You must remember that, even after sunset, the sand and rock are sometimes hot enough to fry you before your brain realizes what has happened. To protect yourself you must learn to crawl in a different way. The humans call it sidewinding, but the Elder Race knows it as spiraling. I will show you how to do this later, when you are feeling better, but remember that spiraling will keep you off hot surfaces. That is the first rule of survival in the desert: stay out of the heat.

"Now you must rest. You will be happier in the desert than any of us, Junior, but you must learn to be patient and clever as well as brave."

"But, Sherahi," the cascabel said in a drowsy voice, "I don't want to wait until it's dark. I'm not afraid of a little sun. I've got to find Dervish. He's disappeared and it's my fault. You left me in charge of them. If I . . ."

"Stop, Junior," Sherahi commanded. "You did well to get us to this place and to force the driver to open the truck. If you hadn't done that, we'd all be dead by now. I haven't told the others yet, but Sandeagozu is only across those mountains on the horizon. I've been here before—in inwittings—and I'm sure of it. You did very well, indeed, Junior."

There was silence and Sherahi saw that her hypnotic control had finally conquered Junior's fevered brain. "Tonight we'll leave this truck and you can explore to your heart's content."

"Will I be able to spiral as well as you, Sherahi?" Junior asked sleepily.

"Better than me, Junior. Far better than I ever could. You'll be able to glide across the sand in a motion so beautiful, so intricate, that it will amaze everyone who sees your tracks." She sent a soothing image of the cascabel winding obliquely across a rippled dune, his sinuous scales and spiral tracks etched with starlight.

Sherahi and Manu were quiet, watching the cascabel's still body.

Manu broke the silence. "He'll be all right, won't he, Sherahi?"

"Yes. Eventually, he'll be fine. But he's burned his skin very badly. Look at how dull his belly plates are. They've lost their sheen already. They'll be blistered by tonight. He won't be able to crawl for a long time."

"Will it hurt?"

"Not if I can prevent it," said Sherahi. "I can't heal him by mind control, but I can make him comfortable. We'll have to carry him, though."

"I'll do that," said Manu. "He's been so good to us that, if Dervish doesn't return, it's the least I can do."

"Let's hope that isn't necessary," said Sherahi. "Now, how long has Dervish been gone?"

"Three nights and two days, Pythoness. I'm worried. Dervish doesn't know how to take care of himself in a desert any better than Junior does. I've had nightmares of his being chased by a spotted cat. I've seen him wandering alone, whimpering. He's full-grown, but he's such a baby. He could get bitten by something and die out there. . . ."

"Don't worry, Manu, he can't have gone far. I'll bring him back.

"Are you feeling well, Manu? Somehow you don't look right."

"I'm thirsty, Sherahi. Very thirsty."

Sherahi sent the image of a stream of cool water flowing down into Manu's mind. She saw it fool him into forgetting his parched throat. "To-night, Manu. We'll drink real water tonight." The langur nodded and bowed his head. "Dervish, Sherahi. You must find him."

Seeking the young coati, Sherahi flung her questing mind out of the truck that held a tangled cargo of withered trees. She saw the desolate highway baking in the sun and the mountains on the horizon, which she had seen so many times before. Sherahi realized exactly where the Culls were and thought, "If only we can get over those mountains."

"Dervish," Sherahi hissed in a voice that sounded like wind in cactus spines. "Come here. Come back to the truck."

She concentrated on Dervish's long-snouted face, with its twitching, ever-curious nose and white-ringed, shoe-button eyes. "Come here, Der-vish. Come back. We miss you. We're worried."

She heard a faint chirrup and followed it to its source, a debris-filled canyon beside a faintly trickling stream. She heard the coati's chirr again and noticed a suspicious-looking hole near the canyon's blind end. The en-trance led to a steep tunnel and down into a dim, shallow burrow. "I'm here, Sherahi," Dervish chittered. "I knew that you'd find me sooner or later."

"Come back, Dervish. Manu is sick with worry."

"No, Sherahi. Not now. It's too hot out. All sensible animals are hav-ing a siesta." Dervish yawned and continued, "Look for me when the stars are up.

"Tell Manu that I'm okay and that I've found a good hiding place for us. And if you promise that you won't tell Manu and spoil my surprise, I'll show you what else I've found."

"I promise," said Sherahi, wondering what trick Dervish had in mind.

"Look," he said, gesturing with his muzzle.

Sherahi's field of vision traveled down from his face, past his shoulder to his flank. Although she couldn't quite believe it, a smaller, unmistakably feminine version of Dervish lay curled up next to him. In the manner of infant squirrels clutching their mother's paws, she held one of Dervish's forefeet tucked firmly beneath her chin.

"Isn't she beautiful?" chittered Dervish softly. "And, Pythoness, she likes me. A lot. She's taught me all kinds of things—about scorpions and spiders and sunburn. . . . Did you know that a chulo like me can get sunburned? That's what we call ourselves—chulos. And hawks. I've learned all about them. She knows an awful lot, Sherahi. I'll tell you all about it tonight."

Without opening her eyes the female coati trilled something to Dervish and cuddled more closely.

"If you'll excuse me, Pythoness," Dervish whispered, "I'm going to go back to my nap." Dervish yawned and curled protectively around his companion, chirruping contentedly. "Nice things, naps," he whispered. "Don't tell Manu. He's going to be so surprised." Dervish tucked his long, banded tail protectively around his mate, closed his eyes and sighed in his underground burrow.

Hollywood, California

It was the premiere of Max Goldman's *Crown of Thorns* in Loew's Hollywood Palladium theater. Even though she'd seen daily rushes of herself and Thurston P. Topping, this was the first time Ruthie had seen the entire movie. "Thank God," she thought as the camera pulled back to show Golgotha and its three crosses silhouetted against a many-fingered sunset. "It's nearly over."

Ruthie was tired of sitting. Her garters bit into the backs of her thighs, the waist of her gold lamé gown was too tight and the theater was stuffy. Thurston P. Topping sat on her left. From the corner of her eye she caught the motion of his head as it drooped forward again and she suppressed a giggle. The idol of female moviegoers was infamous for his ability to catnap between takes, after lunch, during makeup and even in the midst of a party, but Ruthie was amazed that he'd doze at the premiere of the movie that was meant to be his comeback. "But then," she thought, "he probably doesn't care what happens now. He died in the last reel."

Ruthie hitched up one of the crystal-trimmed shoulder straps that continually threatened to slip and surreptitiously watched the drowsy bobbing of Topping's head. Just as his chin grazed his starched, white shirt-front Topping would rouse and lift his head groggily, like a swimmer emerging from a vat of molasses. He'd open his eyes very wide and Ruthie giggled soundlessly as she heard him whisper, "Stop it, Jenny," to the woman who sat on his other side.

"His wife's been poking him to keep him awake," thought Ruthie. "She knows how important this is to his career."

Finally the matinee idol straightened in his chair and coughed. He fished in his cummerbund pocket and Ruthie knew that he was looking for the packet of Sen-Sens that he always carried to mask the smell of alcohol on his breath. Months on the set had familiarized her with his habits and, as Topping methodically shook several of the minute, black breath sweeteners into his palm, Ruthie turned her attention back to the screen.

The odor of anise, which she always associated with her love scenes with Thurston P. Topping, enveloped Ruthie as she saw herself and Mae Burton, the woman who played Judah Ben-Salam's mother. Dressed in leper's rags they knelt at the foot of Jesus' cross. Scabrous leprosy spread like a white fungus across the older woman's mouth and her nose was partially eaten away. There were layers of gray makeup beneath her red-rimmed eyes and she looked like a corpse. With her eyes fixed on Christ, Mae lifted her bandaged hands in prayer. Ruthie remembered the endless pairs of argyle socks that Mae had knitted between takes, her bandages neatly pushed up and fluttering like the raveled sleeves of a worn sweater. Ruthie thought, "I wonder who's wearing those socks now?" Like all the featured players, Mae sat somewhere in the rear of the theater. Ruthie had caught a glimpse of her marcelled hair hours ago. She would have liked to be seated next to Mae. At least that would have been fun. The two had become friends during the filming of the movie, but at premieres all the seats were assigned by rank and billing. Only stars, critics, columnists and the studio brass were allowed to sit in the best seats—along the aisles in the middle of the orchestra.

The camera moved in for a close-up of Christ's bowed head. The crown of thorns bit deeply into his scalp, his hair hung in lank locks and gelatin blood dripped asymmetrically from one temple. "He looks awful," thought Ruthie, trying to remember his name.

The orchestra suddenly stopped playing the swirling background music and Ruthie heard people sniffling in the darkness all around her. On the screen the crucified actor's mouth opened, his eyelids drooped, the whites of his eyes were visible. With great effort he uttered his last line: "It . . . is . . . finished." The subtitle flashed on the screen as his head fell forward, like Thurston Topping finally succumbing to sleep. Ruthie wondered if the actor were unconsciously mimicking the star. A quick, sidelong glance told her that the actor was wide awake now. The Sen-Sens had worked their miracle. His pomaded hair gleamed in the light of the crucifixion. "Whatever else," thought Ruthie, "he's still got his looks."

On the screen Ruthie saw a quick cut to herself and Mae Burton. She remembered how many times this scene had been reshot. Max had demanded that they do it over and over. She could still hear his commands issuing from a cloud of cigar smoke. "No. That's not quite it. Again." Max had fired the director halfway through the movie and had taken on his duties. The cast had found him exacting and hard to please. "Almost but not quite," he would say. "Let's do it again."

Wrapped in towels, Ruthie and Mae would retire to their dressing rooms and an hour later they would be kneeling once more at the foot of the cross. Their retakes had all seemed virtually identical to Ruthie. She had never understood what finally had pleased Max, but had been grateful when it was over and he had said, "Good. That's a print."

On the screen Ruthie's left profile was lit by rapid flashes of light and washes of shadow as lightning clawed the sky behind the crucifix. The crescent patch of leprosy that the makeup man had applied from Ruthie's forehead to her chin was visible for the first time. Ruthie remembered its scaly, bubbly surface. Her counterpart on the screen was so grotesque that Ruthie wanted to look away; nevertheless she watched, as fascinated by her ugliness as a pinfeathered nestling hypnotized by a smooth-talking black mamba. Thunderheads darkened the sky, moving more rapidly than buzzards coming home to roost. Skirling violins, braying French horns and kettledrum thunder accompanied the deluge and tornado that whipped at Ruthie and Mae Burton as they clung to the foot of the cross. Ruthie had a firm grasp on the older woman, who seemed overcome by the furious elements. The earth groaned and opened, revealing grinning skeletons beneath Golgotha, and the rest of the crowd shrieked and scuttled away to cringe in the alleyways. Leaves and debris whirled past the two crouching women and papier-mâché rocks fell all around, but somehow they were unscathed. Braving the storm and earthquake, Ruthie lifted her head to meet the gaze of the dead Christ. Her hair was plastered prettily to her scalp, making her appear even more ethereal. A nimbus played about her head as her wide eyes mutely appealed to the Crucified One and the earth yawned open once more.

The camera was glued to her beatifically radiant face as scenes from the movie flashed in her memory: the chariot race, her snake dance, Jesus preaching on the shores of Galilee, the miracle of the loaves and fishes and, of course, close-ups of that miserable ham, Thurston Topping: his heroic profile and patent-leather hair made even more glamorous by soft focus. Then these celluloid recollections faded from the upper corner of the screen and, as the wind and rain relented, Ruthie turned to Mae Burton. She saw that the leprosy was gone from Mae's face, washed clean by the diluted blood of Christ. Unbelievingly she tore the bandages from the older woman's fingers to see them whole and untainted by the necrotic disease. With trembling fingers Ruthie touched her own face and registered amazement because she, too, had been miraculously cured. Clutching Mae Burton and weeping with inarticulate joy, Ruthie staggered to her feet. The camera recorded the convert's fervor in her wide eyes as she turned Mae Burton to face her. Gripping her by both shoulders, Ruthie testified, "I believe, Mother. What you said all along is true. He is the Son of God." The two women embraced and, as her words filled the screen, they slowly turned to the cross. Mae Burton knelt and reached up to Ruthie, who pushed the wet hair back from her face and knelt beside her, both women gazing fixedly up. The orchestration swelled and the camera rolled back. The final, long shot showed two praying women and three crosses silhouetted against a brilliant black-and-white sunset.

The image froze and the credits began to roll and Ruthie suddenly expelled her breath. She hadn't realized that she'd been holding it so long. She became aware of the sounds of the audience behind her. "They're actually crying," she thought. Then she looked to her left and saw that Max Goldman was crying, too. In the specially padded chair that ensured that the four-foot-eight-inch mogul would sit as tall as everyone else, with his tiny feet perched upon the petit-point stool that followed him everywhere, Max Goldman took a handkerchief from his breast pocket, removed his horn-rimmed glasses and blew his nose loudly and wetly. He looked at Ruthie in the light of the final scene and the movie's credits. His moist, diamond-studded fingers grasped hers and his watery eyes beamed.

"I'm all choked up, baby," he said and wiped his eyes. In a hushed voice he said, "Just think of the profits." He put his handkerchief away and added, "Listen to them. They're eating it up—all of Hollywood. They loved it."

Ruthie smiled and her smile widened as he whispered, "We've got a blockbuster, baby. This'll be the biggest thing since *Birth of a Nation.*"

The lights slowly brightened in the rococo theater and for a moment the audience was quiet. Then a young man in the front row jumped to his feet and began applauding madly, calling, "Bravo. Bravo."

He was joined by others and in moments the entire audience was on its feet, clamoring for the cast and crew of *Crown of Thorns.* Max Goldman lost no time in hustling his stars to the stage. He replaced his horn-rims, took a fresh cigar from his pocket, grabbed Ruthie by the elbow and motioned to Thurston P. Topping to lead the way to the stage, where the heavy curtains were slowly drawing together.

With the huge, silken tassels of the golden brocade curtains swaying behind them the cast of *Crown of Thorns* bowed to the thunderous applause. There were no footlights and Ruthie could see the emotion-choked faces in the audience—even the violin players were wiping their eyes. "Funny," she said to herself, "I didn't think it was all that great." She took her own special bow and heard Max's rasping voice at her elbow. "It's only the beginning, baby. Wait till you see the new script that I've got for you. You're gonna love it, baby. *Jungle Queen*—it was written just for you. Lots of snakes in it."

Ruthie smiled her skyrocket smile and curtsied like a queen, hoping that her shoulder straps would stay in place and that her dress didn't look too wrinkled. She jauntily tossed her white sable wrap around her shoulders and lifted her cheek for Thurston P. Topping's anise-flavored kiss. "I'm a real star now," she thought. "A real star."

Near Coalston, California

"SHERAHI." Manu's voice spoke into the giant python's mind as she lay in the truck, waiting for dusk, which would bring Dervish and relief from this heat. "I know it's none of my business, but . . . tell me what happened to you while we were traveling across the country for all that time. You were gone so long that something exciting must have happened to you."

The serpent was silent and Manu continued, "I haven't wanted to pry into your affairs before, but somehow I have the feeling that this particular inwitting was more important than the others. Am I wrong, Sherahi?"

"No, Manu," said Sherahi. "It was much more important." The big snake shifted her coils and fell silent again.

"Oh," said Manu, feeling that he had been rebuffed for his inquisitiveness. "I guess it is none of my business." Obviously Sherahi was hiding something from him. "Maybe she thinks I'm too stupid to understand," thought the langur. "Our minds are very different, and . . ."

Sherahi saw these thoughts in the old monkey's mind and silently said, "Of course I want to tell you, Manu. And as far as smartness goes, you're the most intelligent mammal that I've ever met. It's just that it's so sad. . . ."

"What's so sad, Sherahi?"

"How they've all dwindled."

"Who?"

"I'm sorry, Manu. I'm not helping. The serpent nats—gods and near gods who have been worshiped for ages by humans and snakes alike. They used to be very powerful, but things have changed. Humans don't believe in

374

them anymore and they've dwindled. Lachesis used to judge the souls of all living beings and tell Atropos when to cut the threads of their lives. He has shriveled into a little, green inchworm. But it's even worse than that. The Great Worm, the nat who once held the cosmic egg in his coils—the spirit who warmed the earth and gave it life—is fossilized. He still has power, but it's been warped and deformed so that now he's hungry for souls.

"A long time ago U Vayu told me of other great nats. They were water spirits and such, but I haven't tried to inwit to them. When the truck was heading west I inwitted to Quetzalcoatl, the Feathered Serpent. I really didn't mean to do it. It was an accident. U Vayu warned me that he might be dangerous, and I was expecting an awful creature, but he wasn't dangerous at all. He was just . . . sad."

"Has he dwindled, too?"

Sherahi sighed. "He's the worst of all, I suppose. Once he had more power than any of the serpent nats but now he's a grotesque, headless, brainless, eyeless colonial worm who lives in perpetual darkness on the bottom of the ocean."

"Why is he the worst of all? Did he try to hurt you?"

"No, Manu. He can't hurt anybody. He's just pathetic. He begged for food—a bit of chocolate or a single coffee bean. How lonely he must be down there in the cold, dark water, with only blind crabs and giant clams for company."

Sherahi's mindspeech broke off and then she continued, "It makes me feel so confused, Manu. All of the things I've believed in turn out to be wrong. Whenever I look for answers, I end up with more questions."

"Maybe there are no answers," Manu said gently in his peculiar brand of mindspeech.

"I don't like that idea," Sherahi replied. "If there are no answers then we are as good as lost."

"Not necessarily, dear Pythoness," said the old langur, smiling kindly at her. "We have each other and we have hope. We know that we're trying to get to Sandeagozu. Everything else is unimportant.

"What does it matter that the serpent nats have dwindled, Sherahi? Would they really have been willing to help us? Weren't they interested in themselves?" He didn't wait for an answer and continued, "We don't need serpent nats, Sherahi. We can make our own myths. Somehow we'll blunder our way to Sandeagozu. I'm sure of it."

"I suppose so," answered the serpent, haltingly. "But it would be so much nicer if there were someone to help. Someone who knew everything and would give us answers that we could trust."

"Ask yourself, Sherahi. You probably know as much as any serpent nat ever did. And you won't try any sneaky tricks. Those nats weren't always kind, were they?"

"No, usually they had other things in mind."

"I thought so," said Manu. "Sherahi, I've been doing some thinking while you were away. And I don't want you to laugh at a foolish old monkey, but I've been looking at the stars each night since Dervish has been gone. I've been so worried that I didn't know what else to do, and when Junior went after him, I was all alone for two nights. I think they were the longest nights I can remember, except for when I was kidnapped by Leftrack when I was a youngster. I was so frightened then that I couldn't sleep for weeks. But then I was inside the ship. There were no stars there. Only Ura, and he tried to kill me.

"Anyway, I've seen the stars now, Sherahi. I don't think I ever saw them when I was free: my tribe went to sleep at sundown. Anyway, I'd never really looked at them.

"Sherahi, there are so many stars up there, spilled across the sky, that they make you feel as small as a spider. So many that they make you want to believe that someone is up there behind the stars, keeping them and the moon and the sun all circling about the earth. Langurs have a saying, though, that I remember from when I was small. Langurs say, 'The stars run blind.'

"'The stars run blind,' Sherahi. Think about it. I never understood what that meant, but I think I've figured it out now. It means that, even though we'd feel happier if there were someone up there behind the stars who keeps things in order, there is really no one looking after things. It means that there is no machine, no nat, no nothing—just the stars and the night and the silence.

"The first night I gazed up at the stars and felt as if I were falling up into the sky. It frightened me and I ran back into the truck to hide. But after thinking about it I have come to think that it's enough to have just all those stars.

"All we have is today. No serpent nats or monkey gods will help us. That's what it means—'the stars run blind.' We must try to be happy with it, Sherahi. You must trust yourself. I do. And I think that together we can get across those mountains to Sandeagozu—somehow."

Sherahi was silent for a long while and then she said, "Thank you, Manu," in mindspeech that was thick with emotion. "I think you're the best friend I've ever had. Even though so many bad things and so many strange things have happened to me since Ruthie brought me to Leftrack's pet shop, I'm awfully glad she did. I'll think about what you said." To herself she added, "And, Manu, no matter if the stars steer blindly or if some uni-maginably powerful nat controls all that we see, I'm going to get you to your tribe in Sandeagozu if it's the last thing I do."

The sky was studded with a few, faint stars and a horned moon when Dervish and his new friend, Nemi, trotted up to the abandoned truck that listed by the side of the deserted highway, sunk up to its axles in sand. A pair of lights could be seen a long way off and the two animals crouched in the shadow of a rear wheel, watching the beams of light approach.

Dervish was so excited to see Manu, Sherahi and Junior that he gathered himself to bound into the truck. Nemi saw this and barked a sharp warning that made him hesitate and look at her questioningly. "It is better to wait and let the lights pass," she said. "We don't want to be seen."

Although Dervish would rather have immediately leaped into the truck, with Nemi at his side, he sighed and obeyed. For some reason it was especially important that Manu see Nemi. Dervish had been amazed when the little female coati had found him wandering in the sun. He'd been dazed, thirsty and exhausted and had become immediately infatuated with her. From the minute that she had pressed her round nose into his ear and snuffled a greeting—even before he had realized that she was a coatimundi like himself—Dervish had thought that there was something wonderfully familiar about this creature that called herself Nemi. He remembered thinking that he had never seen such an enchanting being. Everything about her seemed well formed and graceful. He even loved the way her upper lip didn't quite cover the pointed canines that showed white against her shiny, black lower lip. The sight of her furry flanks disappearing into the vegetation had made him wild with desire. And the smell of her. Like a drugged creature Dervish had staggered after her, inhaling that lovely odor. To Dervish this female coati smelled better than sardines and milk; she smelled better than Sorensen's salty palm and much better than the welcoming nest box that had been his first universe.

As he had stumbled through the underbrush, all Dervish could see of Nemi was the tip of her vertical tail. He recognized it as the twin of his own and for a moment his overheated brain had thought that he was following himself. He remembered seeing the tip of Nemi's tail curl and uncurl above a low thicket, even though the rest of her body was concealed. That tail seemed to beckon and Dervish had struggled to follow. Now he grudgingly obeyed her command to wait quietly, even though he thought that she was being unnecessarily cautious. He settled onto the warm sand beside her and sniffed the fur between her shoulder blades in the way that coatis do— by pressing his nose firmly down into it. If it had been sand or moist earth Dervish's nose would have left a round print.

Impatiently he complained, "I don't see why we have to . . ."

"Hush," Nemi interrupted. "Watch."

Dervish sighed and looked up at the pair of lights on the horizon. They grew larger. There was no sound, though, and Dervish remembered that a few days ago Nemi had told him, "In the desert things are always farther away than you think they are."

"I wonder how far away they are," he thought. There was no wind, and Dervish's nose was not far from Nemi's soft, furry belly. Her perfume enveloped him and he rubbed his face along her side, moving over her ribs to the back of her head. Gently he took her small, rounded ear between his front teeth and nipped it playfully. She was so small, so delicious. He couldn't get close enough.

But Nemi had other ideas. "Not now, Dervish," she growled. In a flash she grabbed the loose skin of his neck in her jaws and held it for a moment, shaking him to get his attention. "Watch," she told him again. "Danger is coming. There'll be time for that later, when we're alone. At home."

The lights in the distance made a continuous swooshing noise now and, as both animals looked up, Nemi whispered, "Whatever you do, don't run toward it. Pretend to be a rock."

The lights and noise increased tenfold. They seemed to call to Dervish in voices that he couldn't quite understand. For an instant he wanted to run forward to greet them, but then he grew frightened as they came closer and closer. Dervish remembered the fire serpents in the cavern below the city and felt as if this creature with the twin lights were searching for him. It was almost upon them. Shadows jumped at the sides of the road and Dervish buried his face in the sand, shutting his eyes and covering his ears with his paws. He was certain that this above-ground fire serpent was headed straight for them. He whimpered with fear and heard Nemi's calm voice, "Don't be scared. It's only a car. It'll pass. Pay no attention to its voice and be still."

The whooshing sound filled his ears. He could hear the creature's voice calling, "Come. Come." Even with his eyes closed the twin spots of light danced, leaving trails and spots of light on the insides of his eyelids. He burrowed beneath Nemi to escape and in the confusion heard her growl, "Stop it, Dervish."

And then as rapidly as it had appeared, the sound diminished, growing smaller and smaller until the roadside was quiet once more. All that Dervish could hear was the pounding of his heart and Nemi's regular breathing.

Still dazzled by the pair of white lights and the noise they had made, Dervish shook the sand from his fur and looked down the road. A pair of eyes glowed red on the horizon, followed by a faint, swooshing noise.

"That was a car, Dervish," Nemi said. "There are people inside. Cars often run along this road—especially at night. They are harmless as long as you stay off the road."

"What happens if you get in their way?"

"Then they trample you and leave you for the vultures," said Nemi, matter-of-factly. "You'll see.

"Now, call your friends, Dervish. We must be going. It's dangerous here in the moonlight."

"Aren't we going inside?" asked Dervish. He had pictured a victorious return, parading Nemi before an astonished Manu.

"Of course not," said Nemi. "There are snakes in there. With your sense of smell you probably can't notice them. But snakes have crawled in there, I'm certain of it. This is one chulo who isn't going within fifty feet of that hole. Tell your friends to come out. And tell them to be careful where they step. We don't want anyone to get bitten."

"Oh, Nemi, don't be such a 'fraidy cat," teased Dervish, batting at her tail. He hadn't told her that his friends included two snakes. For a moment he worried that this might mean trouble, but he dismissed the thought. "Sherahi and Junior would never hurt her," he decided.

As no amount of cajoling would convince Nemi to enter the rear of the truck, Dervish sighed and leaped up to the dark opening. "You're too stubborn, Nemi," he said. Peering inside he chittered, "Manu, Sherahi, Junior. Come out. We're going now and I've got someone for you to meet."

Moments later Manu peered out of the truck. Like a live gargoyle he sat on the apron of the truck, his silver fur washed by bright moonlight, and allowed his eyes to adjust to the light. He heard the sound of chittering below and looked down to see a long-snouted face peering back at him. "I see you've got a new friend, Dervish," Manu said.

Dervish said nothing, but bustled about importantly, urging Manu along with a shove of his muzzle. Dervish had told Nemi that he was traveling with animals that had escaped from a pet shop. Nemi didn't understand much about humans and their ways and Dervish had told her of the adventures that the Culls had had, emphasizing his own heroic deeds. "Nemi," he said matter-of-factly, "this is Manu. He's a langur."

"Oh," Nemi chattered, "is this the one you saved from the giant white lizards?"

Manu looked at Dervish for one long moment and then leaped down to the sand beside Nemi and said to him, "I've been worried about you, Dervish. But I see that you've been well taken care of." To Nemi he said, "Yes, Miss. Dervish saved all of us from those monsters. He was magnificent. We owe him our lives."

Above them Sherahi's huge head and thick, sinuous body began to emerge from the open truck. Manu felt Nemi stiffen and heard her gasp of astonishment.

Sherahi had scryed Nemi's mind and saw the little coati's fear and loathing of snakes. "This isn't going to be easy," she thought as she spoke into Nemi's mind, using the hypnotic, commanding tone that froze rabbits in their tracks and made them welcome the strike that would end their confused, disoriented lives. "Don't be afraid," Sherahi said. "I will not harm you, little friend. Look into my eyes. See how gold they are. Watch them glitter in the moonlight. I am like moonlight. Moonlight cannot hurt you. Neither will I."

Dead branches crackled as Sherahi's enormous body flowed out of the truck and down onto the sand. She kept a firm hold upon Nemi's mind, fearing that just the mere sight of herself would cause Dervish's mate to bolt. As she came near Manu and Nemi, Sherahi lifted her huge head and thick neck, casting a long shadow over them and fnasting the newcomer with a languid, forked tongue. "She must fear me," thought Sherahi. "She must know that, even if she runs away, I will follow and plague her dreams. No matter how deep her burrow, no matter how inaccessible, no matter how cleverly hidden, I will seek her out and find her. Otherwise she will run away and Dervish will follow her, and we need both of them to get to Sandeagozu. But, if thongs of fear bind her to me, she will guide us across those mountains and to Sandeagozu. Then she can go her own way and I will bless her forever."

For a long moment the huge python towered over Nemi, imprinting her image upon the coati's memory. Nemi crouched against the sand, her gaze full of fear and awe.

"There," thought Sherahi, as she lowered herself to the ground. "It is enough. Now I will be in her nightmares and she will take us to Sandeagozu." To Dervish, who had watched all this from the truck, not quite knowing what to do, she said, "Please help Junior. He was injured trying to find you and you'll have to carry him until his skin heals."

"Come," she said to all of them, "we go this way. Sandeagozu is just on the other side of those mountains." Sherahi slithered away from the roadside, with the moonlight glinting in her smooth scales. "Sandeagozu," she thought, "I've seen it a hundred times. We'll be there tomorrow night." She was crawling west as rapidly as she could when she was surprised to hear Nemi and Dervish growling behind her.

"Dervish," Nemi screamed. "Quick. Drop it before it bites you. That's a cascabel."

Sherahi saw that Dervish stood near his mate with Junior held gently between his jaws. Sherahi saw that Junior was still numb from her mind balm. He rattled feebly and tried to curl around Dervish's neck, but didn't have the strength to clasp his tail about his neck in his usual fashion and hung limply from Dervish's jaws. He was babbling something in incoherent mindspeech.

Nemi's fur bristled. She dashed up to Dervish and one of her quick paws batted Junior from his mouth. She was about to seize the little snake and shake the life from him when Manu leaped between them. The langur scooped up Junior and shielded him from Nemi's attack.

"Junior is one of us. Dervish, you should have warned her. Don't you remember how afraid you used to be of him?"

"But he's a cascabel," Nemi said. "A killer. Rattlesnakes are treacherous. They lurk where you least expect them and they prowl all night. Manu, don't let that snake fool you. One that was even littler than that killed my mother. I thought that, even if Dervish were a fool, you seemed to be a reasonable creature, but you're crazier than he is. None of you seems to understand anything. When I think that the two of you have come all this way with two snakes—ugh. It makes me sick to see you let that slimy reptile touch you.

"Please, Manu. Let me kill it. It won't take long. He'll never feel it. He's sick. He's going to die anyway."

Manu turned away from the furious coati, cradling Junior in one arm, putting his body between her and the injured snake. "No, Nemi. I told you, Junior is one of us. He's sick because he tried to find Dervish. Sherahi will heal him. Then you'll see that he's no ordinary rattlesnake."

Manu hurried away from the abandoned truck, Dervish and Nemi, following in the wide track that Sherahi had made in the sand.

The two coatis were left by the roadside, watching Manu and Sherahi move away toward the mountains on the horizon. "This is the strangest, most unnatural thing," Nemi said to herself. "How did I ever get myself into this mess?"

"You don't understand; we've all been through so much," said Dervish.

"But they're snakes, Dervish. No matter what you've been through it doesn't change the fact that snakes kill coatis. We can never be friends with them."

"These snakes are different. You'll see."

"You mean that you actually expect me to travel with you?"

"You promised, Nemi. You promised that you would help us."

"But I didn't know that two of you were snakes."

"All right, Nemi. If that's how you feel, I guess I've got to be going. I guess promises are different to animals that have always been free." Dervish looked longingly at the little female coati and touched the side of her jaw with his nose. Then he sprinted after the others, leaving her alone by the roadside.

Nemi saw Dervish's banded tail disappear through the underbrush.

"Fool," she chittered in rage. "You don't even know how to find water yet. You don't know what's good to eat. Oh, why are you so stupid?"

Moments later Dervish felt something warm and fuzzy leap at him from above and recognized Nemi's luscious perfume. She was almost as strong as Dervish and in moments had wrestled him to the ground; her jaws were buried in his throat. "See," she said. "If I were a cat, you'd be dead now."

"But you're not," said Dervish, delighted that she had changed her mind. "You're a coati and you're going to go to Sandeagozu with us."

"Wait a minute, I never said anything about going to this Sandeagozu with you. I promised that I'd see all of you across the mountains and a promise is a promise. But actually going to Sandeagozu is something different. I'll take you as far as I can, but keep those snakes away from me." Nemi leaped off Dervish and hurried away, playing hide-and-seek in the brush.

"But, Nemi," pleaded Dervish. The female coati paid no attention and he raced after her, chittering, "You'll like them, I know you will, if you'll only give them a chance."

"No," said Nemi firmly as the two coatis trotted past Sherahi in silence. Sherahi saw the thoughts in Nemi's mind and chuckled. The coati thought, "It's bad enough that he's so retarded that he doesn't even know how to open an anthill, but of all the animals in the world, why did he have to pick snakes for his friends?"

Once more Sherahi reinforced the thongs of fear that bound the female coati to the Culls. "She'll see that we get to Sandeagozu," Sherahi thought. "And then she and Dervish can retire to this godforsaken desert to raise their babies and hunt for fat grubs and forget all about giant snakes and white crocodiles and any but the most commonplace adventures."

CHAPTER FOURTEEN

N HER DREAM Sherahi coiled on the crest of a high dune. Her huge head was aloft and the night wind sweeping from the valley below brought a complex mixture of odors to her restlessly flicking tongue. A light fog blanketed the valley, obliterating some of the lights of Sandeagozu and swathing others in rainbow-fringed coronas. Even though Sherahi's distance vision wasn't acute, she thought she could finally see the garden of free animals that they'd traveled so long to find. It was a dark blot on one edge of the rows of lights that marched to the horizon.

"We're over the mountains at last," thought the pythoness as she mentally interpreted the molecular brew that her tongue had sampled. She could fnast strange and terrifying animals—beasts so wondrous that she knew of them only from legends she'd been told during her earliest training in the ancient hibernaculum of her native land. "Such unusual creatures," Sherahi thought, "and most of them are asleep." Her methodical, pythonine mind pictured the haunches of a herd of sleeping zebras, their striped rib cages moving in synchronous inhalations and exhalations. Another bundle of molecules triggered the image of shaggy animals hanging like lumpy fruit in the forked branches of a tree. The males had grotesquely swollen faces, but the females and young looked as wistful as Manu did when he was asleep. Even though they had coarse, uneven, auburn coats instead of his sleek, silver pelt, Sherahi recognized them as Manu's distant relatives. Next she fnasted a combination of warm fur and fish and saw the mental image of a gently snoring huddle of female walruses, all cuddled about the hulking body of their mate. A thick thread of saliva drooled from his bristly upper lip and puddled at the tip of one long, ivory tusk. Sherahi remembered the legend of the single-tusked unicorn and wondered if it, too, slept and dreamed at Sandeagozu.

Without any conscious effort on her part, a portion of that outsized brain, hidden deep beneath her wide forehead, interpreted another sample of the odors brought by the night wind from Sandeagozu and she felt a sharp pang of homesickness as she fnasted the unmistakable combination of smell, size and shape that could only mean elephants. "A whole herd," Sherahi marveled as she saw round-eared babies that slept on their knees within the columnar fortresses formed by their mothers' legs. The adults dozed standing up, swaying slightly, ears flapping irregularly. Their trunks were thrown affectionately across one another's shoulders and Sherahi remembered how her elders had described elephants as earthbound clouds, whose softest tread made the earth tremble. The mental glimpse of the herd of sleeping elephants in Sandeagozu reminded Sherahi of the temples and the orange and lime-green sunsets of her home and made her eager to speak with one of her own kind again. "There must be pythons there," she thought. "They've got every other kind of animal."

She was tensing her mind, preparing to cast it into Sandeagozu to draw and seek a python like herself, when Manu joined her on the crest of the dune and killed her inwit before it began. In her dream Sherahi sighed impatiently, but Manu seemed not to notice. "Mammals are like that," she thought. "So quick-minded that they don't notice details like the songs of tortoises, the thoughts of serpents. They see so little of what goes on around them."

"Sandeagozu," the langur said, panting a little and gesturing with his chin at the lights in the valley below. He sat on his haunches in the moonlight beside her, and Sherahi was shocked to see that the twisted knot of pink scar tissue was gone from the left side of his face. It was hard to believe, but his face was completely coal black and a pair of liquid, black eyes glinted at her in the moonlight. "How elegant you are, Manu," Sherahi thought as he idly groomed sand from his long, streaming tail. "But, how did this happen?" she wondered. From the way that he admired this appendage, holding it up to catch the moonlight on its thick, silver-blond fur, Sherahi knew that the old langur was inordinately proud of it. With a start she remembered, "This isn't right. This can't be right. Manu's tail was cut off long ago. He told me so himself. He has only a stump of a tail left."

But his tail was as plain as the shelf of black eyebrows that jutted above his magically restored eyes. He continued grooming himself as he caught his breath, waiting for the other Culls to join them. Manu made no mention of his changed appearance and Sherahi knew that it would be grossly impolite to broach the subject. Like all primates, langurs had peculiar rules of etiquette and Sherahi knew that it would be as rude as a slap in the face and as threatening as a fixed stare to bring up the subject until he chose to speak of it. Manu acted as if nothing had happened to his appearance. Excitedly he pointed to the dark blot in the maze of lights spread in the valley below and whispered, "I see it.

"That must be Sandeagozu, Sherahi. We've almost made it. Can you tell if my tribe is there? Can you fnast any of them?"

Sherahi was about to try when he quickly changed his mind, saying,

"No, Sherahi. Don't tell me. If they're alive, I'll see them soon enough. I'm not sure that I want to know if I've come all this way for nothing."

As if not allowing himself to dwell on this possibility Manu hastily added, "Do you think they'll recognize me? Do you think I've grown awfully old and scrawny? Once I was the most beautiful langur on the hill. I could have had all of the females that I wanted. But the years have taken my good looks and now the best I can hope for is that they'll just let me live with them."

"What do you mean, Manu?"

"If they don't recognize me—if I don't have the right smell—if they think there's anything odd about me at all, they will all attack."

Sherahi was astounded by such barbarity. "After you've come all this way? Impossible."

"You don't understand, Sherahi. We are governed by tribal rules that have allowed us to prosper over the years. Our tribe protects the helpless little ones and trains the youngsters, but it is closed to outsiders. The top male is very jealous. He kills his rivals."

Suddenly Sherahi had an image of Manu's twisted face ground into the dirt. The silver fur of his neck was torn and bloody. She shook her head to banish this vision, thinking, "This must not happen. Not to Manu."

The langur continued thoughtfully, "Going back to them after all these years has its risks. Tell me honestly, Pythoness, how do you think I look? I must be confident . . . strong."

Sherahi was about to reply that he had never looked better when a familiar voice began to splutter and whine in the darkness behind and below them. Both Culls listened indulgently as the Duchess toiled up the slippery face of the dune, continuously complaining. "You'd think they'd have more sense. You'd think that they'd listen to me just once, but no. That would be too easy.

"They think they're so smart. 'Keep going. Keep going. Just a little farther. Just a little farther.' And now we've spent another night of torture, trudging over sand and stones. My claws are worn to nubbins. I've got a cactus thorn in my foot. My ankles are killing me. And just look at my poor tail feathers. No proper scarlet macaw would be seen in public with these scraggly stubs. They look like they belong to a buzzard who needs a dose of salts."

"She could fly," Manu whispered to Sherahi.

"She's lost the knack," Sherahi replied and smiled in her inscrutable way. Pretending to ignore the Duchess they gazed at the horizon and surreptitiously watched her step sideways up the last few feet of sand. It suddenly occurred to Sherahi that she hadn't seen the Duchess in many months. She thought, "I must ask where she's been all this time and what happened to her when she flew away from the chambers of the white crocodiles." But the thought slipped from Sherahi's mind as the Duchess joined them on the crest of the dune.

The bird craned her neck and peered at the network of lights below, examining the view first with her left and then with her right eye. Her attention was suddenly drawn to the steep incline just below her scaly claws and she gasped in horror. Nictitating membranes filmed each eye and Manu thought that she might faint as she frantically beat her wings to keep from falling.

"Why didn't you warn me that we were so high?" she screamed. "You know how much I hate heights. How many times have I said that I have vermigo? I think I'm going to be sick."

Manu put out an arm to steady the nervous bird. "It's okay, Duchess. Don't be scared. Even if you fell down to that road, way down there, it's only sand. You couldn't hurt yourself if you tried. Besides, that's Sandeagozu down there. Just think, pretty soon you'll be sitting with your own mate on your own nest of little chicks. Isn't that what you've always wanted?"

"Hmph," the Duchess sniffed, pretending to be unimpressed with the panorama of lights spread before her and delicately ignoring what Manu had said about the prospect of a mate in Sandeagozu. Scarlet macaws never discussed sex. "Chicks? Is that what we've come all this way for?"

Sherahi thought she saw a glimmer of laughter in Manu's eyes, but it might have been only starlight. Just then Dervish bounded up the dune with Junior around his neck. "Good," thought Sherahi, "we're finally all together." It occurred to her that it was strange that Dervish was carrying Junior about his neck again. In the months since Nemi had come into his life the coati had refused to come near the cascabel. Manu usually carried Junior now while Nemi and Dervish went ahead, finding a path and scouting for food and water. But in Sherahi's dream Dervish sat right beside her and she was sure that the arrow-shaped silhouette that reared itself between the coati's ears was Junior. Just then she saw it flick a forked tongue at the distant lights and she was certain that the two old traveling companions were together once more.

"Let's not stop now," the Duchess insisted and began to step sideways down the foredune. All the while her cranky baritone voice continued muttering, "Of course it doesn't matter to you that there are scorpions and spiders and vinegarroons and galliwasps all creeping around in the dark just waiting to get me. No, that wouldn't cross your minds.

"If I had any sense I'd find a nice, comfortable perch and roost till morning. That's if there were anything to perch on in this godawful place. Something's always moving—just out of sight. For once I'd like to see what's scuttling away in the shadows. I hate all this stumbling around in the dark more than anything. . . .

". . . but they never listen to me. If I've told them once, I've told them a thousand times that I'm not an owl. But they don't listen. Now, for the last time, all of you: you can eat all you want of those disgusting bloody messes, but if I don't have some nice, clean seeds, I swear—I'll go crazy. Right now I'd give my three longest primaries for a piece of fruit—even a wormy, wrinkled apple."

Sherahi stopped listening to the Duchess's cranky litany and turned her attention to Dervish. "At least he's excited to see Sandeagozu," she thought.

"You've done it, Sherahi," the coati chittered. "We're almost there," he panted and capered on his hind legs and pounced upon the python's coils.

"He's playing like a puppy again," thought Sherahi. "He hasn't done that since he met Nemi."

Then it occurred to Sherahi that the little female coati was not in sight. She looked down the dune, but there was only one set of coati tracks leading to the crest. "That's odd," thought Sherahi. "Nemi's not with him."

Stranger still—a quick scan of Dervish's thoughts showed no recollection of her at all. Dervish hadn't lost Nemi; he didn't even know that she existed.

"How do we get there, Sherahi?" asked Manu. "Do we just walk right into Sandeagozu?"

Sherahi looked below and saw a dark, rectangular shape on the road below the dune. Something deep within told her that this shape was a wagon. "No, Manu," she said, with the feeling that something unimaginably queer was about to happen. "We ride."

The Duchess was ten feet below the other Culls when she lost her footing and began the sandslide that undermined the crest of the dune. Sherahi heard the Duchess screech and saw her head disappear in a flood of moving sand. She saw Manu and Dervish disappear into whirling clouds of sand and felt the sand begin to shift and slip beneath her belly scales as she, too, slid down the steep face of the dune. She tried to keep her head upright as she tumbled; she tried not to think of what would happen to her if she snapped her backbone; she tried to quell the panic that rose in her throat. There was sand in her labial pits and nostrils, but she held her breath and struggled for balance, sliding within the cataract of sand, thinking, "I've come too far. I won't be hurt by a little sand now."

In moments she and the other Culls were hidden in the back of the shadowy wagon as it began to move. Sherahi didn't dare raise her head to see the driver, but next to her she saw that a huge rope was neatly coiled. She gripped it with her belly scales as the wagon began to jolt and bounce down the rutted road. Sherahi was about to warn all of the Culls to hold on tight when she saw Dervish suddenly thrown from the wagon. "Oh, no," she thought. "Not Dervish. He'll be killed beneath the wheels." She imagined the coati's body lying flattened and trampled like so many hapless animals that ventured out onto the road.

"I'll get him," said Manu and leaped over the side of the wagon after the coati.

"No, Manu," Sherahi commanded. But it was too late. The langur was gone.

The road suddenly dipped and, although she didn't understand how it was possible, Sherahi saw that Dervish wasn't hurt after all. He wasn't mangled by the side of the road. Instead, he was in front of the wagon, pulling it down the road faster than ever. He looked identical to the coati that had played with her on the crest of the dune only moments ago, except that now he was ten times as large. This mammoth coati pulled the wagon faster, and more violently than ever it bounced in his wake as he bounded forward. Sherahi saw Junior around his neck like a halter. Manu clung to the coati's back, gripping fistfuls of fur.

"Faster," urged Manu. He turned to look over his shoulder and from her precarious seat in the rear of the wagon, Sherahi saw Manu grin. The moonlight marked his features in grim contrast. With horror, Sherahi saw that Manu's eyes were milk white within his pitch-black face. "He's blind," she thought. "Manu's blind. He can't see where we're going. If he drives Dervish off into that ditch we'll all be killed." Just then Dervish turned his long-snouted face at her and she saw that his eyes were white, too. "How can this be?" thought Sherahi. "How can they both be blind?"

In terror Sherahi clung to the coil of rope in the bed of the wagon and called to the Duchess for help. She saw the bird clinging to the wagon seat above her, beating her wings and screeching ecstatically in the whistling wind. "She thinks that she's flying," thought Sherahi as she tried to find some purchase upon the slick bed of the wagon, but there was nothing for her coils to grip. The wagon was bouncing so high now that she was certain that the next jolt would throw her clear. "The fall will surely kill me," thought Sherahi and she remembered the yellow-and-brown-ringed body of the banded krait thumping its broken life out against the dusty road. "Stop it," she commanded, calling to Manu and Dervish in her most regal mind-speech. But for the first time her words had no effect. "I've lost control," she thought and refused to believe it. Again and again she summoned all of her powers and commanded, "Manu, Dervish. Stop. STOP."

"We can't hear you, Sherahi." Dervish turned back to look at her. His eyes were white like Manu's and his huge, pink tongue lolled from behind enormous, jagged teeth. "We're all blind."

"That's the stupidest thing I ever heard," thought the pythoness. "This can't be happening. It's only a dream."

"Is it?" said the voice of the Duchess, very close to her ear.

Sherahi hadn't realized that the bird was so close and whirled to face her. "Of course," said Sherahi. "I'm dreaming all of this. It's not real. It can't be."

But the jolting continued and Sherahi heard the Duchess say, "Oh good. If it's not real, I'll try it, too."

Then the wagon took another dip and the jolting ceased abruptly. It was as if the road had turned to glass. Sherahi peered over the side of the wagon and saw that the wheels spun in the air. They were high above the road. "We're flying," she thought. She saw Manu, Junior and Dervish on the ground below, staring up at her. "Goodbye, Sherahi," they called. Dervish's banded tail curled high in the moonlight as he danced on his hind legs, reaching for the wagon as it gained altitude. It reminded Sherahi of the way he had once reached for the full moon and discovered, instead, the way out of Leftrack's pet shop. Junior rattled a farewell.

Sherahi looked ahead and saw that a huge scarlet macaw was between the traces of the wagon. With sure, powerful wing beats, the bird pulled the wagon higher and higher into the sky. Far below, the road that led from the desert to Sandeagozu dwindled to a silver ribbon and Sherahi could hear the wind thrumming through the Duchess's pinions.

The macaw screamed in recognition as a flight of parrots swooped out of the night to join them. Their cries were seductive and Sherahi saw the Duchess wriggle free of the wagon's traces. Without a backward look the Duchess flew to join in their midnight aerial acrobatics.

"Come back, Duchess," Sherahi called. She looked down and once more felt the fear that had seized her as she tumbled down the dune, afraid that her backbone would be snapped by the fall.

As the Duchess flew away she called, "You don't need me, Sherahi. I'm going to find my jungle—finally. Besides, it's only a dream. You said so yourself."

Sherahi was alone with the stars. She was almost afraid to breathe lest she upset the wagon and make it tumble from the sky. There was no sensation of movement and as she looked below she could see that the wagon wheels were still. Their spokes were silhouetted against the moonlit landscape below. Above her the stars were motionless, too, painted onto the inside of a huge, cobalt bowl.

"Can it be possible?" thought Sherahi. "Can I believe that harebrained bird?"

She looked at the peaceful landscape below and thought, "I can try."

A feeling of reassuring calm flooded over the pythoness as the wagon began to move again, imperceptibly at first and then gaining momentum. Soon it was soaring through the night sky, a rectangular rollercoaster, dipping down to skim the tops of the leafless trees, frightening a hunting owl, scaring a herd of mule deer who ran away and then stopped to turn and look over their shoulders at this strange apparition.

"I can do it," Sherahi exulted. "I can do it!" The lights of Sandea-gozu were only a glow on the far horizon when Sherahi began to laugh in her slow, cold, mirthless way. A velvety, foreign voice spoke inside her mind, using the familiar tone of ancient reptilian mindspeech that pythons speak only to one another, and Sherahi writhed with delight. She coiled in recognition, feeling the glassy scutes of what she now realized was no mere coil of rope. She laughed again as she said to him, "Did you know, we're running blind?"

"It's the funniest thing I ever heard of," she thought. "We're running blind. We're flying blind. The funniest thing."

"Sherahi," the voice called. "Sherahi."

"He knows my name," she thought. "And I didn't even have to tell him."

The tone suddenly changed and grew more insistent and Sherahi awoke to the sound of him calling her name. Her own laughter was still echoing within her mind. "It's the most wonderful joke in the world," she thought, looking about and not recognizing her surroundings.

"Why is it so dark in here?" she thought. She flicked her tongue right and left, trying to fnast the musky coils that had held hers in the wagon, but there was only the smell of mammals all around. Then she saw the half black, half pink, one-eyed face of Manu staring down at her with concern. It was his voice that had awakened her, saying, "Sherahi—Sherahi? Are you all right?"

As her eyes became accustomed to the darkness Sherahi slowly remembered where she was: underground in a burrow that Nemi and Dervish had dug so that the Culls could escape the hottest hours of the desert day. The two coatis were asleep in one corner. She, Junior and Manu had another all to themselves.

With a shock she realized that the starlit wagon and the view of Sandeagozu that she had seen from the top of a dune were only part of a dream.

"I'm fine, Manu," she said. "I had the strangest dream. We were all in it and we were almost to Sandeagozu. It was so funny, Manu."

"What was, Sherahi?"

"We were flying blind or driving blind. Somehow it was so funny. Such a wonderful joke."

"Uh huh." Manu yawned and turned to his side and went back to sleep, leaving Sherahi wide awake. "It was a dream," she thought, as she remembered that they had been traveling through the desert for what Nemi called "two moons." It was much farther to the mountains around Sandea-gozu than Sherahi had initially thought and now it seemed that they still had far to go. Suddenly she felt very tired as she looked at Manu's gargoyle face and thought, "It was only a dream—but so real."

She thought of telling him about it but as she listened to his regular breathing she reasoned that it might only hurt the langur's feelings, especially the part about his face being restored. "What will happen when his tribe sees him?" she wondered. "He looks so strange—even hideous. They might kill him. I wonder, though—I can't change the way his face actually looks, but I might be able to alter the way his tribe or anyone else sees it. I'll have to think about this."

"Look, Sherahi," said the old langur, propping himself up on one elbow and pointing to a translucent tissue that clung to the rough, rear wall of the burrow. "I think Junior has shed his skin. This must mean that he's finally healed."

"I certainly am," said the cascabel, undulating toward them across the dirt floor of the burrow, the zigzagged pattern on his back working like slow lightning. "And I can travel on my own now. You don't have to carry me anymore, Manu."

In the far corner of the burrow Dervish yawned and stretched and nuzzled Nemi's tightly closed eyes. "Time to get going," he chittered, looking up the tunnel toward the burrow's entrance and sniffing. "The sun's going down. It's going to be a nice evening—not cold at all. We should be able to make good time."

Led by Nemi and Dervish, the Culls abandoned this temporary burrow, as they had abandoned so many others before it. Intent upon traveling quickly, they melted into the desert twilight to join the host of other creatures who hid from the sun's glare and became active only when it slipped below the western horizon and allowed the desert to cool.

The curled tips of Nemi's and Dervish's vertical tails were all that was visible of them as they snuffled ahead into the underbrush, foraging as they traveled. Manu had learned from their example and followed behind, chewing mouthfuls of piñon nuts and an occasional grasshopper that Dervish stunned and left for him to find. Now that Junior was able to travel on his own, the cascabel would hunt for himself, but Sherahi would fast till they reached Sandeagozu. She could go without food for a year and not even feel hungry. Time and again she watched the others feeding greedily and thought, "What a waste of effort—hunting and eating all the time. No wonder the mammals never produced any outstanding thinkers." She had found that if she could avoid direct sunlight and drink deeply once every three or four days, she did not even suffer from thirst. Sherahi was actually enjoying their travel through the desert. This country suited her. It was as stripped bare of nonessential details as her long body itself, and as she slithered along, winding over rock and sand, she thought of the great herds of her reptilian forebears who had traveled through these same canyons, maybe even drinking from rivers that had long since disappeared, becoming extinct just like the heavy-footed sauropods, whose bones silently eroded and revealed themselves in the canyon walls above.

So, once more the Culls resumed their journey through the foothills on the eastern side of the mountains. This night they would traverse rock faces and dry riverbeds, scramble over slippery scree and out of dead-end canyons, always moving west toward the mountains and Sandeagozu. Because of her great size, Sherahi traveled more slowly than the others and her wide trail obliterated their tracks. She lifted her head above the leafless bushes, fixed her gaze upon the black mountain range that fringed the violet horizon and concentrated upon moving muscle and bone as quickly as possible while the darkness protected them and the temperature allowed the Culls to be abroad.

The two men rode into the glare, enveloped in a silence that was broken only by the creaking of saddles and horses' hooves clattering on stone.

After hours it was too much for the white man. "Dagnabit, you crazy half-breed," he spluttered, mopping his florid face with a red bandanna. "Where is it?"

The Indian pointed to the western mountains. They were shrunken by the midday glare and looked very remote. Nothing was real except the wall of heat that the men rode into, the ashy, leafless bushes and the sandstone canyon walls bleached by the sun to a pale, apricot color.

But the white man wasn't looking at the scenery. "I tell you," he continued, raving more to himself than to his impassive guide, "if you've brought me out here on a wild-goose chase, I'll have your hide. Tanned and pinned to the wall."

The Indian said nothing.

"Boy, if this is your idea of a joke—if this *culebra* isn't everything that you said it was—if I've come all this way in this consarned heat for nothin', I swear I'll . . . I'll . . . I don't know what I'll do, but you won't like it. Believe-you-me. You won't like it." He glared at the sweat stain that spread down the middle of the back of the Indian's worn denim shirt, and stuffed his bandanna into a rear pocket. Gritting his teeth against the heat he rode on.

"Just like an Indian for you," he thought. "Doesn't say a word—just keeps riding. He's probably laughing himself silly. Oh, it'll be a big laugh for him. I can hear him tellin' it now: 'How I took D. K. Beasley to see the Great *Culebra*.' I have a bad feeling about this whole ex-pe-dition. A bad feeling."

The Indian rode ahead into the searing heat, slouched in his saddle, motionless except for an occasional flick of the reins against his horse's neck and the restless movements of his eyes. The overwhelming heat allowed him to listen abstractedly to the white man behind him. "Gringos are nuts," he thought. "Who but a crazy gringo would pay me thirty dollars—thirty dollars—to take him all the way out here just to see a track in the sand?"

He thought of the rich couple from Iowa whom he'd taken to the caves of the Old Ones. He snickered as he remembered how they'd nearly killed themselves with heat prostration carrying the bushels of pottery shards that they'd tried to take back with them. He compared them with the man behind him and thought, "Too bad about those two. They weren't so bad, after all." He remembered how surprised they'd been when he'd taken the ladder away and left them there with the Guardians. He could hear them hollering and yelling for miles as he rode away. But then they had quieted down. Sometimes the Guardians took their time. Beneath his hat brim he glanced behind at this white man, who fancied himself a snake hunter, and spat through the gap between his broken front teeth. "Whites," he thought. "They're all nuts."

Restlessly he scanned the horizon, wondering where it would show itself today. Then he saw it: a wide track in the sand that wound along the dry riverbed. It looked as if the Spirit of the River itself had come to life and writhed briefly in the sun. The track climbed out of the river bottom, entered a brushy patch of ground and disappeared on a rock outcropping. It wasn't much, but it would qualify as the proof of the Great *Culebra* that this gringo wanted to see so badly. "There," he said and pointed to the track.

"Where? I don't see it."

"In the dry river."

"Oh, my God," the white man said reverently. "God bless your Irish great-grandmother—you weren't lyin', after all. All them legends must be true." He spurred his horse forward, careful not to damage the trail of the creature that they had been seeking for so many days.

When the Indian caught up with him he was on his knees in the sand with a metal measuring tape. "Got to be thirty—thirty-five—maybe even forty feet long and pretty near as thick-round as a heifer. How long have you known about this thing?"

"My people have always known of the Great Serpent. It has always been here." As if to change the subject he held out his hand and demanded, "Thirty dollars."

But the white man was pacing off the length of the wide tracks in the sand, growing more and more excited. "Twenty-five years in this business and I finally hit pay dirt. This one's worth its weight in gold. I've seen all the snakes this godforsaken country has to offer and I've never come across anything like this." He addressed the tracks directly, saying, "I don't know what you are, but back East they'll pay plenty heap-big money for you."

Softly he said to himself, "Holy Jesus, D. K. Beasley, you're lookin' at your retirement!"

He turned to the mounted Indian and said, "And I'm gonna share it with you, Joe. You'll be rich, too." He began to unstrap the leather case that held his camera and tripod.

The Indian reached for the canteen that hung from his saddle next to the fringed scabbard that held his .30/06. "Thirty dollars," he repeated, fixing his level, brown gaze on the white man, who panted in the blazing sun, his hat pushed back upon his head.

"How can you think of a measly thirty dollars at a time like this? Don't you have any sense of pri-or-i-ties? This is the biggest moment of your life. Don't you realize what you're looking at here, Joe? You're a rich man now. You'll be able to buy yourself a nice spread—herd of pretty cattle— maybe even a Model A. What's thirty dollars—between friends?" He smiled at the Indian for the first time.

"Thirty dollars," Joe Spotted Wolf said resolutely, wiping his mouth on the back of his hand.

The white man stopped fussing with the tripod, looked at the Indian for a long moment and then sighed. "Okay, okay. You sure are hardheaded. Must be the Irish half of you, huh?" He grinned at the Indian and his smile faded in the man's impassive stare. Beasley pulled his hat squarely on his head and withdrew three ten-dollar bills from his wallet. Holding them out to the Indian he said, "Now, get down here and give me a hand with this. I want to get some solid evidence before we go back to town and that telegraph office. Can you tell where it is now? We're going to get some supplies and a wagon and come back here pronto. This is one *culebra* that ain't going to get away from old D. K."

"Just exactly what kind of a deal did you have with my father, Mr. Beasley?" Ehrich Leftrack spoke into the telephone.

"Call me D. K., son. 'Mr. Beasley' sounds mighty formal for an old, leather-bellied snake hunter like me."

"All right, D. K. Please understand, since my father's illness I've had to take things in hand and I'm not completely familiar with all the ins and outs of his dealings. Also, our business has changed somewhat. We are no longer interested in purchasing imported specimens for resale." Ehrich was impressed with the businesslike ring of that phrase. He leaned back in his father's swivel chair and unsuccessfully tried to lift one beefy leg onto the desk in front of him.

"Yeah, I heard about the feds lifting your license, but I'm telling you, son, this is no imported animal. It's right here. Thirty miles to the east of San Diego. And since when does anyone need a license to sell a rattler or a whipsnake or a handful of garters?"

"I see, Mr. Beas—er, D. K. But there's no native snake that's even close to as big as you say this one is. Only boas and pythons grow that large and the rosy boa can't come close to those measurements. As far as I know there's no American snake that's even over twenty feet long. There's certainly none that's thicker around than a telephone pole, as you say this specimen is."

Ehrich didn't add that he wanted nothing whatsoever to do with this or any snake. The memory of the python that had nearly killed his father was still fresh in his mind. Even though it had happened more than a year ago, the mere thought of those coils about his father's chest gave him palpitations.

"Son, I can't explain it any more than I can explain any of the other strange things that I've seen in this country. I could tell you stories that would make your hair stand on end. All true—no fabrications. Why, the things I've seen creeping around the fire at night in the mountains and deserts in these parts would freeze your blood. This is still unexplored territory—wild country. The redskins say there's a band of giants living in the hills and I believe 'em. Heck, we've only been a part of the Union for twenty years or so.

"All I can tell you is that if I were Ira Leftrack's son, I'd catch the first train out west. D. K. Beasley is on the trail of the largest snake known to civilization. And you're the fella who's going to sell it for him. I admit it, son, I'm no good with that end of the business. But I know for sure that the Bronx Zoo has a standing offer of five thousand for a snake this big and God-only-knows how much the Ringling Brothers or Barnum and Bailey might cough up. It's a risk, I'll admit that. But for this kind of money, don't'cha think it's worth it?"

"I don't want to have anything to do with catching snakes," Ehrich said.

"Son, you don't have to lift a finger to be in on this. Catching this monster is my end of it. Selling it is yours. This is the chance of a lifetime, but if you're not interested, I'll call someone who has a little imagination. Someone who can see what this really means.

"Believe-you-me, if anyone had told me that Ira Leftrack's boy would turn his nose up at a chance like this, I'd've never believed it. I always thought you folks had a sixth sense for makin' money."

Ehrich Leftrack reached for the box of chocolates that he kept in his top drawer for emergencies like this. Quickly he popped two nonpareils into his mouth and thought, "Can I believe this crazy man? Will it be good for business?"

"The publicity alone'll be worth a million to you. Ask your father—he'll tell you."

Ehrich had the fleeting image of his father livid and raving incoherently against the restraints of the straitjacket. Last week he'd tried to strangle his nurse. His doctors were talking about shock treatments, definitely hospitalization for life. "I wonder how much that'll be?" Ehrich thought. "Maybe shock treatments will be too much for his heart. People do die from them." He realized that there was an expectant silence on the other end of the phone line and hastily continued, "No, I'm afraid that's impossible."

The chocolate melted reassuringly against his palate, leaving a residue of sugary pellets that gave Ehrich confidence and helped him to decide. "Give me three days, Mr. Beas— I mean, D. K. What did you say the name of that town was?

"In the meantime, I want you to capture that snake. If it's what you say it is, we'll earn a bundle. I assume that your agreement with my father was the usual seventy-thirty?"

"No," lied D. K., "we always split fifty-fifty."

"Sixty-forty," bargained Ehrich Leftrack. "Otherwise it isn't worth my time."

"You've got a deal," said D. K., adding, "You're a hard bargainer, boy. Just like your old man." He smiled as he hung up the phone.

Ehrich said goodbye and replaced the receiver in its cradle. He thoughtfully put two more chocolate wafers on his tongue and savored their rich flavor as they softened to a lovely, thick fudge. "What's sixty percent of five thousand dollars?" he wondered. "Two thousand dollars would pay for medical school and I'd have some left over." Resolutely, Ehrich took pencil and pad from his top desk drawer, picked up the phone again and asked, "Operator, give me the number of the *Brooklyn Star* and the *Los Angeles Herald*."

Later that afternoon Ehrich Leftrack was at Grand Central Terminal. Behind him a porter struggled beneath suitcases and a hamper bulging with necessities for the trip: volumes five and six of A. V. Bracegirdle's *Atlas of Human Neural Anatomy*, as well as a ten-pound box of chocolates, six bottles of cream soda, a salami, a dozen poppy-seed bagels, a pound of lox and cream cheese, a crock of gefilte fish and a brown paper bag filled with rugelach that his mother had made just in case her baby got hungry on his trip across the country.

He gave the porter a nickel tip, loosened his belt and settled into his seat, asking, "Which way to the dining car?"

Even though she distrusted them, Nemi led Dervish's traveling companions through mile after mile of desert, always moving toward the mountains that stood between them and this strange place that they talked about so much. Sandeagozu. She hated the sound of it. "But why do they want to go there so badly, Dervish?" she asked. "It makes no sense for you to go back to humans. They've never been particularly kind to you, have they?"

She wanted to ask Dervish if he were going to this Sandeagozu with the others. Many times she said to him, "I'll take you to the trail up the mountain and point you in the right direction, but no coati in her right mind would go up there." It was as close as she could come to an ultimatum. Nemi wanted Dervish to volunteer to stay with her in her sagebrush and creosote bush desert. The winter flowers were just beginning to blossom. She wanted to show him the whole fields of flowers that would come in the spring and the elf owls and the comical roadrunners. She wanted him to help her raise the little ones that would arrive in a few months. Although she wanted him to stay with her more than anything, Nemi realized that it was probable that Dervish would follow the others across the mountain wall. He was so devoted to the old monkey and that horrid, big snake. "It doesn't make any sense," she said to herself many times. "Chulos belong with chulos." But her opinions didn't seem to make any impression on Dervish.

Through many still afternoons she lay sleepless in the burrow that they had dug for themselves and the others, listening to him breathe as he curled protectively around her. She waited for the hot hours to pass and wondered what she could do to get him to stay. If only he would forget these others, these Culls.

She had considered leading the monkey and those two awful snakes into a trap. It would have been simple to take them up a rock face and then start an "accidental" rockslide. The monkey always foraged behind them and she'd had many opportunities to put the deadly, straw-colored scorpions into his path. But Nemi had hesitated and now could not bring herself to harm Manu. "I should have done it that first night, when we took them away from the truck," she thought. "That was my best chance." Months of travel had endeared Manu to Nemi and, though it might have given her all of Dervish's affections, she was no longer able to kill the langur. She kept her distance from the two snakes, however, and as time passed grew sadly resigned to leading this strange party of exotic animals toward the city that lay beyond the western mountains.

"But I'll miss you, Dervish," she said to herself, as they waited for the hot hours to pass, dozing in the shade of a grove of smoke trees. Nemi had rehearsed her final confrontation with Dervish a thousand times. She pictured herself alone in the desert, watching his silhouette slip out of sight, lost beyond the far mountains. She resolved, "I won't cry. I'll be brave. He'll never know how much he's hurt me."

Sherahi lay nearby. Although she was completely submerged beneath a foot of sand she alertly scanned the intelligence above her. She noted the dozing dream of a horned toad that slept in the comfortably warm layer of sand a few inches beneath the burning surface and marveled that his mind worked in such a birdlike fashion: thought chasing thought like sulfur butterflies battling above a meadow. She also eavesdropped on Nemi. Sherahi saw her restless worry over Dervish. She saw the melodrama that Nemi rehearsed and felt pity for the lovesick female coatimundi.

In Nemi's mind was a firm bond for Dervish, amalgamated out of love and need and loneliness. Sherahi also saw that this bond was a permanent feature in Nemi's mind and was surprised at its strength and the tenacity with which it penetrated all of Nemi's quick thoughts. "I know that there's nothing like this in Dervish's mind. Oh, he likes Nemi well enough, but Manu raised Dervish and I wouldn't be surprised if Dervish thinks of himself as a kind of long-nosed langur."

In Nemi's mind Sherahi saw the image of the little female coati fighting tears as Dervish bounded out of sight, following the Culls up into the mountains. "Nemi is right," Sherahi's slow thoughts milled. "It would be better if Dervish stayed here with her. After all, what'll there be for him in Sandeagozu? Manu will have his tribe and I'll have a consortium of other pythons, but will Dervish ever be happier than he'd be here in this desert with Nemi?"

Sherahi examined Dervish's mind and, as usual, it was filled with thoughts of food. She smiled in her scaly way, remembering that even as a baby Dervish had thought about his stomach first. "Where can it be?" she wondered, peering with distaste beneath thoughts of sugary, prickly-pear fruits, sensations of tart stalks of agave and the crunchy tubers that Nemi had taught him to find. She saw the nauseating smell of the carrion that he had learned to relish, the crunch of grasshopper legs and the minty odor of Indian paint. She saw the memory of the lizards that Nemi had taught him to catch: leopard lizards; banded geckos, with their soft, almost scaleless skin; and little night lizards that tasted more like insects than reptiles. Finally, beneath the sensation of the meaty hind legs of long-tailed jumping mice, she located his attachment for Manu. Beside it she was surprised to find a puddle of fondness for a remarkably handsome, very large snake. She was examining the features of this serpent, thinking how intelligent it looked, when its gold-and-black eyes suddenly flickered in his imagination, and with a start she recognized her own image. "I didn't know that Dervish thought that much of me," Sherahi hissed in amazement. Quite unexpectedly she found that she was pleased with her discovery.

Working quickly while Dervish slept she began to subtly rearrange the features of the langur that he carried in his mind. Soon the forward-looking eyes had been moved to the sides of its head and the rounded chin had been drawn out into a coati's nosy muzzle. Manu's smooth face, with its black and pink skin, had been coated with gray-brown fur and now a pert, white circle surrounded each eye. Dervish would now identify with this new image, which was the exact duplicate of Nemi. Sherahi even sculpted the idiosyncratic curve of her lip and the faint scar on her left cheekbone. So that she could admire her handiwork from a distance, Sherahi straightened up some of the mess in Dervish's mind and placed Nemi's image at the forefront of his thoughts, obscuring the memories of his favorite foods. She sighed contentedly as she surveyed what she had done, thinking, "Now he won't follow us to Sandeagozu. He'll stay here in this desert, where his kind belong. Nemi won't have to actually live through that sad parting that she's rehearsed so many times. Bet she'll be surprised."

Sherahi withdrew her scan from Dervish's mind. As usual when dealing with a mammalian brain, the pythoness was fatigued. She felt soiled by the residue of warm-blooded emotions that stubbornly clung to her ordered, reptilian thought patterns. Although she was fond of Dervish, delving into his mind was like diving into a barrel of rotting fruit and she was glad that this job was finished.

She was trying to cleanse herself of the unpleasant residue from Dervish's thoughts by scanning the minds of cold-blooded creatures in the vicinity, running her mind through the hot sand in the way a skunk-sprayed dog rubs his face against the ground to wipe away the odor, when she detected the sound of small voices calling from the topmost branches of the smoke trees that shaded the ground. She cast her mind aloft and found that the branches were covered with a crowd of incredibly small spiderlings. Their bodies were pale yellow, gaily splotched with red and so minute that twenty of them could have danced the Virginia reel on her rostral scute. The smoke tree looked as though it had grown gossamer hair and many of the little spiders stood on the tips of their eight legs, with the ends of their abdomens pointed toward the sky. "What are they waiting for?" Sherahi wondered. "What can they be doing?"

As she watched their curious posture and listened to their excited cries, the afternoon breeze began to blow. It lofted the silken strands that they spun, carrying them up and out of sight. Each spiderling was now attached to a single, glistening fiber. The bravest of the crowd flexed his claws at once, and clenched them around his strand in an eight-legged fist. Sherahi was astonished to see him float away.

"See," he cried triumphantly. "That's how you do it, you 'fraidy cats. Cummon. It's fun. Goodbye, Mama. Goodbye." His squeaking voice faded and Sherahi lost sight of him as he sailed high above the cholla cacti and creosote bushes into the distance.

The breeze grew stronger and the excitement increased in the crowd of spiderlings. More and more of them grew brave enough to assume the peculiar posture, standing on tiptoe, and more and more of them were carried away by the afternoon breeze. "Whee," they cried. "Rollo was right. It is fun!"

"Goodbye. Goodbye, Mama. Take care of yourself. Tell Papa that we said goodbye. We're sorry that he's not feeling well enough to see us off."

Sherahi chuckled as she saw two fierce infants quarreling. "Look out," said one. "Your silk's getting tangled with mine."

"It's not my fault. You're in my way."

"Now look what you've done. We'll both have to start all over again."

One by one they ballooned out of sight, suspended from their gossamer strands, crying, "Look how high up I am."

"Look how beautiful my balloon is."

Even as they sailed away the two infants continued their quarrel. "Beautiful?" said the first. "You call that beautiful? Look at my balloon. Now, that's beauty."

"No," said his sister. "Your balloon is all scraggly. Look at mine. It's gorgeous."

"Yeah, well, if you don't watch out a bat'll get you."

"Not me. I'm too smart for that. But you'll be gobbled up by a swallow the minute you take off."

"Says who?"

The breeze grew stronger and the quarrel between the two infant spiders was drowned as their sisters and brothers called, "Goodbye. Goodbye, Mama." Singly and in small groups all of the spiderlings sailed out of sight. The voices of the brother and sister could be heard quarreling in the distance. "Watch where you're going, Stupid. Don't you know how to do anything right?"

"Me? You were the one who crashed into me. It's all your fault that we'll have to start all over again. Hurry up. We don't want to be left behind. Mama said that that was a bad thing."

They scrambled to the top of a piñon pine and called, "Goodbye again. Goodbye, Mama." The little voices faded in the distance and Sherahi heard a tearful reply, "Goodbye. Goodbye, my little ones." Then it broke into delicate sobs and sniffles. Sherahi was intrigued and followed the sounds to a small burrow between the roots of the smoke tree. Her questing mind probed the entrance, pushing down a tunnel past the strands of sticky silk that webbed its opening. She peered into the darkness and saw that the walls of the burrow were covered with lustrous silk. A grief-stricken, shiny black spider sat crumpled at the rear of this silken chamber. Her abdomen heaved with each sob. Beside her lay the discarded egg case that until only recently had protected her hatchlings. A number of odd-shaped, silk-wrapped lumps hung from the silken ceiling and they reminded Sherahi of the sausages and hams that used to hang in the window of the butcher shop across from Leftrack's pet shop.

One of these lumps quivered and Sherahi heard it speak: "Don't take on so, lovey," the muffled voice said. "That's the way children are. You've got to expect that they'll leave home. How else do you expect to become a grandparent?"

The spider didn't reply. She only sobbed harder and turned the silken memento of her children over and over with a pair of her legs. Slowly she began to nibble one corner of the precious egg case. She had carried it below her abdomen for months, cherishing the minute, developing spiderlings.

"Such sweet children," she gasped. "I know, Papa, I know they've got to leave us," the spider said between mouthfuls. "I remember when I left my own mother and father. But it's so sad to think of them all floating away. And I know that most of them will perish. They don't know that, of course. I've lied to them in the way that we always lie to our little ones. They believe that they're going on a great adventure out of this dark burrow and up into the bright world. If they knew what was waiting for them they probably wouldn't have the courage to go at all.

"Oh, Papa," she cried, breaking into sobs again, "they're so innocent." She stuffed the last remnant of the egg case between her fangs and combed her eight legs through her hairy mouthparts, sniffling all the while.

"Don't you think that you could untie me now, lovey?" her mate timidly asked. "They've all gone, haven't they? I think I've been in here long enough. Our little charade for their benefit is over and my legs are cramped. You tied me up awfully tight, I must say."

"Well, Papa," the spider sighed, stretching up to gently grasp the silk-wrapped package that trembled ever so slightly between her claws. "I'm afraid that I can't do that. You see, I lied to you, too. And now it's your turn to go on a journey, my dear." Her fangs penetrated the silk and Sherahi saw the outline of the eight legs of the male spider move convulsively against his silken shroud. He gave a little cry and then was still. As the spider hunched over her extravagantly wrapped meal Sherahi saw the red hour-glass clearly delineated on the underside of her abdomen. The pythoness also saw that the spider was weeping again as she began to suck in the partially digested flesh of her mate, murmuring to him coquettishly as if she were speaking to a dinner companion, "How else do you expect to be a grandfather, Papa?"

Sherahi withdrew her scan from the underground burrow. She was glad to hear the Culls stirring in the twilight around her and was anxious to leave the grove of smoke trees and their fierce, subterranean inhabitants. "The more I see of this world," she thought, "the queerer it becomes. It'll be good to get to the pythons in Sandeagozu. At least I'll understand them."

CHAPTER FIFTEEN

ORDLESSLY, JOE SPOTTED WOLF motioned for D. K. Beasley to follow him to the edge of the canyon. In pantomime he made it clear that the snake hunter should make no noise that might alert the animal that they'd tracked for three days and two nights. Excitedly he pointed below, and although D. K. didn't like being ordered about by the half-breed, he obeyed. He knew it was important. He watched the Indian's tense posture and stony expression, thinking, "This's gotta be it."

Following his tracker's example, Beasley silently dismounted, tied his horse to a sand-blasted juniper and began to climb. When he finally reached the top of the mesa he dropped to all fours and, with his binoculars swinging to and fro, stealthily crawled toward a clump of bushes at the edge of the canyon, where Joe Spotted Wolf waited, lying on his belly, peering down intently. The early-morning sun was already strong on Beasley's back. It burned through his shirt and singlet.

"Dammit," he said aloud as a twig snapped beneath his left knee.

Instantly the Indian's hand went up, ordering him to stop. D. K. froze, afraid that another wrong move would scare this animal that he wanted so very badly.

With his eyes fastened to the Indian's hand, Beasley waited for the signal to move ahead. He thought of the wary, enormous snake, imagined it waiting in the canyon below and prayed, "Don't run, snake. That little sound was nothing; just a mule deer picking her teeth with juniper buds." Then Joe Spotted Wolf's hand dropped and Beasley silently crawled to the rim of the canyon floor, taking care to avoid any twigs lurking in his path.

"There," the Indian whispered. "On this side of those rocks."

There was a swirl of movement. Through binoculars D. K. saw a gigantic tail disappear into the canyon floor. It was over in moments and D. K. had the impression of a thick stream of water pouring into thirsty ground. As he watched, something was pushed into the opening and it looked as if the entrance to the burrow had been plugged from the inside.

"What the hell kind of a snake is that?" he thought to himself. "Even a shovelnose doesn't close its burrow like that."

"I'll be damned if I know what that thing is," he whispered, "but we've got it now." He pounded the Indian on the back with glee. "And we're gonna catch it. That's for damn sure."

The heat grew more intense as the two men studied the canyon where the snake had gone to ground. Joe Spotted Wolf envied the snake's cool burrow and thought, "Now the Great *Culebra* sleeps below the earth. He will sleep and dream until the moon is high. It is just as Grandmother said." He looked at the huge track that led to the snake's hiding place. It occurred to him that the moon would be full tonight: the Wolf Moon would watch as they caught this big snake. The Wolf Spirit was his namesake, his guardian. It would not be pleased.

Joe Spotted Wolf fingered the amulet around his neck, remembering the wrinkles around his Grandmother's watermelon-seed eyes. Across the gulf of lost years he said, "I've got to do this, Grandmother." She had been dead for nine years, but Spotted Wolf often spoke to her eyes as they watched him across the fire. He knew that it was a bad idea to try to catch the Great *Culebra*—especially tonight, when the Wolf Moon was high.

He watched the buzzards shaking their rusty-black feathers and stretching those snaky necks that were the color of dried blood. He knew that their bloodshot, black eyes could count the hairs on the back of his hand. Grandmother's voice whispered, "Get out of here, Spotted Wolf. Get away from this white man before it's too late." But then he thought about the things he would buy with the money that Beasley had promised. He saw himself behind the wheel of a car, a Model A with shiny running boards. He saw a pair of new boots to replace his worn-out pair and a fancy suit that had come all the way from St. Louis. He saw the faceless woman he'd be able to buy and thirty head of stocky, red-and-white beef cattle. "What harm could it do?" he wondered. "D. K. said that the whites will give the *Culebra* a cage of gold to live in and all the food he can eat. What else could a snake want—even a magic snake like this one?

"It will be all right," he reassured himself. "The *Culebra* will never know the difference." He stared into the shiny, black eyes that watched him from the shade at the foot of the mesa and said, "Shut up, Grandmother."

Two jackrabbits entered the canyon and began to forage on the salt bushes that were just beginning to put out leaves. On the rim of the opposite canyon the flock of vultures became more active, flapping and airing those rag bags they called feathers. One by one they half-waddled, half-ran toward the canyon rim. Most stopped short and looked around as if they had forgotten what they'd meant to do. A few launched into space and laboriously flew across the chasm, toward the spot where D. K. and Joe Spotted Wolf lay hidden by a screen of bushes. The two men could have touched each vulture as it rose on the column of warm air that rushed up from the superheated rocks below. Buoyed out of the canyon, the buzzards solemnly spiraled out of sight.

In the distance Beasley could see the leaders of the flock angling toward the next rising column of air, moving lazily, as if they had all the time in the world. "It won't be long before they're prospecting for breakfast," Beasley thought and he, too, began to get restless. "We're wasting time," he said. "That snake won't move until nightfall." He got up and motioned to the Indian to follow him down to the horses.

Each drank from his canteen and D. K. said, "Now we've got to catch that thing. You ride into town. Get the wagon and our supplies and get back here as quickly as possible.

"I'll watch to see if he comes out of that hole. If you don't find me here, just follow my trail. I'm sure that snake'll stay hidden until late tonight. We'll have plenty of time to get things set up. We'll fix it so that that critter practically catches hisself."

Beasley watched the Indian lead his horse away. He was always amazed at how silent they could be. Then he unslung his bedroll and pack, and unsaddled his horse. He thought about fixing himself breakfast and then remembered, "That fella Leftrack ought to be in town by now. I'd better tell Spotted Wolf to fetch him. No telling how long this'll take. We might need an extra hand."

He called out to the Indian, who had reached the bottom of the cliff and was about to mount his horse and head for the main road. "And check at the hotel for an Easterner called Ehrich Leftrack. Bring him along." As an afterthought he added, "And stay away from the liquor."

Beasley's words echoed in the canyon below, reverberating over the sandy ground where Sherahi and the other Culls rested. Spotted Wolf heard the echo and winced. He wanted to warn Beasley to shut up, but it was too late. Once again, Grandmother whispered in the dark medicine lodge. The fire illuminated her lined face, turning it into a slit-eyed mask. The image flickered and she said, "You must be careful of what you say, my son. The *Culebra* hears everything we say in the desert. You don't want him to know that you're a fool." All the way to town he was followed by the uncomfortable sensation that he was being watched. It made the hair on the back of his neck prickle and he spurred his horse on, wanting to get away from the scrutiny.

Only after he'd downed three whiskeys and three beers did Joe Spotted Wolf begin to feel better. Once again he confronted that face across the fire and said, "Go to hell, Grandmother."

Secure within the burrow that the coatis had dug to escape the hot hours, Sherahi lay with her chin pressed against the hard-packed earth and waited for sleep. Traveling in the desert night gave the Culls relief from the heat, but each dawn found Sherahi eagerly anticipating the time when Nemi and Dervish would stop and dig, searching for a place to make the burrow that would shelter all from the sun. The lavender dawn would give way to a pale-lemon wash low on the eastern horizon, as Nemi and Dervish made sure that the burrow was large enough and safe. Long before the sky was white-hot and the smoke trees shimmered in the heat, all the Culls would be in their subterranean retreat, hidden from the sun and the skyful of predators.

Sherahi listened to the familiar sound of the other Culls drowsing around her. She was thinking about how surprised Dervish would be when he discovered that he was unable to leave Nemi and follow the others to Sandeagozu when her jawbones brought the sound of nearby hoofbeats to the ears that were buried deep within her skull. Sherahi listened and, like an owl gliding on soundless wings, held her breath so that she could hear better. "It's coming closer," she decided and, even though she was tired, she summoned the energy to cast a message to the pony that cantered across the canyon floor, warning him to come no closer. "Holes," her message hissed. "Ankle-snapping holes. Stay away."

She heard the hoofbeats falter and stop and could sense the fear in the stiff-legged, ears-flattened stance of the pony that capered above, urged forward by the man who crouched on his back.

The Culls had traveled all night and Sherahi was so tired that she hadn't even had the energy to erect and maintain the mental screen that usually hid their retreat. Bone tired, she had followed the others down into the burrow, grateful that their journey was over—at least for another day.

"Not now," she prayed. "I want to sleep." As if in reply, the hoofbeats grew fainter as Joe Spotted Wolf cursed his pony, turned him in a tight semicircle and galloped away.

Worried that it had been a bad mistake not to erect the usual mental screen about their burrow's entrance, Sherahi traced the hoofbeats to the man who rode the pony and scryed his mind. She saw the crazy quilt of his hopes and fears, featherstitched with superstitions from two cultures and embroidered with the Irish Catholicism that was all that his father had given him. She saw the candles flickering in their red glasses on the altar and smelled incense. The sweet-faced statue of the Virgin had a crown of twisted antlers and a rattlesnake coiled in the lace that edged her blue mantle. Desert poppies and foamflowers were strewn below her bare feet. Sherahi saw his guilt at leaving the bespectacled couple from Iowa at the mercy of the Guardians, and his habit of allowing himself to forget everything by drinking too much alcohol. Draped over all of this, like a fat woman sleeping upon a settee that was too small, was his plan to sell the Great *Culebra* and become a rich man.

"Great *Culebra*," Sherahi thought. "That must mean me. Well," she sighed, "I suppose this had to happen sooner or later. We've been lucky to get this far without trouble from humans." She saw Joe Spotted Wolf's amalgam of fear and respect of a white man called D. K. and concluded, "There are two humans following us. Where is the other one?"

She scanned the tops of the rock walls of the canyon and found a dust-covered man asleep in the spare shade of a grove of thirsty junipers. His head was propped against his saddle blanket and his hat was pulled down over his stubbly cheeks. As if she were climbing into a tree hung with lianas and fragile touch-me-not orchids, Sherahi insinuated a path into D. K. Beasley's mind. She saw how he meant to capture the Great *Culebra*, as well as his plan to cheat Spotted Wolf and Ehrich Leftrack.

"Ehrich Leftrack?" Sherahi was astounded. "Can it be the same hairy biped whose father trafficked in animals stolen from their homes? The same boy whose father maimed Manu and caused the Duchess to cannibalize herself with boredom? That human slug who was so afraid to touch me that he poured my medicine down the drain and then lied about it? That worm hoped that I would die of mouth rot so that he could cut me open and see my insides. He even poisoned Manu and his father blamed it all on poor, old Sorensen. Oh, if only I'd strangled both of those Leftracks when I had the chance."

The memory of the elder Leftrack's face turning blue-gray within her coils surfaced slowly in her cold mind and Sherahi remembered how close she'd come to killing him. "This time it's going to be different," she resolved. "This time Ruthie won't be around to stop me. He will pay for all the harm he and his father have done."

Sherahi lashed restlessly in the dark burrow, clenching her coils, imagining how Ehrich Leftrack's hot body would feel within her deadly embrace. Her muscles rippled from head to tail as she imagined how she would squeeze and squeeze, alert for the slightest relaxation of his chest, which would allow her to tighten her scaly vise ever more. Bit by bit she would wring the life from him and then cast him aside, a rag of bruised meat. "Even for a human, Ehrich Leftrack is lower than a rat-tailed maggot. When I'm done with him he'll die like a toad rolled flat by a truck, spitting out his guts into the dirt."

Sherahi thought of how weary all of the Culls were, worn thin with the strain of continual traveling. Manu had lost the well-fed, sleek appearance that six months in the crystal house had imparted. Now he was perpetually tired and loped haltingly behind Nemi and Dervish, a wizened handful of bird bones covered with silver fur. Even Dervish and Nemi had lost weight and Sherahi had noticed that the scales of her belly were dulled and worn from continual slithering over rough ground. "We've come so far," she thought. "We've nearly reached the mountains and Sandeagozu is just on the other side. We've worked too hard to be stopped now. I can't let Leftrack and these others catch us. I swear I'll kill them if they try. No one will keep us from getting to Sandeagozu. No one."

Sherahi's angry thrashing awakened Manu. Sleepy and confused, he huddled against the pair of sleeping coatis and wondered, "What's wrong with Sherahi? Why isn't she asleep, too?"

Before he had been captured Manu had been raised to assume the leadership of his large, tribal family. Even though Leftrack had interfered with this plan many years ago, Manu still remembered the elaborate rules of etiquette that had once ruled his actions. One of the things that the Hanuman langur did not do was eavesdrop. It was impolite and Manu listened to the big snake thrash around in the dark burrow for a long time before deciding to look into her mind and read her thoughts.

In Sherahi's mind, Manu was horrified to see slow, violent millstones that crushed Ehrich Leftrack. "Why is she still thinking about him?" Manu wondered. "Maybe I've gotten it wrong. Maybe it isn't Ehrich Leftrack." The langur took a second look and saw Sherahi rehearse Ehrich Leftrack's death. He also saw the glimmer of an idea to use Junior's venomous talents to dispose of other humans who were following the Culls. Her plan to use Junior instead of killing them herself made Manu smile in spite of himself. He thought, "How like a serpent: Sherahi is always stingy with her energy."

Manu knew that Sherahi could easily kill a human. Murder was as natural to her as stealing ripe mangoes was to him. But he'd never allowed himself to dwell upon the strength of her coils and, of course, it was unthinkable that she might try to hurt him or one of the other Culls. She was their leader and had saved each of them many times since they'd left the pet shop. Ordinarily Manu would have deferred to her judgment and would never have questioned one of her plans. "This is a mistake, though," he thought as he saw the idea to kill the three humans take form in her mind. "If she does this, we'll never get to Sandeagozu alive."

"No, Pythoness." Manu's unspoken thought fell like a withered leaf into the whirling pools of Sherahi's thoughts. In true reptilian fashion she paid no attention and he saw a bloated human face bob to the surface. Hair clung wetly to the man's forehead and Manu saw the face of the fat boy he'd once bitten in Leftrack's pet shop. Manu saw Ehrich Leftrack flail and struggle, but the pythoness had no pity. Relentlessly she submerged him in the turbulent wash of her hatred.

"No, Sherahi," Manu repeated. "You cannot kill him. If you do, it will only be the beginning of terrible trouble for us. More humans will come. We might be able to kill some of them but, sooner or later, even more will come and they will bring dogs and guns. They will have no more pity for us than you do for Leftrack's son."

"What should I do then, Manu? Let them capture me? Do you think you and the others can get all the way to Sandeagozu without my help?"

"You are right, Sherahi," Manu replied, "but you must be cunning. You are dealing with men. Even toad-brained men like Ehrich Leftrack are treacherous. You must be more devious than they are. Somehow you will find a way to either get rid of them or to make them take us to Sandeagozu."

"I don't think I could manage three humans at once. I'm tired, Manu."

"How about one?" asked Manu. "Surely, Sherahi, the most powerful serpent that ever slashed out of an egg can make one limp-willed human do as she wishes."

"Yes, I suppose so," sighed Sherahi. "I could handle them one by one. I could trick them, I suppose. But it would be so much easier to just kill them outright. I'd like that much better."

"That may be, Pythoness," said Manu. "But there is another problem. Have you realized how high those mountains are? I have been looking at them carefully and I believe that they are covered with snow. Tell me, Sherahi, how will we, and especially you, get through ice and snow?"

Sherahi did not reply. Manu knew that her eyes were not good enough to have seen ice and snow on the mountaintops. "I will consider these things, Manu," she sighed and rearranged her coils.

"He is right," Sherahi thought. "It would be a mistake to kill these three humans and leave their bones as a reminder. It would only bring more humans. There must be a way to use them, though. . . . A way that would take advantage of them. Then, when they are no longer needed, I can toss them aside.

"After all," she thought with an internal, scaly smile, "sometimes things that are cast aside get broken. Sometimes they are beyond repair and are lost forever."

———————————————

Ehrich Leftrack gripped the wooden seat of the buckboard and clenched his teeth to keep them from shattering as the wagon jounced along the desert road. Behind him the load of ropes and shovels clattered and his voice shook as he complained, "Do we have to go so fast?"

Joe Spotted Wolf concentrated on driving the team of horses. His only reply was an impassive glance at the fat Easterner who rode on the seat next to him, pale, hatless and sweating in the afternoon sun.

What Spotted Wolf didn't bother to say was that he was anxious to reach D. K. Beasley before sundown. Even at this distance his keen eyes saw the snake hunter silhouetted on the ridge above the canyon. He knew from the set of D. K.'s shoulders that the man was angry that he'd been kept waiting all day.

Joe Spotted Wolf put out one hand and covered Beasley's silhouette with the tip of one grimy fingernail. Giving a cry that was part war whoop and part rebel yell, he slapped the reins and braced himself to keep from losing his balance.

Beasley met the wagon at the foot of the hill. One look at the lathered team and another at Spotted Wolf told him that the Indian had been drinking. "Last time I'll send you to town on your own. Cummon, let's get that stuff down there. We want to set up while there's still light."

He held out his hand to Ehrich and said, "You must be young Leftrack. Pleased to meet you. I'm Dinsmore K. Beasley and this miserable specimen here is Joe Spotted Wolf. His ma was a Navajo squaw and his daddy was an Irish tinker. I s'pose he's got the best and the worst of both.

"Get out of there," he growled to Spotted Wolf. "I'm drivin' now."

Beasley tied his horse to the tail of the wagon, alongside the Indian's pony, and climbed aboard next to Ehrich. Spotted Wolf unsteadily relinquished his seat on the buckboard and collapsed in the midst of the supplies. As soon as Beasley had the wagon rolling toward the entrance to the canyon and had begun a conversation with Leftrack, Spotted Wolf stealthily helped himself to a swig from the bottle of whiskey that he'd hoarded inside his shirt. He was nodding when Beasley stopped the team and shook him roughly by the shoulder, saying, "Wake up, Spotted Wolf, you good-for-nothing excuse for a human being. Hand me down those tools."

Spotted Wolf slumped forward, completely unconscious, and Beasley took the bottle from his hand. With a curse he flung it at the canyon wall. He turned to Ehrich and said, "I guess I'll need your help after all, son. This one's no earthly use to anyone like this."

"I told you," Ehrich said, "I don't want to touch that snake. Our agreement was that you would have it packed and ready to go. I've come all the way out here from New York City. That's five days traveling, sir. I haven't eaten a decent meal since the day I left New York. I arrive in Coalston, am accosted by your friend here, am forced to come out here to the middle of nowhere with him. He nearly kills the both of us driving so recklessly. I didn't even have time to buy a proper hat. I'm tired and hungry and I think I have all the symptoms of sun poisoning. Now you want me to do your job, too." Ehrich rolled his eyes and sighed.

"As soon as we have the snake, Mr. Leftrack," said Beasley in a voice that dripped charm like a beehive leaking honey in the sun, "I'll fry you the finest steak this side of the Trans Pecos.

"Son, you look like a man who appreciates the finer things in life. Tell me, have you ever tasted baking-powder biscuits hot off the griddle? Well, I assure you that you ain't tasted nothin' till you've tucked in a good half dozen of D. K.'s famous baking-powder biscuits. Butter melting and drippin' all down your hand. So light they fly right into your mouth.

"You see the way things are with the Indian. Be a sport, son. I guarantee—you won't regret it."

"I won't have anything to do with the snake. I swear, Mr. Beasley, I won't go within thirty feet of it till it's crated and ready to be loaded onto the railroad car."

"Okay," said Beasley. "Have it your way. But I'll need you to help set up the lines."

Ehrich sighed and loosened his tie and unbuttoned his collar. "Steak, you said?"

"I guarantee, better'n anything Delmonico's has to offer. My special sauce, too—a secret handed down to me by old Grandpappy Beasley. Two gills heavy cream, an egg, a spoonful of fresh-grated horseradish and the secret ingredient."

Ehrich handed him a spade and a shovel and asked, "Secret ingredient?"

"Well," said D. K., "I generally don't tell—but since I knowed your pappy for such a long time, I guess it's safe—you'n me, we're sort of like kin."

D. K. came close to Ehrich and whispered, "Chicken fat."

"Chicken fat?" thought Ehrich. He imagined the taste of a sauce compounded of cream, horseradish and chicken fat and thought, "Of course!" His mouth began to water.

"Now you're talking," he said to Beasley and eagerly handed down the first box of supplies. It began to grow dark as the two men arranged the equipment on the ground next to the wagon according to Beasley's directions.

―――――――――――

From the cool, underground burrow Sherahi watched the two men sweating in the strong sun and smiled at the feeble plan that occupied D. K. Beasley's mind. She watched the snake hunter tie a snag of multiple, running slipknots in a thick rope and observed that this man was no beginner. Sherahi had seen knots such as these before. They had been used by the bad priests who had tried to capture her when she was a baby—only six feet long and naïve about the ways of men. She knew how effective these multiple loops were, how efficiently they trapped and held an unwary snake, not allowing backward or forward movement. She saw Beasley and Ehrich Leftrack approach the closed entrance of the burrow where she and the other Culls lay and felt the vibrations of their heavy footsteps and of the sledgehammer that Beasley used to send long stakes into the ground. "He knows what he's doing," thought Sherahi, "but, still, he's not as smart as he thinks he is."

The sound of hammering awoke Dervish and Nemi.

"What's that?" Dervish chittered, the fur along his spine bristling in fear.

"Men who have come to catch me," Sherahi said into his mind, her voice a ribbon spun of calm concentration. At once Dervish regained his composure and nonchalantly he began to groom the fur between his left hind toes.

"What are we going to do, Dervish?" whimpered Nemi. "We're trapped. This is solid rock beneath us. We can't dig out. They'll get us. Oh, Dervish, I'm afraid. I don't want to die down here. Men pour awful-smelling stuff down burrows to make animals come out. I'm scared, Dervish. I don't want to die down here. What'll we do?"

"Sherahi will take care of everything, Nemi," said Dervish. Protectively he nudged his mate's ear with his cold nose and tried to reassure her. "Now you'll see what I've told you about Sherahi. She can do things that even humans never thought of. You'll see."

"But, Dervish, what if . . ."

"Stop it, Nemi. Trust me. Sherahi will take care of us. She's gotten us out of worse scrapes than this. Come over here and lie down. Pacing back and forth won't help. It'll only tire you out in case we have to run for it and it'll distract the pythoness. We must allow her to concentrate."

Nemi obeyed, but her mind was busy imagining how she'd defend them from these humans. She saw her lip curl and she leaped at their throats. She would bite them if they dared touch her or Dervish. "Shhh," Dervish said, feeling her leg muscles quiver and hearing the growl roll in her chest. "Sherahi won't let them hurt us."

Nemi put her head on Dervish's thickly furred flank and waited in the darkness, wondering how the hideous snake could possibly outwit humans. "It can't be possible," she thought to herself. "Except for ravens, humans are the smartest creatures on earth. Everyone knows that."

Sherahi was busy scrying the minds of the two men above, watching the trap they arranged about the opening to the burrow. The looped line was set so that it would automatically encircle any large animal that emerged from this burrow. A small mammal could easily slip through the snare that was designed to pull tight around the gradually widening body of a long snake. "They know what I look like," thought Sherahi. "At least they think they do."

Sherahi watched through Beasley's eyes as he and Ehrich Leftrack piled boulders and cacti in two long rows leading away from the entrance. "A snake coming out of this burrow will have to go forward. It will automatically be caught in the other snares. As the snake struggles, the snares will tighten and the poor snake will be helpless. They've fixed it so that now the only way for me to leave this place is right through those snares." She couldn't help admiring Beasley's plan and smiled, thinking, "It is more interesting to deal with an intelligent opponent."

"That ought to do it," Beasley said to Ehrich Leftrack as he tied the free ends of the line of snares to a stout Joshua tree. "That'll catch him for sure. All we have to do is sit back and wait."

"How'll we see it?" asked Ehrich, aware of the ruddy light of the sunset.

"Well, we don't want much light. We're not going to track it, you know. But in case we need to, there's a full moon tonight," Beasley answered. "I've tracked plenty of snakes in the dark. I guess I can see as good in the dark as any goddamn cat-eyed snake.

"Let's get some grub while there's enough light to see what this fool's brought for us to eat."

Joe Spotted Wolf was snoring loudly in the rear of the wagon and Beasley lifted the remaining crate of supplies. With a disgusted expression he watched the Indian's saliva make a dark blot on the wooden slats of the wagon below his half-open mouth and Beasley muttered, "Lazy. Good-for-nothing. If I wasn't a Christian soul I'd have a mind to leave you out here for the buzzards."

To Leftrack he said, "Rule number one, Mr. Leftrack: Never. Never depend on an Indian who has a taste for whiskey—especially one who's half Irish. They always let you down."

The two walked back to the vantage point from which they could make dinner and watch the line of snares. "Grab that lantern, will you?" Beasley said.

"What's for dinner?" Ehrich asked, eyeing the heavy box, imagining the thick slabs of steak that Beasley had promised. The Indian would be asleep at dinner time. Perhaps he could ask for an extra share of dinner.

"Beans and rice," D. K. replied. "Bellyful of beans'll give you the strength to manage that big fella."

Later that night, after Ehrich had had thirds and shared the heel of the salami he'd brought from New York, he thought about the big snake and wondered, "What's he going to do once he's caught it?"

It suddenly occurred to Ehrich that there was no box or crate to hold the snake. The silence of the cool desert night was broken by the snores of Joe Spotted Wolf, the wail of a coyote and an owl insistently demanding, "Who-who-who?" Ehrich was about to ask Beasley how he intended to manage this detail when the snake hunter put down his coffee mug and began to behave in a strange, furtive manner.

Wordlessly he crept away from the campfire and toward the burrow. Soundlessly he checked and rechecked the security of the knots that held his snares in place. Once again he pulled with all his strength on the staked lines. They didn't budge. Beasley smiled and returned to the fire and kicked sand on it. "Any time now," he said, looking at the moon, which was high overhead. "Cummon."

Ehrich Leftrack followed the snake hunter to a spot closer to the burrow. He tried to be quiet, but bushes and rocks seemed to leap into his path and he made noises like a bull moose crashing through underbrush to escape a swarm of botflies.

Beasley winced at the noise Leftrack made, thinking with disdain, "City folk. They're worse than Injuns.

"Well," Beasley reconsidered, "at least he's sober."

"Look," he said as Leftrack panted beside him. "There he comes."

"What are we going to do once he's in the snares?"

"Wait till morning, young fella. Wait till morning. You don't want to fool with a snake that size till you can see what you're doin'."

A shadow appeared in the middle of the burrow. As the two men watched, it carefully pushed aside the snare that encircled the mouth of the burrow. Then the shadow hissed and a snake shape elongated leisurely in the moonlight. The two men's sight seemed to grow more acute as the velvety shadow moved on the pale earth. They could see the blotches on its head and neck.

Beasley could see horns of fanned scales that projected over its eyes. Its tongue darted in and out and its shape seemed to shift. He rubbed his eyes and whispered, "I could swear that thing's glowing in the dark. Do you see it, too? Or am I crazy?"

"I see it," said Leftrack. "Maybe we're both crazy."

The belly of the snake glowed with pale-green fire, as if hundreds of fireflies were within each scute. Something caught the moonlight and glittered from between its elaborately sculpted brows. As the vision flowed along the sand the two men saw sparks and gleams about its neck. Gradually their eyes could see the details of a broad, golden collar studded with gems arranged in subtle patterns.

"I've heard about this," said Beasley in a wondering whisper, "but I never thought it could be real. I figured it had to be the firewater talking. Consarn it, though, those crazy Indians was right."

The serpent's head and neck were clear of the burrow now and Ehrich could see the jewels that were embedded down the length of its spine. As the astonished men watched, yard after yard of the Great *Culebra* emerged into the moonlight. The texture and pattern of the jewels changed, but the glitter and flash of gold and faceted stones remained constant.

"Got to be worth millions," said Beasley, drawing his pistol and slapping the cylinder open to check that all bullets were in place. He spun it and said, "Can't let something like this get away." Then he took careful aim at the snake's glittering head.

"Wait," said Leftrack, grabbing Beasley's arm and pulling it down. "Listen to me," he said, not quite knowing where this knowledge came from, but confident that he was right; "wait till it's clear of that hole in the ground. If it goes back down we'll never be able to dig it out."

Beasley eyed Leftrack sharply, surprised at this fat boy's practical knowledge of the ways of snakes. "Maybe I was wrong about you, fella. Mighty good thinkin'. We'll wait."

As the two men watched, the Great *Culebra* continued to flow silently from its burrow, unrolling like the jeweled sash of a Hundu raja. Its huge body tapered and there was a single jewel at the tip of its tail that winked and beckoned to them in the moonlight.

"Hurry, D. K.," said Ehrich. "Shoot. It's getting away."

Beasley took careful aim. He had the jewel-encrusted brow of the serpent in his sights and fired two shots squarely into the beast's head. "Got him right between the eyes," he gloated. "Cummon."

There was a sound of thrashing in the cacti and creosote bushes around the snares and D. K. smiled, happy that he'd thought to erect that impenetrable barrier. "Not even a weevil can get through there," he thought to himself. "Whoopee," he hollered, throwing his hat high into the night sky. He pounded Ehrich on the back, threw his arms around his belly and gleefully lifted him off the ground. "We're rich! Did you see those stones and all that gold? Come on, boy. Don't just stand there with your face hanging out; let's go get it."

By moonlight they hurried across the ground to the burrow, expecting to see the great, jeweled serpent helplessly thrashing in the sand a short distance away. But there was only a broad track that wound sinuously away from the burrow, retreating into the darkness as far as they could see. Sounds came from beyond the place where the track disappeared from sight.

Beasley spotted something winking on the ground and picked up a glittering lump of yellow metal. "Winged him," he said triumphantly. "He's gone off to die by hisself. Probably won't quit till the sun rises. Snakes're like that. Let's take the horses and follow him. He can't go far all shot up like that."

Ehrich was so excited that he forgot to mention to Beasley that he'd never ridden anything wilder than the IRT subway line. But somehow it didn't matter. He felt supremely confident as Beasley handed him the reins of the Indian's pony. He watched Beasley vault into the saddle of his mare

414

and disappear. Still holding the reins, Ehrich climbed into the wagon, tip-toed around Joe Spotted Wolf and somehow clambered aboard the pony. "Giddiap," he said, kicking his heels into the animal's sides, feeling very much like a rugged frontiersman. He held both reins in one hand, grasping the saddle horn with the other, and bounced off into the night in the direction he thought Beasley had taken.

A few minutes of uncomfortable jouncing brought him to his senses. "Whoa, there," Ehrich said, sawing at the reins. "Why am I doing this?" he asked himself. "This is crazy. I can't ride. I don't know where I'm going. I'm not even sure where D. K. Beasley has gone."

Once again the image of the jeweled serpent glittered in his mind. Simultaneously he thought he heard Beasley calling him and turned the pony to the left and lurched away into the night, thinking, "He can't be far away."

"D. K.," Ehrich called eagerly. "Wait for me."

Moments later the echo returned from the cliffs. "D. K.—K.—K. Wait for me—me—me." Ehrich listened and galloped toward the sound.

Below ground Sherahi hissed to the other Culls. "Hurry," she commanded. "I can't keep this up for long. We must get out of here before it all collapses. Dervish, clear the entrance, but don't go out. Come back and listen carefully to my instructions."

Dervish obeyed and a short while later he was back at Sherahi's side. "It's open," he said, but the pythoness didn't immediately respond. A portion of her mind intently controlled Beasley and Ehrich Leftrack, creating the illusion of the brilliantly jeweled and feathered serpent that lured them out across the moonlit desert, making them race away from the Culls, this canyon and each other.

"We're ready, Sherahi," he said, tentatively touching her wide, scaly back with a gentle paw.

Sherahi spoke slowly, as if from a great distance. "Take Nemi with you and find the knot that is tied around the mouth of the burrow. Loosen and untie it."

Sherahi's mind watched as the two animals found the first knot in the looped snare. While Nemi held it still with her handlike paws, Dervish worried the knot with his paws and teeth, growling a little when the knot did not immediately loosen and then chirruping when it began to slide free. She saw Nemi carefully pull the rope away from the entrance to the burrow.

"Now," Sherahi's voice commanded in Dervish's mind, "tunnel beneath those rocks and bushes so that we can all get out of here." Sherahi saw the two coatis look down the avenue of snares bordered by thorns on either side. Purring to his mate, telling her to watch for danger, Dervish began to dig a tunnel that would dive below the hedge of thorn scrub and rock.

All this, while another portion of Sherahi's mind watched Beasley follow the illusion of the wide track she continually created and studded with pieces of fool's gold and worthless copper ore. Simultaneously she saw Leftrack chase phantom hoofbeats that led him deeper into the desert and hoped that soon he would be beyond the reach of potential rescuers, so that she could stop generating the hoofbeats and concentrate on managing the sleeping Indian. "By morning they'll both be lost and confused." She pictured Ehrich Leftrack hallucinating beneath the sun, deluded and befuddled, and she had no pity for him. She imagined Beasley in the morning when the illusory track of the Great *Culebra* would fade. "He has a better chance of surviving in the desert, but still, his chances are slim," she thought impassively. She heard geysers of sand fall onto the desert floor as Nemi and Dervish took turns digging in the tunnel, and she thought about Ehrich Leftrack and the snake hunter, both lost in the desert. "Things that are lost often get damaged," she reminded herself. "Serves them right."

"Come, Manu and Junior," Sherahi called. "Follow me and mind your feet," she warned. "Don't go near those snares." Above ground she followed Nemi's retreating tail into the tunnel that led down and out of the avenue of snares. Surfacing on the other side she began to slither toward the wagon and the sleeping Indian. With effort she ordered, "Hurry, Manu, climb into the wagon. Nemi, Dervish: unroll those blankets and bring them up here."

Sherahi herself lost no time in climbing into the wagon. As she did so, she began to manipulate the malleable mind of the unconscious half-breed who lay in the bed of the wagon. She saw his love of whiskey and, abandoning the ruse of the jeweled serpent for a moment, concentrated all her powers on this human. She made him imagine that a three-quarters-full bottle lay by his side. "Wake up," she commanded, holding her huge head aloft and swaying over his head. His eyelids flickered and, when he was able to focus on the form that hovered above him, he grabbed for the amulet that his grandmother had hung around his neck when he was a child. Sherahi fixed him with her steady, cat-eyed gaze and said, "Drive. As fast as you can to Sandeagozu."

Keeping his eyes on the gigantic serpent, the Indian scuttled to the wagon seat, released the hand brake and grabbed the reins.

Just in time the two coatis appeared, tugging blankets up over the wagon side behind them. "Here, Sherahi," Dervish chittered. "Where should we put them?"

"Anywhere," Sherahi said. Suddenly it was too much for her to grip the Indian's mind as well as communicate with the Culls. Sherahi felt as if she were being pulled asunder and she turned on the pair of coatis and hissed fiercely, "Now get out—both of you—and take Junior with you."

The wagon was already moving and Sherahi didn't have the strength to countermand her order to Joe Spotted Wolf so that the animals could have a proper goodbye. Dervish's mouth dropped open as if he would whine. He looked at Sherahi reproachfully, as if she'd suddenly lunged at him. "But, Sherahi," he faltered. "Manu . . . Sandeagozu."

"Get out, before it's too late," Sherahi hissed again, more vehemently this time. "There's no time. I can't make the wagon stop. Manu and I are going. The three of you are staying here. Goodbye, Junior. You explain it to them."

The two coatis and the little rattlesnake did not move and Sherahi panicked. "They've got to get out of here before it's too late." By moonlight she saw the shocked faces of the other Culls and could feel the wagon gaining momentum. She heard Dervish start to whine and remembered her dream of the flying wagon. And then, from deep within the oldest part of her mind, she felt a power that she had not known she possessed. It gave her the strength to simultaneously create the illusion of the Great *Culebra*, manage the actions of D. K. Beasley and Ehrich Leftrack, as well as enter Joe Spotted Wolf's alcohol-soaked mind and order, "Stop."

The wagon rolled to a halt. Sherahi took a long look at Junior as he lay coiled in a corner of the wagon. "Come, little brother," she said. "It is time for you to leave us. You made it possible for us to get here, but there is no need for you to go to Sandeagozu. This is nearly your home. If you keep traveling south you will find others of your own kind and, perhaps," she said into his flinty, zigzagged thoughts, "you will even find your true name.

"Leave us, Junior," Sherahi urged. "It is time." The other Culls watched the little cascabel angle up the rough wooden sides of the wagon and saw him drop soundlessly to the desert floor. Sherahi saw him slither across the sand, head held high, tongue flicking. Into her mind came Junior's hissing thought, "If I get to choose a name, I have decided that it will be 'Sherahi.'"

"Goodbye, Manu," he said in a voice that sounded like pebbles thrown down a cliff face. "Be careful."

"Now, Dervish," Sherahi said into the coati's mind. "Our journey together is at an end. There is no point in your going with Manu and me to Sandeagozu. You belong here with Nemi."

Dervish cocked his head and looked wistfully first at Sherahi then at Manu. He began to whimper and Sherahi continued, "You will be happy here, Dervish, and soon you'll have many little ones to tell all about sardines and peaches."

"But, Sherahi," the coati whined, his tongue lolling out of his mouth, "Manu . . ."

The langur dashed forward. He reached out one slender-fingered black hand and for a moment touched the fur on Dervish's cheek. The coati turned his head beneath the langur's caress and just as he started to howl, Sherahi said, "Come, Manu, you and I are going now.

"Nemi," she hissed, "take Dervish and go. And hurry."

Sherahi returned to the half-breed who was slumped in the driver's seat and roused him, commanding, "Drive. Drive across the mountains."

She felt the wagon begin to roll again and saw that Dervish and Nemi were still there. "Go," she hissed, "go while there is still time."

The two coatis leaped over the side of the rolling wagon and Sherahi saw Junior angle over to Dervish and coil between his paws. "Explain it to them, Junior," she said. "Make them understand."

With relief Sherahi relinquished contact with their minds and once again spurred D. K. Beasley and Ehrich Leftrack forward across the moonlit sands.

"Goodbye, little cascabel," Sherahi called in the ancient reptilian mindspeech that only Junior could comprehend. "You've earned your freedom ten times over. Be careful.

"Faster," she said to the Indian. She saw that Junior had encircled Dervish's neck as he had so many times before and hoped that he understood and would be able to explain to Dervish.

With effort she nudged the imaginary bottle toward the front seat of the wagon and reminded Joe Spotted Wolf of it. She saw one of his hands grope blindly behind him and he took a long, dry swig of the bottle that seemed to be nearly full again. The wagon reached the main road, moving west toward the mountains and the city that was on the other side. Sherahi looked at Manu as he held onto the side of the wagon and watched the pair of coatis grow smaller before they were swallowed by the night. "Poor Manu," she thought. "This is harder for you than I thought it would be. I fixed Dervish's mind so that he could bear to leave you, but I forgot that you were attached to him, too. I should have realized. . . ." She sent a wave of compassion to the langur, who stared behind even though there was nothing more to see. Then Manu huddled in a corner of the wagon, far away from her. With effort Sherahi read the sadness in his mind.

"It's better this way," she said gently. "The three of them belong here. You and I don't. There's nothing for them in Sandeagozu."

"I know, Sherahi, but it's so sad. I've known Dervish since he was a baby—even before his eyes were open. Remember how he tried to bring me the moon? I guess his kind don't get as attached as langurs do. He didn't even say goodbye."

"If only you knew, Manu," Sherahi thought. "I'll explain it sometime. I must do other things now, though." She turned her mind to controlling the Indian while she sent Beasley and Leftrack racing away across the desert after the glittering phantom snake.

The Indian seemed to have forgotten them. He muttered things to himself and as they reached the foothills of the mountains he slapped the reins hard against the horses' rumps. He sang a tuneless, rhythmic chant and Sherahi saw that it was the Navajo death hymn that his grandmother had sung so many years ago.

"Come, Manu," Sherahi said. "Pull those blankets over both of us. We've got to keep each other warm. Soon we'll be in the mountains and, as you said, it's going to be very cold."

CHAPTER SIXTEEN

San Diego, California

I
T WAS DAWN when the wagon reached the outskirts of the city on the other side of the mountains. Manu had been right. There had been snow in the high passes, but the road had been clear and Sherahi and Manu had huddled together beneath the blankets. Sherahi had made the team of horses gallop, promising them clover and green pastures at the end of the road.

Joe Spotted Wolf was barely conscious. "Why am I doing this?" he wondered as he held onto the reins, swaying in the high driver's seat. "Where is D. K.? What happened to Leftrack?" But these thoughts were only fleeting. He was gripped by a burning desire to reach San Diego. "Why do I want to go there?" he wondered. "Why am I driving these horses so fast? Why does my head hurt so?" But then he was seized by a sudden surge of exhilaration and he stood up in the seat and whipped the horses on. "I have seen the Great *Culebra*," he thought. "I can die now."

The sun was just above the horizon behind them when they arrived at the outskirts of San Diego. Joe Spotted Wolf stopped in front of the ornate, wrought-iron gates of the zoo and thought, "Why do I want to be here?" He parked the wagon and tied the reins to the brake lever, thinking, "What I really want is a cup of coffee and some rest." Then he remembered a diner down by the docks and, holding the empty whiskey bottle by the neck, lurched away in what he thought was the right direction.

Sherahi watched him disappear down the avenue of royal palm trees and said, "Quick, Manu. We're here. This is Sandeagozu. We've got to get inside before the humans arrive. We've made it, Manu. We're at Sandeagozu."

Cautiously Sherahi and Manu slipped between the bars of the high fence that surrounded the zoo. "Where do we go now?" Manu asked. Then he lifted his nose and Sherahi remembered her resolve to change his appearance so that his tribe would accept him. "I've even got to change the way he smells," she thought. "But after controlling those humans all night, this will be easy."

The two Culls crept along a concrete path. They passed the African savanna and Manu noticed that his withered arm looked different. "That's funny," he thought, but he was so excited by the prospect of seeing his tribe again that he didn't bother to question the change. Sherahi was slithering slowly, keeping to the shadows, and Manu ran eagerly ahead and then hurried back to her side. Hesitantly he said, "I think I can find them by myself, Sherahi." Shyly he said, "And if you don't mind, Pythoness, I'd like to do the last bit by myself."

Manu sat alongside the giant python's head and, even though it was forbidden to Hanuman langurs, he ran his hand lightly over Sherahi's glossy-scaled head and neck. "What can I say to you, dear friend?" he said silently. "Perhaps we'll meet again." He looked at her soberly and then withdrew his delicate, black hand. Then he was gone and Sherahi saw him race across the grass, his restored face sniffing alertly. He stopped for a moment and then disappeared over a high, concrete wall.

Through Manu's eyes Sherahi watched the members of his tribe cautiously approach and gather around him in a wary circle. Their curiosity drew them to this strange langur who had mysteriously appeared in their midst, but they were also frightened. Screaming toddlers fell silent. Their enormous-eyed faces peered from their mothers' arms. From the back of the group a young, strong male stared at Manu and began to threaten him open-mouthed, showing long, canine teeth. A withered, barrel-chested female pushed him roughly out of the way, saying, "Calm down. You'll get your chance soon enough." More hesitantly she said in her coughing grunt, "I think I know this langur."

The others watched silently as she crossed the ten feet of rock that separated Manu from the tribe. Tentatively she reached out one spindly arm. Quicker than the eye could follow, she touched his tail and scampered back, out of reach. "He's not a ghost," her old voice cackled. "He's real. And if my brother Manu hadn't been kidnapped by the white men many years ago, I would say that this is him. But it cannot be Manu."

"Is it Manu's ghost?" a little female asked, but the old matriarch had settled into her tale and continued, "When we were on the ship, before most of you were born, Manu was killed by old Ura. Oh, what a temper that one had! The humans had put Manu into the same cage with him. And Manu was trapped. He couldn't get away from Ura. I saw it with my own eyes. When the white man took him away, he was bleeding. It was the last any of us ever saw of my little brother Manu."

"Maybe this is Manu's ghost come to haunt us."

"Don't talk foolishness," the old female said, annoyed. She wondered if this strange langur would let her touch him again. "Can't you see the sun? Can't you hear the birds? It is daytime. Everyone knows that ghosts are asleep now. They only walk at night."

To Manu she said, "Are you Manu's ghost? Tell these silly children who you are. Are you Manu's child?"

"I am Manu himself. And you are my sister Isi. Yes, I am sure that you are Isi, who was always too fat to do a back somersault."

The old female gasped in astonishment. She sat down on her haunches and hugged herself nervously. For long moments she watched Manu. Then, as if she had decided something, she averted her eyes and cautiously approached him, holding out one hand, palm drooping. Gently she touched him on the shoulder before returning to the other langurs. "It is Manu," she said. "Only he could know that."

The langurs didn't move and she said, "Well, go ahead. Don't let him think that we have forgotten our manners. Greet him properly."

This was the signal for the entire group of juveniles and females to pay their respects to Manu, who, without a struggle, assumed the dominant position in his tribe.

"But how is it that you look the same as when we were all in the old country?" Isi asked.

Manu smiled and allowed a six-month-old baby to suck on one of his fingers while a pair of curious yearlings played jump rope with his tail. "That's another story, for another time," he said. "I think because of a friend of mine called Sherahi." Interrupting himself he asked, "Pardon me, Isi, but what's there to eat here in Sandeagozu?"

"Anything you could want, except termites," Isi replied. "Are you hungry, Manu?"

"Starved," the langur replied. When Sherahi left him his mind was filled with the taste of papaya. As she slithered away, a single thought arrowed into Sherahi's mind. Manu's voice said clearly, "Thank you, my dear Pythoness. You did something that made them remember me. I'm home at last."

The big snake thought of the years that the scarred creature had spent huddled in his cage in the shadowy Culls' room at Leftrack's pet shop. "Then Manu was too frightened to even come out of that awful cage," she thought. She remembered how resolutely he had struggled against the white crocodiles, even though he had been sick, almost dead. He had encouraged all of them as they fled from the pet shop. "Dear Manu," Sherahi thought and sighed. "How I will miss you."

Sherahi lay there for a long while, watching the langur and his tribe. She was in no hurry, but the sun had warmed her. "I guess it's time I found my own kind," she thought, lifting her head and fnasting in all directions. "I wonder where the pythons live?" She encountered a familiar, musky smell that seemed to come from a low, windowless building at the bottom of a nearby hill. Eager to see a real snake again, Sherahi undulated across the grass, wondering what in the world pythons were doing inside a building in

Sandeagozu. "All of the animals are supposed to be free here," she thought. "I must be mistaken. Maybe the smell of python is coming from somewhere near that building, but surely they can't be inside of it."

She crawled past an enclosure that held spreading almond trees and heard the raucous morning calls of a crowd of parrots that gossiped in the interlaced branches. "If only the Duchess were here," Sherahi thought, seeing the flash of brilliant blue and scarlet feathers as the large birds groomed themselves with their heavy, curved bills. "She would be happy to have all these friends."

One of the birds spotted Sherahi and began to scream an alarm. Sherahi looked for a place to hide, but there was no cover. She could only duck her head and pray that the bird wouldn't hurt her too much before she could strangle it. From the topmost branches it flew directly at her, gray claws forward, ready to grasp. Sherahi braced herself. She saw the scaly talons reaching for her and expected to feel them dig into her back at any moment, but instead they clenched around the webbing of an almost invisible nylon net that shrouded the parrot enclosure.

"Well, it certainly took you long enough," a familiar voice said. "I thought you'd never get here." Sherahi looked up to see the Duchess gripping the nylon netting. As usual, the bird was boasting. "While the rest of you have been lollygagging, I've fledged a nestful of chicks. Where have you been?"

"Duchess," Sherahi said. "Can it really be you?"

"What other scarlet macaw would be foolish enough to associate with a nasty-looking python like you? Can't you hear the others screaming for me to come away? They think you're dangerous. Imagine that! What dumb birds!"

"Duchess, how did you get here?"

"The humans brought me," the macaw replied. "I've become quite a celebrity 'round here. I've even been in the newspapers and on the radio, but I don't suppose you know what that is."

"Duchess," said Sherahi, "there's so much I want to know about this place."

"Well, all I've got to say is that unless you want them to put you into The Pit with the other loonies, you'd better hide. And quick. It's about time for them to get here. And if you're not careful, they will catch you and throw you in there." The Duchess motioned with her head toward the low building that Sherahi knew held pythons. "Whatever else, you don't want that to happen."

"But, Duchess, I've come all this way to see my own kind. You have your friends, Manu has his, Dervish and Nemi are together . . ."

"Nemi?" asked the Duchess in her usual nosy fashion. "Who's Nemi? What kind of name is that?"

"A coati name. She's Dervish's mate. Their babies will be born in a few months."

"And Junior—what happened to that venomous little viper?" asked the Duchess.

"Unless I miss my guess he's on his way to his home farther south. But the point is that all of you are happy with your own kind while I'm still all alone."

"Suit yourself, Pythoness," said the Duchess, "but I'd stay away from that place if I were you. Whatever else you do, hurry. They'll be coming soon."

The parrots in the tree called to the Duchess and she flew back to join the others. Sherahi saw a large macaw detach itself from the rest of the flock and watched for a moment as he and the Duchess stood facing one another on a limb, heads bobbing. In a moment the Duchess was tenderly grooming his eyelids.

"She can't be right," thought Sherahi. "This is Sandeagozu. Things are different here. It's not just a glorified Leftrack's pet shop. Here all the animals are free. I've got to see these pythons for myself. What does the Duchess know of higher intelligence?"

With her mind questing ahead, like a dog sniffing for hidden pheasants, Sherahi hurried as quickly as she could to the low building that the Duchess had called The Pit.

Sherahi pushed against a heavy glass door and entered the dark building that smelled strongly of snake. The walls of the dim anteroom were covered with the marks that humans called writing, but they meant less to her than patterns of high, distant clouds. She fnasted the small room, learned that it held no living snakes and saw a second pair of glass doors in one wall. She slithered over to them and was pleased when they also swung inward, allowing her to pass inside to a larger, darker space.

She had expected to see open enclosures similar to those that housed groups of birds or mammals outside. "It will be so good to get back onto a comfortable tree perch or coil in a proper cave," she thought. "I'm tired of traveling. It's time I found a place where I can settle for good."

She undulated silently forward, her head aloft and her tongue sampling the air ahead. She was in a wide, hard-surfaced corridor. In the walls were glass panels that enclosed small displays. They reminded her of something she had seen before and she remembered the Animal of the Month exhibit that had been a featured attraction in Leftrack's pet shop. "Where are the pythons?" she wondered. "Perhaps I should think more precisely of what I'm looking for," she considered as she slithered forward. "Now, what will the perfect home for pythons be like?" she asked herself. "Pythons are water creatures, so it'll have a stream and a deep pool full of fish. There'll be a smooth, soft bank for sunning and a dry cave for sleeping. There'll be lots of flowering trees that have sturdy limbs for daytime perches. There'll be birds to stalk and a wide meadow filled with flowers and rabbits. And, I almost forgot, there'll be deer and pigs in the forest who won't mind terribly much if I take a piglet or fawn from time to time. And there'll be elephants to watch and water buffalo and, of course, crocodiles to listen to. And there has to be a pagoda. A huge one with a golden spire and a Buddha guarded by generations of rats. And there must be flowers—flowers of all colors.

"Now, where can it be? I know it's here somewhere."

Sherahi was so intent upon finding this verdant enclosure that she ignored the glassed-in exhibits that held varieties of serpents, most of whom were asleep. As she passed a low window that was half as long as her body she saw something that she couldn't quite believe. It made her stop and widen her elliptical pupils: within the enclosure she saw an obese male Burmese python. He lay loosely coiled near a trough of greenish water. A blue-green fuzz slimed the water's surface and a dead rat lay fetally curled near the python's spine. The wall and floor of his cell were made of the same, hard, glossy substance that covered the floor of the corridor. "There's not even a perch for him to cling to," Sherahi thought as she saw that, except for the water trough and the dead rat, the cage was bare.

Sherahi ducked below the windowsill and cautiously peered at the captive serpent. Like herself, he was an enormous snake. Although he was only three quarters of her size he carried the pattern of dark-bordered blotches on a cream-colored background that was the hallmark of the Burmese python clan. He wore the light, temporal stripes that showed Vishnu's special protection and all over his body was the iridescence that made Burmese pythons gleam as if they had been touched by the same brush that colored the throats of sunbirds, the wings of morpho butterflies and the golden eyes of toads.

As Sherahi watched, a stout tongue flicked from between his closed jaws and Sherahi realized that he had seen her. She could see the stout claws at either corner of his cloacal scale and for a moment she wondered what it would be like to feel the gentle scratch of those spurs. She wondered what his mating embrace would be like and her tail stiffened as she imagined allowing him to penetrate her tightly closed cloaca. Her labial pits quopped and Sherahi combined their sensations with those of the Jacobson's organs within her lower jaw. Her slow, pythonine thoughts reached for his mind and instantly recoiled as if she had touched something hot. Sherahi took one look within this stranger's mind and saw why the Duchess had referred to this place as The Pit. This male python was not merely obese; he was also insane. Meaningless thoughts jangled in his mind like tin cans clattering to frighten crows. Sherahi knew that if she were forced to live with this poor creature, she would go insane, too. This male python should have been using his mental powers to inquire into the nature of the universe—into the meaning of wisdom, of beauty, and the rational mind. At the least he should have been composing poetry, but instead he hummed a tuneless nursery raga and rhymed words. In the characteristic slow, pythonine manner, as if pontificating, his thoughts revolved around the words "rat, cat; cat, sat; sat, bat; bat, mat; mat, fat; fat, hat; hat, nat; nat, that. . . ." He hummed and repeated these words over and over, taking no further notice of Sherahi. Instead of being welcomed by her own kind, as the Duchess and Manu had been, Sherahi was ignored by the only Burmese python in Sandeagozu.

"Don't be alarmed, Pythoness." A stranger's voice spoke within her mind. "Our big friend is quite mad. He's been that way for years. All he ever does is eat and rhyme and hum. See what captivity can do?

"And they'll put you in there with him if you don't get out of here before they come."

Sherahi sought the source of the voice and whirled to see a twenty-foot-long king cobra swaying within an enclosure similar to the one that held the male Burmese python. "That's why they call this place The Pit," the cobra continued, fixing Sherahi with a steady, round black eye.

"But how can this be?" asked Sherahi. "This is Sandeagozu. The animals are supposed to be free. There aren't supposed to be any bars on the cages."

"That's only true for some of the animals here," the cobra replied. "It doesn't apply to us. The humans are too frightened of serpents to let us run free like mammals behind moats or birds with their wings clipped. Buster over there went mad years ago. In fact, except for myself and that disreputable gaggle of crocs and caimans at the end of the line and the pair of ancient Galápagos tortoises in the Children's Zoo, all the reptiles here are crazy. Buster is the worst, but then, he's also the biggest."

"Why is he crazy?" asked Sherahi.

"Boredom, I suppose," replied the cobra, swaying slightly. "Do you know what it's like to spend all your time in a cage? I see that you've had some experiences like that yourself, Pythoness. So you know how much we need variety. They even kill our food for us. Little wonder that most of us go mad."

Sherahi remembered those long days in the tank in the Culls' room at Leftrack's pet shop and said, "I understand."

The cobra continued, "And now, although it's been refreshing to speak with an intelligent being for a change, I really do think you'd better get out of here. Go outside and hide in the bushes until it's dark."

"But where can I go?" wailed Sherahi. "I've come so far to get here. What's left for me?"

426

"Don't worry, Pythoness. You'll figure it out. Now, go."

With one backward glance at the pathetic male python who was now rhyming, "barn, tarn; tarn, farn; farn, carn; carn, marn; marn, narn; narn, sarn; sarn, larn . . ." Sherahi hurried as fast as she could toward the glass doors and freedom.

The morning shift of guards and zoo keepers for the eastern end of the park was walking toward the Reptile House. Sherahi was nosing through the second set of glass doors when the twenty men in green uniforms discovered her. She was so upset and distracted by what she had found in Sandeagozu that she hardly put up any fight at all.

Even though she was distraught, it took all twenty of the men to subdue her. None of them had ever seen such a huge snake. "She's the biggest Burmese in the world," they agreed. "What in the hell is she doing here?" Not having any better place to house her, the keepers temporarily put her into Buster's cell.

Later that morning newspaper reporters and photographers came and took pictures of the sensational serpent who had been caught within the zoo itself.

The headlines read: "MONSTER SNAKE VISITS ZOO." Further down the page was a story headlined: "Mysterious Disappearances: Two Feared Dead in Desert. Indian Sought for Questioning." There was also a feature article in the entertainment section detailing the exciting life and beauty secrets of Naruda, Hollywood's latest darling.

Sherahi lay in Buster's uncomfortable cell and watched scores of humans file past the fingermarked window. She saw them shudder in fear and horror while she listened to Buster rhyming, "zipper, flipper; flipper, dipper; dipper, sipper; sipper, nipper; nipper, gipper; gipper, lipper; lipper, bipper; bipper, zipper."

"How long will it be before I'm doing that, too?" Sherahi wondered and buried her head in her coils and wished she were a thousand miles from Sandeagozu.

The Desert

EHRICH LEFTRACK had been wandering for days when he first saw the village carved into the canyon wall. Confused and exhausted from thirst he took off his shirt, stood up and waved it excitedly. "Help me. Help. Help," he shouted at the square-cut windows that marched in a straight line high on the canyon wall, just beneath its rim. "Help me. Help. Help," he yelled until he was hoarse, but there was no answering call and no one peered out of those black doorways. There was only the sun boring into his forehead; the sun blistering his lips. "They can't see me," Ehrich said to himself. "They can't hear me. It's all right. It's okay. I'll go to them."

He bound his shirt around his head, tying it in place with the sleeves, and began to plod over the stony ground. He tried to remember what the Boy Scout manual had said about survival in the desert, but all that came to his mind was the embroidery on the dog and cat badge that he had earned before they'd kicked him out for eating all the refreshments. Ehrich clearly remembered the pointy-eared cat and the snub-faced Scotty dog and the Scout oath. He stumbled over the floor of the canyon, reciting, "Trustworthy, loyal, helpful, friendly, obedient, brave, clean, reverent . . ." There were ten. What were the other ones? "Trustworthy, loyal, helpful, friendly, obedient, brave, clean and reverent. Why can't I remember?"

Hours later he found himself standing below the village. The heat shimmered in the canyon and he thought of the deep, cool shade within the rock-walled rooms. He looked at the unforgiving landscape and the rimrock seemed to sway in the glare. There was a roaring in his ears and he saw that there wasn't even a bush to crawl under. "I've got to get out of this sun," he thought. "It's doing funny things to my eyes. I think I'm getting sunstroke." He licked his swollen lips and thought, "Maybe there's water up there." He began to climb up the narrow stairs that led up the rock face, thinking, "Even if they're not there now, Indians are smart—they wouldn't build a town where there was no water."

Ehrich toiled upward, panting with exertion, climbing the sandstone stairs on all fours. "Help me. Help me," he whimpered under his breath. "Why won't somebody help me?" But there was no one to hear him and after he slipped and slid down a flight of sand-covered stairs he tried to dig his fat fingers into each stone as best he could. There was no guard rail on the staircase as it snaked upward across the canyon wall, and Ehrich pressed himself into each stair, afraid to look over the edge to see how high he had climbed. "Trustworthy, loyal, helpful, friendly, obedient, brave, clean and reverent. What were the other two?" he asked himself as he saw a vulture fly through the canyon, level with his shoulder.

"Thank God," he said as he saw that he was near the top of the stairs. A wide, sheltered corridor opened above. Ehrich crawled up the last steps and pulled himself back from the cliff edge, glad to be out of the sun and away from the steep drop. For a long time he lay there, panting and listening to the silence. Then he heard a slight scraping sound and saw that two huge sand-colored rattlesnakes were fighting in a spot of sunlight at the end of the corridor. Fascinated and terrified, Ehrich watched the two writhe around one another. He saw them rear up and push against each other, necks intertwined like a caduceus, and he hoped that they wouldn't turn and attack him. "Please, don't let 'em bite me," he prayed. Slowly and silently, hoping not to attract their attention, he struggled to his feet and hurried away from the two rattlers who were enmeshed in their silent, territorial wrestling match. They did not turn to chase him.

Ehrich found himself wandering through a maze of cool, dark, empty rooms hewn into the cliff face. Some had broken pieces of pottery in odd corners and in one Ehrich saw a painted wooden carving stuck into the roof timbers. It was a chalk-white man who had his teeth clenched around a rattlesnake. There were green ovals around his eyes and mouth, and a zig-zag wound around his waist. Tattered, gray feathers were stuck into the back of the carving's hair. As he put it back into the roof beams where he had found it, Ehrich saw a jug that was tucked farther back into the rafters. This jug was not broken and it was painted with lizards chasing one another. Ehrich looked at it a moment before thinking, "Water." He shook it next to his ear, but could only hear a rattling noise. Hoping that no snakes were inside he gingerly removed the clay plug. He squatted down and shook the jar, pouring some of the contents into the dust. "Corn," he thought. "Little, blue kernels of corn. Well, at least I won't starve." He put a few of the grains into his mouth and took the jug with him. "Water," he thought. "I've got to find water."

Ehrich wandered out of these rooms that led one into the next, like a child's game of chutes and ladders, and found himself in a dim passage that opened into a wide, sunlit courtyard. There were ladders and doorways all about. Against one wall he saw a large, circular basin. He heard a dripping sound and smelled the water before he actually saw it. "Thank God," Ehrich said. He put the jug of corn down and dipped both hands into the water. It seemed unbelievably cool—even cold. "Is it poisoned?" he wondered for a moment but did not hesitate to slurp the water from his cupped hands. It tasted so good that he lay with his face in the basin, splashing his head and chest, drinking his fill. "Got to go slow," he said to himself. "Not too much. Don't want to get sick."

Ehrich fell asleep next to the basin in the deserted village and awoke hours later with a terrible hunger. It had been several days since he had eaten and his ordeal in the desert had taken its toll: for the first time in his life the waist of his trousers was loose. Ehrich put his thumbs into his waistband and thought, "I'm hungry. I may be dying of malnutrition." He had thought of catching lizards before and saw one eyeing him suspiciously from a windowsill, but he knew that he wasn't quick enough. Then he remembered the jug of corn.

Experimentally he tossed a few of the grains into his mouth. They were smaller than the yellow corn his mother had served and Ehrich found that, although the kernels were hard and dry, they had a nutty, sweet taste.

They were so hard that he wasn't able to chew them much, but contented himself with swallowing them whole. He washed them down with a lot of water and by the time he had emptied the jug he felt contented and full. He rubbed his stomach with satisfaction and took another long drink from the basin. He filled the jug with water and, feeling better than he had in days, went back to the outer passage, with its view of the canyon, thinking, "I'll see 'em when they come to rescue me. I'll surprise 'em." Exhausted, Ehrich slumped against a comfortable wall and was soon asleep.

It was past midnight when he was awakened by the first pains. "I don't feel so good," he thought. A spasm gripped his abdomen and he tried to make himself burp. "Gas," he thought. "Just gas trapped in the transverse colon. It's painful, but it's nothing serious. I can relieve it if I just lie on the other side." He took a deep breath and gritted his teeth against the pain and carefully tried to roll over onto his other side. As he did so, another, stronger, spasm grabbed his innards. "I'll undo my belt," he gasped. "That always helps." He fumbled with his belt and unbuttoned his trousers, but the pain continued. For hours Ehrich bent double on the ground and clutched his belly, groaning and screaming. "Water," he gasped. "I've got to have water." With effort he found the jug that lay by his side. He uncorked it and drank deeply. "There," he thought. "That's better. Oh, those were the worst pains. I wonder what was in that corn? Thank God it's over."

Then he thought, "Corn—whole-grain—dry. Oh, my God." It suddenly occurred to Ehrich that he had made an awful mistake. "I've got to make myself throw up," he thought. He stuck his finger down his throat and felt his palate heave. He made himself retch several times, but could bring up only water. He felt his insides lurch wildly and his belly bloated even further. "It's too late," he thought. "It's in my intestines already."

Ehrich Leftrack knew exactly what was going to happen to him. Another, even stronger, spasm of pain clutched at his belly and Ehrich wept, "Mama—Mama. Please don't let me die. Please, Mama."

For hours Ehrich lay on his side, doubled up, trying to stop the pain. He grew weak from the effort and the ripping spasms suddenly became just another feature of his universe—like the black-and-white lizards that chased one another around and around the polished terra-cotta jug that lay beside him. Toward morning the pressure in his belly was relieved and he felt a queer, hot sensation as his belly swelled even further. It hurt to touch his skin now and he clutched his hands against his chest. He felt the skin of his belly stretch outward even further. "Oh, my God," he said. "What's happening to me?" Just then a final spasm clawed at his belly and he felt blood thudding in his ears. He gasped, but he could not catch his breath. "I can't breathe. I'm dying," he thought. "This can't happen. Mama—this . . . can't . . ." It was the last thing that Ehrich Leftrack said into the floor of the deserted Hopi village. Swollen grains of blue corn dribbled from the corner of his mouth as the pressure from the expanded grain within his abdomen stifled his heart and lungs and burst his intestines. The vultures found him in the morning.

Hollywood, California

"PLEASE, MAXIE DARLING, be a dear and arrange it for me." Ruthie's sequined dress shimmered as she reached across the table and ran a mauve fingernail around Max Goldman's ear and down his jowl. "Please, Maxie," she whined. "It won't take much time. Just a wave of your hand can arrange everything. And it would be such a little thing for you to call the Publicity Department and have them send reporters and photographers along. I know it's a long shot, but if it is my snake, and it certainly sounds like it may be, just think of the publicity for the new movie."

Goldman chewed his cigar and thought, "How can I tell her that there won't be a new movie? How can I tell her that we won't spend another penny promoting her? How can I tell her that she's all washed up?"

Just then the waiter arrived and announced, "Oysters Rockefeller." He placed a silver platter before each of them and Goldman thought, "Saved by the appetizers."

"I'll think about it," he said, hitching himself up so that he would sit higher in the banquette covered with zebra skin.

"You do that, sweetheart," said Ruthie, wondering, "What's wrong with you, Max?" It was clear that he was no longer as avidly interested in her as he had been at the beginning. Now instead of merely hinting, she had to push and nag and wheedle to get any attention at all. "Maybe it's just that business is off," she thought as she watched him gulp the fourth spinach-draped oyster. "Profits from my first feature film weren't what we had hoped for, but still, *Gator Girl* made money."

Ruthie felt sorry for herself and mourned, "There was a time when all I had to do was wish for something and it would appear. There was a time when he called me 'marquee magic.' " She watched his eyes follow the twitching skirt of the waitress who pushed the dessert cart, patted her hair into place beneath the sequined snood that matched her dress and worried, "Am I losing my looks? Is he looking for another new face?"

"LET'S GET A SHOT of you feeding the crocodiles, Naruda." There was a whirring of cameras and a popping of flashbulbs and Ruthie carefully turned her best side to the photographers, her long, blond mane curling halfway down her back. She wore a pith helmet and a safari outfit and she looked every inch the proper White Hunter. All these photographers were getting a little wearying, though. "Isn't that enough, fellas?" The little man from the Publicity Department bustled in, destroying the rapport that Ruthie was building. "Get out of here, you idiot," Ruthie hissed, her smile clenched between even, studio teeth. "I'll tell them when I've had enough, Bonehead." She lifted her skirt, exposing a yard of silken calf and thigh, and smiled compliantly for the cameras, cooing rhetorically, "Like this?"

The photographers didn't reply, but their cameras spoke for them. "Why did Max send this third-stringer with me?" she wondered. "There was a time when he'd have sent the best, shrewdest, most experienced man on the staff of the Publicity Department to see to it that everything went smoothly. I used to rate the red-carpet treatment; all of a sudden I'm a poor relation. Well," she decided, "who needs help from this Bozo? I've done this a thousand times. I've forgotten more about how to handle photographers than most actresses ever learn." She arched her back and leaned forward, looking knowingly at their lenses. She'd practiced just this pose time and again before her mirror. She knew to the millimeter exactly how much of her breasts she was revealing. "How's this, boys?" she purred.

The moment finally came when Naruda was to be introduced to the Burmese python that she had claimed belonged to her. The San Diego Zoo, however, was not about to relinquish its new prize specimen just because someone claimed it as her own—even if that someone were a Hollywood star. Ruthie spent long moments looking at the snake through the glass of the exhibit. "Well," she said to the Curator of Reptiles, a weedy, academic type whose name she had forgotten the moment they were introduced, "it sure looks like my snake." What she didn't add was that the snake in the exhibit was a third larger than her snake had been. But the markings were the same. "I think it's her," Naruda said. "But I'm not sure. The only way I'll ever find out is to see if she recognizes me."

"How will you do that?" the reptile curator asked, incredulous that this girl should think that a snake, even an intelligent snake like a Burmese python, would be able to remember a human. In his years at the zoo he had observed that the most intelligent reptiles, crocodiles and cobras, seemed to recognize their keepers, but the idea of a python recognizing someone who hadn't seen it for a few years was ludicrous. "Now she's going to get herself bitten," he worried, "and these reporters will make hay out of that." He signaled to the ten burly keepers who stood nearby, holding nets and nooses, just in case the snake should be vicious, and steered the blonde to the door that led to the back of the snake exhibits.

"She hasn't hurt anybody," he said, "but you never know. When we captured her she didn't even struggle."

"Has she eaten since she's been here?" asked Ruthie.

"No, but that doesn't surprise me," the curator replied. "They can go for weeks—months—without eating."

"Big Bertha would only do that when she was unhappy," Ruthie replied.

"Is that what you called her? Big Bertha?"

"Only when she was a baby," Ruthie replied, smiling a special smile and crinkling those famous bottle-green eyes. "Can I see her now?"

"Yes, but be careful. You know about their teeth? You know how fast they can strike?"

"Mr. Curator, before I got into the movie business I did three shows a day with snakes. Believe me, I know about their teeth," returned Ruthie, annoyed that this man doubted her expertise.

"Okay," he replied. "Try. But don't say I didn't warn you."

He opened a small metal door in the rear of the exhibit that held Sherahi and Buster, the insane male Burmese python. Ruthie looked in and saw that the big female was watching her alertly, while the smaller male paid no attention. She watched as the enormous snake flicked a shiny, black tongue in her direction. "Hello, Big Girl," Ruthie said in a soft, confident voice. "Do you remember me?"

Ruthie held out her hand for the snake to smell and the black tongue flicked even faster. The snake held it out straight and quivered its forked ends.

Sherahi considered this fair-haired woman and thought, "Why don't they leave me alone?" She watched this woman's frail hand, with its long, pink fingernails, come closer and fnasted the odor that wafted from her arm and hair. "I know that smell," Sherahi thought and the image of a single-file row of yellow wooden ducks swam in her memory. She remembered Ruthie, a brown-haired girl who danced in a spot of hot-pink light. "The rituals," Sherahi thought. "I had almost forgotten them. But something's wrong. Ruthie's hair wasn't yellow."

She fnasted the woman's hand and concluded that it was the same person. Carefully she listened to Ruthie's voice, which seemed to come from a long distance. "Do you know me, Big Girl? Do you remember? Come, Bertha. Big Bertha."

Sherahi heard the name that she had hated for so many years and suddenly lifted her regal head, returning Ruthie's green gaze with her golden stare. "What took you so long to come back for me, Ruthie?" She thought of asking, "Why did you leave me with those awful people?" but Sherahi already knew that answer. The serpent nats and U Vayu had told her; the Leftracks had already taught her that lesson. Instead, she sent a bolt of fear into the girl's mind, as well as the idea, "You're going to take me out of this place. You need me." Sherahi smiled in her inscrutable way when she saw the actress's plan to take her away from her cage with Buster and away from this zoo.

"Come, old friend," Ruthie said in a much kinder tone, which Sherahi found irresistible. "Come out and show them how we can dance."

As quickly as she could Sherahi bridged the gap to Ruthie's hand and crawled up onto those familiar, warm shoulders. Staggering under the weight of the serpent's head and neck, Ruthie thought, "I can't lift her. She's grown too heavy. Now we can never dance as we used to in the old act."

Sherahi saw this fear flash into Ruthie's mind and withdrew her head. "Make them open this cage," she ordered the girl.

"Please let her out," Ruthie said to the astounded Curator of Reptiles.

"Are you sure she won't try anything dangerous?"

"Mister, I have no idea what she'll do, but if she's my snake she'll remember our old routine. Please. I want to prove it to you. Besides," she drawled, "what can one snake do against twelve big men?"

Moments later the rear door of the python exhibit swung open and Sherahi emerged. She slithered as few of them had ever seen a python move: head four feet above the ground, looking alertly left and right, tongue fnasting the mix of odors that she encountered.

When she was clear of Buster's enclosure she sent a clear message into Ruthie's mind. "Begin. We'll convince them that I belong to you."

Ruthie took off her pith helmet and bound up her long hair. She unbuttoned all but two of the buttons on her long khaki skirt and rolled up her long sleeves and kicked off her shoes. "Now, we'll see," she said to the curator. "Give us some room."

Ruthie began to clap her hands, slowly at first. Then she increased the tempo in the ancient dance that Sherahi had once thought was the sacred dance that women and serpents had always performed. It was a dance that kept the sun swinging about the earth, kept the carpet of stars in its proper place. It was a dance in which beauty and death were inextricably woven to create life.

Sherahi watched Ruthie move before her. The woman's head was thrown back, her eyes were half-closed. "Good," thought the giant serpent, "she's doing exactly as I say. Now, it's my turn. If I can manage it."

Sherahi moved to a spot at the dancer's feet and began to twine

434

around and between her legs, careful to direct the woman's steps so that she was not trodden upon. Sherahi danced the dance of the river of life flowing through the canyons of time. Giving Ruthie the strength of five tigers she began to climb up the woman's body, caressing her in the way she had when they danced in tawdry saloons like the Club Istanbul in Omaha, Nebraska. Except this time they danced not to titillate the sexual palates of a few beer-soaked, would-be big spenders; this time they danced to encourage the earth and all of its creatures. This time they danced as Sherahi thought proper: the real ritual in the old way.

For once the photographers were speechless. Out of wisecracks, and not knowing how to evaluate this spectacle, they merely stared open-mouthed until the studio publicity man came to his senses and remembered his job. He realized that they were witnessing a sensational performance by a small woman and an enormous, frightening serpent.

He nudged one of the dumbfounded photographers, and cameras began to whirr and click and flashbulbs began to pop. Annoyed, Sherahi lifted her head protectively over her partner's head and hissed open-mouthed at the photographers, menacing them into silence, as Ruthie collapsed onto the floor and the dance was over.

"I've never seen anything like that," the Curator of Reptiles said. "There's no question but she's your animal. When you're ready, come to my office and we'll discuss terms."

"I do not discuss terms," said Naruda haughtily, panting with exertion but strangely exhilarated by the experience. It had succeeded beyond her fondest hopes. "My business manager will call you. With your permission, we're leaving."

"How're we going to send that thing, Boss?" one of the keepers asked the Curator of Reptiles.

"Crate and bag, I suppose—same as usual," was his reply.

Sherahi overheard this conversation and sent an immediate thought into Ruthie's mind.

"That won't be necessary," she said. "She'll ride with me."

An hour later Sherahi slithered into the limousine as the chauffeur held the door open. He stood just as far away as the tips of his gloved fingers would reach and anxiously watched the big car settle down onto its shock absorbers, thinking, "I'll have to take it real slow or I'll lose the goddamn gas tank." As the chauffeur watched, yard after yard of python coiled onto the soft, leather seat of Naruda's limousine. Coils spilled onto the floor. Finally, the tail whisked inside and he gingerly closed the door. He made sure to close the glass panel that separated him from the back seat and watched in the rear-view mirror as the movie star fondly stroked the big serpent, whose regal head was coiled so close to her own. He heard Naruda coo, "How could I ever have sold you, my pet?" He wheeled the car away from San Diego Zoo thinking, "Show folk. Hmph."

Sherahi looked into Ruthie's clear, green eyes, framed by this strange, curly, blond hair, and scryed her mind. "The woman is a selfish fool," she thought, "but then, how can she be anything else? She's only human," Sherahi sighed.

Hollywood, California

MAX GOLDMAN removed his horn-rimmed glasses and gestured to the assistant who stood behind his chair. In recent months Max had put on weight and he found it increasingly difficult to pull himself out of his easy chair to his feet. "Help me, you nincompoop," he wheezed.

Once he was on his feet he hurried to the spot on the stage where Naruda lay in a crumpled heap. Sherahi stood guard over her, hissing and swaying slightly, but for some reason Max was unafraid. "Nice snakee," he said and reached for Ruthie's limp hand.

"Sensational. Absolutely sensational. I've never seen anything like it. How did you ever do it, my dear? I never thought you had it in you."

Mervyn LeMarr, Goldman's director, was not far behind him. "Incredible, Naruda. You were the soul of sensuality," he lisped, pushing his hair back from his immaculate forehead and resting his hands on his slim hips. "Frankly, my dear, this makes everything else you've done seem— well, rather ordinary, even pedestrian. But this—this was—simply glorious. You were—*inspired!*"

To Goldman he said, "Max, darling, I can see it all now. Naruda as the Jungle Queen: all the beasts do her bidding. We'll only have to change the script a little and it'll be perfect."

Goldman agreed and ordered: "Story conference at ten A.M. sharp in my office."

Max helped Ruthie to her feet.

"I feel a little tired," she said, leaning upon his shoulder.

"I'm not surprised, darling," he beamed. "After a performance like that, who wouldn't be tired?

"You have a swim and relax. I want you to get plenty of rest because once we start shooting it will be nonstop."

"Yes," LeMarr concurred. "You *must* rest, Naruda, darling," he said, suddenly interested in her welfare. "Our star must shine.

"Now, Max, dear," LeMarr said, turning the fat little producer away from Naruda, "where do you think we should shoot it? Monterey? Fort Lee? Miami?"

Sherahi had returned to the resting coil from which she normally controlled Ruthie's actions. She shot a sudden image into LeMarr's mind: an image of ruined shrines and jade-green vegetation. He said, "Some place with temples would be scenic, don't you think, Max?"

"Yeah," said Goldman. "Some place lousy with temples and monkeys and crocs, even. Get the scouts working on it."

Sherahi scryed Max's mind and found a memory he had of the scent of frangipani—of a market on the Irawaddy where he used to haggle for gems. She kneaded this thought within his mind and saw him take the cigar from his mouth and scratch his chin meditatively.

"Mervyn," he called. "I just had a fantastic idea. Let's go to the jungle and actually film there. On location. It'll be great for publicity and we'll take the press along."

"Do you really think we can do it?"

"Of course we can. *The Jungle Queen* will be the talk of the town before it's even in the can."

"Brilliant, Max. *Absolutely brilliant.*"

"Get on it right away."

"Will do, Max. Will do."

"Come, sweetheart." Goldman extended his hand to Naruda and led her to her private wing of the mansion while Sherahi quietly slipped into her spacious, secure, silk-lined wicker basket to rest and plan.

CHAPTER SEVENTEEN

Falam, Burma

RESSED ONLY IN the ragged, patchwork chamois
costume that revealed and accentuated her lithe figure, with a necklace of
boar tusks and cowrie shells around her neck, Naruda, as the Jungle
Queen, waited for Mervyn LeMarr to begin shooting. Unlike the rest of the
picture, this scene was remarkably simple. All it involved was for Ruthie and
Sherahi to move up a path to the crest of a hill and disappear into the vegetation.

The script read, "Having bid a tearful adieu to Lieutenant Swansby,
and with the knowledge in her deepest heart that they will meet again one
day in a better, kinder future, where their two worlds can harmonize,
Naruda, the Jungle Queen, gives Reggie one last longing look, a look so
filled with longing that in it he hears the ragged cough of the tigress as she
calls to her mate, the measured tread of the peacock kneading the earth
with his desire. He knows that her eyes will burn in his memory down the
long, dark corridors of time that will separate them.

"J.Q.: 'Till we meet again, my darling.'

"He gives a military salute to his beloved, waves and turns away,
unable to control his tears.

"Trailed by her ever-present guardian, Kas, the python, and carrying
Miko, the mischievous chimpanzee, on one hip, the Jungle Queen strides
purposefully up the path and, with one rippling, backward glance, disappears like a blond shadow into the jungle that has always been her home.
THE END."

Goldman had murmured, "There won't be a dry handkerchief in the
house when this one finishes."

"All right, dear." Mervyn LeMarr slapped the riding crop against his
jodhpurs and minced over, very businesslike despite his silk shirt and solar
topee. "This is it. Just the shot of you melting into the forest and we'll wrap
it up." He noticed Naruda's distraction and asked, "Happy, darling?"

"Yes. I'm fine."

"It's just that you seem so far away," said LeMarr with concern.

"Perhaps it's the weather. You simply cannot get sick, dear girl. I *simply cannot* have you coming down with some deadly Burmese plague. When this is all over, you must rest, Naruda, dear. Publicity has scheduled the national tour to begin a month from now."

Like a somnambulist Ruthie replied, "That's nice."

"Are you sure you're all right?"

"I'm fine," Ruthie insisted, wondering why he sounded as if he were speaking subaqueously.

"Okay. Places, everybody. Quiet on the set." The clapper board identified this segment of film and Max shouted, "Action."

Sherahi and Ruthie began to move up the jungle path and the scene was shot without incident.

"Cut," shouted LeMarr. To the crew he said, "That's a wrap. Thank you, ladies and gentlemen. I believe that Mr. Goldman has refreshments for us." He gestured to a canvas tent that was stretched above a table spread with an assortment of sandwiches and luncheon food. Turbaned, silk-clad waiters stood beneath it, holding trays of glasses, and magnums of champagne waited in ice buckets.

Max Goldman struggled out of his canvas director's chair and extended his hand to the pressmen and columnists who waited. "Right this way, ladies and gentlemen." To LeMarr he said, "Get Naruda. Her public awaits."

Mervyn LeMarr found Naruda standing in a glade on the other side of the ridge. She was staring abstractedly at the ground and didn't seem to hear his approach. "Naruda," he called, annoyed at having to be her nursemaid when he should be receiving congratulations from the cast and crew. "The party's just starting and everyone wants to congratulate you."

He came up beside her and saw that she was crying. "What's wrong, now?" he asked, thinking, "I knew that something was wrong. Please, dear God, *don't* let her be pregnant. The whole movie depends upon her public appearances."

He put his hands on her shoulders and shook her. Slowly the green eyes focused.

"What's the matter, dear girl?"

"She's gone," Ruthie replied. "I've called and called but she doesn't come. I've lost her."

LeMarr knew that Naruda was talking about her big snake and said, "Well, she can't have gone far. She doesn't move that fast. We'll get the natives to find her."

"You don't understand," Ruthie said, looking at the impenetrable screen of bamboo plants that surrounded them. "She'll never come back. I know it. She's not an ordinary snake. No one will ever be able to find her again."

"Don't be silly," LeMarr sneered. "These natives are incredibly sharp-eyed. Didn't they find the diamond stud that you dropped in the mud?"

"I know," said Ruthie, "but this is different. She's gone. She doesn't want to be found. She won't let us find her."

"Rubbish. Utter nonsense," LeMarr said. "Be a good girl and come along. Max has champagne just for you. You're overtired. No need to take on so over a snake."

Ruthie let him lead her away from the glade. "I am tired," she thought. "It feels as if I'm waking up from a bad dream. Maybe Mervyn is right. Maybe the natives can find Bertha."

"You're wrong about one thing, though," she said to LeMarr as they were about to join the celebration beneath the tent. "She is no ordinary snake. I don't think I'll ever see her again."

"What does it matter that you've lost your pet," said LeMarr. "You're a big star now. Your days with animal acts are over."

Max Goldman saw them approach and lifted his glass, crying, "To the Jungle Queen." Inwardly he exulted, "And to the biggest little money-maker since *Birth of a Nation*."

Sherahi coiled in the thicket of bamboo a few yards from Ruthie's feet. From where she lay she could see the girl's ankles, and later they were joined by a pair of leather boots. Like a spider hurrying to repair a damaged web, Sherahi concentrated upon reinforcing the mental screen that prevented them from seeing her, even though she was hidden only by a pale-green filigree of bamboo leaves. She reinforced the screen with a murk of confusion that clouded Ruthie's thoughts and kept her from seeing the giant pythoness, even though she came within a foot of her hiding place beneath the bamboo. "You cannot see me," Sherahi intoned. "You are tired. Very tired. You've been working much too hard. You can't see me now and you'll never see me again. Go now," she ordered. "Our time together is finished." She was pleased to see the ankles of the two humans leave her field of view. Concerned that they might send others to look for her, she mentally followed them back to the clearing where the others waited, eating and drinking. She saw them open bottles and pour glasses full of a clear liquid that frothed and bubbled and made them giddy. She spoke directly into Ruthie's mind, saying, "You don't need me now. I am free. Don't bother to look for me. You'll never find me," and released her control of Ruthie's thoughts. It was the first time in months that a major portion of her consciousness didn't manage the actions of humans and, even though Sherahi had been able to control them as she had never thought possible, she was delighted to be free again.

Sherahi waited until nightfall before cautiously nosing her way out of the bamboo thicket. Soundlessly she glided through the dew-spangled grass, leaving a dark, sinuous track in the silvered meadow. She made her way to the river that was at the bottom of the ridge where she had left Ruthie. The water glittered before her and she wanted to swim and scrub the stench of captivity from her scales and find a spot to rest before beginning to search for the place that would become her home. It had been so long since Sherahi had been on her own, with no other beings to consider, that she felt lighthearted and young and strangely alone.

She found a branch that extended out over the water and slid along it, glorying in the scrape of rough bark beneath her belly plates and the smell of leaves crushed by her weight. Her labial pits began to quop and she froze, tongue flicking inquisitively. Something warm-blooded was nearby. Sherahi put her jawbones onto the limb and heard the frantic pattering of the heart of an animal. An eye blinked and beneath the tree Sherahi saw a chaital doe and her spotted fawn, gazing up, their eyes filled with liquid dread at the sight of the python coiled above them.

"Don't worry, Mother," Sherahi said into the frightened doe's mind. "I've been given my freedom tonight. Now I give you yours. I won't harm you. Tell your baby that everything is all right. In gratitude for what I have been given, I promise never to strangle another spotted deer again."

Sherahi wasn't sure if the doe understood and she didn't wait for a reply, but slid into the warm, still water. For a while she swam with her head above the surface. She heard the mouth-watering croak of giant bullfrogs, lovelorn in a pool on the bank, and considered leaving the water to hunt a few of them. It had been a long time since she'd eaten a fat, succulent amphibian, but hauling out of the water would require a lot of energy and she wasn't really hungry. Ruthie had fed her a half-grown goat only two days ago. So, she swam past the chorus of mournful bullfrogs, thinking, "Who but a glutton would consider something so mundane as feeding when I have just escaped from captivity. It's been so long since I was free that I've lost count of the years. U Vayu would be ashamed. He would know to the exact moon. I guess I've grown lax, but it doesn't matter. How lucky I am to be free at last." She laughed and submerged, following the moon's golden path beneath the water.

"I'll find a ruined, abandoned pagoda that's attended by an old, blind monk. He'll wear a saffron-colored robe and his eyes will be as milky as mine are just before I shed my skin. The monk will keep to the old ways and will recognize a sacred python. My pagoda will have generations of rats living in the galleries beneath the stupa. And the peasants' careless piglets and thickheaded young goats will forage nearby. If I take them at night, their owners will know that it is the will of the gods. There'll be stilt-legged water birds that hunch on tangled tree roots and harpoon unlucky fishes. There'll be crocodiles telling tall tales on the sunny banks and convocations of butterflies that sip and giggle at mud puddles. All through the slow, hot afternoons I'll lie in the cave below the bank and eavesdrop. Who knows, there might even be a male python in the neighborhood, but it will have to be one who doesn't like poetry or rhyming words. I've had my fill of that.

"In the dry season I'll find the ancient caves where pythons hibernate and I'll teach those hatchlings who find their names. Then, when spring comes, I'll coil around a beautiful mound of eggs. I'll sing to the little ones who float within those egg worlds and watch their minds grow strong and subtle. There's so much to do and so much time."

Sherahi undulated in the warm water, washing herself free of the smell of Ruthie and of Sandeagozu, of humans and the other Culls. She thought, "It's a lot to ask, but if I try I think I can find such a place. After all, I'm home. We got across the desert and across the mountains to Sandeagozu. The white crocodiles said it was impossible, but we actually got there. Compared to that, finding the perfect pagoda will be easy."